PENGUIN CLASSICS

THE EARTH

EMILE ZOLA, born in Paris in 1840, was brought up at Aix-en-Provence in an atmosphere of struggling poverty after the death of his father in 1847. He was educated at the Collège Bourbon at Aix and then at the Lycée Saint-Louis in Paris. He was obliged to exist by poorly paid clerical jobs after failing his *baccalauréat* in 1859, but early in 1865 he decided to support himself by literature alone. Despite his scientific pretensions Zola was really an emotional writer with rare gifts for evoking vast crowd scenes and for giving life to such great symbols of modern civilization as factories and mines. When not overloaded with detail, his work has tragic grandeur, but he is also capable of a coarse, 'Cockney' type of humour. From his earliest days Zola had contributed critical articles to various newspapers, but his first important novel, *Thérèse Raquin*, was published in 1867, and *Madeleine Férat* in the following year. That same year he began work on a series of novels intended to follow out scientifically the effects of heredity and environment on one family: *Les Rougon-Macquart*. The work contains twenty novels, which appeared between 1871 and 1893, and is the chief monument of the French Naturalist movment. On completion of this series he began a new cycle of novels, *Les Trois Villes: Lourdes, Rome, Paris* (1894–6–8), a violent attack on the Church of Rome; this led to yet another cycle, *Les Quatre Évangiles*. He died in 1902 while working on the fourth of these.

•

DOUGLAS PARMÉE studied at Trinity College, Cambridge, the University of Bonn and the Sorbonne. After serving in RAF Intelligence, he returned to Cambridge as a Lecturer, Fellow and Director of Studies at Queens' College. In recent years he has become best known for his anthologies and translations, mainly from French and German, including Maupassant's *Bel Ami* and Fontane's *Effi Briest* in the Penguin Classics.

ÉMILE ZOLA

THE EARTH

[La Terre]

TRANSLATED WITH AN INTRODUCTION BY
DOUGLAS PARMÉE

PENGUIN BOOKS

Penguin Books Ltd, Harmondsworth, Middlesex, England
Viking Penguin Inc., 40 West 23rd Street, New York, New York 10010, U.S.A.
Penguin Books Australia Ltd, Ringwood, Victoria, Australia
Penguin Books Canada Limited, 2801 John Street, Markham, Ontario, Canada L3R 1B4
Penguin Books (N.Z.) Ltd, 182–190 Wairau Road, Auckland 10, New Zealand

—

This translation first published 1980
Reprinted 1981, 1982, 1984, 1986

—

—

Made and printed in Great Britain by
Hazell Watson & Viney Limited,
Member of the BPCC Group,
Aylesbury, Bucks
Set in Linotype Juliana

INTRODUCTION

ÉMILE ZOLA (1840–1902) first planned his vast cyclical series of novels, under the title *histoire naturelle et sociale d'une famille sous le Second Empire*, in the late sixties of the last century. While Balzac's *Comédie humaine* cast its vast shadow over the project, Zola's cycle, concerning five generations of the Rougon-Macquart family, was intended to be much more overtly and consciously 'scientific'. He had been greatly attracted to the ideas of the positivist philosopher Hippolyte Taine, who particularly stressed the influence of the physical over the psychological. Taine's conclusion that there are three main determinants of personality – *la race* (heredity), *le milieu* (environment) and *le moment* (not only the moment of time but the dynamic momentum of an age) – was eagerly accepted by Zola; and later on, under the influence of the great French physiologist Claude Bernard, he entertained far more nonsensical ideas, for example using the novel as a sort of laboratory to prove certain hypotheses. Fortunately, by the time he came to write *La Terre*, these scientific enthusiasms had considerably waned and despite the fact that a closed, materialistic agricultural community offered great scope for the observation of heredity and environment, Zola managed to resist this obvious temptation. The most superficial reading of his novel makes it plain that psychology is not ruthlessly sacrificed to physiology and that many, indeed most of his characters, despite the material pressures, lead vigorously independent mental and moral lives, often of considerable subtlety. The image of Zola as a depicter of mindless automata is sheer myth.

The idea of a peasant novel seems to have come late to Zola. His preliminary project on the cycle makes no mention of such a work nor is there any trace of it in the first genealogical tree in 1878. The family's representative in *La Terre*, Jean Macquart, was originally intended to figure only in *La Débâcle*, a later novel dealing with the Franco-Prussian war of 1870–71; indeed, in the last chapter of *La Terre* he is seen deciding to join up and 'bash a few Prussians', though in the event he is the one who is bashed.

Readers of *La Terre* who find him interesting – and Zola did his best not to make him too much of a pure accessory, even though he still seems rather unresolved – may like to know that he recovers from his wounds and in *Le Docteur Pascal*, the last novel of the series, he goes back to the land – in the less bleak region of Provence – remarries and rears a family. In *La Terre*, he has one distinguishing moral quality: unlike almost all the others, he is shown as capable of tenderness, in his relation with his future wife Françoise; as Jean is very much the outsider in this village community, is there not a suggestion here that tenderness is a luxury that peasants cannot afford? Be that as it may, the link between *La Terre* and the rest of the series is a tenuous one and the novel seems all the better for the fact that Zola steers clear of too much science and gives freer rein to his imagination.

Not until 1880, then, do we first find mention of *La Terre*, when at its very conception he announces that it is going to be his favourite work. His confidence was well-founded. By 1880 he had already written nearly half of his cycle, covering such fields as provincial life (Plassans, alias Aix-en-Provence); political intrigue in Paris; les Halles, the Parisian central food market (in his younger years Zola was something of a gourmand and his description of piles of French cheese is mouth-watering); the Parisian slums (*L'Assommoir*) and the life of high-class prostitution (*Nana*). Both of these last novels obtained such a *succès de scandale* that he would have been silly not to realize the market value of squalor and eroticism, and such considerations cannot have been completely absent from his mind in writing *La Terre*. However, before *La Terre* was published, he was to write five more novels, including studies of the urban middle classes, of artistic circles (which cost him the friendship of his old friend from Aix, Paul Cézanne) and also perhaps his best known work, *Germinal*, a novel situated in a northern French mining village. In a word, he had ranged very widely and was a master of his craft.

This craft was that of the naturalist, and it is in this light that we must now examine *La Terre*. Leaving aside the scientific pretensions already mentioned, naturalism in the novel revolves around one main concept: impartial truth to life through documentation. It is incumbent on the naturalist to acquire, from all sources – books, people, direct experience – all the knowledge indispensable to the content of his novel : as Zola wrote, 'Take what you know as a starting-point, firmly establish the terrain on which you'll be working.' Only from such a foundation can a novelist exercise his true creative function. How thorough, how systematic and how impartial was Zola in acquiring this knowledge? Our first answer, on the evidence available, is simple : he was not impartial, only partly systematic and his thoroughness was far from scholarly. To counteract such deficiencies, it must be added that he had two outstanding gifts : a genius for noting detail and a powerful creative imagination that could dispense with scholarly thoroughness. As far as knowledge of the peasantry was concerned, he had also a great number of excellent cards in his hand. He had grown up in the provinces, having spent his childhood in Aix-en-Provence. His mother came from a country family settled on the borders of Beauce and Zola speaks of listening avidly to his grandfather's conversation about this region – a factor that may well have weighed with him in his final choice of scene for the novel, after he had rejected certain other parts, such as Brittany, which he described as 'too dismal'. With hindsight, however, we can see how Beauce exactly fitted his bill, with respect to covering as broadly typical a canvas of peasant life as possible and suggesting the general through the particular. Quite apart from its convenient proximity to Paris, Zola found, when he went there for a few days in May 1886 with his plans for the novel already well advanced, precisely what he had hoped for : a smallish village beside a river (Romilly, which became Rognes in the novel), close to a market town (Cloyes in the novel but with similarities to Châteaudun) in which he could set up his middle-class characters, such as a doctor, a veterinary surgeon and a tax-inspector (taxes are very important for smallholders) as well as magistrates and law courts (for the law also plays a big role in *La Terre*). In Beauce there was a wide variety of farmers – large ones, some of them absentee landlords, struggling share-croppers, tenant farmers and peasants, smallholders scratching a laborious living, sometimes from a couple of acres or less of land – and many types of farming – sheep-rearing, small dairy-farming, forage crops and, most important, wheat, the very staff of life, for Beauce was the vast granary of France. There was another crop, smaller in extent but an equally important pillar of French society : the grape. So we find Bread and Wine almost as two protagonists of the novel. The latter in particular provides a lot of good, clean (or at least, not very dirty) fun in the novel: no reader can fail to be fascinated by the chapter devoted to the grape-picking scenes, when the laxative effect of eating too many grapes causes as many petticoats to be lifted as does, later on, for different reasons, the fuddling effect of drinking their juice. Chartres was also near by and useful to Zola not, oddly enough, for its superb cathedral but because it was large and, with its garrison, busy enough to support a brothel or two, which Zola reconnoitred during his visit. Zola's determination to make the novel not unrelievably gloomy is shown, incidentally, by his description of the Beauceron as 'gay', hardly the impression left by a first quick reading of the novel, despite the many moments of rather coarse fun.

Zola had already had far more direct and prolonged contact with French country manners and customs before his brief Beauce trip, although his notes from that trip show much acute and relevant observation. In 1877, following the resounding success of *L'Assommoir,* he had bought a large house in Médan, a village of less than 200 inhabitants, near Paris but not yet engulfed in the suburbs of the capital. He was henceforth to spend up to six months or more there every year. In 1881 he became for a short while (like a number of the characters of *La Terre*) a municipal councillor, although frequently an absentee one. There were farmers on the council and it is interesting to know that during his tenure of office there arose, as in *La Terre*, a question of building a new road and compensating owners for their expropriated land. Zola speaks of the secretiveness and suspicion of the local peasantry and of having as a result to resort to culling information and gossip from his servants. In his preliminary plans, we even find him using one or two local names for his characters.

All in all, therefore, his direct knowledge of French country life was not inconsiderable and probably superior to that of the background of any of his other novels in the series. His documentation from secondary sources is not easy to evaluate. He certainly consulted, if only cursorily, three or four general works on the history of French agriculture and rural population, one of which provided the basis for the long account of the French peasant through the ages (the symbolic Jacques Bonhomme) that occupies

8

such an important position towards the end of the first part of the novel and is clearly intended to place his characters in their proper social, economic and psychological perspective. But it is significant that the work shown by his notes to have most impressed him was a chapter from the very jaundiced *Pensées*, published in 1886, of an Abbé Roux, concerning his parishioners in a little village in the Corrèze. The similarities between Roux's peasants and Zola's are striking: they are tough, harsh and ungrateful, concerned solely with their own short-term interest, understanding only coercion and thus kowtowing to any established authority, superstitious, barely Christian though perhaps deists, childish, deceitful, stoical, mean and greedy (if someone else is paying): in a word, completely self-centred. Such nasty characteristics are understandable in a context of unremitting toil and grinding poverty. Roux's influence is significant, first because it is living source material about aspects of character – already the very stuff of a novel – and secondly because his disabused opinions chime in completely with Zola's temperament, for we must not forget that, despite his insistence on documentation, Zola defined the work of art as *un coin de la création vu à travers un tempérament*.

There remained one further type of source for the indefatigable Zola: direct discussion, through personal contact and correspondence. One of his important sources here was an interview which he engineered with the leading French socialist of the time, Jules Guesde, who enlightened him on many matters that recur constantly in the novel: the dangers inherent in the French system of inheritance, which led to ever-increasing subdivision of the land; the threat of imports of wheat and meat from the vast prairies of North America, undercutting the French market; the reluctance of the French peasant, because of conservatism, lack of capital or the poor profitability of his small plot, to embark on modern methods; in general, the precariousness of the peasants' lot and the miserable rewards for their endless toil. All these are constant threads throughout *La Terre* and there are at least three exponents of left-wing ideas in the novel: the republican 'Jesus Christ', still fired by the ideals of the 1848 Revolution; his buddy, the extremist Canon; and the frustrated, bullying schoolmaster who reveals himself at the end as the most anarchistic of all. Zola is obviously determined to offer not only an historical perspective

9

but glimpses of much broader problems that give an important extra dimension to La Terre, absent from many others of the cycle: a sense not only of the past but also of the future, giving an impression of timelessness in human affairs and matching the perennity of natural phenomena.

Not that Zola was unaware of the importance of le petit fait vrai to lend verisimilitude. Both his earliest notes for the novel and his observations from his trip to Beauce deal with just such petty yet indispensable details: peasants coming out with their lamps to inspect the damage after a hailstorm; a woman and a cow giving birth simultaneously; a father chasing a wayward daughter with his whip; the colour and texture of the soil; the changing light over the plain: all most important to ensure concreteness and vividness. In such a vast work, however, breadth and vigour of imagination, combined with meticulous planning, are equally important assets.

His planning was both broad and precise, as we can learn from his vast wad of notes for La Terre held in the Paris National Library. He starts from the grand premise that the heroine of the novel is Mother Earth herself, in all her moods, and he divides his work into five parts, covering a time-span of some ten years, into which he introduces every aspect of country life: the whole cycle of the seasons with their agricultural counterparts, starting with an autumn sowing and ending with a spring sowing, with, in between, all the manifold seasonal activities of manuring, reaping, haymaking, sheep-shearing and grazing, cattle-breeding, vine-growing, wine-making, all measured against the human cycle of birth, marriage (the first often precedes the second) and death, with the accompanying country events of markets, fairs, weddings, feasts, wakes, funerals and odd festivities that can only be described in the most familiar terms as booze-ups and blow-outs; village pump politics with their envies and jealousies and the basso continuo of crass self-interest; economics – chemicals versus old-fashioned muck (not only animal muck); machinery (liable to break down) against manual labour – the latter generally prevailing, for it is as cheap as muck in family farming; and finally politics, both national (protectionism versus free trade) and personal (the hated institution of ballot for conscription into the army and various ways of avoiding it). All this takes place against the essential backdrop of the weather, devastating hail and murderous summer heat, pallid springs and gorgeous Indian summers, chill winter rains and parched dusty autumns.

Stated in these terms, the novel sounds too carefully organized, but in fact Zola never works abstractly and all these aspects are realized in terms of human character: as Zola himself said, 'I want to write the living poem of the Earth; but in human terms, not symbolically.' For example, it is during the famous episode of autumn sowing that Jean first meets his future wife Françoise, accompanies her back to the farm and watches her take hold of the bull's pizzle and direct it into the cow – an episode that predictably aroused the ire of the prudish; and haymaking, with its mixture of toil and excitement and languor, is the occasion for Françoise, sweating and smelling of hay and *odor di femmina*, to jump down from a stack into Jean's arms, making him for the first time conscious of his desire for her, which grows into love; and during the threshing of the wheat by Françoise and Buteau, the rhythmic beating of their flails and pounding of their hearts smelts them into a single person long before Françoise has the ecstatic realization, after he has raped her, that he is the man she loves. So the set-pieces are also functional, even although we become a trifle bored with being told of the flatness and boundlessness and fertility of Beauce (Zola is rather heavy-handed in his attempts at being poetical); but it is also worth remembering, if we find some repetitiveness in description and in reference to events, that *La Terre* first appeared in serial form and this inevitably leads to repetition from one episode to the other.

For ordinary people (*pace* many linguisticians and others suffering from a surfeit of structuralism and certain other *isms*), important though background is, a novel stands or falls to a great extent by its plot and its characters, both of which must carry conviction. The point of departure of the plot is elegantly simple: an old peasant, Fouan, who has coveted and tended his acres like a man in love with a woman but has become too feeble to continue to look after them properly, decides to divide his land between his three children, so that it will continue to be well farmed. He is to receive from them a pension in return. Two of them, his daughter Fanny, who has already made a good match with a farmer, Delhomme, possessing more land than most, and his good-for-nothing drunkard of an elder son, whose beard and hair have earned him the ironical nickname of Jesus Christ, accept their share immediately; the third, Buteau (a name connoting, in the French *buté*, bloody-minded pigheadedness) for a while refuses, claiming that he has been diddled in the drawing of the lots. From the moment he dispossesses himself, Fouan's fate is sealed: a man without land is a man of no account. Only Delhomme pays him his pension regularly; Jesus Christ never pays him a penny and indeed sponges on him, as well as selling off his share of the precious, hard-earned family land to outside buyers – a heinous crime in such a close-knit community. Buteau eventually takes up his share when the building of a road enhances its value; he also marries his cousin Lise (by whom he has already had a son a couple of years before) because her land runs with his. Buteau is the real anti-hero of the novel: a bully like his father before him, he is also a randy goat, soon eager to add Françoise to his harem, not only because he lusts after her but also to maintain control of her land. He is also wily and a blatant and unrepentant liar, but he has redeeming qualities: he works like a slave – and indeed, like so many of the characters, he is a slave to the land – and he has a blunt joviality and sly sense of humour, even though his grin comes from a mouth framed in the ferocious jaws of a gorilla.

The heroine counterpart to Buteau is his cousin Françoise. It is notoriously difficult to make *jeunes filles* interesting, for 'nice' girls tend to be colourless: but Lise's sister Françoise is far from this. Her distinguishing characteristic, apart from the fresh beauty of her face and her sturdy peasant body, is a sense of justice, largely lacking in the other, completely utilitarian characters, except perhaps in her husband Jean, who, as an outsider, is relatively uncorrupted by the meanness and single-minded egocentricity of the peasantry. Yet even Françoise, as she lies dying, with her belly and unborn child slit by being thrown, deliberately and impulsively, by her sister Lise onto a scythe blade, refuses to make a will in her husband's favour, as in all fairness she should. Why should this be? Zola, like all good novelists, leaves an area of ambiguity: perhaps it is because she has discovered that she loves Lise's husband Buteau, perhaps because Jean is an intruder with no real right to Fouan property? Certainly it is a free personal choice and we are left in doubt as to the outcome until her last breath; we cannot feel that she has been entirely determined by either heredity or environment.

The main plot of the novel thus follows Fouan's downward path. When his wife dies, partly as a result of her son Buteau's brutality, he goes to live with Fanny but cannot bear the constant pinpricks of her cheeseparing meanness; from there he goes on to the Buteaus where he is at first fêted like a lord, for, well-treated, he could prove a profitable milch-cow. However, things go wrong when he takes Françoise's part against the lecherous Buteau, who is pestering her with his far from delicate attentions (he enjoys taking handfuls of her pubic hair). So Fouan moves to Jesus Christ's subterranean hideout in the tumbledown cellars of the old castle, only to move out again in terror when his host and particularly his daughter La Trouille institute hair-raising methods of surreptitiously searching not only his clothes but his body in an endeavour to uncover a packet of bonds that represent his nest-egg, saved from a lifetime of toil. He goes back to Lise where, after a vain attempt to assert himself and a dreadful experience (Zola had King Lear in mind) of exposure to the elements, he is reduced to impotent sullen silence until, enraged at his refusal to die and terrified because he had witnessed Françoise's murder, Lise and Buteau smother him and burn his body to make it appear accidental death: a scene all the more macabre in that, halfway through the burning, Fouan briefly revives and, from his eyes set in his charred face, glares with hatred at the criminal pair. Over-melodramatic? Perhaps: yet at about the time that Zola was launching into his novel, in the autumn of 1886, the trial took place at Blois of a man and his wife accused and found guilty of having thrust the wife's mother into the fireplace and holding her there, alive, until she had burned to death – a *cause célèbre* that Zola could hardly fail to know.

The most illustrious member of this respected Rognes family, which she terrorizes, is old Fouan's sister, Marianne, nicknamed La Grande, so despicable a matriarch as to be almost a caricature: her eyes are like a vulture's, her skeletally thin body shows no trace of her gluttony, and her cold-hearted implacability and meanness are such that when her daughter marries for love against her will and dies leaving two orphaned children, Palmyre and Hilarion, she refuses to have anything to do with them and, despite her relative wealth, lets them subsist in squalor and destitution. Hilarion, a deformed village idiot, is kept alive by his saintly sister, who accepts the hardest tasks in the fields and at the markets to provide for the two of them until, in one of the many unforgettable scenes in the book, she falls exhausted to the ground while harvesting and lies dead, crucified beneath the implacable sun. Her brother and lover (she has given him her body, since no one else could be expected to do so) howls like a dog for the whole night following her death, while La Grande seizes her chance of unpaid domestic labour to take him into her household as a beast of burden. Finally, infuriated as she belabours him for his clumsiness, he attempts to rape her (she is now in her late eighties) and has his skull split open with a cleaver for his pains. At the end of the novel, La Grande survives, serenely convinced that she has many years to live (and we feel she may be right), happy in the thought that she has, in any case, devised such an intricate will that the Fouan family will be at each other's throats for many a long year, enriching the lawyers by trying to sort out its complications.

A notable family, of which one further scion must be briefly mentioned: Fouan's son Jesus Christ does not follow in the family footsteps: he is an amiable, soft-hearted, drunken, lazy, greedy layabout of a poacher, obviously intended to supply some light relief. For example, though having few moral principles himself, he becomes infuriated when his (illegitimate) daughter sleeps around (being kind-hearted like her father) with the lads of the village; he then punishes such a blot on the family escutcheon by pursuing her across country with a horsewhip – a fine object lesson on the lack of deterrent power of corporal punishment. But Jesus Christ's outstanding and most amusing quality is his controlled anal flatulence, monumental in its proportions; he uses it to enliven parties, wins a competition against a presumptuous bumpkin from another village, and on one occasion produces so quintessentially concentrated a fart that it floors a bailiff's man like a gunshot. Zola has let his Rabelaisian imagination run riot, no doubt once more to provide some humorous counterpoint to the grimness of other members of the family.

There are numerous secondary characters, many of whom serve a similar funny or ironical purpose. Such are the Charles, rich retired townsfolk, highly regarded in the village, who are bringing up their granddaughter, as they had brought up their daughter, according to the strictest moral principles in a convent: it so happens that the source of all their considerable wealth (far greater than any peasant could hope to earn by a lifetime of toil) is a family brothel in Chartres. Zola's touch seems a trifle heavy here and the conversion of the shy, blushing virginal granddaughter into an assured married woman, highly efficient as a brothel-keeper, seems oversudden and implausible. Similarly the 'Cognet girl', Jacqueline, who from being the skivvy becomes the mistress of Hourdequin, representative of the progressive large farmer interested in new ideas of chemical fertilizers and machinery, seems almost too much of a nymphomaniac to be true. Zola still had a tendency to see the Scarlet Woman around him, a tendency which only vanished when he had established, a couple of years later, his liaison with his own servant, Jeanne Rozerot.

There are many other vivid, concretely realized, minor characters. We see the comical drunken gamekeeper and bell-ringer Bécu, the constant drinking companion, ironically enough, of the professional poacher Jesus Christ, who enjoys also the favours – perhaps services is the better word, for she is extremely ill-favoured – of the skinny Madame Bécu. There is Berthe, the daughter of one of two feuding innkeepers and their warring wives, nicely contrasted, one nastily bitchy, the other sluggishly apathetic – the lads of the village call her Berthe Not Got Any, for she is rumoured to be bald in parts hardly ever hairless, at least not in western Europe. How do they know, we wonder? And talking of fur, we must not forget that most human of animals – far nicer than some of the villagers – the intelligent donkey Gideon, who can open doors and knows that a good bucketful of wine is well worth drinking, even if it leads to his making an exhibition of himself in front of the shocked hypocritical Charles.

At the more respectable end of the scale there is the likeable priest Godard, the apoplectic and kind-hearted curé of a neighbouring parish ruthlessly exploited by the parishioners of Rognes, too mean to pay for a priest of their own and basically quite indifferent to religion or indeed God, yet insisting on his offering them regular Mass as well as providing them with church christenings, weddings and funerals. Poor Abbé Godard! His Daughters of

Mary are continually becoming pregnant . . . One of them goes off to Paris and becomes a successful high-class tart, although there are hints that she finishes up in hospital with an assortment of nasty diseases. Indeed, although the villagers of Rognes are depicted so unflatteringly, Zola seems to give the impression that both those who leave the village and those who come in from outside are less admirable or vigorous characters than those who, so to speak, grin and bear it. The rather cocky Nénesse, Fanny Delhomme's son, who goes off to the city and ends up as the Charles' son-in-law running the brothel, is far less sympathetic than the honest, bullet-headed Delphin, who stays on the land; the craven, seedy bailiff's man is no match for generous-hearted Jesus Christ, scoundrel that he is; even Jean Macquart himself, gentle, rather clumsy and easily led, is pale beside Françoise and Buteau. Country folk may be dreadful: but here beats a mighty heart that, after all, keeps the whole of France alive with its produce.

So we find in La Terre a lively canvas, grand and broad, peopled by characters who can be almost heroic in their evil and, certainly, humorous in their humanity, and who often have something of each; but is this splendid canvas, worthy of Hieronymus Bosch or Bruegel, painted in over-sombre colours? Or worse, is Zola's picture of French peasants under the Second Empire so nasty as to be obscene? Many of his contemporaries thought so, and while the novel was still appearing in serial form five of his naturalist colleagues and acquaintances launched their celebrated manifesto in which, while quite reasonably exposing some of Zola's more pretentious scientific claims, they attacked him hip and thigh on other grounds. His observation, they cried, was superficial and his technique was out of date. His narrative style was common and flat – they failed to realize that rhetoric or other fine writing needs to be deliberately eschewed in such a slice of life. But above all, they thought, Zola had descended to such depths of filth that La Terre read at times like a collection of scatology. They charitably attributed this wallowing in dirty rubbish first to Zola's kidney trouble, secondly to his excessive chastity (this seems a very French argument) and thirdly (this is perhaps where the shoe really pinched) to his successful preoccupation with writing books that would sell – near-pornography is obviously a means of achieving this end. In this connection, it is amusing to note that one of the signatories of the *Manifeste des cinq* had recently written a book on the long taboo subject of masturbation.

However, our times are less innocent or less hypocritical than the 1880s. No one is likely to be greatly shocked by *La Terre*, which is no more scandalous or obscene than daily reports of happenings in our free media, read by millions. Indeed, from the beginning there were percipient critics who brushed aside the manifesto and, ignoring the brutishness of certain scenes (for when people are treated like animals they will behave like them – or worse), they drew attention to the many positive aspects of the novel: the epic grandeur of the theme of birth and death and rebirth; the sharpness of Zola's observation of people and things; his sombre but intelligent appraisal of so many social, economic and political aspects of the nineteenth century – even if his chronology was faulty, for the sixties were in fact a time of prosperity, not of hardship, for French farmers.

Almost all critics use the term epic of this novel; some – including that outstanding doyen of Zola studies in England, Professor Hemmings, and the equally outstanding French Zola scholar, Guy Robert, who set the standard for all future Zola criticism in his masterly *La Terre d'Émile Zola* – have gone so far as to apply the adjective *tragic* to it. I find it difficult to agree: certainly the novel arouses pity but tragedy implies a tragic flaw in a character punished with undeserved severity. But how could Fouan, loving the land and unable to till it, do otherwise than divide it amongst his children? He did it, in fact, with his eyes open and his children, as it happened – particularly Buteau – were as mean and brutal and ruthless as old Fouan himself is described as having been in his youth. Françoise, too, brings her own fate on her head and she is shown as realizing this herself by refusing to break the unwritten family pact of solidarity and make a will in Jean's favour. In a word, all these characters are so much of the earth, earthy, so much part of the soil, that there can be no question of tragedy, perhaps barely even of pity. With the land, with the soil, everything that is has to be: a hailstorm is a hailstorm, just as rape is just rape and incest just incest – both shown, indeed, as the almost everyday occurrences that they may well be for peasants, events more common than people think, if less common than people say. All these things are built-in necessities of an existence in bondage to that hard and impartial taskmistress, Mother Nature – a taskmistress whom the peasants are shown, rightly or wrongly, as unwilling to exchange for any other.

Nor is everything in the novel pathetic squalor, although any joy is usually sensual rather than spiritual: the peasants can no more afford love than they can afford religion and their relationship to the land is certainly utilitarian rather than aesthetic. But the peasant has other qualities and other rewards. His toil, if it provides little pecuniary reward, receives some compensation from the rich yellow soil of Beauce and the golden glow of its wheat. And if life connotes death, in between the two there is room for many things, not all physical misery or sexual indulgence: there is courage and deep moral satisfaction, and if the novel strikes many a chord of harsh pessimism, it ends on a heroic note; for in the last chapter, in early spring, after old Fouan's grotesque funeral, with its ludicrously petty and superstitious squabbles about the siting of his grave, the reader's eye, like Jean Macquart's, is seized by the green expanse of winter wheat and, as at the beginning, the peasants, like tiny insects dwarfed by the boundless horizon of Beauce, are once again, as they always have done and always will do, making the eternal gesture of the sower casting the good seed on the land.

In retrospect, we can now see that Zola stood at the right point of time to produce what is certainly a masterpiece. Under the influence of realism – the desire to depict, in painting and literature, the hitherto neglected lower-middle and working classes in all their contemporaneity – the urban and rural proletariat had become an accepted subject. Such a depiction, which aimed at objective impartiality, was certain to appear both unflattering and bold: middle-class critics were bound to hold up their hands in horror at, for example, a writer who not only wrote about *coitus interruptus*, but described it in some detail – despite the fact that it must have been a universal practice as the poor man's contraceptive, and an important one when sex was the only free pleasure. So despite academic reservations about the solidity of his research, Zola's detailed, concrete and vivid observation – not necessarily, be it noted, of significant detail but frequently of meaningless detail, all the more effective and real because of its apparently random nature – creates a solid, satisfying effect of immediacy and

18

plausibility. We feel that any appeal to the heroic or to our pity springs from the plain, unvarnished nature of the tale: we might be reminded of Courbet's paintings of the rural proletariat, such as the *Casseurs de pierres*, crouched and awkward at their toilsome yet so necessary task. And this is, I think, ultimately the sort of general image that remains with the modern reader, long after many details have faded from his mind; not so much the set passages, sometimes a trifle ponderous, but the honest, relatively balanced depiction, in its unspoken heroism as well as in its inevitable wretchedness, of a class that is at last granted citizen's rights in the serious novel. How true is this imaginative picture? Let us leave the last word to the inhabitants of Rognes/Romilly themselves. Zola's son-in-law went back there fifty years after the publication of *La Terre*. Were they appalled by the picture Zola had painted of them? Not at all: they knew the work well, they could quote episodes from it. Nowhere did he meet anyone who felt that Zola had blackguarded him and he adds, perhaps maliciously, that if nobody thought of recognizing himself in the novel, people were very ready to discover in it portraits of their neighbours . . .

DOUGLAS PARMÉE

PART ONE

Chapter 1

THAT morning, Jean had slung a blue canvas seedbag round his middle, and was holding it open with his left hand, whilst with his right he took out a handful of wheat and at every third step scattered it broadcast with a sweep of his arm. His heavy shoes sank into the rich, thick soil which clung to them as he strode along rhythmically swaying his body; and through the constant haze of golden seed, each time he cast you could see the red glow of two corporal's stripes on his old regimental tunic, which he was wearing out. He looked preternaturally tall as he walked slowly forward, alone in front of the harrow covering up the grain behind him and which was drawn by a pair of horses urged on by their driver, who kept cracking his long whip around their ears.

The field, situated at Les Cornailles and a bare couple of acres in extent, was not large enough for the owner of La Borderie, Monsieur Hourdequin, to have thought it worth-while to send out his mechanical seeder, which was being used elsewhere. In point of fact, the farm buildings themselves lay only about a mile and a half away in front of Jean as he moved up the field from the south to the north. Pausing at the end of the furrow, he lifted his head and stared blankly as he took a breather.

The low walls and the brown patch of old slate roof seemed lost at the edge of the plain of Beauce which reached out towards Chartres, for beneath the late October sky, vast and overcast, the rich yellow farmland, bare at this time of year, extended for a score of miles or more, its broad stretches of arable alternating with green expanses of clover and lucerne, with no sign of a hillock or a tree as far as the eye could see; everything merged and fell away over the far skyline, as curved and clear-cut as a horizon at sea. Only to the west was the sky fringed by a tiny strip of russet wood. Down the middle went the chalk-white road joining Châteaudun to Orléans, which ran dead straight for a good fifteen

21

miles, geometrically marked by its line of telegraph poles. And that was all, except for three or four wooden windmills, with idle sails, perched on their timber frames. A few villages were scattered about like little islands of stone and in the distance the steeple of an invisible church would emerge from a fold in the ground, hidden in the gentle undulations of this land devoted exclusively to wheat.

Jean now turned back and set off once again, this time from north to south, his left hand still holding open the bag while his right swept through the air and dispersed its cloud of seed. Directly ahead of him now lay the narrow little valley of the Aigre, cutting through the plain like a dyke, while beyond it the flat lands of Beauce began once again, their vast expanses stretching as far as Orléans. The only hint of meadows or shade was a row of tall poplars whose yellowing heads, protruding from the hollow, looked like low bushes, on a level with the banks of the stream.

Of the little village of Rognes, built on the slope, there could be glimpsed only a few rooftops, huddled round the church whose tall steeple, of grey stone, provided a venerable haunt for families of rooks. And to the east, beyond the Loir where the chief town of the canton, Cloyes, lay concealed five miles away, the low hills of the Perche rose up in the distance, purple against the slate-grey sky. This was formerly the region of Dunois which nowadays formed part of the administrative district of Châteaudun : lying between Perche and the extreme edge of Beauce, its poor fertility had earned for it the title of the bad lands.

When Jean reached the end of the field, he stopped once more and cast his eye down along the Aigre, a swift clear stream flowing between meadows parallel to the Cloyes road : and he could see the procession of carts coming in from the country on their Saturday morning market day. Then he turned again and went back up the field. And he continued in this way, up and down, from north to south and then back, always at the same pace and with the same sweeping gesture, enveloped in the living cloud of grain, while behind him at the same gentle, almost meditative, pace, the harrow buried the seed to the sound of the cracking whip. Long spells of wet weather had held up the autumn sowing; the fields had already been newly manured in August and the land had long been ready for the plough, its deep soil, cleaned of unwholesome weeds, ripe to produce its crop of wheat following the rotation of clover and oats. So the fear of the coming frosts, potentially damaging after so much rain, had spurred on the activity of the farmers. The weather had suddenly turned cold and windless and a pitch-black sky spread a sombre, even light over this still ocean of land. They were sowing everywhere: another sower was working three hundred yards away to the left and yet another further along to the right; and for miles around, others and yet others could be seen sinking from sight and receding into the distance over the level ground ahead, tiny black figures, mere lines which grew thinner until they were finally lost from view. But all of them made this same gesture of casting the seed which you could sense floating in the air around them like a living wave. And even in the distance where all was blurred and the scattered sowers could no longer be seen, the plain was still quivering beneath it.

Jean was on his way down the field for the last time when he spied a large brown and white cow coming from Rognes and led on a rope by a girl, barely more than a child. This little cowgirl and her charge were following the path which ran parallel to the valley at the edge of the plateau; and Jean, going up the slope with his back turned, had just finished his sowing when the sound of running mingled with stifled cries made him raise his head as he was untying his seedbag in preparation for leaving. The cow had bolted and was galloping away through a patch of lucerne, followed by the girl, who was making desperate efforts to hold her back. Afraid that she might come to harm, he shouted:

'Let her go!'

She ignored him and continued to hurl breathless abuse at the cow in an angry, scared voice:

'Coliche! Now, Coliche, do be good! Oh, you stupid cow! You silly stupid cow!'

Till then, by dint of running and jumping as fast as her little legs would carry her, she had managed to keep up with the cow. But now she stumbled and fell, picked herself up for a few more steps and then fell down again; and as the animal then took fright, she was dragged along the ground. She was shrieking now and her body was leaving a trail in the lucerne.

'Let her go, for heaven's sake!' Jean kept crying. 'Let her go!' He was shouting automatically, through sheer fright, for by now he was running himself, having at last realized what was wrong: the rope must have caught round her wrist and was being drawn tighter at every jerk. Fortunately, by cutting across a corner of ploughed field he was able to come round in front of the cow and ran towards her so fast that, bemused and scared, she came to a sudden halt. Quickly he undid the rope and made the girl sit up in the grass.

'No bones broken?'

She had not even fainted. She got to her feet, felt herself all over, calmly pulling her skirt up over her thighs to look at her knees, which were smarting; she was still too breathless to speak.

'That's where it caught me, see? Anyway, I'm all in one piece, it's not too bad. My goodness, what a scare. If I'd been on the path I'd have been cut to ribbons.'

And examining the wrist which had been caught in the rope and had a red weal all round it, she moistened it with spittle and sucked it, adding with a sigh of relief and already on her way to recovery:

'Coliche isn't really bad, only she's been giving us trouble all this morning because she's on heat. I'm taking her to the bull at La Borderie.'

'At La Borderie?' Jean repeated. 'That's lucky, I'm going back there myself, I'll come along with you.' He continued to speak to her familiarly, treating her like a little child, since for all her fourteen years she was very slight in build. Meanwhile, with her chin in the air, she was looking up at this sturdy young man with his regular, rounded features and close-cropped brown hair; at twenty-nine, he was already an old man to her.

'Oh, I know who you are, you're the Corporal, the carpenter who's taken a job at Monsieur Hourdequin's.'

Hearing this nickname which the locals had given him, the young man gave a smile; and he in turn looked at her more closely, intrigued by the signs which showed that she was already almost a young woman. Her firm little breasts were starting to fill out; and her deep dark eyes were set in a long face with pink fleshy lips like fresh ripening fruit. She was wearing a skirt and black woollen bodice, and had a round cap on her head; her skin was a dark golden brown, tanned by the sun.

'You must be old Mouche's youngest daughter!' he exclaimed. 'I

24

didn't recognize you. Wasn't your sister going around with Buteau last spring when he was working with me at La Borderie?'

She replied simply:

'Yes, that's right, I'm Françoise. My sister Lise did go out with cousin Buteau and now she's six months pregnant. He cleared off to Orgères, to the Chamade farm.'

'Yes, that's right,' Jean agreed. 'I saw them together.'

And they stood facing each other for a moment in silence, he laughing because he'd caught the two love-birds together one evening behind a haystack, she still moistening her bruised wrist as if her wet lips would relieve the soreness. Meanwhile the cow was calmly tearing up tufts of lucerne in a neighbouring field. The driver had gone off with his harrow, taking a roundabout way to the road. You could hear two rooks cawing as they wheeled monotonously round the steeple. In the dead still air, the angelus bell tolled three times.

'Good Lord! Twelve o'clock already,' exclaimed Jean. 'Let's get a move on.'

Then, catching sight of Coliche in the field:

'I say, your cow's trespassing. Suppose someone saw her. You wait, you stupid cow, I'll show you what's what.'

'No, leave her alone,' said Françoise, stopping him. 'That piece of land belongs to us. She made me fall over on a bit of our own land, the silly cow! All that side belongs to the family as far as Rognes. We go from here over to there, then next to that comes Uncle Fouan's and after that it's my aunt's, La Grande!'

While she was pointing out the various fields, she led the cow back onto the path. It was not until she was holding her by the rope again that she thought of thanking the young man.

'Anyway, I'm terribly grateful to you. Thanks ever so.'

They had started to go along the narrow path which ran beside the valley before branching off into the fields. The last peal of the angelus bell had just died away in the distance and only the rooks were left cawing. And as they followed behind the cow, who was tugging at her rope, neither of them could find anything more to say; they had fallen silent in the way of country people who can walk side by side for hours without exchanging a word. They glanced towards a mechanical seeder as its horses swung round beside them on their right, the driver called out 'Good morning' and they replied 'Good morning', in the same serious tone. Down below to their left, the carts were still going along the road to Cloyes, for the market did not start till one o'clock. They bumped along on their two wheels, like little jumping insects, looking so tiny in the distance that you could make out only the white dot of the women's caps.

'That's Uncle Fouan over there with my Auntie Rose,' said Françoise, catching sight of a carriage no larger than a walnut driving along the road a good mile and a half away.

She had the sailor's or the plainsman's ability to see things and pick out details far away, recognizing a man or an animal when there was nothing to see but a little moving speck in the distance.

'Oh yes, I heard about that,' Jean replied. 'So old Fouan's made up his mind at last, he's going to split up his land between his daughter and his two sons?'

'Yes, he's finally made up his mind, they're all meeting at Monsieur Baillehache's today.'

She was still watching the cart moving away down the road.

'It's no skin off our nose, because it's not going to affect us one way or the other. But there is Buteau. My sister thinks that perhaps he'll marry her, when he's got his share.'

Jean laughed. 'Ah, Buteau's a lad! He and me were pals. He was always ready to lead the girls up the garden path. He can't do without them, though, and if they don't come quietly he's not above using a bit of force.'

'He really is a pig!' Françoise exclaimed forcefully. 'No one plays a dirty trick like that on your cousin by leaving her in the lurch when she's six months pregnant!'

Then with a sudden burst of temper:

'You just wait, Coliche! I'm going to give you something you won't forget! She's at it again, there's no holding her when she's in this state.'

She violently tugged at the cow. At this point the path left the edge of the plateau and the carts disappeared, while they both continued to follow the plain where all they could see was the interminable expanse of farmland stretching away in front of them. The path went along on the level between the arable and the artificial meadows, without a single bush, up to the farm which seemed almost close enough to reach out and touch but which continually retreated under the ashen sky. They had fallen silent again, as if weighed down by this pensive, solemn plain of Beauce, so melancholy and so fertile.

When they reached the big square farmyard of La Borderie, enclosed on three sides by cowsheds, sheepfolds and barns, it was deserted. But a short, pretty, saucy-looking young woman quickly appeared at the kitchen door.

'Well, Jean, aren't we getting anything to eat this morning?'

'I'm on my way, Madame Jacqueline.'

This was the daughter of the local roadmender Cognet and everybody used to call her Cognette at the time when she had been taken on as scullery maid at the age of twelve; but ever since she had been promoted to become not only the farmer's servant but his mistress, she had developed autocratic tendencies and insisted on being treated as a lady.

'Oh, there you are, Françoise,' she went on. 'You've come for the bull . . . Well, you'll have to wait. The cowman's at Cloyes with Monsieur Hourdequin. But he'll be back soon, he should have been here already.'

And as Jean, with some reluctance, was making his way into the kitchen, she put her hand on his waist and jokingly rubbed up against him, unconcerned whether anyone was watching, greedy for love and not satisfied with just her master.

Left alone, Françoise sat waiting patiently on a stone bench in front of the dung-pit which took up a third of the farmyard. She stared blankly at a group of hens warming their feet as they pecked over the low, wide layer of manure which was emitting a slight blue haze in the cool air. Half an hour later when Jean reappeared, finishing off a slice of bread and butter, she was still there. He sat down beside her and as the cow was restless, flicking herself with her tail and lowing, he said at last:

'It's annoying that the cowman hasn't come back yet.'

The girl shrugged her shoulders. She was not in any hurry. Then, after a fresh silence:

'Well, Corporal, everyone calls you just Jean. Is that your only name?'

'No, of course not. I'm Jean Macquart.'

'And you don't come from these parts?'

'No, I'm from Provence, a town called Plassans.'

She had looked up at him to examine him more closely, surprised that anyone could have come from such a faraway place.

'Eighteen months ago, after Solferino,' he went on, 'I got my discharge and came back from Italy and a pal persuaded me to come up here. And then I got fed up with being a carpenter and, what with one thing and another, I stayed on at the farm.'

'I see,' she said without further comment, still watching him with her large dark eyes. But at that moment, Coliche, who was becoming frantic, gave an extra long despairing 'moo' and a hoarse panting could be heard behind the closed cowshed door.

'Good God!' exclaimed Jean. 'Old Caesar's heard her . . . Hark at him talking away in there. Oh, he knows what's what, you can't bring any cow into the yard without him smelling her and knowing what he's got to do!'

He stopped short.

'You know, the cowman must have stayed behind with Monsieur Hourdequin. If you like, I'll get the bull out for you. The two of us could manage together.'

'Yes, that's an idea,' said Françoise, standing up.

As he was opening the door, he asked her:

'How about Coliche? Do we need to tie her up?'

'Tie her up? Goodness no, it's not worth it! She's ready and no mistake, she won't budge an inch!'

When the door was opened, they saw two rows of cows each side of the central passageway, the whole thirty of them, some lying on their litters, others munching beetroot from their trough; and in his corner, one of the bulls, a black and white Friesian, stood straining his head forward, expectantly.

As soon as he was untied, Caesar came slowly out. But suddenly he halted, as though surprised at finding himself in the open air and in broad daylight, and for a minute he stood stock-still, tense, nervously twitching his tail, his outstretched neck swelling as he sniffed the air. Lowing more gently, Coliche stood motionless, staring at him with her big eyes. Then he sidled up to her and abruptly pressed his head roughly against her rump; his tongue was hanging out and pushing her tail to one side, he licked her all the way down her thighs; her skin could be seen rippling and quivering although she kept quite still as she let him do it. Jean

28

and Françoise watched intently, their arms dangling limply at their sides.

And when he was ready, Caesar suddenly heaved himself up on to Coliche, so heavily and violently that the ground shook. She stood firm as he gripped her sides between his two legs. But she was a tall Cotentin cow, too broad and high for a bull of less powerful breed to reach. Caesar felt this and was helplessly trying to raise himself up.

'He's too tiny,' said Françoise.

'Yes, a bit,' said Jean. 'Never mind, he'll manage it in time.'

She shook her head, and as Caesar was still groping and tiring himself, she took a decision.

'It's no good, he's got to be helped. If he doesn't get in properly, it'll be wasted because she won't be able to hold it.'

Carefully, as though undertaking something of great importance, she stepped quickly forward with pursed lips and set face; her concentration made her eyes seem even darker. She had to reach right across with her arm as she grasped the bull's penis firmly in her hand and lifted it up. And when the bull felt that he was near the edge, he gathered his strength and, with one single thrust of his loins, pushed his penis right in. Then it came out again. It was all over; the dibble had planted the seed. As unmoved and as fertile as the earth when it is sown, the cow had stood four square and firm as the male seed spurted within her. Not even the bull's last powerful thrust had unsteadied her. And now he had already slipped down from her back, making the ground shake again.

Françoise had released her grip but was still holding her arm in the air. Finally, she let it drop, saying:

'That's that.'

'And very nice too,' added Jean emphatically, with something of the satisfaction of a good workman seeing a job well and quickly done.

It never entered his head to make the sort of bawdy jokes which the farmhands indulged in when girls used to bring their cows to be covered. This young girl seemed to find it so completely normal and necessary that, in all decency, there was really nothing to laugh about. It was just natural.

But Jacqueline had been standing watching at the door again, and with a typical throaty chuckle she called out cheerfully :

'Hi there, where've you been sticking your hand? I suppose your sweetheart hasn't got an eye at that end !'

Jean gave a guffaw and Françoise, embarrassed, turned suddenly red in the face and to hide her confusion, as Caesar went back of his own accord into the shed and Coliche stood nibbling at some oats growing on the dungheap, she fumbled in her pockets until she found her handkerchief, and undid one of the corners in which she had tied the two francs to pay for the bull.

'Here's your money,' she said. 'And good afternoon to you.'

She went off with her cow and, picking up his bag again, Jean followed her, telling Jacqueline that, in accordance with Monsieur Hourdequin's instructions for his day's work, he was going off to Post Field.

'All right,' she replied, 'the harrow should be down there by now.'

Then, as the young man caught up with the girl and the two of them went off in single file down the narrow path, she called after them in her coarse, fruity voice:

'You won't worry if you both lose your way, will you? She knows how to find it.'

Once more, the farmyard was deserted. This time, neither of them had laughed. They walked on slowly, the silence broken only by their shoes scuffing the stones. All that he could see of her were the little black curls on the nape of her neck, like a child's, under her round cap. Finally, after they had walked about fifty yards, Françoise said soberly :

'It's wrong of her to try and make fun of people, about men. I could have told her . . .'

And she turned towards the young man and looked up mischievously into his eyes :

'It's true, isn't it, that she's deceiving Monsieur Hourdequin, just like she was already married to him? I suppose you might know something about that yourself, mightn't you?'

He looked flustered and a little silly.

'Well, she can please herself, that's her business.'

Françoise had turned round and started walking again.

'Yes, that's true enough. I'm joking because you're almost old enough to be my father and it doesn't really matter . . . But, you see, ever since Buteau played that dirty trick on my sister, I swore that I'd do anything rather than have a sweetheart.'

Jean shook his head and they fell silent. Post Field, a small one, lay at the end of the path, halfway to Rognes. When he reached it, he stopped. The harrow was waiting and a bag of seed had been emptied into a furrow. As he filled his seedbag from it he said :

'Well, goodbye then.'

'Goodbye,' Françoise replied. 'And thanks again.'

But a thought suddenly struck him, and he stood up and shouted after her :

'I say, suppose Coliche misbehaves again, would you like me to come along with you to the farm ?'

She was already some distance away and she turned and called out in her calm voice which echoed over the silent countryside :

'No, there's no need, she won't be any trouble now. She's got all she wanted !'

With his bag of seed slung round his middle, Jean had started walking down the ploughed field, casting the corn with a regular sweep of his hand; and lifting his head, he watched the tiny figure of Françoise growing smaller and smaller as she went far away across the fields, with her large, placid cow lumbering in front. As he turned to come back up the slope she was hidden from sight, but as he went down a second time he could pick her out again, even smaller this time and so slender with her slim waist and white cap that she looked like a daisy. Three times this happened and each time she appeared smaller; then after that, when he looked for her, she must have turned off by the church.

It struck two o'clock. The sky was still dull and grey and icy, as though the sun had been buried beneath shovelfuls of fire-ash for months to come, until next spring. In this general bleakness, you could see a brighter patch in the cloud lighting up the sky towards Orléans, as though the sun were shining somewhere over there, miles and miles away. The steeple of Rognes church stood out against this livid break in the cloud while the village nestled unseen on the hidden slope, which dropped down to the little valley of the Aigre. But to the north, in the direction of Chartres, the skyline still remained clear cut and inky black, like a penstroke cutting across a wash drawing, between the monotonous ash-grey sky and the interminable rolling plain. Since lunchtime, the number of sowers seemed to have increased. Now every tiny plot of land could boast one; they had proliferated like disorderly swarms of black ants toiling confusedly at some giant task quite disproportionate to their size; and even with those further away, you could still distinguish the same stubborn, monotonous gesture, like so many insects, engaged in an implacable struggle against the vast expanse of earth, who finally triumph over their immense task, and over life.

Jean continued sowing until nightfall. After Post Field came Ditch Field and then Crossways Field. Up and down he walked over the ploughed land with steady stride; and as the wheat in his bag diminished, so behind him the good seed fructified the land.

Chapter 2

THE house of Maître Baillehache, the Cloyes notary, was in the
Rue Grouaise on the left of the Châteaudun road. It was a small,
single-storey dwelling at one corner of which hung the cord for
lighting the only lamp in this broad paved street. Deserted during
the week, it came to life on Saturday when people poured into
market from the countryside around. The two resplendent escut-
cheons stood out from afar against the long low chalk-white
buildings; at the back, a narrow garden sloped down to the
Loir.

On this Saturday the office-boy, a pale and puny youngster of
fifteen, had lifted one of the muslin curtains of the main office,
which looked out on to the street, and was watching the passers-
by. The two other clerks, one of them paunchy, old and extremely
grubby, the other younger, gaunt and bilious-looking, were writing
on a very large ebonized pine table; and together with seven or
eight chairs and an iron stove (which was never lit until December, even when snow had fallen by All Hallows) this table con-
stituted the sole furniture of the room. The pigeon-holes covering
the walls, the dirty green cardboard boxes with dented corners,
overflowing with faded yellow files, filled the room with a nauseat-
ing smell of stale ink and ancient dusty papers.

Meanwhile, two peasants, a man and a woman, were sitting
quite still, patiently waiting in respectful silence. The sight of so
much paper and, above all, of these gentlemen writing at high
speed with their pens scratching in unison, inspired solemn
thoughts of money and lawsuits. The woman, thirty-four years old
and very dark, had a pleasant face marred by a big nose. Her toil-
worn hands were crossed over her loose black woollen jacket with
velvet hems; her quick eyes kept darting into every corner of the
room, obviously fascinated by all the property deeds that were
slumbering there; while the man, five years her senior, red-haired
and placid, wearing black trousers and a long brand-new linen
smock, sat holding his round felt hat on his lap, betraying not the
slightest glimmer of thought on his broad, close-shaven, nut-brown.

33

face in which two large china-blue eyes were staring with bovine passivity.

But at this moment a door opened and Maître Baillehache, who had just finished lunching with his brother-in-law, the farmer Hourdequin, appeared, very red in the face, still fresh-looking despite his fifty-five years, with thick lips and little slit eyes whose crinkles gave him the appearance of perpetually smiling. He was wearing spectacles and kept tugging all the time at his long grizzled whiskers.

'Ah, there you are, Delhomme,' he said. 'So old Fouan has decided to share out his property.'

It was the woman who replied:

'That's right, Monsieur Baillehache. We've all arranged to meet here to come to an agreement and for you to tell us what's to be done.'

'Good, Fanny, we'll see to that ... It's only just one o'clock, we'll have to wait for the others.'

He chatted on for a few moments, enquiring about the price of wheat, which had been falling over the past couple of months, and showing the friendly consideration due to a man such as Delhomme, who farmed some fifty acres, had a hired hand and kept three cows. He then went back into his own office.

The clerks had kept their noses to their desk, scratching away more urgently than ever, and once again the Delhommes sat waiting without a movement. This young woman, Fanny, had been lucky to find a sweetheart ready to marry her who was not only a nice young man but rich into the bargain; she had not even been pregnant and could hardly have had expectations of more than eight acres or so from old Fouan, her father. What was more, her husband had not come to regret the marriage because he could never have found a more intelligent or more active helpmate; so much so, indeed, that he followed her lead in everything he did. His own intelligence was strictly limited, although he was always so calm and direct that people in Rognes often thought that it was he who made the decisions.

At this moment the office-boy who was looking out into the street put his hand to his mouth to stifle a laugh and murmured to his neighbour, the clerk who was very dirty and pot-bellied:

'It's Jesus Christ!'

Fanny leaned sharply forward and whispered in her husband's ear:

'Don't forget, leave everything to me ... I'm very fond of Mother and Father but I'm not going to let them rob us, and we must look out for Buteau and that good-for-nothing Hyacinthe.'

She was talking about her two brothers, the elder of whom she had just seen through the window: Hyacinthe was known to all and sundry by his nickname Jesus Christ; a lazy, drunken fellow who on his return from military service – he had fought in Africa – had refused to settle down or accept regular employment and now made his living by poaching and pilfering as though still looting poor defenceless Arabs.

In he came, a tall, strapping, curly-headed, powerfully built man in the full prime of his forty years; his long, pointed, unkempt beard made him look like Jesus Christ but a Christ on whose face life had left its mark; the face of a drunkard not above raping women and waylaying men. He had spent the morning in Cloyes and was already drunk; he wore muddy trousers, a stained and filthy smock, a ragged cap pushed back on his head and he was chewing a cheap, foul-smelling, soggy black cigar. And yet in his bleary handsome eyes you could detect the sense of fun and generosity of heart often met with in dissolute but good-natured rogues.

'Haven't my father and mother arrived yet, then?' he enquired.

And when the thin, bilious-looking clerk replied with an angry shake of his head, he stood for a second looking at the wall, holding his smoking cigar in his hand. He had not bothered even to look at his sister and brother-in-law who, for their part, seemed not to have noticed his arrival. Then, without another word, he went outside and stood waiting on the pavement.

'Oh Jesus Christ, oh Jesus Christ!' chanted the office-boy, looking out towards the street and seemingly more amused than ever by this nickname which reminded him of so many different funny stories.

But five minutes had barely elapsed before the Fouans arrived, slow and cautious in their movements as befitted an elderly couple. The father, formerly so sturdy, had, through age – he was seventy years old – hard work and his devouring and dried-up passion for the soil, become so shrunken that his body was now bent as though anxious to return to that soil which he had owned and coveted so fiercely. Nevertheless, apart from his legs, he was still in good shape, trim with his little white whiskers and neat side-boards and the long family nose which gave a sharp look to his wizened, leathery face. His wife, shadowing him closely and never letting him out of her sight, was shorter and seemed to have re-mained plump; her paunch showed incipient signs of dropsy and her round eyes and mean, round mouth, tightly clenched, with countless tiny pouches and wrinkles, were set in a face the colour of oatmeal. A stupid woman, reduced to a mere submissive and hard-working beast of burden in the family, she had always been afraid of her dictatorial and despotic husband.

'Ah, there you are then!' exclaimed Fanny, standing up.

Delhomme had also risen to his feet. And behind the old couple, Jesus Christ had just appeared, swaying and not saying a word. He stubbed out the end of his cigar and stuffed the foul, smoking weed into a pocket of his tunic.

'So here we are,' said Fouan. 'All except Buteau. Never on time, always wanting to be different, that young fellow-me-lad.'

'I saw him in the market,' Jesus Christ said in his drink-sodden husky voice. 'He's on his way.'

Buteau, aged twenty-seven, the youngest of the family, was so called because of his unruly nature, always rebellious and head-strong in his ideas, which were never shared by anyone else. Even as a lad he had never been able to get on with his parents, and later, having escaped military service by the luck of the draw, he had left home and found a job first at La Borderie and then at La Chamade.

His father was still complaining when in he came, lively and cheerful. He had inherited the large Fouan nose, but in his case it was flat; and in the lower part of his face his jawbones jutted out like those of some great carnivorous beast. He had receding temples and the whole of the top of his head was narrow, while behind the cheerful grey eyes you could detect a latent craftiness and violence. He had his father's ruthless greed and sagacity aggra-vated by his mother's cheeseparing meanness. Every time they quarrelled and his two old parents bitterly admonished him, he would reply: 'You shouldn't have made me that sort of person.'

36

'Look here, it's twelve miles from La Chamade to Cloyes,' he retorted in reply to their protests. 'So what? I've arrived at the same time as you . . . You going to start getting at me again?'

And so they all started quarrelling, bawling at each other in voices used to talking in open spaces, arguing over their business exactly as if they were at home. Hindered in their work, the clerks kept casting sidelong glances at them, when, hearing the uproar, the notary opened his study door and came in again:

'Is everyone here? Come along in!'

The study overlooked the garden, the narrow strip of land running down to the Loir, whose leafless poplars could be seen in the distance. An ornamental black marble clock stood on the mantelshelf between heaps of files; apart from this, there was only a mahogany desk, a filing cabinet and some chairs.

Maître Baillehache promptly sat down at this desk, like a judge on the bench, while his rustic clients filed in one by one, casting hesitant glances at the seats provided and embarrassed as to how and where they were to sit down.

'Do sit down!'

So, urged on by the others, Fouan and Rose found themselves sitting in two chairs in the front; Fanny and Delhomme sat down behind them, also side by side; Buteau took a seat by himself in a corner against the wall while only Hyacinthe remained standing in front of the window with his broad shoulders blocking the light. But losing patience the notary called out, addressing him familiarly by his nickname:

'Do sit down, Jesus Christ.'

He was forced to start the discussion himself:

'Well now, Père Fouan, you've decided to divide your property between your two sons and daughter?'

The old man made no reply, the others sat still, there was complete silence. However, the notary, being accustomed to such protracted deliberations, was in no hurry either. His practice had been in the family for a long time; the Baillehaches had handed it down from father to son in Cloyes for the last two hundred and fifty years and had learned from their peasant clientèle their calculating slyness and plodding caution, which submerged the slightest discussion in long silences and empty phrases. He had opened a penknife and was paring his nails.

37

'Isn't that right? We must assume that you have made up your minds,' he repeated finally, fixing his eyes on the old man.

The latter turned round and gazed at all the others before he replied, groping for the right words.

'Yes, that may be so, Monsieur Baillehache. I mentioned it to you at harvest-time and you told me to think it over a bit longer; and I have thought it over and I can see that it'll have to come to that.'

In halting sentences full of parentheses, he explained the reasons. But something he did not say, although it came through in the emotion that he was trying to conceal, was his immense grief, hidden resentment and appalling heartache at giving up this land which he himself had so greedily cultivated, with a passion that can only be described as lust, and had then added to, with an odd patch of land here and there at the cost of the most squalid avarice. A single piece of land would represent months of a bread-and-cheese existence, spending whole winters without a fire and summers drenched in sweat, with no respite from his toil save a few swigs of water. He had adored his land like a woman who will kill you and for whom you will commit murder. No love for wife or children, nothing human: just the Earth! And now he had grown old and, like his father before him, would have to hand over this mistress to his sons, furious at being so powerless.

'You see, Monsieur Baillehache, one's got to face facts, my legs aren't much good now and my arms aren't much better and blast it, it's the land that suffers. . . It might have been all right if we could have come to an arrangement with our children.'

He cast a glance towards Buteau and Jesus Christ, who were sitting quite still, staring into the distance, as though miles away from what he was saying.

'So what could I do? Take on help, strangers who would just strip us of everything? No, farm-hands cost too much, they eat up all your profit, these days. . . So I just can't go on. Take this last season: out of my twenty acres I hadn't the strength to farm more than a quarter of them, just enough to provide food, wheat for us and grass for our two cows. And it breaks my heart to see all that good land going to waste. Yes, I'd sooner pack it in than see something like that happen.'

38

His voice broke and he made a violent gesture of grief and resignation. Sitting beside him, crushed by half a century of obedience and work, his wife was listening humbly.

'The other day,' he went on, 'while Rose was making her cheese, she pitched headlong into it. As for me, it takes all my strength just to come into market with my cart. And what's more, you can't take the land with you when your time comes. You have to give it up, give it up. And anyway, we've done enough work, we want to die in peace . . . Isn't that right, Rose?'

'That's it, that's God's truth !' the old woman replied.

Once more silence fell, a long silence. The notary had nearly finished paring his nails. Finally he put his penknife down on the desk and said :

'Yes, those are sensible reasons, people often have to decide to give their land away. . . I should add that this represents a saving for a family because taxes on legacies are higher than those on gifts.'

Despite his pretence of indifference, Buteau could not help exclaiming :

'So that's true, Monsieur Baillehache?'

'Certainly it is. You stand to gain some hundreds of francs.'

The other stirred and even Delhomme's face lit up, while their mother and father joined in their satisfaction. Everything was all right; now that money would be saved, the deal could go through.

'All that remains is for me to make the usual comments,' the notary went on. 'Many right-thinking people condemn this way of disposing of property as being immoral because they feel that it destroys the bonds of the family. Indeed, it would be possible to cite most unfortunate situations; children sometimes behave very badly once their parents have divested themselves of their property.'

The two sons and the daughter were listening open-mouthed, blinking their eyes, their cheeks quivering with emotion.

'Then Father can keep the lot if he thinks like that about it,' Fanny snapped touchily.

'We've always done our duty,' said Buteau.

'And we're not afraid of hard work,' added Jesus Christ.

Maître Baillehache silenced them with a gesture.

'Do let me finish ! I know that you're good children and decent

39

workers, and that with you there's certainly no danger that your parents may live to regret what they have done !'

There was no irony in his remark; he was merely repeating the kindly formula that twenty years' exercise of his profession had brought smoothly to his lips. But even though she did not seem to have understood, their mother was looking from her daughter to her sons through her half-closed eyes. She had shown no tenderness to any of the three in their upbringing, treating them with the cold indifference of a housewife who blames her young ones for consuming so much of what she herself was scrimping to save. She bore a grudge against the youngest because he had left home just when he was beginning to earn; she had never been able to see eye to eye with her daughter, irked at having to deal with someone of her own sort, a lively, active girl in whom her father's intelligence had taken the form of pride : and her glance softened only when it settled on her first-born, that rogue who took neither after her nor her husband, a thorough bad lot. He had turned up from God knows where and, perhaps for that very reason, he was her favourite whom she always forgave.

Fouan had also looked at his children one after the other, dimly worried at what they might do with his property. The drunkard's laziness caused him less concern than the greedy love of pleasure of the other two. He shook his trembling head : what was the point of fretting, since it had to be done !

'Now that the decision's been taken to share out the land,' the notary went on, 'we must settle the terms. Are you agreed as to what annuity to pay ?'

At this, everybody suddenly sat still and silent again. Their weather-beaten faces took on the fixed expression and gravity of poker-faced diplomats about to discuss matters involving the fate of an empire. Then they cast a questioning glance at each other; but nobody was ready to speak. Once more it was the old man who explained the situation.

'No, we haven't talked it over yet, Monsieur Baillehache, we've been waiting until we were all gathered together here. . . But it's quite straightforward, isn't it? I've got twenty-five acres, or ten hectares they call it now. So if I let it out, that would be just one thousand francs at forty francs an acre.'

Buteau, the least patient of the three, jerked upright on his chair.

'What did you say? A hundred francs a hectare? Are you trying to have us on, Father?'

And they launched into the first argument, over figures. There was an acre and a half of vines: all right, you could get sixty francs for that. But would anyone ever give that amount for the fifteen acres of arable land and above all for the eight and a half acres of permanent meadow along the bank of the Aigre which produced such poor hay? The arable itself wasn't much to write home about, particularly one bit of it which ran along the edge of the plateau, because the soil was shallower the nearer you came to the valley.

'Really, Father,' said Fanny reproachfully, 'you mustn't try to take advantage of us.'

'It's worth forty francs an acre,' the old man kept repeating stubbornly, slapping his thigh with his hand. 'I can let it for forty francs tomorrow if I want to... And what do you think it's worth then, to you? Let's hear what you say it's worth.'

'It's worth twenty-five francs,' said Buteau.

Beside himself with fury, Fouan was insisting on his price and launching into an extravagant eulogy of his land, such good land that it produced wheat without needing any cultivation at all, when Delhomme, who had hitherto said nothing, spoke up, in his honest way:

'It's worth thirty francs, not a penny more or less.'

The old man immediately calmed down.

'All right! Let's say thirty francs, I'm prepared to make a sacrifice for my children.'

But Rose had tugged her husband's smock and now spoke up herself, to say just one word summing up all her natural meanness:

'No!'

Jesus Christ had lost interest. Ever since his five years spent in Africa, he was no longer concerned about the land. He was keen on one thing only, getting hold of his share and turning it into cash. So he continued to sit swaying gently, with a superior, mocking air.

'I said thirty francs,' Fouan was shouting, 'and I mean thirty francs. My word's always been my bond. Twenty-five acres, let's see, that makes seven hundred and fifty francs, let's say eight hundred in round figures ... eight hundred francs, that's fair.'

Buteau burst into a loud guffaw while Fanny was shaking her head in protest, as though unable to believe her ears. And Monsieur Baillehache, who had been staring vaguely into the garden since the beginning of the argument, now returned to his clients and seemed to be listening to them as he tugged away obsessively at his whiskers and sleepily digested his excellent luncheon.

However, this time the old man was right: it was a fair price. But by now feelings were running high; it was terrifying to see how the children, carried away by their passionate urge to strike the best possible bargain, went on haggling and swearing like crafty peasants buying a pig.

'Eight hundred francs,' sneered Buteau. 'So you want to live like a fine gentleman? Eight hundred francs! It's enough for a family of four! Why don't you admit straight away that you want to eat yourself to death?'

Fouan was still able to control his temper. He considered haggling quite a natural thing and so merely stood firm against this attack, which he had anticipated; his own blood was up as well, and he now spelt out bluntly all his own demands:

'Just a second. That's not everything. We shall keep the house and garden until we die, of course... And as we shan't be harvesting any more crops, we want a barrel of wine every year, a hundred logs of firewood as well as three gallons of milk, a dozen eggs and three cheeses every week.'

'Oh, Father!' Fanny moaned in tones of shocked anguish, 'oh, Father!'

As for Buteau, he considered the discussion over. He had sprung to his feet and was walking up and down gesticulating wildly; he had even jammed his cap onto his head, all ready to leave. Jesus Christ had also stood up, anxious in case all this arguing might prevent the deal from going through. Only Delhomme remained quite unmoved, resting his finger against his nose in an attitude of deep thought and quiet exasperation.

At this point Monsieur Baillehache felt it was necessary to

hasten things along a little. He shook off his torpor and, rummaging even more vigorously in his whiskers, said:

'You know, don't you, that wine and firewood as well as the cheese and eggs are customary?'

But he was cut short by a battery of acid comment:

'Do we drink our own wine? We sell it!'

'Doing damn all and sitting warm and cosy is all very well while your children are tearing their guts out!'

The notary, who had heard all this before, continued placidly:

'All that has nothing to do with it... For God's sake, Jesus Christ, can't you sit down! You're blocking the light, it's getting on my nerves! So you're all agreed, then? You'll pay those items in kind, because otherwise people will think you're being mean... So the only thing that remains to be discussed is the amount of the annuity.'

Delhomme at last indicated that he had something to say. Everyone had sat down again and they all listened attentively as he slowly spoke:

'Excuse me, but what Father is asking seems quite fair to me. We could let him have eight hundred francs since he'd be able to let his property for that amount... But we're not calculating like that. He's not letting his land to us, he's giving it to us, and the calculation we've got to make is how much he and Mother need to live on... That and nothing more, what they need to live on.'

'That's it,' the notary approved, 'that's what they usually take as a basis.'

And another long squabble ensued. The old people's style of living was laid bare, scrutinized and discussed, item by item. They weighed up the bread, the vegetables and the meat; they worked out the clothing, cutting down on the linen and wool, they even probed into the little luxuries, such as their father's pipe tobacco; his daily ration of tuppence was reduced to a penny, after endless recrimination. If you're not going to be working any more, you'll have to learn to economize! And couldn't Mother manage to do without black coffee? It was like their dog, an aged animal, twelve years old, which ate a lot and did nothing in return: it ought to have been liquidated long ago. Having made their calculations once, they went back to revise them, looking for other things to eliminate; two shirts and six handkerchieves a year, a centime off what had been set aside for sugar per day. And by paring away again and again, they reached a figure of five hundred and fifty odd francs, which left them in a state of considerable agitation because they were determined not to go above five hundred francs, in round figures.

But Fanny was becoming tired of all this talk. She was not a bad sort of girl and more compassionate than the men because neither her heart nor her skin had yet been toughened by their hard life in the open air. So having resigned herself to making concessions, she suggested calling a halt to the discussion. Jesus Christ, for his part, shrugged his shoulders. He was very easy about money matters and now that he was feeling maudlin, was even ready to offer to make up the amount out of his own share – though he would never have paid it.

'Well, then,' the daughter asked. 'Are we agreed on five hundred and fifty francs?'

'All right, all right,' he replied. 'They've got to have their bit of fun, the old folk.'

His mother looked at her first-born with a smile, her eyes misty with affection; while his father continued his struggle with his younger son. He had given ground only inch by inch, contesting every reduction, digging in his heels at some of the figures. But beneath his cold and stubborn exterior, inwardly his wrath was rising in the face of the savage determination of his own flesh and blood to suck him dry while still alive. He was forgetting that he had devoured his own father in the same way. His hands were beginning to tremble; he snarled:

'What a nasty lot you are! When I think that I brought you up, and you want to take the bread out of my mouth! It's disgusting. I'm sorry I'm not stiff and cold already. So you won't do the decent thing, you'll not go above five hundred and fifty?'

He was weakening when once again his wife tugged at his sleeve and whispered:

'No, don't accept.'

'That's not quite all,' Buteau said after a moment's hesitation. 'What about the money you've saved up? After all, if you've got some money of your own, surely you're not going to accept ours.'

He glared at his father. He had saved up this shot for the end. The old man had gone very pale.

'What money?' he asked.

'The money you've invested, of course. All those securities you keep hidden away.'

Buteau only suspected the existence of this nest-egg and was trying to find out definitely. One evening he had thought he had seen his father pull out a little roll of papers from behind a mirror. Next day and on the days following, he had kept watch; but nothing had reappeared, there remained just an empty hole.

Fouan had gone very pale; but all at once his face turned bright red as his anger suddenly brimmed over. He rose to his feet with a furious gesture and screamed:

'Christ Almighty! So you go through my pockets now, do you? I've not got one penny invested, not a single farthing! I had to spend too much on you, you miserable lot! But in any case, what business is that of yours, aren't I your father? Aren't I the master?'

In this sudden access of authority, he seemed all at once to have grown taller. For years, all of them, wife and children, had trembled under his rule, the harsh and tyrannical rule of a peasant father over his family. If anyone thought he was finished with, they were mistaken.

'Oh, Father.' Buteau made an attempt to treat it as a joke.

'For Christ's sake shut up,' the old man went on, his hand still raised. 'Shut up or I'll let you have it.'

His younger son stammered and cowered back in his seat. He had felt the wind of the blow and his childhood fears had returned as he raised his elbow to ward it off.

'And as for you, Hyacinthe, take that grin off your face! And Fanny, stop staring!... As sure as God's my witness, I'll make you all hop!'

He stood there, dominating and threatening. His wife sat trembling, afraid that one of his blows might miss its target. Their children sat quite still, holding their breath, cowed.

'Do you hear? I want six hundred francs for my annuity... If not, I'll sell my land. I'll take a life interest on it. Just so that I can blue the lot and you won't get a penny... Are you going to let me have six hundred francs?'

'Of course, Father, we'll give you anything you want,' said Fanny quietly.

'Six hundred francs, I agree,' said Delhomme.

'And as for me,' said Jesus Christ, 'I want what everyone else wants.'

For Buteau, his teeth clenched in resentment, silence seemed to give consent. And still Fouan stood glaring from one to the other with the harsh look of a master determined not to brook any disobedience. Finally, he sat down:

'Very well, then, we're agreed.'

Monsieur Baillehache had sunk back into his torpor and was waiting placidly for the storm to subside. He opened his eyes again and gently summed up:

'Now you've come to an agreement, that's that. Now that I know the terms I'll draw up the deed... On your part, you must have the land surveyed, divide it up and tell the surveyor to send me a note indicating the actual plots. When you've drawn lots for them, all we shall need to do is write down the number which has been drawn against the name of each plot and we can sign.'

He had stood up from his desk to indicate that the meeting was at an end. But they still lingered, discussing and having second thoughts.

Was that really everything? Hadn't anything been forgotten, hadn't they made a bad deal, which there was perhaps still time to go back on?

Three o'clock struck; they had been there almost two hours.

'Please go now,' the notary said in the end. 'There are other people waiting.'

They had to accept his decision; he ushered them out into the main office where numbers of peasants were, in fact, sitting stiffly upright, patiently waiting, whilst the office-boy was watching a dog-fight through the window and the two others were still scratching away with a surly air on official stamped paper.

Outside, the family stood for a moment in the middle of the street.

'If you like,' their father said, 'the survey can be done on Monday, tomorrow.'

They nodded agreement and went down the Rue Grouaise, a few steps apart.

Then, after Fouan and Rose had turned off into the Rue du Temple, towards the church, Fanny and Delhomme went away along the Rue Grande. Buteau had stopped in the Place Saint-Lubin, still wondering whether his father had a hidden nest-egg or not. Jesus Christ, left to his own devices, relit his cigar-end, and lurched into the Jolly Ploughman.

Chapter 3

FOUAN'S house in Rognes was the first one on the road from Cloyes to Bazoches-le-Doyen, which runs through the village. So at seven o'clock on the Monday morning, at daybreak, the old man was just leaving home to go to meet the others, as agreed, in front of the church, when in the doorway of the next house he caught sight of his sister, known as La Grande, already up and about despite her eighty years.

The Fouans had been born and bred here for centuries, like a tough and hardy plant. Former serfs of the Rognes-Bouqueval family, of whom no trace remained except a few half-buried stones of a demolished castle, they must have been freed under Philippe le Bel; and from that time onwards they had become landowners of an acre, or perhaps two, which they bought from the lord of the manor when he was short of cash; and they sweated blood to pay for it at a price ten times its real value. Then the battle had begun, which was to last four long centuries, to defend and enlarge their property, a battle fought with a savage passion passed down from father to son as pieces of land were lost or recovered; a property of derisory proportions, constantly in jeopardy, an inheritance burdened by such onerous taxation that at times it threatened to melt away but whose meadows and arable slowly increased through the Fouans' irresistible hunger for land and their tenacity of purpose, which slowly achieved its goal. Whole generations died in pursuit of their task and the soil grew fat with the sacrifice of many a life; but when the Revolution of 1789 finally established his rights, Joseph-Casimir, the Fouan of the day, owned twenty-one acres wrested from the former manor lands over the space of four centuries.

In 1793 Joseph-Casimir was twenty-seven years old; and on the day when the remainder of the estate was declared to be the property of the nation and sold by auction, he longed to buy more of it. The Rognes-Bouqueval family, having let the last of the castle towers fall down, themselves ruined and crippled by debt, had long since abandoned the tenancies of La Borderie to their creditors, and three-quarters of the land was lying fallow. Above all, adjoining one of the plots, there was a large piece of land which Joseph-Casimir, insatiably covetous like all his family, would have dearly loved to possess. But the harvests had been poor and his savings amounted to barely a hundred crowns hidden in an old jar behind the stove; and in addition, when he had for a moment toyed with the idea of borrowing from a money-lender in Cloyes, he had been seized by misgivings: he was scared at the thought of those properties formerly belonging to the nobility. Who could tell whether they wouldn't have to be returned later on? So, torn between desire and distrust, he had the mortification of seeing La Borderie bought up in the auction, lot by lot, by a rich townsman, Isidore Hourdequin, a former exciseman from Châteaudun, who acquired it for a fifth of its value.

In his old age, Joseph-Casimir divided up his twenty-one acres between his eldest daughter, Marianne, and his two sons, Louis and Michel, seven acres apiece; a younger daughter, Laure, who had learned dressmaking and was employed in Châteaudun, received financial compensation instead. But marriage destroyed this equal distribution. Whereas Marianne Fouan, nicknamed La Grande, married Antoine Péchard, a neighbour who owned roughly eighteen acres, Michel Fouan, whom everyone called Mouche, found himself saddled with a girl whose father eventually left her only two acres of vine. For his part, Louis Fouan had married Rose Maliverne, who had inherited twelve acres, and he had thus finished by owning nineteen acres which he was now about to divide between his own three children.

In the family La Grande was respected and feared, not for her age but for her wealth. Still very erect, very tall, lean, tough and big-boned, she had a long, withered, blood-red neck topped by a gaunt face like that of a bird of prey, in which the family nose had become a terrifying curved beak. Her eyes were round and staring; under her headscarf she was completely hairless but on the other hand she had kept all her teeth and her jaws would have made light work of a diet of stones. She always walked with her stick poised in the air, and never left home without it – a hawthorn stick reserved exclusively for cudgelling animals and people. She had been widowed when still young and had one daughter whom she had turned out of her house because the wretched girl had persisted in marrying, against her mother's wishes, a penniless young man called Vincent Bouteroue; and even now that this son-in-law and her daughter had died in poverty, leaving behind a granddaughter and grandson, Palmyre and Hilarion, already thirty-two and twenty-four years old, she had never relented; she refused to recognize their existence and was letting them starve. Ever since her man's death, she had personally taken over the farming of his land – she had three cows, a pig and a hired hand, whom she fed out of the common feeding trough. Everyone went in deadly terror of her, and nobody would ever dare to disobey her.

Seeing her standing in her doorway, Fouan went over to speak to her and pay his respects. She was ten years older than he and he shared the general deference and admiration which the whole village felt for her hardness, her greed, her zest for living and her single-minded devotion to material possessions.

'I was wanting to see you, La Grande,' he said. 'I wanted to tell you that I've finally made up my mind and I'm on my way up to work out the various lots.'

She made no reply and held on to her stick more tightly in order to brandish it.

'The other evening I wanted to ask your advice but no one answered when I knocked.'

Her harsh voice exploded:

'You're an idiot! I gave you my advice! You're a stupid coward to give up your property as long as you're alive and kicking. . . Wild horses wouldn't have dragged that sort of decision out of me. Seeing other people own what belongs to you, leaving your house and home for the benefit of those wretched children of yours, not on your life!'

'But suppose you're no longer able to farm the land,' Fouan objected, 'and the land is suffering as a result.'

'Well, let it suffer! I'd sooner go along every day and watch the thistles growing than give up one square inch of it!'

She straightened up with her wild look that made her seem like an old vulture which has lost its feathers. Then, tapping him on the shoulder with her stick to emphasize her words, she said:

'Listen to me. . . When you've got nothing left and they've got the lot, your children will push you into the gutter and you'll end up like a tramp with a begging bowl... And when that happens, don't think you can come and knock at my door, because I've given you plenty of warning and it'll be your fault... Do you know what I'll do then? Would you like to know?'

He stood there meekly, waiting with the deferential air of a younger son as she turned and went back into her house and slammed the door violently behind her.

'That's what I'll do... You can die in the gutter!'

For a second, Fouan remained motionless in front of the slammed door. Then, with a gesture of resignation, he went up the pathway leading to the square in front of the church. It was here, in fact, that the Fouans' ancestral home stood; it had been given to Michel, or Mouche as he was called, at the time his father had shared out the estate, whereas Louis's house, down below on the road, had come to him from his wife Rose. Mouche, a widower of long standing, lived alone with his two daughters Lise and Françoise. Soured by his bad luck and smarting even now under the humiliation of having married a poor girl, he was still, forty years later, accusing his brother and sister of having cheated him when drawing the lots; and he never tired of telling how the worst lot had been reserved for him at the bottom of the hat, a story which seemed in the end to have turned out to be true, because he was so argumentative and such a slacker that in his hands his share had diminished by half. The man makes the land, as they say in Beauce.

That morning, Mouche was also standing in his doorway on the look-out when his brother came in at one corner of the square. He was fascinated at the thought that his brother should be dividing up his property, although he had nothing to gain from it; and it stirred old grievances. But in order to pretend that he was totally indifferent, he, too, brusquely turned his back on him and slammed the door.

Fouan had at once caught sight of Delhomme and Jesus Christ, who were standing waiting, twenty paces apart. He went up to the farmer and the latter then came up. Without speaking to each other, all three directed their gaze towards the path which ran along the edge of the plateau.

'There he is,' said Jesus Christ at last. It was Grosbois, the official surveyor, a farmer from the neighbouring little village of Magnolles. His skill at reading and writing had been his downfall. Called upon to undertake surveys over an area from Orgères to as far away as Beaugency, he had let his wife look after his own property and, since he was continually on the move, he had developed such drunken habits that he was now never sober. Very stout and hearty, despite his fifty years, he had a broad, ruddy face, spotted with grog blossoms, and although it was still early he was very badly the worse for drink through having spent the previous night carousing with some wine-growers of Montigny to celebrate the conclusion of a partition of some property amongst the next-of-kin. But this was of no importance; the drunker he was, the clearer his sight became; he had never been known to make a mistake in his measurements or calculations. People listened to him and showed him consideration, for he had the reputation of being a very spiteful customer.

'All right, everybody here?' he said. 'Let's get going.'

He was followed by a dirty, ragged, twelve-year-old urchin carrying the chain under one arm and the stand and the poles over his shoulder, while in his free hand he was swinging the cross-staff in a tattered old cardboard box.

They all set off without waiting for Buteau, whom they had just spied standing motionless beside one field, the largest of all, at the place known as Les Cornailles. This field of roughly five acres adjoined the one where Coliche had dragged Françoise along the ground a few days ago. Thinking there was no point in coming any further, Buteau had stopped here, absorbed in a brown study. As the others came up, they saw him bend down, pick up a handful of soil and then let it slip slowly through his fingers, as though sizing it up and seeing how it smelt.

'Here we are,' said Grosbois, pulling a greasy notebook out of his pocket. 'I've already drawn up a little detailed plan of each bit of land, just as you asked me, Monsieur Fouan. Now we have to divide the whole lot into three parts, and that's what we're going to do together. That's right, isn't it? Now tell me what your ideas are on the subject.'

The light was better now and large masses of cloud went scudding across the livid sky, driven before the icy wind which scourged the sad and dreary plain of Beauce. However, not one of the men seemed aware of these blasts of ocean air which were filling out their smocks like sails and threatening to blow away their hats. All five of them, dressed in their Sunday best in view of the solemnity of the occasion, had now fallen silent. As they stood beside the field set in the middle of this boundless plain, their faces took on the fixed, dreamy look of sailors idly musing on their lonely life spent among the vast expanses of the sea. This flat, fertile plain, easy to cultivate but requiring continuous care, has made its inhabitants cold and reflective; their only passion is for the earth.

'We must split everything into three,' said Buteau in the end.

Grosbois shook his head and an argument ensued. Through his contact with the larger farms, he had been won over by progressive ideas and he sometimes took the liberty of disagreeing with his smallholder clients over the policy of dividing land into excessively small holdings. When you had plots of land no bigger than a pocket handkerchief, didn't it make movement and transport ruinously expensive? Was it proper farming when you had little garden-sized plots where you couldn't use the right rotation or machines? The only sensible thing was to come to some agreement, not cut up a field like a piece of cake; it was sheer murder. If one person was prepared to accept the arable land, the other could take the pasture; and then you could arrange so that every share was equal and the final allocation would be made by drawing lots.

Buteau was still young enough to have kept a sense of humour: he took Grosbois's remarks as a joke:

'And suppose I end up with nothing but pasture, what am I going to eat, grass? That's not good enough, I want a bit of everything, hay for my cow and my horse, wheat and vine for me.'

Fouan nodded approvingly. Successive generations had always split up the land like that; and then each holding would be built up afresh through the acquisition of other land through purchase or marriage.

As the prosperous owner of more than sixty acres, Delhomme could afford to take a broader view, but he did not want to create trouble, he had come along on his wife's behalf merely to ensure that the survey was fairly done. And as for Jesus Christ, he had gone off in pursuit of a flock of larks, his hands full of stones.

As soon as one of them remained fluttering for a couple of seconds motionless against the wind, he would bring it down as skilfully as any primitive savage. He knocked down three of them and stuffed them into his pocket, all bloody as they were.

'That's enough blather,' said Buteau, addressing the surveyor with cheerful familiarity. 'Just you cut it up into three parts. And take care it's not six, because it seems to me that you've got one eye on Chartres and the other on Orléans this morning!'

Offended by this remark, Grosbois drew himself up and retorted with some hauteur:

'Young man, see if you can be as drunk as me and keep your eyes open. . . Is there any clever person here who would like to use my cross-staff instead of me?'

As nobody took up the challenge, with a triumphant air he sharply called out to his boy, who was lost in admiration at Jesus Christ's skill at killing birds; the cross was set up on its stand but as the stakes were being thrust into the ground another dispute arose over the way to divide the field up. The surveyor, supported by Fouan and Delhomme, wanted to divide it up into three strips parallel to the valley of the Aigre, whereas Buteau was demanding that the strips should run at right angles to the valley, on the objection that the soil became progressively shallower going down the slope. In that way, everyone would have a fair share of the poor soil, whilst otherwise the third strip would consist of nothing but poor quality land. But Fouan was becoming annoyed: he insisted that the topsoil was the same all over and pointed out that the previous division of the land between him, Mouche and La Grande had been conducted on the same basis, as was proved by the fact that the third strip would be bordering Mouche's own five-acre plot. For his part, Delhomme made the very valid point that even if that strip were less good, its owner would benefit as soon as they opened up the road which was going to run along the edge of the field, at that very spot.

'Oh yes!' Buteau cried. 'That famous direct route from Rognes to Châteaudun via La Borderie. That's something you'll not see for donkey's years.'

And when they persisted despite his objection, he went on protesting through clenched teeth. Even Jesus Christ had joined them and they all became absorbed in observing Grosbois draw the dividing lines, watching him like hawks as though they suspected him of wanting to cheat by giving one of the strips an extra inch or two. Three times Delhomme went over to put his eye at the slit in the cross-staff head to be quite sure that the wire cut the pole cleanly. Jesus Christ swore at the wretched little boy for not holding the chain properly taut. But Buteau in particular followed the operation step by step, counting every yard and redoing the sums in his own way, mumbling with his lips. And though filled with desire to own the land and with joy at the prospect of finally laying hands on it, another feeling was welling up within him, a dull, bitter rage at not being able to possess the lot : what a lovely field it was – five acres of it all in one piece ! He had insisted on its being carved up so that if he could not be the sole owner, it should at least not belong to anyone else – yet now he felt appalled at such butchery.

Fouan had stood silently watching his property being divided up, his arms dangling at his side.

'That's that,' said Grosbois. 'And between this bit and those over there, you couldn't squeeze ten francs difference out of any of 'em !'

On the plateau there still remained some ten acres of land under the plough but divided into ten fields or more, none of them larger than an acre; one was even less than half an acre and when the surveyor asked sardonically whether he was to split that one up, too, another argument arose. Once more Buteau repeated his instinctive gesture of bending down, taking a handful of earth and holding it up to his face, as if intending to taste it. Then, blissfully wrinkling his nose, he seemed to be suggesting that this was the best of the lot; and letting the soil slip gently through his fingers he said that he would be agreeable if the plot of land could be allotted to him; otherwise, it would have to be split up. . . Annoyed by this, Delhomme and Jesus Christ both refused and demanded their share. 'All right then, an eighth of an acre each, that was the only fair thing to do.' And so all the fields were divided up, so that everyone was certain that none of the three would have any more than the other two.

'Let's go over to the vineyards,' said Fouan.

But as they were going back to the church, he cast one last glance over the immense plain and, as his eye settled for a second

55

on the farm buildings of La Borderie in the distance, he uttered an exclamation of inconsolable grief at the thought of the opportunity they had let slip when the national estates had been sold, so long ago.

'Ah, if only my father had been prepared to go ahead, Grosbois, you'd've been measuring all that !'

His two sons and son-in-law suddenly stopped and turned round to cast a lingering look at the farm's five hundred acres spread out before their eyes :

'Ah well,' grunted Buteau, as he went on his way, 'a fat lot of good that'll do us. And townsfolk always do us down, don't they ?'

It was striking ten o'clock. They quickened their steps because the wind had slackened and a large black cloud had just released its first shower of rain. Rognes's few vineyards lay beyond the church, on the hillside which sloped down to the Aigre. This was where the castle had formerly stood in its park and it was barely a century ago that, encouraged by the success of the vines at near-by Montigny, the Cloyes farmers had had the idea of planting this hillside with vines, since its steep south-facing slope seemed suitable for that purpose. They produced a poorish wine which was, however, pleasantly tart and reminiscent of the light table wines from the region of Orléans. Anyway, none of the inhabitants of Rognes had more than a few patches of vineyard; the richest of them, Delhomme, had six acres; the main crops of the area were cereals and fodder.

They passed round the back of the church and along the side of the former presbytery; then they made their way down to the patchwork of small vineyards.

As they were crossing a stretch of stony ground overgrown with shrubs, they heard a shrill voice coming from a hole :

'Dad, it's raining, I'll bring my geese out !'

It was La Trouille, Jesus Christ's daughter, a twelve-year-old with a tangled mop of hair and as thin and wiry as a holly branch. She had a large mouth, screwed up in its left corner, and staring green eyes; she could easily have been mistaken for a boy, for instead of a dress she wore one of her father's smocks tied round the middle with a piece of string. And if everyone called her the Brat, even though she bore the splendid name of Olympe, it was because Jesus Christ, who used to bawl abuse at her from morning till night, whenever he addressed her always finished by saying: 'You wait, you little brat, I'll give you something you won't forget!'

He had produced this tomboy with the aid of some slut whom he had picked up in a ditch after a fair and then settled in his den, to the great scandal of the village. For nearly three years the couple had lived a cat-and-dog life together and then one night at harvest-time the trollop had taken herself off with another man, just as she had come. The daughter, scarcely weaned, had flourished like the green bay, and ever since she could walk she had prepared the meals for her father, whom she feared and adored. But her real passion was for her geese. At first, she only had two, a goose and a gander which had been abstracted while goslings through a gap in a farmer's hedge. Then, thanks to her motherly care, the flock had prospered and now she had twenty geese which she fed on stolen food.

When La Trouille appeared with her saucy little faunlike face, driving her geese in front of her with a stick, Jesus Christ exploded:

'You get back and see to the dinner or else you'd better look out. And shut up the house, you little brat, in case of burglars!'

Buteau gave a grin and the others were also unable to hide a smile at the thought of Jesus Christ being burgled, for his house was a disused cellar, or three walls of one, below ground, a proper foxhole, set amongst tumbled-down stones and overgrown with old lime trees. It was all that remained of the castle; and when, after a quarrel with his father, the poacher had taken refuge in this retreat among the ruins, which belonged to the parish, he had had to build another wall of dry stones to enclose the cellar, leaving two openings for a window and a door. It was overhung by brambles and the window was hidden behind a tall dog-rose. The locals called it the Castle.

A fresh downpour overtook them but fortunately the vineyard was close by and the division into three was speedily concluded without arousing further disagreement. All that was now left was seven and a half acres of meadow, down by the bank of the Aigre. But at that moment, the rain started falling so heavily that as they were passing by the entrance to an estate the surveyor suggested that they might go in.

'What do you think? Shall we take shelter with Monsieur Charles for a minute?'

Fouan had stopped and was hesitating in awe of his brother-in-law and sister who, having made their fortune, had retired to end their days in this opulent property.

'No, I don't think so,' he said, lowering his voice, 'they have lunch at noon, we'll be disturbing them.'

But Monsieur Charles had appeared on the terrace, under the glass porch, to look at the rain, and recognizing them he called out:

'Won't you come in?'

And as they were all dripping wet, he shouted to them to go round the back and into the kitchen, where he joined them. He was a handsome man of sixty-five, clean-shaven, with heavy lids, lack-lustre eyes, and the dignified, jaundiced face of a judge. Dressed in coarse blue flannel and fur-lined slippers, he wore on his head a priest's cap with the self-assurance of a man who had spent his life in positions requiring tact and authority.

When Laure Fouan, a dressmaker in Châteaudun at the time, had married Charles Badeuil, he was running a small café in the Rue d'Angoulême. Anxious to make money fast, the ambitious young couple moved to Chartres. But at first every venture proved unprofitable; in succession they tried keeping a tavern, a restaurant and even a dry fish-shop; and they were beginning to despair of ever having two pennies to rub together when Monsieur Charles, an enterprising young man, hit on the idea of buying one of the brothels in the Rue aux Juifs, which had fallen on hard times owing to the shortcomings of its staff and its well-earned reputation for lack of cleanliness. He had summed up the situation at a glance: as a county town Chartres needed a reputable establishment providing comfort and safety in line with modern progressive ideas and this need was not being met. In fact by its second year, No. 19, properly modernized with nice curtains and mirrors and equipped with a hand-picked staff, had acquired such an excellent reputation that they had to increase the number of women to six. Army officers, local government officials, in a word the cream of Chartres society, would never dream of patronizing any other establishment. And this success-ful start was maintained thanks to Monsieur Charles's iron hand

and firm, fatherly management; whilst Madame Charles showed extraordinary energy in keeping her eye on everything and ensuring that nothing went astray, although she knew when to turn a blind eye at petty thefts committed by her richer customers.

In less than twenty-five years, the Badeuils accumulated more than 300,000 francs in savings and they then thought that they might realize their lifelong dream of an idyllic old age in the depths of the country among trees, birds and flowers. But they were unable to realize their dream for another two years because they could not find anyone prepared to pay the high price that they had set on No. 19. It was really heartbreaking: here was an establishment to which they had devoted the best years of their lives and they now found themselves forced to let it pass into unknown hands where it might well go downhill. As soon as he first arrived in Chartres, Monsieur Charles had had a daughter, Estelle, whom he sent to school with the Sisters of the Visitation in Châteaudun when he set up in the Rue aux Juifs. It was a pious convent, very strong on moral upbringing, and he left his daughter there until she was eighteen to ensure her total innocence; she spent all her holidays far away from Chartres and never learnt how she came to be so wealthy. And he removed her from the convent only at the time of her marriage to a young excise officer, Hector Vaucogne, a good-looking young man whose sterling qualities were marred by inordinate laziness. She was nearly thirty and had a little girl, Élodie, who was seven, when, having finally learnt the truth and hearing that her father wanted to retire from the business, she asked him, of her own accord, for the first refusal. Why should such a splendid gilt-edged concern go out of the family? Everything was settled, the Vaucognes took over the establishment and by the very first month the Badeuils were delighted and touched to see that their daughter, albeit brought up with quite different ideals, showed herself a very gifted bawdy-house keeper, thus making up for the inertia and total lack of managerial skills of her husband. The parents had retired five years ago to Rognes, where they could look after their granddaughter Élodie, who had been sent in her turn to the convent of the Sisters of the Visitation in Châteaudun to receive a religious education in accordance with the strictest principles of Christian morality.

When Monsieur Charles came into the kitchen where a young maid was beating an omelette and keeping an eye on a pan full of larks frying in butter, they all doffed their hats, even Delhomme and old Fouan, and appeared greatly gratified to shake the hand he offered them.

'My word,' said Grosbois, making himself agreeable, 'what a nice property you have here, Monsieur Charles. And when you think that you got it for a song! Yes, you're a very smart man, Monsieur Charles, a really smart man.'

Monsieur Charles smirked.

'A bit of luck, sheer chance. We decided we liked it and Madame Charles was so keen to end her days in the village where she was born... You know, where sentiment is involved, I've never been able to say no.'

Roseblanche, which was the name of the property, was the folly of a rich citizen of Cloyes who had just spent nearly fifty thousand francs on it when he was struck down by an apoplexy even before the paint had dried. The house was extremely elegant, set halfway up the hill in nearly eight acres of garden sloping down to the Aigre. In such a dreary village on the edge of the dismal plain of Beauce, there were no buyers and Monsieur Charles had picked it up for twenty thousand francs. Here he was able to satisfy, in uninterrupted bliss, his every taste: superb trout and eels caught in the river, lovingly cultivated collections of roses and carnations, and finally birds, a vast aviary full of wild singing birds of all sorts of which he took sole care. The affectionate old couple lived there on their twelve thousand francs a year, in a state of unruffled happiness which he regarded as the just reward of his thirty years of work.

'Isn't that right,' Monsieur Charles added, 'at least people here know who we are?'

'Yes, of course, people know you,' replied the surveyor. 'Your money sees to that.'

And all the others nodded approval.

'Certainly, certainly.'

Then Monsieur Charles told the maid to set out some glasses and he himself went down into the cellar to fetch a couple of bottles of wine. They all sniffed the delicious smell of the larks frying in the pan. And they solemnly drank, rolling the wine round their mouths.

'Goodness me, that doesn't come from these parts! Really lovely!'

'Another drop, your very good health.'

'And yours too!'

As they put down their glasses Madame Charles appeared, a respectable-looking lady of sixty-two, with snow-white hair drawn tightly back from her face; she had the heavy features and big nose of the Fouans, but they were combined with a fresh pink complexion, like that of a gentle old nun who has spent her life in cloistered seclusion. Her twelve-year-old granddaughter, Elodie, who was spending a couple of days' holiday in Rognes, followed her into the room, looking scared and shy as she clung awkwardly to her grandmother's skirts. She was a pallid, plain little girl with a flabby, puffy face and pale wispy hair, a bloodless little creature who was moreover repressed by the virginal innocence of her upbringing to the point of idiocy.

'Well, well, it's you,' said Madame Charles to her brother and her nephews, without enthusiasm, as she slowly offered them an aloof and rather lordly hand.

And then, swinging round and paying them no further attention:

'Do come in, Monsieur Patoir. . . Here he is. . .'

Patoir was the veterinary surgeon from Cloyes, a short, stout, sanguine man, with a military-looking purple face and large mustachios. He had just arrived in his muddy cabriolet in the pouring rain.

'This poor little pet,' she went on, pulling out of the warm oven a basket containing a dying cat, 'this poor little pet started trembling all over yesterday and so I wrote to you. . . Oh, he's not young, he's almost fifteen. . . We had him with us in Chartres for ten years and last year my daughter had to get rid of him because he kept forgetting himself all over the shop, and I brought him here.'

'Shop' was in deference to Elodie, who had been told that her parents kept a confectioner's shop which took up so much of their time that they were unable to have her to stay with them. Moreover, the others did not even smile because the word was current in Rognes, where people used to say that 'the Hourdequins' farm didn't bring in as much as Monsieur Charles's shop'. And they looked wide-eyed at the skinny, yellow, wretched old cat which had lost all its fur; the cat who had purred its way through every single bed in the Rue aux Juifs, tickled and fondled by the plump hands of five or six generations of loose women. For so many years he had been pampered as a favourite pet, at home in the parlour and in the bedrooms, licking up left-over face-cream, drinking out of the toothglasses, a silent, meditative observer of all that was happening as he watched through his narrow pupils ringed with gold.

'So, Monsieur Patoir,' Madame Charles concluded, 'I want you to cure him, please.'

The veterinary surgeon stared with wide-open eyes, wrinkling his nose and lips with a grimace on his cheerful, coarse, puglike face. He exclaimed:

'What on earth! That's what you fetched me out for? Of course, I can cure him for you. Tie a stone round his neck and chuck him in the river!'

Élodie burst into tears while Madame Charles choked with indignation.

'But your little pussy is smelling to high heaven! How can anyone want to keep such a dreadful animal and give the whole house cholera? Chuck him in the river!'

But in the face of the old lady's wrath, he finally sat down and wrote out a prescription, grumbling the while:

'All right then, if you enjoy this sort of stench. . . What's it to me as long as I get paid? Here you are: stick a spoonful of that into his mouth every hour and here's a prescription for two enemas, one tonight, the other tomorrow.'

For the last few minutes, Monsieur Charles had been growing restless because he could see the larks becoming overcooked while the maid, bored with beating the omelette, was standing there with her arms dangling. So he quickly handed Patoir the six-franc fee for his consultation and invited the others to drink up.

'It's lunchtime. All right? Look forward to seeing you. It's not raining now.'

They left regretfully and the veterinary surgeon, as he climbed into his ramshackle old crock, said once again:

'All for a cat that isn't worth the cost of the piece of rope to chuck it in the river! Ah well, I suppose if you're rich. . .'

'If you earn your money through whores then you spend it likewise,' sneered Jesus Christ.

But they all shook their heads in protest, even Buteau, whose face had gone pale with secret envy; and Delhomme said judiciously:

'All the same, if you've succeeded in amassing a pension of twelve thousand francs a year, you can't have been idle or stupid either.'

Patoir whipped up his horse and the others went off down towards the Aigre along the paths that had been turned into streams of water. They had just reached the last seven-odd acres still left to divide when it started to rain again in torrents.

This time, however, they kept on with their task, famished though they were, but determined to finish. Only one disagreement delayed them: it was over the third plot, which was treeless, whereas the other two plots shared a little copse. Nevertheless, everything seemed to be settled and agreed. The surveyor promised to let the notary have his notes so that he could draw up the deeds; and they arranged to meet to draw lots the following Sunday at ten o'clock in their father's house.

As they were going back into Rognes, Jesus Christ suddenly swore:

'You wait, you little brat. I'll give you something!'

Along the verge of the grassy track La Trouille was unhurriedly parading her geese under the driving rain. The gander was waddling along in front of the bedraggled and delighted flock and each time he turned his big yellow beak to the right, all the other big yellow beaks turned likewise. But the little girl took to her heels in fright up the hill, followed by the gaggle of geese, all of them with their long necks outstretched behind the outstretched neck of their gander.

Chapter 4

It so happened that the following Sunday fell on November 1st, All Saints' Day; and nine o'clock was about to strike when Father Godard, the vicar of Bazoches-le-Doyen, who was in charge of the former parish of Rognes, emerged at the top of the slope leading down to the little bridge over the Aigre. Rognes now numbered only about 300 inhabitants – it had earlier been much larger – and it had not had a parish priest of its own for years; nor did it seem anxious to acquire one, since the parish council had housed the gamekeeper in the half-demolished presbytery.

So every Sunday Father Godard walked the one and a half miles between Bazoches-le-Doyen and Rognes. He was short and portly with a neck as red as a turkeycock and so thick that he had to hold his head backwards. He used to force himself to undertake this walk for his health's sake, but this Sunday he was panting with his mouth wide open in a frightening manner; the fat on his florid, apoplectic face had submerged his little grey eyes and pug-nose; and despite the livid, snow-laden sky and the early onset of cold weather after last week's rain, he was swinging his hat in his hand, his bare head covered only with a tangled greying thatch of ginger hair.

The road descended abruptly and on the left bank of the Aigre there were only a few houses before the stone bridge, a sort of suburb which the reverend father hurtled through at top speed. He glanced neither upstream nor downstream at the slow, clear-flowing river which meandered through the meadows between clumps of willows and poplars. The village began on the other bank, with house-fronts lining each side of the street while others clambered haphazardly up the hillside. Immediately beyond the bridge stood the town-hall and the school, housed in a former barn, whitewashed and provided with an extra floor. The priest hesitated for a moment and stuck his head into the empty front hall. Then he turned and seemed to be rapidly scrutinizing two drinking-shops opposite: one of them with a neat front window full of bottles and jars and a little yellow wooden sign above, on which you could read MACQUERON, GROCER, printed in green letters; on the other one, adorned merely with a holly branch, these words: TOBACCO: LENGAIGNE, sprawling in black letters on its rough-cast wall. And he had just made up his mind to take the little street between the two and go up the steep footpath leading to the square in front of the church when he caught sight of an old farmer and stopped.

'Ah, it's you, Fouan... I'm in a hurry, I was wanting to come and see you. What do you think we can do? Your son Buteau can't possibly leave Lise in the condition she's in, getting bigger in front every day for everyone to see... She's a Daughter of Mary, it's scandalous, absolutely scandalous!'

The old man listened with an air of polite deference.

'Yes, Father, but what on earth can I do if Buteau refuses to do anything about it? And we can't blame the lad really, it's no good getting married at his age when you haven't got a bean.'

'But there's the child to think of!'

'Yes, of course... But there isn't any child yet, is there? How can one know? That's the point, it's a bit discouraging to take on a child when you can't afford to pay for a shirt to put on its back!'

He was making the remarks with the sagacious air of an old man full of experience. Then in the same judicious tone, he added:

'Anyway, perhaps something can be done... I'm sharing out my property, we'll be drawing lots later on, after Mass... So when Buteau has got his share, I hope he'll see his way to marrying his cousin.'

'Splendid!' said the priest. 'That's good enough, I'll be relying on you, Fouan.'

But a peal from the bell interrupted him and he asked in consternation:

'That's the second bell, isn't it?'

'No, Father, it's the third.'

'Glory be! That's that oaf Bécu ringing the bell again without waiting for me!'

With an oath, he sped on his way up the path. At the top, he nearly had an attack; he was puffing and blowing like a grampus.

The bell went on tolling, disturbing the rooks who wheeled and cawed round the steeple of the fifteenth-century belfry which bore witness to Rognes's former glory. In front of the wide open door of the church a group of villagers were standing, including the publican Lengaigne, a freethinker, who was smoking his pipe; further along, beside the cemetery wall, Farmer Hourdequin, the mayor, a handsome man with an energetic cast of countenance, was chatting with his deputy, the grocer Macqueron; when the priest greeted them and passed on, they all followed him except Lengaigne, who pointedly turned his back, still sucking his pipe.

In the church to the right of the porch a man was hanging on to a bell-rope, tugging vigorously.

'That's enough, Bécu,' snapped the priest furiously. 'I've told you times without number to wait for me before ringing the third bell.'

The bell-ringer, who was the gamekeeper, dropped back onto his feet, scared at his own disobedience. He was a little man of fifty with an old soldier's square weather-beaten face, grey moustache and goatee beard, as stiff-necked as if he were perpetually being choked by collars that were too tight for him. Already quite far gone in drink, he sprang to attention without venturing an excuse.

In any case, the priest was already on his way up the nave, casting an eye on the pews as he went. It was a small congregation. On the left he could see as yet only Delhomme, attending in his capacity of councillor. On the right, where the women sat, there were at most a dozen people he recognized: Coelina Macqueron, a wiry and high-handed woman; Flore Lengaigne, a stout, flabby, gentle matron, always complaining; Bécu's wife, lanky, swarthy and filthy. But what really angered him was the behaviour of the Daughters of Mary, in the front pew. Françoise was sitting there between two of her friends, Berthe, the Macquerons' girl, a pretty brunette who had received a ladylike education in Cloyes, and Suzanne, the Lengaines' daughter, a plain, saucy blonde whom her parents were going to send to Châteaudun to become an apprentice dressmaker. All three were laughing in an unseemly manner. Next to them, poor pregnant Lise, fat and cheerful, was displaying her scandalous protuberance in front of the altar.

Father Godard was finally making his way into the sacristy when he ran into Delphin and Nénesse who were playfully pushing each other as they prepared the altar cruet. The former, Bécu's boy, an eleven-year-old, was a sun-tanned, strapping young lad, already sturdy in build, fond of working in the fields and glad to play truant to do so; whilst Ernest Delhomme's eldest son, of the same age, was a slim lackadaisical fair-headed boy who always kept a mirror in his pocket.

'Well, you young scamps!' exclaimed the priest. 'Do you think you're in a cowshed?'

And turning towards a tall thin young man, with a pale face sprouting a few ginger hairs, who was tidying his books away on a cupboard shelf, he said:

'Really, Monsieur Lequeu, you might keep them in order when I'm not here!'

This was the village schoolmaster, a country boy who through his education had become imbued with hatred for his class. He used to brutalize his pupils, whom he called savages, and beneath his ceremonious correctness towards the priest and the mayor he concealed progressive ideas. He sang bass in the choir and even looked after the prayer and hymn books but he had categorically refused to be the bell-ringer although this was customary; he considered such a task beneath the dignity of a free man.

'It's not my job to keep discipline in the church,' he retorted. 'But if they were at school, what a clout I'd give them!'

And as the priest, without replying, started hurriedly to put on his alb and stole, he went on:

'Low Mass, I suppose?'

'Of course, and as quickly as possible! I've got to be at Bazoches by ten-thirty for High Mass.'

Lequeu closed the cupboard from which he had just taken an old missal and went out to place it on the altar.

'Come on, come on!' the priest kept saying, to hurry Delphin and Nénesse along.

Sweating and puffing, he went back into the church carrying the chalice and began the service while the cheeky young altar-boys cast sidelong glances at each other. It was a church with a single nave, barrel-vaulted and oak-panelled but falling into disrepair because the municipal council refused to vote any money towards its upkeep: rain came through the broken slates on the roof; there were large areas of badly rotten wood; and in the choir, shut off by an iron railing, a dirty green streak straggled across the fresco in the apse, cutting in two the face of the Eternal Father who was being adored by angels.

When the priest turned towards the congregation with his arms outstretched, he became a trifle calmer when he saw that the numbers had increased: the mayor, his deputy, some municipal councillors, old Fouan and Clou, the blacksmith who played the trombone at choral Eucharist. Lequeu had remained sitting in the front pew, looking dignified. Bécu, drunk as a lord, was at the back, sitting up as stiff as a ramrod. And the women's pews in particular were filling up with Fanny, Rose, La Grande and a number of others, so that the Daughters of Mary had had to move closer together, with their heads bowed over their prayer books. They were now pictures of propriety. But the priest was particularly gratified to catch sight of Monsieur and Madame Charles with their granddaughter Élodie; he was wearing a black frock-coat while his lady had on a green silk dress; both of them were solemn and prosperous-looking, setting an excellent example to all.

However, he was in a hurry to expedite the Mass, gabbling the Latin and hurrying through the responses. For the sermon, he did not go up into the pulpit but sat on a chair in the middle of the choir-stalls, mumbling, losing the thread – and not bothering to recover it: oratory was not his strong point; unable to find words, he would hum and haw and never finish his sentences. This was the reason why the bishop had left him to moulder for twenty-five years in the little parish of Bazoches-le-Doyen. And then he rushed through the rest of the service, so that the bell for the elevation of the host tinkled like some electrical device that was out of order while his *Ite missa est* despatched his flock like a gunshot. Hardly was the church empty than Father Godard reappeared, wearing his hat all askew in his haste. A group of women were stationed in front of the church doors: Coelina, Flore and Bécu's wife, highly offended at having been rushed through the service at such speed. So he wouldn't give them any more of his time because he looked down on them? It was All Souls' Day, too!

'Tell me, Father,' Coelina asked sourly, stopping him, 'do you have a grudge against us since you sent us packing like a bundle of old clothes?'

'What else can I do?' he replied. 'My parishioners are expecting me. . . I can't be in Bazoches and in Rognes at the same time. If you want High Mass you must get a priest of your own.'

This was the perpetual bone of contention between Rognes and Father Godard, the villagers demanding consideration, he keeping to the strict letter of the law, since the parish refused to maintain the church and he was continually disheartened by scandalous goings-on. Pointing to the Daughters of Mary, who were going off together, he went on:

'And anyway, is it decent to have ceremonies where the young people have no respect for God's commandments?'

'I hope that remark's not intended to refer to my daughter,' Coelina said, clenching her teeth.

'Nor to mine, indeed?' added Flore.

'I'm referring to the girl I must be referring to. . . It's as plain as a pikestaff. Look at her, all dressed in white! I can never have a procession here without someone being pregnant. . . It's impossible, you'd try the patience of our Lord himself.'

He flounced off and Bécu's wife, who had said not a word, had to act as peacemaker between the two excited mothers, who were hurling their respective daughters at each other's heads; but she did it with such nasty insinuations that their squabble only increased. Oh yes, that Berthe of yours, with her velvet bodices and her piano, we'll see how she turns out! And what a clever idea to send Suzanne to a dressmaker in Châteaudun where she'd certainly come to no good!

Free at last, Father Godard was on the point of hurrying away when he found himself face to face with the Charles. He swept his hat from his head and gave a radiant smile. In reply Monsieur Charles greeted him with a majestic gesture while Madame made a stately bow. But the priest was fated not to be allowed to leave, for he had still not reached the end of the square before he was stopped again. This time it was a tall woman of some thirty years who looked at least fifty; her hair was sparse, her dull, flat face was yellow and flabby; exhausted and broken-down by excessive toil, she was tottering under the weight of a bundle of firewood.

'Palmyre,' he asked, 'why didn't you come to Mass on All Souls' Day? It's very bad.'

She gave a feeble moan:

'Of course, Father, but what can I do? My brother's cold, it's

69

freezing at home. So I went to pick up a few bits of firewood along under the hedges.'

'La Grande is still as hard-hearted as ever?'

'Oh, she'd sooner die than throw us a log or a crust of bread.'

And she went on in her whining voice about their grandmother, who had turned them out of her house so that she, together with her brother, had had to take shelter in an abandoned stables. Poor Hilarion, with his bandy legs and twisted hare-lip, was quite harmless, despite his age – he was twenty-four – and such a blockhead that nobody would offer him a job. So she had to work for him, which meant working herself to death, for her devoted affection to her invalid brother, her determination in ministering to his needs, and her deep tenderness were as great as any mother's.

As he listened, Father Godard's heavy perspiring face took on an expression of beatific goodness; charity lent beauty to his angry little eyes and sorrow touched his large mouth with grace. This peevish old man, always in a state of violent indignation, had a passionate love for the poor and destitute and he gave them all he had – his money, his underlinen, even his very clothes. In the whole province of Beauce you would not find a priest with a rustier looking cassock or one more darned.

He fumbled uneasily in his pockets and slipped Palmyre a fivefranc piece.

'Here you are, but put it away quickly, it's all I've got. . . And I must speak to La Grande again, since she's so hard-hearted.' And this time, he was able to make his escape. Fortunately, since he was quite out of breath, as he was climbing up the slope on the other side of the Aigre the butcher of his parish, on his way home, picked him up in his cart; and he went jolting along over the edge of the plain, his hat bouncing up and down against the livid light of the sky.

Meanwhile the square in front of the church had emptied and Fouan and Rose had gone back home where Grosbois was already waiting for them. Shortly before ten o'clock Delhomme and Jesus Christ arrived – but they waited in vain for Buteau until twelve o'clock; he was always incalculable and never on time. It was presumed that he had been held up, perhaps over lunch. At first, they thought of going ahead without him, then, secretly afraid of his cantankerousness, it was decided that they should wait and not draw lots until two o'clock, after lunch. Grosbois accepted the Fouans' offer of a slice of bacon and a glass of wine; he then finished off the bottle and started on another one, drunk again, as was his habit.

At two o'clock there was still no sign of Buteau. So entering into the festive spirit of the village on this Sunday holiday, Jesus Christ went off to take a peep into Macqueron's drinking-shop; and he was successful, because the door was suddenly flung open, and Bécu appeared:

'Come on in, you useless man, let me buy you a drink.'

He was still as stiff as a ramrod; in fact the more he drank the more dignified he became. As an old soldier and a drunk himself, he had a secret affection and fellow-feeling for the poacher; but when he was on duty and wearing his official armband, he avoided recognizing him; as he was always likely to catch him red-handed, he was torn between his duty and his feelings. In the pub, once he was drunk, he treated him to a drink like a brother.

'A drop of wine, eh? And if the Arabs keep buggering us about, we'll chop their ears off!'

They sat down at a table and started playing cards; and one bottle followed the other.

Macqueron, with his big face and big moustache, was sitting slumped in a corner twiddling his thumbs. Ever since he had made some money by speculating in the new vineyards at Montigny, which produced a reasonable table wine, he had been overcome by laziness and spent his time shooting and fishing and giving himself superior airs; at the same time he had remained a very dirty man and dressed like a tramp, while his daughter Berthe flounced around in silk dresses. If his wife had been prepared to listen to him, they would have shut up shop, the tavern as well as the store; because as his vanity increased he began nursing secret ambitions of which he himself was as yet scarcely aware; she, however, was a skinflint of the first water and, although he never did a hand's turn himself, he was glad for her to continue serving her jugs of wine in the happy knowledge that it would annoy his neighbour Lengaigne, the tobacconist who also sold drinks. Theirs was a long-standing feud, dormant but always ready to flare up.

However, they had been at peace for some weeks now and it so happened that at this moment Lengaigne came in with his son Victor, a tall, awkward lad who was shortly going to draw lots to decide if he would be called up for military service. The father, a very lanky, dour man with a tiny owl-like head perched on broad bony shoulders, farmed a little land while his wife weighed out the tobacco and fetched wine from the cellar. His importance lay in the fact that he was the village barber, a trade which he had learnt during his military service and one which he exercised in his shop, surrounded by his customers, or in their homes, if they so wished.

'Well now,' he said to Macqueron, as soon as he was through the doorway, 'are we going to have that shave today?'

'Good Lord!' exclaimed Macqueron. 'Yes, I'd asked you to come round. All right, let's do it at once, if you don't mind.'

He took an old shaving-mug down from its hook and fetched some soap and hot water while the other man started sharpening his long cutlass of a razor on a strap fastened to its case. But a shrill shout came from the adjacent grocery shop. It was Coelina:

'Look here, you two!' she cried. 'You're not going to make your mess all over the tables, are you?... I don't want hairs in my glasses!'

This was an allusion to the cleanliness of the tavern next door, where she claimed that you ate more hairs than you drank good wine.

'Get on with your salt and pepper and leave us alone!' retorted Macqueron, irritated at this outburst in front of his customers.

Jesus Christ and Bécu both grinned. That would put her in her place! So they ordered another litre of wine, which she brought without a word, inwardly raging. They were shuffling the cards and then slamming them down as though exchanging punches: 'Trumps! And trumps to you, too!'

Lengaigne had already soaped his customer's face and was holding him by the nose when Lequeu, the village schoolmaster, pushed open the door.

'Good afternoon, gentlemen!'

He remained silently warming his back in front of the stove while young Victor stood behind the card players, absorbed in their game.

'By the way,' said Macqueron, taking advantage of a moment when Lengaigne was wiping some froth off his shoulders, 'just before Mass earlier on, Monsieur Hourdequin brought up the question of the road again. We really ought to make up our minds about something!'

This was the famous direct road from Rognes to Châteaudun which was going to save some five miles, since traffic was now forced to go via Cloyes. The new route would naturally be of great advantage to the farm, and in order to persuade the local council the mayor was relying on the help of his deputy, who was also looking for an early decision. The proposal was, in fact, to link the road up to the lower one, thus making it easier for vehicles to drive up to the church, which at the moment was accessible only by goat tracks. The line of this link road simply followed the narrow alley between the two taverns, widening it by taking advantage of the slope; and as the grocer's property would be opened up, since it would be alongside the new street, its value would be very considerably increased.

'Yes,' he went on, 'apparently the government is waiting for us to vote on it before it can offer us any financial aid. You're in favour, aren't you?'

Lengaigne was a local councillor but he had not even a small piece of garden at the back of his property. He replied:

'A fat lot I care! What good's your road to me?'

And as he tackled the second cheek, scraping away at the skin as if using a grater, he launched into an attack on the farm. These rich townsfolk nowadays were even worse than the old aristocrats: when the share-out took place, they kept the lot, they made the laws to suit themselves and their wealth came at the expense of the wretched plight of the poor! The others were listening embarrassed, yet secretly pleased at his daring words: the age-old and invincible hatred of the land-worker for his landlord.

'It's a good job we're amongst friends,' muttered Macqueron, casting an uneasy glance towards the schoolmaster. 'As for me, I'm a supporter of the government. And our deputy, Monsieur de Chédeville, who's said to be a friend of the Emperor.'

At this Lengaigne brandished his razor wildly in the air:

'And that's another fine one, old Chédeville... Shouldn't a

wealthy man like him, who owns more than twelve hundred acres round Orgères way, make a present of your road to the parish instead of trying to squeeze the money out of us? The old devil. . .'

But the grocer, by now terrified at such talk, protested:

'That's not true, he's a very decent sort and he's not a snob. . . But for him you'd never have got your tobacco shop. What would you have to say if he took it away from you?'

Lengaigne suddenly calmed down and started scraping away at his client's chin again. He had gone too far and was losing his temper; his wife was right when she said that his ideas would get him into trouble. And at that moment Bécu and Jesus Christ started to quarrel. The former tended to become argumentative and nasty in his cups whereas the latter, although a rogue when sober, became more and more mawkish with every glass of wine, like a soft-hearted, good-humoured but drunken apostle. There was also their basic disagreement over politics: the poacher was a republican, a Red as people used to say, who boasted that he had made the women dance to his tune in Cloyes in 1848; the gamekeeper was a rabid Bonapartist who adored the Emperor, whom he claimed to know personally.

'I swear it's true! We once ate a herring salad together. And afterwards he said: Mum's the word, I'm the Emperor. . . I recognized him because of his picture on the five-franc pieces.'

'A likely story!. . . And he's still a swine who beats his wife and never showed any affection for his mother!'

'Shut up, for Christ's sake, or I'll give you a punch on the nose!'

They had to remove the bottle which Bécu was brandishing from his grasp, whilst Jesus Christ, with tears in his eyes, sat waiting for the blow with a smile of resignation on his face. Then they made it up and started playing again. . . 'Trumps and trumps again and I trump the whole lot!'

Macqueron, disturbed by the schoolmaster's pretence of in-difference, finally asked him:

'Monsieur Lequeu, what's your view about the road?'

Lequeu, who was warming his bloodless hands against the stovepipe, gave a sour smile to indicate that his superior position prevented him from speaking frankly.

'I'm not saying anything; it's none of my business.'

At this moment Macqueron went over, dipped his face in a basin of water and, as he dried himself, spluttered:

'Well, listen to me, I'm prepared to do something... Yes, for Christ's sake, if they vote in favour of the road, I'll give my land for nothing!'

The others were dumbfounded by this statement. Even Jesus Christ and Bécu, drunk as they were, looked up. There was a sudden hush; people were looking at him as if he had suddenly taken leave of his senses, while he, excited by the effect he had produced, although his hands were trembling, now he had committed himself, added:

'There'll be a good half an acre... Strike me blind if I don't, cross my heart.'

Lengaigne went off with his son Victor, exasperated and upset at his neighbour's generosity: he wouldn't really miss the land, he'd already rooked everybody pretty thoroughly! Despite the cold, Macqueron took down his gun from the wall and went out to see if he would come across the rabbit which he'd seen the day before at the bottom of his vineyard. There remained only Lequeu, who used to spend all his Sundays there (although he never had a drink), and the two fanatical card players, their heads bent over their cards. Hours went by; other peasants came in and went out again.

At about five o'clock, the door was pushed roughly open and Buteau appeared, followed by Jean. As soon as he caught sight of Jesus Christ, he exclaimed:

'I'd've bet anything... Are you trying to have us on? We've been waiting for you.'

But Jesus Christ, drooling at the mouth, replied with a chuckle:

'No, you old humbug, I've been waiting for you... You've been keeping us waiting ever since this morning.'

Buteau had looked in at La Borderie where Jacqueline, whom he had been tumbling in the hay ever since the age of fifteen, had invited him to stay and have a meal with Jean. Farmer Hourdequin had stayed in Cloyes for lunch after Mass and they had gone on drinking and guzzling until late afternoon, so that the two young men, now inseparable, had only just arrived.

75

Meanwhile Bécu kept bawling that he would pay for the five litres of wine but the game must go on; whilst Jesus Christ, maudlin and bleary-eyed, hauling himself with difficulty out of his chair, followed his brother.

'Wait here,' Buteau said to Jean, 'and come and pick me up in half an hour's time. Remember that you're having supper with me at my father's.'

When the two brothers went into the Fouans' house, everyone was already gathered in the room. Their father was standing up with a hangdog expression on his face. Their mother was sitting knitting mechanically at the table in the middle of the room. Opposite her, Grosbois had eaten and drunk so much that he had dozed off, his eyes half closed; while Fanny and Delhomme were sitting on a couple of low chairs near by, patiently waiting. And, in this smoke-blackened room with its shabby old furniture and the few kitchen utensils worn thin by constant scouring, there was the unusual sight of a blank sheet of paper and pen lying on the table beside the surveyor's hat, a hat of monumental proportions, once black but now a rusty brown, which its owner had carried about with him, come rain, come shine, for the last ten years. Night was falling and in the murky light filtering through the narrow window the hat with its flat rim and urn-like shape assumed a strange significance.

However, ever mindful of his business despite his drunkenness, Grosbois roused himself and mumbled:

'Here we are, then. I was explaining that the deed is all drawn up. I went to see Monsieur Baillehache yesterday and he showed me it. Only the numbers of the lots have been left blank against your names. So now we'll draw and all the lawyer will have to do is to write them in so that you can sign the deed in his office on Saturday.'

He shook himself awake and spoke more loudly.

'Well, I'll get the pieces of paper ready.'

At once the children all quickly gathered round, making no attempt to disguise their mistrust, watching each other like hawks so as not to miss the slightest gesture, as if a conjuror might spirit away their share. First of all, with his thick, trembling, alcoholic's fingers, Grosbois cut the sheet of paper into three, and then, laboriously, on each piece he wrote an enormous 1, 2

76

or 3; looking over his shoulders, they all followed the movement of his pen, even the father and mother nodding their head in satisfaction when they saw that there was no chance of cheating. Slowly the pieces of paper were folded and thrown into the hat.

A solemn silence ensued.

After waiting a good two minutes, Grosbois said:

'Well, make up your minds. . . Who's going to begin?'

Nobody stirred. Night was falling fast and in the gloom the hat seemed to be growing larger.

'In order of age, do you think?' the surveyor suggested. 'You go first, then, Jesus Christ, you're the eldest!'

Jesus Christ good-naturedly stepped forward, but losing his balance he nearly fell flat on his face. He thrust his fist violently into the hat as if he were expecting to pick up a boulder. When he had seized his piece of paper, he had to go to the window to read what was on it.

'Two!' he exclaimed, doubtless thinking that this was a particularly funny number, since he spluttered with laughter.

'Your turn, Fanny,' Grosbois called.

When Fanny put her hand into the hat she was in no hurry. She rummaged in the bottom, moving the papers around and lifting up one after the other.

'You're not allowed to choose,' exclaimed Buteau angrily, in a voice choking with emotion; his face had gone pale when he saw the number his brother had drawn.

'Really? Why not?' she retorted. 'I'm not looking, there's nothing wrong in feeling.'

'Go on,' her father said. 'They're all the same, there's no difference in any of them.'

She finally made her choice and rushed to the window:

'One.'

'Well, Buteau's got number three,' said Fouan. 'Go on, draw it, my boy!'

In the ever deepening gloom, it was impossible to see how contorted the face of the youngest son had become. He burst out angrily:

'I shan't!'

'What do you mean?'

'If you imagine I'm going to accept that, you're mistaken!

That's the third lot, isn't it? The rotten one! I've already told you lots of times that I want the sharing to be done differently. No, I won't! You'd just be making a fool of me! And anyway, do you think I can't see what you're up to? Shouldn't the youngest have drawn lots first? So I won't! I'm not going to draw because I'm being cheated!'

His father and mother watched him throwing his arms about, stamping and banging the table.

'You poor boy, you must have taken leave of your senses,' said Rose.

'Oh yes, mother, I know you never loved me. You'd skin me alive to give my skin to my brother... You all want to do me down!'

Fouan harshly interrupted him.

'Stop talking nonsense! Will you draw or not?'

'I insist we do it all again!'

Everyone protested. Jesus Christ and Fanny clung to their pieces of paper as if someone were trying to take it away from them. Delhomme pointed out that the lots had been drawn fairly and Grosbois, highly offended, talked of leaving if his good faith was being questioned.

'Then I want Father to add another thousand francs to my share from the money he's got hidden away.'

Completely taken aback, the old man was momentarily at a loss for words. Then he collected himself and made towards his son with a terrifying expression.

'What's that you said? So you really want to kill me off, you swine! You wouldn't find a brass farthing even if you pulled down the whole house. Draw your lot, for Christ's sake, or else you'll get nothing!'

Buteau, pigheaded and stubborn, did not even flinch at his father's threatening gesture.

'I won't.'

Once again an embarrassed silence fell. Now the enormous hat sat there, rebuking them and blocking the way with that single piece of paper lying inside it which nobody was willing to take. To end the discussion, the surveyor advised the old man to draw it himself and he solemnly pulled it out and went over to the window to look at it, as if he did not know what was on it.

'Three! You've got the third lot, do you hear? The deed's drawn up and Monsieur Baillehache certainly won't change it, because what's done can't be undone... And since you're going to sleep here, I'll give you tonight to think it over!... Now that's over and done with, let's say no more.'

Plunged into gloom, Buteau made no reply. The others loudly approved and their mother decided to light a candle to lay the table.

And at that moment Jean, on his way to rejoin his friend, caught sight of two shadowy figures, huddled together, standing in the dark deserted road and trying to see what was going on at the Fouans'. From the slate-grey sky, feathery flakes of snow were beginning to fall.

'Oh! You frightened us, Monsieur Jean,' a voice said softly.

Then he recognized Françoise, wearing a hood over her long face with its heavy lips. She was huddled against her sister Lise with her arm round her waist. The two sisters were devoted to each other and were always to be seen together like that, with their arms round each other's necks. Lise, taller and pleasant-looking, despite her coarse features and the incipient flabbiness of her plump figure, had remained cheerful in spite of her misfortune.

'So you're spying?' he said with a smile.

'Well, perhaps,' she replied. 'It interests me to know what's happening in there... To know if it will help Buteau make up his mind.'

Françoise had passed her other arm round her sister's bulging waist and was holding it affectionately.

'If that's possible, the rotten pig!... Once he's got the land, perhaps he'll want a girl with more money!'

But Jean raised their hopes: the share-out must have been decided by now, all the rest would be all right. Then, when he told them that he was going to eat with the old people, Françoise said:

'All right then, we'll meet later on, we'll come round to the evening gathering!'

He watched them disappear into the night. The snow was falling more heavily now and their clothes, merging together, were acquiring a feathery white fringe.

Chapter 5

BY seven o'clock, after supper, the Fouans, Buteau and Jean had gone over to the cowshed to join the two cows which Rose was going to sell. Tied up at the end beside their trough, these two animals filled the shed with the powerful smell and the heat of their bodies and of their litter, whereas the kitchen, with its three miserable logs of wood which had been lit for supper, was already bitterly cold from the early November frosts. So, in winter, the neighbours would gather there on the mud floor and be warm and cosy, with no further effort than bringing in a little round table and a dozen old chairs. Each neighbour provided a candle in turn; broad shadows danced along the bare walls, black with dust, up to the spiders' webs in the roof timbers; and in the background was the warm breath of the cows lying chewing the cud.

La Grande was the first to arrive with her knitting. Taking advantage of her great age, she never provided a candle herself; and she inspired such awe that her brother never dared to remind her of the normal custom. She at once took the best seat and seized the candlestick which she kept to herself because of her bad eyes. Against her chair she had leant her stick, which she never left far away. Little shining specks of snow were melting on the coarse bristles of her scrawny bird-like head.

'Is it snowing?' asked Rose.

'It is,' she answered curtly.

And compressing her thin lips, she took up her knitting after casting a sharp glance in the direction of Jean and Buteau.

Then the others appeared: first of all Fanny, who had brought along her son Nénesse, since Delhomme never came to these gatherings; then, almost at once, Lise and Françoise, laughing as they shook off the snow. But at the sight of Buteau, Lise blushed. He looked at her unabashed.

'How are things since we last met, Lise?'

'Not too bad, thanks.'

'That's good, then.'

Meanwhile Palmyre had surreptitiously slipped in through the half-open door. She was crouching down and staying as far away as possible from her terrible grandmother La Grande when a loud noise outside made her straighten up. She could hear furious stammering, shouts, laughter and boos.

'Those miserable kids are at him again,' she exclaimed.

She leapt towards the door and, suddenly transformed into a bold raging lioness, she rescued her brother Hilarion from the tormenting of La Trouille, Delphin and Nénesse. The latter had just joined the other two, who were shrieking and yelling at the cripple's heels. Hilarion limped in on his deformed legs, quite out of breath and bewildered. His hare-lip was dribbling and he was stammering, unable to explain what was wrong, looking like an ugly village idiot and frail for his age of twenty-four. He was in a temper, furious because he had not been able to catch the young scamps who were chasing him and knock their heads together. Not for the first time, he had met a volley of snowballs.

'Oh, what a fibber,' said La Trouille, all innocence. 'He bit my finger, look.'

At this Hilarion spluttered helplessly as he tried to explain, while Palmyre calmed him down and petted him as she wiped his face with her handkerchief.

'That's enough now,' said Fouan at last. 'Palmyre, you ought to stop him from following you. Make him sit down at least and keep him quiet !. . . And you brats shut up ! We'll take you back to your parents by your ears if you're not careful.'

But as the cripple still kept babbling on, La Grande, her eyes blazing, picked up her stick and struck the table with it so hard that everyone jumped. Terrified, Palmyre and Hilarion subsided and remained still as mice.

The evening now began. Grouped around the solitary candle, the women sewed and knitted or did needlework without a single glance at what they were making. The men sat behind, slowly smoking as they exchanged a few desultory remarks, while in a corner the children, with suppressed giggles, pinched and pushed each other.

Sometimes they would tell stories: the story of the Black Pig who kept guard over a treasure with a red key in his jaws; or the Beast of Orléans who had a man's face, bat's wings, hair reaching

81

to the ground, two horns and two tails, one to catch and the other to kill you; and this monster had eaten a man from Rouen and left only his hat and his boots. At other times, they would launch into endless tales about wolves, the devouring wolves which ravaged Beauce for centuries. Formerly, when Beauce, which is so bare and treeless at the present time, had still a few coppices left from original forests, countless bands of wolves, impelled by hunger, used to come out in the winter to prey on the flocks. They devoured women and children, and the old people of the district could remember that in times of heavy snow the wolves would come into the towns. In Cloyes you could hear them howling on the Place Saint-Georges; in Rognes they would push their noses under the loose doors of cowsheds and sheep pens. Then, one after the other, the same old stories would be told: the miller ambushed by wolves who put them to flight by striking a match; the little girl who ran for two hours pursued by a she-wolf which ate her up when she fell down just as she reached the door of her home; and still more stories, legends of werewolves, of men changed into beasts leaping out onto the shoulders of belated passers-by or running them to death.

But what made the blood of the girls run cold as they sat round in the pale candlelight, and sent them running off to peer wildly into the darkness, was the story of the famous band of criminals from Orgères called the Roasters, whose exploits still made the district shudder with horror sixty years later. There were hundreds of them, beggars, tramps, deserters and pretended hawkers, men, women and children living from theft, murder and vice. They were descended from the old bands of organized armed bandits, who took advantage of the troubles arising out of the Revolution by systematically attacking isolated houses which they burst into by breaking down the doors with battering rams. At nightfall they would come like wolves out of the forest of Dourdan, the scrubland of La Conie, from the dens where they lurked in the woods; and as dusk fell, terror descended on the farms of Beauce, from Étampes to Châteaudun and from Chartres to Orléans. Amongst their legendary atrocities the one most frequently spoken of in Rognes was the sacking of the Millouard farm, only a score of miles away, in the canton of Orgères. On that night, their celebrated leader, Beau François, who had succeeded May Blossom, had with him his lieutenant, Red Auneau, the Big Dragoon, Breton-dry-arse, Longjumeau, One-thumb Jean and fifty more, all with blackened faces. First, they forced all the workers on the farm, the maids, the carters and the shepherd, down the cellar at bayonet-point; then they 'roasted' old Fousset the farmer, whom they had kept separate from the rest. Having stretched his feet out over the glowing embers of the fire, they set light to his beard and all the hair on his body with lighted wisps of straw; then they went back to his feet which they slashed with the point of a knife so that they would cook better. When the old man had been persuaded to reveal the whereabouts of his money, they eventually let him go and made off with an immense amount of loot; Fousset had the strength to crawl to a neighbouring house and did not die until some time later. And the tale invariably ended with the trial and execution in Chartres of the band of the Roasters who had been betrayed by One-eyed Jacques: a mass trial for which it took eighteen months to collect the evidence and in the course of which sixty-four of the accused died in prison from a plague caused by their own filth; a trial which brought one hundred and fifteen prisoners before the assize court (thirty-three of them *in absentia*), which required the jury to answer seven thousand eight hundred questions and led to twenty-three death sentences. On the night of the execution, the executioners of Chartres and Dreux came to blows underneath the blood-stained scaffold while sharing out the condemned men's effects.

So, in connection with a murder which had just been committed over at Janville, Fouan proceeded to relate for the umpteenth time the dreadful events at Millouard: and he had just reached the point when Red Auneau himself was composing his ballad of lament in gaol when the women were horrified by noises in the street, the sound of footsteps and pushing mingled with oaths. Pale-faced, they listened intently, terrified that they might see a sudden invasion of black-faced men. Bravely, Buteau went to the door and opened it:

'Who's that?'

And they saw Bécu and Jesus Christ, who, having quarrelled with Macqueron, had just left the tavern, taking their cards and a candle with them to finish their game elsewhere. They were so drunk and the others had been so frightened that everybody laughed.

'All right, you can come in,' Rose said, smiling at her great scamp of a son. 'Your children are here, you can take them with you when you go.'

Jesus Christ and Bécu sat down on the ground next to the cows, placed the candle between them and went on with their game: 'Trumps and trumps and still more trumps!' But the conversation had moved on and they were now talking about the boys of the village who would be drawing lots for military service, Victor Lengaigne and three others. The women had become serious, they were talking slowly and sadly.

'It's no joke,' said Rose, 'no, it's no joke at all for anybody.'

'Yes, war's a dreadful thing,' said Fouan in a subdued voice. 'It's the ruination of agriculture. . . When the lads go off, it's the strongest who go, you can see it when there's hard work to be done; and when they come back, well, they've changed, their hearts are no longer in ploughing. Cholera's better than war.'

Fanny stopped knitting.

'Well, I don't intend to let Nénesse go,' she declared. 'Monsieur Baillehache explained how to get round it, something like a lottery; several people club together and everyone contributes a certain amount and those whose number turns up are able to buy themselves out.'

'You have to be rich to do that,' remarked La Grande sharply.

But Bécu had overheard a word or two, between two games.

'War? War makes a man of you, by God!. . . If you've never been, you can never understand, that's life, bashing each other about. What d'you think, eh? Those wogs down there. . .'

And he gave a wink with his left eye while Jesus Christ grinned with a knowing air. They had both fought in Africa, the gamekeeper at the beginning of the war, the other man later on at the time of the recent uprisings. So in spite of the difference in time, they both had common memories: cutting off Bedouins' ears and threading them on a string; Bedouin women with their bodies rubbed all over in oil whom you picked up behind the hedgerows and stuffed in every hole. Jesus Christ in particular would often tell a story which used to bring big guffaws from

84

the peasants: a great cow of a woman as yellow as a lemon whom they'd made run about stark-naked with a pipe stuck up her behind.

'For Christ's sake,' said Bécu, addressing Fanny, 'do you want Nénesse to be a cissy?... I'm going to make quite sure that Delphin goes into the army.'

The children had stopped playing. Delphin was looking up; his round, sturdy head already made him seem a proper peasant, young though he was.

'No,' he said bluntly, looking obstinate.

'What did you say? I'll teach you what courage means, you unpatriotic little sod!'

'I don't want to go into the army. I want to stay here.'

The gamekeeper was about to strike him when Buteau intervened.

'Leave the child alone! He's right. Do they need him? There are plenty of others... Anyway, is that how things ought to be, to have to go away from home and get your mug bashed in for a lot of stupid rubbish... I never left the village and I'm none the worse for it!'

He had in fact been lucky in the draw; he was a real landworker and loved it; he had never gone further than Chartres or Orléans or seen anything beyond the flat horizon of Beauce. And he seemed to be proud of it, proud at having his roots in his own patch of land, bound to it like a stubborn hardy tree. He had risen to his feet; the women were watching him.

'When they come back from military service they're all so thin,' Lise said quietly and timidly.

'And how about you, Corporal?' old Rose asked. 'Did you go to foreign parts?'

Jean was a young man who preferred to think rather than talk. He had been quietly smoking his pipe, which he now slowly removed from his mouth.

'Yes, I went quite a long way... But I didn't get as far as the Crimea. I was on the point of going when they took Sebastopol... But later on there was Italy...'

'And what's Italy like?'

The question seemed to surprise him, he hesitated and searched his memory.

'Well, Italy's no different from here. They grow things, they've got woods and rivers. It's the same as everywhere.'

'So you took part in the fighting?'

'Yes, I did some fighting, of course.'

He was sucking at his pipe again, in no hurry to talk, and Françoise looked up, her lips parted, expecting a story. All the women were interested and even La Grande rapped the table again with her stick to stop Hilarion from whining, as La Trouille had hit upon the idea of slyly sticking a pin into his arm.

'Solferino was a hot spot, all right, although it was raining, goodness me how it rained... I hadn't got a dry stitch on me, the water was pouring down my back into my shoes. We certainly got wet and no mistake.'

They waited but he had nothing to add; that was all he had seen of the battle of Solferino. After a minute's silence, he went on in his quiet, sensible way:

'Well, war's not as bad as people think. You draw lots, don't you? You've got to do your duty. As for me, I left the army because I'd sooner be doing something else. All the same, it can be a good thing for someone who doesn't like his job and hates the idea of an enemy coming in and mucking us about in our own country.'

'All the same, it's a nasty business,' concluded old Fouan. 'Everyone ought to defend his own home and that's all.'

Once again silence fell. It was very warm, a damp, living heat that seemed all the stronger because of the powerful smell of the cows' litter. One of the two cows, which had stood up, was dropping her dung and they heard the regular plop-plop as it spread out on the ground. In the gloom of the roof-timbers they could hear the mournful chirruping of a cricket, while the shadows of the women's nimble fingers busy with their knitting seemed like giant spiders' legs dancing along the wall in the all-pervading blackness.

But when Palmyre tried to snuff the candle she did it so awkwardly that it went out. There were startled exclamations, the girls laughed while the children pushed a pin into Hilarion's backside; and they would have been in trouble but for the candle of Jesus Christ and Bécu, who were drowsing over their cards; with its aid they relit the other one, despite its long wick, which had spread out like a red mushroom. Terrified at her clumsiness, Palmyre was trembling like a little girl expecting a thrashing.

'Well now,' said Fouan, 'who's going to read us this, to finish the evening? Corporal, you must be good at reading printed books. . .'

He had been to fetch a greasy little book, one of those books of Bonapartist propaganda which every village and hamlet in France had been flooded with under the Empire. This one had turned up from the pack of some itinerant pedlar and it was a violent attack on the old monarchy, a dramatized history of the peasantry before and after the Revolution, under the doleful title *The Misfortunes and Triumph of Jacques Bonhomme*.

Jean took the book and without any urging started to read in the flat drone of a schoolboy ignoring any punctuation. They listened with rapt attention.

First it was the story of the Gauls, a free people reduced to slavery by the Romans and then conquered by the Franks; the latter, by establishing the feudal system, turned slavery into serfdom. And then the long martyrdom of Jacques Bonhomme began, the martyrdom of the tiller of the soil, exploited and exterminated through the centuries. While the townspeople revolted, founded communes and achieved status as a middle class, the peasant, isolated and possessing nothing, not even himself, did not succeed in freeing himself until later, by buying with his own money the freedom to be a man; and only an illusory freedom at that, for the landowner was hamstrung by vicious and ruinous taxes, his tenure was always precarious, his property burdened with so many tolls and levies that he was left with little more than stones to eat. Then followed a terrifying catalogue of all the dues the wretched peasant had to pay. No one could draw up an accurate and complete list because they were legion; an icy blast that blew from the king, the bishop and the lord all together. Three ravening beasts were devouring the same body: the king had the quit-rent and talliage, the bishop had the tithes, the lord taxed and filled his coffers with everything. And now the common man no longer owned anything, neither land nor water nor fire nor even the air he breathed. He had to pay and keep on paying, pay to live, pay to die, pay for his deeds of contract, his herds, even his pleasure. He paid in order to channel the rainwater from the moat into his land, he paid for the cloud of dust raised by the feet of his sheep along the paths in the summer, during the droughts. Anyone who failed to pay in cash paid with his body and his time, talliable and liable to forced labour at his lord's pleasure, forced to plough and harvest and reap and prune the vine and clean out the moat of his castle, to build and maintain the roads. And then there were payments in kind; and the rights of banality, the mill, the oven, the winepress, which cost him a quarter of his crops; and then watch and guard duty, which, when dungeons were abolished, were commuted into money payments. And then there were the rights of capture, purveyance and lodging, so that when the king or the lord passed through, cottages were ransacked, coverlets and palliasses seized, the inhabitants driven out of their homes and doors and windows wrenched from their frames if the occupant failed to take himself off quickly enough. But the tax most loathed, the one which still aroused the bitterest memories in every hamlet, was the hateful salt tax, with the storehouses full of salt and every family forced to buy a certain quantity of it at a fixed price from the king, an arbitrary and iniquitous revenue that caused rebellion and bloodshed all over France.

'My father,' Fouan broke in, 'could remember salt at nearly a franc a pound. . . Ah, those were hard times!'

Jesus Christ was chuckling in his beard. He tried to bring the conversation round to the more salacious rights, such as the *jus primae noctis*, which the little book was content modestly to hint at.

'How about that? The lord stuck his thigh into the bride's bed and then on the first night he'd stick. . .'

They prevented him from finishing his sentence. The girls, even Lise with her round belly, had blushed violently while La Trouille and the two young scamps stuck their fists into their mouths to stifle their laughter. Hilarion, open-mouthed, was not missing a single word, as if he understood.

Jean continued his reading. Now they were hearing about justice, the threefold justice of king, bishop and lord, crucifying the poor peasant as he sweated over the soil. There was common law and written law and, above all, there was the capricious law of the strongest: no guarantee or appeals, nothing but the supreme power of the sword. Even in later centuries, when the voice of equity was raised in protest, offices were bought and justice was sold. And it was worse when armies had to be recruited, a blood tax which for many a long year was confined only to the lower orders; when they fled into the woods the peasants would be fetched back in chains, driven along by gun butts and enrolled in the army like galley-slaves. They would never gain promotion. A younger son of a noble family used his regiment as a business, rather like a commodity which he had bought; he would put the rank and file up for auction and send the rest of his human cattle off to slaughter. Then finally there were the hunting rights, the right to have a dovecot, the right to shoot rabbits, rights which, even now they have been abolished, have still left a ferment of ill feeling in the hearts of the peasantry. Shooting game was the old feudal prerogative, a fanatical insistence on hereditary rights which gave the lord authority to hunt whenever he wanted and made the villein liable to death if he had the temerity to shoot over his own ground. The wild beast or bird kept in confinement beneath the open sky for the pleasure of one man; fields penned into royal hunts which any game was free to devastate while the owners were not allowed to shoot even a dunnock.

'That's understandable,' muttered Bécu, who used to talk of shooting poachers like rabbits.

But Jesus Christ had pricked up his ears at the sound of the word 'shooting' and was whistling between his teeth with a facetious air. Game belonged to anyone who knew how to kill it.

'Oh deary me,' Rose said simply, with a big sigh.

They were all sad at heart and were slowly becoming oppressed as when they listened to a ghost story. Nor did they always fully understand, and this added to their disquiet. Since those things had happened in the past, they might well happen again in the future.

'Go on your way, poor Jacques Bonhomme,' Jean droned on in his schoolboy voice. 'You must sacrifice yet more sweat and blood, the end of your tribulations is not yet in sight. . .'

Indeed, the whole calvary of the peasant was now unfolded. He had suffered from everything, from man, from the elements and from himself. Under the feudal system, when the nobles set out on the rampage, he was hunted, pursued and carried off as part of the loot. Every private war between one lord and another ruined him, if it did not kill him, his cottage was burnt down, his field laid waste. Later on came the big companies, the worst of the scourges that devastated the countryside, those bands of mercenaries at the service of anyone who could hire them, sometimes for and sometimes against France, killing and burning as they passed and leaving nothing but waste land in their wake. Though towns might hold out, thanks to their walls, the villages were swept away in this mad hurricane of massacre which blew from one end of a century to the next. There were centuries of blood, centuries during which our flatlands, as they were called, resounded with one single, massive cry of pain, of raped women, battered children and hanged men. Then, when there was respite from war, the royal tax-collectors were sufficient torment for the poor wretches on the land, because the number and burden of the taxes was as nothing compared with the brutal capricious methods of collecting them: talliage and salt tax were farmed out and taxes, unjustly allotted in accordance with the merest whim, exacted by armed troops who turned revenue collection into a war levy; so that hardly any of the money reached the coffers of the state, having disappeared on the way, stolen little by little by every dishonest hand through which it passed. And then famine played its part. The idiotic tyranny of the laws hampered trade, prevented the free sale of corn and so brought about dreadful shortages every ten years, either through years of drought or excessive rain, which seemed like punishment from on high. A storm which flooded the rivers, a rainless spring, the slightest cloud or ray of sunshine could affect the crops and carry off thousands of men; terrible seasons of famine, sudden excesses of all sorts, dreadful periods of destitution during which men nibbled the grass beside the ditches, like beasts of the field. And, inevitably, after the wars and famines would come the epidemics which killed off those who'd been spared by hunger or the sword. It was the noisome fruit of ignorance and filth, ever recurring, the Black Death, the Great Plague, which stride like giant skeletons through past centuries, scything down the pale, sad people of the countryside.

So, when his sufferings became unbearable, Jacques Bonhomme

would rise in revolt. He had centuries of fear and submission behind him, his shoulders had become hardened to blows, his soul so crushed that he did not recognize his own degradation. You could beat him and starve him and rob him of everything, year in, year out, before he would abandon his caution and stupidity, his mind filled with all sorts of muddled ideas which he could not properly understand; and this went on until a culmination of injustice and suffering flung him at his master's throat like some infuriated domestic animal who had been subjected to too many thrashings. Constantly, from one century to the next, there came the same explosion of exasperation, the ploughmen of the Jacquerie arming themselves with scythe and pitchfork when nothing remained for them but death. Such were the Christian Bagaudes of Gaul, the Pastoureaux of the time of the Crusades, then later on, the Croquants and the Nu-Pieds hurling themselves against the nobles and the soldiers of the king. After four hundred years, the cry of pain and anger from all the Jacques Bonhommes which still resounds over the devastated fields made the masters quake in their castles. Suppose they were to lose patience once again and claim at last their rightful heritage? And the vision of old surged through the land, of tall, ragged, half-naked fellows, lusting and mad with violence, spreading ruin and destruction in the same way as they have themselves been ruined and destroyed, raping in their turn the wives of those who had raped theirs!

'Rein in your anger, you men and women of the countryside,' Jean read on, in his quiet, careful voice. 'The hour of victory will soon strike on the clock of history...'

Buteau suddenly shrugged his shoulders: what was the point of being rebellious? So that the gendarmes could cart you off to prison? Indeed, since the little book had started talking of their ancestors' revolts, they had all been listening with their eyes cast downwards, not daring to make a gesture, full of distrust even although they were with people whom they knew. These were things which were not to be spoken of aloud, there was no need for anyone to know what they thought about them. When Jesus Christ broke in and exclaimed that when the next time came he would wring several people's necks, Bécu spoke up violently to proclaim that all republicans were pigs; and Fouan had to impose solemn silence, in the sad and serious voice of an old man who knows a great deal but does not wish to talk about it. While the other women seemed to be concerned with their knitting, La Grande said sententiously:

'What you've got, you keep,' although that remark hardly seemed to have any connexion with the reading.

Only Françoise, who had let her book fall onto her lap, was looking at the Corporal in astonishment that he could read for so long without making any mistakes.

'Oh dear, oh dear,' Rose said again, sighing even more deeply.

But now the tone of the book changed and became lyrical in its praise of the Revolution. This was Jacques Bonhomme's triumph, the apotheosis of 1789. After the capture of the Bastille, while the peasants were burning down the castles, the events of the night of August 4th legalized the victories achieved over the centuries by recognizing civil liberty and the equality of man. In the space of one night the tillers of the soil became the equal of their lord and master who, by virtue of ancient title deeds, had been living on the sweat of their brow and devouring the fruits of their sleepless nights. Serfdom was abolished, the privileges of nobility were abolished, ecclesiastical and manorial courts of justice were abolished; all the old rights were commuted into money, there was equal liability to taxation for all; all citizens were to be given equal access to civil and military posts. And the catalogue went on; all the ills of this life seemed to be evaporating one by one in a song of praise for the new Golden Age of the farm labourer which was beginning. There followed a whole page of obsequious flattery, lauding the labourer to the skies as the king and provider of the world. He alone was important, everyone must bow the knee before the holy plough. Then the horrors of 1793 were condemned in the strongest terms and the book launched into an extravagant eulogy of Napoleon, the child of the Revolution who had succeeded in 'dragging it out of the slough of its excesses to bring happiness to all those living from the land'.

'Yes, that's true,' Bécu interjected, as Jean turned over the last page.

'Yes, I agree,' said old Fouan. 'There were still good times to be had when I was a young man. Sure as I sit here, I saw Napoleon once, at Chartres. I was twenty then. We were free, we owned the land, everything seemed wonderful! I remember my father saying to me one day that he used to sow pennies and reap crowns. . . Then we had Louis XVIII, Charles X, Louis Philippe. Things weren't too bad, we had enough to eat, we couldn't complain. . . And now we've got Napoleon III and things were still not too bad until last year. . . All the same. . .'

He tried to keep the rest of the sentence to himself but the words burst out:

'All the same, what's all their liberty and equality done for Rose and me? Are we any better off, after slaving away for fifty years?'

Then, slowly, laboriously, in a few words, he summed up, unconsciously, the whole story they had just heard. The peasant who had for so long cultivated the land for the benefit of the lord of the manor yet who was beaten and stripped like a slave, not even owning his own skin; who had made the land fruitful by his efforts; then the constant, intimate link with the land which makes him love and desire it with a passion such as you might feel for someone else's wife whom you care for and take in your arms but can never possess; that land which, after you have coveted it in such suffering for centuries, you finally obtain by conquest and make your own, the sole joy and light of your life. And this desire which had built up over the centuries, this possession seemingly never to be achieved, explained his love for his own plot, his passion for land, the largest possible amount of land, the rich, heavy lump of soil that you can touch and weigh in your hand. Yet how thankless and indifferent that land was! However much you adored it, its heart was never softened, it would not produce one single extra grain. Too much rain rotted the seed, hail cut down the young wheat, a thunderstorm broke the stalks, two months of drought would stop the ears from filling out, and then there were the insects which gnaw, the frosts that kill, diseases which attack your cattle, and weeds which spread like a canker over the soil: everything could bring ruination, the struggle had to be fought every day; and always you were subject to the whims of ignorance and lived in a perpetual state of alarm. True, he had never spared himself, he had fought tooth and nail, infuriated that work alone was not enough. He had strained every sinew of his body, he had given himself completely to the land and now, after it had barely allowed him to keep body and soul together, it had left him wretched and unsatisfied, ashamed of his senile lack of strength, and it would pass into the arms of another male, without pity for his poor old bones, which it was waiting to receive.

'And that's how it is,' concluded the old man. 'When you're young, you sweat blood, and after all your efforts, when you've at last managed to make ends meet, you're old and it's time to leave... That's it, isn't it, Rose?'

His wife shook her trembling head. Yes, curse it, she'd worked too, more than a man, certainly. Getting up before everybody else, cooking, sweeping, scouring the pots, worn out by a thousand and one jobs, the cows, the pigs, kneading the bread and then not getting to bed until long after everyone else! You had to be strong to survive. And that was her only reward, to have kept going; all you got was wrinkles and, after looking at every farthing, going to bed in the dark and living on bread and water, you could think yourself lucky if you had enough to keep body and soul together in your old age.

'All the same,' Fouan went on, 'we mustn't complain. I've heard tell of places where it's a dog's life to live on the land. In the Perche, for example, there's nothing but rock and stones. In Beauce, the soil is still good, all it needs is to be looked after all the time... But it's not as good as it was. It's getting poorer, that's for sure, there are fields which used to give a hundred and fifty bushels and now don't give more than a hundred... And prices have been going down ever since last year, people say that wheat's been coming in from foreign parts, something evil is happening, what they call a crisis... Can we ever feel free from trouble? Their "one man one vote" doesn't put much meat into your mouth, does it? The tax-man is always sitting on your back and they take your children away from you to send them off to war... No, it's all very well having revolutions, it's always six of one and half a dozen of the other, and a land-worker's still a land-worker!'

Jean was a methodical man and he had been waiting to finish his reading. As silence fell, he went on quietly:

'Happy tiller of the soil, never leave your village for the town

94

where you would have to buy everything, milk, meat and vegetables, and where you would always spend more than you need
because of all the temptations. In the village, haven't you got
sun and air, healthy work and healthy pleasures? Country life
has no equal, yours is real happiness, far from magnificent
palaces; and the proof is that workers in towns come to the country to relax, just as the rich townspeople have only one ideal, to
retire to the country to pick your flowers, to eat fruit straight
from the tree and disport themselves on the grass. Make no mistake, Jacques Bonhomme, money is an empty delusion. The only
real wealth is peace of mind!'

His voice was breaking and the big, tender-hearted young man
had to restrain his emotion, for, having been brought up in the
town, his heart melted at the thought of rustic happiness. The
others remained glum, the women bending over their needles, the
hard-faced men slumped forward. Was the book pulling their leg?
Money was the only good thing there was and they were poverty-
stricken. Then, embarrassed by the silence, pregnant with so
much suffering and resentment, the young man ventured to make
a judicious comment:

'All the same, things would be better with more education. If
people were so unhappy in the past, it was through ignorance.
Nowadays, people know a little more and things are certainly
better. So we ought to know more and more, set up schools
where you can study agriculture.'

But old Fouan, stubbornly set in his ways, fiercely interrupted
him:

'Oh, get along with your science! The more you know, the less
well things go; didn't you hear me say that fifty years ago the
land was producing more? The land is fed up with being mucked
about with. It never gives more than it wants, the crafty old
bitch! And look at Monsieur Hourdequin, who's risked pots of
money on new inventions... No, it's no bloody good, a peasant's
a peasant!'

Ten o'clock was striking and this parting shot put an end to
the conversation like a clap of thunder. Rose went off to fetch a
jar of chestnuts that she had left cooking in the embers of the
kitchen fire: an obligatory treat for Hallowe'en. She even brought
back a couple of litres of white wine to make it a real feast. So

they forgot their troubles, and spirits rose as, with tooth and nail, they set about pulling off the steaming skins of the boiled chestnuts. La Grande had immediately engulfed her share in her pocket, because she could not eat so fast. Bécu and Jesus Christ were tossing theirs into their mouths and swallowing them skin and all, while, plucking up courage, Palmyre was very carefully peeling her share before stuffing them into Hilarion's mouth as though stuffing a goose with corn. As for the children, they were 'making a pudding'. La Trouille pierced a hole in a chestnut with her teeth and then pressed it so that it spurted out for Delphin and Nénesse to lick. It was jolly good. Lise and Françoise decided to do the same. They snuffed the candle for the last time, they drank to the health of all those present. It was much warmer now : a brownish haze was rising from the liquid dung in the litter, the cricket was chirping louder than ever in the flickering shadows of the roof beams, and, not wishing to leave the cows out of the treat, they gave them the chestnut skins which they slowly and gently munched.

At half past ten, they began to leave. First Fanny went off, taking Nénesse with her. Then Jesus Christ and Bécu left, squabbling as the cold outside made them tipsy again. You could hear La Trouille and Delphin supporting their fathers, pushing them and setting them on the right path, like restive animals which cannot find their own way back to their stable. Each time the door slammed an icy blast came in from the snow-covered street. But La Grande was in no hurry as she tied her handkerchief round her neck and pulled on her mittens. She did not once look at Palmyre and Hilarion, who slipped away frightened and shivering in their rags. Finally, she went off to her home next door, loudly slamming her door behind her. Now only Françoise and Lise were left.

'I say, Corporal,' Fouan asked, 'will you take them with you, when you go back to the farm? It's on your way.'

Jean nodded agreement while the two girls tied on their headscarves.

Buteau had stood up and was prowling uneasily to and fro in the cowshed, hard-faced and meditating. He had not said a word since the reading had finished, as though obsessed by what the book had been saying. All those stories of how the land had been so hardly won; why shouldn't he have the lot? He was beginning to find the idea of sharing intolerable. And there were other things as well, muddled ideas, which were chasing each other round his thick skull: anger and pride, a mulish determination not to go back on what he had said and an exacerbated male desire which made him half want something and half not want it, for fear of being taken in. Suddenly he made up his mind.

'I'm off to bed, goodbye!'

'What do you mean, goodbye?'

'Yes, I'll be off to La Chamade before it's light, so goodbye in case I don't see you again.'

His father and mother stood in front of him, side by side.

'Well, what about your share?' asked Fouan. 'Do you accept it?'

Buteau strode towards the door before turning round:

'No!'

The older farmer's whole body shook. He drew himself up in one final outburst of his old authority:

'Very well, then, I disown you... I'll give your brother and sister their shares and I'll rent your share out to them and, when I die, I'll make sure they keep it. So you'll get nothing. Get out!'

Buteau stood firm, defiant and undaunted. Then Rose tried to placate him herself.

'But we love you as much as the others, you silly boy... You're cutting off your nose to spite your face. Won't you accept?'

'No, I won't.'

And he went upstairs to bed.

Outside, Lise and Françoise, still shocked by the scene, walked on for a while in silence. They were holding each other round the waist again and together formed a dark mass in the blue shadows of the snowy night. But as Jean followed them he could soon hear that they were crying. He tried to cheer them up.

'Look, he'll be thinking it over, he'll agree tomorrow.'

'Oh, you don't know what he's like!' exclaimed Lise. 'He'd sooner drop dead than give in. No, there's no hope.'

Then, despairingly:

'So what shall I do with his baby?'

'Well, it's going to have to come out sometime,' said Françoise quietly.

That made them laugh. But they were both too sad and they started crying again.

When Jean had left them at their front door, he continued on his way across the plain. It had stopped snowing and the sky was now bright and clear, dotted with stars, a frosty sky which cast a light as blue and transparent as crystal; and Beauce spread out as far as the eye could see, white and flat and as still as a frozen sea. No breath of wind came from the plain, all he could hear was the steady tramp of his shoes on the frozen earth. The deep and peaceful calm of icy cold reigned supreme. All the things he had been reading kept whirling around in his head, and he took off his cap to cool his brow; he felt an ache behind his ears and the need to stop thinking. The thought of that pregnant girl and her sister worried him, too. He clumped along in his heavy shoes. A bright shooting-star shot across the silent sky.

Over there in the distance, the farm of La Borderie was barely visible, a gentle hump on the white expanse of snow; and when Jean turned off down the side track, he remembered the field that he had sown there a few days before: he looked to the left and recognized it beneath its winding-sheet of snow. It was a thin layer, as light and pure as ermine, marking the ridges of each furrow and telling you, mysteriously, that the earth lay beneath, its limbs now numbed. How gentle the slumber of the seed must be! What peace would lie hidden within this icy bosom until the warmth of morning, the spring sun, roused it into life!

PART TWO

Chapter 1

It was four o'clock and dawn – a rosy dawn in early May – was just beginning to break. As the sky paled, the farm buildings of La Borderie slumbered on, still half in darkness: three long buildings forming three sides of the vast square courtyard, the sheep pen in the rear, the barns on the right and the cowsheds, stables and living quarters on the left. The large gate shutting off the fourth side was closed and fastened with an iron bar. And on the dung-pit a large yellow cockerel was the only sign of life, crowing in a resounding clarion call. A second cock replied and then a third. The call was taken up in the distance from farm to farm all over Beauce.

That night, as on almost every other night, Hourdequin had gone to Jacqueline's bedroom, the little maid's bedroom that he had allowed her to decorate with a floral wallpaper, cambric curtains and mahogany furniture. Despite her ever-increasing power, she had met fierce resistance every time she had attempted to sleep with him in his dead wife's bedroom, which he wished to keep inviolate as a last sign of respect. She was deeply offended by this, realizing full well that she would never really be the mistress of the house until she was sleeping in the old oak fourposter with its red cotton curtains.

As day broke, Jacqueline awoke and she remained lying on her back, wide awake, while the farmer still snored on beside her. In the snug warmth of the bed, her dark eyes were pursuing exciting fancies and her slim, half-naked body throbbed with a sudden wave of desire. Yet the pretty young woman still hesitated; finally she made up her mind and stepped lightly over her master's body, holding her nightdress tucked up and with such agility that he felt nothing; and without making a sound, her hands hot and trembling with sudden lust, she slipped on her petticoat. But she knocked against a chair and he, too, opened his eyes.

'Good Lord, you're getting dressed. . . Where are you going?'

'I'm worried about the bread, I'm going to have a look.'

Hourdequin muttered something and then went back to sleep, surprised and vaguely doubtful at the reason she had given, his head still full of sleep. What a strange idea, the bread didn't need any attention from her at this time of day. He woke up again with a start, seized by a sudden suspicion. Seeing that she was no longer there, he cast a bewildered and rather bleary eye round the maid's room, where he had left his slippers, pipe and razor. So the randy bitch was after a farm-hand again! It took him a couple of minutes to clear his head as he went over the whole story in his mind.

His father, Isidore, was descended from an old peasant family who had made good and risen to the ranks of the bourgeoisie in the sixteenth century. They had all been excisemen: one of them the manager of a salt warehouse in Chartres, another a superintendent in Châteaudun; and Isidore, who had been orphaned when young, found himself with some sixty thousand francs, when, having lost his post at the age of twenty-six as a result of the Revolution, he hit on the idea of making his fortune by exploiting those thieving republican rogues who were selling off the national estates. As he knew the district very well, he sniffed around, did a few sums, and bought the three hundred and seventy acres of La Borderie, all that remained of the former Rognes-Bouqueval demesne, for thirty thousand francs, about a fifth of their real value. Not a single peasant farmer had dared to take the risk with his own money: lawyers and financiers were the only people to profit from this decision of the Revolution. In any case, it was purely a speculative venture, because Isidore had no thought of taking over all the responsibilities of running a farm, but of selling it at its real price at the end of the troubles, thereby making a fivefold profit. But then came the Directoire and the price of property continued to fall, so he was unable to realize the profit which he had hoped for. Left saddled with the land, he now became so imprisoned by it that, since he obstinately refused to let any of it go, he decided to exploit it himself, with the hope of making his fortune this way. At about this time he married the daughter of a neighbouring farmer, who brought him another hundred and twenty-five acres, thereby making him the owner of five hundred acres in all. Thus it was that this townsman of peasant stock went back to agriculture but on a grand scale, a landowning aristocrat replacing the old all-powerful feudal nobility.

His only son, Alexandre, born in 1804 and sent to a private school in Châteaudun, turned out to be a hopeless scholar. He had a passion for farming and preferred to leave school and help his father, thereby disappointing a further hope of the latter, who had wanted to sell up and have his son trained for some liberal profession. The young man was twenty-seven when his father died and he became the owner of La Borderie. He was in favour of new methods; his prime concern when he married was not property but money because, in his view, the chief cause of inefficient farming was lack of capital; and he found the dowry he wanted, fifty thousand francs, by marrying a sister of the notary Baillehache, a spinster of ripe age, five years his senior, extremely ugly but kind and gentle. Then there began his struggle with his five hundred acres, a long struggle which had started cautiously but little by little became more and more feverish as a result of various miscalculations and disappointments; a struggle waged unceasingly from day to day and season to season and which, although it failed to make him rich, enabled him to live on a grand scale like the full-blooded man he was, determined never to deny himself any satisfaction he sought. In recent years, things had become even worse. His wife had produced two children: a boy, who had gone into the army as he hated farming, and had just been promoted captain after the battle of Solferino; and a sensitive charming girl, the apple of his eye, to whom he intended to bequeath La Borderie since his ungrateful son had chosen a life of adventure. And then, in the middle of the harvest, he lost his wife. The following autumn, his daughter died. It was a terrible blow. Since his son, the captain, did not put in an appearance even once a year, the father found himself suddenly alone, his future a blank now that he no longer had the incentive of working for posterity. But if his heart bled inwardly, he stood firm, fierce and autocratic that he was. When the peasant farmers jeered at his machinery and hoped disaster would overtake this townsman foolhardy enough to try his hand at their trade, he dug in his heels. And anyway, what else could he do? The land held him in an ever tighter grip: all his work and the capital he had committed held him increasingly a prisoner and the only way out now was to be overtaken by some disaster.

The burly Hourdequin, with his broad ruddy face and only his tiny, refined hands as a reminder of his middle-class origins, had always been a despot where sexual relations with his servants were concerned. Even when his wife was alive, he went through the lot, as a matter of course, without a second thought, as his due. If the daughters of poor peasants sometimes escape by going away to learn dressmaking, none of the girls who go into service on farms avoid falling into the clutches of some man, either the farm-hands or their master. When Jacqueline was taken on at La Borderie as an act of charity, Madame Hourdequin was still alive; her father Cognet, an old drunkard, used to thrash her and she was so skinny and wretched-looking that you could see her bones through her rags. And people thought her so ugly that little boys would boo her. She looked no more than fifteen years old, though in fact she was at least eighteen. She became the skivvy of the household and was given all the dirty jobs, washing up, looking after the farmyard, cleaning out the animals, which made her filthier than ever, as grubby a girl as you would find anywhere. However, after the death of the farmer's wife, she seemed to spruce herself up. All the farm-hands tumbled her in the hay; not a single man passed through the farmyard gate without climbing on top of her; and one day, when she had gone down into the cellar with Hourdequin, although he had till then held back, he too tried to have a go at this ugly little slattern; but she offered such furious resistance and scratched and bit so much that he was forced to leave her alone. From that moment onwards her success was assured. She held out for six months and then surrendered her bare flesh inch by inch. She had levitated from the farmyard to the kitchen as the official servant; next, she took on a skivvy to help her, and then, now quite the lady, had a maid to serve her. Now the former little slut had developed into a shrewd, pretty, firm-breasted, very dark brunette, whose thinness belied the wiry strength of her limbs. She was flirtatious and extravagant and smothered herself in scent, although she was still at heart rather a grubby girl. All the same, the people of Rognes and the farmers in the neighbourhood were still surprised at the affair: how on earth could a rich man have fallen for such a little slip of a girl, not even plump or pretty, in fact for that Cognet girl, the daughter of that drunkard Cognet whom everyone had seen breaking stones for the last twenty years! What a fine father-in-law that would be! And such a notorious trollop! And they failed to realize that this trollop was their vengeance, the revenge of the village against the farm, of the wretched farm labourer against the prosperous bourgeois who had become a big landowner. At the dangerous age of fifty-five, Hourdequin was going soft, a victim of his lust and feeling the need for Jacqueline in the same way as someone has a physical need for bread and water. When she wanted to be very nice to him, she would snuggle up to him like a cat to caress and pleasure him with an eagerness and lack of shame or scruple that would have brought a blush to the cheek of a whore, and, in return for such moments, he would beg her not to leave when he had quarrelled with her and, in a sudden explosion of outrage and revolt, had threatened to throw her out of the house.

Last night, for example, he had slapped her face when she had made a scene in order to sleep in the bed in which his wife had died; and she had kept him at arm's length, giving him a slap whenever he tried to approach her, because although she continued to treat herself to the farm-hands she kept him strictly rationed, whipping up his desire so as to increase her power over him. And so as he lay that morning in this warm, stuffy room among the untidy bed clothes where he could still smell her scent, he was once more overcome by anger and desire. He had long sensed that she was continually betraying him. He jumped out of bed and said out loud:

'Ah, if I catch you at it, you bitch!'

He quickly dressed and went downstairs. Jacqueline had hurried out through the silent house, still barely light in the early dawn. As she went through the farmyard, she drew back for a second when she saw that old Soulas the shepherd was already up... But she was in too excited a state to stop.

Why worry! She kept away from the stables containing the farm's fifteen horses, where the farm's drivers slept, and went round the back, to the corner where Jean slept on some straw, with a blanket and not even a sheet. All breathless and shivering, she gave him a hug as he lay there asleep and, silencing him with a kiss, she whispered softly:

'It's me, you silly. Don't be afraid... Come on, quickly...'

But he was scared, for he never wanted to do it here because of the danger of being caught. The ladder leading to the hayloft was close at hand, so they climbed up it, leaving the trap-door open, and fell in each other's arms into the hay.

'Oh, you silly boy, you silly boy,' said Jacqueline rapturously, in her husky voice that seemed to come from deep down in her body.

Jean Macquart had been at the farm for nearly two years. After leaving the army, he had landed up in Bazoches-le-Doyen with a friend, a carpenter like himself, and he had started working again for this man's father, a small village contractor who employed two or three workmen; but his heart was no longer in his job, his seven years of military service had left him empty, out of practice, and tired of wielding a saw or a plane, so that he seemed to have become a different man. In Plassans in the old days, he had hammered away, never having any gift for learning and barely knowing the three Rs, although he was very serious-minded, hardworking and determined to achieve a position of independence away from his dreadful family. Old Macquart had kept him completely subservient, like a daughter, took his girls away from under his nose, and every Saturday went to the workshop gate to help himself to his pay. So when his mother had succumbed to exhaustion and brutality, he followed the example of his sister Gervaise, who had just gone off to Paris with her lover; he ran away from home, too, to avoid having to keep his good-for-nothing father. And now he could no longer recognize himself, not that he, too, had become lazy, but the army had broadened his mind: politics, for example, which used to bore him, now interested him a great deal and he argued to himself over equality and fraternity. And then there was the habit of loafing around, the idleness and coarseness of the guardroom, the somnolent existence of garrison life, the wild rough-and-tumble of war. So he would down his tools and idly think about his Italian campaign, feeling an urgent need to rest, a longing to stretch out on the grass and forget everything.

One morning, his employer sent him to do some repairs at La Borderie. There was a good month's work, bedrooms to be refloored and doors and windows to be made good all over the house. He liked it up there and managed to take six weeks over the job. Meanwhile, his employer died and his son, who had married, left to set up his business where his wife's parents were living. Jean stayed on at La Borderie, working for himself; there was always a bit of rotten wood needing replacing somewhere; then, as they were starting the harvest, he lent a hand and stayed on another six weeks; so that the farmer, seeing how well he was taking to farming, finally took him on permanently. In less than a year the former carpenter had become a good farm-hand, carting, ploughing, sowing and scything, peacefully working on the land in which he hoped finally to satisfy his need to relax. . . So he had done with sawing and planing. And he seemed a born farmer, with his slow, equable temperament, his love of fixed, regular tasks and his bovine placidity inherited from his mother. At first he was delighted, enjoying the countryside that peasants themselves never look at, enjoying it through sentimental memories of things he had read, ideas of simplicity, virtue and perfect bliss which you find in little moral tales written for children.

If truth be known, there was another reason why he liked the farm. While he was mending the doors, the Cognet girl had come to visit him and opened her legs amongst the shavings on the floor. It was she in fact who led him on, unable to resist the sturdy limbs of such a well-built young man, whose massive regular features gave promise of vigorous sexual prowess. He succumbed and went on succumbing, for fear of appearing stupid, and tormented in his turn by his need for this vicious little creature who was so adept at arousing a man's desires. But secretly his native decency had been protesting. It wasn't right to go with Monsieur Hourdequin's girl in view of the debt of gratitude he felt towards him. Of course, he invented reasons: she wasn't the farmer's wife, she was nothing but a little trollop; and since she slept around with so many other men, he might just as well enjoy the pleasure as leave it to them. But these excuses did not prevent him from becoming more and more uneasy as he saw the farmer becoming fonder and fonder of her. It would certainly all end badly.

In the hayloft, Jean and Jacqueline were breathing as quietly as possible when his alert ear heard the ladder creak. He leapt to his feet and, at the risk of breaking his neck, jumped down through the hole through which the fodder was thrown. . . At that very moment, Hourdequin's head appeared at the other end on a level with the opening of the trap-door. With one glance he took in the vague figure of a man disappearing and the woman's belly as she lay there with open legs. He was so wild with rage that he did not think of climbing down to see who the lover was, and with a slap on the face which would have felled an ox he knocked Jacqueline down as she was rising to her knees.

'You whore!'

She screamed back, furiously denying what was so obvious.

'It's not true!'

He was tempted to stamp his heel on the belly which he had seen naked and exposed in her frenzied animal lust.

'I saw him. . . Tell me the truth or I'll kill you!'

'No, I won't. It's not true.'

And when she finally managed to stand up, with her skirt properly adjusted, she became insolent, brazenly determined to rely on her complete mastery over him.

'Anyway, what business is it of yours? Am I your wife? Since you don't want me to sleep in your bed, I'm free to sleep where I like.'

She spoke in her husky, caressing voice, as though making fun of him.

'Go on, get out of the way, I want to get down. . . I'll be leaving this evening.'

'You'll leave straight away.'

'No, tonight. . . It'll give you time to think it over!'

He was still quivering and beside himself with rage, not knowing where to vent his wrath. Even though he no longer had the courage to throw her out of the house at once, what immense pleasure it would have given him to boot out her lover! But how could he catch him now? He had gone straight up to the hayloft, following the trail of open doors, and when he came down the four carters in the stables were getting dressed, as was Jean in his little corner. Which one of the five was it? It might as well be this one as that, or perhaps the whole lot, one after another. All the same, he hoped that the man would betray himself as he issued his instructions for the morning's work; they were all to work inside the farm; nor did he go out himself but roamed round the building, with clenched fists, casting sidelong glances here and there, longing to lay into someone.

After seven o'clock breakfast, his irritated visit of inspection put the whole household in fear and trembling. At La Borderie there were the five drivers for five ploughs, three threshers, two cowmen who worked in the farmyard, one shepherd and a boy to look after the pigs, twelve hands in all in addition to the maid-servant. First of all he took the latter to task because she had failed to hang the oven shovels up on the ceiling after use. Then he explored the two barns, one for oats and the second one, an immense building as tall as a church, for wheat, with doors sixteen feet wide; here he told off the threshers, whose flails, he asserted, were cutting the straw too fine. Then he went on through the cowshed, infuriated to see that it was in good order, with the central gangway properly washed and the troughs clean. He failed to find any way of getting at the cowmen but, checking the water tanks, which they also looked after, he noticed that one of the downpipes was blocked by a sparrow's nest. As in every farm in Beauce, the rainwater from the roofs was jealously collected with the help of a complicated system of guttering. So he gruffly enquired whether they were going to let him die of thirst because of a few sparrows. The storm finally broke when he came to the drivers. Although the fifteen horses in the stable had been given fresh litter, he began shouting that it was disgusting to let them lie in such filthy conditions. Then, ashamed of his unfairness and still more exasperated, as he was visiting the furthest reaches of the farm buildings, the four sheds where the instruments and tools were kept, he was delighted to see a plough with both handles broken. He flew into a rage. Did those five buggers positively enjoy smashing up his equipment? He'd pay the whole lot off, all five of them, yes, all five, so that no one would feel hard done by. While he was abusing them, he watched them searchingly, hoping for one of them to turn pale or tremble and give himself away. No one stirred and he went away with a despairing gesture.

As he was completing his tour of inspection at the sheep-pen, Hourdequin thought he might question the old shepherd, Soulas, a man of sixty-five who had been working on the farm for half a century without ever saving a penny of his pay, all squandered by his wife, a loose-living drunken woman whom he had, quite recently, at last had the pleasure of burying. He was very much afraid that he might soon be dismissed because of his age. His master might perhaps be able to help him; but who could tell whether a master might not die first? And did they ever give you anything for a pipe of baccy or a drop of drink? Moreover, he had made an enemy of Jacqueline, whom he loathed with all the hatred of a jealous old servant disgusted by the rapid rise to fortune of a newcomer. When she now ordered him about, he could not bear the thought that he had seen her in rags sitting in the dung. She would certainly have dismissed him had she felt powerful enough, and that made him cautious, for he wanted to keep his job. So he avoided falling foul of her although he felt certain of his master's support.

The sheep-pen occupied the entire rear of the farmyard, one single covered building ninety yards long in which the eight hundred sheep belonging to the farm were kept separated by hurdles: in one part the ewes, in various groups; in another the lambs; in yet a third, the rams. The male lambs were castrated when two months old and reared for sale, whereas the females were kept in order to provide replacements for the ewes, the oldest of which were sold each year; and the rams covered the young ewes at regular intervals. They were crossbred Leicesters and merinos, splendid animals, gentle and stupid-looking, with heavy heads and big round noses like violently passionate men. When you went into the sheep-pen you felt suffocated by the powerful smell of ammonia rising from the litter, where fresh straw was piled on top of the old for three months on end. There were hooks along the walls so that the racks could be raised as the level of the manure rose. Yet it was airy, with wide windows, and the floor of the hayloft above was made of movable beams, some of which would be removed as the amount of fodder diminished. Moreover, it was said that the organic heat provided by these soft, warm, fermenting layers of straw were necessary for the proper growth of the sheep.

As Hourdequin pushed open one of the doors he caught a glimpse of Jacqueline disappearing through another. She had also thought of Soulas and was uneasy because she was sure that she had been sighted on her way to Jean; but the old man had not responded and did not seem to understand why, contrary to her usual custom, she was making herself agreeable to him. But the sight of the young woman leaving the sheepfold where she would normally never go added fuel to the farmer's uncertainty.

'Well, Soulas,' he asked. 'Anything new this morning?'

The shepherd, a very tall, lean man with a long, wrinkled face, as though rough-hewn out of a heart of oak, replied slowly :

'No, sir, nothing new at all except that the shearers are coming to start work presently.'

The farmer chatted for a moment in order not to appear to be questioning him. The sheep, which had been kept there ever since the first frosts of Hallowmas, would shortly be let out, about the middle of May, as soon as they could be taken into the clover. The cows, however, were not generally taken out to pasture before the end of the harvest. This plain of Beauce, dry and without any natural pasture though it was, produced good meat nonetheless; and if there was no beef breeding, it was due to sheer laziness and conservatism. And indeed, each farm fattened only five or six pigs for their own consumption.

Hourdequin was stroking the ewes with his hot hand as they came running up, lifting their heads and showing their pale, soft eyes; while the lambs penned in further along scampered up bleating to press against the hurdles.

'Well, old Soulas, so you haven't seen anything this morning?' he asked again, looking him straight in the eyes.

The old man had seen something, but what was the point of saying anything? His dead wife, the tipsy slut, had taught him all about vicious females and male stupidity. Perhaps it was possible that even if he gave the Cognet girl away, she might prove the stronger of the two and then they would take it out on him, so as to get rid of an awkward witness.

'Didn't see anything, nothing at all!' he repeated, blank-faced, without twitching an eyelid.

When Hourdequin walked across the farmyard again he noticed Jacqueline still lurking around, nervously trying to eavesdrop and afraid of what might have been said in the sheepfold. She was pretending to see to her poultry, all the six hundred chicken, ducks and pigeons who fluttered and squawked and scratched at the dung-pit, creating an incessant din, and when the boy who looked after the pigs upset a bucket of clean water that he was carrying over to them, she even relieved her feelings by clipping him round the ear. But one glance at the farmer reassured her: he knew nothing, the old man had kept a still tongue in his head. She could afford to be more brazen than ever.

So at lunchtime she was aggressively cheerful. The heavy work had not yet begun and so there were only four meals a day, bread and milk at seven o'clock, toasted bread at noon, bread and cheese at four o'clock and soup and bacon at midnight. They ate in the kitchen, an immense room containing a long table with benches along each side. The only sign of progress was a kitchen range occupying one corner of the vast chimney-piece. At the end, you could see the black opening of the oven; and there were shining saucepans and ancient utensils hanging tidily along the smoke-blackened walls. As the maid, a fat ugly girl, had baked that morning, a lovely smell of warm bread was wafting from the open bread-bin.

'So you've lost your appetite this morning?' Jacqueline asked Hourdequin saucily as he came in last.

Ever since the death of his wife and daughter he took his meals with his servants, as in olden days; he sat at one end, on a chair, while his servant and mistress did the same at the other end. There were fourteen in all and the maid served them.

When the farmer had sat down without replying, Jacqueline told the maid to take care of the toast. These were slices of toasted bread, broken into a soup plate, then soaked in wine and sweetened with lap, which was the old name for molasses. She asked for another spoonful and pretended to make a fuss of the men; all the time she kept making jokes which aroused loud guffaws. Every sentence had a double meaning and she reminded them that she was leaving that evening: easy come, easy go, and if this was your last chance, you'd be sorry if you didn't put your finger in the sauce for the last time. The shepherd was eating with a blank look while the farmer said nothing, and did not seem to understand either. In order not to betray himself, Jean was obliged to laugh with the others, despite his annoyance; he was not at all proud of his conduct in all this.

After lunch, Hourdequin gave his instructions for the afternoon. There were only one or two small jobs to finish outside: they were rolling the oats and finishing the ploughing of the fallow land, before beginning to cut the lucerne and the clover. So he kept two men back, Jean and one other, to clean out the hayloft. He himself, now almost at the end of his tether, with his ears buzzing from the rush of blood to his head and feeling very miserable, started to wander around without knowing what to do to calm his nerves. The sheep-shearers had settled down under one of the open barns, in a corner of the farmyard. He went over and stood watching them.

There were five of them, gaunt, yellow-faced fellows crouching down with their long shining steel shears. The shepherd brought along the ewes with their feet tied, like goatskins, and lined them up on the mud floor of the hangar where all they could do was lift their heads and bleat. Then, when one of the shearers caught hold of one, she would stop bleating and submit in her bulky thick coat which had a hard black outer crust of grease and dust. Then, with a rapid snip of the shears, she came out of her fleece like a hand out of a glove, fresh and pink amidst her golden, snow-like inner wool. Held on its back between the knees of a tall lean man, a ewe with its thighs held apart and head held straight up was displaying its white belly, which was hidden and quivering like the skin of someone being undressed. The shearers were paid three sous per animal and a good workman could shear twenty a day.

Absorbed in his thoughts, Hourdequin was remembering that the price of wool had fallen to eight sous a pound; and he would have to sell it quickly before it dried out too much, which made it lose weight. The previous year, sheep-pest had decimated the flocks in Beauce. Everything was going from bad to worse, ruin was staring him in the face, the land had become bankrupt ever since the price of corn had begun to fall steadily every month. And preoccupied with all his farming problems, he left the farmyard, where he was finding it difficult to breathe freely, and went out to survey his land. His quarrels with the Cognet girl always ended like this: after having blustered and clenched his fists, he would throw up the sponge and go away sick at heart to seek the only consolation he could find, the sight of his wheat and oats, a sea of green stretching out to infinity.

God, how he had come to love that land, with a passion which went far beyond the grasping avarice of a peasant, with a passion that was sentimental and almost intellectual, recognizing in it the Great Mother who had given him life and substance and to whose bosom he would return. At first, brought up on the land as a boy, his dislike of school and his urge to make a bonfire of all his books had sprung from the freedom he enjoyed, his wonderful rides across country gulping intoxicating draughts of the fresh air that blew from every quarter of the horizon. Later, having succeeded his father, his love of the land had grown into a deep, mature affection, as if he had become wedded to it in order to make it fructify. And this affection had continued to grow as he devoted all his time and money to it, his whole life, as to a good and fruitful wife whose whims and even whose betrayals he always forgave. Often he would lose patience when she was in one of her bad moods, when she devoured his seed and then, because of too much or too little water, refused to give a harvest; at such times, he was seized by doubt and he would even accuse himself of being an incompetent, or impotent male; if the land had not brought forth a child, the fault must be his. It was since then that the idea of adopting new methods had kept running through his head and had led him to experiment, full of regrets that he had been a dunce at school and had not followed courses at one of the agricultural colleges that both his father and he had made fun of. So many of his attempts were fruitless, so many experiments ended in failure; and his farm-hands damaged his machines and the artificial fertilizers on the market were a fraud! All his money had been swallowed up, La Borderie barely provided him with his daily bread and soon the agricultural crisis would finish him off. Never mind, he would stay on, held prisoner by his own land, and he would bury his bones there, wedded to it to the bitter end.

That day, as soon as he was away from the farm, he thought of his son the captain. What a good job they could have made of it, the pair of them together. But he immediately put aside the thought of that idiot who preferred the sword to the ploughshare. No, he was childless now, he'd finish his days all alone. Then his mind turned to his neighbours, particularly the Coquarts, farmers who cultivated their land at Saint Just themselves, the father and mother, three sons and two daughters; and they were not doing much better, either. At La Chamade, Farmer Robiquet, whose lease was running out, had given up manuring his fields and was letting the estate go to rack and ruin. That's how it was, there was trouble all round, the only thing to do was to work till you dropped and not complain. Moreover, little by little, as he walked beside them, he found himself being gently lulled by these large green fields. A few April showers had brought the fodder crops on splendidly. The pink of the clover delighted him and he forgot everything else. Now he took a short cut over the ploughed land to see how his two carters were doing: the earth stuck to his shoes, he could feel how rich and fertile it was, almost as though it wanted to cling to him and embrace him; and once more he felt completely won over by it, he was recovering the strength and joy he had felt as a young man of thirty. Did any woman exist apart from the earth? Was the Cognet girl or any of the others of the slightest importance? They were merely a sort of plate, which anyone could eat out of and which you have to put up with as long as it's clean enough! Such a convincing excuse to explain his need for such a slut put the finishing touch to his good humour. He went for a three-hour walk and cracked a joke with a girl, the Coquarts' maid, in fact, who was coming back from Cloyes on a donkey and showing her legs.

When Hourdequin came back to the farm, Jacqueline was in the farmyard saying goodbye to all the cats. There was always a whole host of them, a dozen, fifteen, twenty, nobody knew exactly, because the females had their litters in odd corners in the straw and then reappeared followed by five or six kittens. Next, Jacqueline went over to the kennels of the two sheepdogs, Emperor and Massacre, who could not bear her and growled.

Despite all these farewells from the animals, supper was no different from usual. The farmer ate and chatted normally. Then, when the day was over, there was no further question of anyone leaving. Everyone went off to bed and the farm sank quietly into darkness.

And that night, Jacqueline slept in the bedroom of the late Madame Hourdequin. It was the best bedroom, with a large bed in an alcove papered in red. It had a wardrobe, a bedside table, a high-backed Louis XV bedroom chair, and over the little mahogany bureau there glittered all the medals won by the farmer at agricultural shows, framed in a glass case. When the girl climbed into the marriage bed in her nightgown, she stretched herself out with her sensual, husky laugh and spread out her arms and thighs to take complete possession of it.

Next day, when she went and draped herself on Jean's shoulders, he pushed her away. Now that the affair was becoming serious, it would be a dirty trick to behave like that and he refused to have anything more to do with it.

Chapter 2

A FEW days later, Jean was coming back from Cloyes one evening when, a mile or so away from Rognes, he was struck by the strange behaviour of a farm-cart in front of him. It seemed to be empty, for there was no one on the seat and the horse was making its own leisurely way back to its stable, like a homing animal left to itself. The young man was thus easily able to catch up with it. He stopped it and raised himself to look into the cart: there was a man lying on the floor, a short, fat old man who had fallen on his back; his face was so red that it looked almost black.

Jean was so surprised that he exclaimed out loud:

'It's a man! Is he asleep or is he drunk? My goodness, it's old Mouche, the father of those two girls up there! Good Lord, I think he's had it! What a business!'

But although he had had a sudden stroke, Mouche was still breathing faintly, but with difficulty. So Jean laid him flat, with his head raised, got into the driver's seat and whipped the horse up to a trot to take the dying man back home before he died on his hands.

When he arrived at the square in front of the church, whom should he see but Françoise standing in her doorway. She was amazed to see the young man in their cart driving their horse.

'What's up?' she enquired.

'Your father's not very well.'

'Where is he?'

'Have a look.'

She climbed onto a wheel and looked. For a second, she was stunned with surprise, seeming not to understand as she saw the convulsed purple face looking as though one half of it had been pulled violently upwards. Night was falling and a large tawny-yellow cloud cast a fiery light over the dying man.

Suddenly, she started to sob and ran off to tell her sister.

'Lise! Lise! Oh dear!'

Left alone, Jean hesitated. They could hardly leave the old man lying on the floor of his cart. The house was three steps down from the level of the square and it did not seem easy to go down into this dark hole. Then he saw that on the side facing the road, on the left, there was another door opening into the yard, at the same level. This courtyard, quite large, was enclosed by a quick-set hedge; two thirds of it were covered by a murky brown pond and there was half an acre of fruit and vegetable garden at the back. He let go of the horse, which went in of its own accord and stopped in front of its stable beside the cowshed where there were two cows.

Now Françoise and Lise appeared, weeping and crying out. The latter had given birth four months ago; she had been suckling her baby and in her bewilderment and surprise was still holding him in her arms; and he was screaming too. Françoise climbed up onto a wheel again and Lise on the other one; their cries of distress became even shriller, while on the floor of the cart Mouche was still breathing wheezily.

'Daddy, do say something! What's the matter? For goodness' sake, what's wrong with you! Is it your head that makes you not say anything? Oh, Daddy, do speak, do say something!'

'Get down, it's better to pull him out of there,' Jean said sensibly.

Instead of helping him, they merely exclaimed more loudly than ever. Fortunately, the wife of their neighbour Frimat, hearing the noise, appeared on the scene. She was a gaunt, lanky old woman who had been looking after her paralysed husband for the last two years and keeping him by cultivating their single acre of land with as much determination as any male. Quite unperturbed, she seemed to find the situation completely normal and lent a hand like a man. Jean grasped Mouche by the shoulders and dragged him until Frimat's wife was able to catch hold of his legs. Then they lifted him into the house.

'Where shall we put him?' asked the old woman.

The two girls, who were following them quite bewildered, did not know: their father had a little bedroom upstairs, partitioned off from the loft; and it was hardly possible to carry him up there. On the ground floor, beyond the kitchen, was the big bedroom containing two beds which their father had made over to them. It was pitch-dark in the kitchen and the young man and the old

116

woman stood waiting, their arms aching, not daring to go any further for fear of tripping over the furniture.

'Come on, we can't stand here all day !'

Finally Françoise lit a candle and at that moment in came the wife of Bécu the gamekeeper, scenting that something was amiss, probably warned by that mysterious force which makes any news spread like wildfire through a village.

'Goodness me, what's up with the poor man? Oh, I see, he's had a fit. Quick, sit him down on a chair.'

But Frimat's wife thought differently. What's the point of sitting a man down if he can't sit upright? The best thing would be to lay him down on one of his daughters' beds. They were beginning to squabble about it when Fanny appeared with Nénesse: she had heard what had happened as she was buying some vermicelli at Macqueron's and had come to see, full of concern for her cousins.

So they deposited Mouche onto a chair next to the table on which the candle was burning. His chin fell onto his chest, his arms and legs hung limply down. Through the twitching on the left side of his face his eye had opened, and through the corner of his twisted mouth he was wheezing more than ever. Silence fell; death was lurking in this damp room with its peeling walls and large black fireplace.

Jean was still standing there, embarrassed, while the two girls and the three women, their hands dangling at their sides, continued to watch the old man.

'I'll go and fetch the doctor, if you like,' he suggested uncertainly.

Bécu's wife shook her head; none of the others answered: if it turned out to be nothing, why spend money for the doctor to come? And if it was the end, what good could the doctor do?

'Vulnerary's good,' said Frimat's wife.

'I've got some spirits of camphor,' said Fanny in a low voice.

'That's good, too,' declared Bécu's wife.

Quite at a loss, Lise and Françoise were listening, unable to make up their mind what to do, one dandling her baby Jules, the other awkwardly holding a cupful of water that her father had refused to drink. Seeing this, Fanny spoke abruptly to Nénesse, who was fascinatedly watching the contorted expression on the dying man's face.

'Run back to the house and ask for the little bottle of spirits of camphor in the cupboard on the left. . . You understand? In the cupboard on the left. And go to Grandpa Fouan and your aunt La Grande and tell them that Uncle Mouche is very poorly. . . Go on, off with you, quick !'

When the little boy had scampered off, the women continued to discuss the case. Bécu's wife knew a man who had been saved by having the soles of his feet tickled for three hours. Frimat's wife, remembering that she still had some lime tea from the two sous' worth she had bought for her husband last winter, went off to fetch it, and she was just bringing back her little bag of it and Lise was lighting a fire, having first handed her baby to Françoise, when Nénesse reappeared.

'Grandpa Fouan was in bed. . . La Grande said if Uncle Mouche hadn't drunk so much he wouldn't feel so sick.'

But Fanny was examining the bottle and exclaimed :

'You silly boy, I told you on the left ! You've brought the eau de Cologne !'

'That's good, too,' said Bécu's wife once more.

They made the old man drink a cup of lime tea by forcing a spoon between his clenched teeth. Then they rubbed his head with eau de Cologne. And still he wasn't any better, it was enough to make you despair. His face turned even blacker, they had to lift him up in the chair because he was slumping forward and threatening to fall flat on the floor.

'Oh,' said Nénesse, who had gone back to the door, 'I don't know if it's going to rain. . . The sky's a funny colour.'

'Yes,' said Jean, 'I saw a nasty big cloud coming up.'

And as if reminded of his first idea :

'Never mind, I'll still go and fetch the doctor if you like.'

Lise and Françoise were looking at each other anxiously. Finally, with the generosity of youth, the latter said :

'Yes, Corporal, you go to Cloyes to fetch Monsieur Finet. . . It shan't be said that we didn't do what was right.'

In the confusion, they had not even unhitched the horse and Jean had only to jump into the seat of the cart. There was a clatter of wheels and he was gone. Frimat's wife then mentioned the priest; but the others made a sign to show that they were having trouble enough as it was. And when Nénesse proposed to walk the two miles to Bazoches-le-Doyen, his mother snapped at him: of course she wouldn't let him go off on a night like this, with such a dreadful angry red sky. Anyway, since the old man couldn't understand or answer, they might just as well disturb the priest for a block of stone.

The painted cuckoo-clock struck ten. They were surprised to think they'd been there more than two hours without being able to do anything! But nobody talked of giving up, fascinated as they were by the spectacle of the old man and determined to stay until the end. There was a ten-pound loaf on the bread-board, with a knife. First the girls, ravenous despite their distress, mechanically cut themselves slices of bread that they ate dry, without noticing; then the three women followed suit, the loaf got smaller and smaller, there was always one or other of them who was cutting into it and munching. By now they had lit another candle and they had not even remembered to snuff the old one. It was a dismal sight, this poor peasant's bare, gloomy room, filled with the death-rattle of the body slumped beside the table.

All of a sudden, half an hour after Jean had left, Mouche tipped over and fell on the floor. He was dead.

'Didn't I say so? Yet you had to send for the doctor!' Bécu's wife remarked acidly.

Françoise and Lise burst into tears again; the two tender-hearted girls adored each other and now they instinctively flung themselves into each other's arms, stammering disjointed phrases:

'Oh dear God, there's only us two now. It's all over, there's just us two now... Oh dear God, what's going to become of us?'

But they couldn't leave the dead man lying on the floor, so Frimat's wife and Bécu's wife did what was necessary straight away. As they did not dare move the body, they took the mattress from one of the beds, brought it in and laid Mouche on it, covering him with a sheet up to his chin. Meanwhile, Fanny lit the tallow candles in the two other candlesticks and put them on the ground, like church candles, at each side of his head. That was all that was needed for the moment, except that the left eye which they had closed three times with their thumb persisted in opening again and seemed to be looking at everybody out of that twisted,

purple face which stood out boldly against the pale canvas mattress cover.

Lise had eventually put Jules to bed and the wake began. Twice
Fanny and Bécu's wife said they were going, because Frimat's wife
was offering to look after the two girls; but they did not go;
they stayed chatting in whispers, casting sideways glances at the
dead man; while Nénesse, who had got hold of the eau de Cologne
bottle, was emptying vast quantities of it over his hands and hair.

It struck twelve o'clock. Bécu's wife raised her voice.

'And what about Doctor Finet, eh? He gives you plenty of time
to peg out. More than two hours to fetch him over from Cloyes.'

The door opening into the yard had been left open and a gust of
air came in, blowing out the candles at each side of the dead man.
All were terrified, and as they were relighting the candles the
stormy blast came again, more frightening than before, and a
long swelling roar arose from the furthest reaches of the dark
countryside. It was like the thundering hooves of a ravaging army
approaching with branches creaking and groaning and the fields
moaning as they were rent asunder. The women had run to the
door and saw a lurid, copper-coloured mass of cloud writhing
across the livid sky. Suddenly there was a rattle of gunfire and a
shower of bullets which lashed and rebounded on the ground at
their feet.

And then they uttered their cry of disaster and distress.

'Hail! A hailstorm!'

Pale and sick with shock, they stood and watched the calamity.
It lasted a bare ten minutes. There was no thunder, but great
flashes of lightning seemed to be running incessantly along the
ground in broad bands of phosphorescent blue; the darkness of the
night was now lit up by countless pale streaks of hail hurtling
down like jets of glass. The noise was deafening, like machine-
gun fire or a train rushing at full speed over an endless metal
bridge. The wind was gusting furiously and the slanting hailstones scythed down like bullets everything in their path, piling
up until they covered the whole ground with a layer of white.

'Oh God, it's hail! Oh, what a disaster! Look, they're as big
as hen's eggs!'

They did not dare to go into the yard to pick any up. The gale
was increasing in violence; all the panes of glass in the windows

were smashed; and the force of the hailstones was such that one hit and broke a jar, while others came rolling in up to the mattress on which the dead man lay.

'They'd be less than five to a pound,' said Bécu's wife, weighing them in her hand.

Fanny and Frimat's wife made a despairing gesture:

'Everything's gone, it's a massacre.'

It was all over. They could hear the disastrous storm thundering away at great speed and a deathly hush fell. Above the cloud, the sky was now as black as ink. A slight, persistent rain was falling, soundlessly. On the ground, only the thick layer of hailstones could be discerned, a livid sheet which seemed to be gleaming with a pale half-light, like millions of tiny, endlessly glimmering nightlights.

Nénesse had rushed outside and come back with a jagged and irregular block of ice, as big as his fist; and Frimat's wife, who was fidgeting, could not resist the temptation of going out to look as well.

'I'm going to get my lamp,' she said. 'I must see what damage there is.'

Fanny restrained her impatience for a few minutes longer and continued her lamentations. Oh, what a business! What dreadful damage to the vegetables and fruit-trees! The wheat and oats and barley weren't tall enough to have suffered much. But oh dear, what about the vines! And standing in the doorway she tried to peer through the impenetrable darkness of the night, trembling in a fever of uncertainty and imagining the countryside shot to pieces and bleeding from its wounds.

'Well, girls,' she said in the end, 'I'm going to borrow a lamp from you and run and have a quick look at our vines.'

She lit one of the two lamps and disappeared with Nénesse. Bécu did not own any land and so his wife was not really concerned but she was sighing and offering up prayers out of sheer habit, being always ready to moan. Even she felt drawn by curiosity to keep going back to the door; and she stayed there, watching with great interest as she saw the whole village becoming dotted with little stars of light. Between the cowshed and a barn, you could look out over the whole of Rognes from the farmyard. No doubt the hailstorm had aroused the peasants and they were all equally impatient to go and see their plot of land and too anxious to wait until morning. So one by one the lamps appeared, until there were dozens of them dancing and darting here and there. And Bécu's wife, knowing where each house was, was able to give a name to each lamp she saw.

'Goodness, that's La Grande's light going on and they're coming out of Fouan's and that's Macqueron over there and Lengaigne next door. Gracious heavens, all those poor people, it's heartbreaking. . . Well, it can't be helped, off I go !'

Lise and Françoise remained alone with their father's corpse. The rain continued to pour down and little gusts of damp air came in along the floor, making the candles run. They should have closed the door but neither of them thought of it for they, too, were preoccupied and shaken by the tragedy outside, despite their own bereavement. Wasn't it bad enough to have death in your home? God destroyed everything, you didn't even know if you'd be left a crust of bread to eat.

'Poor Father,' murmured Françoise. 'How worried he'd've been ! It's a good thing that he didn't see it.'

And as her sister picked up their second lamp :

'Where are you going?'

'I was thinking about the peas and beans. I'll be back in a minute.'

Lise ran across the yard in the rain and went into the kitchen-garden. Françoise was left alone with the old man. Even she was standing in the doorway, excitedly watching the lamps going to and fro in the dark. It was heartbreaking.

'Well? What's it like?' she cried. 'What's happened?'

There was no reply, the lamp was moving about faster and faster, as if panic-stricken.

'The beans have been stripped, haven't they?. . . And have the peas been damaged?. . . And how about the fruit and lettuce, for goodness' sake?'

But when she distinctly heard a horrified cry of dismay, her mind was made up. She gathered up her skirts and ran out into the rain to join her sister. And the dead man was left alone in the empty kitchen, all stiff under his sheet between the two sad, smoky candles. His left eye still remained stubbornly open, staring at the old timbered ceiling.

The little plot offered indeed a dreadful scene of devastation; and how heartrending were their cries of dismay, as the extent of the disaster was dimly perceived in the wavering light of the lamps! The glass of the sisters' lamp was so streaming with rain that they could hardly see as they walked around holding it close to the ground; in its narrow beam of light they could vaguely make out that the beans and peas had been cut down to the ground and the lettuce slashed and chopped about so much that no one could imagine using their leaves. But above all it was the trees which had suffered: the smaller branches and the fruit had been cut off as though with a knife; even the trunks were so battered that sap was oozing out of the holes in the bark. And further on in the vineyards it was worse; furious oaths mingled with wails of lament in the light of dozens of bobbing lamps. The plants seemed to have been mown down, the bunches of blossom were scattered all over the ground with broken branches and vine tendrils; not only would that year's vintage be ruined but the vinestocks themselves, stripped of their leaves, would wither and die. Nobody noticed the rain; a dog was howling dismally; women were bursting into tears, as though at the graveside. Despite their rivalry, Macqueron and Lengaigne were helping each other to illuminate their respective plots, going from one to the other uttering cries of 'Christ Almighty!' as they saw one ruined plant after another in the brief dim glimpse they had before darkness again swallowed it up. Although he was now landless, old Fouan wanted to have a look and was becoming annoyed. Gradually tempers were rising: was it possible to lose the fruit of a whole year's work in the space of a quarter of an hour? What had they done to deserve such punishment? There was no security or justice but just senseless, haphazard calamity bringing death and destruction to everyone. Suddenly La Grande bent down to pick up some stones and flung them furiously into the air as though to smash open the invisible sky. And she screamed:

'You dirty pig up there! Why can't you leave us alone?'

In the kitchen, Mouche, left alone on his mattress, was watching the ceiling with his one staring eye when two vehicles stopped in front of the door. It was Jean bringing Monsieur Finet, for whom he had had to wait three hours at the doctor's house; he had come back in the cart while Finet had brought his own gig.

The doctor, tall and thin with the jaundiced look of a man who has failed to achieve his ambitions, went brusquely in. At the bottom of his heart, he loathed his village clientèle, whom he blamed for his own mediocrity.

'What, nobody here?... Has he recovered?'

Then, catching sight of the body:

'No, it's too late! I told you so, I didn't want to come. It's always the same old story, they send for me when they're dead.'

He was annoyed at having been called out at night to no purpose; and as Lise and Françoise came in just at that moment, his exasperation knew no bounds when he heard that they had waited two hours before sending for him.

'Then you're responsible for his death, damn it all!... How stupid can you be? Eau de Cologne and lime tea for a stroke... And no one with him, either. True, he's not likely to run away...'

'But Doctor,' stammered Lise in tears, 'it's because of the hailstorm.'

Interested by this remark, Finet calmed down. Really? There'd been a hailstorm? Through spending his life amongst villagers, he had ended by developing their obsessions. Jean had joined them, and they both exclaimed in astonishment because they had not seen a single hailstone on their way from Cloyes. The people there had been spared and a few miles away they had been devastated. That was the truth of it! What bad luck to be in the wrong direction! And as Fanny now came back with the lamp and Bécu's and Frimat's wives followed, all three of them tearful and full of details of all the dreadful things they had seen, the doctor solemnly declared:

'What a misfortune, what a terrible misfortune. There's no greater misfortune for the farmer.'

He was interrupted by a muffled sound, a sort of gurgling. It came from the dead man, lying there forgotten between the two candles. They all stopped talking and the women made the sign of the cross.

Chapter 3

A MONTH went by. Old Fouan, who had been appointed Françoise's guardian, as she was just entering her fifteenth year, persuaded her and her sister Lise, ten years her senior, to rent their land to their cousin Delhomme, except for a bit of meadow, so that it would be properly cultivated and looked after. Now that the two girls were alone, with neither father nor brother, they would have had to take on a farm-hand, and with the rising cost of labour this was ruinously expensive. In any case, Delhomme was only doing it as a favour and promised to give up the lease as soon as one of them married, which would mean dividing their property between the two of them.

However, although they also let their cousin have their horse, which they no longer needed, Lise and Françoise kept their two cows, Coliche and Blanchette, and their donkey Gideon. Similarly, they kept their half acre of kitchen-garden, which the elder girl undertook to look after while the younger sister would take charge of the animals. So there was still work to do there; but, thank God, they were in good health. They would be able to see the thing through.

The first few weeks were very hard because they had to make good the damage caused by the hail by digging up and replanting the vegetables; and this is what led Jean to lend them a hand. A relationship had been developing between him and them since he had brought their dying father home. The day after the funeral, he dropped in to see how they were. Then he dropped in again for a chat, gradually getting to know them better and generally being helpful, so that one afternoon he relieved Lise of her spade and finished digging over a patch of ground for her. From that time onwards, he was accepted as a friend and spent with them all the time he was not working up at the farm. He became one of the household, in the Fouans' old ancestral home, built three centuries ago and to which the family devoted a sort of cult. During Mouche's lifetime, whenever he used to complain at having been badly treated in his share and accused his brother and sister of robbing him, they would reply: 'What about the house? Hasn't he got that?'

But what a poor ramshackle old house it was, shaky, sunken, full of cracks and held together all over with bits of wood and plaster. It had presumably been originally built in blocks of stone and earth; later on two of the walls were redone in mortar; and finally, at the turn of the century, they reluctantly replaced the thatch with slates, little slates that were now all falling to pieces. This was how it had endured and it continued to do so. It was built a yard below the surrounding level, as they all were in the old days, no doubt for extra warmth; this had the disadvantage that when there was a heavy storm, the water all came in; so, sweep how you might, the earth floor of this sort of cellar always had mud in the corners. But above all, it had been cleverly sited, with its back to the north, to the immense plain of Beauce and the terrible winter gales; on that side the kitchen had merely a tiny gable window, level with the road and strongly shuttered. It looked like one of those fishermen's shacks at the edge of the Atlantic in which there is not one single chink opening onto the sea. After centuries of pushing, the winds of Beauce had given the house a tilt and it leant forward like those very old women whose backs can no longer hold them upright.

Jean soon learnt every nook and cranny. He helped to clean out the dead man's bedroom, formerly part of the hayloft, a corner boarded off and containing only an old chest full of straw serving as a bed, a chair and a table. Downstairs, he never ventured further than the kitchen and avoided following the two sisters into their bedroom; through its ever-open door you could see their two beds in an alcove, a tall walnut wardrobe and a superb carved round table, doubtless a relic stolen from the castle in days gone by. Beyond this room there was another, so damp that their father disliked having to keep the potatoes in there because they sprouted at once. But their lives were spent in the kitchen, a vast smoke-blackened room where generation after generation of Fouans had succeeded each other over a period of three centuries. It reeked of hard labour and meagre rations, the constant effort of a breed of men who had barely avoided starvation by dint of back-breaking toil and who had never had a spare penny-piece from one year's end to the other. A doorway opened straight out onto the cowshed; the cows were part of the family; and when this door was shut, you could still keep an eye on them by means of a pane of glass set in the wall. Next there were the stables, where only Gideon was left, then a shed and a woodpile. Thus you never needed to go out of doors; you could slip from one place to the next. Outside, the pond was filled by the rain and provided all the water there was for the animals and for watering the garden. You had to go down to the public fountain on the road every morning to fetch up drinking water.

Jean enjoyed being there without thinking overmuch as to the reason why he kept coming. Lise, a cheerful round body, always made him welcome. All the same, at the age of twenty-five she was no longer young and she was becoming plain, especially since the birth of her baby. But she had big sturdy arms and she worked with such a will, laughing and talking at the top of her voice, that she was a pleasure to watch. Jean kept his distance and never spoke to her as familiarly as he used to address Françoise, who at fifteen still seemed to him a child. The open air and hard work had not yet taken their toll on her and she still had her long pretty face, her stubborn little forehead, dark silent eyes and thick lips, the upper one already precociously hairy; and little girl though she seemed, she was a woman too, and as her sister used to say, you wouldn't need to tickle her too hard to give her a baby. As their mother had died, Lise had brought her up and from this had sprung their great affection for each other, lively and vociferous on the older sister's part, passionate yet restrained with the younger one. Young Françoise had a great reputation for having a mind of her own. Any unfairness exasperated her. Once she had said 'That's mine, that's yours', she would have died at the stake rather than change her mind; and apart from anything else, her reason for adoring Lise was that she felt that she owed it to her. Otherwise she was a reasonable girl, well-behaved, pure in mind but at that awkward age when girls are listless, lazy and somewhat greedy. One day, she started addressing Jean in the same familiar way as he used with her, treating him as a friend, much older indeed but a good sort who played with her and sometimes teased her by deliberately making untrue and unfair remarks because it amused him to see her spluttering with anger.

One Sunday in June, on an afternoon that was already baking hot, Lise was in the garden weeding peas; she had put Jules under a plum-tree where he had gone off to sleep. The burning sun was falling directly on her back and, breathing heavily, she was tugging away at the weeds when a voice came from behind the hedge.

'What's all this? Working even on a Sunday?'

She had recognized the voice and straightened up, her arms and face all red, but still ready to laugh.

'Well, not on a Sunday more than any other day. Someone's got to do the work!'

It was Jean. He walked along the hedge and came into the yard.

'You leave it, I'll do it in two shakes of a lamb's tail!'

But she did not let him: she would soon have finished; and anyway, if she wasn't doing that, she'd be doing something else: how could anyone stay idle? Although she got up at four o'clock every morning and sat sewing by candlelight at night, she never came to the end of her chores.

Not wishing to irritate her, he sat down in the shade of the plum-tree, taking care not to sit on Jules. He watched her bending over again, with her bottom in the air pulling up her skirt and showing her hefty legs, while with her face close to the ground she worked away with her arms, not worrying about the rush of blood to her head which was making her neck swell.

'It's a good job,' he said, 'that you're solidly built.'

She seemed proud of it and gave a pleased laugh. And he was laughing too, and genuinely admiring her, for she had the strength and the spirit of a man. No lewd thoughts crossed his mind as he watched her bottom stuck up in the air and the muscular calves of this woman on all fours sweating and smelling like an animal on heat. He was merely reflecting that with limbs like that you really could get through a lot of work. Certainly a woman built like that could pull her weight with any man in the house.

There was no doubt an association of ideas in his mind as he blurted out a piece of news that he had promised to keep to himself.

'I saw Buteau a couple of days ago.'

Lise slowly straightened up but she had no time to question him because, recognizing Jean's voice, Françoise had come out of the dairy at the back of the cowshed, her bare arms white with milk, to add an angry comment.

'You saw him, did you? What a pig he is !'

Her ever-increasing dislike of her cousin made her no longer able to hear his name without a feeling of outraged decency, as if she had to avenge a personal wrong.

'Of course he's a pig,' said Lise calmly, 'but there's nothing to be gained by calling him it now.'

With her hands on her hips she went on, in a serious voice:

'Well, what has Buteau got to say for himself?'

'Nothing really,' replied Jean, embarrassed and annoyed with himself at having let his tongue wag too freely. 'We spoke about his business, and his father talking all the time about cutting him out of his will; and Buteau says he's got plenty of time because the old man's tough and anyway he doesn't give a damn.'

'Does he know that Jesus Christ and Fanny have signed the agreement and taken up their share?'

'Yes, he knows that and he knows that old Fouan has rented out to Delhomme the share that he refused to accept and he knows that Monsieur Baillehache is so furious that he's sworn he'll never allow any lots to be drawn in future unless the papers have been signed beforehand. Yes, he knows that it's all been settled.'

'And he still hasn't got anything to say?'

'No, he's not saying anything.'

Lise silently bent down and took a few steps to pull up some weeds, showing only the big round expanse of her bottom. Then, twisting her neck, she said, with her head held downwards:

'Would you like to know what I think, Corporal?... Well, that's it, I'm left with Jules on my hands.'

Jean, who until now had been holding out hopes for her, nodded agreement.

'Yes, confound it, I think you're right.'

And he glanced at Jules, whom he had forgotten. The tiny mite, wrapped in his swaddling-clothes, was still asleep, with his little face all quiet in the light. That was the problem, that little lad! Otherwise, why shouldn't he have married Lise himself, since she was now free? The thought had just come to him suddenly, while watching her at work. Perhaps he loved her and it was the pleasure of seeing her that brought him to the house? All the same, he felt surprised because he had never desired her and never even joked with her as he did with Françoise, for example. And at that very moment, lifting his eyes, he saw Françoise standing there in the sun with her eyes gleaming with such a passionate fury and with such a funny look in them that he had to laugh in confusion at his discovery.

But at that moment, a bugle call, a strange tarantara, was heard, and abandoning her peas, Lise exclaimed:

'Ah, that's Lambourdieu, I want to order a sun-bonnet from him.'

On the other side of the hedgerow, on the road there appeared a short little man blowing a bugle and leading a long, tall cart drawn by a grey horse. It was Lambourdieu, a big shopkeeper of Cloyes who little by little had added hosiery, haberdashery, boots and shoes and even ironmongery to his original draper's business: a whole bazaar which he hawked around all the villages within a radius of fifteen miles or so. In the end the villagers found themselves buying everything from him, from saucepans to wedding-dresses. His cart opened up and folded flat, revealing rows and rows of drawers, like the display counters of a proper shop.

When Lambourdieu had taken the order for the sun-bonnet, he added:

'You wouldn't like a lovely headscarf in the meantime?'

He pulled them out of a cardboard box and flourished them in the sunlight: splendid red scarves decorated with gold-coloured leaves.

'How about that, eh? Dirt cheap at three francs! Five francs for two!'

Lise and Françoise reached out over the hawthorn hedge where Jules's napkins were drying and covetously turned them over in their hands. But they were sensible girls, they didn't need them – why spend money? And so they were just handing them back when Jean suddenly made up his mind that he wanted to marry Lise, despite her baby. So, to further his suit, he cried:

'No, keep it, let me make you a present of it! No, don't offend me, it's because we're good friends, I really mean it!'

He had not said anything to Françoise, and as he noticed her still trying to hand the scarf back, he felt a sudden twinge of sadness when he thought he detected that she had gone pale and that her mouth had dropped:

'You too, of course, silly. Keep it. I insist, you mustn't pull that horrid face !'

Under attack, the two sisters defended themselves, laughing. Lambourdieu had already reached across the hedge for the money and pocketed the five francs. He went off, the horse set off behind him with the long cart and the raucous bugle fanfare died away round a bend in the road.

Jean at once thought of pressing home his advantage with Lise and making a proposal of marriage when an untoward incident prevented him. The stable door must have been badly closed, because suddenly there was Gideon the donkey in the middle of the kitchen-garden, gaily cropping a bed of carrots. This donkey, a big animal, ruddy-brown and sturdy, with a big grey cross on his back, was very mischievous and fond of playing tricks. He was able to lift latches with his mouth and he would come in to help himself to bread in the kitchen; and when he was told off for being so naughty, you could see that he understood by the way he wagged his long ears. As soon as he realized that he had been discovered, he assumed a casual, bland expression; and when he was threatened by word and gesture he took himself off, but instead of going back into the yard he trotted away across the paths to the bottom of the garden. So they had to chase him in earnest, and when Françoise finally caught him he crouched and drew in his neck and his legs to make himself heavier and more difficult to tug. There was nothing she could do, either by kicks or coaxing. Jean had to take a hand and hustle him along with his strong masculine arms, because ever since he had been in the care of two women Gideon had developed a supreme contempt for them. The noise had woken Jules up and he was screaming. The opportunity had been lost and the young man had to go away without saying anything that day.

A week went by and Jean had been overcome by such a fit of shyness that he now no longer felt bold enough to say anything. This was not because it seemed a silly thing to do: on the contrary, on thinking it over, he had seen all the advantages more clearly. Both sides could only be the gainers. He had no property but she had the problem of the baby: that evened things out; and he was not being selfish, he was planning as much for her happiness as for his own. Moreover, getting married would force him to leave the farm and he would be rid of Jacqueline's wiles to which he had been cowardly enough to succumb and whom he was now seeing again. So his mind was firmly made up and he was merely waiting for the opportunity to make his proposal, rehearsing in his mind the words he would choose, for even the army had not cured him of his fear of women.

So one day, at about four o'clock in the afternoon, Jean slipped away from the farm, determined to speak to Lise at last. He had chosen this time because it was when Françoise used to take her cows for their evening grazing and he could have Lise to himself. But at first he was greatly put out to discover Frimat's wife installed in the kitchen and, like the good neighbour she was, helping Lise with her washing. The day before, the two sisters had put it to soak and since early morning the bleaching water, scented with orris roots, had been boiling in a cauldron hanging on the hook over a bright fire of poplar logs. And now Lise, with her arms bare, her skirt tucked up and armed with a yellow earthenware jug, was taking water out of the cauldron and pouring it onto the washing which filled the copper: sheets at the bottom, then cloths and shifts and nightdresses and, on top, still more sheets. So Frimat's wife was not having very much to do, but she sat chatting, content, every five minutes, to remove and empty into the cauldron the bucket underneath the tub which was collecting the water constantly dripping from the washing.

Jean sat patiently waiting for her to go. But she stayed on, talking about her husband, the paralytic who could only move one hand. It was a great affliction. They had never been rich, but while he was able to work he used to rent land to farm; whereas now she had great difficulty in cultivating on her own the acre of land which they owned; and she worked like a slave, collecting the droppings on the road to manure it, since they had no livestock, looking after her lettuces, her peas, her beans and even watering her three plum-trees and two apricots, and ending up with quite a sizable profit from this one acre, so much so that she went off to the market at Cloyes every Saturday bent double under the weight of two enormous baskets, quite apart from the heavy vegetables which a neighbour took in for her on his cart. She rarely returned without two or three five-franc pieces, particularly in the fruit season. But she continually complained of shortage of manure: neither the droppings which she collected from the road nor the sweepings from the few rabbits and chickens which she reared gave her enough. So she had resorted to using what she and her husband themselves produced, that much-despised human manure that even peasants find disgusting. The fact became known and she was teased about it: they called her Old Ma Poohpooh and this nickname did her no good at the market. In Cloyes, housewives had been known to turn up their noses in disgust at her superb carrots and cabbages. She was greatly grieved by this but it also made her furious.

'Look, Corporal, you tell me, is it reasonable?... Aren't we allowed to use everything God provides? And then they say that animal manure is cleaner!... No, it's just jealousy, the people in Rognes have got a grudge against me because my vegetables grow better. Tell me, Corporal, does it disgust you?'

Embarrassed, Jean replied:

'Well, I don't find it very appetizing. We're not used to it, perhaps it's all in the mind.'

Such frankness distressed the old woman. Although not a gossip, she could not conceal her bitterness:

'I see what it is, they've already turned you against me. Ah, if you only knew how spiteful people are, if you could guess all the things they say about you!'

And she launched into all the tittle-tattle of Rognes on the subject of the young man. First of all they had disliked him because he was a workman who sawed and planed wood instead of tilling the soil. Then, when he became a ploughman, they accused him of taking the bread out of their mouths in a job where he didn't belong. Did anyone know where he had come from? Hadn't he been up to some mischief or other so that he didn't dare to go back home? And they were spying on him and the Cognet girl, and people said that one fine day the pair of them would slip something into Hourdequin's soup so as to rob him.

'What a nasty lot!' exclaimed Jean, livid with indignation.

Lise was taking a jugful of boiling bleach from the cauldron and when she heard mention of Jacqueline, whom she herself used to joke about sometimes, she started laughing.

'And since I've started, I might as well go on to the end,'

Frimat's wife continued. 'Well, there's no end to the horrors they talk about, since you've been coming here. Last week, you gave both of them a silk scarf, didn't you, and they wore them at Mass on Sunday. It's disgusting, they say that you go to bed with both of them!'

At this, trembling but with his mind suddenly made up, Jean stood up and said:

'Listen, Madame Frimat, I'll answer that here and now. I'm not ashamed. Yes, I'm going to ask Lise if she'll marry me. . . Do you hear what I'm saying, Lise? I'm asking you, and if you say yes, you'll make me a very happy man.'

At that moment she was just emptying her jug into the copper. But she did not hurry, she carefully poured it over the washing before she turned towards him, with her bare arms wet with steam, looked him in the face and said seriously:

'Do you really mean it?'

'Yes, I really mean it.'

She did not seem surprised. It was something quite natural. However, she would not say yes or no; there was obviously something in her mind that was worrying her.

'You mustn't say no because of the Cognet girl,' he said, 'because she. . .'

She stopped him with a gesture; she knew very well that what went on at the farm was of no importance.

'There's also the fact that I've only got what I stand up in whereas you've got this house and land.'

Once again, she made a gesture to say that in her position, with a child, she took the same view as he did, those things balanced each other out.

'No, it's not all that,' she said finally. 'But there's Buteau.'

'But since he doesn't want to.'

'Of course, and we're no longer friends, because he's behaved so badly. . . All the same, you must consult Buteau.'

Jean thought this over for a good minute. Then, in his reasonable way:

'If you like. . . I ought to, because of the child.'

And Frimat's wife, who was also solemnly emptying the overflow bucket into the cauldron, felt it incumbent on her to approve such a step, while still favouring Jean, a decent young man, not rough and stubborn like the other one: and at that moment they heard Françoise coming back with the two cows.

'I say, Lise,' she shouted, 'come and see... Coliche has hurt her foot.'

They all went out and when she saw the animal limping with its left front foot bruised and bleeding, Lise flew into a rage, one of those sudden rages which she used to vent on her sister when she was young and had done something wrong.

'Another bit of your carelessness, I suppose? ... You went to sleep in the grass like last time.'

'No, I didn't, I promise... I don't know what she can have done. I'd fastened her to the stake, she must have caught her foot in the rope.'

'Don't lie to me... You'll kill my cow one day.'

Françoise's dark eyes glowered. She went very pale as she spluttered indignantly:

'Your cow, your cow! You might at least say our cow.'

'What do you mean, our cow? A cow belonging to a little girl like you?'

'Yes, half of everything here belongs to me. I've got the right to half of it and to mess it up if I feel like it!'

And the two sisters stood glaring threateningly at each other, sudden enemies. In their many years of fondness for each other, this was their first painful quarrel, sparked off by ideas of 'yours and mine', one of them irritated by her younger sister's rebelliousness, the other stubborn and violent when faced by injustice. But now the older sister gave in and went into the kitchen for fear of slapping her sister's face. And when the latter, after shutting the cows into their shed, came back and went to the breadbin to cut herself a slice of bread, there was silence.

Meanwhile, Lise had calmed down. The sight of her sister, tense and sulky, now made her feel sorry. She broke this silence first, trying to end their quarrel by introducing a piece of unexpected news.

'What do you think? Jean's just asked me to marry him.'

Françoise, who was eating standing up in front of the window, showed complete indifference and did not even turn round.

'Why should I care?'

'You should care because he'd be your brother-in-law and I want to know if you like him.'

She shrugged her shoulders.

'Why like him? Him or Buteau as long as I don't have to sleep with them. . . But there's one thing I should like to say : I think it's all a bit disgusting !' She went out to finish eating her bread in the yard.

Jean hid his embarrassment by trying to laugh, as if this was the petulant outburst of a spoilt child; whilst Frimat's wife declared that when she was a girl, they'd have thrashed such a young hussy till they drew blood. Lise looked serious and remained silent for a moment, busying herself again with her washing. Finally she said :

'Well, Corporal, let's leave it like that, I'm not saying yes and I'm not saying no. . . It's haymaking time, I'll be seeing our family, I'll make enquiries, I'll know what's what. And we'll come to some decision. . . Is that all right with you?'

'Yes, that's all right with me.'

They shook hands on it. Her whole person, soaked in warm steam, had a smell of good housewifery, a smell of bleach and orris root.

Chapter 4

FOR the last two days Jean had been driving the mechanical reaper on the few acres of meadow belonging to La Borderie down by the Aigre. The regular clatter of the blades had been heard from dawn till dusk and this morning he was coming to the end of his task and the last line of swathes was dropping on the ground behind the wheels in a fine layer of tender green stems. As the farm had no mechanical tedder, he had been allowed to take on two hands to do the tossing, Palmyre, who was working like a Trojan, and Françoise, who had accepted the job half jokingly, amused at the thought of doing this sort of work. They had been there since five o'clock in the morning, spreading out with their pitchforks the grass that had half dried out and been heaped up in stooks the evening before to protect it from the night dew. The sun had risen in a clear, burning sky, but the breeze was cool. Just the weather to produce good hay.

When Jean came back after lunch with his two haymakers, the hay of the first acre he had mown was ready, crisp and dry to the touch.

'I say,' he called out. 'We'll turn it over just once more and then we'll start making the ricks this evening.'

Dressed in a grey linen dress, Françoise had tied a blue handkerchief over her head, with one end hanging down over her neck and two corners flapping loosely over her cheeks to protect her face from the glare of the sun. Swinging her fork, she picked up the grass and flung it into the wind which carried it away in a pale golden shower. The wisps flew about in the air giving off a powerful penetrating smell, the smell of new-mown grass and withered flowers. As she walked along through this continual cloud of hay, she was very hot and full of high spirits.

'Ah, my girl,' Palmyre said in her doleful voice, 'anyone can see you're young... You'll feel it in your arms tomorrow.'

But they were not alone, the whole of Rognes was mowing and tossing the hay in the meadows all around. Delhomme had arrived before daybreak because grass is more tender to cut when it is soaked in dew, whereas it hardens up under the heat of the sun. You could hear it now, tough and crackling under the scythe as he swung it continuously to and fro with his bare arms. Closer still, next to the farm meadows, there were two small fields, one belonging to Macqueron, the other to Lengaigne. In the first one, all dressed up in a flounced dress and a straw hat, Berthe had joined the other girls haymaking, to pass the time; but she was already tired and leaning on her fork in the shade of a willow. In the other one, Victor, who was reaping for his father, had sat down and was dressing his scythe with a hammer on an anvil held between his knees. For the last five minutes the only sound that you could hear in the quivering, silent air was this persistent hammering, the quick taps of the hammer on the blade. At that moment, Françoise came up close to Berthe.

'Had enough?'

'For the moment, I'm just beginning. When you're not used to it. . .'

They chatted, talking about Suzanne, Victor's sister, whom the Lengaignes had apprenticed to a dressmaker's in Châteaudun and who had run away after six months to lead a gay life in Chartres. It was said that she had gone off with a lawyer's clerk and all the girls in Rognes were secretly gossiping about it amongst themselves and imagining all the details. A gay life meant orgies of redcurrant syrup and soda-water amidst a riot of men, dozens of them, getting up you in the backrooms of wine-shops.

'Yes, my dear, that's what it's like. . . I bet they're letting her have it good and proper !'

Françoise was listening to the older girl wide-eyed, quite flabbergasted.

'What a queer sort of fun,' she said at last. 'But if she doesn't come back the Lengaignes will be left on their own, because Victor's going to be conscripted.'

Berthe shared her father's dislike of the Lengaignes; she shrugged her shoulders: Lengaigne didn't care; all he was sorry about was that his daughter hadn't stayed at home to attract more customers to his own shop by sleeping with them. Hadn't one of her uncles, an old man of forty, already had her before she went off to Châteaudun, one day while they were scraping carrots together? And lowering her voice, Berthe described in detail how it had happened. Françoise found it so funny that she bent double trying to stifle her laughter.

'Oh, I say, isn't it silly to do things like that to each other!'

She started work again and moved away, lifting up her fork-fuls of grass and shaking them in the sun. You could still hear the persistent sound of the hammer tapping on the scythe. And a few minutes later, as she came up to the young man sitting there, she spoke to him:

'So you're going to be a soldier?'

'Oh, I don't leave till October... I've lots of time, there's no hurry.'

She was trying to refrain from questioning him about his sister but her curiosity overcame her.

'Is it true what they say about Suzanne being in Chartres?'

'Seems so... If she likes it there...'

Seeing Lequeu come strolling up in the distance, seemingly by chance, he went on quickly:

'Well, well! There's someone after Macqueron's daughter... What did I tell you? He's stopping and poking his nose into her hair... Go on, you dirty old clown, sniff away, you'll never get nearer than the smell!'

Françoise laughed again and Victor, sharing the family dislike, started taking Berthe to pieces. Of course the schoolmaster wasn't much of a man, with his bad temper and always clouting the children as well as being a sly old devil who never spoke his mind honestly, the sort who'd make up to the daughter so as to lay hands on her father's money. But Berthe wasn't a particularly nice person either, in spite of all her grand airs and boarding-school education. All right, she wore flounced skirts and velvet bodices and stuffed towels down her backside to make it look bigger, but underneath she wasn't any better, quite the opposite in fact, she knew a thing or two, you'd learn more going to a boarding-school in Cloyes than you would staying at home and looking after the cows. There was no danger of her getting herself landed with a child; she preferred to ruin her health all by herself.

'How do you mean?' Françoise asked, not understanding what he was saying.

He explained with a movement of his hand. She stopped laughing and said, seriously and without embarrassment:

'So that's why she's always making dirty remarks and pushing herself so close up against you.'

Victor had begun hammering his blade again. He grinned and said, in the gaps between his hammering:

'And then you know. Not got any.'

'Not got any?'

'Berthe, of course! "Not Got Any" is the nickname the boys have given her because she hasn't grown any.'

'Any what?'

'Hair all over. . . Hers is just like a little girl's, as smooth as a billiard ball. . .'

'You're fibbing.'

'I'm telling you!'

'Have you had a look?'

'No, I haven't, but others have.'

'Which others?'

'Oh, boys who've sworn blind to boys I know.'

'And where did they have a look? How did they do it?'

'Good Lord, like anyone can see when they've got eyes in their head and when they spy on her through a crack in the door. How do I know? If they haven't gone with her, there are times and places when you pull your skirts up, aren't there?'

'Of course, if they've been watching out specially.'

'Anyway, what's it matter? Apparently it looks so silly, it's so ugly, all bare like those horrid little spadgers without feathers holding open their beaks in the nest, really horrid, enough to make you sick all over it!'

Hereupon Françoise was once more attacked by a fit of giggles at this funny idea of sparrows without feathers. Then she quietened down and went on tossing the hay but only until she saw her sister coming down to the meadow. Lise went up to Jean and explained that she was off to see her uncle about Buteau. This step had been agreed between them three days ago and she promised to come back again to tell him the reply. As she went off, Victor was still hammering away, and in the glare of the vast clear blue sky Françoise, Palmyre and the other women went on tossing the grass again and again and again, while Lequeu was

140

most obligingly giving Berthe a lesson by sticking the fork into the grass, lifting it up and lowering it again with the stilted precision of a soldier on parade. In the distance, the reapers were lunging forward without a pause, all in the same rhythm, their bodies swaying from the hips and their scythes swinging steadily to and fro. Delhomme had stopped for a minute and was standing still, much taller than all the rest. He had taken his honing stone out of the cowhorn filled with water hanging from his belt and with long rapid sweeps was sharpening his scythe on it. Then once again he bent forward and you could hear the sharpened blade make a crisper sound as it bit into the grass.

Lise had arrived at the Fouans' house. At first she was afraid there was nobody at home because the place seemed so dead. Rose had got rid of her two cows, the old man had just sold his horse and so there were no animals, no work being done, nothing stirring at all in the empty buildings and farmyard. However, the door opened when she pushed it and, going into the room, dark and still despite all the cheerful activity outside, Lise found old Fouan standing up and just finishing a piece of bread and cheese while his wife sat idly watching him.

'Good morning, Auntie. . . I hope everything's all right?'

'Yes, my dear,' the old woman replied, her face lighting up with pleasure at the visit. 'Ever since we've been retired and come up in the world, we've nothing else to do but enjoy ourselves from morning till night.'

Lise was anxious to make herself agreeable to her uncle as well:

'And you haven't lost your appetite, Uncle, I see.'

'Oh,' he answered. 'It's not that I'm hungry. . . It's just that having a bite to eat keeps you busy, it helps to pass the time.'

He looked so miserable that Rose started exclaiming again how happy they were at not having to work anymore. Yes, they'd really earned that, it wasn't any too soon to be able to watch other people working away while they had their pension. . . Getting up late, twiddling your thumbs, not having anything to worry about, not a care in the world, what a change that made, it was sheer heaven. Encouraged by these remarks, Fouan livened up too and waxed even more enthusiastic than his wife. And yet underneath this forced gaiety and excitement you could sense the utter boredom, the excruciating idleness that had been tormenting these two old people ever since their arms, suddenly stricken with inertia, were going rusty for lack of use, like old machines in a scrapyard.

Finally Lise ventured to mention the reason of her visit.

'Uncle, someone told me that you'd seen Buteau.'

'Buteau's a blasted nuisance!' cried Fouan in a sudden outburst of rage, without giving her time to finish. 'If he hadn't been as obstinate as a mule, I shouldn't have had that trouble with Fanny.'

It was the first disagreement between him and his children, which he had been keeping to himself but which had left a bitter feeling behind, as he had just shown by his outburst. When he had put Buteau's share into the hands of Delhomme, he had asked him to pay rent for it at thirty francs the acre whereas Delhomme simply wanted to pay him a double pension, two hundred francs for his share and two hundred for Buteau's. This was a fair arrangement and the old man was furious at being caught in the wrong.

'What trouble?' enquired Lise. 'Aren't the Delhommes paying you?'

'Oh, yes, certainly,' replied Rose. 'Every quarter at noon precisely, the money's there on the table. All the same, there are ways of paying, aren't there? And Father is sensitive and would like a little courtesy at least. Fanny comes here with the air of someone going to the bailiff, like she was being robbed.'

'Yes,' the old man added. 'They pay up and that's all. I don't think that's enough, myself. They should show some consideration. Is their money just like settling a debt? That makes us nothing but creditors. And yet we're wrong to complain. If they only all paid up!'

He broke off and an embarrassed silence ensued. Always ready to defend the scamp who was the apple of her eye, his wife was pained by this allusion to Jesus Christ, who had not paid a penny-piece and was drinking his way through his share, which he was mortgaging piecemeal. She was afraid that this second grievance might be revealed, so she hurriedly said:

'Don't get het up about trifles! Since we're happy, what does the rest matter? If you've got enough, that's all you need.'

She had never stood up to him like this before. He glared at her.

'You're talking too much, woman!... I've nothing against being happy but I won't be buggered about!'

So she shrank back again into her chair and sat idly there while he finished off his bread, rolling the last piece round his mouth for a long time to make the most of it. The dismal room relapsed into its slumber.

'Well,' Lise continued, 'I'd like to know what Buteau intends doing about me and his son. I haven't been pestering him much and it's time something was decided.'

The two old folk remained completely silent. She directed her question to her uncle:

'Since you saw him, he must have mentioned me. What did he say about it?'

'Nothing, he didn't once open his mouth on the subject... And there's nothing to say, after all. The priest is on at me all the time to arrange something, as if anything can be arranged if the bridegroom won't play!'

Lise was turning this over uncertainly in her mind.

'Do you think he'll agree one day?'

'He might still do that.'

'And you think he would marry me?'

'There's a possibility.'

'So you advise me to wait?'

'Well, it's up to you, everyone does as he thinks fit.'

She made no reply, unwilling to mention Jean's proposal and not knowing how to obtain a definite answer. Then she made a final attempt:

'You see, I'm getting really upset not knowing where I stand. I must have an answer one way or the other. Uncle, please won't you go and ask Buteau?'

Fouan shrugged his shoulders.

'In the first place, I'm never going to talk to that awkward young bugger again... And secondly, you silly girl, aren't you being a bit simple? Why make the pigheaded so-and-so say no now when he can always say no later on? So leave him alone, to say yes one day, if it's in his interest to do so.'

'That's right,' added Rose simply, happy to be able to echo her husband's words again.

And Lise could get nothing more definite out of them. She left

143

and closed the door of the room, which sank back into its previous torpor. Once again, the house seemed empty.

In the meadows down by the Aigre, Jean and his two helpers had started making the first haystack.

Françoise was building it by standing in the centre on a stook and arranging in a circle the forkfuls of hay brought by the young man and Palmyre. Little by little, it rose up, taller and taller, while she still stood in the middle, putting new trusses of hay under her feet as the wall around her began to reach her knees. The stack was beginning to take shape. It was already over six feet high; Palmyre and Jean had to reach up with their forks; and the operation did not proceed without a good deal of laughter caused by the pleasure of being in the open and the loud jokes they kept making amidst this wonderful smell of new-mown hay. In particular Françoise, whose scarf had slipped off her head, exposing it to the sun and leaving her hair loose and tangled with grass, was as happy as a lark as she sank into this moving pile of hay reaching up to her thighs. She plunged her bare arms in as each forkful was tossed up to her, covering her in a shower of dry grass, and she disappeared, pretending to be submerged in the swirling hay.

'Oh dear, it's pricking me !'

'Where?'

'Under my skirt, up here.'

'Look out, it's a spider. Keep your legs closed !'

And he laughed louder than ever as he made saucy remarks which made them split their sides, too. In the distance, Delhomme, disturbed by this frivolity, turned his head to look for a moment while still continuing to swing his scythe. That little scallywag must be doing a lot of work, playing about like that ! They spoilt girls these days, they only worked for the fun of it ! And he continued on his way, rapidly cutting his swathes, leaving a hollow wake behind him. The sun was sinking towards the horizon and the swathes left by the reapers were spreading out wider and wider. Victor had stopped hammering his scythe but did not seem to be in any great hurry; and when La Trouille went by with her geese he slipped slyly away after her to the shelter of a thick row of willows along the bank of the river.

'Well done,' shouted Jean. 'He's going to sharpen his tool again. The grinder's waiting for him.'

This remark sent Françoise into another fit of laughter.

'He's too old for her.'

'Too old?. . . You just listen, you can hear them sharpening up together.'

And with his lips, he made the hissing sound of a grindstone scraping against the edge of a blade, so that even Palmyre, clasping herself as if she had stomach ache, said :

'What's up with Jean today, he's so funny !'

They were tossing the forkfuls of grass higher and higher and the haystack was now quite tall. They joked about Lequeu and Berthe, who had finally sat down. Perhaps 'Not Got Any' was being tickled at long range, with a piece of straw; anyway, even if the schoolmaster might be warming the oven, somebody else would eat the cake.

'Isn't he a dirty man?' Palmyre said again. She was never able to laugh but she was choking with amusement. Then Jean teased her.

'And to think that you've reached the age of thirty-two without ever having a tumble in the hay !'

'Not me, never !'

'How's that, didn't any boy ever relieve you of it?'

'No, never, never.'

Her long, miserable face, already tired, worn out and blank through excessive work, had gone all pale and serious; the only thing ever alive in it was her eyes, shining with deep devotion like those of a faithful old bitch. Perhaps her thoughts had gone back to her sad, unhappy, friendless and loveless life, the life of a beast of burden mercilessly whipped during the day and ready to drop with fatigue in the stable every night; and she stood motionless, her hands on her fork, her eyes far away amidst the countryside which she never even saw.

There was silence. Françoise remained still, listening on top of the stack while Jean, who was also taking a breather, continued to poke fun, hesitating to mention what was on the tip of his tongue. Then he blurted out :

'So it's all lies, what they say about you sleeping with your brother?'

Palmyre's pale face suddenly became purple, making her look young again. She stammered with annoyance and confusion, vainly trying to find words to deny what he had said.

'Oh ! They're wicked. . . If anyone can believe. . .'

At this Françoise and Jean burst out laughing and both started talking at once, pressing and bullying her. After all, in the tumbledown cowshed where she and her brother lived there was hardly room to move without falling on top of each other. Their mattresses were touching, they must sometimes get into the wrong one in the dark.

'Come on, it's true, isn't it? Admit it. Anyway, people know it's true.'

Completely taken aback, Palmyre jerked herself upright and was so distressed that she lost her temper.

'Even if it is true, what's it got to do with you? The poor boy doesn't get much pleasure out of life. I'm his sister, so I could be his wife, since he can't stand girls.'

As she made this confession two tears ran down her cheeks, in her maternal pity for the cripple which did not stop short of incest. After earning his bread during the day, surely she could give him that as well at night, since nobody else was prepared to offer him that pleasure, even though it would have cost them nothing. And such dim-witted creatures living so close to the soil, who had perhaps never known love, would always be incapable of explaining how it had happened; a sudden instinctive approach without any premeditation or agreement, he tormented and little more than an animal, she passive and ready to accept anything; and afterwards neither of them could resist the pleasure of keeping each other warm in the cruel cold of their hovel.

'She's right, what's it got to do with us?' Jean said good-naturedly, sad to see her so upset. 'It's their own business, it's nothing to do with anyone else.'

In any case, something else was happening to distract them. Jesus Christ had just come down from the Castle, the former cellar halfway up the slope in the undergrowth where he lived, and from the road above he was shouting at the top of his voice for La Trouille, swearing and screaming that his slut of a daughter had disappeared again two hours ago without bothering to get his supper.

'Your daughter's in the willows,' shouted Jean. 'She's watching the moon together with Victor.'

Jesus Christ waved his fists in the air.

'That God-forsaken bitch! Bringing disgrace on the family. I'll get my whip.'

He ran back up the hill to fetch his whip, a long horsewhip which he kept hanging beside the door on the left for such occasions.

But La Trouille must have been listening. Under the leaves you could hear a sound of rustling and someone running away; two minutes later, Victor nonchalantly strolled out. He examined his scythe and set to work at last. And when Jean called out to him from a distance to enquire whether he'd had an attack of the gripes, he replied:

'Correct!'

The haystack was now nearly finished, more than twelve feet tall and solid, looking like a round beehive. Palmyre's long thin arms were tossing up the last trusses and standing at the top Françoise stood out tall against the pale sky, tawny in the light of the setting sun. She was quite out of breath and trembling from her efforts, soaked in sweat with her hair sticking to her skin, and with her clothes in such disorder that her bodice was gaping open, showing her hard little breasts, while her skirt had come unhooked and was slipping down over her hips.

'Oh, I say, isn't it high. . . It's making me giddy.'

And she gave a little shaky laugh, hesitating because she was afraid to come down, sticking one foot out and then quickly drawing it back.

'No, it's too high. Go and fetch a ladder.'

'Don't be silly,' said Jean. 'Sit down and let yourself slide.'

'No, I'm frightened, I can't.'

There followed cries and shouts of encouragement mingled with rude jokes: Don't come face downwards, you might end up with a bump in the front! On your backside, unless you've got chilblains on it! And standing down below, he was becoming excited as he looked up at the girl and could see her legs; and filled with an unconscious male urge to seize hold of her and press her close against him, he was slowly becoming exasperated because she was so far out of his reach.

'But I promise you won't break anything! Jump and I'll catch you in my arms.' He was standing under the haystack, holding out his arms and offering his chest for her to jump onto. And when she finally made up her mind and let herself go, closing her eyes, she fell so suddenly as she slid down the slippery slope of hay that she knocked him over, straddling him with her thighs round his ribs. She lay on the ground with her skirts round her thighs, roaring with laughter and gasping that she hadn't hurt herself. But when he felt her all hot and sweaty against his face, he seized hold of her.

Intoxicated by this acrid woman's smell and the overpowering scent of hay floating in the air, his whole body became taut in a sudden fury of desire. And there was something else as well, a deep unrecognized passion for this girl, a long-standing fondness of heart and body, born of their games and horseplay and reaching a climax in this desire to possess her, here and now, in the grass.

'Jean, that's enough! You're crushing my ribs!'

She was still laughing, imagining that he was playing. And seeing Palmyre staring with wide-open eyes, he gave a start and stood up, trembling with the bewildered look of a drunkard suddenly sobering up at the sight of a gaping hole in front of him. What had happened? So it wasn't Lise he wanted but this little girl! The idea of Lise's body lying against his own had never made his heart beat any faster, whereas the mere thought of kissing Françoise sent the blood racing through his veins. He knew now why he so much enjoyed visiting the two sisters and helping them. But the girl was still only a child! He felt disheartened and ashamed.

At that very moment Lise came back from the Fouans. On her way she had been thinking. She would have preferred Buteau because, after all, he was the father of her child. The old couple were right, why try and rush him? If Buteau one day said no, Jean would still be there to say yes.

She went up to Jean and said straight away:

'No news, Uncle doesn't know anything. Let's wait.'

Still scared and shaking, Jean was looking at her uncomprehendingly. Then he remembered: their marriage, the brat,

Buteau's consent, all these things which two hours earlier he had thought of as beneficial to both her and him. He said hastily:

'Yes, of course, let's wait, that's the best thing.'

Night was falling and already a distant star was shining in the dark-red sky. In the deepening twilight only the round shapes of the first haystacks could be dimly perceived, breaking up the flat expanse of the meadows. But in the calm air, the warm scents rising from the earth were all the stronger, each sound louder, more resonantly clear and musical. They were the voices of men and women, faint sounds of laughter, a snorting horse, the clink of a tool; while, still obstinately working on their patch of meadow, the reapers continued their unremitting task, and from this scene of toil, which could no longer be seen, still the long regular hiss of the scythe rose into the air.

Chapter 5

Two years had passed, two active and monotonous years of life on the land, and in the inevitable succession of the seasons Rognes had followed the same eternal recurrence of all things, the same rhythm of work and sleep.

Down below at the roadside, on the corner by the school, there was a fountain of spring-water where all the village women used to come to fetch their drinking-water, since the houses only had ponds for their cattle and for watering their plots of land. At six o'clock in the evening all the latest news of the village was exchanged; everything that had happened, however trivial, was related and commented on endlessly: so-and-so had had meat for lunch; so-and-so's daughter had been pregnant since Candlemas; and in the course of the two years, the same tittle-tattle had followed the passage of the seasons, being repeated again and again, always about babies appearing too soon, wives being beaten, a great deal of hard work to produce a great deal of poverty. So much had happened, yet it added up to nothing at all!

The Fouans, who had been such a source of comment when they handed over their property, had gone on quietly stagnating, so quietly that hardly anyone talked about them anymore. The situation had not changed: Buteau was digging his heels in and he was still not keen to marry Mouche's elder daughter who was bringing up his child. It was Jean who had been accused of sleeping with Lise but perhaps he wasn't sleeping with her after all; in that case why did he go on visiting the two sisters? There was something fishy there. And on some days the session round the fountain would have been dull without the rivalry between Coelina Macqueron and Flore Lengaigne – which Bécu's wife kept stirring up under the pretext of pouring oil on troubled waters. Then, in the middle of a slack period, two big events had just burst on the community: the coming elections and the famous question of the road between Rognes and Châteaudun. These whipped up a gale of gossip. The jugs of water stood lined up waiting while their owners refused to leave. One Saturday evening, they almost came to blows.

It so happened that, the following day, Monsieur de Chédeville, the outgoing deputy, was lunching with Hourdequin at La Borderie. He was conducting his electoral campaign and showing great consideration to the latter, who had a good deal of influence on the countryfolk of the canton. He was, however, certain to be re-elected since he was the official candidate. As he had once been to Compiègne, everyone in his constituency knew him as 'the Emperor's friend'; and that was enough, they called him that as if he slept at the Tuileries every night. This Monsieur de Chédeville, a ladies' man in his younger days and a leading light under Louis Philippe, had, deep down, retained Orléanist sympathies. He had squandered his substance on women and now possessed only his farm, La Chamade, near Orgères, but he never set foot there except at election-time and was, moreover, dissatisfied with the drop in farm revenue since he had had the practical but belated idea of restoring his fortunes in business. Tall and still elegant, tightly buttoned up in his close-fitting coat, he dyed his hair; but he was now settling down, although his eyes still lit up at the sight of a bit of skirt, however sluttish the wearer, and he was preparing, so he said, some important speeches on agricultural questions.

Hourdequin had had a violent quarrel with Jacqueline the day before because she wanted to be present at the lunch.

'Your deputy, your deputy! Do you think I'd eat him? So you're ashamed of me?'

But he remained firm and the table was laid for two only. Jacqueline was sulking, despite Monsieur de Chédeville's gallant manner; he had caught a glimpse of her, had understood the situation and kept continually glancing towards the kitchen whither she had retired in high dudgeon.

Lunch was coming to an end: an omelette followed by fresh trout from the Aigre, and roast pigeon.

'What's ruining us', said Monsieur de Chédeville, 'is this free trade that the Emperor is so keen on. Of course, things went well after the 1861 treaties; people said it was an economic miracle. But it's now that the real effects are being felt. Look how prices are falling all round. I'm a protectionist, we must be defended against foreign competition.'

Hourdequin had stopped eating and was leaning back in his chair with a vacant look on his face. He said slowly:

'Wheat sells at under two and a half francs a bushel and costs over two francs to produce. If it drops any more we're ruined. And America is increasing her production of cereals every year. They threaten to flood the market. Then what will become of us? Look, I've always been one for progress and science and freedom. Well, I'm beginning to waver, 'pon my soul! No, we mustn't starve, we've got to be protected!'

He tackled his pigeon wing again as he went on:

'You know that your opponent Monsieur Rochefontaine, the owner of the building firm at Châteaudun, is a fervent free trader?'

They talked for a moment about this opponent, an industrialist who employed twelve hundred workmen, a tall, energetic, intelligent young man, very wealthy, who would have been happy to support the Emperor but was so offended at not being backed by the *préfet* that he had insisted on standing as an independent. He had no chance at all, for the peasants treated anyone who was not on the winning side as a public enemy.

'Yes, damn it,' Monsieur de Chédeville said, 'all he wants is for bread to be dirt cheap so that he can pay his workers less.'

The farmer, who was about to pour himself another glass of claret, put the bottle back on the table.

'That's the dreadful thing,' he exclaimed. 'On the one hand we farmers need to sell our corn at an economic price, and on the other the industrialists want to push prices down so that they can pay lower wages. It's open warfare and how's it going to end, tell me that?'

And indeed it was the frightening problem of the day, an antagonism that was pulling the framework of society apart. The question was quite beyond the mental powers of our aging ladies' man, who contented himself with nodding his head with an evasive gesture.

Hourdequin filled his glass and emptied it in one gulp.

'There's no end to it. . . If the farmer gets a good price for his wheat, the worker starves, if the worker gets enough to eat, the peasant goes hungry. So what, then? I don't know, let's gobble each other up!'

Then, with his elbows on the table, he launched fiercely into his pet subject and, as he unburdened himself, from a certain ironic vibration in his voice you could detect his secret contempt for this landowner who not only did not farm himself but knew nothing about the land which provided his livelihood.

'You asked me to supply you with a few facts for your speech. Well, first of all, it's your fault if La Chamade is losing money. Your tenant Robiquet is letting things slide because his lease is coming to an end and he suspects that you intend to increase it. You never put in an appearance, they treat you as a joke and they rob you, it's absolutely natural. In addition, there's a simpler reason why you're going to rack and ruin: it's because we're all going that way, the whole of Beauce is becoming exhausted. Yes, our fertile Beauce, the all-providing mother, the granary of France!'

He went on. For example, in his youth, the Perche, on the other side of the Loir, was a poor area, thinly cultivated, with hardly any wheat, and its inhabitants used to come over to Cloyes, Châteaudun and Bonneval as hired hands for the harvest. Today, thanks to the constant rise in labour costs, the Perche was prospering and would soon have overtaken Beauce, apart from the fact that it was growing rich through breeding live-stock, so that the markets of Mondoubleau, Saint-Calais and Courtalain provided the lowland plain with horses, cattle and pigs, while Beauce made its living from breeding sheep. Two years ago, when they had been decimated by the pest, there had been a terrible crisis, and if the disease had continued Beauce would have been destroyed.

And he launched out on his own story, his thirty-year-long struggle with the land which had left him poor. He'd always been short of capital, he'd never been able to improve some of his land as he would have liked, the only thing that didn't cost too much was marling the soil and nobody bothered to do it, apart from himself. It was the same with fertilizers, people only used farmyard manure, which was inadequate; all his neighbours laughed at him when they saw him trying out chemical fertilizers, whose poor quality, in fact, often justified their laughter. In spite of his own ideas on crop rotation, he had been forced to adopt the local triennial system, without any fallow period, ever since the practice of artificial meadowland and the cultivation of fodder crops had spread. Only one machine, the threshing machine, was beginning to be accepted. Everywhere you could see the deadly, inevitable inroads of habit and inertia; and if he, progressive and intelligent as he was, was affected by this, what would the thick-headed, completely conservative small landowners do? Any peasant would sooner starve than pick up a handful of his soil and take it to be analysed by a chemist who would tell him what it lacked or what it had too much of, what fertilizer it needed, what crop would do well on it. For centuries the peasant had been robbing the soil without ever a thought of putting something back in, except the manure of his two cows and a horse, and sparingly at that; the rest was left to chance, the seed cast in any old field and sprouting at random, and if it didn't sprout it was God who got the blame. If the day were to come at last when the peasant farmer was properly educated and adopted rational, scientific methods of agriculture, then production would double. Until then, in his ignorance and pigheadedness and without a penn'orth of capital, he would destroy the good earth. And this was why Beauce, that age-old granary of France, flat and water-less, whose only wealth was its wheat, was dying of exhaustion, inch by inch, tired of being bled dry and feeding a population of idiots.

'Everything's going to buggery,' he exclaimed coarsely. 'The next generation will see the land go bankrupt. Did you know that these days our small farmers, who used to pinch and scrape to save enough to buy a bit of land that they had had their eye on for years, now invest in stocks and shares, Spanish or Portu-guese or even Mexican? And they wouldn't risk a five-franc piece to improve a couple of acres of land. They've lost confidence, the old men trudge along in their ruts like broken-down animals while the young men and girls think only of getting away from looking after cows or getting their hands dirty with a plough and go off as soon as they can to the towns. . . But the worst thing is that education, do you remember, that wonderful education that was going to be our salvation? Well, all it does is to speed up this emigration and depopulation of the countryside by making children stupidly conceived and obsessed with material comfort. Take Rognes, for example, they've got a schoolmaster, a man called Lequeu, a country lad full of resentment against the land where he might have ended up as a farm labourer. Well, how can he possibly make his pupils like their lot when every day he calls them savages and barbarians and tells them to go back to their dung-pit with all the contempt of someone with a bit of book-learning? The cure, yes, by heavens, the cure of course, would be to have other kinds of school, a practical education of graduated courses in agriculture... There you are, *monsieur le député*, there's a fact for you. Make a point of it, our salvation can perhaps come from proper schooling, if there's still time!'

Monsieur de Chédeville, not paying much attention and uneasy at this massive and violent display of information, hurriedly replied:

'Of course, of course.'

And as the maid brought in the dessert, a cream cheese and fruit, leaving the kitchen door wide open, he caught a glimpse of Jacqueline's pretty profile and bent forward, winking and fidgeting to attract the attention of such an agreeable young woman; and then he said in his carefully modulated voice, that of a former lady-killer:

'But you've said nothing about the smallholder?'

He trotted out all the fashionable ideas: the smallholder, born of the Revolution of '89, protected by the law and destined to regenerate agriculture; in a word, everyone becoming a land-owner and using his intelligence and energy in the cultivation of his own little plot of land.

'Tell that to the marines!' said Hourdequin. 'In the first place, smallholdings existed before the Revolution and to almost the same extent as now. Secondly, there's a lot that can be said about parcelling out land into smallholdings, both for and against.'

Once again, elbows on table and cracking cherry stones between his teeth, he launched into the details. In Beauce, the smallholding, the estate of less than fifty acres, represented eighty per cent. For some time now almost all the day-labourers, the ones who hired themselves out to the farmers, had been buying up small pieces of land when the big estates were broken up and cultivating them in their spare time. This was, of course, a very good thing because the labourer could now feel he had a stake in the land. And another thing in favour of smallholdings was that it made for better education and gave a man a sense of personal dignity and pride. Finally, it produced proportionately more and of better quality, since the owner devoted all his energies to it. But think of all the disadvantages! First of all, the superior production of the smallholding was the result of excessively hard labour; the father, mother and the children had to kill themselves with work. In addition, the large number of small plots involved a great deal of transport, thus damaging the tracks and paths and increasing the costs of production, apart from wasting time. As for using machines, it would seem impossible when the plots were too small, apart from the disadvantage of making a three-year system of rotation inevitable, something which was certainly scientifically inadvisable because it was illogical to expect two cereal crops, oats and wheat, in succession. In a word, excessive division of the land seemed dangerous, so much so that after passing laws in its favour immediately after the Revolution, in the fear that the big estates might be reconstituted, the situation now was that exchanges of land were being encouraged by giving tax relief on them.

'Listen to me,' he went on. 'There's a struggle growing up between large- and small-scale farming and it's getting more acute. Some farmers, like myself, are in favour of large-scale farming because it seems to be in line with scientific progress, with its increasing use of machinery and a large capital turnover... On the other hand there are those who believe only in individual effort and so favour smallholdings, with some sort of miniature farming in mind where everyone produces his own manure and looks after his quarter of an acre, sifting his seeds one by one, giving them the soil they require and then growing each plant separately under cloches... Who's going to win? I'm damned if I can guess! Of course, I realize, as you were saying, that every year big farms go bust all round here and get split up so that they fall into the hands of gangs of ruffians, and so smallholding is certainly gaining ground. I know another case in Rognes, a very curious one, of an old woman who has less than an acre and succeeds in producing a very decent living for herself and her husband, with even a luxury or two. The villagers have nicknamed

156

her Old Ma Poohpooh because she doesn't mind emptying her chamber-pot – and her husband's – over her vegetables, which is a method used by the Chinese, apparently. But it's really not much more than gardening, I can't see cereals growing on plots no bigger than a cabbage-patch; and if the small farmer has got to produce a bit of everything in order to be self-sufficient, what's going to become of the people here, who can only produce wheat if Beauce is cut up into a patchwork? Well, time alone will tell whether the future lies in large-scale or small-scale. . .'

He broke off and shouted:

'Have we got to wait all day for our coffee?'

Then, lighting his pipe, he concluded:

'Unless, of course, they're neither of them going to survive, and they're being killed off at this very minute. . . You must realize, *monsieur le député*, that agriculture is on its deathbed and it will die if no one comes to its support. It's being crushed out of existence by taxes, foreign competition, the continual increase in labour costs, the flight of capital into industry and the Stock Exchange. Oh, I know, there's no shortage of promises, every-body's full of them: *préfets*, ministers, the Emperor. . . And then the dust settles and nothing happens. . . Do you want to know the real truth of the matter? Nowadays, any farmer who is keeping his head above water is doing it by spending either his own money or somebody else's. As for me, I've got a little fat to live on, I'm all right. But I know farmers who are borrowing at six per cent while their land is giving them a return of three per cent, at best. Inevitably they'll go under. A farmer who starts borrowing is sunk, he'll not even be left with his shirt. Even the other week one of my neighbours was expelled, the father, mother and four children all thrown onto the street, after the lawyers had gobbled up his cattle, his land and his house. And yet we've been pro-mised an agricultural credit scheme at reasonable rates for years! What's happened to it? It's discouraging even for the hard workers, they're going to ask themselves twice before they give their wives a baby. . . No, thanks! Another mouth to feed, an-other poor little wretch who'd be born to starve! When people haven't got enough bread for everyone, they stop having children and the nation goes to pot!'

Visibly comforted, Monsieur de Chédeville ventured an uneasy smile as he murmured:

'You don't paint a pretty picture.'

'That's true, there are days when I'd chuck up everything,' Hourdequin replied cheerfully. 'And these worries have been with me these last thirty years, too... I don't know why I kept on, I should have sold up the farm and tried something else. I suppose it's habit and possibly the hope that things will change. And then there's an insatiable urge, one might as well admit it. Once the land gets you by the short hair, the bitch won't let go. There you are, just look over there, it's probably stupid but I feel consoled when I can see that.'

He pointed to a silver cup, protected from the flies by a piece of muslin, the first prize in an agricultural show. These agricultural shows where he never failed to win prizes were a constant spur to his vanity and one of the reasons for his persistence. Despite the fact that his guest was obviously tired, he lingered over his coffee; and then, pouring brandy into his cup for the third time, he took out his watch and sprang to his feet.

'Good God! Two o'clock and I've got a meeting of the municipal council!... Yes, it's a question of a road. We're quite happy to pay half but we'd like a government subsidy for the rest.'

Monsieur de Chédeville, happy at being released, had got up from table:

'Look, I can help you there, I'll get your subsidy for you. Would you like me to take you to Rognes in my gig, since you're in a hurry?'

'Splendid.'

The vehicle had been left standing in the middle of the yard and Hourdequin went out to have it hitched up. When he came back, the deputy was no longer there and he finally found him in the kitchen. He had pushed open the door and he was standing smiling in front of a beaming Jacqueline and offering her compliments at such close range that their faces were almost touching; the pair of them had sniffed each other out, had come to an understanding and were telling each other so quite plainly with their eyes.

When Monsieur de Chédeville had climbed into his gig, Jacqueline detained Hourdequin for a moment to whisper in his ear:

'Well? He's nicer than you, he doesn't think I ought to be hidden away !'

On the way, as the carriage was passing between wheat fields, the farmer came back again to his perpetual concern, the land. Now he started supplying written notes and figures, because for the last few years he had been keeping accounts. In the whole of Beauce there were not three farmers who did this, and the smallholders, the peasant farmers, would shrug their shoulders without even understanding. Yet only by keeping accounts could a clear picture of the situation be obtained, showing which products were showing a profit and which a loss; in addition, it showed the cost price and consequently the sale price. With Hourdequin, every farm-hand, every animal, every crop, even every tool had a page to itself, in two columns, debit and credit, so that he was kept continually informed as to the result of his operations, good or bad.

'At least,' he said with a guffaw, 'I can know how I'm being ruined.'

But he broke off with a muttered oath. For the last few minutes, as the gig was proceeding towards Rognes, he had been trying to see exactly what was happening in the distance, at the roadside. Although it was Sunday, he had sent one of his farm-hands out to toss some lucerne which needed doing urgently, and had provided him with a mechanical tedder of a new type which he had recently acquired. And the unsuspecting farm-hand, failing to recognize his master in the unfamiliar vehicle, was poking fun at his piece of machinery with three villagers whom he had stopped as they were passing by.

'Look at that for a dud article,' he was saying. 'It breaks the grass up and poisons it. Three sheep have died as a result of it already, word of honour.'

The peasants were grinning and examining the tedding machine as if it were a queer, malevolent beast. One of them declared :

'It's all an invention of the devil against us poor folk. . . What'll our wives do if they're not needed for haymaking?'

'Christ, the farm owners couldn't care less,' the farm-hand said, kicking the machine. 'Gee up, dead bones !'

Hourdequin had heard all this. Thrusting his body half out of the gig, he shouted :

'Get back to the farm, Zéphyrin, you're sacked !'

The farm-hand stood gaping and the three peasants went off with derisive laughter, making loud insulting remarks.

'There you are !' said Hourdequin, falling back into his seat. 'You saw that... Anyone would think that all these new agricultural instruments burn their hands. They call me a townsman, they work less hard on my farm than on the others with the excuse that I can afford to pay more; and they've got the support of my neighbours, the other farmers, who accuse me of teaching the local people bad methods of work; they're furious with me because they say they'll soon be unable to find anyone who can work in the good old way.'

The gig was just going into Rognes along the Bazoches-le-Doyen road when the deputy caught sight of Father Godard coming out of Macqueron's place where he had been to lunch that Sunday after Mass. Chédeville remembered his electioneering concerns and asked :

'And how about religious feeling in the country districts?'

'Oh, they go to church and that's about all,' Hourdequin replied casually.

He stopped the gig in front of Macqueron's tavern, where the landlord himself had remained in the doorway with the priest, and he introduced the deputy mayor, who was dressed in his short, greasy old overcoat. But at this, Coelina came bustling up, looking very clean in her cotton dress and propelling her daughter in front of her. Berthe, the pride of the family, was dressed like a young lady, in a silk gown with little mauve stripes. Meanwhile, the village, seemingly dead and completely idle on this fine Sunday afternoon, was rousing itself in surprise at this extraordinary visitation. Villagers were coming out of their houses one by one and children were peering from behind their mothers' skirts. There was much hustle and bustle at Lengaigne's particularly; he poked his head out, razor in hand, while his wife Flore broke off from weighing four pennyworth of tobacco to stick her nose to the window. They were both cut to the quick to see the gentleman getting out of his gig in front of their rival's door. And so, gradually, people began to come up, groups were forming, Rognes was already aware, from one end of the village to the other, of the important occasion.

'*Monsieur le député*,' Macqueron kept saying, embarrassed and red in the face, 'it's really a great honour.'

But Monsieur de Chédeville was carried away by Berthe's pretty face and was not listening, while her limpid eyes set in their pale circles of blue looked at him boldly. Her mother gave her age and said where she had been to school, while the girl herself, smiling and welcoming, invited Monsieur de Chédeville to come in, if he felt so inclined.

'But of course, my dear girl!' he exclaimed. Meanwhile, Father Godard had buttonholed Hourdequin and was once again begging him to persuade the municipal council to vote the necessary funds so that Rognes could have a resident priest of its own. He repeated this performance every six months, together with his reasons: the effort it involved for him and his continual squabbles with the villagers, quite apart from the interests of religion.

'You mustn't say no,' he said sharply as he saw the farmer make an evasive gesture. 'Mention it anyway, I'll be expecting an answer.'

And as Monsieur de Chédeville was just about to follow Berthe, he hurried over and stopped him, in his simple, determined way.

'Excuse me, *monsieur le député*. The poor church in this village is in such a state!... I'd like to show it to you, you must help me to get it done up... Nobody listens to me. Please come and see.'

Greatly annoyed, the aging Lothario was resisting when, hearing from Macqueron that several of the councillors were already in the town-hall and had been waiting for the last half hour, Hourdequin said, in his unceremonious way:

'That's right, you go and take a look at the church. That'll kill time until I've finished and then you can take me back to the farm.'

Monsieur de Chédeville was forced to follow the priest. The groups of people had grown and several villagers set off behind him. They were beginning to pluck up courage and they all had something in mind to ask him.

When Hourdequin and Macqueron went up into the council-room, they found three councillors waiting, Delhomme and two others. It was a vast, whitewashed room containing only a long pine table and a dozen straw-bottomed chairs; fastened to the wall between the two windows looking onto the road was a cupboard in which were kept the archives, together with odd official documents; and on shelves round the walls there were piles of canvas fire-buckets, the gift of a rich villager for which they had been unable to find a storage place; in any case, they were a useless encumbrance because there were no pumps.

'I'm sorry I'm late, gentlemen,' said Hourdequin politely. 'I had Monsieur de Chédeville to lunch.'

There was no reaction and it was not clear whether his apology was accepted. They had seen the deputy arrive from the window and had strong feelings about the coming election; but it would have been a mistake to mention it out of turn.

'Damn,' said the farmer. 'There are only five of us, we haven't got a quorum.'

Fortunately Lengaigne came in. At first he had been determined not to go to the council meeting because he was not interested in the question of the new road; he was even hoping that his absence would prevent any vote being taken. Then, bitten by curiosity at the appearance of Monsieur de Chédeville, he had decided to come along, to learn what was happening.

'Good! That makes six of us, so we can take a vote,' exclaimed the mayor.

And since Lequeu, who acted as secretary, now arrived, red-faced and sulky, with the minute book under his arm, the session could now begin. But Delhomme had started talking in an undertone to his neighbour, Clou, the blacksmith, a tall, dark, gaunt man; they stopped when they realized that the others were listening. But they had all overheard a name, that of the independent candidate, Monsieur Rochefontaine, and after tentatively sounding each other they all now launched, by word or innuendo or disgusted expressions, into an attack on this candidate, whom they did not even know. They were in favour of the maintenance of order, the status quo and the obedience to authority which made for a stable market. Did this gentleman fancy himself to be stronger than the government? Would he succeed in raising the price of wheat to three and a half francs a bushel? It was a blasted impertinence to send out pamphlets, promising more butter than bread when you had no commitments to anything or anybody. They even went so far as to call him an adventurer, a dishonest man combing the villages in order to steal their votes, just as he would make off with their money. Hourdequin could have explained to them that as a free trader Monsieur Roche-fontaine had, basically, the same ideas as the Emperor but he deliberately let Macqueron give vent to his violent Bonapartist sympathies and Delhomme put forward his sensible, narrow-minded views; while Lengaigne, forced to keep his mouth shut because he held a tobacco licence, was grumbling away in a corner and muttering about his own brand of muddled republicanism. Although Monsieur de Chédeville's name was not once mentioned, the whole conversation pointed to him and showed how completely they were ready to truckle to his position as the official candidate.

'Well, gentlemen,' the mayor said at last, 'suppose we start?'

He had sat down at the table in the chairman's place, on a rather wider chair with a back and arms. Only his deputy sat down beside him. The four councillors remained standing, two leaning against the window-sill.

However, Lequeu had handed a piece of paper to the mayor and whispered something in his ear; then he left the room with a dignified air.

'Gentlemen,' said Hourdequin, 'the schoolmaster has given me a letter for us.'

He read it out. It was a request for a salary rise of thirty francs a year in view of all the work he had to undertake. Everyone was frowning. They were always reluctant to spend the commune's money, almost as though it came out of their own pockets, and especially to spend money on the school. They did not even discuss it but gave a blank refusal.

'Good! We'll tell him he's got to wait. He's in too much of a hurry, that young man. And now let's start on this question of the road.'

'I'm sorry, Mr Mayor,' Macqueron interrupted. 'I'd like to say a word about the matter of the parish priest.'

Taken aback, Hourdequin now understood why Father Godard had been lunching at the inn. Macqueron was certainly ambitious: what were his motives in pushing himself forward like this? In any case, his proposal met the same fate as that of the schoolmaster. He vainly tried to prove that they had money enough to afford their own priest and that it was really rather disreputable to make do with Bazoches-le-Doyen's leftovers. No, it was out of the question, they'd have to repair the presbytery, it would cost too much to have a priest of their own: half an hour every Sunday from the present one was ample.

Offended by his deputy's initiative, the mayor summed up:

'There's no case, the council has already taken a decision on this. . . And now to our road. We must decide something at last. . . Delhomme, would you be so kind as to ask Lequeu to come back? Does the damned fellow think we're going to spend the whole afternoon discussing his letter?'

Lequeu was waiting on the stairs. He came solemnly in; and since they did not inform him of the fate of his request, he remained tight-lipped and uneasy, full of unuttered insults: these blasted peasants! What a set! They sent him to fetch the plan of the road from the cupboard and spread it out on the table.

This plan was well known to the council. It had been lying about in the cupboard for years. Nonetheless, they all gathered round and, resting their elbows on the table, they examined it once again. The mayor listed the advantages for Rognes: a gently sloping street which would allow carriages to drive up to the church and then a saving of five miles compared with the present Châteaudun road which passed through Cloyes; and the commune would only have to pay for less than two miles of it since the neighbouring village of Blanville had already approved the other section, up to where it would join the main road from Châteaudun to Orléans. They listened to him, staring at the plan meanwhile, and nobody said a word. What had prevented the project from going through was above all the question of compensation. Each councillor could see there was a lot of money to be made out of it and was concerned to discover whether any part of his own land would be affected and if he could sell some of it to the commune, at a hundred francs a pole. And if he was not going to be able to sell any part of a field belonging to him, why should he vote in favour of putting money in someone else's pocket? And as for the gentle slope and the saving in distance, fiddlesticks! His horse would have a harder pull, that's all!

So Hourdequin did not need to invite discussion in order to know their opinions. He himself was keen on the new road merely because it would pass by his farm and give access to a number of his fields. Similarly, Macqueron and Delhomme, who also had land lying beside the route, were pressing in favour. That made three supporters but neither Clou nor the other councillor had anything to gain; and as for Lengaigne, he was violently opposed to the plan, first because there was nothing in it for him and secondly because he was incensed at the thought that his rival, the deputy, would be the gainer. If Clou and the other councillor were undecided and voted against, that would be three to three. Hourdequin became uneasy. The discussion finally began.

'What's the point? What's the point?' Lengaigne kept repeating. 'We've already got a road. It's just for the fun of spending money, robbing Peter to pay Paul... Incidentally, you promised to hand over your piece of land for nothing.'

This crafty remark was addressed to Macqueron. But the latter, bitterly regretting his fit of generosity, stoutly denied what he had said:

'I didn't promise anything... Who told you that?'

'Who? You yourself, damn it! And in the presence of witnesses. Here now, Monsieur Lequeu was present, he can say... Isn't that the case, Monsieur Lequeu?'

The schoolmaster, furious at having to wait to learn his fate, made an abrupt dismissive gesture. What interest had all this dirty business of theirs for him!

'Well, really,' Lengaigne went on. 'If there's no honesty left in the world, we might as well all go back to the jungle! No, I'm not going to have anything to do with your road! It's highway robbery!'

Seeing that things were going badly, the mayor hastened to intervene.

'All this is just gossip. It's not for us to go into private squabbles... We must be guided by the public interest, the common good.'

'Of course,' agreed Delhomme, sensibly. 'The new road will be of great value for the whole of the community... Only there are things we want to know. The *préfet* keeps on saying: Vote a sum of money and then we'll see what the government can do for you. And if he were to do nothing, what's the point of wasting our time voting?'

At this juncture, Hourdequin felt the moment ripe to announce his big news, which he had been holding in reserve:

'In this connection, gentlemen, I have to inform you that Monsieur de Chédeville has given his word that he will obtain a subsidy from the government to cover half the cost... You know that he is a friend of the Emperor's. All he'll need to do is mention us, over coffee.'

Even Lengaigne was shaken by this and a blissful look spread over everyone's face, as if at the sight of the Blessed Sacrament. And at any rate the re-election of the outgoing deputy was now assured: the friend of the Emperor was the right man at the source and fount of money and jobs, the man who was known, who was honourable and powerful, the master! There were nods of approval all round the table. These things were obvious, why bother to say them?

All the same, Hourdequin remained concerned at Clou's silence. He stood up and looked out of the window. Spying the game-keeper, he instructed him to go and find old Loiseau and bring him along, dead or alive. This man Loiseau was a deaf old peasant, Macqueron's uncle; the latter had had him elected to the council but he never turned up at any meeting because, he said, it was too much of a bother. His son worked at La Borderie and he was completely in Hourdequin's pocket. So as soon as he appeared, in a fluster, all the mayor had to do was to shout into his ear that it was the question of the road. Everyone was already awkwardly scribbling on his voting paper; head down and elbows spread out so that no one else could read. Then they proceeded to the vote of half the cost, in a little whitewood box, like a church collecting-box. There was a superb majority, six for and only one against, Lengaigne. That wretched fellow Clou had voted the right way. And the meeting came to an end after everyone had signed the minute book which the schoolmaster had prepared in advance, leaving a blank space for the result of the vote. Then they all clumped off downstairs at the double, without shaking hands or saying goodbye.

'Oh, I was forgetting,' Hourdequin said to Lequeu, who was still waiting. 'Your request for a rise was turned down. The council felt that too much is being spent on the school already.'

'Gang of savages,' exclaimed the young man, seething with anger, as soon as he was alone. 'Go on back to your pigsty!'

The meeting had lasted two hours and Hourdequin found Monsieur de Chédeville standing in front of the town-hall, where he had only just returned from his tour of the village. First of all the priest had not spared him the smallest details of the decrepitude of the church: the hole in the roof, the broken stained-glass, the bare walls. Then, as he was finally making his escape from the vestry which needed repainting, the villagers, now completely recovered from their shyness, fought over him to gain a hearing, tugging him this way and that, full of requests and complaints or asking for favours. One of them dragged him off to the village pond, which was no longer regularly cleaned out through lack of funds; another wanted a covered public washplace on the Aigre, at a spot which he showed him; a third asked for the street to be widened in front of his door so that he could turn his cart round; there was even one old woman who, after forcing the deputy into her house, showed him her swollen legs and asked him if he didn't know a cure for that in Paris. Flustered and out of breath, he still kept a good-humoured smile on his face and was full of promises. Ah, he was a good sort, not too stuck up to talk to us poor folk!

'Well, are we off?' asked Hourdequin. 'They're expecting me up at the farm.'

But at that moment, Coelina came hurrying to her doorway with her daughter Berthe, begging Monsieur de Chédeville to come in for a second; and he would not have asked for anything better, relieved to be able to relax and delighted to see these disingenuously limpid eyes with their circles round them:

'No, we can't,' the farmer said. 'We're late as it is. Some other time.'

And he bustled the bewildered deputy into the gig, meanwhile informing the priest, who was still standing there, that the council had taken no new decision about the question of the parish priest. The coachman whipped up his horse and the carriage shot off, surrounded by the delighted, friendly villagers. The furious priest was left to walk the two miles from Rognes to Bazoches-le-Doyen by himself.

167

A fortnight later, Monsieur de Chédeville was elected with a large majority; and by the end of August he had kept his promise and the commune received its subsidy for the new road. Work started on it at once.

The evening the first stone was turned, Coelina, the dark, lean wife of Macqueron, was at the fountain listening to Bécu's lanky wife, who was talking endlessly, her hands clasped under her apron. For the last week, the tremendous repercussions of the new road had revolutionized the fountain gossip; all they could talk about was the money that some people were going to receive and the backbiting fury of those who weren't. And every day Bécu's wife kept Coelina up to date with what Flore Lengaigne had to say about it; not to set them at odds with each other, of course, but so they could explain their views to each other, which was the best way to agree. Women lost all count of time as they stood there with their arms dangling and their full water jugs at their feet.

'So you see,' she said, 'it was all arranged between the mayor and his deputy, so they could have a good rake-off on their land. And she also said your husband didn't keep his promises. . .'

At this moment, Flore came out of her house carrying her jug. When she came up, stout and flabby, Coelina, hands on hips, with her prickly sense of fair play, and always ready with foul language, started to give her a piece of her mind, throwing her slut of a daughter in her face and accusing her herself of sleeping with her own customers; while the tearful down-at-heel Flore merely kept muttering:

'What a bitch ! What a bitch !'

Bécu's wife rushed between them and tried to make them embrace, which nearly made them come to blows. Then she added another piece of news:

'I say, talking about that, did you know that Mouche's daughters are going to get five hundred francs?'

'It's not possible.'

The quarrel was forgotten there and then and they all gathered round, abandoning their jugs. Yes, it was true. Up at Les Cornailles, the road passed alongside the field belonging to the Mouche girls and they would have to cut off the verge over a distance of two hundred and fifty yards; and at two francs a yard, that worked out at five hundred francs, and with access to the road the land would also increase in value. It was a stroke of luck.

'But in that case,' said Flore, 'Lise will become quite a good match, with her little boy... That big innocent the Corporal knew what he was doing after all when he kept persisting.'

'Unless,' added Coelina, 'Buteau doesn't take his place... His share is also going to do pretty well, out of the road.'

Bécu's wife turned round, nudging with her elbow:

'Look out. Not a word!'

Lise herself was approaching, cheerfully swinging her jug. And they all began lining up at the fountain again.

Chapter 6

LISE and Françoise had got rid of Blanchette, who had become too fat and too old for calving; and they had resolved to go to Cloyes that Saturday to buy another cow at the market. Jean volunteered to take them there in one of the farm-carts. He had asked to have the afternoon off and Hourdequin had given him permission to have the cart, in view of the rumour that the young man and the elder Mouche girl were thinking of getting married. In fact, they had decided to marry; at least, Jean had promised to approach Buteau on the matter in the course of the following week. A decision had to be taken at last between one or other of them.

So they left at one o'clock, Jean sitting in front with Lise while Françoise sat by herself on the back seat. He kept turning round and smiling at her; he could feel her warm knees against his back. What a pity she was fifteen years younger than he! And if, after much reflection and procrastination he was resigned to marrying the older sister, the reason was probably, at the bottom of his heart, the thought of living as one of the family, close to the younger one. And also, you just let matters slide and do lots of things without knowing why, just because one day you've said that you would!

As they entered Cloyes, he put on the safety ratchet and set the horse up the steep slope by the cemetery; and as they came up to the crossing formed by the Rue Grande and the Rue Grouaise, intending to leave the cart at the Jolly Ploughman, Jean suddenly pointed towards a man's back disappearing down the latter street.

'I say, that looks like Buteau.'

'It is,' said Lise. 'I expect he's going to see Monsieur Baille-hache. Do you think he's going to accept his share?'

Jean cracked his whip and laughed:

'You can never tell, he's such a crafty customer!'

Buteau had pretended not to see them although he had recognized them in the distance. He was walking along with a stoop, and they watched him disappear, both thinking to themselves that they would be able to clear matters up, although neither spoke. In the courtyard of the Jolly Ploughman, Françoise, who had not said a word, was the first to jump down by way of one of the wheels. The courtyard was already full of unhitched carts resting on their shafts and the old inn was bustling and humming with activity.

'Well, shall we go?' enquired Jean when he came back after stabling his horse.

'Certainly, straight away.'

However, after leaving the inn, instead of going through the Rue du Temple straight to the cattle market, the three of them loitered, stopping here and there along the Rue Grande, among the fruit and vegetable sellers on each side of the street. Jean was wearing a silk cap and a large blue smock over black worsted trousers; the girls were also in their Sunday best, their hair caught up in their little round caps and wearing similar dresses, dark fleecy woollen bodices over steel-grey skirts with large pink striped cotton aprons. They were not walking arm-in-arm but in single file, their hands dangling and elbowed by the crowd. Servants and housewives were jostling each other in front of the peasant women squatting beside the one or two open baskets which they had brought in and simply dumped on the ground. They recognized Frimat's wife, her wrists aching from carrying her two baskets overflowing with all sorts of produce, lettuce, beans, plums and even three live rabbits. An old man had just emptied out a cartload of potatoes, which he was selling by the bushel. Two women, a mother and daughter, the latter, Norine by name, well known for her easy virtue, were spreading cod and salted and red herrings on a rickety table, tipping out their barrels so that people's throats were caught by their powerful smell of brine. And the Rue Grande, normally deserted during the week despite its fine shops, its chemists, ironmongers and above all its smart fancy goods store, Lambourdieu's Bazaar, was never wide enough on Saturdays when the shops were packed out and the roadway blocked with the stalls overflowing onto it.

Followed by Jean, Lise and Françoise made their leisurely way to the poultry market in the Rue Beaudonnière. Vast crates had come in from the farms full of crowing cockerels and scared ducks pushing their necks through the openwork sides. In other crates dead chickens, already plucked, were lying several layers deep. And the country women were out in force here too, each bringing along her five or six pounds of butter, her few dozen eggs and her large low fat, small medium fat and mature full fat cheeses, ash-grey in colour. A number of them had come with two brace of hens with their claws tied together. Ladies were bargaining and there was a throng of people round a big arrival of eggs outside the inn, the Poulterers' Arms. And amongst the men unloading the eggs, whom should they see but Palmyre; on Saturday, when there was no work in Rognes, she hired her services out in Cloyes, carting loads until her back was ready to break.

'She certainly earns her keep!' Jean remarked. People were still crowding in. Carriages were arriving along the Mondoubleau road, the horses trotting over the bridge one after the other. The gentle curves of the Loir stretched out on both sides as it flowed along level with the meadows, while in the gardens of the houses on the left, lilac and laburnum branches were dangling in the water. Upstream there was a bark mill loudly ticking away and a tall flour mill, an immense building perpetually covered in white flour from its blowers set in the roof.

'Well?' Jean asked again. 'Shall we go?'

'Yes, let's.'

And they came back to the Rue Grande and stopped in the Place Saint-Lubin, opposite the town-hall, where the corn market was held. Lengaigne had brought along four sacks and was standing there with his hands in his pockets. Hourdequin was gesticulating angrily as he stood talking in the middle of a group of silent, downcast peasants. They had been expecting a rise; but even at eighteen francs the price was weakening and they were afraid that by the end of the day it would have dropped another twenty centimes. Macqueron went by with his daughter Berthe holding his arm; she was wearing a rather shabby short coat, a muslin dress and a posy of roses and lilies of the valley on her hat.

As Lise and Françoise, after turning into the Rue du Temple, were going along beside Saint George's church, against the wall of which were the stalls of the itinerant vendors of haberdashery, ironmongery and all sorts of materials, they exclaimed :

'Oh, it's Aunt Rose!'

And it was indeed old Fouan's wife, whom her daughter Fanny, having some oats to deliver for her husband, had brought along with her in her cart as a treat. They were both standing waiting in front of a perambulating knife-grinder who was sharpening the old woman's scissors. . . She had been having them sharpened by him for the last thirty years.

'Well, well. It's you!'

Fanny turned round and, recognizing Jean, added:

'You're having a stroll round, are you?'

However, hearing that the cousins were going to buy a cow to replace Blanchette, their interest was aroused and they went along with them, the oats now having been delivered. Left to his own devices, Jean followed behind the women walking four abreast; and so they arrived at the Place Saint-Georges.

This vast square lay behind the apse of the church and was dominated by its old stone clock-tower. It was enclosed all round by bushy lime-trees and two sides were shut off by chains attached to stone posts; the two other sides had long wooden bars to which the animals were tethered. On this side of the square, overlooking some gardens, grass was growing like a meadow, whereas on the opposite side, alongside two roads lined with inns, the Saint George, the Good Harvesters and the Oak, it was hard and trodden down, full of whirling dust.

Lise and Françoise, together with the others, had difficulty in crossing the centre of the square, which was packed with people. Amidst the confused mass of smocks of every shade of blue, ranging from the harsh blue of new linen to the pale blue of those faded by many a washday, the only thing you could pick out was the white round specks of little caps. A few ladies were parading with shiny silk parasols. There was laughter and sudden shouts which were lost in the steady buzz of voices, broken by horses neighing and the lowing of cows. Suddenly a donkey brayed very loudly:

'This way!' said Lise, looking round.

The horses were at the far end, fastened to the bar, their bare coats rippling, attached merely by a rope round their neck and their tail. On the left the cows were almost entirely free, held only by their owners who kept them moving around to show them off.

173

Groups of people were stopping to look at them; at such moments there was no laughter and very little was said.

The women immediately stopped to scrutinize a black and white Cotentin cow that a man and his wife had come to sell; the woman, very dark and with a stubborn look, was standing in front holding the animal; he was standing behind, stolid and motionless. They examined her with deep concentration for a good five minutes, but without exchanging a word or even a glance; then they walked on and stopped similarly to look at another cow twenty yards further on. This one, black and enormous, was being offered for sale by a girl, barely more than a child, pretty-looking, holding a hazel switch. Then they went on again and stopped another seven or eight times, for just as long, without saying a word, going all the way along the cows on sale. And then at the end they came back to the first cow and once again became absorbed in contemplation.

This time, however, it was a more serious scrutiny. They were standing in line and peering keenly, trying to see what lay beneath the skin of the Cotentin. The woman selling her cow said nothing either but kept her eyes elsewhere, as if she had not seen them come back and take their stand. However, Fanny went forward and suddenly whispered something to Lise. Old Rose and Françoise also exchanged a remark in a low voice. Then they fell silent again and continued their still appraisal.

'How much?' Lise asked suddenly.

'Four hundred francs!' the farmer's wife replied.

They pretended to take fright, and as they were looking round for Jean, to their surprise they found him just behind them with Buteau, both chatting together like old friends. Buteau had come over from La Chamade to buy a young pig and was in the middle of bargaining for one. The pigs were in a movable pen at the rear of the cart in which they had come; they were nipping at each other with their teeth and emitting ear-splitting squeals.

'Twenty-two francs?'

'No, thirty.'

'You can stuff that.'

And full of cheerful good humour he came over to the women, laughing with amusement at the look on the faces of his mother, sister and two cousins, exactly as if he had seen them only yesterday. Moreover, they too remained quite unmoved, seemingly ready to ignore their two years of quarrelling and estrangement. Only his mother, who had been told that he had first been seen in the Rue Grouaise, looked at him narrowly, trying to discover why he had gone to see the lawyer. But nothing of this was to be seen and neither uttered a single word on the subject.

'Well, cousin,' he went on, 'it seems you're buying a cow? Jean was telling me. And look, there's one over there, there's not a sounder one in the market, a real good beast!'

He was pointing in fact at the black and white Cotentin.

'Not at four hundred francs, thank you,' muttered Françoise.

'Four hundred francs for you, my little chickabiddy!' he said, slapping her jokingly on the back.

But she was annoyed and angrily slapped him back.

'Leave me alone, will you! I don't play about with men.'

He laughed all the more and turned towards Lise, who was looking rather pale and serious.

'And how about you, would you like me to try my hand? I bet you I'll get her for three hundred francs. Will you bet me five francs?'

'That's all right with me. . . If you feel like trying.'

Rose and Fanny nodded agreement, because they knew that he was a really tough bargainer, stubborn, insolent, a liar and a thief, ready to sell anything at three times its value and to get everything for nothing. So the women let him go on ahead with Jean while they lagged behind so that they did not seem to be together.

The throng round the livestock was growing as groups moved out of the centre of the square, which was in the sun, to go under the trees. People were coming and going all the time; the blue smocks looked darker under the shadow of the lime-trees while the leaves cast green flecks on the florid faces. But no one was buying yet; not a single sale had been made although the market had been going for an hour. People were meditating, thinking things over. But a great disturbance suddenly stirred the warm air above their heads. Two horses tied side by side were rearing up and biting each other, whinnying furiously, their hooves scraping on the paving-stones. People were scared and some women took fright, but by dint of many oaths and a great cracking of whips like rifle shots, peace was restored. And on the ground, in the space left empty by the panic, a band of pigeons swooped down and scuttled here and there, pecking at the grains of oats in the dung.

'Well, old girl, what's your price?' Buteau asked the farmer's wife.

She had observed the stratagem and she repeated calmly:

'Four hundred francs.'

At first he took it as a joke and said teasingly to the husband, who was still silently keeping in the background:

'I say, old boy, is the missus thrown in at that price?'

But while indulging in these pleasantries he was examining the cow closely; he saw that she had everything needed to make a good milch-cow: lean of head with slender horns, large eyes, a largish, thickly veined belly, fairly light limbs and a thin, very high set tail. He bent down and made sure that the udders were long and the dugs supple and properly placed, with a good orifice. Then, resting one hand on the cow's rump, he began to bargain, running his hand mechanically over the bones:

'Four hundred francs, eh? You must be joking... How about three hundred?' And his hand was checking the bones to see if they were strong and well jointed. His hand moved lower and slipped between the cow's thighs, where the skin, a beautiful saffron-yellow, gave promise of an abundant supply of milk.

'Did we say three hundred?'

'No, four hundred,' replied the woman.

He turned to go, came back and she decided to start talking:

'Go on, she's a fine beast all round. She'll be two years old on Trinity Sunday and she'll be calving in a fortnight's time. She's just the cow you're looking for.'

'Three hundred,' he repeated.

Then, as he was walking away, she glanced at her husband and cried:

'Look, I don't want to hang about. I'll let you have her for three hundred and fifty, on the nail.'

He stopped and began to run the cow down: she was badly built, had a weak back, had obviously had something wrong with her and you'd have to keep her for two years at a loss. Finally, he claimed that she had an injured foot, which was untrue. He was lying for the sake of it, with blatant insincerity, in the hope of annoying and bewildering the woman. But she shrugged her shoulders.

'Three hundred francs.'

'No, three fifty.'

She let him walk away. He went back to the women, told them that she was beginning to nibble and that he was going to bargain for another one. And they all went and stood by the tall black cow that the pretty girl was holding on a rope. This one was, in fact, three hundred francs. He seemed to find it not too much, went into raptures of delight and then suddenly went back to the first one.

'So that's your last word, I've got to take my money elsewhere!'

'Of course I would if I could but it's just not possible! You must have the guts to back your fancy.'

And bending down she took a handful of udder:

'Just look how lovely that is!'

He refused to agree and repeated:

'Three hundred francs.'

'No, three fifty.'

That seemed to put an end to it. Buteau took hold of Jean's arm to show that he had lost interest. The women came up in a state of excitement; they thought the cow was worth the three hundred and fifty francs. Françoise in particular liked the look of her and talked of buying at that price. But Buteau was annoyed: who would think of letting himself be robbed like that? And he held out for nearly an hour, to the great anxiety of his cousins, who trembled with apprehension each time a buyer stopped in front of the cow. And Buteau never let her out of his sight, either; but that was how you played it, you had to have strong nerves. Certainly no one was going to put his hand into his pocket as quickly as that: they'd see if there was an idiot about stupid enough to pay more than three hundred for it. And it was a fact that no one showed the colour of their money, even though the market was coming to an end.

Now they were putting some horses through their paces on the highway. One of them, all white, was galloping, excited by the deep-throated cry of a man who was holding onto the halter and running along beside it; while the veterinary surgeon Patoir, red-faced and bloated, was standing beside the buyer in a corner of the square, hands in pockets, watching and offering loud advice. The taverns were buzzing with a continual flood of customers who were going in, coming out and going in again, interminably arguing and bargaining. The bustle and noise had reached a deafening height: separated from its mother, a calf was bleating incessantly; dogs – black terriers and large yellow spaniels – were running around and yelping as someone in the crowd trod on their paws; and when there was a sudden silence, the only sound to be heard was a flock of rooks disturbed by the noise, cawing and wheeling round the top of the steeple. And dominating the warm smell of livestock, from a neighbouring blacksmith's, where the peasants were taking advantage of market day to have their horses shod, there arose a pestilential odour of burnt hoof.

'Well, three hundred?' Buteau repeated indefatigably.

'No, three fifty.'

Then, as there was another buyer there also bargaining, he took the cow by the jaws and forced them open, to see her teeth. Then he pulled a face and let them go. And at that very moment the animal chose to defecate, and as the dung plopped on the yard Buteau followed it with his eyes and looked even more disgusted. Dismayed, the other buyer, a tall, pallid man, moved on.

'I'm no longer interested,' said Buteau, 'her blood's tainted.'

This time the woman made the mistake of losing her temper and calling him names; this was what he wanted and he replied with a flood of abuse. People gathered round laughing. Behind his wife, her husband still made no move. Eventually, he touched her elbow and suddenly she cried:

'Will you take her for three twenty?'

'No, three hundred!'

He was walking off again when she called him back, choking with anger:

'All right, take her away, blast you! But by Christ, next time I'd as soon punch your ugly mug for you!'

She was beside herself and quivering with rage. He was roaring with laughter and affably offering to sleep with her to make up the difference.

Lise had come up straight away. She drew the woman aside behind a tree-trunk and gave her the three hundred francs. Françoise had already taken possession of the cow, but Jean had to push the animal from behind to make her move. They had been hanging about for a couple of hours and Rose and Fanny had been waiting to see the outcome without a word or sign of impatience. Finally, as they were moving off they looked round for Buteau, who had disappeared, and found him giving the pigman a friendly tap on the shoulder. He had just bought his piglet for twenty francs; and to pay him, he first of all counted the money out in his pocket, pulled out the exact amount and then counted it again in his half-closed palm. Then there was a great to-do when he tried to force the pig into a sack which he had brought along under his smock. The sack was rotten and split so that the pig's legs came through, and its snout as well. So he slung it over his shoulders as it was, wriggling, snorting and squealing horribly.

'I say, Lise, what about my five francs?' he demanded. 'I won my bet.'

She handed him the money, thinking that he would not accept it. But he did and promptly pocketed it. Slowly they all made their way back to the Jolly Ploughman.

The market was at an end. Coins were flashing in the sunlight and rattling on the innkeepers' tables. Everything was being hurriedly settled up at the last minute. In the corner of the square only a few animals remained unsold. The crowd had gradually drifted back towards the Rue Grande where the fruit and vegetable sellers were clearing up and removing their empty baskets from the roadway. Similarly, the only thing left in the poultry market was straw and feathers. Carts were already leaving, in the inns horses were being hitched up and their reins untied from the rings in the pavements. All the roads out of town were filled with spinning wheels and blue smocks were billowing in the wind as the carts jolted over the sets.

Lengaigne passed by, his black pony at the trot; he had taken advantage of his excursion to buy a scythe. Macqueron and his daughter Berthe were still shopping. As for Frimat's wife, she was going home on foot with as big a load as she had come with, because she had filled her baskets with dung from the streets. In the chemist's in the Rue Grande, amidst all the gilt decoration, poor exhausted Palmyre was standing waiting to pick up some medicine for her brother, who had been ill for the past week: some foul concoction that would take half her hard-earned two francs. But the leisurely progress of the Mouche girls and their companions was speeded up by a glimpse of a very drunk Jesus Christ, reeling across the whole breadth of the street. They had heard that he'd been borrowing money that morning by mortgaging his last piece of land. He was laughing to himself and you could hear the five-franc pieces jingling in his big pockets.

When they finally reached the Jolly Ploughman Buteau said cheerfully, in an ingenuous voice:

'Are you off then? Look, Lise, suppose you and your sister stayed on and had a bite to eat with me?'

She was taken aback, and as she looked towards Jean Buteau added:

'Jean can join us too, I'd like him to.'

Rose and Fanny exchanged a glance. The young man certainly had something in mind, although his expression was still giving nothing away. Never mind! They mustn't put any obstacles in his way.

'All right,' said Fanny. 'You stay... I'll be off with Mother. We're expected.'

Françoise, who was still holding the cow, said curtly:

'I'm going too.'

And she refused to be persuaded. She was fed up with the inn, she wanted to get the cow home straight away. They had to give in because she was making herself thoroughly disagreeable. As soon as they had hitched up, the cow was tied to the back of the cart and the three women got in.

Only then did Rose, who had been waiting for her son to speak out, pluck up the courage to ask her son: 'You've no message for your father?'

'Nothing at all,' Buteau replied.

She was looking him full in the eyes and pressed him:

'So there's nothing new?'

'When there's anything new, you'll learn all about it when the time comes.'

Fanny flicked her horse and it went ambling off, pulling the cow along behind, with her neck outstretched. Lise remained on her own, between Buteau and Jean.

By six o'clock, the three of them were seated at table in one of the inn rooms which opened off the café. Without telling anyone whether he was the host, Buteau had gone behind into the kitchen and ordered an omelette and a rabbit. Meanwhile Lise had been urging Jean to speak to Buteau and clear their situation up in order to save himself another trip. But by now, after finishing off the omelette, they were busy with the rabbit fricassée and the embarrassed young man had still done nothing about it. In any case, the other man hardly seemed to be thinking of such matters. He was eating hungrily and guffawing with laughter as he kept giving his cousin or his pal a friendly push with his knee under the table. Then the conversation turned to more serious matters, they talked about Rognes and the new road, and although the five hundred franc compensation and the increased value of the land was never mentioned, it added hidden weight to all that they were now saying. Buteau started playing the fool again and toasted them, while one could see in his grey eyes the thought of a profitable deal now that his third share was worth accepting and his former girl friend, whose field next door to his had nearly doubled in value, well worth marrying.

'For Christ's sake,' he shouted, 'aren't we going to get any coffee?'

'Three coffees,' Jean ordered.

They spent an hour sipping and emptying their small carafe of brandy and still Buteau had not declared his hand. He kept beating about the bush and dragging things out as though still bargaining for the cow. In his heart of hearts he had already taken his decision but, all the same, you had to see what was what. Suddenly he turned to Lise and said :

'Why didn't you bring the littl'un along?'

She started to laugh, realizing that this time all was well. She leant over and gave him a happy little slap, with merely the good-humoured remark :

'Lord, what a skunk you are !'

That was all. He was grinning too. The marriage was settled.

Jean, who until this moment had been embarrassed, now joined in their laughter with a look of relief. He even finally unburdened himself :

'You know that it's a good thing for you that you're coming back to Lise. I was going to replace you.'

'Yes, people told me that. Oh, I wasn't worrying, you'd have given me notice, probably.'

'Well, of course... And in any case it's better that it's with you, because of the little lad. That's what we always said, wasn't it, Lise?'

'Always, and that's the honest truth!'

All three faces were flushed with emotion and their joy was free of any jealousy; this was particularly the case with Jean, who was quite surprised at being a marriage-broker. And when Buteau exclaimed that, for Christ's sake, they ought to have one last drink, he ordered some beer. Elbows on table, with Lise sitting between them, they were now talking about the recent rains that had flattened the wheat.

But in the neighbouring coffee-room, sitting at a table with an old peasant, equally drunk, Jesus Christ was creating an unholy din. Indeed, neither of them, sitting in their smocks in the smoky glow of the lamps and drinking, smoking and spitting, could open his mouth without shouting; but Jesus Christ's ear-splitting voice drowned all the others. He was playing cards and a dispute had just broken out between him and his partner over the last hand, which the latter calmly but firmly asserted he had won, despite the fact that he seemed to be in the wrong. The quarrel went on and on and the enraged Jesus Christ was starting to shout so loudly that the proprietor intervened. Then he stood up and with drunken obstinacy went round from table to table showing his cards for the other customers to judge. He was getting on everyone's nerves. Then he started bawling again and went back to the old man, who was quite unperturbed at being in the wrong and listened to his abuse with stoical complacency.

'You cowardly idle bugger! Come on outside and I'll show you!'

Then suddenly Jesus Christ sat down again in his chair opposite the other man and quietened down:

'I tell you what. I know a game. You have to bet, right? Will you take me on?'

He had pulled a handful of five-franc pieces, fifteen or twenty of them, out of his pocket and piled them all up in a heap in front of him:

'This is what it is. . . You do the same as me.'

Intrigued, the old man took out his purse without a word and made an identical pile.

'Now look, I take one off your pile and here goes !'

He picked up the coin, solemnly placed it on his tongue like a eucharistic host, and swallowed it at one go.

'Now it's your turn, take one off my heap. And the one who swallows most from the other pile keeps them. That's the game !'

Wide-eyed, the old man accepted and with some difficulty disposed of his first coin. But Jesus Christ was bolting them down like prunes, loudly asserting meanwhile that there was no need to rush. When he reached five, a murmur ran through the café and a circle of people gathered round, spellbound with admiration : 'Good God, what a gob the bloke's got to tuck 'em away like that !' The old man was just swallowing his fourth coin when he tumbled over backwards, purple in the face, choking and gasping; for a moment they thought he was dead. Jesus Christ stood up, quite unperturbed, with a sardonic look on his face; he had stowed away ten five-franc pieces in his own stomach so at any rate he was thirty francs to the good.

Buteau, afraid that he might become involved if the old man failed to recover, had left the table, and as he stood gazing vaguely at the walls of the room with no mention of paying, even although the invitation had come from him, Jean settled the bill. This put the rogue into an even better humour. In the courtyard, once they had hitched up, he took his friend by the shoulders :

'You know, I want you to come. The marriage will be in three weeks' time. . . I've been to see the lawyer and I've signed the deeds, the papers will all be ready by then.'

And he helped Lise into his own cart :

'Up you come, I'll take you home ! I'll go via Rognes, it won't be much further.'

Accepting the situation, Jean climbed into his cart by himself and followed them. Cloyes had returned to its deathlike torpor and was slumbering in the light of its street-lamps, which were shining like yellow stars. Nothing remained of the bustle of the market but the stumbling footstep of some belated drunken peasant. Then the road stretched out ahead in complete darkness.

However, eventually he caught sight of the other cart with the future husband and wife. It would be better that way, it was the best solution. And he whistled loudly in the cool night, filled with a blissful feeling of freedom.

Chapter 7

ONCE again, haymaking time had come round; the weather was very warm, the sky blue, with a cooling breeze; and the wedding had been fixed for Midsummer Day, which that year fell on a Saturday.

The Fouans had strongly advised Buteau to begin by inviting La Grande, the head of the family. Like the rich and fearsome queen she was, she demanded special consideration. So one evening Buteau and Lise set off, both in their Sunday best, to invite her to the ceremony and to the lunch afterwards, which was going to be held in the bride's house. La Grande was sitting knitting in her kitchen by herself, and, continuing to ply her needles, she stared at them, letting them explain their mission and repeat themselves three times before replying in her shrill voice:

'To the wedding? Certainly not! What would I be doing at a wedding? It's all right for those who like enjoying themselves!'

They had seen her face, the colour and texture of old parchment, flush with pleasure at the idea of this free binge and they felt certain she would accept; but convention required that she must be persuaded.

'Oh, Auntie, really, we can't possibly do without you.'

'No, I'm not up to that sort of thing. How can I find the time? And I've got nothing to wear. It all costs money... I can get along without going to a wedding!'

They had to repeat the invitation a dozen times before she eventually said grumpily:

'All right, since you won't take no for an answer, I'll come. But I wouldn't go out of my way for anybody else!'

Then, when she saw that they were not ready to go, an inner conflict took place, because in such cases it is customary to offer a glass of wine. She decided to go down to the cellar although she had a bottle that was already started. The fact was that for these occasions she had some leftover bottles of wine that had gone off and which she could not drink herself because it was so sour; she called it her special family wine. She filled two glasses and

185

watched her nephew and niece so closely that they were forced to drain them with a straight face in order not to offend her. They left her with their throats burning.

That same evening Buteau and Lise went to Roseblanche, the Charles' house. But there they arrived at a moment of high tragedy.

Monsieur Charles was in his garden in a state of great agitation. No doubt something had happened to give him a violent shock while he was tidying up a climbing rose, because he had secateurs in his hand and the ladder was still leaning against the wall. However, he made an effort and asked them into the drawing-room, where Élodie was sitting demurely at her embroidery.

'So you're getting married in a week's time. That's splendid. . . But I'm afraid we can't come because Madame Charles has gone to spend a fortnight in Chartres.'

He raised his heavy lids and glanced towards the little girl.

'You see, when there's a lot of business at fair-time, Madame Charles goes and lends my daughter a hand. You know, business is business, and there are days when the shop is obviously packed out. And although Estelle now knows the job thoroughly, it's still a great help to have her mother there; the more so as our son-in-law Vaucogne is hardly any use at all. And Madame Charles enjoys going back. After all, when you've spent thirty years of your life in a place it means something.'

He became sentimental and his eyes were full of tears as his mind went back on the distant past. And what he said was true; despite their prosperous, cosy, comfortably furnished villa, full of flowers and birds and sun, his wife often felt a nostalgia for their little house in the Rue aux Juifs. Shutting her eyes, she could see the old quarter of Chartres tumbling down from the cathedral square to the banks of the Eure. When she arrived, she would go down the Rue de la Pie and the Rue Porte-Cendreuse, then, after the Rues des Ecuyers, to take the shortest route, she would go down the steps of the Tertre du Pied-Plat; and on the bottom step you could see No. 19 at the corner of the Rue aux Juifs and the Rue de la Planche-aux-Carpes, white-fronted with its green shutters always closed. They were two wretched little streets and for thirty years she had looked on miserable hovels and their squalid occupants, with the gutter in the middle of the street full of murky water. And how many weeks and months on end she had spent there in the dark rooms without ever crossing the threshold. She still felt proud of the divans and mirrors in the parlour, the mahogany and linen sheets in the bedrooms, all this luxury, comfortable yet discreet, which they had created by their unaided labours and to which they owed their wealth. She felt a pang of sadness as she recalled certain cosy little corners, the pervading scent of toilet water, that special smell throughout the whole house which had become part of her whole being, like a nostalgic memory. So she looked forward to the times when there was great pressure of work and she would go off happily, looking years younger, after two big kisses from her granddaughter which she promised to pass on to the little girl's mother as soon as she arrived at the confectioner's shop that evening.

'What a nuisance, what a nuisance,' Buteau was saying, really annoyed at the thought that the Charles would not be coming.

'Suppose Cousin Lise wrote to her aunt asking her to come back?'

Élodie, who was rising fifteen, lifted her anaemic, puffy, virginal face with its wispy hair; she was so thin-blooded that good country air seemed only to make her more sickly.

'Oh no,' she said in a soft voice, 'Grandma told me definitely that she would need more than two weeks at the sweet-shop. She's even going to bring me back a bag of sweets if I'm a good girl.'

It was a pious pretence. After each trip she was given some sugared almonds which she believed had been made in her parents' shop.

'Well,' suggested Lise, 'why not come without her, Uncle, bring Élodie along with you !'

But Monsieur Charles had stopped listening and was becoming agitated again. He kept going up to the window and appeared to be on the look-out for someone, meanwhile holding back his anger which seemed on the point of exploding. Then, unable to restrain himself any longer, he sent the girl out of the room.

'Go away and play for a minute, my pet.'

After she had left, accustomed to being sent out of the room when grown-ups were talking, he planted himself in the middle

187

of the room with his arms crossed, his firm, fat, yellow judge's face quivering with indignation.

'Can you imagine? Have you ever seen such abominable conduct... I was tidying up my rose-tree and I climbed up to the top rung and without thinking looked over the top and what do I see?... Honorine, yes, my maid Honorine, with a man on top of her and her legs in the air, up to their disgusting tricks... The dirty pigs, right under my wall!'

He was finding difficulty in breathing and started walking up and down, waving his arms about in noble gestures of execration.

'I'm waiting for her to come in so that I can send her packing, the depraved creature... We can't keep a single one, they all get pregnant. After six months, like clockwork, they become impossible to keep on in a decent family, with their bellies sticking out... And this one I actually caught at it and wasn't she enjoying it, too! It really is the end, there's no limit to their filthy conduct.'

Dumbfounded, Buteau and Lise deferentially echoed his indignation.

'No, it's certainly not decent, not decent at all.'

Once more he stopped in front of them:

'And can you imagine Élodie climbing up on the ladder and discovering that! That innocent little girl who knows nothing about anything, we even try to keep watch over her thoughts. It makes one shudder, it really does! What a shock if Madame Charles had been here.'

And at that very moment, looking out of the window he caught sight of his granddaughter inquisitively putting her foot in the lowest rung of the ladder. He rushed over and shouted to her in a voice trembling with anguish, as if he had seen her standing on the verge of a precipice:

'Élodie! Élodie! Get down, go away from there, for goodness' sake!'

His legs gave way and he collapsed into an armchair, continuing to complain about the shameless behaviour of maids. Hadn't they caught one of them in the chicken-run showing their little girl what a hen's backside was like! It was worrying enough, outside, to have to protect her from the villagers' coarseness and the cynical behaviour of the animals: but it really made him lose heart if there was a constant source of immorality in his own house.

'She's coming in,' he said suddenly. 'You'll see.'

He rang the bell and sat waiting sternly for Honorine to appear, having with difficulty regained his air of calm and dignity.

'Honorine, pack your bags and leave at once. I'll pay you a week's wages in lieu of notice.'

The maid, a puny skinny girl, looking miserably ashamed, mumbled apologetically as she tried to explain.

'It's no good, you should be grateful I'm not going to turn you over to the police for indecent behaviour.'

This was too much for Honorine to stomach:

'I suppose it's because you didn't get your cut?'

He sprang to his full height and pointed imperiously towards the door. Then, when she had gone, he violently relieved his feelings.

'Can you imagine that whore bringing disgrace to my house?'

'Yes, what a whore she is, a real whore,' echoed Lise and Buteau obligingly.

And the latter went on:

'So it's agreed, Uncle, you'll come with Élodie?'

Monsieur Charles was still quivering. He went over to look at himself in the mirror, with a worried look; and came back re-assured.

'Come where? Oh yes, to your wedding... Yes, I'm very glad you're getting married... Yes, I'll be there, you can rely on me. But I can't promise to bring Élodie because at a wedding, you know, there's a lot of loose talk. Ah, that trollop! I turned her out and no mistake! I can't stand women who give trouble! Goodbye, I'll be there, don't worry.'

Buteau and Lise then went to the Delhommes, who accepted after the customary refusal and persuasion. The only member of the family left was Jesus Christ. But he was really becoming unbearable, at loggerheads with everyone and thinking up the most disgusting stories to discredit his relatives; so they decided not to include him, despite their apprehension in case he took his revenge by some monstrous piece of behaviour.

Rognes was all agog: this long-deferred wedding was an event. Hourdequin, the mayor, took the trouble to attend the ceremony but refused the invitation for the wedding-feast in the evening because it so happened that he had to spend that night in Chartres for a lawsuit; he promised that Madame Jacqueline would come, since they were so kind as to invite her. For a moment they had considered inviting Father Godard as a really distinguished guest. However, hardly had the marriage been mentioned when the priest lost his temper because they wanted the ceremony on Saint John's Day. He had to take High Mass at Bazoches-le-Doyen for a foundation; so how could they expect him to be at Rognes in the morning? At that, the three women, Lise, Rose and Fanny, all dug in their heels; they made no mention of any invitation and he was forced to give in; and he came over at noon, so infuriated that he dispatched their Mass in such a bad-tempered way that they were deeply offended.

In any case, after discussion, they had decided that the wedding would be a very simple family affair, because of the situation of the bride, with her son now nearly three years old. All the same, they had ordered a pie and dessert from the cake-shop at Cloyes, resigning themselves to extravagant expenditure on the dessert, to show that when the occasion demanded they could be open-handed. So there would be a raised cake, a double quantity of cream and four platefuls of cakes and *petits fours*, just like the wedding of the Coquarts' eldest girl, the farmers at Saint Juste. They themselves would provide a cream soup, chitterlings, four fried chickens, four fricasséed rabbits, roast beef and veal. And that would be for fifteen people or so; they did not yet know the exact number. Anything left over could be eaten up the next day.

After a slightly hazy start the clouds dispersed and the day ended up clear and pleasantly warm. The table had been laid in the middle of the vast kitchen, opposite the fire and the oven where the meat was roasting and the sauces bubbling. The fire was making the room so hot that they had left the two windows and door wide open, letting in the sharp scent of fresh-mown hay.

Rose and Fanny had been helping the Mouche girls ever since the previous day. At three o'clock there was great excitement when the pastryman's cart appeared: all the women in the village came to their doorsteps to look and at that very moment La Grande arrived in advance; she sat down, gripped her stick between her knees and her hard eyes never left the food. Such extravagance should be forbidden! She had eaten nothing that morning in order to leave more room for the meal in the evening.

The men, Buteau, Jean who had been best man, old Fouan and Delhomme, together with his son Nénesse, all in tail-coats and black trousers with tall silk hats, which never once left their heads, were playing cork penny in the courtyard. Monsieur Charles arrived alone, having taken Élodie back to her school in Châteaudun the day before; and without joining in, he watched the game and made some judicious comments.

But when everything was ready at six o'clock, they had to wait for Jacqueline. The women let down their skirts, which they had tucked up with pins in order not to dirty them at the stove. Lise wore a blue dress, Françoise a pink one, in garish-coloured silk which was no longer fashionable but which Lambourdieu had sold them at twice their proper value as being the latest thing from Paris. Old Madame Fouan had brought out the purple poplin dress which she had been parading at every wedding in the district for the last forty years, while Fanny, in green, had put on all her jewellery, her watch and chain, a brooch, rings for her fingers and earrings. Every minute one of the women ran out up the road to the corner of the church to see if the lady from the farm was coming. The meat was beginning to burn, the thick soup, which they had made the mistake of serving, was going cold in the plates. Finally, there was a shout:

'Here she comes! Here she comes!'

And the gig appeared. Jacqueline sprang lightly down. She looked charming, having had the good taste, pretty as she was, to wear a simple white cretonne dress with red spots but without a single jewel on her bare flesh except brilliants in her ears, a present from Hourdequin which had caused a great stir among the local farmers. But they were surprised to see, when they had helped her put her carriage away, that she did not send the farm-hand who had driven her over back to the farm. This was an individual by the name of Tron, a sort of giant, white of skin and red of hair, with a childlike manner. He came from the Perche and had been working at La Borderie as a farm-hand for the last fortnight.

'Tron's staying, by the way,' she said gaily. 'He'll be taking me home.'

In Beauce, they were not very fond of people from the Perche; they accused them of being shifty and untrustworthy. They exchanged glances: this big oaf was the Cognet girl's latest fancy man, was he? Buteau, who had been very agreeable and full of fun all the morning, replied:

'Of course he can stay! Anyone who's with you. . .'

Lise gave the order to begin and they all elbowed their way noisily to the table. They were three chairs short so they quickly fetched a couple of stools that had lost their stuffing and put a piece of board across them. Spoons were already clattering against the bottoms of the plates. The soup was cold and covered with blobs of congealing fat. Nobody minded and old Fouan pointed out that it would be warming up in their stomachs, a remark which sent everyone into fits of laughter. Then the slaughter began as everything vanished down their throats: the chickens, the rabbits, the meat were paraded and devoured with a terrible crunching and gnashing of teeth. . . Frugal eaters at home, they ate like pigs in other people's houses. La Grande said not a word, in order to leave more time for eating as she munched away without a single pause. It was frightening to see what this lean, flat-chested octegenarian could tuck away without the slightest sign of swelling. It had been agreed that Françoise and Fanny should do the serving so that the bride could remain in her seat, but in fact she was unable to restrain herself and kept getting up all the time, tucking up her sleeves and keeping her eyes open to pour out gravy or take a piece of meat off its spit. In any case, the whole table soon started to take part; there was always someone standing up to cut himself some bread or trying to help himself to a bit more of something. Buteau had assumed responsibility for the wine but soon found he could not keep up; true, he had taken the precaution of tapping a cask of wine in order to save time corking and uncorking bottles; nonetheless, they did not give him time to eat and Jean had to help him in filling the litre bottles, while Delhomme, rooted to his seat, declared in judicious tones that liquid refreshment was necessary to avoid choking over your food. When they brought in the pie, as big as a plough-wheel, a solemn hush fell, and the forcemeat balls were particularly admired; while Monsieur Charles politely gave his word of honour that he had never seen a finer one in Chartres. At that, old Fouan, in high spirits, produced another witticism:

'I say, if you stuck that on your bum it would clear up all the wrinkles.'

The whole company exploded, particularly Jacqueline, who had tears in her eyes. She was spluttering and trying to add something that was lost in her laughter.

The bride and groom were sitting facing each other, Buteau between his mother and La Grande, Lise between old Fouan and Monsieur Charles; the other guests sat where they pleased, Jacqueline next to Tron, who was devouring her with gently stupid eyes, Jean close to Françoise with only little Jules between them, as they had promised to look after him; but the pie immediately produced a violent attack of indigestion and the bride had to put him to bed. So Jean and Françoise finished the meal sitting side by side. She was very lively, flushed from the big fire in the hearth, tired out but over-excited. He was very attentive and tried to stand up to help her but she kept slipping away, and had the additional task of handling Buteau, who was much given to teasing when in a good mood and had been plaguing her ever since the meal began. He was pinching her as she went by and she would give him an infuriated slap; then she would find some pretext to stand up as if she liked being pinched again and giving him another slap. She complained that her behind was black and blue all over.

'Why not stay here?' Jean kept saying.

'No, I won't,' she cried. 'He mustn't think that I'm his as well, just because Lise is.'

When it was quite dark, they lit six tallow candles. They had been eating since three and they finally launched onto the dessert at about ten o'clock. From then on they drank coffee, not one or two cups but big bowlfuls of it all the time. The jokes became more pointed: coffee gives you energy, just the thing to liven men up who sleep too soundly; and each time one of the married guests took a gulp, everyone held their sides with laughter.

'You'd better drink a lot,' Fanny said to Delhomme, with a loud laugh, forgetting her usual reserve.

He blushed and soberly offered the excuse that he had to work so hard, while their son Nénesse, open-mouthed, laughed too amidst the shrieks and thigh-slapping that followed their revelation of a marital secret. In any case the lad had eaten so much that he was ready to burst. He disappeared and was found at the end of the evening asleep beside the two cows.

It was in fact La Grande who held out longest. At midnight she was still tucking into the *petits fours*, silently despairing because she would never finish them off. They had wiped out the cream jugs and swept up the crumbs of the raised cake. And as their drunkenness increased and they let themselves go more and more, with their bodices unhooked and trouser belts loosened, they moved around, chatting in little groups around the table stained with wine and gravy. Attempts to sing had faded out and only old Rose, bleary-eyed, was continuing to hum a bawdy song from another age, a refrain from her youth, keeping time with her shaking head. And as there were not enough people for dancing, the men preferred to go on drinking spirits and smoking, tapping out the dottles of their pipes onto the tablecloth. In one corner, Fanny and Delhomme, watched by Jean and Tron, were working out to the nearest sou what the financial situation of the newly-weds would be, as well as their expectations. They went on endlessly, evaluating every inch of land, for they knew how much everybody in Rognes was worth, down to the value of the bed-linen. At the other end of the room Jacqueline had cornered Monsieur Charles and was looking at him with an irresistible smile, her charming, perverse eyes shining with curiosity. She was questioning him about Chartres.

'So it's amusing, is it? You can have fun there?'

In reply, he spoke appreciatively of the 'promenade', an avenue of old trees encircling Chartres and providing a green shady walk all round the town. Down below, particularly along the bank of the Eure, the boulevards were very cool in summer. Then there was the cathedral: he expatiated on the cathedral, like a knowledgeable man with a respect for religion. Yes, indeed, it was an outstandingly fine monument, too large now in an age of declining faith, standing almost always empty in its deserted square which only the shadowy figures of a few pious women were to be seen crossing during the week; and he had felt all the melancholy desolation of such vast abandoned buildings one Sunday when he had gone in as he was passing, at Vespers; it was freezing cold and he could not see very clearly because of the stained-glass windows, so that he had to accustom himself to the dark before he was able to distinguish two groups of little girls from boarding-schools, looking quite lost, like a handful of ants, and singing in their piping voices under the vaulted roof. Oh, it was really heartbreaking to see the churches being deserted for the taverns!

Jacqueline, surprised, continued to watch him closely, still with the same smile on her face. In the end she said in a low voice:

'But how about the women in Chartres?'

He understood what she meant and looked very solemn; but expanding under the influence of the drunkenness all around them, he unbosomed himself. She had sidled up to him, very pink, with little gurgling laughs, as though wanting to enter into the secret of these men out on the spree every evening. But it was not as she had imagined it; he was telling her what hard work it was, for in his cups he was maudlin and avuncular. But he livened up when she told him how, for fun, she had once gone to have a look at the brothel at the junction of the Rue Davignes and the Rue Loiseau in Châteaudun, a ramshackle little house with closed, rotting shutters. At the back, in the badly kept garden, a big ball of silvered glass reflected the wall of the house, while in front of the skylight, in the attic which had been turned into a dovecot, pigeons were flying around cooing in the sun. On that particular day children were playing on the doorstep, and over the wall of the adjacent cavalry barracks you could hear orders being given. He interrupted indignantly. Yes indeed, he knew that place, the women were disgusting and overworked, they didn't even have mirrors downstairs. Filthy hovels like that brought discredit on the trade.

He finally regained his composure. 'What can you expect from a sub-prefecture?' he said philosophically, with the tolerant resignation of a man whose mind is above such things.

It was now one o'clock and there was talk of going home to bed. When you'd already had a child there was not really much point, was there, in standing on ceremony to get between the sheets? It was like those practical jokes such as itching powder or the collapsing bedstead, toys that bark when you squeeze them, that sort of thing would really have been too late in the day for them. The best thing was to have one for the road and say goodnight.

At that moment, Lise and Fanny gave a cry. A big lump of filth had just been thrown through the open window, a handful of dung picked up from under the hedges, and the women's dresses had been thoroughly bespattered from top to bottom. Who was the dirty pig who had done it? They ran out and looked in the square and the street behind the wall; nobody to be seen. Anyway, everyone agreed that it was Jesus Christ taking his revenge for not being invited.

The Fouans and Delhommes left and Monsieur Charles as well. La Grande walked round the table to see if there was anything left, then she also decided to leave, after telling Jean that the Buteaus would finish in the gutter.

While the others were stumbling drunkenly around over the stones, you could hear her firm heavy footsteps and the regular tapping of her stick as she went off home along the path.

Tron had hitched up the gig for Madame Jacqueline, and as she was climbing in she turned round:

'Are you coming back with us, Jean? ... I don't think you are, are you?'

The young man, who was about to get in, changed his mind, happy to leave her alone with his fellow farm-hand. He watched her snuggle up against the large body of her new lover and could not refrain from laughing once they had disappeared. He would be going back on foot and went to sit down for a second on the stone bench in the courtyard, next to Françoise who had also sat down there, bemused by the heat and fatigue and waiting for the rest to go. The Buteaus had already gone up to bed and she had promised to shut everything up before retiring herself.

'Oh, isn't it lovely here!' she murmured after a good five minutes' silence.

And silence fell again, marvellously peaceful. The night sky was dotted with stars; it was beautifully cool. The scent of hay was so strong as it rose from the meadows along the Aigre that it filled the air with a fragrance of wild flowers.

'Yes, it's lovely,' Jean finally replied. 'It makes you feel good.'

She made no reply and he realized that she had fallen asleep.

She was slipping down and leaning against his shoulder. And so he stayed for another hour, with all kinds of ideas running vaguely through his head. Lustful thoughts came into his mind but not for long. She was too young and it seemed to him that, if he waited, she alone would grow older and come closer to him.

'I say, Françoise, it's bedtime. We'll catch cold.'

She woke with a start.

'Yes, that's true, we'll be better in bed ... Goodnight, Jean.'

'Goodnight, Françoise.'

PART THREE

Chapter 1

So now at last Buteau had his share of the land on which he had been casting such covetous eyes for two and a half years, even while obstinately refusing to accept it in a frenzy of mingled longing and resentment. He himself did not understand why he had been so stubborn when at heart he had been longing to sign the deed of transfer; but he was afraid of making a fool's bargain and he could not reconcile himself to the idea of not inheriting everything, all the nineteen acres which had now been carved up and dispersed. Ever since his acceptance, his passion had been satisfied in the fierce joy of owning his land; and his joy was increased by the thought that he had got the better of his sister and brother, for now that the new road ran alongside his land, his share was worth more. Every time he met them he greeted them with a malicious twinkle in his eye, which said:

'I diddled them in the end!'

And that was not all. He was also delighted at his long deferred marriage, which had brought him another five acres, adjacent to his own. The thought that it would be necessary for the two sisters to share out their own inheritance never entered his head, or if it did, he thought of it as so far in the future that he hoped in the meantime to find a way of avoiding it. Including Françoise's share, he had eight acres of ordinary arable, four of wheat and roughly two and a half of vine; and he was going to keep them, he would sooner be torn limb from limb and, above all, he would never give up the Cornailles plot, next to the road, which now comprised nearly seven and a half acres. Neither his brother nor sister had anything comparable and his face glowed with pride whenever he spoke of it.

A year passed by and this first year of ownership was sheer delight for Buteau. Never had he ploughed so deeply when he was working for others: this was his land and he wished to force his way into it and make it fruitful, like a woman. At night he would come home exhausted with his ploughshare shining like silver. In March he harrowed his wheat and in April his oats, with endless care and unstinting exertion. When there was no further work to do in his fields he would go back and contemplate them like a lover. He would go the rounds, bending down and, with his usual gesture, picking up a handful, a whole lump of rich soil which he enjoyed crumbling and letting slip between his fingers, particularly pleased when he could feel that it was neither too dry nor too wet, with the good smell of bread on its way.

And as he watched, the plain of Beauce spread out its carpet of green from November to July, from the moment when the first green spikes poke through till the time the lofty stalks turn yellow. Without leaving the house he devoured it lovingly with his eyes; he had unbarricaded the back kitchen window, which overlooked the plain : and he would station himself there and look out over twenty-five miles of bare plateau spread out beneath the bowl of the sky. Not a single tree, nothing but the telegraph poles along the road from Châteaudun to Orléans stretching in one straight line as far as the eye could see. At first there was nothing to see on the broad brown fields but barely perceptible touches of green along the ground. Then this tender green grew bolder, more velvety, and became almost uniform in colour. Then the wisps of corn grew and thickened out until each plant took on its special hue; he could pick out from afar the yellowy green of wheat, the blue-green of oats, the grey-green of the rye, in fields stretching out in all directions as far as the horizon, amid the red patches of clover. This is the time when Beauce is lovely, dressed in youthful spring attire, uniform and refreshing to the eye in its monotony : the stalks grew longer and turned into a sea, a sea of grain, heaving and deep and limitless. On mornings when the weather was fine a pink mist would melt away, and as the sun rose higher in the limpid air, a gentle wind would blow in steady gusts, hollowing the fields out into waves which started on the skyline and swept along until they died away on the further horizon. The fields quivered and grew paler, the wheat was shot through with tints of old gold, the oats were tinged with blue whilst the rye trembled with glints of purple.

And as one undulation followed the next the fields heaved ceaselessly under the ocean breath. As evening fell, the walls of the distant houses in the sun's rays looked like white sails and the steeples reared up like masts from the folds of the earth. It grew cold and damp and the increasing gloom heightened the impression of a murmuring open sea; and a wood vanishing in the distance was like part of a sinking continent.

In bad weather, too, Buteau looked out over Beauce, spread out at his feet, like a fisherman on a cliff looking down at the raging sea and at the tempest taking the bread from his mouth. He saw a violent storm and the livid murky light of a dark cloud, with the rolling thunder and the fiery red flashes of lightning along the tips of the grass. He saw a whirlwind coming more than a dozen miles away, first as a thin tawny yellow cloud spinning like a rope and then a howling, monstrous mass hurtling towards him, leaving behind it devastated crops, a wake two miles wide, all cut and broken down, razed to the ground. His own fields had not suffered and he commiserated with those whose had with secret gratification. And as the wheat grew tall, his pleasure increased. Already a grey little village had disappeared on the skyline like an island swallowed up by the rising tide of green. There now remained only the roofs of La Borderie which were submerged in their turn. All that was left was a windmill with its sails, like a piece of wreckage. Everywhere there was wheat, a vast green sea of wheat, invading and flooding the whole land.

'By God,' he would say every evening as he sat down to eat, 'if the summer isn't too dry, we shan't go short of bread!'

The Buteaus were now settled in. The couple had taken over the large bedroom downstairs and Françoise had to make do with the small upstairs bedroom, formerly her father's but which had been cleaned out and furnished with a trestle bed, an old chest of drawers, a table and two chairs. She took care of the cows and led her life as before. However, in this peaceful existence there was a hidden source of disagreement, the question of the sharing out of the two sisters' estate which had been left in suspense. Immediately after the elder sister's marriage, old Fouan, the younger girl's guardian, had insisted that the property should now be divided to avoid any trouble later on. But Buteau had protested. What was the point? Françoise was too young, she didn't need her land and had anything really been changed? She was living with her sister as before, she had board and lodging and her clothes were being paid for. In fact, she had certainly nothing to complain about. At all these reasons the old man shook his head: you never knew what might happen, the best thing was to get everything straight; and the girl herself was insistent that she wanted to know what her share was, even if she then left her brother-in-law in charge of it. But the latter, with his heartiness, his blustering good humour and his determination, had had his way. The subject was dropped and he kept harping all the time on the joys of family life, with everyone living happily together.

'I'm all for friendly feelings, that's what we need!'

And, in fact, for the first ten months there had never been any quarrel either between the sisters or in the household. Then, slowly, things turned sour. It began with fits of ill humour. There were sulks and hard words and underneath it all the thought of 'mine and yours' continued to simmer and gradually spoilt their friendly relationship.

Certainly nothing remained of the mutual affection or admiration that Lise and Françoise used to feel. Nobody ever saw them now with their arms round each other's waists, draped in the same shawl, going for an evening walk. It was as though they had been separated; there was a growing coldness between the two. Ever since a male had come on the scene, it seemed to Françoise that her sister was being taken away from her. She had hitherto shared everything with Lise; but she did not share the man and so he had become the foreign body, the obstacle blocking the way to her heart where she was now living alone. She would go away without kissing her sister when Buteau had kissed her, offended as though someone else had drunk out of her glass. Where ownership was concerned she still held with passionate conviction to her childhood notions of 'that's mine, that's yours', and since her sister now belonged to someone else she would surrender her, but she did want what was hers, half the land and half the house.

There was another reason for Françoise's anger which she herself would have been unable to formulate. Till now, with her father a widower, the house had been chilly and lacking love, with nothing to disturb her peace of mind. Now it was occupied by a male, a coarse male used to lifting up girls' skirts under hedges; who made the house shake with his boisterous love-making and whose grunts and gasps could be heard through the cracks in the panelling. She knew all about it, she had learnt it from watching animals and she was disgusted and exasperated. During the day, she preferred to go out and let them get on with their beastliness undisturbed. At night, if they began to romp about after supper, she would call out to them to wait at least until she had finished the washing up. And she would flounce up to her bedroom, slamming the doors and muttering inarticulate insults between her clenched teeth : filthy swine ! filthy swine ! In spite of everything, she still imagined she could hear what was going on downstairs. With her head buried in her pillow and her sheet pulled up to her eyes, she would tremble in a fever of revolt, hallucinated by the agonizing visions and sounds of her budding sexuality.

The worst thing was that, seeing her so preoccupied by all this, Buteau kept teasing her for fun. Well, how about it? What would she have to say when it came to her turn? Lise would laugh too, seeing no harm in it. And then he would explain his own ideas on the subject : since God had provided everyone with this pleasure that cost nothing, it was quite legitimate to get a bellyful of it, as much as you could; but beware of children, they didn't want any more of them ! People always had too many of them when they weren't married, through sheer stupidity. Take Jules, for example, what a terrible surprise he had been but he had to accept it. But when you were married, you had to take things seriously, he'd sooner be gelded like a cat than have another one. No thanks ! Another mouth to feed in a house where people were hungry enough already. So he kept his eye open and took care when he was with his wife, who was so fat, the saucy bitch, that she'd swallow it up like a shot, he would say, adding that he believed in ploughing but not sowing. Wheat, yes, as much wheat as the belly of the earth could produce, but no more brats, never again !

And through constantly hearing all these details and being surrounded by this sexual activity that she could sense and almost touch, Françoise became more and more disturbed. People said that her character was changing and indeed she was continually subject to inexplicable fits of moodiness: cheerful, then sad and then sullen and bad-tempered. In the morning she looked darkly at Buteau when he unconcernedly walked half naked through the kitchen. She and her sister would quarrel over trifles, over a cup that she had just broken: wasn't it her cup as well, or at least half of it? Couldn't she break half of everything if she felt like it? On all such questions of ownership, their squabbles became embittered and their resentment would last for several days.

At about this time Buteau himself went through a dreadfully black period. The land was suffering from a terrible drought, with not a drop of rain having fallen for six weeks; and he would come back with his fists clenched, distracted at the sight of his crops in jeopardy, his rye stunted, his oats scanty and his wheat scorched before it was formed. It made him positively ill, like the wheat itself, with contractions of the stomach, cramp in his limbs, shrunken and bent with worry and anger. And so one morning, for the first time, he crossed swords with Françoise. It was warm and he had left his shirt open and his trousers unbuttoned, ready to fall off his backside, after having a wash at the well; and as he was sitting down to his soup, Françoise, who was serving him, went round behind him for a moment. Finally she exploded, red in the face:

'Look, tuck in your shirt, it's not decent.'

He was in a bad humour and lost his temper:

'For Christ's sake, can't you leave me alone? If you don't like it, don't look. . . Perhaps you're keen to try a bit of it, you snivelling brat, since you're always on about it!'

She stammered and blushed still more when Lise made the mistake of adding:

'He's quite right, you're becoming a damned nuisance. . . Clear out if you don't feel free at home.'

'All right, I'll clear out,' Françoise said furiously and she went out, slamming the door.

But the following day, Buteau had become cheerful, conciliatory and good-humoured. During the night, it had clouded over and for the last twelve hours a warm, gentle, penetrating rain had been falling, the sort of summer rain that revives the countryside; and he had opened the window onto the plain, and as soon as it was dawn he stood there watching the water with his hands in his pockets, beaming as he kept saying:

'We'll be in the money now that God's doing the work for us. Yes, damn it, this sort of day, when you just sit doing nothing, is worth all those days working like a black and getting nothing for it.'

The rain was still pouring down, on and on, slowly and gently; and he could hear Beauce drinking it up, thirsty Beauce that had no springs or rivers of its own. Everywhere there was a babbling and gurgling of water, full of comfort and joy. Everything was soaking up the downpour and growing green again. Once again the wheat was young and healthy, firm and straight, its head held high with the ears all ready to swell to immense size, bursting with flour. And like the earth and the wheat, he was drinking it in through every pore, relaxed and refreshed and cured, exclaiming loudly as he went back to look out of his window:

'Go on! Get on with it! It's raining five-franc pieces.'

Suddenly he heard the door open and, turning round, he was surprised to recognize old Fouan.

'Goodness me, it's you, Father. Have you been frog hunting?'

After struggling with a big blue umbrella, the old man came in, leaving his clogs on the doorstep.

'What a soaking,' he said simply. 'It's wonderful, just what we wanted.'

Ever since his land had been finally split up a year ago, with the transfer signed, sealed and delivered, he had only one occupation left, which was to go round looking at it. He could always be seen prowling round it and taking an interest, sad or cheerful according to the state of the crops, loudly telling off his children because things were not being done as they used to be and it was their fault if things were going badly. The rain had cheered him up, too.

'So you've just dropped in to see us on the way?' Buteau asked.

Françoise, who had not said anything as yet, stepped forward and said flatly:

'No, I asked Uncle to come.'

Lise was standing at the table shelling peas; she stopped with a sudden scowl and stood waiting, her hands dangling. Buteau, who had first of all clenched his fist, assumed his jocular air again, determined not to become annoyed.

'Yes,' the old man slowly explained. 'Young Françoise came to have a talk with me yesterday. . . You can see I was right to want to settle everything straight away. If everyone has his share, there's no cause to fall out, in fact it's the opposite, it stops squabbling. . . And the time has come to put things in order once and for all. After all, she has the right to know exactly what's hers. Otherwise I'd be to blame. . . So we'll fix a day when we can all go to see Monsieur Baillehache.'

But Lise was unable to restrain herself any longer:

'Why doesn't she set the police on to us? Anyone would think we're robbing her, for heaven's sake! Do I go about telling people she's bloody impossible to get on with?'

Françoise was about to reply in similar vein when Buteau, who had playfully caught hold of her from behind, exclaimed:

'What a lot of nonsense. . . We rag each other but we're still fond of each other really. That would be a fine thing if sisters couldn't agree!'

The girl shook herself free and the quarrel was about to start again when Buteau uttered an exclamation of pleasure as he saw the door open again.

'Jean! Good Lord, you're soaked! You look like a poodle.'

In fact Jean had come over from the farm at the double as he frequently did and had merely tossed a sack over his shoulders to protect himself; and he was wet through, dripping and steaming and laughing himself in his good-humoured way. While he was shaking himself dry, Buteau went back to the window and was beaming even more as he watched the unflagging downpour.

'Ah, it's still falling, what a blessing! It's really wonderful, all this rain.'

Then, turning round:

'You've come just at the right moment, those two were at each other's throats. . . Françoise wants her share so that she can leave us.'

'Really? That little sprat!' cried Jean, taken aback.

His desire had grown into a fierce, secret passion and his only satisfaction was to be able to see her in that house where he was welcomed as a friend. He would have asked her to marry him a score of times if he had not thought that he was too old for such a young girl; and though he kept on waiting, the fifteen years' difference did not seem to grow any smaller. No one seemed to imagine that he might be thinking of her, neither she herself nor her sister nor her brother-in-law. Indeed, it was for this reason that the latter made him so welcome, without fear of any consequences.

'Little sprat's the word,' he said with a fatherly shrug of his shoulders.

But Françoise was not placated:

'I want my share,' she said obstinately, staring at the ground.

'It would be the most sensible thing to do,' old Fouan muttered.

Then Jean took her gently by the wrists and drew her against his knees, and held her there, his hands trembling at the feel of her flesh, and he spoke to her in his kind, quiet voice, which quivered with emotion as he begged her to stay. Where would she go? Into service with strangers in Cloyes or Châteaudun? Wasn't she better off in this house where she had grown up, surrounded by people who loved her? She listened to him and her heart began to soften, too, because although she hardly thought of him as a sweetheart, she was usually glad to obey him, largely because they were friends and also because she was slightly scared of him since she thought him a very serious person.

'I want my share,' she repeated, less emphatically, 'but I'm not saying that I'll leave.'

'What a silly girl you are,' Buteau interrupted. 'What on earth will you do with your share if you stay on here? You've got everything you need, just like your sister and me. Why do you want half of it? It's enough to make a cat laugh! Listen to me. We'll let you have your share the day you get married!'

Jean had been watching Françoise intently; now his eyes wavered, as if his heart had missed a beat.

'You heard what I said? On your wedding-day.'

She still made no reply and hung her head.

'And now why not go and kiss your sister, Françoise? That'd be a nice thing to do.'

In her fat, bumbling, cheerful way, Lise was still good-hearted, and she shed a tear when Françoise put her hands round her neck.

Delighted at having postponed the evil day, Buteau exclaimed that a drink was what was needed, for Christ's sake. He fetched five glasses, uncorked a bottle and went back to fetch another one. The blood had risen to Fouan's tanned old cheeks as he explained that as far as he was concerned, he had felt in duty bound. They all drank, the women as well as the men, to each and everyone's health.

'It's good stuff, wine!' said Buteau, banging his glass down on the table. 'But you can say what you like, it's not as good as the water out there... Look at it, it's still teeming down all the time. Oh, it's wonderful.'

And they all stood beaming beside the window, in a sort of religious ecstasy, watching the warm, gentle rain pouring endlessly down as if they could already see the tall green wheat growing under this benison of water.

ONE day that summer, Rose, who had been suffering from giddiness and trouble with her legs, sent for her grand-niece Palmyre to wash out the house. Fouan was out prowling round the fields as usual, and while the poor girl, wet through, slaved away on her knees, scrubbing, the old woman followed her round, both of them harping on the same old themes.

First, there was Palmyre's own miserable state: her brother Hilarion had now taken to beating her. Yes, this innocent cripple had turned nasty, and as he didn't realize his own strength, with fists like footballs, she was always afraid he might kill her whenever he caught hold of her. But she did not want anyone to interfere. She would send them away and succeeded in calming him down by her endless, inexhaustible affection for him. The other evening there had been a scandal that was still being talked about by the whole of Rognes; she had been beaten up so badly that the neighbours had come round and found him indulging in all sorts of disgusting practices.

'Tell me, Palmyre,' Rose asked, trying to draw her out, 'was it because that beast wanted to rape you?'

Palmyre stopped scrubbing, still squatting in her soaked, tattered old clothes, and replied angrily, without answering the question:

'What business was it of anybody? Why did they need to come snooping in our house? We're not robbing anyone!'

'That's all very well,' the old woman replied, 'but if you sleep together as people say, then it's very wrong.'

For a moment the poor girl said nothing, looking vacantly into space, her face drawn with suffering: then, bending double again, she mumbled between each sweep of her skinny arms:

'I wonder if it really is so wrong? The priest sent for me to tell me that we would go to hell. But surely not my poor darling. He's an innocent creature, Father, I replied, a young man who doesn't know any more about life than a three-weeks-old bairn, and he would have died if I hadn't brought him up and being what he is he's hardly known any happiness! As for me, it's my business, isn't it? The day he decides to strangle me in one of these fits of rage he's been having recently, then I'll see if the good Lord will forgive me.'

Seeing that she would not be discovering any fresh details and having long known the truth, Rose concluded philosophically:

'When things go one way then they don't go the other. All the same, it's no sort of life for you, my girl.'

And she complained that everyone had their own cross to bear; for example, hadn't she and her man had to put up with so much misery since they'd been kind-hearted enough to strip themselves of everything for their children? On this subject, nothing could stop her. It was a perpetual cause for complaint for her.

'God knows, in the end you can get used to lack of consideration. When your children are swine, they're swine. But if only they'd pay us the pension they owe us...'

And for the twentieth time she explained that only Delhomme brought along his fifty francs every quarter, oh yes, on the dot. As for Buteau, he was always late and trying to beat them down: for example, although the payment was ten days overdue, she was still waiting: he'd promised to come and settle up that very evening. As for Jesus Christ, that was a simpler matter, he just didn't pay a thing, they'd never seen the colour of his money. And that very morning hadn't he had the cheek to send La Trouille round and she'd started snivelling and asking for a loan of five francs to make a broth for her father, who was ill. Well, they knew what sort of illness he'd got: a great big hole under his nose! They'd given the little hussy a warm reception and told her to go home and let her father know that if he didn't bring his fifty francs along that very evening like his brother Buteau, they'd have the bailiffs on him.

'Just to scare him like, because the poor boy's not really bad,' Rose added, her heart already softening towards her favoured firstborn.

At dusk, when Fouan had come back for supper, she started up again at table while he sat eating in silence, all downcast. How on earth was it possible that out of six hundred francs they had only Delhomme's two hundred, barely a hundred from Buteau, nothing at all from Jesus Christ, adding up to just half

210

the amount of the pension! And the dirty lot had signed at the notary's, it was in writing and legal! They didn't give a tinker's damn for legality!

Palmyre, just finishing wiping off the kitchen floor in the dark, gave the same reply to every complaint, like a doleful refrain:

'Yes, everyone's got his cross to bear and you die on it!'

Rose was just making up her mind to light up when La Grande came in with her knitting. On the long summer evenings they did not foregather, but in order to save even an inch of candle she would come and spend the evening with her brother before groping her way to bed in the dark. She immediately settled down and Palmyre, who still had some pots and pans to scour, relapsed into silence, upset by the sight of her grandmother.

'If you need some hot water, Palmyre,' said Rose, 'start a new bundle of wood.'

She restrained herself for a moment and tried to talk about something else, because the Fouans avoided recriminations when La Grande was there, knowing that she enjoyed hearing them complain out loud at having handed over their property. But her anger overcame her caution.

'And anyway, put on the whole bundle of firewood, if you can call it firewood. Bits of dead twig and hedge clippings! Fanny must be scraping at the bottom of her woodpile to be giving us rubbish like that!'

At this, Fouan, who had remained sitting at table with a glass-ful of wine in front of him, broke the silence into which he seemed to have deliberately sunk. He flared up angrily:

'For God's sake stop going on about your firewood! We know it's lousy! What about me with this dog's piss that Delhomme lets me have for wine?'

He raised his glass and looked at it in the light of the candle.

'You see? What the devil has he put in it? It's not even the bottom of the barrel. And Delhomme's a decent man! The two others would rather let us die of thirst than go and fetch us a bottle of water out of the river!'

Finally, he decided to drink his wine up in one gulp, only to spit it out violently.

'God, what rot-gut! Perhaps it's so as to get rid of me as soon as possible!'

And now Fouan and Rose gave full rein to their resentment, pouring their hearts out to relieve their bitter feelings. Each in turn told their tale of woe and recrimination. The dozen and a half pints of milk per week, for example: well, they didn't even get a dozen; and although it may not have been blessed by the priest, there was certainly a good dose of holy water in it. It was like the eggs – they certainly must have been on special order from the hens, because you never saw such small eggs in Cloyes market; they really were odd eggs and they'd taken so long to reach them that they went rotten on the way. And as for the cheese, heaven help us, it gave Rose belly-ache every time she had any. She hurried off to find one, because she was anxious to let Palmyre try a piece. Well, wasn't it really dreadful? Didn't it cry out for vengeance? They must be adding flour to it or perhaps even plaster. And now it was Fouan's turn to complain that he could only smoke a penn'orth of tobacco a day and Rose immediately chimed in to bewail her black coffee, which she had been forced to give up; and then, in chorus, both of them accused their children of being responsible for the death of their dog, old and infirm, which they had decided to drown yesterday, because he now cost too much for them to keep.

'I gave them everything I had,' the old man cried, 'and now the bastards don't give a damn for me! ... Ah, it makes us so mad, it'll be the death of both of us.'

They stopped at last and La Grande, who had not opened her mouth, looked at them one after the other with her wicked, round, birdlike eyes:

'You asked for it,' she said.

But at that very moment Buteau came in. Palmyre had finished her task and took advantage of this to make her escape, with the couple of coppers Rose had just slipped into her hand. And Buteau stood stock-still in the middle of the room, silent and wary, for a countryman never likes to be the first to speak. Two minutes went by. His father was forced to broach the matter.

'Well, you've come at last, that's a good thing... You've been keeping us waiting these last ten days.'

His son was shifting from foot to foot.

'Well, you can only do what's possible. We haven't always got bread in the oven.'

'That's true, but at that rate, if it takes too long, then we could be starving while you're eating yours. You signed on the dotted line, you ought to pay us on the dot!'

Seeing that his father was becoming annoyed, Buteau tried to joke:

'So I'm too late, am I? Well, I'd better go away again in that case! It's not a very agreeable thing, having to hand over money. Some people manage to get by without doing it.'

This allusion to Jesus Christ upset Rose and she timidly tugged her husband's coat. He restrained himself and said:

'All right, hand over the fifty francs. I've got the receipt ready.'

Unhurriedly, Buteau fumbled in his pocket. He had looked annoyed on seeing La Grande there and seemed embarrassed by her presence. She had stopped her knitting on his arrival and was watching closely for the money to appear. His father and mother had also come nearer and were looking at their son's hand. And beneath the gaze of these three staring pairs of eyes he reluctantly produced the first five-franc piece.

'One,' he said putting it down on the table. The other coins appeared, each more slowly than its predecessor as he continued to count them out loud, with increasing reluctance. After the fifth, he stopped and had to search very carefully to find the next one, and then exclaimed, loudly and firmly:

'And that makes six!'

The Fouans waited but no more coins were forthcoming.

'That's six,' his father said in the end. 'We need ten. Are you trying to have us on? Last quarter it was forty and now it's thirty!'

Buteau immediately started moaning: things were all going wrong: the price of wheat had dropped again, the oats were in poor shape. Even his horse had a swollen belly and they'd had to send for the vet twice. In a word, it was a disaster and he just didn't know how to make ends meet.

'That's none of my business,' the old man retorted in a fury. 'Give me my fifty francs or I'll have the law on you.'

Then he calmed down a little when he thought he could accept the six five-franc pieces as an advance; he said he would alter the receipt accordingly.

But Buteau quickly grabbed the money he had placed on the table.

'Oh no! None of that! I want my receipt for the lot. If you won't give it me, I'll be off. If I'm still going to be in your debt, then it's not worth me giving you the shirt off my back!'

And a terrible scene ensued, father and son both refusing to budge and flinging the same words in each other's face again and again, Fouan exasperated at not having pocketed the money straight away, the other man gripping it tightly in his hand and determined not to let go until he had his receipt. Once more Rose had to tug at her husband's coat and once again he gave in.

'All right, you dirty thief, here you are, here's your receipt! I ought to stick it on your mug with a punch on the nose... Now hand over the money.'

Unclenching their fists, they made the exchange and now the row was over Buteau started to laugh. He went off, affable and contented, wishing everyone a good night. Fouan had sat down exhausted at the table. Then, before going back to her knitting, La Grande spat two words at him:

'Bloody fool!'

Silence fell and then the door opened and Jesus Christ came in. Having been warned by La Trouille that his brother was going to pay up that evening, he had kept watch on the road and waited until the latter had left before presenting himself in his turn. The gentle expression on his face was merely a maudlin hangover from the previous day. He was barely through the doorway before his eyes lighted on the six five-franc pieces that Fouan had been incautious enough to put back onto the table.

'Oh, it's Hyacinthe!' exclaimed Rose, pleased to see him.

'Yes, it's me! Good evening all!'

And he came in, not once taking his eyes off the pieces of silver shining, moonlike, in the candlelight. His father, turning his head, gave an uneasy start as he saw what his son was looking at and smartly put a plate on top to hide them. Too late!

'Bloody fool,' he said to himself, irritated at his thoughtlessness. 'La Grande's right.'

Then out loud he snapped:

'It's a good job you've come to pay me because, as sure as I'm sitting here, I was going to set the bailiffs on you tomorrow.'

'Yes, La Trouille told me that,' wailed Jesus Christ penitently, 'and so I took the trouble to come over to see you because I can't imagine you want to be the death of me. You said something about paying but, good God, how can anyone pay if they haven't even got enough bread to eat? ... We've sold up everything, oh, I'm not joking, come round and see for yourselves if you think I'm joking. I've no sheets on the beds, no more furniture, nothing at all. .. And what's more, I'm not at all well.'

His father gave a sneer of disbelief, which the other man disregarded.

'It may not show very much but the truth is that there's something wrong with my inside. I keep coughing. I feel really bad... If only I could have a cup of hot beef tea. But if you haven't got any, you just go under, don't you? That's the truth of it. Of course I'd pay you if I had the money. Just tell me where I can get some so that I can give something and start making myself a mouthful of stew. I haven't seen any meat these last two weeks.'

Rose's heart was beginning to melt while Fouan was becoming more and more annoyed.

'You've drunk it all, you idle good-for-nothing, it's your own fault! Lovely land that had been in the family for years and years and you've mortgaged the lot! Yes, you and your trollop of a daughter have been on the spree for months and now it's all over and you can die in the gutter!'

Jesus Christ did not wait to hear any more; he burst out sobbing:

'That's not the way a father ought to talk. It's unnatural to deny your own son. I've got a kind heart, I have, it'll be the ruin of me... If you hadn't got the money, I'd understand. But you have, so how can you refuse charity to your own flesh and blood? ... I'll go and beg elsewhere and what a fine thing that'll be!'

And each time he uttered a sentence between his sobs, he cast a sidelong glance at the plate, which sent a shiver down the old man's back. And now, pretending to choke, he broke into ear-splitting shrieks like a man having his throat slit.

Greatly distressed and unable to resist his sobs, Rose clasped her hands and begged Fouan:

'Oh, husband, please.'

But, still refusing to give in, he cut her short:

'No, I won't, he's having us on. Stop making all that row! You stupid bugger! What's the point of caterwauling like that? You'll bring the neighbours around, you're driving us all crazy.'

The only effect of this was to cause the drunkard to scream all the louder. He bellowed:

'I haven't told you everything... The bailiffs are coming to-morrow to foreclose on me, for an IOU I gave Lambourdieu. I'm a rotten swine, I'm bringing disgrace on the family, I'm going to put an end to it all... Yes, I'm just a swine, I'm only fit to go and jump in the Aigre... If only I had thirty francs.'

Exasperated and completely overcome by this scene, Fouan gave a start at the mention of thirty francs. He removed the plate. What was the point since the bugger could see how many coins there were through the plate?

'So you want the lot? Do be sensible, for God's sake... Here you are, you're getting on my nerves, take half and clear off and don't come back.'

Miraculously cured, Jesus Christ seemed to be debating with himself and then said:

'No, fifteen francs is too little, it won't be enough. Make it twenty and I'll leave you in peace.'

Then, having laid hands on the four five-franc pieces, he made them all laugh with his account of the trick he had played on Bécu by putting false ground lines in the protected section of the Aigre, so that the gamekeeper had fallen in when he tried to pull them up. And finally he left after accepting a glass of Delhomme's poor wine; and he called him a dirty dog for having the nerve to send his father such muck.

'He's rather nice really,' said Rose when the door had closed behind him.

La Grande had stood up, folding up her knitting and about to go. She gave a long hard look at her sister-in-law and then at her brother; then she in her turn left, not before finally relieving her anger by shouting at them:

'Not one penny, you bloody fools! Never ask me for a single penny!'

Outside, she met Buteau, who had been at Macqueron's and

had been surprised to see Jesus Christ come in, very cheerful, with a pocket jingling with five-franc pieces. He had a vague suspicion of what had happened.

'That's right, that dirty loafer's gone off with your money. Ah, he's going to enjoy wetting his whistle at your expense!'

Beside himself with rage, Buteau hammered on the Fouans' door with both fists. If they had not opened it, he would have battered it down. The two old folk were already going to bed, his mother had taken off her dress and cap and was in her petticoats, her grey hair falling over her ears. And when they finally decided to open up, he flung himself between the two of them screaming in a voice choking with rage:

'My money, my money!'

They were frightened and drew back bewildered, not yet understanding what was wrong.

'Do you think that I'm going to squeeze myself dry for that lousy brother of mine? He does bugger all and I'm supposed to take it lying down. Oh no I won't!'

Fouan made an attempt to deny it but the other man roughly cut him short.

'So now you're trying to lie to me? I'm telling you he's got my money. I could feel it, I heard it jingling in the bastard's pocket! My money that I've sweated blood to earn, my money that he's going to spend on drink! And if that's not true, you show it to me! If you've still got those five-franc pieces, show me them. I know which they were, I'll recognize them. Show me them!'

And he kept obstinately repeating the same phrase a score of times, whipping himself up into a frenzy. He even started thumping his fist on the table, demanding to see the coins at once, swearing that he wouldn't take them back but just wanted to see them. Then, as the trembling old couple could only stand there stammering, he exploded in fury:

'He's got them, that's for sure! God strike me dead if I ever bring you another penny! I was prepared to bleed myself dry for you two but as for helping that swine, I'd sooner have my right arm cut off!'

But his father was now beginning to lose his temper, too.

'That's enough of that. It's no business of yours what I do with my money, I can spend it as I like.'

'What's that?' said Buteau walking towards him with his fists clenched, livid with rage. 'So you want me to speak my mind, do you? ... Well, I think it's a shit's trick, yes, a real shit's trick to squeeze money out of your children when it's absolutely certain you've enough to live on. Oh, don't try and deny it! You've got a nest-egg tucked away somewhere. I know you have.'

Shattered, the old man tried to force his son to leave but all his former authority had gone. Feebly sawing the air, he stammered:

'No, I haven't got a brass farthing... Will you fuck off!'

'Suppose I look? Suppose I look?' Buteau repeated, starting to open drawers and tap on the walls.

At this Rose, terrified at the thought that father and son might come to blows, hung on her son's shoulders crying brokenly:

'Do you want to be the death of us, you miserable boy?'

Buteau suddenly turned towards her, seized her by the wrist, and thrusting his head against hers, without heeding her tired, worn face or her grey hair, he screamed:

'It's all your fault. It's you who gave Hyacinthe the money. You've never loved me, you're an old witch!'

And he pushed her away so violently that she reeled back and with a dull moan slid down against the wall. He looked at her for a moment, slumped forward like a limp rag; then he left with a wild look, slamming the door and blaspheming:

'Christ All-bloody-mighty!'

Next day, Rose was unable to leave her bed. They sent for Doctor Finet. He came three times but there was nothing he could do and on his third visit, seeing that she was at death's door, he drew Fouan on one side and asked as a favour whether he might not draw up the death certificate and leave it with him straight away: this would save him a further call, it was a practice he used in outlying districts. However, she lasted for another thirty-six hours. When asked about his wife, Fouan explained that it was the result of work and old age and once a body was worn out there was nothing else to do but to leave. But in Rognes, where the story was known, everyone said that it was shock. The funeral was attended by large numbers of people and Buteau and the rest of the family behaved very well.

And when the hole in the churchyard had been filled in, old Fouan went back alone to the house where for fifty years they had lived and suffered. He ate some bread and cheese without sitting down and then he prowled round the empty buildings and garden, not knowing how to calm his grief. Unable to think of anything else to do, he went out and made his way up to the plateau to see if the wheat was growing in the fields that had once been his.

Chapter 3

AND so for a whole year Fouan lived like this in silence in his deserted house. He could always be found roaming around with trembling hands, never sitting down, doing nothing. He would stay for hours contemplating the rotting old manger in the cowshed and then go and stand by the door of the empty barn, as though plunged in a daydream. His garden kept him partly occupied; but his strength was failing, his stoop more pronounced as if the earth were drawing him into its bosom; on two occasions they had had to help him when he had fallen flat on his face in his lettuces.

Ever since Jesus Christ had been given those twenty francs, only Delhomme had continued to pay him his pension, for Buteau firmly refused to hand over another penny: he would sooner be taken to court than see his money making its way into his rascally brother's pocket. Indeed, the latter was still managing to extract unwilling charity from his father, who could never resist his son's tears.

At this point, seeing the old man so abandoned, exploited and desperately lonely, Delhomme hit upon the idea of offering to take him into his own home. Why not sell his house and come and live with his daughter? He would have everything he wanted and it would no longer be necessary to pay him his two hundred francs pension. Next day, having heard of this offer, Buteau rushed round to make a similar one, with a great display of filial duty. He didn't have the money to provide any luxuries, of course, but since it was for his father and nobody else, he could come along and get bed and board, in comfort. In his heart, he must have felt that his sister was trying to inveigle the old man into her house with the ulterior motive of laying hands on his alleged nest-egg. Buteau himself, however, was beginning to doubt the existence of this money which he had been vainly trying to track down. And being very much in two minds, it was pride which led him to offer asylum to his father, relying on the latter's probable refusal. He was unhappy at the thought that he might perhaps accept Delhomme's hospitality. In the event, Fouan showed extreme reluctance and indeed fear at both these suggestions. No, it was better to eat a crust of bread in your own home than meat in someone else's, it tasted less bitter. He'd lived there and there he'd die.

Things continued like this until mid July, Saint Swithin's Day, which was the feast of Rognes's patron saint. A fair normally set up a tent for dancing in the meadows down by the Aigre and on the roadway opposite the town-hall there were three stalls, a shooting-gallery, a bazaar selling everything, including ribbons, and a lottery wheel which gave sticks of barley-sugar as prizes. So on that day Monsieur Baillehache, who was lunching at La Borderie, had stopped to have a chat with Delhomme and was persuaded to accompany him to old Fouan's house to try to make him see reason. Ever since Rose's death, the lawyer had also been advising the old man that it was pointless to go on living in a house that was now too large for him and that he should sell up and go and live with his daughter. The house was worth at least three thousand francs and Baillehache even offered to hold the money on his behalf and pay him a small pension out of it, for any little extra he might be needing.

They found the old man in his usual state of bewilderment, loafing aimlessly about, standing stupidly in front of a pile of wood which needed sawing but lacking the strength to do it. That morning his poor old hands were trembling worse than ever because the day before he had suffered badly at the hands of Jesus Christ, who, wanting to wheedle twenty francs out of him to spend on the next day's festivities, had pulled out every stop, bellowing enough to drive the old man crazy, squirming about all over the floor and threatening to stab himself with a cutlass which he had slipped up his sleeve for the occasion. And the old man had handed over the twenty francs, as he confessed to the lawyer straight away with an anxious look.

'Well, what would you have done? As for me, I just can't stand it, I can't put up with it any longer.'

Monsieur Baillehache seized the opportunity thus offered:

'You mustn't put up with it, it'll be the death of you. At your age it's not sensible to live alone, and if you don't want to be squeezed dry you must listen to your daughter, sell up and go and live with her.'

'That's your advice, too, is it?' mumbled Fouan.

He was furtively watching Delhomme, who was pretending not to interfere, but seeing his father-in-law's suspicious glance he too spoke up.

'You know, Father, I'm keeping quiet because you may be thinking it's in my interest to take you in... But heaven knows it won't be, it'll be a great upset for us... Only, you see, it annoys me to see you in such poor shape when you could be so comfortable.'

'All right, all right,' the old man replied. 'I'll think about it a bit longer. When I've made up my mind I'll let you know, don't worry.'

And neither Delhomme nor the lawyer could get anything more out of him. He complained that people were trying to rush him; but his obstinate refusal, even at the cost of his own comfort, was the old man's final attempt to hold on to the fading remnants of his former authority. Apart from his vague dread of being homeless, over and above having lost his land, he was saying no because everyone wanted him to say yes. So there must be something in it for those buggers? He'd say yes when he wanted to.

The previous night a delighted Jesus Christ had been silly enough to show La Trouille his four five-franc pieces and as a result had gone to sleep clutching them in his fist, because last time the young hussy, taking advantage of the fact that he had come home tipsy, had sneaked one from under the bolster and claimed that he must have lost it. On waking up, he had a terrible shock because he had let go of the coins while sleeping; but he discovered that he had been keeping them cosy under his behind and was suddenly filled with great rejoicing, licking his lips in anticipation of blueing the lot at Lengaigne's; it was a holiday and only an idiot would have any money left in his pockets at the end of the day.

Throughout that morning, La Trouille vainly tried to wheedle some money out of him, just a little bit, she said. He refused to listen and did not even thank her for the omelette she made for him with eggs she had stolen. No, being fond of your father

just wasn't enough: money was men's business. So she crossly
flung on her clothes, a blue poplin dress, a present dating from
more affluent days, and said she was going to have a good time,
too. And before she was twenty yards from the door, she turned
round and shouted:

'Father, Father, take a look at this!'

Between her slim fingers she was holding up a fine, glittering
five-franc piece. Thinking he had been robbed, Jesus Christ went
pale and rummaged in his pockets. But the twenty francs were
still there, the little tramp must have been doing some business
with her geese; so he gave an appreciative grin at her sharpness
and let her make herself scarce.

There was only one point on which Jesus Christ was strict:
morality. So he was very angry half an hour later when, just as
he was closing his door to go off himself, a peasant in his Sunday
best hailed him from the road below.

'Jesus Christ! Jesus Christ!'

'What do you want?'

'Your daughter's lying on her back.'

'So what?'

'Only that there's a man on top of her.'

'Where?'

'In the ditch down at the corner of Guillaume's field.'

He brandished his fists to heaven in fury.

'Good! Thanks! I'll go and get my whip! ... God-forsaken
little bitch, bringing disgrace on the family!'

He ran back into his house to unhook the big horsewhip which
he kept hanging on the left, behind the door, especially for such
occasions; and tucking it under his arm he went off, creeping
along under the hedge like a man out shooting, so as to take the
lovebirds unawares. But when he came out at the end in the
road, he was spied by Nénesse, who was keeping watch on a heap
of stones. It was Delphin who was on top of La Trouille, in fact,
they were taking it in turns, one to keep *cave* while the other
had his fun.

'Look out,' yelled Nénesse. 'It's Jesus Christ!'

He had seen the whip and he took to his heels over the fields,
running like a hare.

In the bottom of the grassy ditch, La Trouille quickly tipped

Delphin off her; but she still had the presence of mind to hand him the five-franc piece.

'Hide it in your shirt, you can let me have it back later. And now clear off quick, for Pete's sake !'

Jesus Christ came thundering up, furiously cracking his long whip round his head, like rifle fire.

'You hussy you, you trollop. I'm going to make you dance !'

In his rage at seeing the gamekeeper's son, he missed him as he scrambled away on all fours through the brambles with his breeches half down. She was all tangled up, with her skirts in the air, and was in no position to deny what was happening. He gave her a lash round her thighs which brought her to her feet and dragged her out of the ditch. Then the pursuit began.

'Take that, you slut ! And see if that'll stuff it for you !'

Without saying a word, La Trouille, used to this sort of chase, took off like a scalded cat. Her father's normal tactics were to drive her back to the house and then shut her in. So she was trying to make for the open country, hoping to tire him out. This time she nearly succeeded, thanks to a chance meeting. A moment earlier, Monsieur Charles and Élodie, whom he was taking to see the fair, had stopped in their tracks in the middle of the road. They had seen everything, the girl wide-eyed and stupefied with amazement, her father blushing for shame and bursting with respectable indignation. And worst of all, recognizing him, La Trouille shamelessly tried to put herself under his protection. He pushed her off, but the whip was after her and to avoid it she circled round her uncle and cousin, while her father, swearing like a trooper, abused her for her conduct as he followed her round, fiercely cracking his whip with all his might. Caught up in this disreputable circle, the only thing that the dazed and confused Monsieur Charles could do was to hide Élodie's face in his waistcoat. And so bewildered was he that he, too, started hurling abuse :

'Get off, you dirty little slut ! God, what have I done to deserve such a family in this Christ-forsaken village ?'

Forced into the open, La Trouille realized that she was lost. One whiplash caught her under the armpits and spun her round like a top; the next one removed a lock of her hair and flung her down onto the ground. After that, with no further escape possible, she had only one thought in mind : to make for shelter as rapidly as possible. Leaping over hedges and across ditches, she cut through the vineyards, nearly impaling herself on the stakes. But her legs were too short to keep up the struggle and the blows rained down on her plump shoulders and backside, still throbbing from her amorous antics, and all over her precocious little body. She even began to treat it as a joke, thinking it rather fun to be tickled so roughly. When she reached home and took refuge in a corner where the long whip could no longer reach her, she was even laughing, in a nervous, excited way.

'Hand over your five francs,' said her father. 'That'll teach you.'

She swore that she had lost them during the chase, whereupon he gave an incredulous snort and searched her. When he found nothing he exploded again :

'So you've given them to your fancy boy? Christ, how stupid can you be ! You let them stuff you and then pay them for it !'

Beside himself with anger, he went out, shouting as he locked her in that she would have to stay there on her own until the following day because he didn't intend to come home himself.

Once his back was turned, La Trouille examined her body for weals : there were only two or three, so she tidied her hair, put on her clothes again and calmly undid the lock, a task in which she had acquired a certain knack. Then she made herself scarce without even bothering to close the door behind her : if any burglars came, they'd be wasting their time anyway ! She knew where to find Nénesse and Delphin, in a little copse down by the Aigre. And, indeed, they were waiting for her there : this time it was the turn of her cousin Nénesse. He had three francs and the other lad only six sous. When Delphin gave her back her five francs, she decided, like the kind-hearted girl she was, that they'd blue it all together. They went back to the fair and she paid for some macaroons for them, after buying herself a big red satin bow which she stuck into her hair.

Meanwhile, just as he was arriving at Lengaigne's, Jesus Christ met Bécu wearing his newly polished badge on a smart tunic. He took him fiercely to task :

'I say, you, is that the way you're supposed to do your rounds? Do you know where I found your son Delphin?'

'Where?'

'On top of my daughter. I'll write to the *préfet* to get you sacked, you dirty pig with your pig of a son!'

Bécu immediately flared up.

'Your bloody daughter spends all her time with her legs in the air! ... So she's been leading Delphin astray, has she? Bugger me if I don't have the gendarmes on her.'

'You just try, you old shit.'

The two men stood glaring angrily at each other. Then suddenly they both calmed down.

'We must talk it over, let's go in and have a drink,' said Jesus Christ.

'No money,' said Bécu.

At that, the other man, in high spirits, took the first of his five-franc pieces out of his pocket, flipped it over and screwed it into his eye.

'How about that, eh? Let's demolish it, you happy man! ... In you come, shitface. The drinks are on me, you stand treat for me often enough.'

Grinning broadly, they propelled each other with hearty slaps into Lengaigne's tap-room. That year Lengaigne had hit on an idea: as the fair owner had refused to put up his tent in disgust at not having covered his expenses the year before, the enterprising innkeeper had converted the barn next to his shop, which had a carriage gateway opening onto the road, into a dance-hall; he had even pierced a communicating door in the wall dividing the two rooms. In this way he had succeeded in attracting the custom of the whole village and Macqueron, his rival across the road, was furious because he had no customers at all.

'Two litres of wine and make it snappy,' shouted Jesus Christ. 'One for each of us!'

But as Flore, both delighted and flustered at this influx of customers, was serving him, Jesus Christ realized that he had interrupted Lengaigne in the middle of a letter which he was reading out loud, surrounded by a group of villagers. In answer to his question, the landlord replied grandly that it was a letter from his son Victor, who was doing his military service.

'Ha! Ha! Good lad,' said Bécu, intrigued. 'And what's he got to say for himself? Start from the beginning again.'

So Lengaigne began again:

'Dear Mum and Dad, this is to tell you that our regiment's been in Lille in Flanders, for a month less one week. It's not a bad place except that wine is dear, you have to pay up to sixteen sous a litre. . .'

And the four pages of the letter, written in a painstaking hand, contained little else: the same detail recurred again and again, in ever longer sentences. Moreover, everyone present exclaimed in horror at each mention of the price of wine: what dreadful places these were! Bloody army! Near the end of the letter there was a vague attempt to wheedle some money out of his parents; could he have twelve francs to replace a pair of shoes he had lost?

'Ha! Ha! There's a lively lad!' exclaimed the gamekeeper again. 'God damn it, he's a man now!'

When the two litres had been consumed, Jesus Christ ordered two more; wine in bottle at a franc apiece. He was paying as he ordered, to surprise everybody, slamming down his money on the table and causing a tremendous stir. When the first five-franc piece had been drunk, he pulled out the second one, screwed it in his eye again and shouted that when it was all gone there was still some where that came from. And so the afternoon went by and the boozing peasants jostled each other as they came and went amidst the rising tide of drunkenness. Never anything but serious and gloomy during the week, they were now all shouting, spitting vigorously and banging their fists on the tables. One man, tall and thin, decided to have a shave and Lengaigne at once sat him down amongst the other customers and scraped away at his hide with his razor so roughly that it sounded like someone scouring the bristles of a pig. Another man followed him, amidst general hilarity. And tongues were wagging; people were laughing about Macqueron, who was afraid to show his face now. Wasn't it the fault of this dud deputy mayor himself if the fair owner had refused to put up his marquee in Rognes? Something could have been arranged. But naturally he was more concerned in voting for roads that would make the land he was handing over worth three times as much. This remark raised a howl of laughter. Fat Flore, for whom this day was the high point of her career, kept running to the door and bursting into derisive laughter each time she saw Coelina peering out behind the windows opposite, her face green with envy.

'Madame Lengaigne, we want some cigars,' bellowed Jesus Christ. 'Expensive ones. Ten cents each!'

As night was falling and the paraffin lamps were being lit, Bécu's wife came in looking for her man. But a tremendous game of cards had just started.

'Aren't you coming? Look, it's after eight. We've got to eat, you know.'

He gave her a majestic drunken stare.

'Go and get stuffed!'

At that, Jesus Christ broke in.

'Madame Bécu, allow me to invite you. How about it? We'll have a blow-out, just the three of us... Did you hear what I said, boss? The best you've got: some ham, rabbit, cheese, fruit! ... And don't be afraid. Come and have a look... Look out!'

He pretended to be rummaging at length in his pockets. Then suddenly he produced his third five-franc piece and held it up in the air.

'Cuckoo! There it is!'

Everyone split their sides with laughter and one fat man nearly had a fit. What a wag that Jesus Christ was! And some of them jokingly felt him to see if he'd got coins secreted all over his carcass which he could go on producing until his thirst was quenched.

'I say, old girl,' he kept saying to Bécu's wife, while they were eating. 'How about a spot of bed together, if the old man doesn't object? What d'you say, eh?'

She was very dirty, because she said she hadn't known she was going to be invited to stay; and she was laughing away, with her grimy, ratlike face, as thin as a rusty old rake, while the enterprising Jesus Christ did not hesitate to seize her bare thighs under the table. Her husband, dead drunk, was spluttering and grinning and bellowing that the slut could easily take on the pair of them.

It was ten o'clock and the dance began. Through the communicating door you could see the glare of the four lamps fastened to the roof timbers with wire. The blacksmith Clou was there with his trombone, as well as the nephew of a ropemaker of Bazoches-le-Doyen who was playing the violin. You did not pay to go in but each dance cost two sous. The earth floor of the barn had been sprayed with water to settle the dust. When the band was not playing you could hear the steady, sharp crack of rifles from the shooting-gallery. And the normally gloomy roadway was ablaze with the reflectors of the two other stalls, the bazaar sparkling with gilt and the tombola decorated with mirrors and draped in red like a chapel.

'Ah, there's my little girly-wirly!' cried Jesus Christ with tears in his eyes.

It was La Trouille, coming into the room followed by Delphin and Nénesse; nor did her father seem surprised at seeing her there, although he had locked her in at home. In addition to the bright red bow in her hair, she was wearing a thick necklace of false coral round her neck, with beads made of sealing-wax, blood-red against her brown skin. All three of them, tired of roaming round the stalls, were blown-up and torpid from a surfeit of sweets. Dressed in a smock and capless, with his dishevelled bullet head, Delphin had the wild look of someone who only likes the open air. Young though he was, Nénesse already had a yearning for city slickness and he was sheathed in a suit bought from Lambourdieu, the sort of tight reach-me-downs turned out by the hundred by cheap Paris tailors; and he was wearing a bowler hat to show his contempt and loathing for village life.

'My girly!' piped Jesus Christ, 'My little girly, come and try a drop of this... It's good, isn't it?'

He gave her a drink out of his glass while Bécu's wife asked Delphin sternly:

'What's happened to your cap?'

'I lost it.'

'Lost it! Let me get at you!'

But Bécu, gratified at the thought of his son's precocious amorous exploits, grinningly intervened.

'Leave the boy alone! He's growing up. So, you rapscallions, you've been having it off together, you little imp of Satan, you!'

'Go away and play,' said Jesus Christ finally, with a fatherly air. 'And be good children.'

'They're tight as owls,' said Nénesse in disgust as they went back into the dance-hall.

La Trouille started laughing:

'Good God, of course they are! That's what I was relying on. That's why they were nice to us.'

The dance was livening up; all you could hear was Clou's trombone booming away and drowning the squeaky little violinist. The earth floor had been over-watered and was turning into mud under the heavy tramp of the dancers; and soon, from beneath the swirling petticoats and the large sweaty patches under the armpits of jackets and bodices, there arose a powerful stench of goat reinforced by the acrid smell of the smoky lamps. But in the interval between two quadrilles, there was a stir when Berthe, the Macquerons' daughter, came in wearing a silk foulard dress, similar to those worn by the tax-collector's daughters in Cloyes on Saint Lubin's Day. Good Lord! Had the girl's parents let her come or had she slipped away behind their backs? And people noticed that she was dancing only with the wheelwright's son whom her father had forbidden her to meet because of a family feud. People were joking about it: so she was getting tired of ruining her health on her own!

A moment earlier, although he was very tipsy, Jesus Christ had caught sight of Lequeu's unprepossessing features as he was standing by the communicating door watching Berthe bouncing up and down in the arms of her beau. He could not refrain from making a comment.

'I say, Monsieur Lequeu, aren't you going to take a turn with your sweetheart?'

'Who's that supposed to be?' demanded the schoolmaster angrily, his sallow face going livid.

'The girl with the pretty saucy eyes over there, of course.'

Furious at having been found out, Lequeu spun on his heels without saying a word and stood motionless with his back towards him in the attitude of arrogant contempt into which he often cautiously withdrew. And as Lengaigne came up at this moment, Jesus Christ collared him. Well, he'd told that slimy bugger off good and proper, hadn't he? They'd teach him all about rich girls! It wasn't as if Not Got Any was as smart as all that, because she'd only got hair on her head; and urged on by

230

drink he talked about it as if he had seen it himself. Everyone knew it, from Cloyes to Châteaudun, all the young men joked about it. Not one single hair, honest Injun! She was as bald as a billiard ball down you know where. Flabbergasted at such a phenomenon, they all craned their necks to contemplate Berthe with a grimace of disgust as they followed her with their eyes each time she came dancing by, all white under her billowing skirts.

'Well, you old rogue,' said Jesus Christ, addressing Lengaigne familiarly. 'It's not like your daughter, is it? She's got some.'

And looking pleased with himself, Lengaigne replied:

'She certainly has!'

Suzanne was now living in Paris and had moved up in the world, people said. Her father would speak discreetly of 'a very good job'. But farmers were still coming in and when one of them, a tenant farmer, asked him about Victor, he produced his letter again. 'Dear Mum and Dad, this is to tell you that our regiment's been in Lille in Flanders...' They listened and people who had already heard it five or six times before gathered round again. And it really was nearly a franc a litre, yes, sixteen whole sous!

'What a dreadful place,' said Bécu again.

At this moment, Jean appeared. He went straight over to look at the dancing, as though looking for someone. Then he came back, disappointed and uneasy. For the last two months he had not dared to make such frequent visits to Buteau's house because he felt that Buteau was cold, almost hostile. No doubt he had failed to hide his feelings for Françoise, his friendship for her which was growing into an obsession, and his former mate had noticed it. And that must have irritated him by upsetting his calculations.

'Good evening to you,' said Jean, stopping at a table where Fouan and Delhomme were sharing a bottle of beer.

'Would you care to join us, Corporal?' said Delhomme politely.

Jean accepted, and when he had drunk to their health:

'It's odd that Buteau hasn't turned up.'

'Talk of the devil,' said Fouan.

And in fact, Buteau was just coming through the door, but on his own. He went slowly round the room, shaking hands here and there, then he came up to the table where his father and brother-in-law were sitting but refused to sit down himself or have a drink.

'Lise and Françoise aren't coming to the dance?' enquired Jean finally, in a voice that trembled slightly.

Buteau stared at him with his little hard eyes.

'Françoise has gone to bed, that's the best place when you're young.'

But they broke off, intrigued by a scene near by. It was Jesus Christ squabbling with Flore. He was asking for a litre of rum to make hot grog, and she was refusing to bring it.

'No, that's your lot, you're drunk enough.'

'Hey, what's that she's fussing about? D'you think you're not going to get your money, you silly old woman? I'll buy up your whole caboodle if you like! Look, all I've got to do is blow my nose.'

He had hidden his fourth five-franc piece in the palm of his hand and he now squeezed his nose between two fingers, blew violently and pretended to extract the coin which he then displayed beneath their gaze like a monstrance.

'That's what comes out of my nose when I've got a cold!'

The walls rang with applause and Flore had to admit defeat and bring the litre of rum and some sugar. A salad bowl was needed as well. And then the amazing Jesus Christ held the whole room agog as he stirred the punch with his elbows jutting out and his red face lit up by the flames, which added the final blast of heat to a room that was already overheated by the smoky fumes of the lamps and the men's pipes. But suddenly Buteau, exasperated by the sight of the money, burst out:

'You pig, aren't you ashamed of boozing away all the money that you've stolen from Father?'

His brother took it as a joke.

'Ah, so it's you, my baby brother. You must be short of a drink to be talking balls like that.'

'I'm telling you you're a shit and you'll end up in jug. And anyway, it's you who broke Mother's heart.'

Choking with laughter, the drunk slammed his spoon violently into the salad bowl so that it erupted into flames like a volcano.

'All right, all right, that's your story. Of course it's my fault unless it's yours.'

232

'And I'm telling you that wasters like you don't deserve the wheat to grow. When I think that our land, all the land that our forefathers worked so hard to leave to us, has been mortgaged by you and handed over to other people... You dirty swine, what have you done with your land?'

At this, Jesus Christ suddenly came to life. The flames of his punch were subsiding, he sat up and leant back in his chair, seeing that all the other people drinking had fallen silent and were watching to see how he would react.

'The land?' he bellowed. 'The land doesn't give a brass farthing for you. You're just a slave to it, you bloody fool. It takes away all your pleasure, all your strength, your whole life... It doesn't even make you rich! While I, who despise it and sit there with folded arms and give it a kick up the arse now and again, I live like a prince, as you can see, I just drink... Yes, bloody hell!'

The villagers laughed again while Buteau, taken aback by such a sharp attack, could only falter:

'You good-for-nothing waster! You don't do any work and you're proud of it.'

Jesus Christ was now well launched:

'The land makes me sick. There must really be something wrong with you to go on believing in it... Does it really exist? It's mine, it's yours, it's nobody's. Didn't it belong to the old man? And didn't he have to chop it up to give it to us? And won't you have to chop it up to give it to your children? So what? It comes and goes, it gets larger and smaller – and especially smaller. You even think it's wonderful to have six acres when Father had nineteen... Well, as for me, I was fed up, it wasn't enough for me, so I've squandered the lot. And anyway, baby brother, I only like sound investments and land is collapsing. I wouldn't invest a penny in it, it's a bad job, a bloody disaster that's going to clean out the lot of you. Bankrupts ... all being taken for a ride.'

A deathly silence was gradually settling on the whole room. People had stopped laughing and the peasants were looking uneasily at this tall drunken devil who was pouring out his odd jumble of ideas, the ideas of an old African trooper, a rolling stone, a tap-room politician. Above all it was the 1848 revolutionary talking, the humanitarian communist still praying at the altar of the Revolution of 1789.

'Liberty, equality and fraternity! We've got to get back to the Revolution! We were diddled. The middle classes took the lot and, by God, we'll make them hand it back! Isn't one man as good as the next? For example, is it fair that that jackanapes up at La Borderie has all that land and I don't have any? I want my right, I want my share, everybody must have his share.'

Bécu, too drunk to defend the powers that be, was nodding approvingly, without understanding. But with a sudden flash of good sense he raised an objection:

'Yes, that's all very well, but the King's the King. What's mine isn't yours.'

A murmur of approval ran through the room and Buteau returned to the fray:

'Why listen to him, he ought to be put down?'

People began laughing again and Jesus Christ completely lost control of himself. He stood up, banging his fists on the table:

'You just wait! ... I'll have a word with you, you dirty coward. I know you're very bold today because you've got the mayor on your side and the deputy mayor and our tuppenny ha'penny representative in Parliament. And you lick his boots and you're stupid enough to think that he's the big man and he'll help you sell your wheat. Well, let me tell you that I've got nothing to sell and you and the mayor and his deputy and Chédeville and the gendarmes can all lick my arse! ... It'll be our turn to be the big men tomorrow and it won't only be me, it'll be all the poor buggers who've had enough of being starved and it'll be you as well when you've got tired of feeding the townsfolk, and not having enough bread to eat yourselves! The landowners will be wiped out! We'll smash 'em and the land will be for anyone who can take it. Can you understand, baby brother? I'll take your land and I'll shit on it!'

'Come on out and I'll shoot you like a dog!' shouted Buteau, so infuriated that he went out slamming the door.

After listening with an impenetrable air, Lequeu had already left, being a civil servant who could not risk compromising himself any longer. Fouan and Delhomme were sitting abashed, hiding their faces in their tankards, knowing that if they intervened, the drunkard would bawl all the louder. At the neighbouring tables, the peasants were starting to become annoyed: so their property wasn't their own, someone would come and take it away from them? And they were growling and all ready to set on this communist and chuck him out when Jean stood up. He had not once taken his eyes off him or missed a single word, listening with a serious face as though trying to discover what truth there was in these ideas which revolted him.

'You'd be wiser not to talk like that, Jesus Christ,' he said quietly. 'They're not things that ought to be said, and if you happen to be right, it's not very clever of you to say them, because you're putting yourself in the wrong.'

Hearing this sensible, cool-headed comment, Jesus Christ immediately relapsed into calm. He sank back into his chair, remarking that he didn't really give a bugger. And he started playing his tricks again, kissing Bécu's wife, whose husband, overcome by drink, had gone to sleep with his head on the table. He finished off his grog, drinking it out of the salad bowl. In the thick smoky atmosphere, people were laughing again.

Dancing was still going on at the far end of the barn; Clou was still blowing thunderously into his trombone, drowning the quavering sound of the young violinist. Sweat was pouring off everybody and adding its own rank smell to the reeking smoky lamps. All you could see was La Trouille's red bow as she swirled round and round in the arms of Nénesse and Delphin, in turn. Berthe was still there too, still faithful to her beau and dancing with no one else. Young men whom she had refused to dance with sat sneering in a corner; well, if that dope didn't mind if she hadn't got any, she was right to stick by him, because there were plenty of others who would certainly wait for her to grow some before thinking of marrying her, in spite of all her money.

'Let's go to bed,' Fouan said to Jean and Delhomme.

Then, once they were outside and Jean had left them, the old man walked on in silence, seemingly turning over in his mind what he had just heard; and then, suddenly, as if this had decided him, he turned towards his son-in-law.

'I'll be selling my house and moving in with you. It's agreed. Goodbye.'

He walked slowly home, all alone. But his heart was full and his feet were stumbling on the dark road and in his grief and sorrow he was swaying like a drunken man. He was already landless and soon he would be homeless. It seemed to him that his old roof timbers were being sawn through and the slates removed from over his head. Henceforth, he had not even a stone to shelter under, he would wander through the countryside continually, night and day, like a pauper, and if it rained the cold rain would pour down on him, incessantly.

Chapter 4

BY five o'clock in the morning the mighty August sun had
already risen above the horizon and the ripe wheat of Beauce lay
unfolded beneath a fiery sky. Ever since the last summer showers,
the expanse of green had turned slowly yellow as it grew taller.
Now it had become a radiant golden ocean which seemed to reflect the glowing air, an ocean surging flamelike at the slightest
puff of air. Nothing but wheat, with no sign of house or tree; a
boundless stretch of wheat. At times beneath the heat a leaden
calm would descend on the ears of corn and a heavy scent of fruit-
fulness rose from the earth. Parturition was near; you could feel
the swelling seed, warm and heavy, forcing its way out of the
common matrix. And looking at this plain and this gigantic
harvest, you felt uneasy lest that minute insect, man, lost in
such vastness, might lack the power to complete his task.

Up at La Borderie, after finishing off his rye, Hourdequin had
for the last week been tackling the wheat. Last season, his
mechanical harvester had broken down and in desperation at his
uncooperative farm-hands, beginning even to have doubts himself as to the efficiency of machines, he had been obliged, as a
precaution, to take on a team of harvesters, ever since Ascension
Day. In accordance with custom, he had hired them in Mondoubleau, in the Perche: a foreman, a tall gaunt man, five other
reapers, and six female gatherers, four women and two girls.
They had just come to Cloyes by cart, and his own cart had gone
over to pick them up. They were all sleeping in the sheep-pens,
empty at this time of the year, the girls, the women and the men
all jumbled together in the straw, half naked because of the intense heat.

This was the hardest time of the year for Jacqueline. Her work
went on from sunrise to sunset, for the farm-workers had to show
a leg at three o'clock in the morning and crawled back into the
straw at about ten o'clock at night. And she had to be first up to
prepare their bowl of soup at four o'clock, just as she was last in
bed after serving the main meal – bacon, beef and cabbage – at

nine o'clock. In between, there were three other meals, bread and cheese for breakfast, another bowl of soup at noon and bread and milk at teatime : five meals in all and big ones at that, washed down with wine and cider, because harvesters work hard and expect to be well fed. But she was always cheerful, as though inspired, her muscles like whipcord, and as lithe as a cat; and her boundless energy was all the more surprising since she was wearing Tron out with her sexual demands, for this tall, rough cowman, colossus though he was, had a soft skin that filled her with uncontrollable lust. She had made a sort of pet of him, taking him along into the barns and the hayloft, as well as into the sheep-pen now that the shepherd, whom she had suspected of spying on her, was sleeping out with his sheep. She had orgies of lust, especially at night, which left her buoyant and alert, and bubbling over with energy. Hourdequin neither saw nor knew anything of all this. He was in the grip of his annual harvest fever, a special fever which was the high point of his passionate love of the land, when he went about trembling inwardly, with throbbing heart and head on fire, moved to the depths of his being by the ripe falling ears of wheat.

The nights were so scorching hot that year that sometimes Jean was unable to stay in the loft beside the stables where he used to sleep. He would go out and lie down fully dressed on the stone floor of the farmyard. And it was not only the unbearable animal heat of the horses and the smell of their litter which drove him out; it was sleeplessness, with the image of Françoise dancing continually before his eyes, the obsession that she was coming to him and that he was taking her in his arms and smothering her with desire. Now that Jacqueline had other preoccupations and left him alone, his friendly feeling for the young girl had grown into a frenzy of desire. A score of times, lying half-awake in torment, he had sworn to himself that next day he would go down and possess her, and then as soon as he had got up and dipped his head in a bucket of cold water he thought it disgusting, he was too old for her; and the following night he would be tormented again. When the harvesters arrived, he recognized amongst them a woman married to one of the reapers, whom he had tumbled in the hay two years ago, before her marriage. One night he was in such a state that he slipped into the sheep-pen and pulled her out by her feet from between her husband and her brother, who were snoring with their mouths open. She made no resistance. Stealthily, in the stifling darkness, he had greedily slaked his lust on the bare earth that, despite all the raking, still reeked so strongly of ammonia from the sheep who had spent the winter there that his eyes filled with tears. And ever since, for the last twenty days, he had come back every night.

From the second week of August, the work went ahead. The reapers had started from the fields lying to the north and were working their way down to the ones along the Aigre valley; sheaf by sheaf, the vast expanse of wheat fell beneath the semicircular sweep of the scythes. These tiny insects, submerged in this gigantic labour, were winning the day. Behind their slowly advancing line, the level earth was reappearing under the hard stubble through which the women gatherers were slowly wading, head downwards. It was the time of year when the mournful, lonely plain of Beauce was at its gayest, full of people and enlivened by the constant flow of workers, carts and horses. As far as the eye could see, the teams were working away in the same rhythm, moving along sideways with the same sweep of the arm, sometimes so close to each other that you could hear the hiss of the steel, while others stretched out in long black lines, like trails of ants, right up to the skyline. And in every direction, holes were appearing as in a moth-eaten piece of torn cloth. Strip by strip beneath this antlike activity, Beauce was being bereft of its cloak, the sole adornment of its summer, and left all at once desolate and bare.

For the last few days, the heat had been overpowering, and on one day in particular, when Jean was carting sheaves near the Buteaus' land into one of the farm's fields where they were going to build a tall stack, some twenty-five feet high and containing three thousand trusses. The stubble was crackling in the drought and, above it, the still ears of wheat as yet uncut, in the burning air, seemed to be glowing with their own flame in the shimmering light of the sun. And not one leaf to offer a touch of cool shade, nothing but the foreshortened shadows of the men on the ground. Since morning, soaked with sweat beneath the fiery sky, Jean had been loading and unloading his cart, without uttering a word but at each trip casting a glance towards the field where

Françoise, bent double, was gathering the sheaves behind Buteau who was scything.

Buteau had had to take on Palmyre to help. Françoise could never have coped by herself and Lise could do little, being eight months pregnant. Buteau was exasperated by this pregnancy. He'd taken so many precautions, too! How the devil did that little brat come to be where he was? He kept bullying his wife, accusing her of having done it deliberately, and would moan for hours, as if some tramp or stray animal had slipped into the house to eat them out of house and home; and after eight months he had reached the stage where he could not bear to look at her belly without insulting her: you and your pudden! How bloody stupid can you get! It'd be the ruination of them. That morning she had come along to help in the binding but he had sent her home in a fury at her ponderous clumsiness. She was to come back with the tea at four o'clock.

'My Christ!' said Buteau, who was determined to finish one corner of the field. 'My back's breaking and I'm as dry as a bone.'

He straightened up; his feet were bare in their big shoes and he was dressed in a shirt and canvas overalls, his shirt open and hanging out, revealing the sweaty hairs on his chest down to his navel.

'I must have another drink!'

He went and fetched a litre bottle of cider which he had tucked away under his jacket. Then, having taken two gulps of the luke-warm liquid, he thought of the girl.

'Thirsty?'

'Yes.'

Françoise put the bottle to her lips and took a long draught; she was not squeamish. And as she lent backwards, arching her back, with her breasts pressing hard against her flimsy dress, he watched her. She too was steaming with perspiration in her cotton print dress, half undone, with her bodice unbuttoned at the top showing her white flesh. Under the blue handkerchief protecting her head and neck, her eyes seemed very large, set in her flushed, taciturn face.

Without adding a word he went back to work, swaying his hips as he cut down a swathe with each stroke of his scythe, the rhythmical swish of steel marking each stride, while she bent over again and followed him, holding the sickle in her right hand to cut off an armful of ears of wheat from amongst the thistles and gathering them up at regular intervals, every three steps, into loose sheaves. When he straightened up just long enough to wipe his brow with the back of his hand and could see that she had fallen too far behind, with her buttocks sticking up in the air and her head level with the ground, in the posture of a female offering herself, he would call out harshly :

'Lazybones ! There's no time to waste !'

In the neighbouring field, where the straw of the sheaves had been drying for the last three days, Palmyre was busy binding them up; nobody was keeping an eye on her because, under the pretext that she was no longer strong, already old and worn out, and so he would be losing money were he to pay her one and a half francs, the normal rate for young women, Buteau had taken her on at so much per hundred sheaves. She had even had to beseech him to hire her services and he had agreed to do it only at a cut-throat wage with the resigned air of a Christian offering charity. The wretched woman would lift three or four loose sheaves, all that her thin arms could hold, and then bind them firmly with a twist of straw which she had made ready. She was completely exhausted by this work of binding, which was so hard that it was normally reserved for men only; the constant heavy load crushed her chest and her arms were tired out by having to hold together so bulky a burden and tie the straw tightly round it. In the morning she had brought along a bottle which she would go and fill up every hour from a filthy stagnant pond near by, and she would drink despite the diarrhoea which was slowly eating away her insides ever since the onset of the heat, weakened as she was already by constant overwork.

But the blue bowl of the sky had grown pale, as if white hot; and from it the sun was showering molten embers. It was the oppressive, prostrating hour after lunch, siesta-time. Delhomme and his team, who had been busily building sheaves into straw-hives, four down below and one on top as a roof, had now vanished, all lying down at the bottom of some fold in the ground. For a moment Fouan, who had moved in with his son-in-law, having sold his house a fortnight ago, could still be seen standing up; but then he too had to lie down and could be seen no longer.

And against the empty horizon and the background of gleaming stubble there remained only the lean figure of La Grande in the distance examining a tall haystack that her farm-hands had started to build amidst the tiny host of half-made straw-hives. She looked like a tree toughened by age and now impervious to the sun, erect and terrifying with not a bead of perspiration anywhere, and full of wrath towards all these people who were asleep.

'God, I'm baking,' said Buteau, and turning towards Françoise he added :

'Let's lie down, shall we?'

He looked round unsuccessfully for some shade. The sun was beating down pitilessly with not even a bush for shelter anywhere. In the end he noticed at the end of the field, in a sort of small ditch, a narrow brown streak of shade cast by some wheat as yet uncut.

'Hi, Palmyre !' he called. 'Are you going to do the same?'

She was fifty yards away and called back in a voice barely more than a whisper by the time it reached him.

'No, I can't, I haven't got time.'

She was the only person left working in the whole scorching plain. If she did not take back her one and a half francs that evening, Hilarion would beat her, because not only was he killing her with his brutal love-making but now he was taking her money as well, to get drunk on cheap brandy. But her strength was deserting her at last. Flat as a board, back and front, as though planed down by toil, her body was creaking ready to break each time she picked up a new sheaf. With her ashen face pitted like an old coin, she looked nearly double her thirty-five years, and the burning sun was draining the last few drops of her life in her final despairing effort as she toiled like a beast of burden about to collapse and die.

Buteau and Françoise had lain down side by side, and now that they were no longer active, lying in sweaty silence with their eyes closed, the steam was rising from their bodies. They immediately fell into a leaden slumber which lasted an hour, with the sweat pouring from every limb in the still, heavy, sweltering heat. When Françoise opened her eyes, she saw Buteau lying on his side watching her with a frown on his face. She closed her eyes and pretended to drop off again. Although he had not yet said anything to her, she sensed that he wanted her, now that he had seen her grow up and turn into a woman. The thought upset her; would that dirty beast really dare when every night she could hear him taking his pleasure with her sister? Never had she felt so irritated by this randy goat. Would he dare? And she lay waiting, wanting him without realizing it and yet ready to strangle him if he were to lay hands on her.

Suddenly, as she was lying with her eyes tightly closed, Buteau caught hold of her.

'You beast! You beast!' she stammered, pushing him away.

'Stupid. Let yourself go! They're all asleep, there's nobody looking.'

At that moment, Palmyre's pale deathlike face peered over the wheat, looking towards the noise. But no one ever paid attention to her; it was as if a cow had turned her head in their direction. And in fact she went back unconcernedly to her sheaves. Once more you could hear her bones creaking with every effort.

'Go on, stupid. Lise won't know anything about it.'

Hearing her sister's name, Françoise, who was beginning to weaken and admit defeat, summoned up fresh energy. And now she refused to give in and struck him with both fists and kicked with her bare legs, which he had already exposed up to her hips. This man wasn't her man! Why have somebody else's leftovers?

'Take my sister, you dirty beast! Stuff her as much as you like, give her a baby every night.'

Her blows began to make Buteau lose his temper and, thinking that she was merely afraid of the consequences, he started to remonstrate with her:

'Don't be damned stupid! I swear I'll pull it out so you don't have a baby.'

Then she kicked him in the crutch and, forced to let her go, he pushed her away so roughly that she stifled a cry of pain.

But the game now had to end, for when he stood up Buteau saw Lise coming back with the tea. He went to meet her and engaged her attention for a moment, to give Françoise time to pull her skirt down. The thought that she was going to give him away made him feel sorry that he hadn't knocked her out with the heel of his shoe. But she said nothing and merely sat down in the middle of the sheaves with a sulky expression on her face.

And when he started reaping again, she sat idly there, looking very high and mighty.

'What's up?' asked Lise, who was also lying down, tired by her errand. 'Aren't you going to work?'

'No, I'm fed up,' she answered crossly.

Not daring to take her to task, Buteau pitched into his wife. What the devil did she think she was doing lying there like a sow warming her belly in the sun? That was a fine thing, that was, a real pumpkin to ripen up! She laughed at the expression, for at heart she was still a fat cheerful village gossip and perhaps it really was true that the sun was ripening and helping the mite along; and she stretched out her great fat belly under the blazing sky so that it looked like a seed protruding from the fertile earth. But he was not joking. He roughly told her to stand up and try and help him. Hampered by this enormous bulk hanging down between her thighs, she had to kneel down and pick up the ears sideways, puffing and blowing like some monster as her belly flopped over to the right.

'You might as well go home if you're not going to do anything,' she said to her sister. 'You can get supper ready.'

Françoise walked off without saying a word. The heat was still stifling but Beauce was once more full of activity; as far as the horizon the numberless little black dots making up the teams were swarming like ants. Delhomme was finishing off his straw-hives with his two farm-hands, while La Grande stood watching her own stack growing taller and taller, leaning on her stick, all ready to lay it about the head of any slacker. Fouan went over to take a look at it and then came back and stood absorbed, watching his son-in-law working, before wandering off, heavy-footed, like an old man full of memories and regrets. Françoise, with her head buzzing and not properly recovered from the shock, was going along the new road when a voice hailed her.

'This way! Come and see.'

It was Jean, half-hidden behind the sheaves which he had been carting from the fields near by all the morning. He had just un-loaded his cart and the two horses were standing waiting motion-less in the sun. They were not going to make the main stack until the next day and he had simply built three walls with the sheaves, to form a little private den of straw.

'It's me, come on in!'

Without thinking, Françoise obeyed. She did not even bother to look back; had she done so, she would have seen Buteau peering after her in surprise at seeing her leave the road.

Jean said jokingly:

'Aren't you a bit hoity-toity to go by like that without saying hallo to your friends?'

'What can you expect if you keep yourself hidden away?' she replied.

He complained that he no longer felt welcome at the Buteaus. But she was in no mind to listen and replied very briefly. Without being invited, she had sunk down on the straw at the end of the little den, as though tired out. Her mind and body had room for only one sensation, intense and physical: that man's assault on her at the edge of the field, his hot hands that she could still feel holding her thighs in a vicelike grip, his smell still pursuing her, his amorous advances that she was still anticipating with bated breath and a thrill of fear and repressed desire. She shut her eyes: she could hardly breathe.

Jean had stopped talking too. The sight of her lying back in an attitude of surrender sent the blood coursing through his veins. He had not engineered this meeting, he was fighting back his feelings, thinking that it would be wrong to take advantage of such a child. But the throbbing of his heart confused him; he had been lusting after her so much and the thought of possessing her aroused all the wild feverish imaginings which had filled his sleepless nights. He lay down beside her, at first merely taking her hand, and then both her hands which he crushed in his own, not even venturing to press them to his lips. She made no attempt to withdraw them but opened her eyes, bewildered, looking at him unsmiling and unashamed, her mouth falling nervously open in bewilderment. And it was this mute gaze, almost a look of pain, which sent him suddenly berserk. He thrust his hand under her skirt and caught hold of her thighs, like the other man.

'No, please don't,' she faltered. 'It's wrong.'

But she made no resistance and her only sound was a cry of pain. The ground seemed to be giving way beneath her and her head was spinning: was it the other man who had come back? There was the same brutality, the same acrid male odour of someone who had been working hard in the sun. Bewildered, her dark, stubbornly closed eyes shot with streaks of light, she was stammering confusedly, not knowing what she said.

'You mustn't give me a baby ! Pull it out !'

He gave a sudden jerk and, thwarted of its purpose, the sperm spurted out onto the ripe wheat, spilling over into the ever-willing, eternally fruitful earth, always ready to embrace every seed.

Stupefied, Françoise opened her eyes without saying a word or making a movement. Was it all over already, was that all the pleasure there was in it? Only the pain remained. And her mind went back to the other man, unconsciously regretting his frustrated desire. She felt irritated by Jean lying beside her. Why had she given in like that? He was old, she didn't love him. And he did not stir either, bemused by this strange adventure. Finally, he made a gesture of annoyance and tried without success to say something. Then, even more embarrassed, he decided to kiss her but she shrank away; she no longer wanted to be touched by him.

'I must go,' he said in a low voice. 'You stay here for a moment.'

She made no reply, looking vaguely up at the sky.

'All right? Wait five minutes so that you're not seen coming out at the same time as me.'

At last she spoke :

'All right, off you go !'

And that was all. He cracked his whip, swore at the horses and trudged off, head down, beside his cart.

Meanwhile, Buteau was surprised at having lost Françoise behind the sheaves and when he saw Jean going off, he became suspicious. Without saying anything to Lise, he went off, bending double like a hunter taking cover. Then he sprang into the middle of the little straw den. Françoise was still lying stupefied and inert, looking at the sky, her legs all exposed. There was no point in denying what had happened and she made no attempt to do so.

'So that's it, you dirty slut, you sleep with that tramp and you kick me in the balls... Christ Almighty ! We'll see about that.'

He had already taken hold of her and his flushed face showed her that he was going to take advantage of the situation. Why shouldn't he be the next one on the list? As soon as she felt his burning hands on her again, she felt the same repulsion as before. Now he was actually there, her previous longing had vanished and she no longer wanted him; she did not understand herself why she was so capricious but her whole being was protesting with vindictive jealousy.

'Leave me alone, you beast! I'll bite you.'

Once again he was forced to desist. But he was stuttering with rage, infuriated at the thought of the pleasure he was missing.

'Oh yes, I suspected you were having it off together. I should have kicked him out long ago. You dirty little bitch, letting that bugger stuff you.'

And the flow of filth went on and on, with every foul expression he could think of, describing what she had done in terms so crude as to leave her feeling naked and ashamed. But although she was equally furious, she controlled herself and, pale and composed, replied calmly and curtly to every obscenity he uttered.

'What business is it of yours? If I like it, aren't I free to do it?'

'All right, I'm going to turn you out of the house, then! Straight away, as soon as we get back. I'm going to tell Lise about the whole affair, how I found you with your skirt up over your head, and you can go and get stuffed somewhere else, since you're so fond of it!'

He was pushing her along in front of him, back to the field where his wife was waiting.

'You can tell Lise. I'll do it if I want to.'

'If you want to, eh? Well, we'll see about that. I'll kick you out on your arse!'

As a short cut, she had to cross the Cornailles field, which had not yet been divided between her and her sister, the field which he had always delayed splitting up, and with a sudden shock, an agonizing idea sprang into his mind: in a flash of insight, he had seen the field cut up into two, if he were to turn her out; she would have half and she might even give it to her lover. The thought chilled him and immediately his exasperation came down to earth. No, that would be stupid, you shouldn't throw everything overboard because a girl turned you down for once. There are plenty of other fish in the sea; whereas when you've got a bit of land, the thing is to hang on to it.

He had stopped talking and started walking more slowly, annoyed and not knowing how to make up for his violence before they reached his wife. Finally he said :

'What I can't stand is ill will, I was irritated because you seem to dislike me... Apart from that, I'm not really anxious to cause my wife trouble, in her present state.'

The thought crossed her mind that he was afraid that she would give him away to Lise too.

'Well, you can be sure of one thing, if you tell her, so shall I.'

'Oh, I'm not frightened of that,' he replied jauntily. 'I'll tell her that you're lying, that you're taking your revenge because I caught you out.'

Finally, as they were coming up to Lise, he added hurriedly :

'So we'll keep it quiet, eh ? We'll talk it over again some other time.'

But Lise was beginning to be surprised : why was Françoise coming back with Buteau? He explained that the lazy girl had gone off to sulk behind a haystack over there. In any case, a hoarse cry suddenly interrupted them and cut the matter short.

'What was that? Was someone shouting?'

It was a terrifying cry, a long gasping scream, like an animal being slaughtered. It rose and died away in the implacably blazing sun.

'What was that? It must have been a horse breaking its leg.'

They turned and saw Palmyre still standing in the stubble amidst the sheaves of a nearby field. In her trembling arms, she was holding one final bundle of sheaves against her flat chest and trying to bind them. But with another agonizing cry of distress, even more strangled and frightening, she dropped everything, spun round and fell onto the wheat, struck down by the sun under which she had been roasting for the last twelve hours.

Lise and Françoise rushed towards her while Buteau followed at a more leisurely pace; and everyone else came running up from the neighbouring fields, Delhomme and his men, Fouan who had been lurking round and La Grande who was hitting at stones with the end of her stick.

'What's happened?'

'Palmyre's had a fit.'

248

'I saw her fall from over there.'

'Oh, heavens above !'

And they all looked at her with the awe which sickness arouses in every peasant, but without daring to come too close. She was lying face upwards, her arms flung out as though crucified on the earth in whose service she had so quickly been destroyed and which was now completing her destruction. She must have broken a blood-vessel. There was a trickle of blood from her mouth. But she was dying more of exhaustion, like an overworked animal, lying amidst the stubble so desiccated and annihilated that she was no more than a sexless, fleshless piece of limp rag, faintly breathing her last amidst the rich, fruitful harvest.

However, at last her grandmother, La Grande, who had repudiated her and never spoke to her, ventured nearer :

'I think she's dead.'

And she poked her with her stick. The body, staring wide-eyed and sightless at the blazing sun, with its mouth open to the winds of space, made no movement. The trickle of blood was clotting on its chin. Then, bending down, the grandmother added :

'Yes, she's dead all right. Well, it's better than being a burden on other people.'

Everyone stood shocked and motionless. Could she be touched without sending for the mayor? First of all they whispered and then began speaking more loudly so as to make themselves heard.

'I'll go and fetch my ladder from the haystack over there,' Delhomme said finally. 'We can use it as a litter... You ought never to leave a dead person lying on the ground, it's wrong.'

But when he came back with the ladder and they wanted to put some sheaves on it to provide a bed for the corpse, Buteau protested.

'You'll get your wheat back !'

'I should damn well hope so !'

Rather ashamed at his meanness, Lise added two bundles of straw for a pillow and they lifted Palmyre's body onto it, while Françoise, in a sort of daze, dumbfounded by this death that had suddenly come out of the blue at the same time as her first encounter with a man, could not take her eyes off the corpse, full of sadness but above all of surprise that this could once have been a woman. Together with Fouan, she stayed on guard until it was time to go, and the old man said nothing, either, but seemed to be thinking that it was the lucky ones who die.

At sundown, when work comes to an end, two men came to pick up the litter. It was not a heavy load and there was little need for anyone to relieve them. Nonetheless, other people came along with them and formed a sort of procession. They cut across country, to avoid the longer distance by the road. The body was beginning to stiffen on the sheaves and under its head ears of corn swung up and down and to and fro to the rhythm of the steps. The sky was now living on borrowed heat, a heavy copper-coloured glow in the blue heavens. On the horizon, on the other side of the Loir, the oblique rays of the sun, now bathed in mist, shone with a low, even light across the fields. Everything seemed yellow, that golden yellow of an evening of good harvesting. The wheat that was still standing bore plumes of pink flame; the bristly stubble shone in delicate wisps of red; and on all sides the mounds of the haystacks loomed up like fleecy waves on the golden sea, stretching to infinity, becoming preternaturally tall as, with one side still afire, the other already in the dark, they cast their shadow far into the distance across the plain. A great peace descended; the only sound, high in the heavens, was the chirping of a lark. No one spoke amongst the work-weary labourers who followed along, their heads cast down, resigned, like a herd of cattle. And all that could be heard was the squeak of the ladder swaying under the dead body that they were bringing home amid the ripened corn.

That evening, Hourdequin paid off his workers who had completed their contract. The men took home one hundred and twenty francs and the women sixty as a reward for their month's work. It was a good year, not too much flattened wheat, which chips the blade of the scythe, and no storm during the reaping. So there was clamorous applause when the foreman and his team presented Jacqueline, who was treated as the mistress of the house, with the traditional cross of plaited straw; and the final farewell feast was very gay. They disposed of three legs of mutton and five rabbits and the drinking went on so late that everyone went to bed the worse for drink. Tipsy herself, Jacqueline was nearly caught by Hourdequin as she was hanging round Tron's neck. Befuddled, Jean flung himself on the straw of his loft, but despite his tiredness he was unable to sleep, for the image of Françoise returned to torment him. He was surprised and almost annoyed by this because he had not felt much pleasure at possessing her, despite all the long sleepless nights when he had desired her. Since it had happened, he felt flat and empty; and he could have sworn that he would never want to do it again. But hardly had he gone to bed than she appeared once more before his mind's eye and his body awoke once more in a frenzy of lustful images; he had had little enjoyment from the act but every detail now revived to excite his desire. How could he arrange to have her again, how could he get hold of her tomorrow and the days following, for ever? A rustling beside him made him start, a woman was slipping in beside him, it was the woman from the Perche, the sheaf-gatherer who was surprised because he had not come to fetch her on this, her last night. At first he pushed her off and then he caught hold of her and squeezed the breath out of her; but it was the other woman he was clasping in his arms and would have held tight against himself, limb to limb, until all her bones were crushed and she had fainted in his arms.

At this very same moment, Françoise awoke with a start, got up and opened the window of her attic for a breath of air. She had dreamt that people were fighting and that dogs were biting away at the door below. As soon as the air had cooled her somewhat, her thoughts came back to the two men, one of whom desired her, the other who had possessed her; and her thoughts went no further, she simply let the ideas go round and round in her head without attempting to come to any conclusion. But suddenly she pricked up her ears: was it a dream after all? A dog was howling in the distance down by the Aigre. Then she remembered: it was Hilarion who, since nightfall, had been howling beside Palmyre's dead body. People had tried to drive him away and he had clung on, biting and snapping and refusing to leave the remains of the sister who was his wife, his all; and he kept on howling and howling endlessly, until it filled the whole night. Trembling, Françoise remained listening for a long while.

Chapter 5

'I DO hope Coliche doesn't have her calf at the same time as me,' Lise would say every morning.

And she would drag her enormous belly along to the cowshed and stand lost in thought, anxiously watching the cow whose belly had grown enormous too. Never had a cow had such a swollen belly, as round as a barrel and perched on top of legs that seemed to have grown thinner. The nine months would be up exactly on Saint Fiacre's Day, because Françoise had carefully noted the date when she had taken her to the bull. Unfortunately, it was Lise who was not so certain within a few days either way. The baby had materialized so oddly that she was unable to know exactly. But it would certainly be making its appearance around Saint Fiacre's Day, perhaps the day before, perhaps the day after. And she kept on repeating dolefully:

'I do hope Coliche doesn't have her calf at the same time as me! What a nuisance that would be. Good heavens, we'd really be in the soup!'

Coliche was the spoilt darling of the household where she had now been for the last ten years. She had become one of the family. The Buteaus took refuge beside her because they had no other heating than her warm body. And the cow herself was very affectionate, particularly towards Françoise. She would lick her with her rough tongue until she almost drew blood and take a corner of her skirt between her teeth to make her come and stay beside her. So as her time drew near they took particular care of her: hot soup, little outings at the right time of the day, and attention at all times. It was not only that they loved her; she also represented five hundred francs and milk, butter and cheese, a real fortune that would disappear if they lost her.

A fortnight had gone by since the harvest. Françoise had resumed her normal life in the household as if nothing had happened between her and Buteau. He seemed to have forgotten and she herself was trying not to think about such disturbing things. She had seen Jean and warned him not to come to the house. He hung about under the hedgerows looking for her and implored her to slip away and come and meet him in certain ditches which he described to her. But she was scared and kept refusing, hiding her coldness under a cloak of caution: later on, when she wouldn't be needed so much at home. And one evening when he came on her unexpectedly as she was going down to buy some sugar at Macqueron's, she stubbornly refused to follow him behind the church and would talk of nothing but Coliche all the time, and how her bones were beginning to give way and her behind opening up, proof positive, as he himself confirmed, that her calf was nearly due.

Then what should happen but on the very eve of Saint Fiacre's Day, after dinner, Lise was crippled by griping pains as she was standing in the cowshed with her sister watching the cow, which was also standing with her thighs apart because of her swollen belly and gently lowing because she too was in pain:

'I told you so,' she cried angrily, 'now we are in the soup!'

Bent double, holding her belly in both hands and squeezing it hard as a punishment, she launched into loud recriminations: for Christ's sake, don't bother me now! You could at least have waited! It felt like flies biting her down the side and the pains, starting in her back, shot right down to her knees. She stamped her foot and refused to go and lie down, repeating that she would push it back in.

At about ten o'clock, when young Jules had been put to bed, Buteau decided to go to sleep himself, annoyed that nothing was happening. He left Lise and Françoise in the cowshed, patiently watching over Coliche, whose pains were getting worse. They were both getting worried because there did not appear to be much progress, even although the bones seemed to have moved into the right position. Now that the passage was all ready, why didn't the calf come? They stroked her and encouraged her and brought her sweets and sugar, which she refused, hanging her head and violently jerking her hindquarters. At midnight Lise, who had till now been writhing in pain, suddenly felt relief: for her it had just been a false alarm, a few stray pains, but she was convinced that it was she who had forced the baby back in, as if she had stopped herself from emptying her bowels. And she and her sister kept watch over Coliche all night, relieving her by applying burning hot flannels to her skin, whilst Rougette, the other cow which they had bought at Cloyes market, surprised by the lighted candle, watched them with her big drowsy blue-black eyes.

At daybreak, seeing that there was still nothing happening, Françoise decided to go and fetch their neighbour, Frimat's wife. She was the recognized expert and had helped so many cows that people were always ready to call her in for difficult cases, to avoid sending for the veterinary surgeon. As soon as she arrived, she pulled a face :

'She doesn't look too good,' she muttered. 'How long has she been like that?'

'About twelve hours.'

The old woman continued to circle round behind the cow, sticking her nose in everywhere, with little jerks of her chin and a grim expression which scared the other two women.

'Anyway,' she said finally, 'here's the sac coming. We must wait and see.'

So they spent the whole day watching the sac forming as it filled up and was pushed out by the waters. They studied it, measured it, assessed it : a bag that was as good as any other, after all, even if it was too long and big. But at nine o'clock, progress halted again and the bag hung down, stationary and pitiful, swinging to and fro like a pendulum moved by the convulsive quivering of the cow whose condition was visibly deteriorating.

When Buteau came in from the fields for lunch he was scared, too, and talked of fetching the vet, despite his qualms at the thought of what it would cost him.

'A vet?' said Frimat's wife acidly. 'So you want him to kill the poor beast, do you, like old Saucisse's cow, right under their very noses? No, look, I'm going to burst the sac and I'll go in and fetch your calf out myself.'

'But Monsieur Patoir doesn't like you to burst the sac,' Françoise pointed out. 'He says that the water in it helps.'

Frimat's wife shrugged her shoulders. Patoir was an ass ! And she cut the bag with a stroke of her scissors. The waters poured out like water through a sluice-gate, and as they failed to jump back in time, they were all splashed. For a moment, Coliche breathed more freely and the old woman said triumphantly, 'I told you so!' She smeared her right hand with butter and inserted it to try to discover the exact position of the calf. She slowly felt around inside. Lise and Françoise looked on, blinking anxiously. Buteau, who had not gone back to work, was himself waiting breathlessly, without a movement.

'I can feel the feet,' she murmured, 'but there's no head... That's not very good when you can't feel the head.'

She had to withdraw her hand. Coliche had such a violent contraction that the legs appeared. That was something, at least, and the Buteaus sighed in relief: at the sight of these feet they felt that a bit of their calf was on its way, and they at once had only one idea in mind, which was to pull it out, so that they could have all of it straight away, as if afraid that it might go back in and not come out again.

'Better not rush her,' said Frimat's wife cautiously. 'It'll come out in the end.'

Françoise agreed. But Buteau was becoming excited and kept continually catching hold of the feet, annoyed that they were not becoming any longer. All of a sudden, he took a piece of rope and tied a strong knot in it, helped by his wife who was as excited as he was; and as Bécu's wife, always with a nose for something out of the ordinary, came in at that very moment, they all hung onto the rope and pulled, first Buteau, then Frimat's wife, then Bécu's wife, Françoise and even Lise, crouching down with her big belly.

'Heave ho!' Buteau was crying. 'All together! Ah, the brute, he hasn't budged an inch, he's stuck. Come out, you bugger!'

The women, breathless and bathed in perspiration, were repeating: 'Heave ho! Come out, you bugger!'

But then an accident occurred. The old piece of rope, half rotten, broke and they all fell head over heels in the litter, shouting and swearing.

'It doesn't matter, there's no harm done,' said Lise, as they hurried to pick her up where she had tumbled against the wall.

However, hardly was she on her feet than she came over dizzy and had to sit down. A quarter of an hour later she was sitting holding her stomach with the same violent, regular pains that she had had the evening before. And she had thought she'd made it go back in! But what real bad luck it was that the cow was so slow and she had started up again, so strongly that she might even be first. You can't escape fate, it must have been written that they would both give birth together. She was heaving great sighs and a quarrel broke out between her and her husband. Why had she joined them in tugging, for Christ's sake? What business of hers was someone else's sac? Empty your own first, for God's sake! She was in such pain that she returned his insults: dirty beast, if he hadn't filled her up it wouldn't be giving her all that trouble now.

'That's just talk,' remarked Frimat's wife. 'It won't get you anywhere.'

And Bécu's wife added:

'But it does make you feel better.'

Fortunately, they had got rid of young Jules by sending him off to Cousin Delhomme's. It was three o'clock, the house was all upside-down: on the one hand there was Lise, who insisted on sitting on an old chair, writhing and groaning, on the other Coliche, who kept making the same sort of sound, trembling and sweating and looking worse and worse. The second cow, Rougette, had started lowing with fright. Then Françoise lost her head and, swearing and shouting, Buteau suggested having another tug. They called in two neighbours and the six of them set to pulling as if they were uprooting an oak, using a new rope which did not break. But Coliche swayed, fell on her side in the straw and lay stretched out gasping pitifully.

'The bugger, we shan't get him,' said Buteau, covered in sweat, 'and we'll lose the bloody cow as well.'

Françoise clasped her hands and implored him to go and fetch Monsieur Patoir. 'It doesn't matter what it costs, go and fetch him!'

He was looking glum, but after a final struggle, without saying a word, he got out his cart.

Ever since they had mentioned Patoir's name, Frimat's wife had been pretending to have nothing further to do with the cow but she now became concerned about Lise. She was also an expert on childbirth and all her neighbours had passed through her hands. She seemed worried and she imparted her fears to

Bécu's wife, who called Buteau back as he was hitching up the cart.

'I say, your wife's in great pain. How about bringing a doctor as well?'

His eyes nearly popped out of his head and for a moment he was at a loss for words. What? Someone else who wanted to be petted and pampered! He certainly wasn't going to pay for everybody!

'Don't do it,' cried Lise between two spasms. 'I can manage. We haven't got money to fling down the drain.'

Buteau hastily whipped up his horse and as night was falling the cart disappeared down the road to Cloyes. When Patoir arrived a couple of hours later, he found everything at the same stage, Coliche at her last gasp, still lying on her side, and Lise half slipping off her chair and wriggling like a worm. All this had now been going on for twenty-four hours.

'Which one's mine?' enquired the vet, who was something of a wag.

And then, turning to Lise, he added familiarly:

'Well, old girl, if it's not you, will you do me the favour of popping straight into bed? You need to.'

She did not reply and made no move to go. He was already examining the cow.

'What the devil! She's in a pretty poor state, your cow. You always send for me too late. And you've been tugging at it, I can see that, eh? You'd sooner have split her in two than wait, wouldn't you, you clumsy lot!'

They all stood, listening respectfully, and full of gloom, with hangdog expressions. Patoir took off his coat, tucked up his sleeves and pushed the feet back in, after tying them together with a cord, in order to be able to retrieve them. Then he thrust his right hand in.

'Of course,' he said after a moment. 'It's just what I thought. The head's twisted backwards to the left, you could have pulled until doomsday and not got it out. And let me tell you, your calf's a goner. I'm not anxious to cut my fingers on his toothy-pegs trying to turn him round. In any case, I couldn't manage it even then and I'd risk damaging your cow.'

Françoise burst into tears.

'Oh, Monsieur Patoir, please save our cow. Poor old Coliche is so fond of me.'

And both Lise, pale in the face as a sudden spasm seized her, and Buteau, himself fit as a fiddle and normally so hard-hearted about other people's misfortunes, added their own lamentations and supplications:

'Please save our cow, she's been giving us such lovely milk for years and years. Do save her, Monsieur Patoir.'

'You realize that I'll have to cut the calf up?'

'Oh, damn the calf! Save our cow, Monsieur Patoir.'

So the surgeon, who had brought along a big blue apron, asked to borrow some canvas trousers and, having stripped off completely in a corner behind Rougette, he simply slipped on the trousers and tied the apron round his waist. When he reappeared in this scanty outfit, short and stout with his nice, friendly pugface, Coliche raised her head and stopped moaning, doubtless in surprise. But everyone was too tense to smile.

'Light some candles!'

He stuck four of them on the ground and lay down in the straw on his stomach, behind the cow which could no longer get up. For a second he lay flat on the ground with his head stuck between the animal's thighs. Then he decided to pull the feet out with the cord and examined them closely. He lifted himself onto one elbow and was taking a lancet out of a small oblong bag when a hoarse moan made him sit up in surprise.

'What's that? Oh, you're still there, old girl? I said to myself: that's not the cow.'

It was Lise with agonizing labour pains and pushing hard.

'For goodness' sake, go and do your job next door, will you, and let me do mine here? It's putting me off and getting on my nerves, damn it, hearing you pushing away behind me... Look, is there anyone with common sense around? Take her away, some of you!'

Frimat's wife took one arm and Bécu's the other and together they finally got Lise into her bedroom. She slumped down between them with no further strength to resist. But as they went through the kitchen, lit by one solitary candle, she insisted that they leave all the doors open: she would not be so far away like that. Frimat's wife had already made up the childbed in the usual country manner: a sheet thrown over a bundle of straw and three chairs turned on their sides in the middle of the room. Lise crouched down, spread out her legs and leant back against one chair, with her right leg against the second one and her left against the third. She had not even undressed; she was bracing her feet in her floppy old slippers and her blue stockings came up to her knees, her skirt, pulled high over her chest, exposed her enormous belly and her very white, fat thighs, so spreadeagled that you could see right up inside her.

Buteau and Françoise had stayed in the cowshed, squatting down on their haunches, each holding a candle close for Patoir, who had lain down again and was cutting through the calf's left hock with his lancet. He detached the skin, tugged at the shoulder and loosened it until it came right away. But Françoise went pale and nearly fainted; dropping her candle, she ran off crying:

'Poor old Coliche... I can't look at it!'

Patoir lost his temper, especially as he had to stand up and put out an incipient blaze caused by the falling candle.

'Silly little girl! You'd take her for a princess to be squeamish like that!... She'll make roast pork of us!'

Françoise ran away and flung herself down in a chair in the room where Lise was in labour; her extraordinary spreadeagled posture made no impression on her, as though she found it quite natural after what she had just seen. Brushing away the sight of all that living flesh being sliced up, in a faltering voice she described what they were doing to the cow.

'That won't do, I must go back,' Lise said at once, and despite her pains she half raised herself among the chairs.

But the two older women angrily held her down.

'Now, will you stay still! What on earth's taken possession of you?' And Frimat's wife added:

'Look! Now you've burst your sac, too!'

And the waters had indeed spurted out suddenly and been immediately soaked up by the straw under the sheet; and the final effort to expel the baby began. Her bare belly continued pushing instinctively, expanding like a balloon about to burst while her legs in their blue stockings bent up and straightened out convulsively like a frog diving.

'I tell you what,' Bécu's wife went on. 'To keep you quiet I'll go over myself and let you know what's happening.'

After that, she kept running to and fro from the room to the cowshed; but in the end, to save herself the journey, she stood in the middle of the kitchen and shouted. The veterinary surgeon was continuing his operation in the litter soaked in blood and slimy mucus, a foul and laborious job which left him in a revolting state, filthy from top to toe.

'It's going all right,' Bécu's wife was shouting. 'Keep on pushing, no worry... We've got the other shoulder. And now they're tugging off the head. He's got the head, goodness me what a head. And it's all over now, the body came out in one go.'

Lise was greeting each stage of the operation with a heart-rending sigh and it was difficult to say whether it was for herself or the calf. But suddenly Buteau brought in the head to show her. Everyone exclaimed out loud :

'Oh, what a lovely calf !'

Without stopping in her labour and still pushing harder than ever, with her muscles all tense and her thighs swollen, she seemed inconsolably sad.

'Oh, goodness, what bad luck ! Oh goodness, what a lovely calf ! What bad luck, such a lovely calf, so lovely a calf, we've never seen a lovelier one !'

Françoise was wailing, too, and all their expressions of grief seemed so aggressive and full of veiled criticism that Patoir took offence. He came rushing into the room, but had the decency to stop at the doorway.

'I say, you there, don't say I didn't warn you. You begged me on bended knees to save your cow... I know you, you crafty lot. You're not to go about saying that I was responsible for killing your calf, d'you understand ?'

'Of course, of course,' Buteau mumbled, going back with him into the cowshed. 'All the same, it was you who cut it out.'

As Lise sat between her three chairs on the ground, ripples were running under her skin, starting from her waist, and ending at the top of her thighs, as her flesh kept stretching more and more. And Françoise, who had hitherto been too disconsolate to look, was suddenly flabbergasted as she stood in front of her sister and saw her nakedness, foreshortened so that all she could see were her knees drawn up at an angle on each side of her balloon of a belly, with a round cavity in between. It was so unexpected and distorted and enormous that she was not even embarrassed. She could never have imagined anything like it, this gaping hole like a barrel with the top knocked in or a wide-open skylight in a hayloft for tossing the hay through, with a curly black rim of bushy ivy round it; and then she noticed another, smaller ball, the baby's head moving in and out with every push, like a jack-in-the-box, and she was seized with such a violent urge to laugh that she had to cough in order not to appear callous.

'Not much longer,' promised Frimat's wife, 'keep going, it's nearly there.'

She was kneeling down between Lise's legs, watching the baby and ready to catch it. But it was being awkward, as Buteau would say; it even disappeared altogether for a moment and you might have thought it had gone back in. Only then was Françoise able to tear her eyes away from this fascinating sight, like an oven door staring her in the face; and she at once became embarrassed, so she walked round to take hold of her sister's hand, feeling sorry for Lise now that she had looked away.

'Oh, poor Lise, it's hard going.'

'Oh yes, it is, and nobody's got any sympathy for me. . . If only someone was sorry for me. . . Oh dear, it's beginning again, won't he ever come out!'

This could have gone on for some time, but suddenly there were cries of astonishment from the cowshed. It was Patoir who, surprised that Coliche was still twisting and lowing, suspected that there might be a second calf; and in fact when he thrust his hand in again he brought another one out, this time without any trouble, like taking a handkerchief out of his pocket. Always one for a joke, he was so amused that he lost all sense of propriety and rushed into the bedroom carrying the calf, followed by Buteau, who was also laughing.

'Well, old girl, you wanted one and here it is.'

And it was laughable to see him stark-naked under his apron, his arms, face and entire body spattered with dung and the calf still dripping wet, looking drunk with its heavy head and surprised expression.

Amidst the delighted cries of everyone, as soon as Lise saw him she was seized by an interminable and uncontrollable fit of hysterical laughter.

'Oh God, he's funny! Oh, it's silly of you to make me laugh like this! Oh dear, how it's hurting me, I'm splitting. No, please don't make me laugh any more, I just can't stand it, it'll finish me.'

Her laughter was rumbling away in her fat bosom and down into her stomach where it echoed like a gale of wind. She was all distended and the child's head had started pumping to and fro again, like a cannon-ball about to be fired.

But the climax came when, putting the calf down at his feet, Patoir tried to wipe the perspiration from his forehead with the back of his hand. He left behind a large trail of cowdung, like a scar, and everyone split their sides with laughter while Lise choked and uttered shrill cackles like a hen laying an egg.

'That's enough, you funny man, you'll be the death of me! Stop it, damn you, I can't take any more... Oh, heavens, it's bursting...'

The vast hole gaped even wider, so that you could have imagined that Frimat's wife, still kneeling there, was going to fall into it, and all at once, like a human cannon-ball, the baby shot out, all red, with its extremities pale and dripping wet. All they heard was the glug-glug of a vast bottle being emptied, then the newborn child started bawling while its mother went on laughing even more, shaking like a deflating goatskin bottle. So there were cries at one end and laughter at the other. And Buteau was slapping his thighs and Bécu's wife holding her sides, Patoir burst into loud guffaws and even Françoise, whose hand had been crushed by Lise during the final push, finally gave way to her feelings too, still seeing in her mind's eye her sister's hole, like a cathedral big enough to house the whole of her husband.

'It's a girl!' said Frimat's wife.

'No, it can't be,' said Lise. 'I don't want her, I want a boy.'

'All right, I'll send her back and you can start on a boy tomorrow.'

This time they were almost sick with laughter. Then, as the

calf was still lying on the floor in front of her, Lise, slowly re-
gaining her composure, said sadly :

'The other calf was such a lovely one... We really should
have had two of them.'

Patoir went off after giving Coliche three litres of sweetened
wine. Frimat's wife undressed Lise and put her to bed in the
bedroom while, helped by Françoise, Bécu's wife removed the
straw and swept up. In ten minutes everything was tidy again
and you would never have imagined that a birth had just taken
place had it not been for the constant wailing of the baby girl
who was being washed in warm water. But once she had been
wrapped up and put into her cradle, she slowly quietened down;
and her mother, now completely exhausted, slept like a log, her
red face looking almost black against the rough unbleached linen
sheets.

At about eleven o'clock, after the two neighbours had left,
Françoise told Buteau that he had better go and rest in the
loft... She had spread a mattress on the ground for the night
since she intended to sleep near her sister. He made no reply and
finished off his pipe in silence. A great calm had settled over the
house and the only sound was Lise's heavy breathing as she slept.
Then, as Françoise was kneeling down on her mattress in the
shadow at the foot of the bed itself, Buteau, still not saying a
word, suddenly came up behind her and tipped her over. She
turned round and his tense flushed face immediately told her
what was happening. He was at it again, he hadn't given up the
idea of having her, and his desire must have been very strong
for him suddenly to want her like that, beside his wife, after
such unappetizing sights. She pushed him away and he fell over
backwards. Panting, the two struggled in silence.

'What's up with you?' he said with a grin, lowering his
voice. 'I can cope with the two of you.'

He knew her well and was sure she would never cry out. And
in fact she was resisting without uttering a word, too proud to
involve her sister and not wanting anyone to meddle in her
business, not even Lise. He was crushing her and on the point
of overpowering her.

'It'd be so nice. As we're living in the same house, we'd always
be together.'

But then he had to restrain a cry of pain. Silently, she had sunk her nails into his neck. Now he became really angry and mentioned Jean's name.

'If you think you're going to marry that blackguard of yours. . . Never, not until you come of age.'

This time, as he was coarsely groping with his hand right up her skirt, she gave him such a kick between his legs that he yelled in pain. He sprang to his feet, casting a scared look towards the bed. His wife was still asleep and breathing gently. Nonetheless, he went away, with a menacing wave of his fist.

When Françoise had stretched out on the mattress, she lay with her eyes open, in the great stillness which had descended on the room. Never would she let him do it, she wouldn't do it even if she wanted to. And she felt surprised, because the idea that she might marry Jean had not till now entered her head.

Chapter 6

For the last two days Jean had been working in the fields Hourdequin owned close to Rognes, where the farmer had set up a steam threshing machine, hired from a mechanic from Châteaudun who took it round the villages between Bonneval and Cloyes. The young man fetched the sheaves from the near-by stacks with his cart and two horses and then carried the grain away to the farm; while the machine puffed and blew from morning till night, sending up a golden cloud of dust in the sunlight and filling the surrounding countryside with its incessant loud rumble.

Sick at heart, Jean was racking his brains to see how he could have Françoise again. A month had already gone by since he had held her in his arms, at the very spot where he was threshing the wheat, and now she was scared and avoiding him. He despaired of ever having her again and his lust was growing into an obsession. As he drove his horses, he would ask himself why he shouldn't just go to the Buteaus and ask for her hand in marriage. As yet there had been no open or definitive quarrel between them. He always called out a greeting to them when he went by. And once the idea had entered his head that marriage was the only way of possessing her again, he soon persuaded himself that it was his duty and it would be wrong of him not to marry her.

All the same, when Jean went back to his machine the following morning, he felt apprehensive. He would never have dared make the approach had he not seen Buteau and Françoise going off to work in the fields together. He thought that as Lise had always been friendly disposed towards him, he would be less scared of her, so he handed his horses over to a friend and slipped away.

'Hallo, Jean, so it's you,' Lise cried cheerfully, now thoroughly recovered from the birth of her daughter. 'We haven't seen you for ages. What's up?'

He apologized and then, with the abruptness often found in

shy people, he explained the purpose of his visit. At first she might have imagined that it was herself he was making advances to, because he reminded her that he had been in love with her and would have been happy to marry her. Then he added quickly:

'And that's why I'd be happy to marry Françoise, if anyone asked me to.'

She looked at him in such surprise that he faltered:

'Oh, I know that's not the way to do it... I just wanted to tell you.'

'Well, I never!' she said in the end... 'I'm surprised because I didn't really expect it, seeing the difference in age... But first of all we must find out what Françoise thinks about it all.'

He had gone along with the intention of admitting everything, so that he would be forced to marry Françoise. But at the last moment, he had qualms. If Françoise hadn't confessed to her sister and nobody knew about it, had he the right to mention it first? He felt discouraged and ashamed at being thirty-three years old.

'Of course,' he mumbled, 'we'd talk to her about it, nobody would force her.'

Meanwhile, now that her surprise was over, Lise was looking at him in her cheerful way and it was plain that the prospect was quite to her liking. She was even inviting.

'It'll be up to her, Jean. I don't agree with Buteau that she's too young. She's rising eighteen and sturdy enough to take on two men rather than one... And then it's all very well being fond of each other as sisters, you know, but now that she's a young woman I'd sooner have a servant who I could give orders to. If she says yes, then you marry her. You're a good sort and there's many a good tune played on an old fiddle.'

It was a cry from the heart, revealing the slow breach which was inexorably opening between her and her younger sister, a hostility that sprang from the aggravations of daily life, a dull hatred and jealousy which had been simmering inside her ever since there was a male in the house, with all his demands and appetites.

In delight Jean gave her a big kiss on both cheeks when she added:

'And we're baptizing our little girl today and the family are

266

coming to dinner this evening... Come along and you can ask old Fouan, who's her guardian, if Françoise will have you.'

'All right,' he cried, 'see you this evening !'

And he strode back to his horses and drove them hard all day to the music of his whip, which cracked like the guns they let off on the morning of a village holiday.

The Buteaus were indeed finally having their daughter baptized, after many delays. First of all, Lise had insisted on being quite recovered, so that she could fully enjoy the party. Then, being ambitious, she was determined to have the Charles as godparents; and when they condescendingly agreed, it had been necessary to wait while Madame Charles lent her daughter a hand in the business: it was September and fair-time and the house in the Rue aux Juifs was working overtime. And as Lise had explained to Jean, it was going to be a purely family gathering: Fouan, La Grande and the Delhommes, in addition to the two godparents.

But at the last minute, great difficulties had arisen with Father Godard, who was conducting a running feud with Rognes. He had tried to bear his soul in patience and accept the four miles he had to walk every time he held Mass, and the galling demands of a village which was basically irreligious, as long as there was hope that the town council would eventually offer itself the luxury of becoming a parish. But his patience was exhausted and he could no longer deceive himself. Every year the council rejected the proposal to repair the presbytery and the mayor, Hourdequin, claimed that the budget was already too high. The only person who showed any consideration for the priesthood was the deputy mayor, Macqueron, who had secret ambitions of his own. And so since there was no longer any point in humouring the village, the priest was treating it without compunction, paring the services to the bone, with no extra prayers thrown in or indulgences such as candles or incense. As a result, he was perpetually squabbling with the women of the village. In June especially there had almost been a pitched battle over the question of first communion. There were five children, two girls and three boys, in the catechism classes which he held every Sunday after Mass; and since it would have meant coming back to confess them, he had insisted on their going to him at Bazoches-le-Doyen. This caused a first uproar amongst the women; thanks very much! Two miles there and two miles back! And who knows what would happen when boys and girls were left by themselves, going about together like that? And then the storm broke – a storm of terrifying dimensions – when he bluntly refused to perform the ceremony in Rognes, High Mass and the rest. He was going to perform it in his own parish, the five children were free to come along if they so wished. For a fortnight, the women at the fountain were almost speechless with wrath: so he would baptize them, marry them and bury them in the village but he wasn't prepared to give them communion there! He stuck to his guns, said just a low Mass, despatched the five communicants at the double and refused to offer a single flower or an extra oremus in consolation; and he even sent them packing when, aggrieved at such a travesty of this solemn ceremony, they begged him with tears in their eyes to sing Vespers. Nothing at all! He was giving them what he was in duty bound to give, they could have had High Mass, Vespers and anything else they wanted at Bazoches if they hadn't been so unruly and in rebellion against the Lord. Ever since this incident, there was imminent danger of a complete break between Father Godard and Rognes and the slightest clash could bring disaster.

When Lise went to see the priest to arrange for her daughter's baptism, he suggested one Sunday after Mass but she asked if he would come back at two o'clock on Tuesday because the godmother wouldn't be back from Chartres until that morning. He finally agreed, warning them to be on time, because, he added firmly, he wasn't prepared to wait for them one second, not one second.

On Tuesday, Father Godard arrived at the church punctually at two o'clock, out of breath from his walk and wet from a sudden shower. There was nobody in sight except Hilarion, who was at the entrance of the nave, clearing out a corner of the baptistery littered with old paving-stones which had always been there. Ever since his sister's death, the cripple had been living on public funds and the priest, who used to slip him a franc now and again, had had the idea of keeping him occupied by cleaning out this corner, something he had thought of having done many a time but had never got round to doing. He stood watching for a few minutes and then gave an angry start.

'Good gracious, what do they take me for? It's ten past two already.'

As he was looking across the square at the Buteaus' house, silent and dead, he caught sight of the gamekeeper standing waiting in the porch, smoking his pipe.

'Go on, ring the bell, Bécu,' he cried. 'That'll fetch them along, the slowcoaches.'

Bécu started tugging away, very drunk as always. The priest went to put on his surplice. He had already written up the register the previous Sunday and was intending to hurry through the service by himself, without the assistance of the choirboys, who drove him frantic. When everything was ready, he again lost patience. A further ten minutes went by and the bell continued to toll persistently and infuriatingly in the utter stillness of the deserted village.

'What on earth are they up to? We'll have to drag them along by their ears.'

At last he saw La Grande come out of the Buteaus', walking with her usual gait of an evil old queen, as straight and dry as an old stick, despite her eighty-five years. The family was in a state of great perturbation, for all the guests had arrived except the godmother, whom they had been vainly expecting ever since the morning, and an embarrassed Monsieur Charles kept saying that it was most surprising, because he had received a letter only the evening before; perhaps Madame Charles had been held up at Cloyes; she would surely be along any minute now. Uneasy because she knew that the priest disliked being kept waiting, Lise had finally thought of sending La Grande along to ask him to be patient a little longer.

'Well?' he asked when she was still some distance away. 'Is it going to be for today or tomorrow? I suppose you imagine that God can wait for you?'

'They're on their way, Father, they're on their way,' retorted the old woman, as cool as a cucumber.

At that very moment, Hilarion, who was carrying the last few pieces of paving out, passed by clasping an enormous stone against his midriff. He was rolling on his crooked legs but he was built like a bridge and strong as an ox and showed no sign of dropping it. Dribbles were running from his hare-lip but there was not a drop of sweat on his leathery skin.

Outraged at La Grande's unconcern, Father Godard tackled her:

'Tell me, La Grande, since I've got you on your own, do you think it's kind of you, seeing you're so rich, to let your only grandson turn into a beggar?'

She replied roughly:

'His mother disobeyed me. Her son means nothing to me.'

'Well, I've warned you before and I warn you again, you'll go to hell if you don't show charity. He'd have starved the other day if I hadn't given him something and today I've had to think up something for him to do.'

On hearing the word hell, La Grande gave a thin smile. As she used to say, she knew all too well that, for the poor, hell was here below. But, rather than the priest's threats, it was the sight of Hilarion carrying the flagstones that had given her an idea. She was surprised, she would never have imagined that he could be so strong, with his bow legs:

'If he wants work,' she said at last, 'I might perhaps be able to find him some after all.'

'He belongs in your house, La Grande, take him in.'

'We'll see, send him round tomorrow.'

Hilarion had understood what was being said and started trembling so violently that he nearly crushed his feet by dropping his last piece of paving-stone outside. And as he went away he gave his grandmother a furtive look, like a scared, beaten, defeated animal.

Another half an hour passed. Bécu had grown tired of tolling the bell and had gone back to his pipe. And La Grande stood there silent and unmoved as though her mere presence was an adequate token of the respect due to the priest. Meanwhile the latter, with rising exasperation, kept going to the door of the church to glare in the direction of the Buteaus' house on the other side of the empty square.

'Go on, ring the bell, Bécu!' he shouted suddenly. 'If they're not here within three minutes, I'm off.'

Then, as the bell began furiously tolling again, sending the venerable rooks cawing into the air, the Buteaus and their guests could be seen filing out of the house one by one and crossing the square. Lise was at her wits' end. As there was still no trace of the godmother, they had decided to make their way slowly towards the church, hoping to give her a chance of catching up with them. The distance was not much more than a hundred yards and Father Godard pitched into them straight away.

'Please tell me if you're doing this for fun, will you? I've done it to oblige you and now you've kept me waiting an hour! Let's get on with it.'

And he pushed all of them towards the baptistery, the mother carrying the baby, her father, the grandfather Fouan, Uncle Delhomme, Aunt Fanny and even Monsieur Charles, looking every inch the godfather in his black morning coat.

'Please, Father Godard,' asked Buteau with an exaggerated humility hiding more than a little derision, 'could we possibly prevail on your kindness to wait just a little while longer?'

'What do you mean, wait longer?'

'For the godmother, Father.'

Father Godard looked as if he might have a fit. Red as a turkeycock, he choked:

'Get another one!'

They all looked at each other; Delhomme and Fanny shook their heads and Fouan said firmly:

'We can't do that, it would be a silly thing to do.'

'You must accept our apologies, Father,' said Monsieur Charles, feeling that his superior status and upbringing compelled him to offer an explanation. 'In a way it's our fault but not our fault. My wife has written to say definitely that she will be back this morning. She's in Chartres.'

Father Godard caught his breath, beside himself with rage and this time he could restrain himself no longer.

'In Chartres, in Chartres... I'm sorry that you're involved in this, Monsieur Charles. But this can't go on, I absolutely refuse to put up with it any longer.'

He exploded:

'You can't think up enough insults to offer the good Lord, in the person of his servant, can you? Every time I come to Rognes, I'm given another slap in the face. Well, I'm going and I shan't

271

come back. You can tell your mayor you can find your own priest and pay him if you want one. I'll speak to my bishop about it, I'll tell him what you're like, I know he'll understand. Oh yes, we'll see who'll be punished. You can live without a priest, like the beasts in the fields.'

They were all listening to him with the curiosity and, if the truth were known, the utter indifference of practical people who had lost their fear of his God of wrath and chastisement. Why be frightened and deferential and seek pardon when the idea of the devil now merely made them laugh and they no longer believed in an avenging Lord who sent the wind and the hail and the thunder? It was just a waste of time; it was much more sensible to keep your respect for the forces of law and order: they were stronger.

Father Godard could see that Buteau was jeering, that La Grande was full of disdain and even Delhomme and Fouan were quite unimpressed beneath their pretence of solemn deference; and seeing his flock slipping from his grasp was the last straw.

'I know quite well that your cows are more religious than you. Goodbye! And you can dip your child in the duckpond to baptize him, you heathen savages.'

He rushed away to the vestry, flung off his surplice, rushed back through the church and was gone like the wind, leaving the christening party standing staring, open-mouthed and speechless.

But worst of all, at that moment, just as Father Godard was hurrying down Macqueron's new street, they saw coming along the road a carriage containing Madame Charles and Élodie. The former explained that she had stopped off at Châteaudun to see her little darling and she had promised to take her away for a couple of days' holiday. She was very sorry at arriving so late, she hadn't even driven over to Roseblanche to drop her luggage.

'We must run after Father Godard,' said Lise. 'It's only dogs who aren't baptized.'

Buteau set off at a run and they heard him bounding down Macqueron's street like the priest. But the latter had a good start and had crossed the bridge and was at the top of the slope before he caught sight of Buteau coming round a bend in the road.

'Father Godard! Father Godard!'

He finally turned round and waited for him to come up.

'Well?'

'The godmother's arrived. You can't refuse to baptize some-one!'

For a brief moment he stood stock-still. Then, at the same furious pace, he set off down the hill after Buteau and it was like this that they went back into the church without exchanging a word. He gabbled through the service, rushed the godparents through their credo, anointed the baby, put on the salt, poured over the water, still fuming. In next to no time, they were signing the register.

'Oh, Father,' said Madame Charles, 'I brought you a box of sweets but it's in my trunk.'

He thanked her with a gesture and went off, not before saying again, as he looked at all of them:

'And this time it's really goodbye!'

Quite breathless from the speed of the ceremony, the Buteaus and their guests watched him disappear round the corner of the square, his black cassock swirling in the air. The whole village was out in the fields; there were just three little boys hoping for some sugared almonds. The only sound breaking the silence was the distant, unceasing rumble of the threshing machine.

As soon as they had gone back to Buteau's house, where the carriage had been left with the trunk, everyone agreed that they would have a drink and then come back in the evening for dinner. It was only four o'clock, what could they have found to do together until seven? So when the glasses and the two bottles of wine had been put on the kitchen table, Madame Charles insisted on having her trunk fetched down, so that she could give her presents. From it she produced, rather too late, the baby's dress and bonnet and then six boxes of sweets, which she gave to the baby's mother.

'Are they from Mummy's shop?' enquired Élodie, who was standing watching them.

Only momentarily embarrassed, Madame Charles replied calmly:

'No, my pet, your mother doesn't sell that sort.'

Then, turning to Lise:

'You know, I also thought of some linen for you. There's

nothing more useful than old linen... I asked my daughter and I've ransacked all her cupboards.'

On hearing the word linen, the whole family gathered round, Françoise, La Grande, the Delhommes and even Fouan. Standing in a circle round the trunk, they watched the old lady unpack a whole bundle of linen, fresh from the wash but still smelling strongly of musk. First of all there were some fine linen sheets, in tatters, and then some torn women's shifts, from which the lace had plainly been ripped.

Madame Charles unfolded them and shook them out as she explained:

'Well, the sheets aren't new, you know. They must have been used for five years or more and in the long run they get worn where the body rubs. As you can see, they've got a big hole in the middle; but the edges are still good, you can cut lots of things out of them.'

They all peered at them and ran their fingers over them, nodding approvingly, particularly the women, La Grande and Fanny, whose tight lips betrayed their secret envy. As for Buteau, he laughed to himself, titillated by lewd thoughts which he re-frained from uttering for the sake of propriety; whereas Fouan and Delhomme looked very solemn, showing due respect for fine linen, the other true sort of wealth after land.

'As for the shifts,' Madame Charles continued, proceeding to unfold them, 'just look at them, they're not a bit worn... Well, they're a bit torn, of course, they get really rough treatment and as you can't always stitch them together again because it eventually makes them bulky and look rather poverty-stricken, so we prefer to throw them away as old linen. But you can find some use for them, Lise.'

'I'll wear them,' the farmer's wife exclaimed. 'I don't mind if my shift's been mended.'

'And as for me,' said Buteau, winking mischievously, 'I wouldn't mind if you made me some handkerchieves out of them.'

This time they laughed openly, and then Élodie, who had not missed a single sheet or shift, exclaimed:

'Oh, what a funny smell! Isn't it strong! Is that all Mummy's linen?'

Without a moment's hesitation, Madame Charles replied:

'Of course it is, darling. That's to say, it belonged to the girls in the shop. You need a lot when you're in business.'

As soon as Lise, helped by Françoise, had tumbled it all into her wardrobe, they at last had their drink, toasting the baby who had been christened Laure, after her godmother. Then they relaxed and chatted for a while and, sitting on the trunk, Monsieur Charles could be overheard questioning his wife, too impatient to wait until he was alone with her, in his anxiety to hear how things were going down in Chartres. He was still very much interested and his thoughts constantly dwelt on this house which he had expended so much energy on setting up and which he now greatly missed. The news was not good. Of course, their daughter Estelle was a woman of character and brains; but their son-in-law Vaucogne, that flabby loafer Achille, was definitely failing to back her up. He spent all day and every day smoking his pipes and letting everything get broken-down and dirty: the bedroom curtains were full of stains, the mirror in the little red drawing-room was cracked, the washstand jugs and basins were all chipped and he didn't do a hand's turn; and a man's hand was so necessary if the furniture in a house was to be kept decent! At each fresh piece of damage his wife told him about, Monsieur Charles gave a sigh, his shoulders drooped and his face grew paler. One final complaint, whispered in a quieter voice, was the last straw:

'And do you know, he takes the girl in No. 5, a fat one, upstairs himself.'

'What did you say?'

'Oh yes, I'm sure of it, I saw them.'

Trembling with exasperation, Monsieur Charles clenched his fist in a sudden outburst of indignation.

'The scoundrel! Tiring out his staff and frittering away his profits! . . . Oh, that's the end!'

Madame Charles motioned to him to be quiet, for Élodie was coming back from the farmyard where she had been to look at the hens. They drank another bottle, the trunk was loaded back onto the carriage and the Charles walked back behind it. And everyone else left to see if all was well at home until it was time for dinner.

As soon as they had gone, Buteau, unhappy at having wasted

275

an afternoon, stripped off his jacket and started threshing in the corner of the farmyard that was paved, for he needed a bag of wheat. But he soon became bored with threshing alone; in order to warm to the job, he needed the rhythm of two flails beating in time. So he called to Françoise, who often helped him at threshing, for she had as strong a back and as powerful arms as any young man. Although this primitive method of threshing was slow and tiring, he had always refused to buy a horse-mill, saying like all the other smallholders that he preferred to thresh from one day to the next, according to his needs.

'Hi, Françoise, are you coming?'

Lise was keeping an eye on a veal stew with carrots and, having asked her sister to do the same with a saddle of pork on a spit, she was not keen to let her go. But Buteau was in a bad mood and talked of giving the pair of them a drubbing:

'Bloody women! I'll bash you over the head with your blasted saucepans! There's got to be one breadwinner in the house, otherwise you and that lot would eat us out of house and home.'

So Françoise, who had already changed into dirty old clothes for cooking, was obliged to join him. She picked up a long-handled flail with a dogwood swingle attached by leather straps. It was her own flail, rubbed smooth and bound with cord to prevent her hand slipping. She swung it two-handed over her head and thwacked the whole length of the swingle down onto the sheaf. And she kept doing it again and again, lifting it high in the air, swinging it back as though on a hinge and then bringing it down with the regular rhythm of a blacksmith, while on the other side Buteau was doing the same, alternating with her. They soon warmed up and started to beat faster; all you could see were these swinging pieces of wood which sprang up again each time and swung round the back of their heads like birds soaring with their legs tied together.

After ten minutes, Buteau gave a shout, the flails stopped and he turned the sheaf. Then the flailing began again. After a further ten minutes, he called another halt and opened up the sheaf. Six times it was pounded by the flails before all the ears had released their grain and he tied up the straw. The sheaves followed one after the other and for two hours the only sound in the house was the regular whack of the flails dominated by the never-ending rumble of the mechanical thresher.

Françoise's cheeks were flushed, her wrists swollen, her skin burning; her body, all aglow, set the air quivering all around her. She was breathing heavily through her open mouth. Wisps of straw had caught in the dishevelled curls of her hair. At each upward swing of the flail, her right knee tightened her skirt and her taut round breast and hip pressed against the material so that all the curves of her sturdy body were revealed as though she were naked. One of the buttons of her bodice had torn off. Beneath the tan of her neck, Buteau could see her white flesh swelling with each swing of her arms and strong, muscular shoulders. It seemed to make him more excited, like a lustful woman thrusting and wriggling; and as the flails kept going, the hail of grain danced under the thwack-thwack of the two panting threshers.

At a quarter to seven, as dusk was falling, Fouan and the Delhommes appeared.

'We can't stop yet,' Buteau shouted, without pausing. 'Keep it up, Françoise!'

She kept at it, threshing harder than ever, carried away by the noise and the effort. And that was how Jean came upon them when he in his turn arrived, having obtained permission to eat out. He felt a sudden pang of jealousy and looked at them almost as if he had caught them unawares, two helpmates joined together in this hot, tiring task, one bone and one flesh as they struck at the right time and place, both of them so dishevelled and glowing with sweat that they seemed to be begetting a child rather than threshing wheat. Perhaps Françoise, threshing away so eagerly, had the same feeling, because she suddenly stopped, all embarrassed. Thereupon Buteau, turning round, stood stock-still in surprise and anger.

'What are you doing here?'

But at that very moment Lise came down ahead of Fouan and the Delhommes. They all came up together and she said brightly:

'Oh yes, I forgot to tell you, I saw him this morning and invited him to come.'

Her husband's flushed face took on such a frightening look that she hastened to add:

'I've got an idea, Father, that he wants to ask you something.'
'What is it?' asked the old man.

Jean was blushing and stammering, vexed that the matter should be raised like this so abruptly and in front of everyone. In any case, Buteau broke in first, for the smiling look which Lise had given Françoise told him well enough what it was all about.

'Are you having us on? She's not for you, you dirty old man.'

Buteau's coarse remark gave Jean courage to speak up.

'It's this, old Fouan, it's quite simple... As you're Françoise's guardian, I have to ask you if I can have her, don't I? If she'd like me, then I'd like her. I'd like to marry her.'

Françoise was so astounded that she dropped her flail. Although she must have been expecting it, she would never have thought that Jean would dare to ask straight out, like that. Why hadn't he mentioned it to her first? She felt she was being rushed and she could not have said whether it was hope or fear that was making her tremble. So she stood between the two men, in her unbuttoned bodice, her blood coursing so hotly through her body that they could even feel the warmth themselves.

Buteau gave Fouan no time to reply. He went on with growing fury:

'You've got a cheek too. An old man of thirty-three marrying a girl of eighteen? Fifteen years' difference, that's all! How disgusting can you be! We'll find some tender little lasses for you, you leathery old bugger!'

Jean was beginning to become annoyed.

'What's it got to do with you, if I want her and she wants me?'

And he turned towards Françoise, to make her say something. But still tense and scared, she did not seem to understand. She could not say no, yet she did not say yes. Moreover, Buteau was looking daggers at her, daring her to say yes. If she were to marry, he would lose her and he would lose the land as well. The sudden realization of this consequence made his rage boil over.

'Look, Father, and you, Delhomme, don't you find it disgusting for this little girl to go to this old devil here who doesn't even belong here, a rolling stone who comes from God knows where? A rotten carpenter who became a farm labourer because he had something shady to hide, I'll be bound.'

He was giving vent to all his hatred of the worker from the town.

'So what? If I want her and she wants me,' Jean repeated, restraining himself and remembering that, out of consideration for her, he had promised himself that Françoise must be the first to tell what had happened between them. 'Say something, Françoise.'

'It's true,' cried Lise, anxious to marry off her sister and be rid of her. 'What right have you to talk, if they like each other? She doesn't need your consent, if she wasn't so nice she'd send you packing... Why can't you shut up?'

Then Buteau saw that what he feared would happen if the girl were to talk. Particularly, he was afraid that if the relationship became known, their marriage would appear the sensible thing to do. At that very moment La Grande came into the yard, followed by the Charles, who were coming back with Élodie. He motioned to them to come over, not knowing what he would say. Then, puffing out his cheeks, he thought of something and, shaking his fist threateningly at his wife and sister-in-law, he screamed:

'You fucking cows! Yes, cows and bitches the pair of them! Shall I tell you? I sleep with both of them! And suppose that's why they both bugger me about? I'm telling you, with the pair of them, the dirty trollops!'

The words hit the Charles full in the face as they stood gaping. Madame Charles hurriedly interposed her body in front of Élodie, who was listening, and pushing her towards the garden she too shouted in a very loud voice:

'Come and see the lettuces and cabbages. Oh, aren't they lovely!'

Buteau ranted on, inventing details, describing how as soon as one of them had had her oats, it was time for the other one to come and get stuffed; and he poured it all out, in the coarsest terms, a flood of sewage, words so obscene that they are never spoken. Merely surprised at this sudden outburst, Lise simply shrugged her shoulders, repeating:

'He's mad. Stark staring mad.'

'Tell him he's lying,' Jean exclaimed to Françoise.

'Of course he's lying,' said Françoise calmly.

279

'Oh, so I'm lying,' Buteau said. 'So it's not true that during the harvest you were crying out for it? But now it's my turn to make you dance, you couple of sluts!'

Jean was paralysed and bewildered by such insane audacity. How could he now explain that he had had Françoise? It seemed a nasty thing to do, especially as she was giving him no help. Moreover the others, the Delhommes, Fouan and La Grande, were holding back. They hadn't seemed surprised, they were obviously thinking that if the young rip was in fact going to bed with the pair of them, it was up to him to do what he liked with them. When you've got certain rights, you have to exercise them.

Seeing this and feeling secure in his position of undisputed possession, Buteau smelt victory. He turned to Jean:

'And you, young fellow-me-lad, just keep your nose out of my affairs in future... And to start with, fuck off! ... So you won't? You just wait!'

He picked up his flail and whirled the swingle round his head. Jean only just had time to catch hold of the other one, Françoise's, to defend himself. The others shouted and tried to separate them: but the two men looked so terrifying that they drew back. The long handles had a reach of several yards and their blows cleared the yard. They stood alone in the middle, at some distance from each other, making wide sweeps with their swingles. Their teeth were clenched; not a word was spoken. The only sound was the sharp crack of wood on wood as they parried the blows.

Buteau had struck first and as Jean was still bending down he would have had his head split open had he not jerked himself backwards. At once, tensing his muscles, he quickly lifted his flail and brought it down like a thresher smashing the grain from the ear. But the other man had already struck again and the two dogwood swingles bounced back on their leather straps like a wild flight of wounded birds. Three times they clashed. All that could be seen was the threatening staves, swirling and whistling through the air at the end of their handles, in readiness to flash down and split open a skull.

However, Delhomme and Fouan were just rushing to intervene when the women gave a shriek. Jean had rolled over into the straw, caught off his guard by a sweeping blow along the ground, which had hit him on the legs, fortunately not with full force.

He sprang to his feet flourishing his flail and with his rage compounded by pain, swept his swingle in a wide arc so that it came down to the right whereas Buteau was expecting it from the left. An inch to one side and Buteau would have been brained; but the blow brushed diagonally past his ear and landed full on his arm; the bone snapped in two with a sound of breaking glass.

'You murderer!' screamed Buteau. 'He's killed me!'

With wild, bloodshot eyes Jean let go of his weapon. Then for a moment he looked at them all, as though bewildered by all that had just happened so rapidly; and then he went off, limping, with a furious, despairing gesture.

When he went round the corner of the house, making for the plain, he caught sight of La Trouille, who had been watching the battle over the garden hedge. She was still chortling over it, for she had been lurking around since neither she nor her father had been invited to the christening party. Wouldn't Jesus Christ be amused by this nice little family party ending with his brother's arm being broken! She found it so funny that she was squirming about as though being tickled and ready to lie down on her back like a cat.

'Oh, Corporal, what a whack!' she exclaimed. 'The bone went crack! What a lark!'

He slowed down without making any reply, looking quite overcome. She followed him, whistling up her geese which she had brought along with her as a pretext for loitering and listening under walls. Without thinking, he was making his way back to the threshing machine which was still working in the failing light. He was thinking to himself that it was all over, he could never visit the Buteaus again nor would they let him have Françoise. How stupid it was! All in the space of ten minutes: a quarrel he had not sought and that unfortunate blow at the very moment when things were going well! And now, there would never be another chance! The rumble of the machine in the dusk went on and on like a mournful lament.

But at the corner of the crossroads an encounter took place: La Trouille's geese, on their way home, found themselves face to face with old Saucisse's geese making their own way down to the village. The two ganders in the lead suddenly stopped, resting their weight on one leg and stretching their yellow beaks towards each other; and the beaks of each flock all pointed in the same direction as their leaders', as they rested their bodies on the same leg. For a split second, they all stood stock-still, like two armed patrols on reconnaissance exchanging the password. Then, round-eyed and satisfied, one of the ganders went straight on while the other one swung left; and each flock followed its leader, pit-patting about their business in the same uniform waddle.

PART FOUR

Chapter 1

EVER since May, after shearing the sheep and selling the lambs, Soulas the shepherd had been taking out the whole of the La Borderie flock, nearly four hundred in all, which he looked after by himself with the help of the young pigherd Auguste and his two fearsome dogs, Emperor and Massacre. Until August his flock would be feeding on the fallow land, in the meadows of clover and lucerne or else on the uncultivated roadside verges; and barely three weeks ago, immediately after the harvest, he had finally penned them on the stubble, for the last few scorching, sunny days of September.

It was the hateful season when Beauce was stripped and desolate and its bare fields stretched out without a single tuft of green. The earth was cracked, completely parched by the summer heat and drought, and as all plant growth disappeared, all that was left was the dirty stain of dead weeds and the fields of hard, bristly stubble stretching away to the horizon in all directions, so that the mournful, desolate plain looked as though it had been devastated by some universal fire which had left a murky yellow gleam behind on the ground, a sinister shining yellow, like the lurid glow of a storm. Everything was yellow, but a yellow that was fearfully sad, with baked earth, shorn-off wheat stalks, cart tracks rutted and worn bare by the wheels. At the slightest gust of wind, vast clouds of dust flew up, covering the banks and hedges with powder. And the blue sky and blazing sun were but one more element of sadness gazing down on this scene of desolation.

And in fact there was a high wind that day, with sudden warm gusts of air which sent great clouds scudding across the sky, and when the sun broke through it was like glowing red-hot iron, burning the skin. Ever since morning Soulas had been waiting for water for himself and his flock; it was to be brought up from the farm, because the stubble where he was pasturing was to the north of Rognes, far from any pond. In the pen, formed by hurdles attached to stakes stuck into the ground, the sheep were lying panting on their bellies, while the two dogs, stretched out outside the pen, were panting too, with their tongues hanging out. To have a little shade, the shepherd had sat down against the little two-wheeled hut that he pushed about each time he changed the pen and which was his bedroom, wardrobe and larder. But by twelve o'clock, the sun was high in the sky and he stood up, looking into the distance to see if Auguste was coming back from the farm where he had sent him to find out why the water-cart had not come.

At last the little pigherd appeared, shouting :

'They're on their way, they hadn't got any horses this morning.'

'Well, stupid, didn't you bring a bottle of water back with you?'

'No, I didn't think of it. I did have a drink myself.'

Soulas gave him a cuff, which the boy ducked. He was swearing but decided to eat even without a drink, although his throat was as dry as a lime-kiln. Keeping a weather-eye open, Auguste, in response to Soulas's orders, went and fetched the week-old bread, old nuts and dry cheese out of the cart, and both of them started to eat, closely watched by the dogs who came and sat down in front of them, snapping up the odd crust which was so hard that it sounded like a dry bone when they cracked it between their jaws. Despite his seventy years, the shepherd's gums were as active as the pigherd's teeth. He was still straight-backed, tough and as knotty as a hawthorn stick, his face even more gnarled and worn, as though hewn from a tree, and with a tangled mop of faded earth-coloured hair. And the little pigherd got his clout after all, a cuff which sent him flat on his face in the cart just as he was unsuspectingly putting away the remains of the bread and cheese.

'Take that, you little devil, there's more where that came from.'

By two o'clock still nothing had appeared. It was hotter than ever, and quite unbearable during the occasional lulls when the wind dropped altogether. And then the wind would blow up tiny whirlwinds of dust, stifling and blinding, to exacerbate his agonizing thirst. The shepherd, waiting with stoical patience, without complaint, finally gave a grunt of satisfaction.

'They're not too soon, for God's sake!'

Two carts, scarcely the size of a fist, had just appeared on the horizon at the edge of the plain; in the first one, driven by Jean, Soulas had recognized the barrel of water, whilst the second one, driven by Tron, was loaded with bags of wheat that he was taking over to a mill whose tall timber structure could be seen some couple of furlongs away. This last cart stopped on the road and Tron accompanied the other man up over the stubble to the sheep-pen, on the pretext of lending a hand but in reality to relax and have a short chat.

'So you wanted us all to croak with thirst,' the shepherd called out.

And the sheep themselves, having smelt the water, made a disorderly rush towards the hurdles, plaintively bleating.

'Wait a sec!' Jean replied. 'There's enough for everyone!'

They set up the trough at once and filled it from a wooden runnel; and as it had a leak, the dogs were able to lick the water up as it dripped through; while unable to wait, the shepherd and the little pigherd drank out of the runnel itself. The whole flock trooped along and the only sound to be heard was the welcome bubbling of the water, and the glug-glug of thirsty throats, as man and beast happily splashed and soaked it up.

'Well, now,' said Soulas eventually, having recovered his good humour, 'if you were kind you'd give me a hand to shift the pen along a bit.'

Jean and Tron agreed. In the big areas of stubble the pen would not remain in the same place for more than two or three days, just time for the sheep to crop the weeds, before moving on; and this system had the additional advantage of manuring the land, section by section. While the shepherd and his dogs looked after the sheep, the two men and the little pigherd pulled up the stakes and moved the hurdles fifty yards further on and then fastened them again in a big square into which the sheep moved of their own accord, before it was completely closed in.

Despite his age, Soulas pushed his cart along to bring it closer to the pen. Then, referring to Jean, he said:

'What's up with him? You'd think he was going to his own funeral.'

And as the young man, who was sick at heart ever since he

thought he had lost Françoise, sadly shook his head, Soulas added:

'Eh? There must be a woman behind it! ... Ah, those bitches, they ought all to have their necks wrung.'

Tron was a handsome fellow, built like a colossus and with a cheerful ingenuous air. He gave a laugh:

'People say that when they're past it.'

'I'm past it, I'm past it, am I?' repeated the shepherd scornfully. 'Have I ever tried with you? And let me tell you, sonny, there's one woman you'd do better to keep away from, that'll end in trouble, never fear!'

This reference to his relationship with Jacqueline made the farm-hand blush to the roots of his hair. Soulas had caught them at it one morning behind some bags of oats at the end of the barn and, consumed with hatred for this former scullery-maid who now treated her former companions so shabbily, he had finally decided to open his master's eyes; but hardly had he started talking when his master gave him such a terrifying look that he had stopped short and decided not to say anything more until Jacqueline pushed him to the end of his tether by getting him dismissed. And so they lived like cat and dog, he afraid of being discarded like a useless old animal, she waiting until she was powerful enough to force Hourdequin to do it, for he was fond of his shepherd. In the whole of Beauce there was not one shepherd better at pasturing his sheep, without loss or damage, and cropping a field so close that not a blade of grass was left.

Yielding to the urge to talk which sometimes seizes people who live solitary lives, the old man went on:

'Ah, if my bitch of a wife hadn't drunk up all my pay every week before drinking herself to death, I'd've left the farm like a shot to get away from all that filth. That Cognet girl! She works harder with her bum than with her hands and her soft skin's got her further than her brains. When you think that the master lets her sleep in the same bed as our poor dead mistress and that she's wheedled him into eating alone with her, as if she really was his wife! I expect that she'll chuck us all out one day, as soon as she can, and him too, I reckon. A slut who's slept around with the scum of the earth.'

At every sentence, Tron was clenching his fists more tightly in one of his terrible repressed rages which were all the more terrifying because of his immense strength.

'That's enough!' he exclaimed. 'If you were still a man, I'd've shut you up long ago... She's got more decency in her little finger than you in your whole body.'

But Soulas merely grinned and shrugged his shoulders, and though he never laughed his face suddenly creaked into a cackle like a rusty old pulley.

'You silly booby, you're as stupid as she's clever! She could display her virginity in a show-case and you'd believe it. I'm telling you that every Tom, Dick and Harry has got across her. I get around, I've only got to keep my eyes open and don't need to look far to see the girls who get stuffed. But you'd never believe how often I've seen her getting stuffed, it's so often. Look, there was the old hunchback Matheas who's died since, he had her in the stables when she was just fourteen; and later on when she was kneading bread that young rapscallion of a pigherd Guillaume, he's in the army now, had her actually leaning against the trough, and all the farm-hands that have come and gone have had her in the straw, on sacks on the ground, in every corner you can think of. And there's no need to look so far. If you're interested, there's someone here that I noticed in the hayloft one morning, busy doing a few press-ups!'

He cackled again and the sidelong look he gave Jean greatly embarrassed the latter, who had been sitting with hunched shoulders in silence ever since the conversation had come round to Jacqueline.

'Don't let anybody try and lay a hand on her now,' growled Tron like an angry dog afraid of losing its bone. 'If he did, that'd be the last thing he'd ever do.'

Soulas scrutinized him for a second, surprised by this savage exhibition of jealousy. Then, relapsing into one of his long vacant silences, he said in his laconic way:

'That's your business, son.'

When Tron had gone back to the cart that he was driving to the mill, Jean stayed with the shepherd for a moment to help him drive in some of the stakes with his mallet; and seeing that he was so quiet and sad, the latter started talking again:

'At least it's not the Cognet girl who's upsetting you?'

The young man shook his head vigorously.

'So it's someone else? Who is it then, since I've never seen you together?'

Jean was looking at old Soulas and thinking that in such matters old people can often give sound advice. So he yielded to his desire to unburden himself and told him all about it, how he'd had Françoise and why, after his scuffle with Buteau, he was afraid of never seeing her again. He had even been scared for a while that Buteau might sue him because of his broken arm which, although already well on the mend, was preventing him from working. But no doubt Buteau had thought that it's never wise to let the law poke its nose into private affairs.

'So you stuffed Françoise did you?' the shepherd asked.

'Just once.'

He looked solemn, giving the matter thought, and then stated:

'You must go and tell Fouan. Perhaps he'll let you have her.'

Jean was surprised because it had not crossed his mind to take such a simple step. The pen was now set up and he left, deciding to go and see the old man that very evening. And as he went off behind his empty cart, Soulas took up his watch again, a thin, lean, vertical, grey bar standing out against the flat line of the plain. The little pigherd had sat down between the two dogs in the shade of the tiny hut on wheels. The wind had suddenly dropped and the storm had slid away towards the east. It was very warm and the sun was sparkling in the pure blue sky.

That evening Jean left work an hour early and went to see old Fouan at the Delhommes', before dinner. As he went down the slope, he saw them removing the leaves in their vineyard, to let the sun into the bunches of grapes; rain had fallen at the end of the last moon and as the grapes were not ripening properly it was important to take full advantage of this last autumn sunlight. As the old man was not there, the young man hurried on, hoping to be able to speak to him alone, which he preferred. The Delhommes' house was at the other end of Rognes, beyond the bridge, a little farmhouse which had had more barns and sheds built on recently, forming three irregular blocks enclosing a fairly large farmyard which was swept out every morning and where even the dungheaps were straight as a die.

'Good evening, old Fouan!' Jean called out from the road, in a rather uncertain voice.

The old man was sitting in the yard with a stick between his legs and his head hanging down. However, when Jean called again, he raised his head and recognized him.

'Oh, it's you, Corporal. So you were passing by?'

And he gave him such a friendly, unforced welcome, without any resentment, that the young man went in. But at first he did not dare mention or raise the matter; his courage was evaporating at the thought of telling him straight out about how he'd tumbled Françoise in the hay. They talked about the fine weather and how good it was for the vines. Another week of sun and the wine would be good. Then the young man tried a little flattery:

'You're really sitting pretty now. I don't know a single farmer better off than you.'

'Yes, of course.'

'What it is to have children like yours, you'd have to go a long way to find better ones!'

'Yes, of course... Only, you know, they've all got their own ideas.'

He looked gloomier than ever. Ever since he had been living with the Delhommes, Buteau was refusing to pay his pension, saying that he didn't want any money of his to go to his sister. Jesus Christ had never paid out a penny and now that Delhomme was offering him bed and board, he too had stopped paying his father-in-law anything. But it was not lack of money that Fouan was complaining of, particularly as he was receiving one hundred and fifty francs a year from Maître Baillehache, exactly twelve and a half francs a month, from the sale of his house. Out of this he could afford to buy himself a few luxuries, his ha'porth of tobacco every morning, a little drop at Lengaigne's and a cup of coffee at Macqueron's, because the thrifty Fanny only produced coffee or brandy from her cupboard for medicinal purposes. And yet in spite of everything, although he could afford his little pleasures in the village and lacked for nothing in his daughter's house, he did not feel at home there and spent all his time grieving.

'Yes, indeed,' Jean said, not realizing that he was touching a sore spot, 'when you're living in someone else's house, it's not like your own home.'

'That's right, that's exactly it,' grunted Fouan.

Then, rising to his feet as if seized by a spirit of revolt:

'We're going to have a drink. I presume I've got the right to offer a friend a drink.'

But as soon as they had reached the door, he became scared:

'Wipe your feet, Corporal, because, you see, they make a lot of fuss about being clean.'

Jean went in awkwardly, anxious to tell his story before the others returned. He was surprised at the tidiness of the kitchen: the copper pans were glistening, there was not a speck of dust on the furniture and the floor was worn down through much scrubbing. It was all spotlessly clean and cold, as if uninhabited. Over a fire damped down with ash, yesterday's cabbage soup was keeping warm.

'Here's how!' the old man said, having fetched an opened bottle and a couple of glasses out of the sideboard.

His hand was shaking a little as he drank, for he was frightened at what he had done. He put his glass down with a daredevil air and added suddenly:

'Suppose I told you that Fanny hasn't spoken to me for two days, because I spat? Spat, eh? Doesn't everyone spit? Of course I spit when I want to. No, I'd just as soon bugger off as be pestered like that.'

And serving himself another glass, he poured out his heart, so pleased to have found someone in whom to confide that Jean could not get a word in edgeways. They were only trivial little complaints; he was just an angry old man who was being expected to be faultless and was having to conform to other people's habits. But he would not have been more affected by bullying or downright bad treatment. For him, any remark repeated in too sharp a tone was the equivalent of a slap in the face; and his daughter, too, was excessively sensitive and suspicious, with the vanity of an honest farmer's wife who took offence and sulked at the slightest misunderstanding; so that relations between her and her father were becoming more strained every day. Whereas at the time the property was divided, she had certainly been the nicest of the children, now she was turning sour and really beginning to persecute him, always after him with a cloth or dustpan and brush, telling him off for everything he did and everything he failed to do. Nothing really serious, merely constant pinpricks which eventually reduced him to tears when he was sitting all alone in a corner.

'You must be patient,' Jean kept saying at each complaint. 'If you try hard enough, you can always get along.'

But Fouan, who had lit a candle, was growing excited and indignant.

'No, I've had enough ! Oh, if I'd only known what to expect here ! I'd've been better dead the day I sold my house. But they're mistaken if they think they've got me. I'd sooner break stones by the roadside.'

He choked and had to sit down, at last giving Jean the opportunity to tell his story.

'I say, old Fouan, I wanted to see you because of that business, you remember? I was very sorry, but I had to defend myself, didn't I, because he was attacking me. But the fact remains that we'd reached an understanding, and in view of everything, you're the only person who can arrange it. You could go to Buteau and explain it to him.'

The old man looked solemn. He was nodding his chin and looking embarrassed, wondering how to reply, when he was saved by the return of the Delhommes. They did not seem surprised at seeing Jean in their house and offered their usual friendly welcome. But at her first glance Fanny had seen the bottle and two glasses on the table. She removed them and said sharply, the first words she had addressed to him for forty-eight hours:

'Father, you know very well that I don't allow that.'

Fouan jumped up, trembling with fury at this remark made in front of others.

'What is it now? For Christ's sake, aren't I allowed to offer a friend a glass of wine? Go on, lock your wine away, I'll drink water !'

At this remark, it was her turn to be terribly offended at being accused of meanness. Her face went pale and she replied:

'You can drink the lot and drink yourself to death for all I care. But what I won't allow is you dirtying my table and your wet glasses making round marks on it, like a common drinking-shop !'

Her father's eyes filled with tears. He had the last word:

'A little less cleanliness and a little more kindness wouldn't go amiss, my daughter.'

And as she roughly wiped the table, he went over and stood at the window looking out into the dark night, shaking with silent despair.

Careful not to take sides, Delhomme had simply shown his approval of his wife's firm, sensible attitude by saying nothing.

'You've no idea the trouble old people cause you. They're full of fads and bad habits and they'd sooner die than change them. He's no longer got the strength to make himself really unpleasant. All the same, I'd sooner have four cows to look after than one old man.'

Jean and Delhomme nodded agreement. But she was interrupted by the sudden arrival of Nénesse, dressed like a young man-about-town in a jacket and fancy trousers, bought off the peg from Lambourdieu, and wearing a tiny stiff felt hat. He had a long neck, hair cut short at the back and, with his swagger, blue eyes and flabby face, he had the shady look of a tart. He had always had a horror of the land and he was off to Chartres next day to work in a restaurant with a dance band. His parents had long been opposing his refusal to follow in his father's footsteps but his mother had at last been prevailed upon to persuade his father. And ever since the morning Nénesse had been celebrating his imminent departure with the lads of the village.

For a split second he seemed rather put out at seeing a stranger. Then he took the bull by the horns:

'I say, Father, I'm going to invite them to dinner at Macqueron's. I'll need some money.'

Fanny glared at him and opened her mouth to refuse. But she was so vain that Jean's presence held her back. Of course they could find twenty francs for their son without trouble! And without a word she went off, with a disapproving look.

'Are you with friends, then?' his father asked him.

He had caught sight of a shadow in the doorway. He went over and, recognizing the young man who was standing outside, he said:

'Ah! It's you, Delphin, come on in, my boy.'

Delphin sidled in, with an apologetic air. 'Good evening all.'

He was in a blue smock and overalls and heavy ploughing shoes, tieless, and with his face already weather-beaten.

'Well, my lad,' said Delhomme, who thought highly of him, 'are you going to be off to Chartres one of these days, too?'

Delphin stared in surprise, then he said forcefully:

'Good God no! I'd die if I had to live in a town!'

As Delhomme glanced sideways at his son, the other boy, not wanting to let his friend down, went on:

'It's all right for Nénesse to go because he likes fine clothes and he can play the cornet!'

Delhomme gave a smile because he was inordinately proud of his son's skill on the cornet. And Fanny now came back with a handful of two-franc pieces and slowly counted out ten of them into Nénesse's palm. They were all white, having been hidden in a pile of wheat. She did not trust her cupboard and she used to secrete her money in small sums all over the house, in the corn, in the charcoal, in the sand; the money was sometimes one colour and sometimes another, white, black or yellow.

'That'll do,' said Nénesse, as a form of thanks. 'Coming, Delphin?'

And the two lively lads made themselves scarce and you could hear them laughing as they went off.

Jean emptied his glass, seeing that Fouan, who had kept his back to the room all the time, was leaving his post at the window to go into the yard. He took his leave and found the old man standing outside in the pitch-black darkness.

'Look, old Fouan, will you go and see Buteau to get Françoise for me? You're the boss, all you need to do is to speak up.'

In the gloom, the old man was repeating in a jerky voice:

'I can't, I can't.'

Then he exploded and confessed he'd had enough of the Delhommes, tomorrow he'd go and live with the Buteaus, who had offered to take him in. If his son beat him it would hurt him less than his daughter's constant pinpricks, which were killing him.

Exasperated at this new complication, Jean finally told the truth:

'I must tell you, old Fouan, Françoise and I went to bed together.'

The old man merely exclaimed:

'Ah !'

Then after a moment's thought:

'Is she pregnant?'

Although he was certain that she couldn't be, because he'd cheated, Jean replied:

'She might be.'

'In that case, you only need wait. If she's pregnant, we'll see.'

At that moment, Fanny appeared in the doorway to tell her father the soup was ready. But he turned round and yelled at her:

'You can shove your soup up your arse ! I'm going to bed !'

And he went up to bed, supperless, furious with pique.

Jean made his way slowly back to the farm, in such a torment of grief that he found himself up on the plateau without realizing how he had reached it. It was sultry and the dark blue sky was spangled with stars. In the still air you could once again sense a storm approaching and passing by far away to the east, where you could see sheet-lightning. And lifting his head he saw hundreds of glowing eyes looking at him on his left, like flaring candles, following the sound of his footsteps. It was the sheep in their pens beside which he was passing.

Soulas called out in his slow voice:

'Well, my boy?'

The dogs stretched out on the ground had not stirred, scenting that it was someone from the farm. Driven out of the hut by the heat, the little pigherd had gone to sleep in a furrow. And only the shepherd remained on his feet in the level plain wrapped in darkness.

'Well, my boy, what happened?'

Without even stopping, Jean replied:

'He said that if the girl's pregnant, we'll see.'

He was already past the pen when old Soulas's voice, sounding solemn in the vast silence, caught up with him:

'He's right, you'll have to wait.'

And so Jean continued on his way.

Plunged in leaden slumber, Beauce stretched out endlessly. The smell of burning in the air and the chirping of crickets spluttering like embers on their ash told of scorched stubble and stripped baked earth, of silent desolation. Only shadowy haystacks reared up against the bare and melancholy plain. Every twenty seconds, sudden purple streaks of lightning flashed sadly on the distant horizon.

Chapter 2

NEXT day, Fouan moved in with the Buteaus. His move caused
no upheaval: two bundles of old clothes which the old man insisted on carrying himself, in two trips. The Delhommes tried to
extract an explanation but in vain. He left without uttering a
word.

The Buteaus gave him the large downstairs room behind the
kitchen which till then had been used for storing potatoes and
beetroot for the cows. The worst thing was that the only light
came from a fanlight set high in the wall, which made the room
as dim as a cellar. And the earth floor, the heaps of vegetables
and the rubbish in the corners made the bare damp plaster walls
stream with yellow beads of moisture. Nor did they bother to
move anything but merely cleared a corner to put the iron bedstead, chair and plain wooden table. The old man seemed
delighted.

Buteau was triumphant. He had been wild with jealousy ever
since Fouan had been with the Delhommes, because he knew what
people were saying in Rognes: of course it was no hardship for
the Delhommes to board and lodge their father; but as for the
Buteaus, well, they just didn't have the wherewithal. So at the
beginning they kept urging him to eat, merely to fatten him up
and prove that there was no shortage of food in their house. And
then there was the hundred and fifty franc annuity from the sale
of his house which he would certainly pass on to the child who
had been looking after him. In addition, now that he was no
longer keeping him, Delhomme would no doubt start paying him
the annual two hundred franc pension again, which he in fact
did. Buteau was relying on those two hundred francs. He had
worked everything out and he had said to himself that he would
have the credit of being a good son without having to put his hand
in his pocket and with the expectation of further reward later on
– apart from the nest-egg that he still suspected his father of
possessing, although he had never succeeded in ascertaining
whether it in fact existed.

For Fouan, it was a real honeymoon. He was well treated and paraded before the neighbours: how about that? Wasn't he in fine fettle? Did he look as if he was fading away? The two children, Laure and Jules, were always scrambling round his feet and wrapped themselves round his heart, giving him something to do. But above all he was happy to be able to go back to his old man's fads and fancies and to feel freer in a household which was more easy-going. Although she was a good housewife, and clean, Lise was much less fussy and sensitive than Fanny and he could spit where he wanted, come and go as he pleased and eat at all hours, having the peasant habit of never passing by a loaf of bread without cutting himself a slice, according to the way his work was going. Three months went by like this; then December came and in the terrible frosts the water in the jug at the bottom of his bed froze; but he made no complaint, not even when with the thaw his room became soaking wet, with water streaming off the walls like a downpour of rain. He thought all this perfectly natural, having spent his whole life in similar hardship. As long as he had his baccy, his coffee, and no one to bother him, he used to say, he was the king of the world.

Things started to go wrong when, one bright sunny day, coming back to his room to pick up his pipe when he was thought to have gone out, Fouan found Buteau tumbling Françoise on top of the potatoes. The girl, who had been defending herself staunchly, without uttering a word, picked herself up and left the room after collecting the beetroot that she had come to fetch for her cows. The old man, face to face with his son, expressed his annoyance:

'You dirty pig, with that girl and your wife round the corner, too! And she didn't want to, I could see her struggling.'

But Buteau, still red in the face and panting, refused to accept the rebuke:

'What the hell are you interfering for? Look the other way and keep your trap shut or there'll be trouble!'

Ever since Lise's confinement and the fight with Jean, Buteau had once more been furiously pursuing Françoise. He had waited until his arm was properly set and now he would leap on her in every corner of the house, certain that if he could have her just once she would then be his as often as he wished. Wasn't that

297

the best way of putting off her marriage and keeping both the girl and the land as well? These two desires were even becoming fused into a wild refusal to give up anything he held, so that his passion to own the field was matched by his frustrated lust and exacerbated by the girl's resistance. His wife was becoming enormous, a great lump of a woman; and she was breast-feeding so that Laure was always sucking away at one nipple or the other, whereas this other girl, his little sister-in-law, smelt fresh and young and her breasts were as firm and supple as the udders of a heifer. In any case, he wouldn't sneeze at either of them: that would give him two, one soft one and one hard, each agreeable in her own way. He was a good enough cock for two hens and he saw himself as a pasha, pampered and petted and surfeited with pleasure. Why shouldn't he marry both the sisters if they agreed? That would be a proper way to cement their friendship and avoid dividing their property, which he viewed with dread, as though someone were threatening to cut off one of his limbs.

And so, as soon as they were alone anywhere for a minute, in the cowshed or the kitchen, Buteau would spring to the attack and Françoise would defend herself tooth and nail. And there was always the same scenario: he pushed his arm up her skirt and caught hold of a handful of naked flesh and hair, as when mounting an animal; she, sombre-eyed and clenching her teeth, would force him to let go with a well directed punch between the legs. And no word was ever spoken, the only sound was their panting breaths and muffled gasps, their quiet scuffling; he restrained his cry of pain and she would pull down her skirts and go limping off, her parts bruised and tingling, still with the feeling of his five fingers digging into her flesh. And this would happen with Lise in the room next door, or even in the same room, with her back turned as she tidied away some sheets in a cupboard, as though his wife's presence excited him. He was certain that the proud obstinate young girl would never utter a sound.

But ever since old Fouan had seen them on the heap of potatoes, quarrels had arisen. He had gone and told Lise bluntly what he had seen so that she could prevent her husband from continuing, but she, after telling him roundly to mind his own business, had flared up and blamed her young sister: it was her fault if she excited men! Because everyone knew that all men were beasts!

That night, however, she had such a row with Buteau that next morning she appeared with a half-closed black eye as the result of a badly aimed punch in the course of the argument. From that moment onwards, tempers rose and this spread to all concerned; there were always two of them squabbling, either the husband or the sister and the other sister, unless they were all three at each other's throats.

And at the same time, Lise's and Françoise's unconscious hatred for each other slowly grew. For no apparent reason their former fondness was turning into resentment, leading to continual clashes between them. Basically the only cause was Buteau, whose presence had become a hidden seed of destruction. Françoise would have long since succumbed to the excitement he aroused in her had she not sworn to herself never to give in to her feelings each time he laid hands on her. It was her obstinate sense of justice, never to give up anything of her own and never to take anything from anybody else: but it was costing her dear. Also, she was angry at feeling jealous and loathing her sister because she had the man whom she would have died rather than share with anyone else, had he been hers. When he used to pursue her with his trousers undone, exposing himself, she would spit on it and tell him to take it back to his wife, spit and all : it was her way of relieving the desire which she was holding back, as if to show her anguish and contempt for a pleasure that could not be hers by spitting in her sister's face. As for Lise, she was not jealous because she was certain that Buteau was merely boasting when he had screamed that he enjoyed the services of both of them; not that she thought him incapable of doing it, but she was convinced that her sister's pride would never let her give in. And her only grudge against her was that her continued refusal was turning the house into a hell. The stouter she became, the more she settled down comfortably into her fat, satisfied with life and selfishly greedy in her enjoyment, wanting to be the centre of cheerfulness all around her. How could you possibly squabble like that and poison your existence when you had everything to make you happy? Oh, what a silly little bitch, whose cussedness was the only fly in the ointment !

Every night as she went to bed she would exclaim to Buteau :

'She's my sister but she'd better not start leading you on again or I'll chuck her out!'

But he did not see things like that.

'That'd be a fine thing! The whole village would be after us. Bloody women! I'll give you both a ducking in the pond to cool you off together!'

Two months went by and Lise, all upset and driven to distraction, could have sugared her coffee twice and still not enjoyed it, to use her own expression. She could recognize the days when her sister had resisted a fresh attack by her husband by his increasing foul temper, so much so that she lived in fear of Buteau's failures, watching anxiously when he slyly crept up behind her sister's skirts because she knew that he would then reappear bullying, letting fly all round and turning the whole house upside-down. Days such as these were quite unbearable and she could not forgive that obstinate little hussy who did nothing to smooth things down.

One day in particular things were dreadful. Buteau had gone down into the cellar with Françoise to fetch some cider and he came up in such a state and so infuriated that for a trifle, just because his soup was too hot, he smashed the plate against the wall and went off after giving Lise a backhander that would have felled an ox.

She picked herself up in tears, bleeding and with a swollen cheek, and flung herself on her sister, shrieking:

'You bitch! Why won't you go to bed with him? I've had enough, I'm going to leave if you're so pigheaded and I get beaten up because of it!'

Françoise was listening to her, pale and shocked.

'As sure as God's my witness, I'd sooner do that! Perhaps then he'll leave us alone!'

She had fallen into a chair, whimpering; and her whole fat, collapsing body showed that she was giving up the struggle and had only one wish: to be happy even if it meant sharing with Françoise. She wouldn't feel deprived as long as she had her share. People had silly ideas about that sort of thing. It wasn't as if it was like a piece of bread that is used up if you eat it. Oughtn't they to reach an agreement, come together for the sake of harmony, in fact live like one family?

'Look, why don't you want to?'

Choking with anger and disgust, Françoise merely cried:

'You're more revolting than him!'

And she went off sobbing into the cowshed where Coliche watched her with her large cloudy eyes. It wasn't the thing itself that made her so indignant, but the easy acceptance of it, the willingness to let him have his fun for the sake of peace and quiet. If she had had a man of her own, she would never have given an inch, not one little bit! Her resentment against her sister turned into contempt and she made the vow that she would rather die than give in now.

But from that day onwards, things grew worse and Françoise became the household drudge, the beast of burden which gets all the kicks. She was reduced to the role of skivvy, loaded with all the heavy work, continually grumbled at, bullied and knocked about. Lise now allowed her not one single hour of leisure, she had her out of bed before dawn and kept her up so late at night that the poor girl sometimes was too tired to undress before she fell asleep. Buteau slyly tormented her and took liberties with her, slapping her bottom, pinching her thighs, all sorts of excruciating attentions which left her bleeding and with her eyes full of tears but still obstinately silent. He would snigger and take some consolation from it when he saw her weakening and holding back a cry of pain at his brutal treatment. Her whole body was black and blue, covered in scratches and bruises. When her sister was there, she made it a point of honour not even to flinch in order to deny the fact, as if it were not true that this man's fingers were digging into her flesh. But sometimes she was unable to control the instinctive reaction of her muscles and she would swing a blow at his face, and then there were scuffles and Buteau gave her a thrashing while Lise would belabour the pair of them with her clog on the pretence of separating them. The baby girl Laure and her brother Jules would scream. All the dogs around barked and the neighbours would feel sorry. Ah, poor girl, she needed a lot of pluck to stay on in that inferno!

Everyone in Rognes was in fact astonished that Françoise did not run away. Some wiseacres wagged their heads with a knowing look: she was not yet of age, she still had eighteen months to wait; and if she ran away and put herself in the wrong, without taking her property with her, well, it was sensible of her to think twice about it. If only old Fouan, her guardian, would support her ! But he himself was hardly sitting pretty in his son's house. He was keeping quiet because he was afraid of getting his nose dirty. In any case, the plucky, defiant young girl, proud to rely only on herself, had forbidden him to interfere in her affairs.

By now, every quarrel ended with the same abuse.

'But why don't you bugger off ? Just bugger off !'

'Yes, I know that's what you're hoping. Earlier on I was stupid, I wanted to go. But now I'll stay on even if you kill me. I'm waiting for my share, I want my land and my house and I'm going to have them, I'll have the lot !'

In the early days, Buteau had been afraid that Jean had given Françoise a baby. Since he had caught them in the straw, he had been calculating the days, he kept casting sidelong glances at her to see if there was any sign of a bulge, for the arrival of a child would have meant marriage, which would have spoilt everything. She remained unworried because she knew quite well that she could not be pregnant. But when she noticed that he was interested in her waistline, she was amused and deliberately pushed her stomach out to make him believe that it was getting bigger. Now each time he caught hold of her she could tell that he was feeling her and measuring her with his fingers; so, in the end, she would say firmly :

'Yes, there it is ! He's growing bigger !'

One morning she even padded herself round the waist with some folded dusters. That evening there was almost a slaughter and she was seized by terror when she saw the murderous looks he gave her. If she really had a baby on the way, the brute would certainly have given her a foul blow in order to kill it. So she stopped her tricks and held her stomach in. She even caught him once in her room, rummaging in her underwear, to make sure all was well.

'Why not have one ?' he jeered.

And, pale-faced and furious, she retorted :

'If I don't have one, it's because I don't want to.'

And she was speaking the truth, for she was obstinately refusing to go with Jean again. This did not prevent Buteau from gloating in triumph. He started attacking Jean : what a fine lover he must be, I don't think! There really must be something wrong with him if he couldn't give her a baby. He could catch someone unawares and break their arm but he hadn't even got the guts to do the job properly with a girl! And he would make slighting comments and unpleasant sardonic remarks about leaks in the bottom of her pot.

When Jean learnt how Buteau was treating her, he talked about coming and punching his nose; and he was always on the look-out for Françoise and begging her to go with him: they'd see if he couldn't give her a baby, and a real whopper at that! Now his desire for her was reinforced by anger. But each time she found a new excuse, unable to overcome her reluctance to start doing that sort of thing again with him. She didn't dislike him, it was just that she didn't like him in that way; and she really could not have wanted him very much not to weaken and give herself when he took her in his arms behind a hedge, still flushed and furious from one of Buteau's onslaughts. What a beast he was! And she would talk excitedly and passionately about nothing else but his beastliness and then become all frigid as soon as Jean wanted to take advantage of her and possess her. No, she wouldn't, it made her feel ashamed! One day when she was really hard pressed, she put him off and said they would do it later, on their marriage-night. It was the first time that she had committed herself because she avoided replying directly whenever he had asked her to be his wife. From that moment, it was understood that he would marry her but only when she had come of age, as soon as she could insist on a settlement and come into possession of her property. He was struck by her sound reasoning; he started preaching patience and stopped tormenting her, except at moments when his need for a little fun became too overpowering. She was relieved and reassured by the vagueness of this distant commitment and she would merely catch hold of his hands to stop him and look at him beseechingly with her pretty eyes, like a tender-hearted woman not wanting to risk having a baby from anyone but her husband.

Although finally convinced that she was not pregnant, Buteau was now scared that she might become so if she went back to Jean. Despite his blustering comments about him, he was inwardly trembling because he heard on all hands that the latter was swearing that he would fill Françoise up to the brim until there had never been a more pregnant girl. So he kept watch on her from morning till night, demanding to know how she had spent every minute of her time, tying her down and threatening to beat her like some fractious domestic animal needing to be restrained; and this was a fresh torment, to feel either her sister or her brother-in-law always after her; she could not even go to the dung-pit to relieve herself without seeing someone spying on her. At night they would shut her up in her bedroom; and one evening after a dispute, she found the shutter of her dormer window padlocked. Then, since she still managed to slip away, she had to submit to odious scenes when she came back, interrogations and sometimes medical examinations, with her sister half undressing her while her husband held her by the shoulders. All this brought Jean and her closer together and she came to the point of making rendezvous with him, delighted at defying the other two. Perhaps she might even have given herself to him if she had felt that they were actually on her track. In any case, she finally gave him a promise of marriage and she swore on all that was sacred that Buteau was lying when he had said that he went to bed with both of them, pretending to be cock of the roost and claiming things that were not true at all. Although slightly doubtful, because basically it seemed possible and natural, Jean seemed to believe her. And when they said goodbye, they kissed each other, like very good friends, so much so that she made him her confidant and guide, trying to see him in moments of emergency and not daring to undertake anything without his approval. He now never laid hands on her at all and looked on her as just a good friend whose interests he shared.

Now, whenever Françoise came running to meet Jean behind a wall, the conversation was always the same: she would savagely undo her bodice or pull up her skirt and say:

'Look, that beast's been pinching me again.'

He would look, while remaining cool and determined:

'We'll pay him back for that. You must show it to the neighbours. But above all, don't retaliate. We'll get justice once we've got right on our side.'

'And my sister aids and abets him, you know! Yesterday, when he jumped on me, she just cleared off instead of throwing a bucket of cold water over him!'

'Your sister'll come to a bad end with that bloke. It's all right. If you don't want to, he can't do it, that's for sure. And as for the rest, what's that to us? If we stick together, he can't win.'

Although he avoided interfering, old Fouan was involved in all these quarrels. If he said nothing, they forced him to take sides; if he went out, he would come back to a household all upset and his appearance was often the signal for a further outbreak. Up till then he had not really suffered, physically; but now he began to go short, his bread was meted out and the little luxuries vanished. He was no longer overfed as he was during the early days; a slice of bread cut too thick brought a sharp rebuke: what a bottomless pit! So the less you worked the more you stuffed, it seems! They kept watch and took his money off him every quarter when he came back from Cloyes with the allowance Monsieur Baillehache made him out of the three thousand francs from the sale of the house. Françoise was even reduced to stealing a few pence from her sister to buy him tobacco because they did not give her any money either. And finally the old man was very badly off in his damp bedroom ever since he had broken a pane of glass in the fanlight and it had been plugged with straw to avoid the expense of having a new piece of glass put in. Those miserable children were all the same! He grumbled from morning till night, bitterly regretting having left the Delhommes and in despair at falling out of the frying-pan into the fire. But he kept his regret to himself and only revealed it when caught off his guard, because he knew that Fanny had said: 'Dad'll be round on his hands and knees asking us to take him back.' And so that was the end, something he would never forget, like an ever-open wound. He would rather starve or die in anger with the Buteaus than go back humiliated to the Delhommes.

It so happened that one day when Fouan was walking back from Cloyes after collecting his money from his lawyer and had sat down to rest in a ditch, Jesus Christ, who was strolling around examining rabbit burrows, caught sight of him very absorbed in counting five-franc pieces into his handkerchief. He immediately crouched down, crept along and came to a spot where he could

look down on his father. And lying flat on the ground, he was
surprised to see him carefully wrap up a considerable sum of
money, perhaps as much as eighty francs in his handkerchief. His
eyes glinted and he gave a woolfish grin. His old idea of a secret
nest-egg had immediately sprung to mind. The old man had obviously some bonds tucked away somewhere and took advantage of
his quarterly visit to Monsieur Baillehache to collect the interest.
Jesus Christ's first thought was to wheedle twenty francs out of
his father by blubbering. But then that seemed to him too petty
and a more ambitious scheme began to take shape in his mind.
He slid away like a snake as gently as he had come, so that having
returned to the road Fouan had no suspicions when he met him a
hundred yards further on, walking with the casual air of a young
fellow also on his way back to Rognes. They finished the journey
together, chatting; the father inevitably came round to the topic
of the Buteaus, a heartless lot, and he accused them of starving
him; and his son, his eyes full of tears, good-naturedly offered to
rescue him from such scum by taking him in himself. Why not
come? It would be fun, there was never a dull moment with him!
La Trouille cooked for two, she would cook for three. And damned
good cooking, too, when they had the money.

Surprised and vaguely suspicious at this proposal, Fouan refused. No, he was too old to keep running about from one person
to another, changing his habits every year.

'Well, Father, you know I mean it, think it over. Anyhow, you
can always be sure you won't find yourself on the street. When
you've had your fill of those swine, come up to the Castle.'

And Jesus Christ left him, puzzled and intrigued and wondering what the old boy could be blueing his money on, since he
obviously had quite a lot. A pile of five-franc pieces like that, four
times a year, must add up to at least three hundred francs. And
if he wasn't blueing it, then he must be saving it? That would be
worth looking into. That'd be a really tidy sum!

That day, a mild, damp November day, when Fouan came home,
Buteau tried to relieve him of the thirty-seven francs and fifty
centimes that he received every three months from the sale of his
house. It had been agreed, in any case, that the old man should
hand them over, as well as the two hundred francs a year from
the Delhommes. But this time, a five-franc piece had found its

way in with the ones he had tied up in his handkerchief, and after he had turned out his pockets and produced only thirty-two francs and fifty centimes his son flew into a rage, accused his father of cheating and squandering the five francs on drink and foul practices of some sort or other. Startled and keeping his hand on his handkerchief, with the secret fear that they might search him, his father was stammering an explanation and swearing to heaven that he must have lost it when he had blown his nose. Once again, the household was in an uproar until the evening.

Buteau was in a particularly savage mood because as he was coming back with his harrow he had caught a glimpse of Jean and Françoise slipping behind a wall. The latter had gone out on the pretext of fetching grass for her cows and had failed to reappear because she suspected the sort of welcome she would receive. Night was already falling and Buteau kept furiously going out into the yard and down the road to watch out for that slut coming back from her fancy man. He was swearing loudly and shouting abuse without noticing old Fouan on the stone bench where he had gone to calm down after the quarrel and take a breath of warm air, for this mild sunny November was really springlike.

A sound of clogs was heard coming up the slope and Françoise appeared, bent double under an enormous bundle of grass tied in a piece of old canvas cloth on her shoulders. She was gasping and sweating, half hidden under her load.

'Well, you Christ-forsaken little whore!' yelled Buteau. 'If you think you can make a fool of me and spend two hours being upped by your lover when there's work to do here!'

And he tipped her up into the bundle of grass, which had fallen on the ground, and flung himself on her just as Lise came out of the house to pitch into her as well:

'Well, you bloody shirker, just come here and feel my foot up your behind! Aren't you ashamed of yourself?'

But Buteau had already thrust his arm up her skirt and grabbed a handful of her flesh. His rages always used to turn into a sudden frenzy of desire. While he was lifting her skirts on the grass, he grunted and gasped, all purple and bloated in the face:

'Bloody trollop, this time it's my turn. God strike me blind if I don't have you after him!'

307

A furious struggle began. In the dark, old Fouan could not see exactly what was happening. But he did see Lise standing watching and doing nothing; while her husband, sprawling at full length and continually being unsaddled, still kept trying without success until finally he relieved himself as best he could without caring where.

When he had finished, Françoise at last jerked herself free, panting and stammering:

'Beast! Beast! Dirty beast! You couldn't manage it, that doesn't count. I don't give a damn for that! You'll never do it, never, never, never!'

Triumphantly she took a handful of grass and wiped her thigh, her whole body trembling, as if it too had been partly satisfied by her obstinate refusal. And then, with a gesture of bravado, she flung the handful of grass at her sister's feet:

'Here you are! That's yours and it's not your fault if I can give it back to you!'

Lise slapped her across her mouth to keep her quiet when old Fouan, utterly disgusted, stood up flourishing his stick and intervened:

'Dirty swine, the pair of you! Leave her alone, will you? That's enough.'

Lights were coming on in the houses all around, people were beginning to be uneasy at this dreadful uproar and Buteau hurriedly pushed his father and the girl into the kitchen at the back where there was a candle alight, revealing Laure and Jules crouching terrified in a corner. Lise came in too, not saying a word, startled by the old man's sudden appearance in the dark. He went on, addressing his daughter.

'You really are too disgusting and stupid. You were watching, I saw you.'

With all his strength Buteau banged his fist down on the edge of the table:

'Shut up! That's enough; I'll bash the first person who opens his mouth.'

'And suppose I don't want to shut up?' asked Fouan, in a quivering voice. 'Will you bash me?'

'You or anyone else. You're getting on my wick!'

Françoise bravely put herself between the two men.

'Please, Uncle, don't interfere. You can see that I'm big enough to defend myself.'

But the old man pushed her aside:

'No, leave me alone, this doesn't concern you, it's my business.'

And raising his stick:

'So you'd strike me, would you, you dirty swine! We'll have to see about that. I might want to give you a thrashing myself.'

Buteau quickly snatched his stick from him and flung it under the cupboard, then, with a wild look in his eyes, he stuck his face under the old man's nose and jeered:

'Will you shut your bloody trap? If you think I'm going to put up with your airs and graces, you're mistaken! Just look at me, I'll show you what I'm made of!'

The two men stood glaring at each other in silence, each trying to outstare the other. Since he had come into his property, the son had broadened out and stood thickset and sturdy on his legs, his jaws protruding even more like a bulldog's beneath his narrow receding skull; whereas his father, broken by sixty years of toil, had become even more desiccated and bent; his only strong remaining feature was his enormous nose.

'What you're made of?' repeated Fouan. 'I know that only too well because I made you.'

Buteau sneered:

'That's your fault. But now I'm here and it's my turn. I take after you, I don't like people mucking me about. And once again, shut your trap or there'll be trouble.'

'Trouble for you. I would never have dared speak to my father like that.'

'Oh, I like that. You'd've done him in, if he hadn't died first.'

'That's a lie, you dirty swine! And by Christ, you'll take that back straight away.'

Once again Françoise tried to place herself between the two and, in despair at this new upset, even Lise made an effort. But the two men brushed them aside in order to stand closer to each other, breathing fire and brimstone, father against son, the brutal authority of one confronting the same brutal authority bequeathed to his offspring.

Fouan tried to make himself taller in an attempt to achieve his former absolute mastery as head of the family. For half a century, he had spread fear and trembling amongst his wife, his children and his beasts at the time when he possessed not only power but wealth.

'Say that you were lying, you swine, say that you were lying or I'll make you dance as sure as this candle is lighting us.'

He raised his hand, threatening him with the same gesture that had made them cower in the past.

In his youth, Buteau's teeth would have chattered as he shrank back, with elbow raised to parry the blow; but now he merely shrugged his shoulders with an insulting, insolent air:

'If you think you can frighten me like that! That sort of lark was all right when you were the master.'

'I am the master, I'm your father.'

'Oh, for God's sake, you silly old man. You're nothing at all. So shut your trap, for Christ's sake.'

And as the old man's shaking hand came down to strike him, he caught it in mid-air and held it, crushing it in his grip.

'You obstinate old bugger, so I'll have to lose my temper to get it into your thick head that we don't give a damn for you now! Are you any good to anybody? You're just an expense, that's all! Once you've had your day and handed your land on to some-one else, you kick the bucket and stop buggering them about.'

He was shaking his father to emphasize his words, and then, with a final jerk, he flung him backwards, stumbling and trembling, into a chair beside the window. And the old man remained there, unable to breathe for a minute, beaten and humiliated, his authority destroyed. This was the end, he was of no account since he had handed over his property.

There was utter silence. Everyone stood with their hands dangling by their sides. The children had not uttered a sound, for fear of a clout. Then they all set to work again as though nothing had happened.

'What about the grass?' Lise enquired. 'Is it going to be left in the yard?'

'I'll go and put it under cover,' Françoise replied.

When she had come in and they had had dinner, Buteau, in-corrigible, put his hand into her bodice to find a flea which she said was biting her. She now showed no annoyance and even made a joke.

'No, it's not there, it's somewhere else where you'd get bitten.'

Fouan had not stirred, sitting stiff and silent in his dark corner. Two large tears were running down his cheeks. He was thinking of the evening when he had left the Delhommes; and the same thing was happening again, the same humiliation now that he was no longer the master. They had called out three times to tell him the soup was on the table; he would refuse to come. Suddenly he stood up and disappeared into his bedroom. Next day, at dawn, he left the Buteaus and settled in with Jesus Christ.

JESUS CHRIST was a very flatulent man and in his house many winds did blow, arousing much merriment. No, there was never a dull moment where he was, for he never broke wind without making some funny remark to accompany it. He would have nothing to do with those timid ones, muffled between your buttocks, clumsy, half-hearted little puffs of air. His were always honest explosions, as rousing and hearty as a cannon; and each time, with a jaunty, free and easy lift of his thigh, he would call out to his daughter, in a stern, commanding voice:

'La Trouille, come here at once, for heaven's sake!'   ,

She would come rushing up and it would go off like a gunshot in the empty air with a vibration that made her jump.

'Go on, after it! And give it a bite to see if it's got any knots in it.'

At other times, when she came in, he would give her his hand:

'Pull hard, little girl! Make it go bang!' And as soon as the explosion had occurred, with the blast of an overloaded mine:

'Ah! That was a hard one, thanks all the same.'

Or else he would put an imaginary gun to his shoulder and take long aim; then, after it had gone off:

'Go and fetch it back, lazybones!'

La Trouille would fall on her backside, choking with laughter. It was a never-ending, ever-increasing pleasure; although she knew the drill and expected the final thunderous roar, he still always managed to surprise her with his lively boisterous comments. What a clown her father was! Sometimes he said it was a lodger who wouldn't pay his rent and whom he was evicting, at other times he would turn round with surprise and give a solemn wave of his hand, as if returning the greeting of a tableful of friends; and at other times again he would produce a whole bunch of farts, one for the priest, one for the mayor and one for the ladies. The fellow seemed to be able to produce them out of his behind at will, like a musical box; so much so that at the Jolly Ploughman in Cloyes they would make a bet: 'I'll buy you a drink if you can do six'; and he would do six, he never lost. It was becoming a sort of fame and La Trouille was proud and amused, splitting her sides in anticipation every time he lifted his thigh and watching him with the mingled awe and affection he inspired in her.

And on the evening old Fouan settled in at the Castle, which was the name given to the former cellar where the poacher had gone to earth, the very first meal that the little girl served her father and grandfather, deferentially standing behind them like a maid, was given its duly resounding and cheerful musical accompaniment. The old man had provided five francs and there were delicious mouth-watering smells of kidney beans and veal and onion stew being cooked by the girl. As she was bringing in the beans, she nearly dropped the dish, with uncontrollable laughter. Before sitting down, Jesus Christ had let off three carefully timed rattlers.

'A salvo to celebrate! Let the feast begin!'

Then, collecting his strength, he let out a fourth enormous, insulting, single fart:

'That's for those dirty Buteaus! They can have it for supper!'

Fouan's face, which had been gloomy since he arrived, broke into a grin. He gave an approving nod of the head. It made him feel at home, for people used to say that he, too, had been a wag in his day; and his children had grown up listening quietly to their father's artillery barrage at home. He leant his elbows on the table and felt a wave of well-being creep over him as he sat opposite his hulking great son, who was looking at him with tears in his eyes in his rascally, good-humoured way.

'Ah, Dad, what a lovely life we're going to have, bugger me if we're not. You'll see how things are here, I promise to buck you up! When you're pushing up the daisies, it'll be a fat lot of good having gone short now, won't it?'

Shaken in his sober habits of a lifetime and feeling the need to forget his sorrows, Fouan ended by agreeing:

'Yes, it's better to blue the lot than leave anything to that other bunch. Here's to your very good health, lad!'

La Trouille was serving the veal and onions. Silence fell, and in order to keep the conversation going Jesus Christ let off a long-drawn-out one which modulated *cantabile* through the seat of his chair like a human voice. He immediately turned to his daughter and enquired in a serious voice:

'What did you say?'

She did not say anything for she was forced to sit down holding her sides. But the last straw was when the father and son finally let themselves go, after demolishing the veal and the cheese, as they sat smoking with a large bottle of spirits between them. They had stopped talking; their mouths were thick and coated, they were very drunk.

Jesus Christ slowly lifted a buttock, let off a rouser and then looked towards the door shouting:

'Come in!'

This provoked Fouan, who had been feeling vexed at playing second fiddle the whole evening. Suddenly rediscovering his lost youth, he raised his buttock and let off a rouser in his turn, crying:

'Here I am!'

They both clasped hands, leaning forward nose to nose, laughing and slobbering. That was a good one, that was! And it was too good for La Trouille, who had fallen squirming on the floor, laughing so frantically that she too let out a fart, but such a gentle musical one that it sounded like a tiny fife compared to the two men's full orchestra. Jesus Christ sprang up indignantly and, with a tragic gesture of authority and disgust, exclaimed:

'Leave the room, dirty girl! Leave the room, malodorous wench! God help me, I'll teach you to respect your father and grandfather.'

He would never tolerate such familiarity. It was for adults only! And he fanned the air with his hand, pretending to be asphyxiated by this flute-like puff of wind; his own, he claimed, smelt only of gunpowder. Then as the culprit, very red in the face and upset at having forgotten herself, started arguing and denying what had happened, he pushed her out of the room:

'You filthy little girl, go and shake out your skirts. You can come back in an hour's time when you've had an airing.'

From that day on, a life of fun and games began. The old man was given the girl's bedroom, one of the compartments in the former cellar, divided into two by a wooden partition; and she had obligingly withdrawn into an excavation at the end, a sort of rear section where there were said to be vast underground rooms blocked off by falling rocks. The worst thing was that this fox-hole of a castle was becoming buried more and more every year by stones brought down by the heavy winter rains as they ran off the steep slope; indeed the hovel, with its old foundations and patched up with dry stones, would have been carried away but for the thick roots of the ancient lime-trees growing above. But with the arrival of spring it became a delightfully cool retreat, a grotto hidden under bramble and hawthorn bushes. The dog-rose covering the window was dotted with pink flowers and even the door had its curtain of wild honeysuckle, which you pushed aside in order to go in.

Of course La Trouille did not have kidney beans and veal and onions to cook every day. That happened only when the old man had coughed up a five-franc piece and Jesus Christ, while not over-discreet, was careful not to push him too far; he preferred to wheedle money out of him by playing on his feelings and his greed. They would spend the first few days of every month feast-ing, once the old man had collected the sixteen francs of his pen-sion from the Delhommes; and they would really let themselves go every quarter when the lawyer gave Fouan his allowance of thirty-seven francs fifty centimes. At first Fouan would hand over his five-franc pieces only as the money ran out, unable to break with his inveterate avarice; then gradually he fell into the hands of his rascally son, amused and bemused by his extraordinary gift for story-telling, sometimes even reduced to tears, so that he would hand over two or three francs at a time. He began to fall into glutonous habits, saying to himself that it was better to squander the lot with good grace since it would all be squandered sooner or later anyway. In any case, it must be said in Jesus Christ's favour that if he was robbing the old man, at least he gave him his fair share and kept him amused. At first, touched by all his good cheer, he closed his eyes to the thought of the nest-egg and made no attempt to enquire about it. His father was free to enjoy himself as he liked and as long as he was paying for these celebrations he could not reasonably be asked to do anything more. And it was only during the second half of each month, when the old man's pockets were empty, that he would let his mind wander onto the subject of the money he had once glimpsed before it had been hidden away somewhere. But there was not a farthing to be squeezed out of him! Jesus Christ would grumble at his daughter when she served a dish of mashed potatoes without butter and he would draw in his belt and think how stupid it was, really, to go short and hide your money away. One day that nest-egg would have to be brought to light and demolished!

All the same, even on these miserable evenings when the great hulking rogue would sit stretching himself in annoyance, he would not be too down-hearted and would relieve himself with some windy comment, cheering everybody up with a splendid heavy barrage as though he had had a decent meal.

'And that's for the turnips, La Trouille, and some butter, damn it all!'

Fouan was not bored even when things became difficult towards the end of the month, because it was then that the father and daughter went out in search of something to put in the pot. The first time La Trouille came back with a hen which she had hooked from over a wall, he had been cross. On a second occasion, he had had to laugh heartily too, one morning when she had hidden up a tree dangling a hook baited with meat in the middle of a flock of ducks; one of them had suddenly rushed at it and swallowed it whole, hook, line and meat; and then with a sharp tug it had disappeared into the air, stifled without a cry. It was a trifle dishonest, of course, but when animals are living in the open, surely they ought to belong to anyone who can catch them; as long as you don't steal money, well, really, you can hardly be called a thief. After this incident, he began to take an interest in the little scamp's marauding expeditions, which were almost unbelievable: a sack of potatoes whose owner had helped her carry himself; grazing cows milked into a bottle; even the washerwomen's washing, which she sank in the Aigre by means of stones and came back at night to dive in and fetch out. She was to be seen on every highway and byway, for her geese provided her with a permanent excuse for roaming the countryside on the look-out for some opportunity, spending hours at times beside a ditch with the sleepy air of a goosegirl letting her flock forage around; she even used her geese as dogs to warn her, for the gander would hiss as soon as some intruder threatened to catch her unawares. She was now eighteen years old and she had hardly grown at all since she was twelve, still as lithe and slim as a branch of young poplar and goatlike with her green slits of eyes and her wide mouth, twisted to the left. Her little childish breasts, under her father's old smocks, had become harder rather than larger. A real tomboy, who only liked her animals and thought nothing about men. This did not prevent her, after a friendly tussle with some young village boy, from ending up on her back; this was something quite natural, that was the point of it and it wasn't important anyway. Fortunately, she only had dealings with young scallywags of her own age, otherwise it would have been disgusting; but the staid, older men of the village left her alone, finding her not plump enough for their taste. In fact, as her grandfather used to say with amused admiration, apart from the fact that she was a thief and not quite as decent-living as she might have been, she really was an amusing girl and not as black as she was painted.

But above all Fouan enjoyed following Jesus Christ as he prowled round the fields. Every peasant has a poacher hidden inside him and he was interested in the snares and the ground lines, all sorts of primitive tricks, the continual war of wits waged against the gamekeeper and the gendarmes. As soon as the braided caps and brown crossbelts appeared from the road, moving along above the wheat, father and son seemed to be stretched out on a bank asleep; then suddenly the son would crawl along the ditch on all fours and check the traps while his father, with the innocent air of a harmless old man, kept an eye on the crossbelts and caps receding into the distance. There were superb trout to be found in the Aigre that you could sell for two francs or more to a fishmonger in Châteaudun; the trouble was that you had to watch them for hours because they were very wily. The two often went as far as the Loir as well, in whose muddy bottom there were lovely eels to be found. When the fish were not biting, Jesus Christ had hit on a more convenient method of fishing in the fish-cages of the townsfolk who lived beside the river. But this was little more than a pastime, because his real passion was hunting. His depredations extended a dozen miles or more around; and everything was fair game, quail as well as partridge and starlings as well as larks. He rarely used a gun, which can be heard a long way off. Not one single clutch of partridge nesting in the clover or

317

lucerne would escape his notice, so that he knew the exact time and place when the young birds could be caught by hand, still drowsy and wet with dew. He had specially prepared snares for larks and quail and he would cast stones into the thick clouds of starlings that seem to come in with the autumn winds. For the last twenty years he had been exterminating the game of the whole region so that there was not a rabbit left in the coverts on the slopes of the Aigre, to the great fury of the local hunters. Only the hares managed to evade his tender mercies; there were not many of them and they could make their escape over the plain where it was dangerous to pursue them. He dreamt longingly of the few hares still to be found at La Borderie and he would risk gaol in order to have a shot at one of them, now and again. When he saw his son taking his gun, Fouan stayed at home: it was too stupid, he'd end up being pinched, as sure as fate.

And of course one day this did happen. It must be said that farmer Hourdequin, exasperated at the destruction of the game on his estate, had given Bécu the strictest orders, so, irritated at never managing to lay hands on anyone, the gamekeeper had taken to sleeping in a hayrick, to keep a look-out. And one morning at daybreak he was awakened with a start by a shot, the flash of which passed under his very nose. It was Jesus Christ, lying in wait behind a heap of straw, who had just killed a hare, at almost point-blank range.

'Ah, it's you, blast you!' cried the gamekeeper, seizing the gun which Jesus Christ had leant against the rick while he was picking up the hare. 'I might have known it was you, you scum!'

When drinking, they were boon companions; but out in the fields they were at daggers drawn, with Bécu always on the point of catching Jesus Christ, who was equally determined to punch the former's nose.

'Yes, it's me, sod you! Give me back my gun.'

Bécu was already in two minds about his capture. As a rule, when he saw Jesus Christ going to the left, he was glad to turn off right. What's the point of stirring up trouble between friends? But this time his duty was plain and he could not possibly turn a blind eye. And anyway, when someone's been caught red-handed he can at least be polite.

'Your gun, you dirty dog! I'm going to hang onto it and de-

318

posit it at the town-hall. And don't make a move or try and be clever or else I'll blow your guts out with the other barrel!'

Weaponless, Jesus Christ hesitated to attack him, despite his anger. Then, when he saw him making for the village, he started following him, still carrying his hare dangling from his hand. They both walked for a quarter of an hour without exchanging a word, looking daggers at each other. Any minute hostilities seemed inevitable, yet both were becoming increasingly worried. What a stupid bloody encounter!

As they were coming up behind the church, a stone's throw from the Castle, the poacher made one final attempt.

'Come on, old man, don't be stupid, come and have a drink at home with me.'

'No, I must make my report,' the gamekeeper replied stiffly.

And he refused to budge, like an old soldier sticking strictly to his orders. However, he did stop and eventually, as the other man caught hold of his arm to persuade him to come along with him, he said:

'All right then, if you've got pen and ink. It doesn't really matter where we do it as long as I make my report.'

When Bécu arrived at the Castle the sun was rising and old Fouan, already smoking his pipe on the doorstep, realized what had happened and was worried, the more so as the situation was still very serious. They unearthed the ink and a rusty old pen and the gamekeeper embarked on his terrible struggle to find the right words, sprawling with his elbows on the table. But at the same time, at a word from her father, La Trouille fetched three glasses and a litre of wine; and by the time he had written five lines, the exhausted Bécu, having lost his way in the details of his account of the incident, was ready to take a long gulp. So, little by little, the situation became less tense. A second litre made its appearance, followed by a third. Two hours later the three men, with their heads together, were fiercely engaged in friendly conversation: they were very drunk and had completely forgotten the morning's affair.

'You old cuckold!' Jesus Christ was yelling. 'You know I go to bed with your old woman.'

It was true. Ever since the village feast, he had been tumbling Bécu's wife unceremoniously in any old corner, using such endearing expressions as 'old bag'. But Bécu was aggressive when drunk, and lost his temper. He might accept the situation when sober, but in his cups he took offence. He flourished an empty bottle and screamed :

'You bollocking dirty shit !'

The bottle smashed against the wall, missing Jesus Christ who was sitting there slobbering, with a bleary maudlin look on his face. To appease the outraged husband, it was decided that they would all stay and eat the hare straight away together. Whenever La Trouille cooked a jugged hare, the delicious smell reached as far as the other end of the village. It was a wonderful celebration and lasted the whole day. They were still sitting sucking away at the bones when night fell, so they lighted two tallow candles and continued. Fouan produced three franc pieces and sent the girl to buy a litre of brandy. They were still sipping it when all the village was in bed and asleep. Jesus Christ, who kept groping for a light, caught hold of the report the gamekeeper had started to write, now covered in wine and gravy stains.

'Oh, yes, we've got to finish it off,' he mumbled, with a drunken belly laugh.

He was looking at it and wondering what joke he could play, something to express his whole contempt for the written word and the law. Suddenly he raised his thigh, slipped the paper underneath and let off a meaty one on it, the sort he described as having a mortar at the end of it.

'And now it's signed !'

Everyone burst into laughter, including Bécu. What fun they had that night at the Castle !

At about this time, Jesus Christ made a friend. One evening, when he had gone to earth in a ditch to let the gendarmes pass, he found himself sharing the place with a fellow who was also not keen on being seen. They started talking. He was called Leroi, a good sort who went by the name of Canon; a journeyman carpenter, he had left Paris a couple of years ago as a result of some trouble with the police and he preferred living in the country, wandering from village to village, working a week here and a week there, offering his services to one farm and then another, when the farmer did not want him. Now work was difficult to find and he was on the road, begging, living on stolen fruit and vegetables and glad to have leave to sleep in a haystack. If the truth be told, he was hardly the sort of man to inspire much confidence, being ragged, filthy and very ugly; wasted by vice and poverty and with such a pale, thin face and sparse beard that women locked their doors at the mere sight of him. What was worse, he talked in an outrageous manner of chopping off the heads of the rich and being able to have the time of his life one fine day with other people's wine and wives; threats which he uttered in a sombre voice, waving his fists as he expressed the revolutionary ideas which he had picked up in the poorer suburbs of Paris; a never-ending flow of inflammatory social demands which filled the country folk with bewilderment and awe. For the last two years he had turned up at farms at dusk, asking for a corner to sleep in in the straw. He would sit down by the fire and make their blood curdle with his terrifying talk; then he would disappear the following day and reappear a week later at the same dismal hour of evening and utter the same prophecies of death and destruction. And so the farmers would now no longer take him in because of the terror and anger aroused by the sinister visions of this footloose vagrant. Jesus Christ and Canon hit it off together straightaway.

'God, how stupid I was,' the former exclaimed, 'not to have cleaned out the lot of them in Cloyes in 1848! Come along, old man, let's crack a bottle.'

He took him back to the Castle and put him up for the night, full of deference for all his talk and thinking how superior he was to know so much, with his ideas on how to reform society in one fell swoop. Two days later, Canon left; then, after a week, he was back again but left at dawn. And from then on he dropped in at the Castle every so often, eating and snoring as if the place belonged to him, and swearing each time he came that the bourgeois would be liquidated before three months were up. One night when her father was out on the prowl, he tried to tumble his host's daughter but, blushing with shame, La Trouille indignantly scratched and bit him so hard that he had to let go. 'What did he take her for, the dirty old man?' He called her a silly little girl.

Fouan was not very fond of Canon either. He accused him of being a loafer and wanting things that would land him up on the scaffold. When that scoundrel was there, the old man was so unhappy that he preferred to smoke his pipe outside. In any case, he was once more running into difficulties and no longer enjoying his guzzling sessions with his son so much, ever since a serious point of disagreement had arisen between them. Up till now, Jesus Christ had been selling off his share of the land, bit by bit, only to his brother Buteau or his brother-in-law Delhomme, and each time Fouan, whose signature was required, had given it without question, since the land was staying in the family. But now the question of the last field had arisen. The poacher had used it as security to borrow money and the man who had lent it was talking of having it put up to auction because he hadn't seen a single penny of the interest that had been agreed. When consulted, Monsieur Baillehache had recommended Jesus Christ to sell it himself as quickly as possible, unless he wanted to run into heavy expense. Unfortunately, neither Buteau nor Delhomme wanted to buy it as they were furious at the old man's letting himself be swindled by his rascally elder son and were determined to have nothing to do with any matter as long as Fouan continued to live there. And so the field was going to be sold by legal authority and the papers were all being drawn up. It was the first piece of land ever to be leaving the family and the old man spent sleepless nights as a result. Land that his father and grandfather had coveted so fiercely and acquired by dint of such hardship! Land that had been kept and guarded as jealously as if it had been a wife. Fancy seeing legal proceedings eat into it, fancy seeing it lose its value, and fall into the possession of someone else, a neighbour, for half its real value! He trembled with fury and was so heartbroken that he sobbed like a child! Oh, what a swine Jesus Christ was.

Terrible scenes took place between father and son. The latter would refuse to reply and let the tragic old man stand there, screaming his reproaches and wailing with grief, until he was exhausted.

'Yes, you're a murderer, it's like taking a knife and cutting a piece of flesh out of my body. Such a good field, you couldn't find a better! Anything will grow in it, you only need to breathe on it! You cowardly good-for-nothing, not raising a finger to stop someone else having it! Yes, for Christ's sake, someone else! That's what I can't stand. Haven't you got any guts at all, you bloody soak? And it's all because you've drunk it all, you dirty idle bastard!'

Then, when his father was too breathless and tired to go on, his son replied calmly:

'It's so stupid, to torment yourself like that, old man! Punch me on the nose, if you feel it'll relieve you. But you're not being very philosophical, you know. Look, you can't eat earth, can you? If they put a plate of it in front of you, what a face you'd pull, wouldn't you? I used it to borrow money because that's my way of growing five-franc pieces on it. And now they'll sell it, after all, they sold Jesus Christ, didn't they? And if we get a few pennies out of it, we'll blue them on drink, that's real wisdom. Good God, once you're dead you'll get all the land you want.'

But father and son were in agreement on one thing: they both detested the bailiff, a certain Vimeux, a seedy-looking little man who was given all the unpleasant chores which his colleagues at Cloyes did not want. One evening, Vimeux gingerly made his way up to the Castle to deliver a writ. Vimeux was a very grubby little shrimp of a man with a tiny yellow tuft of beard from which emerged a red nose and a pair of rheumy eyes. Always dressed like a gentleman, in a hat, a frock-coat and black trousers, dreadfully worn and stained, he was celebrated in the region for the frightful drubbings he had received at the hands of the peasants when delivering notice of proceedings against them, in remote areas where he was defenceless. There were many legends about him, thrashings and involuntary duckings in ponds, a mile-long chase at the point of a pitchfork, a sound spanking administered, with his trousers down, by a mother and her daughter.

It so happened that Jesus Christ was just coming home with his gun; and old Fouan, who was sitting on a tree-trunk smoking his pipe, grunted angrily:

'Look at the shame you're bringing on us, you good-for-nothing.'

'Just wait and see,' the poacher said, clenching his teeth.

But seeing that he had a gun, Vimeux had stopped dead, some thirty yards away. The whole of his pitiful, black, dirty, correctly dressed person was trembling with fear.

'Monsieur Jesus Christ,' he quavered, 'I've come on that little matter you know about. I'll put it down here. A very good evening to you!'

He put the writ down on a stone and was already retreating backwards rapidly when Jesus Christ shouted:

'Look, you bloody pen-pusher, you'd better learn some manners! Bring your bit of paper over here!'

And as he stood stock-still, so scared that he hardly knew whether to go backwards or forwards, the other man pointed the gun at him:

'If you don't hurry up, you'll get lead poisoning. Come along, pick up your piece of paper and bring it here. Nearer than that, right here, you dirty little funk, or I'll shoot.'

Paralysed, livid with fright, the bailiff was stumbling on his tiny legs. He looked imploringly at old Fouan but with the savage resentment all peasants feel against the cost of legal proceedings and the law's official representative, the latter merely went on quietly puffing at his pipe.

'Ah, there we are at last, that's a good fellow. Now hand over your bit of paper. Oh no, not like that, you must be a bit more forthcoming. Hand it over properly, as if you really meant it, for Christ's sake! And be polite. Yes, that's more like it.'

Petrified by these jocular remarks which the hulking great fellow was delivering with a malicious grin on his face, Vimeux stood blinking, awaiting the threatened punch or slap across the face.

'And now, turn·round.'

He realized what was going to happen and warily did not stir.

'Turn round or else I'll do it for you.'

He saw that there was nothing else to do and, pitifully, he turned and without being asked offered his little behind, as scrawny as that of a famished cat. Jesus Christ took a run and landed his foot fairly and squarely on the target with such force that the bailiff's man went sprawling on his face, a good four yards away. And then, painfully rising to his feet, he took desperately to his heels, pursued by the shout:

'Look out! I'm going to fire!'

Jesus Christ had put the gun to his shoulder but was content merely to lift his thigh and let out such a loud bang that Vimeux fell flat on his face again, terrified by the report. This time his black hat had gone spinning off among the boulders. He chased after it, picked it up and set off faster than ever, pursued by a further series of bangs, one after the other, a whole volley accompanied by gusts of laughter that completed his discomfiture. He hurtled down the slope hopping like an insect and the valley was still re-echoing with Jesus Christ's artillery barrage when he was a good hundred yards away. The whole countryside was reverberating and the final one, a real tear-arse, followed the bailiff as he disappeared into Rognes, now no bigger than an ant. La Trouille had run up on hearing the noise and was holding her sides as she lay on the ground cackling like a hen. Old Fouan had taken his pipe out of his mouth to laugh more freely. Ah, what a card Jesus Christ was! A proper waster but by God he was funny!

All the same, the following week the old man had to make up his mind to agree to sign the authority for the sale of his land. Monsieur Baillehache had found a buyer and the most sensible thing was to follow his advice. So it was agreed that father and son would go into Cloyes on the third Saturday of September, the day before Saint Lubin's Day, one of the town's two feast-days. The father was also hoping to take advantage of the trip to pick up from the tax-collector the interest on the bonds he kept hidden away, which had been accumulating since July; and he was relying on slipping away from his son in the course of the festivities. They would use the same vehicle for outward and return journeys – Shanks's pony.

As Fouan and Jesus Christ were standing at the level crossing just outside Cloyes waiting for a train to pass, Buteau and Lise came up in their cart. A quarrel broke out immediately between the two brothers, who hurled abuse at each other until the barrier was raised; and even when his horse was carrying him off down the slope on the other side, Buteau turned round with his smock bellying in the wind and shouted further remarks better left unsaid.

'Shut your trap, you bloody slacker,' Jesus Christ bawled with all his might, using his hands as a megaphone: 'It's me who's feeding your father.'

Fouan spent an unpleasant time at Monsieur Baillehache's office in the Rue Grouaise, the more so as it was packed with people wanting to take advantage of market day and he had to wait nearly two hours. It reminded him of the day when he had come along to settle the distribution of his property; certainly he'd have done better to go and hang himself, that Saturday. When the lawyer finally saw them and he had to sign, the old man got out his glasses and wiped them; but his eyes were watering so much that they misted up, and his hand was trembling so that they had to put his fingers in the right place on the paper and he made a big blot of ink as he signed. He found the whole business such a strain that he kept trembling and sweating, casting bewildered glances all around him, like someone who has just had his leg cut off in an operation and is still looking for it. Monsieur Baillehache took Jesus Christ severely to task and he sent them both away with a legal homily: selling property was immoral, the state would certainly be increasing the legal costs in order to discourage people from selling rather than bequeathing it to their children.

Once outside, Fouan left Jesus Christ at the door of the Jolly Ploughman, in the midst of the market-day throng. The latter agreed with alacrity, not without a sly grin, for he suspected what the old man was up to. And indeed his father made his way straight to the Rue Beaudonnière where the tax-collector Monsieur Hardy had his office in a cheerful little house, with a courtyard in front and a garden at the back. He was a stout, jovial, rubicund man with a well-kempt black beard, held in awe by all the peasants who accused him of misleading them with all sorts of tall stories. His office was a narrow room, divided into two by a rail: he sat on one side, they on the other. Often there were a dozen of them standing packed like sardines. At the moment there happened to be only Buteau, who had just arrived.

Buteau could never agree to pay his taxes in one instalment. When he received the demand in March, he was in a bad temper for a whole week. He would angrily scrutinize the land tax, his income tax, the tax on personal estate, the door and window tax; but his main source of anger was the special rate, which went up every year, he claimed. Then he would wait to receive the first demand, which was free of charge. That gave him a week's grace. After that, he would pay in monthly instalments when he went to market; and each month he suffered the same torment; his

326

sufferings even started the night before and he would take his money along as if going to the guillotine. The blasted government! What a gang of thieves they were!

'Ah, it's you,' said Monsieur Hardy cheerfully. 'I'm glad you came, I was just going to work out your additional charges.'

'That would have been the end,' grunted Buteau. 'And you know I'm not going to pay the extra six francs of land tax that you added on. It's just not fair.'

The tax-collector laughed.

'Oh yes, you tell that tale every month. I've already explained to you that your income must have increased because you've planted your former meadow down by the Aigre. We base ourselves on that.'

But Buteau argued fiercely: his income gone up? It was like his meadow, which used to be two hundred and eighty poles and which was now only two hundred and seventy-two, ever since the Aigre had changed its course and removed eight of them. Well, he was still paying on two hundred and eighty, did he call that justice? Monsieur Hardy replied calmly that that was a matter for the survey people and didn't concern him. Buteau would have to wait until the next survey. And under the pretence of explaining the matter again, he smothered him in figures and technical expressions that Buteau could not understand. Then, in his hearty way, he added:

'Well, if you like, don't pay, I don't give a damn. The bailiff will be round to see you.'

Scared and taken aback, Buteau swallowed his anger. When you're the underdog, you have to submit; and his fear increased still more his long-standing hatred of this faceless and complicated authority which he could feel weighing him down, the administrators and the law courts, all these townee layabouts, as he was wont to call them. He slowly pulled out his purse. His thick fingers were trembling. He had been paid a good deal of small coin at the market that morning and he felt each sou carefully before putting it down in front of him. He counted out the money three times, all in five-centime pieces, which made him even more broken-hearted at having to hand over such a large pile of money. In the end, just as he was watching the tax-collector put the money into the till, old Fouan appeared.

The old man had not recognized his son from the back and was startled when he turned round.

'And how are things with you, Monsieur Hardy?' he stammered. 'I was just going by and I thought I might drop in to pass the time of day. We hardly ever see each other these days.'

Buteau was not taken in by this. He said goodbye and left as though in a hurry; and then, five minutes later, he came back, pretending he had forgotten to ask for some information, at the very moment the tax-collector was paying out on his desk a quarter's interest, seventy-two francs in five-franc pieces. Buteau's eyes gleamed but he avoided looking at his father and pretended not to see him throw a handkerchief over them, gather them up into it like a fisherman hauling in his net, and stuff them into his pocket. This time they left together, Fouan very perplexed and casting furtive glances at his son, Buteau in high good humour and showing a sudden affection for his father: they could go along together and he offered to take him home in his cart. He went back with him to the Jolly Ploughman.

Jesus Christ was there with young Sabot, from Brinqueville, a wine-grower, another well-known joker, who could also produce enough wind to turn a windmill. So, having met, the pair of them had just made a bet of ten bottles of wine for the one who would blow out the greatest number of candles. With much guffawing, their friends went off with them, in great excitement, into the back room and formed a circle round them. One went into action on the left, the other on the right, trousers down, aiming with their backsides and hitting the mark each time. However, Sabot had managed ten and Jesus Christ nine, having run short of wind on one occasion. He was very cross about this; his reputation was at stake. Go to it! Would Rognes let itself be beaten by Brinqueville? And he blew stronger than any blacksmith's bellows had ever blown: nine! ten! eleven! twelve! The town drummer of Cloyes, who was relighting the candles, was almost blown away himself. With a great effort, Sabot had reached ten and was exhausted and windless when Jesus Christ triumphantly let off two more, calling on the drummer to light those two for the grand finale. The drummer lit them and they burned with a lovely golden yellow light, like a glowing sun rising in all its glory.

'Ah, that bugger, Jesus Christ! What a gut that man's got! He takes the biscuit!'

Their friends were screaming and doubled up with laughter, in admiration not unmixed with jealousy because, after all, you had to be pretty solidly built to hold all that wind and let it out as and when you liked. They spent two hours drinking the ten litres, talking of nothing else all the time.

While his brother was putting on his trousers again, Buteau had given him a friendly slap on his backside and good relations seemed to be restored by this flattering family victory. Looking years younger, old Fouan told a story about his childhood, at the time when the Cossacks were in Beauce and one of them had gone to sleep beside the Aigre with his mouth open and he had shoved one in his gob which gave him a taste of shit up to his eyeballs. The market was coming to an end and everyone went off very drunk.

And then Buteau actually took Fouan and Jesus Christ back in his cart while Lise, with whom Buteau had had a quiet word, made herself agreeable, too. No more squabbling, they couldn't do too much for their father. But the elder brother, who was now sobering up, was busy thinking to himself: as his younger brother was being so pleasant, it must mean that the sod had uncovered the mystery, at the tax-collector's? In that case, hang on a second! If he, the black sheep of the family, had been decent enough to leave the nest-egg alone, he certainly wasn't going to be stupid enough to let the old man go back to the other couple. He would make sure of that, quite gently, without making a fuss, since the family now seemed set on being reconciled.

When they arrived at Rognes and the old man tried to get down, the two brothers scurried round to help, each trying to show more respect and affection than the other.

'Lean on me, Father.'

'Give me your hand, Father.'

They helped him down to the ground. And standing between the two of them, he felt scared, knowing in his heart that he had been found out, without any shadow of a doubt.

'What's up with you? Why are you all being so kind?'

He was terrified by the way they were looking at him. He would have preferred them to be disrespectful, as usual. Ah, what bloody bad luck! Was he going to run into trouble now they knew he had some money? Disconsolately, he went back to the Castle.

It so happened that Canon, who had not been seen for the last two months, was sitting on a stone waiting for Jesus Christ. As soon as he caught sight of him, he cried out:

'I say, your daughter's down in the Pouillards' wood with a man on top of her.'

Purple-faced with indignation, her father exploded:

'The little slut, disgracing me again!'

And taking down his long horsewhip from its hook behind the door, he dashed down the rocky slope to the little wood. But whenever she was on her back, La Trouille's geese kept guard for her like good watchdogs. The gander at once scented her father and came up with all his flock. Threatening with lifted wings and stretching out his neck, he uttered a series of shrill hisses while, lined up in battle order, the geese all stretched out their necks too, with their large yellow beaks wide open ready to peck him. There was a crack of the whip and the sound of escaping animals: La Trouille had been warned and made herself scarce.

After he had hung up his whip again, Jesus Christ seemed to be overcome by a melancholy, philosophical mood. Perhaps his daughter's persistently shameless behaviour had made him take a more understanding view of human passion? Perhaps he had merely seen the vanity of fame after his triumph at Cloyes? He shook his unhappy head, the head of a drunken, scrounging, crucified Christ, and said to Canon:

'Would you like to know something? The whole thing's not worth a fart!'

And, lifting his thigh, he let one go thundering over the village, now swathed in shadow, as though to shatter the earth beneath his contempt.

Chapter 4

IT was early October and the wine harvest was about to begin; a splendid week of feasting when quarrelsome families usually became reconciled over jugs of new wine. For a whole week Rognes would reek of grapes; people ate so many that women lifted their skirts and men dropped their trousers under every hedge and lovers stained with grape juice greedily exchanged kisses among the vines. In the end, there were lots of drunken men and pregnant girls.

The very day after their return from Cloyes, Jesus Christ started his search for his father's nest-egg, because the old man might not carry his money about on him and he must have secreted his bonds in some little corner or other. But although La Trouille helped him and they turned the whole house upside down, at first they met with no success, despite their astuteness and long experience of scrounging; but a week later, when he was lifting down a cracked old disused saucepan, the poacher discovered underneath some lentils a bundle of paper carefully wrapped up in the sort of oilcloth used to line hats. But no trace of cash : the old man had no doubt tucked his money away somewhere else : and it must be a pretty large sum because his father hadn't spent a penny for the last five years. But it was certainly the bonds, three hundred francs' worth of five per cent. As Jesus Christ was counting them over and examining them he discovered another sheet of paper, a stamped document which left him lost in amazement when he read it. Good God ! So that's where the money was going !

It was an incredible story. A fortnight after splitting up his property at the lawyer's, heartbroken at the thought of no longer having any possessions of his own, not even one square inch of wheatland, Fouan had become distraught. No, he couldn't possibly go on living like that, it'd be the death of him. And so he had done something completely idiotic, comparable to the idiocy of an infatuated old man who sacrifices his last penny to creep furtively back to an unfaithful slut of a woman. And he, who had been so sharp in his day, had let himself be taken in by his friend, old Saucisse. He must have been really frantic to own some property and completely at the mercy of that fierce urge which overtakes old men who have toiled all their lives to make the land fruitful. So frantic was he that he had signed an agreement with old Saucisse whereby the latter made over an acre of land after his death, in exchange for a daily payment of seventy-five centimes for the rest of his natural life. Fancy making an agreement like that at the age of seventy-six, when the vendor is ten years younger than yourself! The truth was that, at about that time, Saucisse, the old rogue, had taken to his bed, coughing as if about to breathe his last, and blinded by his desire the other man stupidly took himself to be the cleverer of the two and was anxious to strike a good bargain. Be that as it may, it all goes to show that if you've got an urge, for a wench or a field, you'd do better to take to your bed than sign a piece of paper. The seventy-five centimes had now been paid over every morning for the last five years; and the more he paid out, the more fiercely Fouan became attached to that bit of land and longed to lay hands on it. To think that, having disposed of all the problems of his long working life, he had nothing else to do but die in peace and quiet while watching other people work themselves to skin and bone to cultivate the land, and then he'd gone back to let himself be killed by it! Alas, men are not very wise and old men are no wiser than young ones.

For a second, Jesus Christ thought of pocketing everything, the agreement as well as the bonds. But then his courage failed him; after doing something like that he would have to go underground. It wouldn't be like money that you can make off with, knowing that there'll be more later on; so he infuriatedly put the papers back under the lentils in the saucepan. But he was so exasperated that he could not keep the matter to himself. By next day, Rognes knew all about old Saucisse and the seventy-five centimes a day he was getting for an acre of rather ordinary land which was certainly not worth three thousand francs; and over five years, that meant that fourteen hundred francs had already been paid, and if the old rascal were to survive another five years, he would have his field as well as the money. They pulled Fouan's legs; but whereas no one had bothered to look at him ever since his sole possession in the world had been his old body, people now greeted him and showed him consideration because he was known to be man of substance, with land and private means.

The family's attitude in particular seemed to have swung round. Fanny, who had been very cool towards her father since he had offended her by going to live with her rascally elder brother instead of coming back to live with her, brought him some linen, some of Delhomme's discarded shirts. But Fouan harshly reminded her of the remark that was still rankling with him – 'Dad'll be round on bended knees to ask us to take him back' – by welcoming her with the comment: 'So you're coming on bended knees to have me back.' The phrase stuck in her throat. When she was home, in her pride, she wept for shame and vexation, for this farmer's wife was so sensitive that a glance could offend her. Decent, hard-working and rich, she was coming to dislike the whole village. Delhomme had to promise that in future he would hand over their allowance to the old man, because she swore she would never speak to him again.

As for Buteau, he astounded everyone by visiting the Castle one day, in order, so he said, to pay his respects to his father. Jesus Christ, with a grin, produced a bottle of spirits and they all had a drink together. But his amusement turned to sheer amazement when his brother spread a row of ten five-franc pieces on the table, saying:

'Father, we really must settle our accounts. Here's your last quarter's allowance.'

The bloody sharper! When he hadn't given his father a penny for years, he must surely be intending to swindle him by showing him the colour of his money once again! Anyway, Buteau immediately warded off the old man's hand as he was about to catch hold of the coins and picked them up again himself.

'Not so fast! It was just to show you that I've got them. I'll keep them for you; you know where to find them.'

Jesus Christ was beginning to see what was happening and he became annoyed:

'Look, if you're trying to entice Dad away...'

Buteau passed the matter off lightly:

'You're not jealous, are you? If I had Father one week and you the next, it would only be natural, wouldn't it? Eh, Father, how

333

about cutting yourself in two? And meanwhile, your very good health!'

As he was leaving he invited them to join in the grape-picking in his vineyard the following day. They'd stuff themselves with grapes until they were bursting. In fact, he was so pleasant that the other two conceded that, though a real rogue, he was an amusing one as long as you didn't let yourself be taken in by him. They showed their pleasure by going part of the way home with him.

And as it happened, at the bottom of the hill they met Monsieur and Madame Charles and Élodie, going back to Roseblanche, their estate, after taking a walk along the Aigre. All three were in mourning for Madame Estelle, as they called the little girl's mother, who had died in July, of overwork, for every time her mother came back from Chartres she would say that her daughter was really working herself to death in her efforts to maintain the good reputation of the establishment in the Rue aux Juifs which her slacker of a husband was neglecting more and more. And how moving the funeral had been for Monsieur Charles who had not dared bring Élodie along, and indeed had not told his granddaughter the news until three days after her mother had been laid to rest. What a pang he had felt that morning when, after years of absence, he had seen the house on the corner of the Rue de la Planche-aux-Carpes, No. 19, with its yellow distempered walls and green shutters, always kept shut, his whole life's work in fact, now draped in black, its little door open and its entrance blocked by the coffin, with candles at each corner. What really touched him was the sympathy shown by the whole quarter. When the coffin was carried out of the entrance onto the pavement, all the women neighbours made the sign of the cross. They went to the church amid scenes of much devotion. The five inmates of the house were there, dressed in dark clothes and looking most respectable, as was commented on that evening in Chartres. One of them even wept at the graveside. In a word, Monsieur Charles was completely satisfied from that point of view; but imagine how unhappy he was the following day, when he questioned his son-in-law Vaucogne and went round the house. It was already looking shabby and you could sense the lack of male authority from all sorts of abuses that he would never have tolerated in his day. All the same, he was pleased to see that the decent attitude of the five women in the funeral procession had been favourably noticed in the town and that the establishment did a roaring trade that whole week. When he left No. 19, full of anxious thoughts, he did not hide them from Hector: now that Estelle was no longer at the helm, it was up to him to mend his ways and get down to work if he did not want to squander his daughter's estate.

Buteau immediately invited them to come grape-picking the following day, but they refused, being in mourning. They all looked dismal and apathetic. However, they did agree to come along to try the new wine.

'It'll be something for Élodie to do,' said Madame Charles. 'There's so little to amuse her here, now that we've taken her away from school. But what can one do? She can't always be at her books.'

Élodie was listening with her eyes downcast and blushing, for no reason. She had grown very tall and pale, like a lily wilting in the shade.

'Well, what are you going to do with her now she's a grown-up girl?' asked Buteau.

She blushed even redder as her grandmother replied:

'Ah well, we don't really know... She'll have to think things over, we'll not try to force her.'

But Fouan had drawn Monsieur Charles on one side and asked interestedly:

'How's the business going?'

He shrugged his shoulders disconsolately:

'Pooh! I've seen someone from Chartres this very morning. That's why we're so fed up. It's the end. There's fighting in the corridors and they're not even paying, because there's no one keeping an eye open!'

He folded his arms and took a deep breath to recover from the shock of this new scandal, yet another grievance against his son-in-law which he had still not come to terms with since hearing of it that morning.

'And would you believe it? The scoundrel spends his time in cafés! In cafés, when he's got one on the spot.'

'Then it's all up,' said Jesus Christ emphatically, who had been listening.

They stopped talking because Madame Charles came up with Élodie and Buteau. They now started talking about the deceased woman and the girl said how sad she was at not having been able to take a final farewell from her dear mother. She added in her simple way:

'But apparently it all happened so suddenly and there was so much work at the confectioner's.'

'Yes, for christenings,' Madame Charles said hastily, winking at the others.

But no one smiled, they all nodded their heads sympathetically. And the girl, looking down at a ring she was wearing, kissed it with tears in her eyes.

'This is the only thing I have of hers. Grandma took it off her finger to put it on mine. She had worn it for twenty years and I shall wear it as long as I live.'

It was an old wedding-ring, a coarse example of the jeweller's art, so worn that the ornamental bands had been almost obliterated. You realized that the hand on which it had become so scratched had not shrunk from any kind of work, busily washing out chamber-pots and making beds, scrubbing, wiping, dusting, poking around in every corner. And the ring had so many tales to tell, its gold had rubbed up against so many secrets, that the men stared at it with flared nostrils, without a word.

'When you've worn it out as much as your mother,' said Monsieur Charles, in a voice suddenly choking with emotion, 'then you'll have earned your rest. If it could talk, it would teach you how you earn money by hard work and discipline.'

In tears, Élodie once more pressed her lips to the ring.

'You know,' Madame Charles went on, 'I want you to use tha' wedding-ring when we marry you.'

But when she heard that, in her highly emotional state, the very thought of marriage shocked her so much and filled her with such confusion that she flung herself distractedly upon her grandmother's chest to hide her face. The latter smiled and tried to calm her:

'Now, now, my little pet, don't be ashamed. You must get used to the idea, there's nothing wrong in it. I wouldn't say anything

336

nasty while you're there, you know that. Your cousin Buteau was asking a moment ago what we're going to do with you. Well, we'll start by finding you a nice husband. Come along now, don't keep rubbing against my shawl. You'll irritate your skin.'

Then, with a look of profound satisfaction, she whispered to the others:

'See how well brought up she is! She doesn't know anything about anything!'

'Ah, if we hadn't got our little angel,' said Monsieur Charles in conclusion, 'we should really have been so sad, because of what I was telling you. And I've had trouble with my roses and my carnations this year and I don't know what's happened to my aviary, all my birds are sick. My only consolation is fishing, I caught a three-pound trout yesterday. But I'm right, aren't I? People live in the country so as to be happy.'

They took their leave. The Charles again promised to come and taste the new wine. Fouan, Buteau and Jesus Christ walked on a few paces in silence and then the old man summed up their thoughts.

'He'll be a lucky man who gets her, with the house and all, won't he?'

The town crier of Rognes had played the roll on his drum for the grape-harvest to begin and on Monday morning everyone was astir, because each villager had his patch of vine and no family would ever have thought of not going along to harvest their grapes on the hillside above the Aigre. But the final excitement for the village was that, the night before, the parish priest, whom the town council had finally decided was a luxury they could afford, had arrived at the church after dark. It was so dark, indeed, that they had not been able to see him properly. So tongues were wagging, the more so as this was really a tasty topic.

After his final quarrel with Rognes, Father Godard had obstinately refused to set foot there again. He baptized, confessed and married anyone who was prepared to come to see him at Bazoches-le-Doyen; as for the dead, they would doubtless have become shrivelled-up corpses while waiting for him but this will never be known, since nobody took it into his head to die during this great schism. He had told his bishop that he preferred to be unfrocked rather than take the sacraments to such an abomination of desolation, where he was so ill received, a lot of lascivious drunkards and damned, one and all, since they no longer believed in the devil; and the bishop obviously supported him, because he made no move until this rebellious flock showed contrition. So Rognes was without a priest: no more Mass, nothing at all, like heathens. At first there had been some surprise; but on the whole they didn't really seem worse off than before. They grew used to it, there was no more rain or wind than there had been before and, what is more, there was a considerable saving on the local budget. So, as a priest was not indispensable and experience showed that it did no harm to the crops nor did it cause premature death, they might just as well do without one for good. Many people held this view, not only awkward customers like Lengaigne but even sensible men who were able to work things out, like Delhomme for example. However, there were also many people who were troubled at not having a priest. Not that they were more religious than the others; why worry about a God who was just a figure of fun whom nobody would take seriously! But not having a priest made it seem as if you were too poor or too mean to pay for one, in a word, you seemed the lowest of the low, of no account at all, people who wouldn't spend a penny except when they had to. Magnolles, which had only two hundred and eighty-three inhabitants, ten less than Rognes, supported a priest, a fact which they flaunted in front of their neighbours so provocatively that it would certainly have led to blows. And then there were the women who had certain habits. Not one of them would ever have agreed to be wedded or buried without a priest. Even the men sometimes went to church, on grand occasions, because everyone went. In a word, there always have been priests and, unless you really didn't give a damn, you had to have one.

Naturally, the town council had the matter on their agenda. Hourdequin the mayor who, although not a practising Catholic, supported religion as a principle of authority, committed the political blunder of being neutral, in the hope of mediating. It was a poor commune, why should they burden the budget, already pretty large for their size, with the extra expense of doing up the presbytery? It was at this moment that Macqueron, the deputy mayor, hitherto a priest-hater, became the leader of the malcontents who felt humiliated at not having a priest of their own.

338

Macqueron must by this time have conceived the idea of ousting the mayor and taking his place, and moreover people were saying that he had become the agent of Monsieur Rochefontaine, the factory-owner from Châteaudun who was once again going to stand against Monsieur de Chédeville at the forthcoming elections. And Hourdequin was tired, he had many problems on his farm and was taking little interest in the council meetings, leaving more and more to his deputy; so that the latter was able to carry the town council with him and they voted the requisite sum to make the commune into a parish. Ever since, at the time when the new road was being built, he had insisted on being paid for the expropriation of his land, although he had promised to hand it over for nothing, the councillors, although calling him a swindler, had started showing him great consideration. Only Lengaigne protested at this decision which would deliver the village into the hands of the Jesuits. Bécu grumbled too, now that he had to leave the presbytery and its garden and move into a hovel. It took a month for replastering, replacing the glass and mending the slate roof, and so at last, the night before, the priest had been able to settle in at the tiny, newly distempered presbytery.

By dawn, wagons were on their way to the hill, each carrying four or five big casks with the top knocked in, all sluice-gates open, as they said. Women and girls were sitting inside, with their baskets, while the men walked beside, whipping up their horses. There was a whole line of them and everyone was laughing and shouting and chatting together, from one cart to the next.

Lengaigne's happened by chance to be following the Macquerons', so that Flore and Coelina, who had not been on speaking terms for the last six months, now made up their quarrel. Flore had Bécu's wife with her and her neighbour had her daughter Berthe. The conversation at once came round to the new priest. In the cool morning air they bandied their remarks to and fro to the steady clip-clop of the horses' hooves.

'I saw him helping to get his luggage down.'

'Oh, what's he like?'

'Well, it was dark. He seemed to me very long and thin, a bit dismal and not very strong. About thirty, I suppose. He looked very gentle.'

'And from what they say, he's been in Auvergne, in the

mountains, where you're snowed under for two-thirds of the year.'

'Good Lord! Well, he's going to like it here, I should think.'

'Certainly he will! And do you know, he's called Madeleine.'

'No, it's Madeline.'

'Well, Madeleine or Madeline, it's not a man's name, at any rate.'

'Perhaps he'll come and look in on us while we're grape-picking. Macqueron promised to bring him along.'

'Goodness me! We must look out for him.'

The carts stopped at the bottom of the slope, on the road that followed the Aigre. And in each little vineyard, the women were busy between the rows of stakes, walking along bent double, with their bottoms sticking up in the air, cutting off the bunches with their bill-hooks and putting them in baskets. As for the men, they had enough to do emptying the baskets into their panniers and taking them down to unload them into the open casks. As soon as all the casks in a cart were full, they were taken away to be tipped into the vats and then brought back to repeat the operation.

That morning, there was such a heavy dew that the women's dresses became soaked at once. Fortunately the weather was superb and the sun dried them out. There had been no rain for the last three weeks and the grapes, which they had given up for lost because of the wet summer, had suddenly ripened and become sweet; and this was why the superb sunshine, very warm for the time of year, was making everyone cheerful as they shouted and grinned, cracking broad jokes which made the girls shriek with laughter.

'That Coelina!' exclaimed Flore to Bécu's wife, straightening up and looking at Macqueron's wife, in the neighbouring vineyard. 'She was so proud of her Berthe because of her ladylike complexion! And now she's going all sallow and dreadfully dried up.'

'Well, that's it,' said Bécu's wife. That's what happens when girls don't get married off! They're very silly not to let her marry the wheelwright's son. And what's more, from what they say, she's ruining herself with her bad habits!'

She bent down and started cutting the bunches again. Then, waggling her behind:

'That doesn't prevent the schoolmaster from sniffing around still.'

'Good God!' exclaimed Flore. 'That Lequeu would pick up pennies from a cow-pat with his nose. And here he is, coming to help them, the cunning little so-and-so!'

They stopped talking, for Victor, who had just returned from military service a fortnight ago, was emptying their baskets into Delphin's pannier; the latter had been hired by the old snake-in-the-grass Lengaigne for the duration of the grape harvest on the pretext that he was needed in the shop. And Delphin, who was attached to the soil like a young oak tree and had never left Rognes, was open-mouthed in amazement at the sight of Victor, jaunty and cynical and delighted at making such an impression on him. He had changed so much, with his moustaches and little goatee beard, his forage cap that he was still fond of wearing and his mocking manner, that nobody recognized him. But if the young fellow thought that Delphin envied him, he was much mistaken. Despite all Victor's tales of his garrison exploits, his fabricated accounts of wine, women and song, the peasant would shake his head, aghast in his heart of hearts, and not tempted in the least. Oh no, you'd lose so much if you had to leave your little niche! He had already twice refused a proposal from Nénesse to come and get rich in a restaurant in Chartres.

'But, you old cripple, how about when you're called up?'

'Called up? I'm going to draw the right number!'

And Victor could get nothing more out of him, despite such scornful remarks as: 'You coward, when you're built like a bridge!' And as he talked, he continued to empty the baskets into his friend's pannier without the latter's showing any sign of strain. And then, jokingly, he pointed to Berthe and added, with a knowing look:

'Well, has she got any since I've been away?'

Delphin gave a guffaw because this phenomenon of the Macquerons' daughter was still the man source of amusement with the young men of the village.

'Ah, I haven't had a peep. Perhaps it grew in the spring.'

'Well, I shan't be watering it,' concluded Victor, pulling a face. 'You might as well get yourself a frog. And anyway, it can't be very healthy, you must catch cold there, unless you wear a wig.'

At that, Delphin was so amused that the pannier nearly slipped off his back and as he went down and tipped it into the cask you could still hear him choking with laughter.

In the Macquerons' vineyard, Berthe was still acting the young lady, using little scissors instead of a bill-hook, frightened of thorns and wasps and quite disconsolate because her fine shoes were soaked in dew and wouldn't dry. And she was reluctantly accepting the attentions of Lequeu, whom she loathed, because she was flattered at being courted by the only man of education in the village. Finally he took out his handkerchief to wipe her shoes. But their attention was drawn to an unexpected apparition:

'Heavens above!' exclaimed Berthe, under her breath. 'What a dress! Someone told me she had come home yesterday at the same time as the priest.'

It was the Lengaignes' daughter, Suzanne, who had suddenly decided to show her face in her village after spending three riotous years in Paris. Having arrived the day before, she had slept late, letting her mother and brother go off to pick grapes and promising herself to join them later so as to sweep in amongst all the villagers at work and overwhelm them with the splendour of her Parisian toilette. And in fact, she did cause an extraordinary sensation, for she had put on a blue silk dress so deep in colour that the sky looked positively pale. In the transparent air she stood out in the strong sunlight amidst the greeny-yellow vine leaves and looked gorgeously opulent and triumphant. She at once started to talk and laugh very loudly, nibbling at bunches of grapes which she held up and lowered into her mouth, joking with Delphin and her brother Victor, who seemed very proud of her, amazing Bécu's wife and her mother who stood there, moist-eyed, with their arms hanging limp with admiration. Moreover, this admiration was shared by the grape-pickers from all the adjacent vineyards: work had stopped and everyone was watching her, barely recognizing her now that she had filled out and become so much prettier. She had been rather plain and was now a very attractive wench, doubtless because of the way she had framed her face in little blond curls. And their scrutiny turned to admiration and respect when they saw her in her expensive get-up, looking so plump, cheerful and prosperous.

Coelina was standing tight-lipped, green with envy, between Berthe and Lequeu, and she could not refrain from commenting:

'Isn't she posh! Flore goes about telling everybody that her daughter's got servants and carriages in Paris. It's probably quite true because you need a lot of money to deck yourself out like that.'

'Well,' said Lequeu, trying to be agreeable, 'we all know how that sort of woman earns her money.'

'What does it matter how they earn it?' replied Coelina bitterly. 'They've still got it.'

But at that moment Suzanne caught sight of Berthe and, remembering her as one of the Daughters of Mary like herself, went up to speak to her in a very friendly way:

'Good morning. I hope you're well?'

And looking at her closely and seeing her unhealthy complexion, she preened herself, all peaches and cream, and said again, with a laugh:

'I do hope you're well.'

'Yes, thanks, very well,' Berthe replied, embarrassed and outmatched.

That day, victory belonged to the Lengaignes; for the Macquerons it was humiliating defeat. Beside herself, Coelina was comparing her skinny, sallow daughter, already wrinkled, with the fresh, pink, good-looking daughter of her neighbours. Was that fair? A lewd woman who went to bed with men night and day and never did a stroke! And a proper young girl who slept by herself and looked as worn out as if she'd had three pregnancies! No, there was no point in being a good girl, it just wasn't worth staying at home and living a decent life with your parents!

In fact, Suzanne was fêted by all the grape-pickers. She went over to hug children whom she had known as babies; she thrilled old men by recalling memories of their past. Once you've made your pile, you can do what you like, you're independent of everybody. And it proved she still had a good heart, not to look down on her family and come back and see her friends now she was rich.

At eleven, everybody sat down and ate bread and cheese. It wasn't that people were hungry, because they'd been stuffing

343

grapes ever since dawn and their gullets were coated in sugar and their paunches as swollen and round as barrels; and the grapes churning round inside were as good as a purge; even now, every minute a girl had to slip off behind a hedge. Of course, this caused great amusement, the men stood up and sent them on their way with shouts of 'Oh! Oh! Oh!' In a word everyone was cheerful and friendly; it was good, honest, healthy fun.

And just as they were finishing the bread and cheese, Macqueron appeared on the road below with Father Madeline. Suzanne was immediately forgotten and all eyes turned towards the priest. To be honest, the first impression was not very favourable: he was a real beanpole of a man and as dismal as an undertaker. All the same, he stopped to pay his compliments at every vineyard, with a friendly word for everyone, and in the end it was agreed that he was very polite and gentle, not a forceful man, in fact. They'd be able to get round him, at least, not like that awkward customer Father Godard. People began to snigger a little behind his back. He had reached the top of the slope and was standing looking at the immense flat grey expanse of Beauce with a feeling almost of fear and a desperate melancholy which filled his eyes with tears, large, clear eyes of a man bred in mountains and used to the narrow horizons and gorges of Auvergne.

Buteau's vineyard happened to be near by. Lise and Françoise were cutting the bunches and Jesus Christ, who had not failed to bring his father along with him, was already drunk with the grapes he had been stuffing while pretending to see to the emptying of the baskets into the panniers. They were fermenting so strongly inside him and blowing him up with so much gas that wind was coming out of every hole. And stimulated by the presence of a priest, he forgot himself.

'You oaf!' shouted Buteau. 'Can't you wait till the priest has gone?'

But Jesus Christ refused to be rebuked. He replied like someone who knows his manners, when required:

'It wasn't meant for him, it was to please me.'

Old Fouan had taken a seat on the ground, as he used to say; he was tired and happy because of the good weather and fine harvest. He was grinning to himself because La Grande, who had the neighbouring vineyard, had just come over to greet him; she, too, had started showing him consideration again, ever since she knew he had private means. Then she suddenly hurried away as she saw her grandson Hilarion greedily taking advantage of her absence to cram himself with grapes, and went after him with her stick: like a pig at its trough, wasting more than he was picking!

'There's a woman who's going to give a lot of pleasure when she pegs out,' Buteau said, sitting down beside his father for a second, to be agreeable. 'What a way to treat an innocent young fellow like him, because he's as strong as an ox and just as stupid.'

Then he went on to attack the Delhommes, who were working lower down, beside the road. They had the finest vineyard in the district, nearly five acres in one piece, and there were a good ten people working on it. Their vines were so well cultivated that the bunches were larger than those in any of their neighbours' fields, and they were so proud of them that they seemed to be keeping apart from the other grape-pickers, not even amused by the sudden gripes that were sending the girls scuttling away under the hedge. It would have been too exhausting to climb up and greet their father, no doubt, because they didn't seem to know he was there. That silly ass Delhomme, a real booby, so keen on good work and fair play, and that shrew Fanny, always making a fuss over the tiniest little fart, and expecting people to look up to her like a saint without ever recognizing the dirty tricks she was playing on other people.

'The truth is, Father,' Buteau went on, 'that I'm fond of you whereas my brother and sister aren't. You know I still can't get over the fact that we parted over such footling things.'

And he put the blame onto Françoise, whose head had been turned by Jean. But she had calmed down now. If she started up again, he was going to cool her off in the duck-pond.

'Look, Father, just think it over. Why not come back to us?'

Fouan prudently said nothing. He had been expecting this offer which his younger son was at last making, and he was anxious not to say either yes or no, because you could never tell. Then Buteau went on, after making sure that his brother was at the other end of the vineyard:

'Aren't I right? You don't really belong in that place with

345

that blackguard Jesus Christ. One of these fine mornings, you'll probably find yourself getting your throat cut. And look, I'll give you your board and lodging and I'll still pay your pension !'

The old man blinked in amazement. But as he still said nothing, his son increased the stakes :

'And little luxuries, coffee, a drop of spirits, two penn'orth of tobacco, any little extra you want !'

This was too much of a good thing. Fouan was scared. True, things were not going too well at Jesus Christ's. But suppose the same fuss started again at the Buteaus'?

He merely said : 'We'll have to see,' and stood up to put an end to the conversation.

They went on picking until nightfall. The carts kept continually taking away the full casks and bringing them back empty. In the vineyards, now bathed in the golden sunset, the baskets and panniers sped to and fro under the vast rose-pink sky, amidst the growing intoxication of shifting so much grape. And Berthe was taken short and did not even have time to disappear : her mother and Lequeu had to stand in front to hide her while she evacuated among the vine stakes. She was seen from the next vineyard and Victor and Delphin offered to take her some paper; but Flore and Bécu's wife refused to let them because there are certain limits beyond which decent folk don't go. Finally, everyone went home. The Delhommes led the way, La Grande made Hilarion pull her cart alongside the horse, the Lengaignes and the Macquerons were fraternizing, forgetting their rivalry in the maudlin state of the semi-inebriated.

The exchange of compliments between Father Madeline and Suzanne had been particularly noticed : seeing her better dressed, he no doubt took her for a lady, so that they walked along side by side, he very attentive, she behaving as though butter wouldn't melt in her mouth and asking him what time Mass would be on Sunday. Behind them came Jesus Christ who, priest-hater that he was, started getting up to his disgusting antics again, with drunken ribaldry. Every five steps he would lift his leg and let off. Suzanne, the hussy, had to bite her lips to prevent herself from laughing, while the priest pretended not to hear; and so they solemnly continued to exchange pious remarks to this musical accompaniment as they brought up the rear of the cavalcade of grape-pickers.

As they finally reached Rognes, Buteau and Fouan, feeling ashamed of Jesus Christ, tried to make him keep quiet. But he still kept going, insisting that the priest would be very wrong to take offence.

'For Christ's sake, I keep on telling you, it's not meant for anyone else, it's just for me!'

The following week, there was Buteau's invitation to taste his new wine. The Charles, Fouan, Jesus Christ and four or five other people were to come at seven o'clock to eat a leg of mutton, nuts and cheese, a proper meal. During the day, Buteau had put his wine in cask, six barrels which he had filled from the tap of the vat. But some neighbours were not so far advanced: one of them, still picking his grapes, had been treading them since morning, stark-naked; another one, armed with a stick, was watching the fermentation and pushing the head down into the seething must; a third, who had a press, was squeezing the skins and stalks and depositing them in a steaming pile in his yard. And it was the same in every house, reeking vats, streaming presses, casks over-flowing and all over Rognes the fumes of wine filled every corner and the smell alone was enough to make you drunk.

That day, just as he was leaving the Castle, Fouan had a pre-monition and took his bonds out of the saucepan of lentils. He might just as well secrete them about his person because he thought he had seen Jesus Christ and La Trouille gazing upwards into the air with a funny look in their eyes. All three set off early and arrived at the Buteaus' at the same time as the Charles.

It was a full moon, so large and clear that it was almost as bright as day, and as he went into the yard, Fouan noticed Gideon the donkey with his nose stuck into a little tub. He was not surprised to see him wandering loose because the crafty animal could easily open latches with his mouth; but he was intrigued by the tub, so he went over and recognized it as being from the cellar where it had been left full of wine from the press while the casks were being filled. And that damned donkey was emptying it!

'Buteau, come here! Your donkey's up to something!'

Buteau appeared in the kitchen doorway.

'What is it?'

'He's drunk the lot!'

Amidst all the hubbub, Gideon was calmly going on draining the last drop. He had probably been drinking away like this for the last quarter of an hour, because the little tub held a good twenty litres. He had drunk the lot and his belly was as round as a goatskin and tight as a drum, and when he raised his head, wine poured out of his nose, a drunkard's nose, for a red streak under the eyes showed how far he had stuck his nose in.

'Ah, the thief!' yelled Buteau, rushing up. 'He's up to his tricks again. He's worse than a waggonload of monkeys.'

When he was being rebuked for his bad habits, Gideon usually stuck his ears out at an angle and showed complete indifference. This time, dazed and losing all respect, he positively leered and waggled his rump to express unrepentant pleasure at his debauchery; and when his master gave him a push, he stumbled and Fouan had to prop him up with his shoulder to prevent him from falling.

'But the blasted animal's blind drunk!'

'Real sozzled, you might say,' said Jesus Christ, gazing at him with an admiringly fraternal eye. 'A whole tub at one go, what a thirst!'

Buteau, however, was not particularly amused and neither were Lise and Françoise, who, hearing the noise, came hurrying up. First of all, there was the loss of the wine, and worse than the loss was the embarrassment caused by such bad behaviour on the part of their donkey in front of the Charles, who were pursing their lips in disapproval, because of Élodie. And the final discomfiture was that Suzanne and Berthe happened to be walking past and met Father Madeline; and all three stood waiting to see what would happen. A real nuisance, it was, with all these grand folk watching with their eyes popping out!

'Give him a push, Father,' whispered Buteau. 'Let's get him into the stable quickly.'

Fouan pushed; but Gideon was happy to stay where he was and he refused to budge, albeit with cheerful good humour, like a good-natured drunk, with a twinkle in his bleary eye and drooling as he curled up his lip. He stayed put, bracing himself on his wobbly legs and straightening up at each push, as though enjoying the joke. But when Buteau started pushing as well, it did not take long for him to tip over sideways, with his hooves in the air; and then he rolled over onto his back and started braying loudly as if to show his complete contempt for all the spectators.

'Ah, you dirty beast, you idle good-for-nothing, I'll teach you to drink yourself sick,' yelled Buteau, laying into him with his heels.

Jesus Christ compassionately intervened.

'Come along. You can't expect him to be reasonable when he's drunk. Of course he doesn't understand, you'd do better to try and get him back into his stable.'

The Charles had moved away, completely shocked by such a crazy, ill-behaved animal; while Élodie had gone very red and was averting her eyes as if she were witnessing some indecent spectacle. At the entrance to the yard, the priest, Suzanne and Berthe were showing disapproval by their attitude. Some neighbours appeared and started making loud jocular comments. Lise and Françoise were ready to weep with shame.

Meanwhile, hiding his rage, Buteau was attempting to lift Gideon back onto his feet, aided by Fouan and Jesus Christ. It was no easy task, because with all the contents of the tub swilling around inside him, the fellow was a tidy weight, and no sooner had they got him onto his four feet and even succeeded in persuading him to move two or three yards forward then he suddenly buckled at the back and fell over again. And they would have to take him right across the yard to reach the stable. They would never manage it. What was to be done?

'Bloody hell! Bloody hell!' the three men kept swearing as they looked at the donkey from all angles, at a loss how to set about it.

Jesus Christ suggested leaning him up against the shed and from there working round the wall of the house up to the stable. At first it succeeded, although the donkey was scratching himself against the plaster. Unfortunately, this scratching must probably have become too painful, for suddenly shaking himself free from the hands which were holding him against the wall, he kicked up his heels and started prancing about.

Fouan nearly fell flat on his face and the two brothers were shouting:

'Hold him! Hold him!'

Then, in the bright moonlight, Gideon was seen lashing out, bucking wildly all round the yard with his long ears flopping madly. His belly had been too much shaken up and he was feeling sick. He suddenly halted and retched, with his head reeling. He tried to gallop off again but his legs failed him and he stood motionless with his neck stuck out, his ribs shaking with dreadful convulsions. And then, reeling like a drunkard relieving himself and jerking his head forward with every effort, he vomited like a man.

The villagers gathered in the gateway were roaring with laughter while the squeamish Father Madeline, standing between Suzanne and Berthe, went pale and they led him away, full of indignation. But it was particularly the offended attitude of the Charles which showed how such an exhibition by a donkey was contrary to decent behaviour and even to the ordinary civility owed to any passer-by. Weeping heartbroken tears, Élodie had flung herself round her grandmother's neck, asking if the donkey was going to die. And despite Monsieur Charles's imperious injunctions to stop, delivered in the magisterial tones which had always been obeyed in the past in No. 19, the donkey went on and on, flooding the whole yard in a lake of red vomit, which flowed away into the pond. And then he slipped and fell sprawling into it, his legs spread out; and no drunk lying flat out in a street could have looked more disgusting. The wretched beast seemed to be doing it deliberately to bring disgrace on his masters. It was too much, Lise and Françoise ran off, hiding their eyes, and took shelter in the house.

'That's enough! Cart him away!'

And indeed, there was nothing else to be done because Gideon, now drowsy and as limp as a wet rag, was going to sleep. Buteau hastily fetched a litter and half a dozen men helped him to lift the donkey onto it. And they took him away, with his legs dangling, snoring so heartily already that he still seemed to be braying and showing his low opinion of mankind.

This incident naturally spoilt the meal at first; but soon everyone had recovered and in the end the new wine was celebrated so heartily that by eleven o'clock everybody was like the donkey. Every minute someone had to go out into the yard to relieve himself.

Old Fouan was very merry. Perhaps he might do well to go back to his younger son after all, because the wine would be good, that year. He had had to go out like the others and he was turning all this over in his head, in the dark, when he heard Lise and Buteau, who had gone out behind him, crouching down side by side under the hedge squabbling because the husband was blaming his wife for not showing enough affection towards his father. She was a stupid little goose! They'd got to butter the old man up so that he'd come back and then they could wheedle his nest-egg out of him. Suddenly stone-cold sober, Fouan felt to make sure that no one had stolen his bonds from his pocket; and when they had all kissed and said goodnight, and he was back at the Castle, he was determined not to move out from there. But that very night, he saw a sight which made his blood run cold: La Trouille prowling round his bedroom in her shift, going through his trousers and smock and even looking in his shoes. Jesus Christ had evidently noticed that the nest-egg had disappeared from the saucepan of lentils and had sent his daughter in search of it, so that they could wheedle it out of him, to use Buteau's expression.

What he had seen went churning round in Fouan's head and gave him no rest. He got up and opened the window. Rognes was bathed in white moonlight and from the village the smell of wine was rising up, mingling with it the smell of those other things they had been gingerly stepping over along the walls for the last week, the whole powerful odour of the grape harvest. What was he to do? Where should he go? Now, he was determined never to let his miserable money out of his sight for a second, he'd sew it into his very skin! And then, as the breeze blew the smell into his face, his mind turned to Gideon; tough beasts, those donkeys; they could take ten times as much pleasure as any man and still not be any the worse for it. Never mind, if he was going to be robbed by his elder son and by the younger one, he hadn't any choice. The best thing to do was to stay on at the Castle, keep his eyes skinned and wait and see! His old frame was trembling at the thought.

Chapter 5

MONTHS went by, winter came and went, followed by spring, and life in Rognes continued much as before; it needed years for anything to seem to happen, in this dreary life of never-ending toil. In July, in the sweltering heat of the doldrums, the coming elections did however cause a great stir in the village. This time, beneath the surface, there were important issues at stake. People were discussing them and waiting for the candidates to make their electioneering visits.

And it so happened that on the Sunday for which the visit of Monsieur Rochefontaine, the factory-owner from Châteaudun, had been announced, a terrible row took place at the Buteaus between Lise and Françoise. The result showed that, even when things do not seem to be changing, they none the less are, for the last link between the two sisters, always near breaking-point yet continually repaired, had worn so thin in their daily squabbles that this time it broke once and for all, with no chance of repair, and for the most trivial of causes.

That morning, when Françoise was bringing her cows home, she had stopped to chat for a moment with Jean in front of the church. It must be admitted that she was being deliberately provocative in doing so, right in front of the house, intending to exasperate the Buteaus. So when she reached home, Lise shouted at her:

'Look, when you meet your men, you might choose somewhere else than under our window!'

Buteau was listening, sharpening a bill-hook.

'My men indeed! I see too much of them here,' retorted Françoise. 'And there's one of them that, if I'd wanted, I wouldn't be seeing under our window but in your bed, the dirty beast!'

This reference to Buteau put Lise beside herself with rage. She had long had only one thought in mind, throwing her sister out so as to have a quiet life at home, even if it meant splitting up her property. This was why she put up with Buteau's thrashings, for he thought differently and was determined to pursue his schemes to the bitter end, still nursing hopes of going to bed with his young sister-in-law, as long as they both had the wherewithal to do it. Lise was irritated at not being mistress in her own house and tortured by a strange kind of jealousy, so that, while quite ready to let her husband tumble her younger sister and to settle the question once and for all, she was furious at seeing him rutting after the little bitch, whom she had come to loathe because of her youth, her hard little breasts and her white skin, which you could see when she rolled up her sleeves. And, although willing to give him free rein, she would have liked him to destroy all this youth and beauty, and even have helped him to do so, not because she had qualms about sharing him but because she suffered from the growing rivalry between her sister and herself and it was making her life miserable to see that Françoise was better looking and would give him greater pleasure.

'You slut!' she screamed. 'It's you who's leading him on! If you weren't always hanging around him, he wouldn't keep sniffing round your dirty bum, which you're too young to wipe properly anyway.'

Disgusted by this lying insinuation, Françoise went very pale. With cold fury she replied calmly:

'Good, that's all I wanted to hear. Only a fortnight longer, and I'll not be troubling you any more, if that's what you want. In a fortnight's time I'm twenty-one, and I'll be off like a shot.'

'Oh, so you're keen to come of age, are you, you've worked it all out so as to cause us trouble! Well, you little bitch, you're not going to leave in a fortnight's time, you're going to leave now, straight away. Fuck off!'

'Well, I must say. . . Macqueron needs someone, he'll be glad of me. Goodbye!'

And Françoise left as simply as that, nothing else took place between them. Buteau dropped the bill-hook he was sharpening and rushed over to restore peace between them again, with a couple of clouts as usual. But he was too late; the only thing he succeeded in doing was punching his wife's nose, which started bleeding. Damned women! Just what he'd been so afraid of and trying to prevent for so long! The girl clearing out and starting a lot of real trouble. And he could see everything slipping out of his grasp and getting away, the girl as well as the land.

'I'll go along to the Macquerons later on,' he shouted. 'She's got to come back, even if I have to bring her back with my boot up her arse!'

That Sunday, the Macquerons were in a turmoil because they were expecting one of the candidates, Monsieur Rochefontaine, the owner of the workshops at Châteaudum. During the last parliament, Monsieur de Chédeville had caused dissatisfaction, some said because he had too openly sympathized with the Orléanist faction, others because he had scandalized the imperial court by his affair with the young wife of one of the parliamentary ushers, who had become infatuated with him despite his age. Whatever the reason, the *préfet* had withdrawn his support and transferred it to the former opposition candidate, Monsieur Rochefontaine, whose factory had recently been visited by a minister and who had written a pamphlet on free trade which had attracted the favourable notice of the Emperor. Irritated at being left in the lurch, Monsieur de Chédeville had decided to stand, for he needed his post of deputy to further certain business transactions, being no longer able to manage on the rents he drew from La Chamade, which was mortgaged and in a bad way. Thus, by a strange quirk of fate, the situation had been reversed, with the large landowner now standing as the unofficial candidate.

Although he was mayor, Hourdequin had remained faithful to Monsieur de Chédeville; he was determined to ignore any official instructions and ready to fight to the bitter end if forced. In the first place, he thought it the decent thing not to turn like a weathercock at the slightest breeze from the *préfet*; and furthermore, as between the protectionist and the free trader, he had finally come to think that, in the catastrophic agricultural crisis, his interests were best served by the former. For some time now, the worries caused by Jacqueline and the problems of his farm had been preventing him from devoting proper attention to his duties as mayor, so that his deputy Macqueron had been left to look after the routine matters on the council. He was therefore surprised, when his interest in the election prompted him to play a more active part as chairman of the town council, to find them resentful and hostile.

It was Macqueron's doing: his crafty and underhand machinations were at last bearing fruit. This slovenly, grubby peasant, who had become rich and idle and was now bored stiff by his useless, idle existence, had gradually hit upon one final ambition to occupy his leisure : to become mayor. So he had undermined Hourdequin by exploiting the perennial hatred, innate in all the inhabitants of Rognes, against the former lords of the manor and against the sons of rich townsfolk who now owned their land. He'd got that land for nothing, that's for sure ! Nothing but daylight robbery at the time of the Revolution ! There was no danger that some poor wretch might be able to pick up a bargain, scum like that always came along when they were tired of making their pile in other ways ! Quite apart from the fact that there were some pretty nasty things taking place up at La Borderie. There was that disgusting Cognet girl; and her master positively enjoyed picking her out of the dirty straw where she'd been sleeping with all his farm-hands ! All this aroused feeling and in the crudest possible terms went the rounds of the whole district, exciting the indignation even of people who would have tumbled their own daughter or sold her, had it been worth the trouble. So that the municipal councillors had reached the stage of saying that rich bourgeois ought to stay at home and swindle and fornicate amongst themselves; but for a farming village, you needed a peasant as mayor. It was, in fact, on the subject of the elections that Hourdequin first met the resistance which took him by surprise. When he mentioned Monsieur de Chédeville, he saw stony faces all around him. When Macqueron had seen that Hourdequin was continuing to support the candidate who had lost favour, he had said to himself that here was the right place to do battle and an excellent opportunity to do Hourdequin down. He therefore supported the *préfet*'s choice, Monsieur Rochefontaine, loudly proclaiming that all men of goodwill should support the government. This statement alone sufficed, without any need to indoctrinate the council members, because fearful of being swept out of office they were always for the winning side and determined to support the powers that be to ensure that nothing should ever change and wheat should continue to fetch a good price. The decent, fair-minded Delhomme, who was of this opinion, carried Clou and the others with him : and Hourdequin's position was finally compromised by the fact that his only supporter was Lengaigne, who was exasperated by Macqueron's growing importance. Slanderous accusations were made; Hourdequin was a 'Red', one of that riff-raff who wanted a republic and to do away with the peasantry; so that even Father Madeline became alarmed and, imagining that the deputy had been the moving spirit in establishing his parish, he too supported Monsieur Rochefontaine, despite the fact that the bishop secretly favoured Monsieur de Chédeville. But there was one final blow for the mayor: there was a rumour that at the time of opening up the famous direct route between Rognes and Châteaudun, he had pocketed half the subsidy. How had he done it? No one elucidated that point, it was just a mysterious and odious business. When asked about it, Macqueron put on a scared look, both pained and discreet, like a man who thinks that it is improper to talk about certain things: in fact, he had simply made it up. In a word, the commune was in a turmoil and the municipal council split in two, with the deputy and all the councillors except Lengaigne on one side and the mayor on the other. Only then did he realize the gravity of the situation.

A fortnight earlier Macqueron had already made a special trip to Châteaudun and grovelled to Monsieur Rochefontaine. He had begged him not to call on anyone else but himself should he condescend to come to Rognes. And this was why on this Sunday the innkeeper kept constantly coming out into the street after lunch on the look-out for his candidate. He had warned Delhomme, Clou and certain other municipal councillors who were possessing their souls in patience, over a bottle of wine. Old Fouan and Bécu were also there, playing cards, as well as Lequeu, busily occupied in reading a paper he had brought along, for he made a point of never being seen to drink. But there were two customers who gave the deputy mayor cause for concern, Jesus Christ and his rolling stone of a crony, the worker Canon, sitting opposite each other and hilariously imbibing a bottle of spirits. He kept casting furtive glances at them and trying to throw them out, unsuccessfully because, contrary to their normal habits, they were not being rowdy: they merely seemed not to be giving a damn for anyone. It struck three and still Monsieur Rochefontaine had not arrived although he had promised to be there at two o'clock.

'Coelina,' Macqueron called anxiously to his wife, 'have you brought up the claret to offer a drink later on?'

Coelina, who was serving, made an anguished gesture; she had forgotten and her husband hurriedly made his way down to the cellar himself. In the room next door, the door of which was always open, was the haberdashery, and Berthe, looking like a fashionable shop-assistant, was showing three peasant women some pink ribbon; whilst Françoise, already at work, was dusting out shelf-compartments, although it was Sunday. Puffed up with self-importance, the deputy had immediately taken her on, flattered by her putting herself under his protection. His wife was, in fact, looking for an assistant. He would offer her board and lodging until he succeeded in reconciling her with the Buteaus, though she was threatening to kill herself if she was forced to go back there.

Suddenly a landau drawn by two superb percherons drew up in front of the door. Out of it climbed Monsieur de Rochefontaine, who was alone; he was both surprised and offended to see no one there. He was debating whether to go into the inn when Macqueron came up from the cellar with a bottle in each hand. Filled with great confusion and despair, not knowing how to get rid of the bottles, he stammered:

'Oh, Monsieur Rochefontaine, what bad luck! I've been waiting here doing nothing since two o'clock; and the minute I go down to the cellar, yes, with you in mind, Monsieur Rochefontaine... May I offer you a glass of wine, your Honour?'

Monsieur Rochefontaine, who was not yet an honourable member, but merely a parliamentary candidate, should have taken pity on the poor man's bewilderment but it seemed merely to make him more annoyed. He was a tall young man, in his late thirties, with close-cropped hair and a neatly trimmed beard, correctly and soberly dressed. He had a cold, brusque manner and a clipped autocratic way of speaking; every inch a man used to command and expect obedience from his twelve hundred employees. He seemed, indeed, determined to stand no more nonsense from these peasants.

Coelina and Berthe now hurried up, the latter with her bright, bold eyes and her tired lids.

'Please come in, Monsieur, do us the honour.'

357

But one penetrating glance had sufficed for Monsieur Rochefontaine to see through her, size her up and judge her. However, he did go in but refused to sit down.

'Here are our friends from the council,' Macqueron went on, now recovering his composure. 'They're very pleased to make your acquaintance, aren't you, gentlemen? Very pleased!'

Delhomme, Clou and the others had risen to their feet, startled at Monsieur Rochefontaine's stiff demeanour. And they listened in complete silence to the things he had decided to say to them, his theories which were shared by the Emperor, above all his progressive ideas which had led official opinion to favour him and reject the views of the outgoing candidate. Then he promised them roads, railways, canals, yes, a canal across Beauce to irrigate this thirsty land which had been parched for centuries. The peasants were listening in a daze, open-mouthed. What was he saying? Water for their fields, now? He went on and concluded by threatening those who voted the wrong way with official sanctions and inclement weather. They all looked at each other. Here was someone who was going to shake them up and whom it would be better to be on good terms with.

'Certainly, certainly,' Macqueron kept saying at the end of every sentence, although rather uneasy at his brusqueness of manner.

But Bécu was wagging his chin approvingly at this no-nonsense military approach and old Fouan was staring wide-eyed, seeming to say : 'There's a man for you.' Even Lequeu, normally so lethargic, had gone very red in the face, although it was difficult to say whether it was with pleasure or rage. Only the two rapscallions, Jesus Christ and his pal Canon, showed obvious contempt, although feeling so superior they merely sneered and shrugged their shoulders.

As soon as he had finished speaking, Monsieur Rochefontaine made for the door. The deputy mayor uttered a disconsolate cry :

'Oh, Monsieur Rochefontaine, surely you'll do us the honour of joining us in a glass of wine?'

'No, thanks, I'm late as it is. I'm expected at Magnelles, Bazoches, a score of other places. Good afternoon to you !'

At this Berthe did not even come to the door with him; and back in her haberdashery, she said to Françoise:

'What a boor! I'd vote for the other one, the old man.'

Monsieur Rochefontaine had just climbed back into his landau when he heard the crack of a whip. Looking round, he saw Hourdequin in his modest gig, driven by Jean. The farmer had heard of the factory-owner's visit purely by chance, one of his drivers having met the landau on the road; and he had hurried along to see the danger face to face, all the more uneasy because, for the last week, he had been unsuccessfully urging Monsieur de Chédeville to make an appearance, the deputy being at the time no doubt tangled up in some woman's skirts, perhaps even with the pretty wife of the parliamentary usher.

'Well, well, it's you,' he called cheerfully to Monsieur Rochefontaine. 'I didn't know you'd started electioneering already.'

The two carriages were wheel to wheel. Neither of the men got out and they chatted for a few minutes, after leaning over to shake hands. They were acquainted, for they had occasionally lunched together at the home of the mayor of Châteaudun.

'So you're against me?' asked Monsieur Rochefontaine suddenly, in his brusque way.

Being the mayor, Hourdequin was hoping not to have to commit himself too openly and was momentarily taken aback to see how well this fellow was informed. But he was no weakling either and he replied with a laugh, trying to pass the matter off amicably:

'I'm not against anybody, I'm for myself. The man for me is the one who'll protect me. When I think that wheat is down to sixteen francs, which is exactly what it costs me to produce! One might just as well down tools and kick the bucket!'

The other man immediately flared up:

'Oh yes, I know, you want protection, don't you? A surcharge, prohibitive duties on foreign wheat so that French wheat producers can double their prices! So Frenchmen will be famished, the quartern loaf will cost two francs and the poor will starve! How can a progressive like yourself have the nerve to want to go back to such a monstrous state of affairs!'

'A progressive, a progressive,' replied Hourdequin, still in the same bantering tone. 'Well, I suppose I am, but it's costing me so much that I shall soon not be able to afford such a luxury. Machines and artificial fertilizer and all these modern methods are all very well and all very rational but they've got one grave disadvantage and that is that, with the best reasoning in the world, they lead straight to ruin.'

'That's because you're impatient, you expect science to provide you with all the answers straight away and you become so discouraged at all the necessary research and experimentation that you even have doubts about the results already achieved and start throwing everything overboard!'

'That's as may be. So you're saying that all I'm doing is experimenting, am I right? So I'm to get a decoration for that and other simpletons are to follow on after me!'

Hourdequin gave a loud guffaw at his own joke, which seemed to him to conclude the argument. Monsieur Rochefontaine said sharply:

'So you want the working man to starve?'

'Not at all! I want the farm labourer to earn a living.'

'But I employ twelve hundred workers and I can't raise their wages without going bankrupt. If wheat cost thirty francs, they'd be dying like flies.'

'And how about me? Don't I employ hired labour as well? With wheat at sixteen francs, we have to draw in our belts, there are poor devils kicking the bucket in every ditch in the countryside.'

Then he added, still with a laugh:

'Ah well! Everyone rides his own hobby-horse! If you get my bread cheap, then French agriculture will be ruined, and if you don't get it cheap, then French industry might as well pack up. Your labour costs go up, the price of manufactured goods goes up, all my tools, my clothes, everything I need. Ah, what a mess we'll all land up in!'

The two of them, the farmer and the industrialist, the protectionist and the free-trader, stared each other in the face, one with a sly, good-humoured chuckle, the other with blunt hostility. This was the modern form of warfare, the confrontation which faces us today, in the economic struggle for existence.

'We'll force the peasant to feed the workers,' said Monsieur Rochefontaine.

'But first of all,' insisted Hourdequin, 'you must make sure that the peasant has enough to eat.'

He now at last sprang out of his gig and Rochefontaine was just calling out the name of a village to his driver when Macqueron, annoyed at seeing that his friends from the council had been listening on the doorstep, called out that they must all have a glass of wine together; but once again the candidate refused and without shaking hands with anyone sank back into the seat of his landau and the two big percherons trotted briskly away.

On the opposite corner, standing in his doorway stropping his razor, Lengaigne had observed the whole scene. He gave an offensive laugh and said loudly, for all his neighbours to hear:

'Kiss my arse and say thank you!'

Hourdequin did go in and accept a glass of wine. As soon as Jean had tied the horse to one of the shutters, he followed his master. Françoise quietly beckoned him over to the haberdashery and told him what had happened and why she had left; he was so affected by her story and so afraid of compromising her in front of the others that he merely whispered to her that they must see each other to arrange what was to be done before he went away. He sat down on a bench in the tap-room.

'Well, damn it all, you're not very choosy if you vote for that young fellow!' cried Hourdequin, putting down his glass.

His encounter with Monsieur Rochefontaine had made him determined to oppose him openly, even if it meant defeat. So he made no attempt to pull his punches, he compared him to Monsieur de Chédeville, such a decent sort, not a bit snobbish, always happy to oblige, a real old-fashioned French aristocrat! Whereas that tall, stuck-up martinet, that modern-style millionaire, well? ... See how he looked down on people and even refused to drink the local wine, no doubt because he was afraid of being poisoned! They really must see that he was impossible! You don't change a decent horse for a boss-eyed one!

'Tell me what you've got against Monsieur de Chédeville? He's been representing you for years, he's always suited you up till now. And now you're deserting him for a fellow whom you used to describe as a scoundrel at the last elections, when the government opposed him! Just think back, for heaven's sake!'

Not wanting to commit himself directly, Macqueron was pretending to be helping his wife serve. The peasants had all listened with stony faces, and not a pucker of an eyelid revealed their secret thoughts. It was Delhomme who replied:

'Well, when you don't know somebody...'

'But you do really know that fellow now! You've just heard him say that he wants cheap wheat and that he'll vote for foreign wheat to come in and undercut ours. I've already explained to you that it's going to be a complete disaster. And if you're stupid enough to believe everything that he promised you for later on... well, all right, vote for him, he won't give a damn for you afterwards.'

A vague smile had appeared on Delhomme's leathery face, and in a few slow sentences, he revealed all the dormant craftiness concealed underneath his straightforward, limited intelligence:

'He can say what he wants to say and we can believe what we want to believe. Whether it's him or someone else, well, what the devil! We've only got one concern and that is for a government strong enough to keep business going; and in that case, if we don't want to make a mistake, the best thing is to provide the government with the representative they want. As far as we're concerned, it's quite enough for him to be friendly with the Emperor.'

At this last remark, Hourdequin was quite dumbfounded. But previously it had been Monsieur de Chédeville who was friendly with the Emperor! What a slave race, always prepared to follow its lord and master, who flogs it and feeds it; still as abject in its congenital selfishness as it ever was, unable to see or know anything beyond its daily ration of bread!

'Well, I swear that the day that Rochefontaine fellow is elected, I'll hand in my resignation, so help me God! Do you take me for a mountebank, saying "Yes, sir, no, sir, three bags full, sir"? If those blasted republicans were in the Tuileries, I bet you'd support them!'

Macqueron's eyes had lit up. At last he was home and dry. The mayor had just signed his own death-warrant, because, unpopular as he was, the mayor's statement would certainly make the village vote against Monsieur de Chédeville.

But at that moment Jesus Christ, who had been sitting forgotten in a corner with his friend Canon, gave such a loud laugh that everyone looked at him. Resting his elbows on the table and cupping his chin in his hands, he was jeering contemptuously at the villagers present and repeating:

'Bunch of cunts! Bunch of cunts!'

And it was at that word that Buteau came in. As soon as he was through the door, a quick glance showed him that Françoise was in the haberdashery and he immediately recognized Jean sitting against the wall, listening while he was waiting for his master. 'Good, the girl and her lover were both there, now we'd see!'

'Well, well, here's my brother, the biggest cunt of the lot!' shouted Jesus Christ.

There were threatening rumbles from the others and people spoke of chucking him out when Leroi, otherwise known as Canon, intervened, in his rasping, working-class accent which had been heard spouting arguments in every socialist meeting in Paris:

'Shut your mug, old boy! They're not as stupid as they seem. Listen to me, you lot, you land-workers, what would you say if you saw a notice stuck up on the door of the town-hall opposite, printed in large capital letters: THE REVOLUTIONARY COMMUNE OF PARIS: First, all taxes are abolished; secondly, military service is abolished. Well, what would you say, you clodhoppers?'

The effect was so extraordinary that Delhomme, Fouan, Clou and Bécu sat wide-eyed and open-mouthed. Lequeu dropped his paper, Hourdequin, who was about to leave, came back in again, while Buteau, forgetting all about Françoise, sat down on the corner of a table. And they all looked at this ruffian, this rolling stone, the terror of the countryside, who lived on blackmailed charity and pilfering. The other week they had chased him off La Borderie where he had turned up like a ghost as night was falling. This was why he was at the moment sleeping at that rascal Jesus Christ's place, where he would disappear next day, perhaps.

'I can see that it wouldn't be too bad,' he went on with a smile.

'No, it wouldn't, damn it,' confessed Buteau. 'When you think that only yesterday I took some more money to the tax-collector. There's no end to it, they'd take the shirt off our backs.'

'And not to see our lads having to go away, by God,' exclaimed

Delhomme. 'I'm paying for Nénesse's exemption, so I know what it costs.'

'Apart from the fact,' added Fouan, 'that if you haven't got the money they take them away and send them off to be killed.'

Canon laughed and nodded triumphantly:

'So you see,' he said to Jesus Christ, 'they're not as stupid as all that, these clodhoppers!'

Then, turning back, he said:

'People keep dinning into our ears that you're conservative, that you won't let things get done. Yes, you're conservative in your own interests, aren't you? So you will let things get done, and you will help to do anything that'll pay dividends, isn't that right? To hang onto your money and your children, you'd do all sorts of things! Otherwise, you'd be right idiots!'

They had all stopped drinking and an uneasy look was beginning to spread over their dull faces. He continued in his bantering tone, smiling in anticipation at the effect that he was about to produce.

'And that's why I'm not worried. I've got to know you while you've been throwing stones at me to drive me away. As this bigwig was saying, you'll be with us, the Reds and the Commies, once we've taken over the Tuileries.'

'Oh no we shan't, never!' Buteau, Delhomme and the others all exclaimed together.

Hourdequin, who had been listening intently, shrugged his shoulders:

'You're wasting your breath, old man!'

But Canon was still smiling with the blind faith of a believer. He was leaning backwards, unconsciously rubbing one shoulder after the other against the wall like a cat caressing itself. And he explained what he meant by this mysterious revolution which he had been going round preaching from farm to farm without being properly understood, to the terror of both servants and masters. First of all, their Paris comrades could seize power: it might take place without fuss, they'd have to shoot fewer people than they thought, the whole show was so rotten it would collapse on its own. Then, the very evening they gained control, private incomes would be abolished, there'd be no more interest paid out by the state, all large fortunes would be confiscated, so that all capital and the means of production would return to the nation and a new society would be organized, a vast financial, industrial and commercial undertaking where work and welfare would be fairly distributed. In the countryside, it would be even easier. They'd begin by expropriating the landowners, they would seize the land...

'Just try,' Hourdequin interrupted. 'You'll be met by pitch-forks, not one single smallholder would let you take even a hand-ful of soil.'

'Did I say that we must grind down the poor?' jeered Canon. 'We'd have to be really silly to quarrel with the small land-owners. Oh dear me no, at first we shan't interfere with the land of those poor wretches who are killing themselves trying to scrape together a few more acres. All that we'll do is to take the five hundred acres of bigwigs like you who make their labourers sweat to earn money for you. No, damn it, I can't see any of your neighbours coming along with pitchforks to defend you. They'll be all too pleased!'

Macqueron gave a guffaw, as if taking the whole thing as a joke, and the others followed suit while the farmer went pale as he sensed this age-old feud: this rogue was right, there wasn't a single peasant, however decent, who wouldn't have helped turn him out of La Borderie.

'So as an owner of ten acres,' Buteau asked seriously, 'I shall be able to keep them, no one will come and take them off me?'

'Of course not, comrade. Only we're certain that later on, when you see what results have been achieved, all around you, on the nationalized farms, you'll come of your own accord, without being asked, to add your own bit of land to them. Large-scale agriculture, with lots of capital, machines and all sorts of other things, everything that science has got to offer. I don't under-stand such things; but you ought to hear the people in Paris who can explain pat that agriculture is done for if we don't decide to do it like that. Yes, you'll hand over the land of your own accord.'

Unable to follow this reasoning, Buteau made a gesture of blank incredulity, albeit reassured by the thought that nobody would be wanting anything from him. Meanwhile, pricking up his ears at this man's confused account of large-scale state agriculture, Hourdequin had been listening patiently. The others were waiting for the end, like people watching a show. Lequeu's pale face had been growing increasingly purple and he had twice opened his mouth to intervene, although each time he had prudently thought better of it.

'And what about my share?' shouted Jesus Christ suddenly. 'Everybody must have his share. Liberty, equality and fraternity for ever!'

Hearing this, Canon lost his temper and lifted his hand as though about to strike his friend.

'For Christ's sake, stop nattering about your liberty, equality and fraternity! Who needs liberty? What a joke! So you want us to end up in the pockets of the bourgeois again? Oh, no, the people are going to be forced to be happy in spite of themselves! So you'd be happy to have equality and fraternity with a bailiff's man? You sucker! It's because they swallowed all that crap that you republicans mucked everything up in 1848!'

Quite at a loss, Jesus Christ said he supported the Great Revolution of '89.

'You make me puke, do shut up! '89, '93, what a lovely sound! Just a pack of lies that people din into our ears! What good is all that nonsense compared with what still needs doing? You'll see, when the people have become the masters, and it won't be long, everything's collapsing and I promise you that our century, as they call it, will end with a bigger splash even than the last one. A real clean-out, a clean sweep of everything such as you've never seen!'

Everyone sat aghast and even that drunk Jesus Christ shrank back frightened and repelled at the thought that they were no longer brothers-in-arms. Jean, who had hitherto been listening with interest, made a gesture of protest, too. But Canon had risen to his feet with his eyes blazing and his face lit up in prophetic ecstasy.

'And it must come, it's bound to come, just like a stone you throw up has to come down. And it's not got anything to do with that old rubbish of priests and the afterlife and law and justice which no one's ever seen, any more than anyone's ever seen God! No, there's just the need we all have to be happy. Eh, you there, just tell yourself that we're all going to get together so that everybody will have a wonderful time with as little work as possible. Machines will do the work for us and all we'll have to do is to supervise them for four hours a day : we may even be able to just sit back and fold our arms. And all the pleasure you want, every one of our needs fostered and satisfied, meat, wine, women and three times as much of them as we have today, because we'll be stronger and healthier. No more poverty, no more sickness, no more old age because we'll be better organized, life will be easier with good hospitals and good old people's homes. A paradise on earth ! The whole of science devoted to taking it easy. Real enjoyment at last !'

Buteau enthusiastically banged his fist on the table, yelling :

'No fucking taxes ! No fucking military service ! No fucking idiots ! Nothing but pleasure, I'll sign on !'

'Of course,' said Delhomme. 'It'd be against our own interest not to sign.'

Fouan nodded approval and so did Macqueron, Clou and the others. Bécu, dazed at hearing all his authoritarian ideas turned upside down, went over and asked Hourdequin in a whisper whether this ruffian ought not to be locked up for attacking the Emperor. But the farmer shrugged his shoulders and calmed him down. Happiness ! Yes, people were dreaming of achieving it through science just as they used to dream about achieving it through the law; well, perhaps it was more logical but it certainly wasn't going to happen tomorrow. Just as he was leaving again, calling out to Jean who had been listening intently to the discussion, Lequeu, who had been restraining himself, although bursting to intervene, suddenly exploded angrily :

'Unless,' he exclaimed in his shrill voice, 'you've all kicked the bucket before all these splendid things happen. Either starved to death or shot by the police if hunger makes you obstreperous.'

They were looking at him uncomprehendingly.

'Certainly, if wheat continues to come in from America, in fifty years' time there won't be a single smallholder left in France. How can our land compare with theirs? We shall hardly be able to get going on organizing our agriculture before we're flooded with corn. I'm reading a book which tells the whole story, you're sunk.'

But as he let fly, he suddenly became aware of all the scared faces looking at him. He did not even finish his sentence but ended with a furious gesture and pretended to go back to reading his paper.

'It's certainly all that wheat from America which will sink you,' said Canon, 'as long as the people don't seize all the big estates.'

'And my view,' said Hourdequin in conclusion, 'is that that wheat mustn't be allowed to come in. And now, vote for Monsieur Rochefontaine if you're tired of me on the town council and you want wheat at fifteen francs.'

He climbed back into his gig, followed by Jean. Then, as the latter was whipping up the horse, after exchanging a stealthy look with Françoise, he said to his master:

'One shouldn't think too much about all that sort of thing,' at which Hourdequin nodded approvingly.

In front of the inn, Macqueron was eagerly whispering to Delhomme, while Canon, who had relapsed into his previous air of complete unconcern, was finishing off the brandy and pulling the leg of the abashed Jesus Christ, calling him 'Miss 1793'. Buteau had fallen into a brown study and suddenly realizing that Jean had left, he was surprised to see Françoise still standing at the door of the tap-room, where she, together with Berthe, had come to listen. He was irritated at having wasted his time talking politics when he had more serious matters in hand. Dirty things, politics, you couldn't help getting involved. He took Coelina into a corner and had a long argument with her; in the end she persuaded him not to make a row then and there; it would be better for Françoise to go back of her own accord, once they had calmed her down; and then he left too, threatening to come back with a rope and a stick if she couldn't be persuaded.

The following Sunday, Monsieur Rochefontaine was elected and Hourdequin sent in his resignation to the *préfet*; Macqueron, as proud as a peacock and puffed up with his success, finally became mayor.

That same evening, Lengaigne was caught with his trousers down outside the doorway of his triumphant rival. He shouted defiantly:

'Now we're governed by shits, I can shit where I like!'

Chapter 6

A WEEK passed and still Françoise obstinately refused to go back
to her sister. A dreadful scene took place in the street with
Buteau dragging her along by her hair until she bit him so hard
in the thumb that he had to let go; but Macqueron took fright
and turned the girl out, too, on the grounds that as the representative of law and order he could no longer encourage such
rebelliousness.

But La Grande happened to be passing and she took Françoise
in. She was now eighty-eight and her sole occupation, as death
drew near, was to leave her wealth to her next-of-kin in such a
way as to ensure endless litigation: she had drawn up an extra-
ordinarily involved and deliberately complicated will in which,
under the pretence of being fair to all, she would force them to
tear each other apart; her idea was that, since she couldn't take it
with her, she could at least die with the consolation that her
bequests would poison the lives of her heirs. Thus her greatest
pleasure was watching her family scratching each other's eyes
out. So she was eager to set her niece up in her own home, restraining her instinctive meanness with the thought that she
would get a lot of work out of the girl in exchange for a few
crusts of bread. That very evening, she set Françoise to scrub her
stairs and kitchen. Then, when Buteau appeared, she stood fast
and met him like an old bird of prey, with a vicious beak all
ready to peck; and the man who had blustered that he would
wreck the Macquerons' house now stood there scared and at a
loss for words, paralysed by the hopes of what he might inherit
and too frightened to cross swords with the awesome La Grande.

'I need Françoise, and I intend to keep her here because she
doesn't like it at yours... Anyway, she's coming of age and
you're going to have to pay her her due. We'll talk about that
shortly.'

Buteau left in a rage, terrified at the thought of all the trouble
ahead.

A week later, in fact, Françoise had her twenty-first birthday.

It was about the middle of August. Now she was her own mistress. But she had really exchanged one drudgery for another, for she, too, went in dread of her mean, hard-hearted aunt as she slaved away in her house where everything was expected to shine without any help except from water and elbow-grease. One day she unthinkingly gave some corn to the hens and nearly had her skull cracked open with her aunt's stick. People used to say that in her anxiety to spare her horse, La Grande would yoke her grandson Hilarion to the plough; and even if that story was invented, it was true that she really did treat him like an animal, hitting him, cruelly overworking him and taking advantage of his brute force to leave him flattened and totally exhausted; moreover feeding him so badly, with crusts of bread and left-overs, like her pig, that he was always ravenous and completely terror-stricken. When Françoise realized that she was intended to become the second beast of burden, she had only one wish: to get away. And it was at this point that she suddenly decided that she must get married.

Quite simply, she wanted to put an end to the whole business. With her intractable sense of justice which had already bedevilled her as a child, she would have killed herself rather than return to her sister's home. Her cause was the only fair one and she despised herself for having been patient for so long; she said nothing about Buteau, all her strictures were reserved for Lise, for without her they would have been able to continue sharing the home. Now that the link was broken, and thoroughly broken, her only thought was to obtain possession of her property, her rightful share of the inheritance. It preyed on her mind from morning till night and she kept losing her temper at the thought of all the long drawn-out formalities. Really! That's mine, that's yours, surely you could settle the whole matter in three minutes. Perhaps it was because people were ganging up to rob her? She was suspicious of the whole family, and so she came to the conclusion that only a man, a husband, could extricate her from all this. Of course, Jean didn't own a square inch of land and he was fifteen years older than she was. But there was no other young man interested in marrying her and perhaps no one would risk it, fearing trouble from Buteau, of whom everyone in Rognes was so afraid that nobody was anxious to have him as an enemy.

What else? She had been with Jean, which didn't mean very much because it had only happened that once; but he was very gentle and very decent. It might as well be him because she didn't love anybody else and she wanted someone or other to defend her; and this would infuriate Buteau, too. She would have a man of her own.

As for Jean, he still felt very friendly towards her, although his desire for her had died down considerably, through having wanted her for so long. All the same, he had kept on seeing her, in his gentle, friendly way, because he considered himself her man and they had exchanged promises. He had waited patiently until she came of age, respecting her wish not to be hurried and in fact preventing her from causing trouble at her sister's. Now she could show more than adequate reasons to have all reasonable people on her side. So while criticizing her for her violent departure, he kept telling her that she now held all the cards. And as soon as she wanted to discuss other things, he would be ready. So one evening when he had come to meet her behind La Grande's cowshed, the marriage was arranged. There was a rotten old gate opening on to a blind corner and they were both leaning against it, he outside, she on the other side with the liquid manure flowing between their legs.

She mentioned it first:

'You know, Corporal,' she said, looking him straight in the eyes, 'if you're still willing, I am, now.'

He looked at her too and replied slowly:

'I hadn't mentioned it before because I might have seemed to be after your money. But you're right, now's the time.'

Silence fell. The girl's hand was resting on the gate and he put his hand over it. Then he went on:

'And you mustn't be bothered by the thought of the Cognet girl, because of all the stories about... I haven't even touched her for the last three years.'

'Well, it's the same with me,' she said. 'I don't want the thought of Buteau to worry you. The dirty beast goes about telling everyone that he's had me. Perhaps you even think so yourself?'

'Everyone in the village thinks so,' he said gently, evading the question.

Then, as she still kept looking at him:

'Yes, I did think so. And I could understand it really, because I know what the fellow's like and you couldn't do anything else but give in.'

'Oh, he tried hard enough all right, he felt me all over. But if I swear that he never went all the way, will you believe me?'

'Yes, I believe you.'

To show how pleased he was, he took hold of her hand and clutched it tightly in his, leaning his arm on the gate. Realizing that the flow of manure from the cowshed was wetting his shoes, he shifted his legs.

'You seemed to be so willing to stay on in his house, you might have liked him catching hold of you.'

She became embarrassed and her honest, straightforward gaze wavered.

'Particularly as you didn't want to have anything to do with me either, d'you remember? Never mind, I was furious that I hadn't given you a baby but now I think it's better that's still to come. It's more decent like that.'

He broke off to point out that she was standing in the muck.

'Look, you're getting wet.'

She moved her feet back too, and said in conclusion:

'All right then, it's agreed.'

'It's agreed, fix any date that suits you.'

They did not even kiss but shook hands like good friends over the gate. Then each of them went their own way.

That evening, when Françoise mentioned her intention of marrying Jean, explaining that she needed a man to help her to obtain her inheritance, La Grande at first said nothing, but her eyes opened wide as she sat there, straight-backed. She was weighing the profit and loss and the pleasure she would enjoy. Not until next day did she express her approval of the marriage. She had spent the whole night awake on her straw mattress, turning the matter over in her mind. She hardly ever slept and she would not close her eyes all night, thinking up unpleasant things to do to her family. This marriage seemed to her so full of consequences for everybody that she was fired with youthful ardour. She could already foresee the slightest difficulties and she intended to complicate them until they became disastrous.

So much so that she informed her niece that, out of friendship, she would take charge of the whole affair. She emphasized these words with an awesome flourish of her stick; since the girl was being deserted, she would be a mother to her; and she would show them what's what!

First of all, La Grande sent for her brother Fouan, to give an account of his guardianship. But the old man was incapable of explaining anything. It wasn't his fault if he'd been appointed her guardian; and anyway, since Monsieur Baillehache had done everything, she'd have to go to Monsieur Baillehache. Moreover, as soon as he realized that the Buteaus were under fire, his confusion became even greater. Age and the realization of his vulnerability had unmanned him, leaving him dazed and at everyone's mercy. Why quarrel with the Buteaus, anyway? He had nearly gone back to them twice already after spending his nights trembling with fear at seeing Jesus Christ and La Trouille prowling round his bedroom, even thrusting their bare arms under his bolster to try and steal his bonds. Surely they'd end by trying to murder him up at the Castle unless he made himself scarce one night. Unable to get anything out of him, La Grande sent him away in abject fear, threatening him that he'd end up in court if he'd laid hands on any of the girl's share of the property. Next, she put the fear of God into Delhomme, as a member of the board of guardians; he went away so upset that Fanny, behind his back, hurriedly went round to say that they would sooner be out of pocket than have any court case. Things were going well; it was beginning to be amusing.

The question was whether it was better to embark on settling the estate or to go ahead straight away with the marriage. La Grande thought it over for two nights and then decided in favour of an immediate marriage: with Françoise married to Jean and having a husband to help her claim her fair share, the Buteaus would be even more harassed. So she rushed to and fro like a two-year-old, saw to her niece's papers, got Jean to hand over his, arranged everything at the town-hall and the church; and her keenness even extended to lending the young couple the necessary money, although they had to sign a paper providing for repayment with interest at one hundred per cent. What really cut her to the quick was all the glasses of wine she had to offer in the course of making these arrangements; but she had her special brand of wine reserved for the family, so vinegary and undrinkable that people drank it with the greatest caution. She decided against a wedding-breakfast, because of the difficulties between the family : only Mass and a glass of the special to drink the health of the bride and groom. The Charles refused her invitation on the pretext of the trouble that their son-in-law was causing them, whilst Fouan, ill at ease, took to his bed and gave out that he was not well. So Delhomme was the only relative present and expressed his readiness to act as one of the witnesses for Jean, of whom he approved. For his part, the groom invited only his witnesses, his employer Hourdequin and one of the labourers from the farm. Rognes was all agog, with everyone on their doorstep to see this marriage which had been rushed through at such speed and promised so much strife. At the town-hall, Macqueron, all puffed-up with his own importance, spun out the formalities in the presence of his predecessor. In church there was an unfortunate incident when Father Madeline fainted during the ceremony. He was ailing, for, living in the flat plain of Beauce, he missed his mountain air, as well as being heart-broken at the irreligiousness of his new parishioners and so upset by the constant gossiping and squabbling of the women that he no longer even dared threaten them with hellfire. They had sensed that he was a weakling and were taking advantage of him, even bullying him over matters concerning the services. However, Coelina and Flore and all of them heartily commiserated with him for falling head-first onto the altar, at the same time asserting that it foreboded the early demise of the wedding couple.

It had been decided that Françoise would continue to live with La Grande until the property had been divided, because she had firmly made up her mind, determined and pigheaded as she was, that she wanted the house. What was the point of moving into lodgings for a fortnight? Jean would in the meantime remain working up at the farm and simply come back to spend the night with her. Their wedding-night was very sad and stupid, although they were not unhappy at being together at last. Whilst he was taking her, she burst into sobs, although he was not hurting her, on the contrary he was doing it very gently. The worst thing was

374

that between her sobs she kept telling him that she had nothing against him and that she didn't even know why she was crying like that. Somewhat naturally, such behaviour was hardly calculated to fill a man with great ardour. And though he took her once again and held her in his arms, they felt no pleasure, even less than on the first occasion, in the haystack. He explained to her that if you didn't do things like that straight away, they went flat. Anyway, despite this uneasiness and embarrassment that had made them both feel rather squeamish, there was no trace of ill-feeling, and as they were unable to sleep they spent the rest of the night deciding on all the things they would do once they had the house and the land.

The very next day, Françoise demanded a settlement of her inheritance. But La Grande was now no longer so keen: in the first place, she wanted to prolong the pleasure of extracting blood from the family by constant pinpricks; in addition, she had been benefiting so much from the girl and her husband, who paid for his room by giving her two hours' work every evening, that she was in no hurry for them to leave and set up on their own. All the same, she had to go and ask the Buteaus what their ideas were on the question of the settlement. She herself, speaking for Françoise, demanded the house, half the arable land and half the meadow; she was ready to relinquish any claim on the vineyard, which she estimated as being roughly worth the house. It was on the whole a fair and reasonable arrangement which, if accepted, would have avoided any need to have recourse to the law, which always takes a good slice of the proceeds. Buteau had been given quite a turn when he saw La Grande come in, for he had to treat her gently because of her money; but he could not bear to hear any more. He stormed out, afraid of spoiling his chances by pitching into her. Left alone, Lise, red as a turkey-cock, was stammering with rage:

'The house? That shameless, worthless hussy who didn't even come and see me when she got married, she wants the house, does she? Well, Aunt, you can go and tell her from me that she'll have the house over my dead body!'

La Grande was unmoved.

'All right, all right! No need to make such a fuss. You want the house, too. Well, that's reasonable. We'll have to see.'

And for the next three days she shuttled between the two sisters, telling each of them in turn the foolish things that they were saying to each other and bringing them to such a pitch of exasperation that they both nearly had to take to their beds. And she never wearied of telling them all the time how much she loved them both and how grateful her nieces ought to be to her for having undertaken such a thankless task. Finally, it was settled that the land should be split between them but that the house, the furniture, and the farm animals should be auctioned, since they could not agree. Each of the two sisters swore she would buy the house whatever it cost, even if she had to sell the clothes off her back.

So Grosbois came to survey the property and divide it into two. There were two and a half acres of pasture, another two and a half of vine and five of arable; it was this last field that Buteau had insistently refused to give up because it abutted onto the land which he had received from his father, making a field of nearly seven and a half acres in all, something which not a single farmer in Rognes owned. So when Grosbois set up his cross-staff and his stakes, his fury can be readily imagined. La Grande was there to keep a watchful eye on things, since Jean had preferred not to come for fear of becoming involved in a fight. Indeed, an argument started up at once because Buteau wanted the line drawn parallel to the Aigre so that his field would still join onto whichever piece fell to his lot; whereas his aunt was insistent that the dividing-line should be drawn at right angles, with the sole purpose of annoying him. She carried the day while he clenched his fists in a constant rage.

'So if I draw the first lot, for Christ's sake, I'll be cut in two, with one bit on one side and my field on the other.'

'Well, young man, it's up to you to pick the right one.'

Buteau had been in a continual rage for the last month. In the first place, the girl was slipping from his grasp; ever since he had no longer had the opportunity of catching hold of her flesh under her skirt, while still nursing the hope of possessing her completely one day, he had been crazy with repressed desire; and after her marriage, the thought of the other man holding her in his arms in bed, lying on top of her and taking his pleasure as he liked, had finally sent him into a frenzy of lust. And now his land was being torn from his arms for the other man to own, too. It was like having a limb cut off. As for the girl, well, there were other opportunities; but this didn't apply to the land, land which he regarded as his own and had sworn never to hand over! He saw red and kept turning over ways and means in his mind, with vague ideas of violence and murder which only his terror of the police prevented him from putting into action.

Finally, a meeting took place in Monsieur Baillehache's office when Buteau and Lise for the first time came face to face with Françoise and Jean, whom La Grande had accompanied for the pleasure of it, on the pretext of preventing things from turning nasty. In tense silence, all five of them went into the room. The Buteaus sat down on the right. Jean remained standing behind Françoise on the left, as though to show that he was not taking any part but was merely there to authorize his wife. Their aunt, tall and thin, took her seat in the middle, turning her vicious beak towards one group and the other, with a wide-eyed, satisfied look. The two sisters, hard-faced, had exchanged neither word nor look, like complete strangers. The men exchanged one swift, piercing glance, with eyes glinting like knives.

'Well now, my friends,' said Monsieur Baillehache, calmly ignoring the warlike atmosphere, 'let's settle the division of the land first of all, since you've all agreed on that.'

This time he insisted that they sign first. The deed was already drawn up and all that was needed was to fill in the numbers of the lots against the names; everyone had to sign before drawing the lots, which he proceeded to have done at once to avoid trouble.

Françoise drew number two, so Lise had to take number one and Buteau turned purple as the blood rushed to his swollen face. Never any luck! Now his land was cut in two! That slut of a younger sister and her man had their piece stuck in the middle, right across his own field!

'Christ Almighty!' he swore between clenched teeth. 'Christ All-bloody-mighty!'

The lawyer asked him to control himself until he was outside.

'The point is, that cuts us off, up on the plain,' Lise pointed out, without looking at her sister. 'Perhaps it might be possible to agree to make an exchange. It would suit us and it wouldn't hurt anybody.'

'No,' snapped Françoise.

La Grande nodded approval : it was bad luck to change something decreed by chance. And this quirk of fate amused her, whereas Jean, standing behind, did not stir and was so determined not to become involved that his face expressed nothing.

'Come on now,' the lawyer continued, 'let's try and finish, don't let's waste time.'

The two sisters had agreed to commission him to arrange for the auction, in one lot, of the house, furniture and animals. The sale was advertised to take place on the second Sunday of the month; it would take place in his office and the conditions of sale stated that the purchaser could enter into possession immediately after the auction. Then, after the sale, the lawyer would see to the settlement of the various accounts between the co-legatees. This was all accepted without discussion.

But at that moment Fouan, who was expected to appear as the guardian, was introduced by a clerk, who also prevented Jesus Christ from coming in because the rogue was so drunk. Although Françoise had been of age for a month, no account of his guardianship had yet been rendered and this was complicating matters. It had now become necessary to do so in order to relieve the old man of his responsibilities. He looked at the two groups with his little, staring eyes; and he was trembling, increasingly scared of being compromised and hauled before the courts.

The lawyer read out the statement of account. Everyone listened, blinking anxiously when they failed to understand something, and fearful, if they overlooked it, that it might turn out to be something crucial.

'Has anyone any further claims to make?' Monsieur Baillehache inquired when he had finished.

They looked startled. Claims? Had they missed anything and were they losing something as a result?

'Excuse me,' La Grande said abruptly, 'but that's not fair on Françoise, not at all fair, and my brother must be turning a blind eye not to see she's being robbed.'

Fouan stammered :

'What do you mean? What's all this about? I haven't taken a penny-piece from her, so help me God I haven't.'

'I'm saying that since her sister's marriage, which is nearly five years ago, she's been working in the family as a servant and they owe her wages.'

At this unexpected blow, Buteau jerked upright on his chair. Lise choked:

'Wages? What d'you mean? Wages to a sister? That really would be a dirty trick!'

Monsieur Baillehache had to impose silence and informed them that a girl under age had every right to claim wages if she wished.

'Yes, I do wish,' said Françoise. 'I want everything owing to me.'

'And how about her food, then?' Buteau shouted, beside himself. 'She never held back on the grub. You just feel her, she's not got as fat as that from licking the walls, the lazybones.'

'And linen and clothes?' Lise went on furiously. 'And the washing? She made her shift dirty in two days with all her sweat.'

'If I was sweating that much, it was because I was working!' Françoise snapped back.

'Sweat dries, it isn't dirty,' added La Grande.

Monsieur Baillehache intervened yet again. He explained that this all had to be calculated, wages on one side and board and lodging on the other. He had a pen in his hand and tried to work it out with the information they supplied. But it was a frightful task. Supported by La Grande, Françoise was very demanding, setting a high price on her services and giving a list of all the work she had done in the house, with the cows, and the housework and the washing-up, and then in the fields, where her brother-in-law Buteau gave her man's work to do. For their part, in exasperation the Buteaus exaggerated their expenses, including meals and clothes (which they lied about) and even claiming money back for presents they had given her for Christmas and so on. All the same, despite their tough bargaining, they still ended up owing one hundred and eighty-six francs. Their hands were quivering and their eyes bloodshot as they searched around for other things to charge.

They were about to accept the figure when Buteau exclaimed:

'Just a sec! What about the doctor when she missed her period? He came twice, that makes six francs.'

La Grande was unwilling to accept this successful appeal by the other two and she bullied Fouan to remember how many days' work the girl had done for the farm, during the time he was living in the house. Was it five or six days, at one and a half francs a day? Françoise kept shouting six and Lise five, as fiercely as if it were stones they were throwing at each other. And the dazed old man was agreeing first with one and then with the other, beating his forehead with his fists. Françoise won and the final total was one hundred and eighty-nine francs.

'Well, that really is all, this time?' asked the lawyer.

Buteau sat on his chair, seeming completely exhausted and overwhelmed by this sum, which appeared to be increasing all the time, but now having given up the struggle in the belief that nothing worse could possibly happen. He muttered glumly:

'If you want the shirt off my back, here it is.'

But La Grande had been holding back one final, dreadful blow, very simple but substantial, something that everybody else had forgotten.

'But what about the five hundred francs compensation for the road up there?'

Buteau jumped to his feet, open-mouthed, with his eyes starting out of his head. But there was nothing to be said: he had undeniably received the money and he would have to give half of it back. He thought for a moment; then, finding no way out, his head in a turmoil, he suddenly rushed madly towards Jean:

'You dirty swine, you've ruined our friendship! But for you we'd still be living all together in one cosy happy family!'

Jean, who had till now kept sensibly silent, was forced to defend himself:

'Don't touch me or I'll hit back!'

Françoise and Lise swiftly rose to their feet and each stood in front of her man, their faces full of their ever-growing hatred, their nails bared all ready to scratch each other's eyes out. And a general scuffle which neither La Grande nor Fouan seemed tempted to stop would surely have sent fists and hair flying if the lawyer's professional phlegm had not deserted him:

'For God's sake! Wait till you're outside! It's so annoying when people can't agree without fighting!'

When, still quivering, they had all subsided, he added:

'So you're agreed, aren't you? Well, I'll draw up the statement of account of the guardianship, which you can sign, and then we'll go ahead with the sale of the house and that'll clear everything up. Now be off with you and try to be sensible. Stupid actions can often cost a great deal of money.'

This remark finally calmed them down. But as they were leaving, Jesus Christ, who had been waiting for his father, insulted the whole family, screaming that it was a real scandal to involve a poor old man in all this dirty business, so as to rob him, that was for sure; and, maudlin with drink, he took him off in the same way as he had come, on the straw of a cart which he had borrowed from a neighbour. The Buteaus went off one way, and La Grande took Jean and Françoise along to the Jolly Ploughman, where she had a black coffee at their expense. She was radiant.

'I really enjoyed myself,' was her summing up, as she pocketed the unused sugar.

And that very same day, La Grande had an idea. On arriving in Rognes, she hurried round to make an arrangement with old Saucisse, who was said to be one of her old flames. As the Buteaus had sworn that they would push up the bidding against Françoise even if it meant spending their last penny, she had said to herself that if her old former sweetheart pushed it up, too, the others would perhaps not suspect anything and would let him buy it, because he happened to own the neighbouring property and he might be wanting to extend it. He at once agreed, in exchange for a present. So at the auction, on the second Sunday of the month, things turned out as she had anticipated. In the offices of Monsieur Baillehache, once more Françoise and Jean were gathered on one side and the Buteaus on the other, with La Grande and a few other farmers who had come along with the vague idea of buying if it went for a song. But in four or five quick bids, Lise and Françoise pushed the price up to three thousand five hundred francs, which was what the house was worth. Françoise stopped at three thousand eight. Then old Saucisse stepped in and pulled four thousand out of the bag, followed by four thousand five. The Buteaus looked at each other in consternation : this was impossible; and their blood ran cold at the thought of all that money. But Lise still let herself be pushed up to five thousand : however, she was finally crushed when the old farmer jumped straight up to five thousand two. That was the end, the house was knocked down to him at five thousand two hundred francs. The Buteaus gave a derisive laugh : it would be a tidy sum for them and at least Françoise and her miserable man had been beaten.

All the same, when Lise came back to Rognes and went into the old home where she had been born and spent all her life, she began to sob. Buteau had a tight feeling in his throat, too, and relieved his emotion by pitching into her, swearing that while he would have spent his last farthing, those heartless women would only loosen their purse-strings or open their legs for a spot of fun. He was lying, for it was he who had stopped her; and they had a fight. What a shame it was for that ancestral home of the Fouans, built three centuries ago and now tottering and cracked and sunk, patched up all over, and tipping forward head-first under the fierce winds blowing across the plain of Beauce. To think that the family had been living there for three hundred years and they had ended by loving and honouring it like a real relic of the past, so that it had become one of the most important parts of the inheritance. Buteau landed Lise a slap across the face that sent her flying, she sprang up and kicked out, nearly breaking his leg.

Next day, it was something else : the storm broke. As old Saucisse went along in the morning to make the obligatory declaration, by noon Rognes had learnt that he had bought the house on behalf of Françoise, on Jean's authority : and not only the house but the furniture, as well as Gideon and Coliche. From the Buteaus there rose a scream of pain and distress as though a thunderbolt had fallen. They both lay writhing and yelling in tears on the floor, frantic with despair at being bested and taken in by that little slut. What really made them wild with rage was that people were laughing about them in the village for having been so simple. Christ, to have been taken in like that and let yourself be kicked out of your own home before you had time to turn round. No, by God, they'd see about that.

When La Grande came round that very evening on Françoise's behalf to come to a polite agreement with Buteau as to the
day when he was expecting to move out, Buteau, throwing
caution to the winds, turned her out and replied with just one
word : Shit !

She went happily away, merely calling to him that they would
be sending the bailiffs along. And so, the very next day, looking
pale and anxious and even shabbier than usual, Vimeux came
gingerly up the street, watched by all the neighbouring gossips.
No one answered, so he knocked more loudly and timidly called
out that it was the summons requiring them to leave. At that the
attic window opened and a voice yelled the same single mono-
syllable :

'Shit !'

And a chamber-pot full of the stuff was emptied out. Spattered
from head to foot, Vimeux was forced to go away with the
summons undelivered. This incident is remembered with glee in
Rognes, to this very day.

La Grande immediately took Jean to Châteaudun to see a
solicitor. He explained that it would take at least five days to
evict them : the provisional injunction, the order made by the
court, the warrant from the clerk of the court and then the final
eviction, for which the bailiff's man would be helped by the
police if necessary. La Grande pressed him to speed up the pro-
cess by one day and, when she got back to Rognes, which was
on Tuesday, she announced to all and sundry that the Buteaus
would be thrown out into the street on Saturday evening at the
point of the sword, like thieves, unless they had previously left
the house peaceably.

When the news came to Buteau's ears, he shook his fist in
wild defiance. He shouted to anyone prepared to listen that they'd
have to fetch him out dead and that the soldiers would have to
knock the house down before they could drag him out. And in
the village, they could not tell whether he was pretending to be
mad or whether he really was, because his rage took such extravagant forms. He drove about at a gallop, standing in the front of
his cart, without a word of warning to stand clear or making
any reply to anyone; he had even been seen at night all over
the village, coming back from Lord knows where. He had

slashed out with his whip at one man who had approached him. He spread terror everywhere and the village was soon in a continual state of alarm. One morning it was realized that he had barricaded himself in; and fearful cries came from behind the locked doors, screams which seemed to be coming from Lise and her two children. The neighbours were so upset that they held a council of war and finally an old peasant bravely agreed to lean a ladder against the wall and climb up to see. But the window was opened and Buteau tipped the ladder backwards so that the old man nearly broke his legs. Aren't I free to do what I want in my own house? He was brandishing his fists and shouting that he'd do them all in if they disturbed him again. The worst thing was that Lise appeared too, with her two brats, swearing and accusing everyone of sticking their nose into things that didn't concern them. After that, nobody dared to interfere. But at every fresh sound their anxiety increased and people listened in fear and trembling to the dreadful things they could hear in the street. There were wiseacres who thought that he knew perfectly well what he was doing. Others were quite certain that he was going out of his mind and that it would end in a tragedy. No one ever knew exactly.

On Friday, the day before the expected eviction, there was one particularly affecting scene. Meeting his father near the church, Buteau started crying bitterly and fell on his knees in front of him, asking his forgiveness for having been such a bad son in the past. Perhaps this was why he was being punished now. He implored him to come back and live with them, he seemed to think that this was the only way to end his bad luck. Annoyed by his bawling and surprised at his apparent repentance, Fouan agreed to do so when all the family squabbles had been settled.

Finally, Saturday came. Buteau's state had become more and more disturbed, he had been hitching up and unhitching his cart without rhyme or reason from morning till night, and people hurriedly moved out of his way as he drove wildly round, all the more bewildered because of the pointlessness of his actions. On Saturday he hitched up again at eight o'clock in the morning but, instead of driving, he merely stood in the doorway shouting to his neighbours as they passed, jeering and sobbing, and broadcasting his plight in the crudest terms. It really was funny, wasn't it, to be buggered about by a bitch who'd been your trollop for the last five years! Yes, just a whore! And his wife as well. Two proper whores, that pair of sisters, who would fight to be the first one to be fucked by him! He kept returning to this lie in the most disgusting detail, taking his revenge. Lise came out and a dreadful quarrel flared up: he gave her a thrashing in public and sent her back into the house, calmed and pacified, feeling relieved himself because he had really let himself go. And he stood waiting on his doorstep, taunting and insulting the law and all its minions. Perhaps they had gone and got fucked on the way? He was exultant, they wouldn't be coming now.

It wasn't until four o'clock that Vimeux appeared with two gendarmes. Buteau went pale and quickly shut the door leading into the yard. Perhaps he had never imagined that they would pursue the matter to the bitter end. The house became as silent as the grave. Arrogant now that he had the protection of the gendarmes, Vimeux banged with both fists on the door. There was no answer. The gendarmes intervened and battered on the old door with the butts of their rifles. They had been followed by a long queue of men, women and children: the whole of Rognes had turned out in anticipation of the expected scene. And suddenly the gate opened and Buteau was seen standing at the front of his cart whipping up his horse and galloping straight for the crowd. As cries of fright arose, he yelled:

'I'm going to drown myself! I'm going to drown myself!'

There was nothing left for him to do but to put an end to everything; he'd throw himself into the Aigre with his cart, his horse, the lot!

'Mind out! I'm going to drown myself!'

At the sight of his swirling whip and galloping horse the frightened spectators dispersed. But just as he was hurtling away down the slope at a speed likely to smash his wheels to smithereens, some men rushed after it to hold it back. That pigheaded bastard was quite capable of taking a dip in the river just to annoy everybody... They caught up with it but they had a struggle, hanging on to the horse's head and jumping up into the cart. When they had fetched him back, he kept grimly silent, his teeth clenched, his whole body tense, impotently submitting to fate, in wild, mute protest.

At this moment, La Grande brought Françoise and Jean along to take possession of the house. Buteau merely stared them full in the face with the same sombre look with which he was now contemplating the culmination of his misfortunes. But now it was Lise's turn to shout and fling her arms about like a mad-woman. The gendarmes repeatedly told her to take her things and clear off. So she had to obey, since her husband wasn't man enough to defend her by standing up to them. With hands on hips, she now pitched into him:

'You bloody weakling, letting us be thrown into the street! Haven't you got any guts? Why don't you set about those dirty pigs? You're just a coward, you're not a man!'

As she was shouting this in his face, infuriated by his passive attitude, he finally pushed her away so roughly that she screamed. But all he did was to give her the same sombre look and remain grimly silent.

'Come along, old girl, hurry up,' said Vimeux triumphantly. 'We're not going to leave until you've handed over the keys to the new owners.'

At that, in a sudden burst of rage, Lise began to move out. She and Buteau had already taken many things, the tools and the heavy kitchen utensils, over to Frimat's wife three days before; and people realized that they had in fact expected eviction because, in order to give themselves time to look round, they had come to an agreement with the old woman to rent her house, which was too large for her, leaving her with merely the bedroom for her paralysed husband. Since the furniture and the animals had been sold with the house, all that Lise had to do was to remove her bed-linen, her mattresses and her personal belongings. Everything was thrown out through the door and the windows while the two children wept bitterly, thinking their last day had come. Laure was clinging to her mother's skirts and Jules lay sprawling on the heap of belongings piled up in the middle of the yard. As Buteau was not lifting a hand to help her, the gendarmes kindly started loading the baggage into the cart.

But trouble arose again when Lise noticed Françoise and Jean standing waiting behind La Grande. She rushed over and all the resentment which had been building up inside her suddenly exploded.

'So you've come to watch with your pig of a husband, have you, you dirty slut? Well, you can see how we're suffering, it's like drinking our blood. You thief, you thief, you thief!'

She was choking on the word and she hurled it at her sister each time she brought some fresh article into the yard. Tight-lipped and pale, with her eyes blazing, Françoise made no reply; she was pretending, insultingly, to be watching what was happening carefully, to make sure that nothing of hers was removed. And at that very moment, she recognized a kitchen stool which had been included in the sale.

'That's mine,' she snapped.

'Yours? Then you can go and fetch it,' her sister replied, flinging it into the pond.

The house was free. Buteau took the horse's bridle, Lise collected the two children, her only two remaining bundles, Jules on her right arm, Laure on her left, went up to Françoise and spat in her face.

'There you are! That's yours, too!'

Françoise immediately spat back.

'And that's for you.'

And still glaring venomously at each other as they slowly wiped their faces, the two sisters took their leave, full of hatred and parted for ever with only the enmity of their impetuous Fouan blood as their sole remaining link.

At the end, Buteau shouted his parting words, with a menacing wave of his fist:

'We'll be back soon!'

La Grande went after them to see the matter through to the end, determined, now that they were down and out, to turn against the others who seemed to be dropping her so quickly and were too happy, in any case. Groups of people stood around for a long time talking in undertones. Françoise and Jean had gone into the empty house.

Just as the Buteaus were busy unpacking their things at Frimat's place, they were surprised to see old Fouan appear and ask in a scared, breathless voice, looking behind him as if pursued by some malefactor:

'Have you got a corner for me? I'd like to spend the night.'

He had run all the way from the Castle, pursued by a dreadful fear. Every time he woke up at night he would see the thin, boyish figure of La Trouille, in her scanty shift, prowling round his bedroom in search of the bonds which he had finally decided to hide outside, in a hole in the rock which he had then blocked up with earth. Jesus Christ used to send the little hussy in because she was so lithe and light-footed in her bare feet that she could glide everywhere, between the chairs, under the bed, like a snake; and she was thrilled by the search, for being convinced that the old man carried them on his person when he was dressed, she was furious at being unable to discover where he deposited them when he went to bed; there was certainly nothing in the bed, for her thin arm had gently inserted itself and groped around there, so skilfully that her grandfather could barely detect its rustling. But that day, after lunch, he had suddenly come over faint and fallen down, dazed, beside the table. And when he came to, still so shaken that he had not opened his eyes, he was lying on the ground in the same place and had the strange feeling that he was being undressed by Jesus Christ and La Trouille. Instead of coming to his aid, the devils had had only one thought – to take advantage of the situation and quickly search him. The girl particularly was angry and rough, no longer making any attempt to be gentle, tugging away at his coat and trousers and, God save us, even prying into his naked flesh, in every hole, to make sure he hadn't stuffed his nest-egg away there. She was turning him over with her two hands, pulling his legs apart, as though rummaging in an old empty pocket. Not a thing! Where was his hiding-place? It was enough to make you want to open him up and search inside! He was so terrified of being murdered if he stirred that he continued to pretend to be unconscious, keeping his eyes closed and his arms and legs limp. But once he was free he had taken to his heels, fully determined not to spend the night at the Castle.

'Well, have you got a corner to put me up?' he asked again.

Buteau had cheered up at the unexpected return of his father. It meant more money coming in.

'But of course, old man! We'll squeeze together a bit! It'll bring us luck. Ah! God knows how rich I'd be if a kind heart was the only thing needed!'

Françoise and Jean went slowly into the empty house. Darkness was falling and a last melancholy glimmer of light lit up the silent rooms. Everything seemed so old under this venerable roof, which had provided shelter for her wretched toiling ancestors over some three centuries, that there was the same solemn atmosphere that you feel in the shadow of old village churches. The doors had been left open and a blast of wind seemed to have blown through the timbers; chairs were lying in disorder on the floor, relics of the catastrophe of the eviction. The house seemed dead.

Slowly Françoise wandered round the house, looking at everything. Confused memories and vague emotions were stirring within her. Over there, she had played when a child. It was in this kitchen, beside this table, that her father had died. In the bedroom, standing beside the bed now stripped of its mattress, she thought of Lise and Buteau and the nights when they would make love so energetically that their gasps could be heard through the ceiling. Would they be continuing to torment her, even now? She could still sense Buteau's presence. Here, he had seized hold of her one evening and she had bitten him. And there as well. And over there. At every corner she was beset by disturbing thoughts.

Then, turning round, she was surprised to see Jean there. What was this stranger doing in her house? He looked embarrassed, like a mere visitor, not daring to touch anything. She was seized by a dreadful sensation of loneliness and despair at not having a greater feeling of rejoicing on her victory. She would have imagined herself coming in, shouting with joy and exulting behind her sister's back. And yet the house was causing her no pleasure; disquiet was growing at her heart. Perhaps it was because of the mournful, fading light? Long after nightfall, she and her man roamed about in the darkness from one room to the next without even the courage to light a candle.

But a sound brought them back into the kitchen and they laughed to see Gideon who, having found his way in as usual, was rummaging in the open sideboard. Old Coliche was lowing next door, at the far end of her shed.

Then Jean took Françoise into his arms and gently kissed her, as though to say that they were going to be happy, despite everything.

PART FIVE

Chapter 1

BEFORE the winter ploughing starts, Beauce is covered in manure as far as the eye can see. Under the pale September skies, from dawn till dusk, carts brimming over with steaming piles of old litter would make their way slowly along the country roads as though delivering heat itself to the land. On all sides the fields were covered with little heaps, a sort of heaving, surging, sea of manure from cowshed and stable, whilst in some of them the piles had been spread out and the soil could be seen from afar stained with the dark, flowing tide of dung. The whole future growth of spring was borne along on this fermenting flood of liquid, matter was decomposing and returning to Mother Earth; death would be producing a rebirth. And from one end of the vast plain to the other, you could smell the stench of all this animal excrement from which man's daily bread would come.

One afternoon Jean drove a big cartload of manure out to his Cornailles field. Françoise and he had now been settled in for a whole month and their lives had taken on the active, monotonous tenor of the countryside. As he came up, he caught sight of Buteau in the next field with a fork, spreading out the heaps of manure deposited there a week ago. The two men exchanged a furtive look. They often met and found themselves forced to work side by side because they were neighbours; and Buteau suffered particularly because Françoise's share had been cut out of his own seven-and-a-half-acre field, leaving him with two separate sections to right and left, thereby forcing him to make a continual detour when passing from one to the other. They never spoke. Perhaps one day, when a quarrel broke out between them, they would slaughter each other.

Meanwhile Jean had started unloading his cart. Standing up to his waist in the manure, he was forking it out when Hourdequin came along the road, having been going his rounds ever since noon. The farmer had kept pleasant memories of his former labourer and he stopped for a chat. He looked old and his face was lined with worry, caused not only by his farm.

'Why haven't you tried phosphate, Jean?'

And, without waiting for a reply, he launched into a long monologue, as though wishing to relieve his mind. The whole secret of farming was in manure and fertilizers. He had tried everything; indeed he had just been passing through that mad craze for fertilizers which often seizes farmers. He had experimented with one thing and another, various sorts of grass, leaves, vine pressings, rape-seed and colza cake; and then bonemeal, meatmeal and dry powdered blood; his great grief was to have been unable to try real liquid blood, there being no abattoirs in the district. Now he had taken to using road-sweepings, muck from ditches, clinker and ash, and above all, wool-waste which he bought from a cloth manufacturer in Châteaudun. His principle was that anything coming out of the land is good to go back into it. He had built huge compost-pits behind his farm, filled with all the refuse of the whole district, any odd shovelfuls of muck, dead animals, decomposing dog-droppings or filth drained from ponds. It was a real gold-mine.

'I've sometimes had good results with phosphates,' he added.

'You can be caught out with that sort of thing,' Jean said.

'Yes, of course, if you take pot-luck with the commercial travellers who work the little country markets. On every market, there ought to be an expert chemist with the job of analysing all these chemical fertilizers, which are so often adulterated. The future certainly lies with that sort of fertilizer but we'll all have kicked the bucket before then. You have to be brave enough to suffer on behalf of all the others.'

The stench of the manure that Jean was turning had cheered him up a little. He adored its promise of fertility and was sniffing it with the relish of a man smelling a randy woman.

'Of course,' he went on after a pause, 'there's nothing like good farm muck. The trouble is there's never enough of it. And then again people spoil it, they don't know either how to prepare it or use it. Look at yours, for example, it's been dried up by the sun. You haven't been covering it.'

And when Jean confessed to him that he was still using the

Buteaus' old pit, in front of the cowshed. Hourdequin attacked him for his conservatism. For some years now he had been putting turf and earth over the bottom of his pit, and in addition he had arranged a system of pipes so that his liquid-manure heap received all the household slops, the urine of both animals and people, all the farm sewage, in fact; and twice a week liquid manure was pumped over the middle heap. And, finally, he had taken to emptying out the latrines as a precious source of fertilizer.

'Yes, there you are! It's stupid to waste God's good gifts! For a long time, I was like the peasants, I had qualms about it. But now Old Ma Poohpooh has converted me. You know Old Ma Poohpooh, don't you, she's your neighbour. Well, she's the only one who's got it right. Those cabbages of hers where she empties her chamber-pot are superb, really outstanding for size, and flavour too. You can't deny it, everything depends on that.'

Jean laughed as he jumped out of his empty cart and began piling his manure up into little heaps. Hourdequin followed him amid the clouds of steam swirling all around them.

'When you think that the night-soil of Paris alone would fertilize seventy-five thousand acres. They've worked it out, and at present it goes to waste, they only use a very small part of it in powder form. Think of that! Seventy-five thousand acres! Think what that would do to Beauce, can't you see it covered with manure and all the wheat that would grow?'

He made an expansive gesture, embracing the immense flat plain of Beauce. Enthusiastically, he drew a picture of the whole of Paris opening the floodgates of its sewers and releasing their fertilizing flood of human manure while streams of liquid dung came pouring through brimming channels and covering every field. And bathed in sunshine, this ocean of excreta would rise up and up, its stench invigorated by the steady breezes of the plain. The great city would be restoring to the land the life which it had received from it. The soil would soak up these riches and the fertile, bloated land would lavish giant harvests of good wheaten bread.

'We might have to take to the boats then,' said Jean, both amused and disgusted at this original idea of submerging plains under floods of night-soil.

But at that moment the sound of a voice made him look round.

He was surprised to see Lise standing in her cart drawn up beside the road and shouting at the top of her voice to Buteau:

'Listen, I'm off to Cloyes to fetch Monsieur Finet. Father's collapsed in his bedroom. I think he's kicking the bucket. Go back and have a look.'

And without even waiting for a reply, she whipped up her horse and drove off, growing smaller and smaller as she bounced away along the straight road.

Buteau leisurely finished spreading the last of the heaps. So his father was ill, what a bloody nuisance! Perhaps it was just a trick to get special attention! Then he thought that it must after all be quite serious for his wife to incur the expense of fetching in a doctor, so he put on his jacket.

'He's mean with his manure, that fellow,' muttered Hourdequin, intrigued by the manure on the next field. 'Stingy farmer, stingy land. And a nasty piece of work whom you'd better be careful of, after all that trouble between you. How can you expect things to be all right when there are so many rogues and bitches in the world? The land's fed up with us, that's the truth.'

He went off to La Borderie, disconsolate again, just as Buteau was clumping away heavy-footed back to Rognes. Left to himself, Jean finished off his job, depositing forkfuls of manure at ten-yard intervals, making the fumes of ammonia even more pungent. There were other steaming heaps in the distance, clouding the horizon in a fine bluish haze. The whole of Beauce would remain like this, warm and pungent, until the frosts.

The Buteaus were still living with the Frimats, occupying the whole of the house except for the downstairs back room, which Frimat's wife had kept for herself and her husband. The Buteaus felt cramped and, above all, they missed their kitchen-garden, for Frimat's wife had naturally retained her own little patch which enabled her to feed her husband and even offer him a few little luxuries. They would have moved out into larger accommodation had they not realized that their presence was a source of exasperation for Françoise. As the two properties were separated only by a party-wall, they would talk at the top of their voices, loud enough to be heard, saying that they were only camping out there and would certainly be returning to their old house at the first opportunity. So it was pointless to go to the bother of making another move, wasn't it? Why and how they might manage it, they made no attempt to explain to each other and it was this crazy certainty and utter confidence, based on unknown factors, that upset Françoise so much and spoilt her pleasure at having become the owner of the house; quite apart from the fact that, now and again, her sister Lise would prop a ladder against the wall to shout abuse at her. Ever since the final settlement of accounts in Monsieur Baillehache's office, she had been saying that she'd been robbed and would stand in her backyard interminably hurling foul accusations over the wall.

When Buteau finally reached home, he found Fouan lying sprawled on his bed in his little corner behind the kitchen, under the hayloft stairs. The two children were looking after him; Jules, now eight, and Laure, three, were playing at making streams by emptying the old man's jug on the floor.

'Well, what's all this?' asked Buteau, standing beside his bed.

Fouan had regained consciousness. His wide-open eyes slowly turned and stared; but his head did not turn. He seemed as though turned to stone.

'Look here now, Father, there's too much work to be done, you mustn't play the fool! You can't pack up today.'

And as Laure and Jules now succeeded in breaking the jug, he clouted them, making them both yell. The old man did not blink an eyelid but kept staring through his wide-open eyes. So there was nothing to be done, since the old boy couldn't stir his stumps or himself. We'll see what the doctor says. He was sorry he had left his field and set about splitting some logs in front of the door, in order not to be idle.

In any case, Lise came back almost at once with Monsieur Finet, who spent a long time examining the sick man, while she and her husband watched anxiously. If the old man died straight away, his death would have been a good riddance; but now it might last a long time. That could cost a pretty penny, and if he were to peg out before they had laid hands on his nest-egg, Fanny and Jesus Christ would surely make a fuss. The doctor's silence confirmed their anxiety. When he sat down in the kitchen to write a prescription, they decided to question him.

'So it's serious, is it? Might last a week, eh? Heavens, what a long prescription! What's all that you're writing?'

Monsieur Finet made no reply: he was used to this sort of interrogation by peasants bewildered and upset by the sight of illness, and he had taken the wise decision of treating them like horses, refusing to enter into conversation with them. He was very familiar with the common forms of illness and usually managed to cure them, better than a cleverer doctor would have done. But since he blamed his patients for having ruined his career, he treated them roughly, thereby making them all the more deferential, despite their constant suspicions as to the effectiveness of his potions. Would the good that they did be worth the money they cost?

'So you think that with all that lot he'll get better?' Buteau went on, scared at the length of the prescription.

The doctor merely shrugged his shoulders. He had gone back to look at the sick man, intrigued to discover a little fever after this slight stroke. He took his pulse again, with his eyes on his watch, not even bothering to ask any questions of the old man, who was looking at him with his bewildered air. And as he left, he simply said:

'It'll take three weeks. I'll look in tomorrow. Don't be surprised if he's a trifle delirious tonight.'

Three weeks! These were the only words that the Buteaus heard and they filled them with consternation. What a lot of money if they had a similar list of medicine every day! The worst thing was that now Buteau had to take his cart and rush off to the chemist's at Cloyes. It was a Saturday; Frimat's wife, coming back from selling her vegetables, found Lise alone and so disconsolate that she was just standing there doing nothing. And the old woman was equally disconsolate when she heard what had happened: she never had any luck, she could at least have taken advantage of the doctor's visit to ask about her old man into the bargain, if it hadn't been market day. The news had already spread through Rognes, because La Trouille had the impertinence to appear and refused to leave until she had felt her grandfather's hand. She went back and told Jesus Christ that he wasn't dead, at any rate. Hard on the heels of this shameless little hussy, La Grande appeared, obviously sent by Fanny. The old woman took up her position at her brother's bedside and summed him up by the freshness of his eyes, like the eels from the Aigre. She went away with a sniff, apparently disappointed that it wouldn't be this time. After this, the family paid no further attention. What was the point, seeing that the odds were that he would recover?

Till midnight the house was in confusion. Buteau had come back in a nasty mood. There were mustard plasters for his legs, a potion to take hourly and, if he improved, a purge for the following morning. Frimat's wife lent a willing hand but at ten o'clock, dropping with sleep and not greatly concerned, she went to bed. Buteau would have liked to do the same and started bullying Lise. What on earth were they doing there? Certainly watching the old man wouldn't help him to get better. He was now wandering in his head, rambling away out loud, seemingly imagining he was out in the fields, working as hard as he had in the distant days of his prime. And Lise, disturbed at hearing her father mumbling these incoherent old stories, as though dead and buried and returning from the grave, was just about to follow her husband, who was undressing, when she thought she would tidy up the sick man's clothes, which had been left on a chair. She shook them carefully, after thoroughly searching through the pockets, where she found nothing but an old knife and some string. Then, just as she was hanging them up at the back of the wall-cupboard, there, staring her in the face, she saw a little bundle of papers lying in the middle of a shelf. Her heart missed a beat: it was the nest-egg, that nest-egg for which they had been on the look-out for the last month, which they had been searching for in all sorts of extraordinary places and which was now lying there for all to see under her very nose! Had the old man been changing his hiding-place when the stroke had laid him low?

'Buteau! Buteau!' she called in such a strained voice that he hurried in, wearing only his shirt, thinking that his father was breathing his last.

He too was left breathless at first. Then the pair of them were seized by such a frenzy of joy that they joined hands and, face to face, capered up and down like goats, oblivious of the sick man who, now with eyes closed and with his head sunk deep in his pillow, was still rambling on, continually losing the thread in his delirium. He was ploughing.

'Come along, you old nag, come along. It's as dry as a bone, curse it, it's like rock ! It's back-breaking, I'll have to buy another one ! Gee up ! damn you !'

'Sh !' whispered Lise, turning round with a sudden start.

'Oh, for God's sake,' Buteau replied. 'How can he know? Can't you hear him raving?'

They sat down beside the bed, their legs giving way under the shock of their joy.

'Anyway,' she went on, 'nobody will be able to accuse us of having searched him, because, God's my witness, I wasn't really thinking of his money. It just jumped into my hand. Let's have a look.'

He was already undoing the bundle and counting out loud.

'Two hundred and thirty and seventy, that's exactly three hundred. Yes, that's it. I'd worked it out right, because of that quarterly payment, those fifteen five-franc pieces, that time at the tax-collector's. It's the five per cents. Isn't it funny to think of those shabby little bits of paper being as good as real money !'

But Lise shushed him again, scared at a sudden outburst of mirth from the old man, who had perhaps now reached the Great Harvest in the reign of Charles X, the one which they hadn't been able to store for lack of space.

'What a lot ! What a lot ! It's stupid, what a lot there is ! God save me, when there's a lot, there surely is a lot !'

And his choking laughter sounded like a death-rattle. His mirth must have been hidden deep inside him, because no sign of it was to be seen on his rigid face.

'It's just foolish thoughts running through his mind,' said Buteau, with a shrug.

Silence fell. They were both looking at the papers and thinking.

'Well, what shall we do?' whispered Lise in the end. 'We'll have to put them back, I suppose?'

But he made a vigorous gesture of refusal.

'Oh, yes, of course we must put them back. If not, he'll start looking for them and screaming the house down and we'll be in a fine mess with those other swine in the family.'

She interrupted him again, shocked at hearing her father sobbing with despair and misery, from the bottom of his heart, tears which seemed to sum up his whole life but without rhyme or reason, because he merely kept repeating :

398

'I'm buggered! I'm buggered! I'm buggered!'

'And do you think,' Buteau went on fiercely, 'that I'm going to leave these papers with that old man who's going off his rocker? So that he can burn them or tear them up, oh, no, that's not on!'

'Yes, that's true,' she murmured.

'Well, that's enough, now let's go to bed. If he asks for them, I'll answer him, I know what to say. And the others had better not cause any trouble!'

They went to bed after hiding the papers under the marble top of an old chest of drawers, which seemed safer than a locked drawer. Left alone, in the dark in case a candle caused a fire, their father continued to rave and sob deliriously all night.

Next day, Monsieur Finet found him quieter, better than he had hoped. Ah, these old carthorses, they're as tough as nails! The fever which he had feared seemed not to have materialized. He ordered iron, quinine, rich man's drugs, the cost of which once again threw the couple into consternation; and as he was leaving he was tackled by Frimat's wife, who had been lying in wait for him.

'My dear woman, I've already told you that your husband's just a cabbage, no more, no less. I'm not a gardener, for goodness' sake! You know what the end will be, don't you? And the sooner the better for him and for you.'

He whipped up his horse and she sank down on a boulder in tears. Certainly twelve years was a long time to have been looking after her husband; and as she grew older her strength was flagging, so that she was terrified that she might no longer be able to tend her little garden; all the same, she felt sick at heart at the thought of losing her paralytic old husband, who had relapsed into childhood and whom she carried about, changed and pampered with delicacies. Even his good arm was becoming paralysed now and it was she who had to stick his pipe in his mouth.

At the end of a week, Monsieur Finet was surprised to see Fouan on his legs, a trifle weak but determined to walk because, he said, the way to stop yourself dying is not to want to. And behind the doctor's back, Buteau gave a sly grin because he had destroyed all the prescriptions after the first one, claiming that the safest thing was to let the illness cure itself. However, on market day, Lise was soft-hearted enough to bring back a potion which had been prescribed the day before; and as the doctor came in on Monday for the last time, Buteau told him that the old man had nearly had a relapse:

'I don't know what they'd put in that bottle of yours but it made him bloody ill.'

That was the evening when Fouan decided to speak out. Ever since he had been up, he had been roaming around the house with an anxious look; his mind was a blank and he could no longer remember where on earth he had hidden his papers. He ferreted and rummaged about everywhere, desperately probing his memory. Then vaguely he recalled something: perhaps he hadn't hidden them after all, but left them there on the shelf? But if he was mistaken and nobody had taken them, wouldn't he be letting the cat out of the bag and admitting the existence of this hard-earned nest-egg which he had been hiding with such care ever since? He struggled with himself for another two days, torn between anger at this sudden disappearance and the need to keep his mouth shut. But the facts were becoming clearer in his mind, he could remember that on the morning of his stroke he had put the packet down, intending to slip it into a gap behind a beam in the ceiling, which he had noticed as he was lying in bed. So, feeling miserable and robbed, he finally spoke his mind.

They had finished their evening bowl of soup. Lise was putting the plates away and Buteau was rocking to and fro on his chair with a facetious look on his face; he had been watching his father closely ever since he had left his bed and was waiting to see what would happen, realizing from his father's unhappy, overwrought look that the time had come. And, in fact, the old man, his legs weak and tottering from walking up and down, suddenly stopped short in front of his son.

'What about my papers?' he asked, in a hoarse, strangled voice.

Buteau blinked and looked extremely surprised, as though failing to understand.

'What's that about papers? What papers?'

'My money!' growled the old man, drawing himself up menacingly.

'Your money? So now it seems you've got some money? You were swearing blind that we'd cost you so much that you hadn't got a penny left! So you've got some money, you crafty old man!'

He was still rocking on his chair with an amused grin on his face, pleased at his own cleverness, because he had been the first to sniff out the nest-egg, long ago.

Fouan was quivering in every limb.

'Give it back to me.'

'So I'm to give it back to you! Have I got it? Do I even know where it is, this money of yours?'

'You've stolen it! Give it back to me or, by Christ, I'll make you!'

And despite his age, he seized him by the shoulders and shook him. But at this his son stood up and caught hold of his father himself, not violently but merely to shout at him:

'Yes, I've got it and I'm going to keep it. I'm going to keep it for you, you understand, you silly old man, because you're going off your rocker! And that's the truth, it really was time to take the papers off you, you were going to tear them up. Isn't that right, Lise, he was tearing them up?'

'Yes, sure as I stand here. When people don't know what they're doing!'

On hearing this, Fouan was shocked and frightened. Was he really mad and not able to remember things? If he had tried to destroy the papers, like a little boy playing with picture-cards, then he was fouling his own nest and ready to be put down. He subsided, defeated and in tears. He faltered:

'Do give them back, please.'

'No.'

'Give them back, I'm better now.'

'No, I won't! So that you can wipe your arse or light your pipe with them? No thanks!'

And from then on, the Buteaus persisted in refusing to hand over the bonds. Moreover, they talked about the matter quite openly, making a very dramatic scene of it, how they had come and snatched them out of the old man's hands at the very moment when he was starting to tear them up. One evening, they even showed Frimat's wife the beginning of the tear. Who could possibly hold it against them for preventing such a disaster, good money torn to pieces and lost for everybody ! Other people loudly approved their action, although in their heart of hearts they suspected them of lying. Jesus Christ in particular was in a permanent state of fury : to think that this nest-egg, which he had vainly tried to find in his own home, had been uncovered by the others straight away ! And he had once held them in his own hand and been stupid enough to have scruples ! Really, it wasn't worth having the reputation of being a rogue ! Anyway, he swore he'd make his brother settle up when the old man pegged out. Fanny, too, was saying that the account would have to be settled. But the Buteaus said nothing to the contrary; unless, of course, the old man took his money back and disposed of it...

For his part, Fouan hobbled round the village telling everyone his story and would even buttonhole passers-by to complain about his miserable lot. One morning, he went into the yard next door, to see his niece.

She was helping Jean load manure into a cart. He was standing in the pit, tossing up forkfuls which she was stamping on to bed it down. The old man propped himself on his stick and began his tale of woe:

'Well, isn't it annoying, it's my money which they've taken and refuse to give me back ! What would you do about it?'

Françoise let him repeat his question three times. She was vexed that he had called on her like this and was giving him a cool reception because she wanted to avoid any possible cause of dispute with the Buteaus.

'You know, Uncle,' she replied in the end, 'it's really no concern of ours, we're only too glad to have got away from that horrible lot.'

And she turned her back on him and went on treading down the manure, which reached up to her thighs and almost submerged her as her husband kept throwing up forkful after forkful. Then she disappeared in the middle of the cloud of steam, relaxed and contented in the asphyxiating fumes stirred up from the dung-pit.

'Because I'm not mad, am I?' Fouan went on, seeming not to have heard her. 'You can see I'm not. They ought to give me back my money. Do *you* think I'd be capable of destroying it?'

Françoise and Jean made no reply.

'I'd have to be mad, wouldn't I? And I'm not mad, you could bear witness to that, couldn't you?'

She suddenly straightened up on top of the load of manure, looking very tall, strong and healthy, as if she had been growing in it and giving off this rich, fertile smell from her own person. With her arms akimbo and her rounded bosom, she had become every inch a woman.

'Now, Uncle, that's enough! I told you not to get us mixed up in all this nasty business. And, incidentally, since we're talking about it, I think you'd do as well not to call on us any more.'

'So you're sending me away?' the old man asked, trembling as he spoke.

Jean felt he ought to intervene.

'No, it's just that we don't want any squabbles. We'd be at each other's throats for three whole days, if they were to see you here. Everyone wants a quiet life, don't they?'

Fouan did not stir, looking from one to the other with his poor pale eyes. Then he went off.

'Well, if I need any help, I shall know where not to come.'

So they let him go away, not very happily because they were not really lacking in heart. But what could they do? It wouldn't have helped him at all and it would certainly have made them lose their appetite and given them sleepless nights. While her husband went to fetch his whip, she carefully shovelled up the odd pieces of manure from the ground and tossed them into the cart.

Next day a violent row broke out between Fouan and Buteau. In any case, the altercation over the bonds kept recurring every day, with one of them obstinately repeating his eternal 'Give them back' like an obsession and the other man refusing with his equally invariable 'Sod you!' But things were gradually growing worse, above all since the old man had started searching to see where his son might have hidden the nest-egg. Now it was his turn to go through the whole house, probing the woodwork of the cupboards and tapping the walls, to see if they sounded hollow. His eyes kept continually darting from one corner to the other, with one single idea in mind; and as soon as he was on his own, he would get the children out of the way and start rummaging again with the passion of a young lad who suddenly hurls himself on the maid as soon as his parents have gone out. On this particular day, as Buteau came home unexpectedly, he saw Fouan lying flat on the floor with his head under the chest of drawers, looking to see if there was a hiding-place there. Buteau was beside himself with rage, because his father was getting warm: what he was looking for underneath was in fact hidden on top, as it was sealed beneath the heavy marble slab.

'Christ Almighty, you crazy idiot! You're turning into a snake now! For God's sake get up!'

He pulled him out by his legs and jerked him to his feet.

'Have you finished poking your nose into every little hole, confound you? I've had enough of you, combing the whole house through!'

Annoyed at having been caught, Fouan looked at him and in a sudden outburst of rage said:

'Give them back to me!'

'Sod you!' Buteau bawled back.

'Well, I can't stand it here, I'm going.'

'Good, so sod off, and the best of luck! And, by Christ, if you come back, it's because you've got no guts!'

He took him by the arm and hustled him out.

Chapter 2

FOUAN went off down the slope. His anger had suddenly evaporated and, when he reached the road at the bottom, he stopped, bewildered at finding himself out of doors and not knowing where to go. The church clock chimed three; the wind struck cold on this dull, raw, autumn day; and he was shivering because in his hasty departure he had not even picked up his hat; fortunately he had his stick. First he set off along the road to Cloyes; then, after a moment, he asked himself what he would do in that direction and turned back towards Rognes, shuffling along as usual. When he reached Macqueron's he thought of having a drink; but, on feeling in his pockets, he realized he hadn't a penny on him, and being scared that people might have already heard what had happened he felt loath to show his face. And in fact it seemed to him that Lengaigne, who was standing in his doorway, was looking at him superciliously, as people look at tramps. Lequeu was watching him through one of the school windows but made no sign of greeting. It was understandable, everyone would be despising him again now that he had once more been stripped of everything – and this time not only stripped but skint.

When he reached the bridge, Fouan leant back for a moment against the parapet. He was worried that it would soon be nightfall. Where could he sleep? Not even a roof over his head. As the Bécus' dog went by, it filled him with envy: there at least was an animal that knew of a hole in the straw to crawl into. He thought confusedly, his mind dulled now that his anger had passed. He had closed his eyelids and was trying to recall some sheltered corner, protected from the cold. Everything was becoming nightmarish, the whole countryside kept flitting through his mind, bare and swept with icy blasts. But in a sudden burst of energy he shook his head and roused himself. He mustn't give up like this. They wouldn't let an old man die in the streets.

Without thinking he crossed the bridge and found himself standing beside the Delhommes' little farmhouse. As soon as he realized this, he turned and went round to the back of the house in order not to be seen. Once there, he stopped again and leant against the wall of the cowshed in which he could hear his daughter Fanny talking. Could he have been thinking of going back to her? He himself would have been unable to answer the question; his feet had carried him there automatically. He could see the inside of the house as clearly as if he had gone in, the kitchen to the left, his bedroom on the first floor, at the end of the hayloft. He was overcome by emotion, his legs gave way and he would have collapsed had he not been supported by the wall. For a long time he stood motionless, his old back braced against the house. Fanny was still talking in the cowshed but he could not distinguish what she was saying: perhaps it was this loud, muffled noise which had stirred his feelings. But she must have been berating a servant, for she raised her voice and he heard her sharp grating tone as, without resorting to abuse, she addressed the unfortunate girl so insultingly that she was sobbing. And he was suffering; his moment of emotion had passed and he steeled himself, certain that, had he pushed open the door, his daughter would have greeted him in that same acid voice. He could still hear her saying: 'Father will be back on his hands and knees asking to be taken in!' – the remark which had cut every link between them for ever, like the stroke of an axe. No, he'd rather starve or sleep under a hedge than see her triumphant look, the look of a righteous woman.

In order to keep away from the road, since he felt that everyone was spying on him, Fouan walked up the right bank of the Aigre beyond the bridge and was soon amongst the vineyards. He must have been thinking of making for the plain, thereby avoiding the village. However, on the way he had to pass by the Castle, to which his legs seemed to have carried him instinctively, like those old carthorses who find their way back to the stables where their oats await them. The climb had left him out of breath, so he sat down to recover and think things over. Certainly, if he were to say to Jesus Christ: 'I'm going to take Buteau to court, please help me,' the rascal would have received him with open arse and that evening they would have had a damned good blow-out. In fact, the smells of just such a feast, some drunken bout which had been going on since that morning, were reaching him in his little hideout. Tempted by hunger, he crept nearer and recognized

Canon's voice and sniffed the fragrant smell of baked red haricot beans which La Trouille prepared so skilfully when her father wished to celebrate his friend's appearance on the scene. Why shouldn't he go in and enjoy himself with those two rogues whom he could hear bellowing away in their cosy smoke-laden den, so drunk that he felt envious? A sudden explosion from Jesus Christ went straight to his heart and he was reaching out to open the door when La Trouille's shrill laugh turned him to stone. It was she whom he dreaded now, and he could still see her skinny figure, stark-naked under her shift, hurling herself on him and prying into every hidden recess of his body like a vulture. So what good would it do him if her father were to help him get his papers back now? She'd be there waiting to strip him of them again. Suddenly, the door opened, the little tramp was taking a look, having sensed someone prowling around outside. He had just time to retreat rapidly behind some bushes, and as he glimpsed her green eyes glinting in the failing light he made himself scarce.

When Fouan had climbed up onto the level plateau he felt a sort of relief: here he was safe from the others and was happy to be alone, even if he died as a result. For a long time, he wandered aimlessly about the plain. Night was falling and he was buffeted by the icy wind. Some of the gusts were so strong that they took his breath away and he had to turn his back, bare-headed, with his wispy white hair blowing wildly in the wind. It struck six o'clock; everybody in Rognes would be eating; and his limbs felt so weak that he could walk only very slowly. Between the gusts a heavy shower of rain pelted down and soaked him to the skin; he walked on and was twice soaked again. Then, without knowing how he had found his way there, he realized that he was standing in the square in front of the church, beside the old family house of the Fouans.

No, he couldn't take refuge there, they'd driven him out. The rain was now streaming down again so hard that suddenly he lost heart. He had gone up to the side door with his eye on the kitchen from which the smell of cabbage soup was rising. Impelled by the physical need for food and warmth, the whole of his poor old body was crying out to submit. But above the champing of jaws he heard an exchange of words that stopped him short.

'Suppose Father doesn't come back?'

'Forget it ! He's too keen on his grub not to come back when he's hungry !'

Fouan shrank back, afraid that they might catch sight of him at the door, like a beaten dog crawling back to his platter. So overcome by shame was he that he was filled with a fierce resolve to creep into some corner and give up the ghost. They'd see if he was so keen on his grub ! He went down the slope once more and collapsed on the end of a beam outside Clou's smithy. His legs were no longer able to support him and he gave himself up for lost in the dark beside the deserted road where there was not a soul to be seen, for the evening gatherings had already begun and the bad weather was keeping everyone indoors. The rain had made the wind drop and water was now teeming down in torrents. He did not feel strong enough to stand up and seek refuge. With his stick between his knees, his bare skull streaming with water, he sat motionless, stupefied by his wretched plight. He could not even think; but that was how things were when you had neither children nor home nor nothing, you tightened your belt and slept in the open. Nine o'clock struck and then ten. The rain kept pouring down, turning his old bones to water. But suddenly lamps appeared, moving rapidly down the street : the gatherings were breaking up and he roused himself again as he recognized La Grande, who had been saving the cost of a candle by spending the evening at the Delhommes'. His bones creaked as he laboriously rose to his feet and followed her at a distance, but not fast enough to catch her up before she went indoors. With sinking heart he hesitated in front of her closed door. Finally, he could not contain his wretchedness any longer. He knocked.

It must be said that he had picked the wrong moment, for La Grande was in a foul temper, as a result of an unfortunate event the previous week which had quite put her out. One evening, when she was alone with her grandson Hilarion, she had hit on the good idea of getting him to split some logs for her, a little extra chore before she sent him off to sleep in the straw; and as he showed little enthusiasm for the job, she stood beside the woodpile abusing him. Up till then, in his craven awe of his grandmother, this stupid, deformed brute with the muscles of an ox had allowed her to exploit his strength quite mercilessly, without even daring to raise his eyes to look her in the face. But for the last few days she should have taken warning, because beneath his gawky exterior he was seething inwardly and becoming restive under the heavy burden of work she was demanding of him. She made the mistake of trying to hurry him along by tapping the back of his neck with her stick. He dropped his axe and looked at her. Irritated by such impertinence, she had started to belabour him all over, back, thighs, everywhere, when suddenly he flung himself on her. She thought that he was going to throw her down, stamp on her and strangle her, but it was something else. Ever since the death of his sister he had been deprived of sexual intercourse and his anger took the form of wild lust, with no account of age or kinship, hardly even of gender. This brute was raping his eighty-nine-year-old grandmother, whose body was as dry as a stick and whose only feminine attribute was the curved slit in her old carcass. But the old girl was still tough and determined to resist; she managed to catch hold of the axe and split his skull open. Hearing her cries, her neighbours hurried round and she told them what had happened in detail: another second and he'd have made it, the lout was right at its very edge. Hilarion did not die until the following day. The magistrate came; then there was the funeral; in a word, a whole pack of trouble from which she had now fortunately recovered, feeling quite composed but cut to the quick by people's ingratitude and fully determined never to do any more favours for members of her family.

Fouan had to knock three times, so timorously that La Grande could not hear him. Finally, she came back to the door and decided to ask who was there.

'It's me.'

'Who's me?'

'Me, your brother.'

She had doubtless recognized his voice straight away but was not hurrying herself, wanting to make him explain. Silence fell. She asked him again:

'What d'you want?'

He was trembling, not daring to reply. Then she roughly opened the door; but as he went to go in, she barred the way with her skinny arms, leaving him in the street in the dreary, driving rain which was still streaming down.

'I know what you want. They came and told me during the wake. So you've been stupid enough to get snaffled again, you couldn't even hang on to the money you'd salted away and now you want me to get you out of trouble, don't you?'

Then, seeing that he was stammering excuses and explanations, she added angrily:

'As if I hadn't warned you. Didn't I tell you time and again that it was stupid and cowardly to give up your land? It's a good thing that you've been reduced to what I said, driven out by your nasty children and wandering about like a beggar in the night with not even a stone of your own to rest your head on!'

He held out his hands imploringly and tried to force his way in. She stood her ground and insisted on having her say to the end:

'No, you don't! Go and ask the people who've robbed you for somewhere to sleep. I don't owe you anything. The family would accuse me of interfering again. Anyway, that's not the point, you handed over all your property and I'll never forgive you.'

And drawing herself up to her full height, with her scrawny neck and round vulture's eyes, she slammed the door in his face:

'You've asked for it so now go and die in the gutter!'

Fouan stood there, rigid and motionless, in front of her pitiless door while the rain continued to beat steadily down. In the end, he turned and vanished into the inky darkness, swamped in the steady icy downpour from the heavens.

Where did he go? He never properly remembered. His feet were slipping in the puddles as he groped his way, trying not to collide with trees and walls. He could no longer think, he no longer knew anything at all; this part of the village whose every stone was familiar seemed like some strange remote and terrible place where he felt like a stranger who had lost his way and was unable to find it again. He turned off to the left and then, afraid of tripping into holes, he went to the right and stopped, shivering, feeling threatened on all sides. He came to a fence, which he followed until he reached a little door which opened. He stumbled and fell down into a hole. He was comfortable there, the rain couldn't reach him and it was warm; but a grunt warned him that he had disturbed a pig, which, thinking there was some food about, was already pushing its snout into his ribs. A scuffle ensued and he was so weak that, fearing the pig might eat him, he retreated. Unable to go any further, he lay down beside the door, curling himself up into a ball under the protection of the eaves. Nevertheless water still kept dripping onto his soaking legs and in his damp clothes his body felt frozen in the icy winds. He envied the pig and would have gone back if he had not heard it sniffing voraciously behind his back and biting away at the door.

At daybreak, Fouan roused from the uneasy slumber in which he had sunk. Once more shame overtook him, shame at the thought that everyone in the district knew what had happened, that his name was being bandied about along the highways and byways, like a pauper's. When you're destitute, there's no justice and you must expect no pity! He slipped along the hedgerows, anxiously expecting a window to open and some early-rising woman to catch sight of him. It was still raining and he made for the plain and hid under a stack. And he spent the whole day like this, shifting from one shelter to the next, in such a state of fright that he would change his cover every couple of hours, imagining that he had been discovered. He was obsessed by only one idea: how long would he take to die? He was suffering from the cold now but he was tortured by hunger; he would certainly die of starvation. Just one more night and one more day, perhaps? As long as it was light, he did not weaken, preferring to end like this rather than go back to the Buteaus. But, as dusk fell, he was seized by a dreadful anguish, a horror of having to spend another night under this implacable downpour. Once more, the cold penetrated into his very bones and unbearable hunger was gnawing at his vitals. As soon as the sky had become quite dark, he felt as if he were being carried away and drowned in the streaming blackness; all thought had left him, his legs kept moving automatically, like an animal's; and thus it was that, quite unconsciously, he found himself standing in the Buteaus' kitchen, having pushed open the door.

Buteau and Lise were just finishing up yesterday's cabbage soup. Hearing the sound, Buteau had looked round and was watching Fouan as he stood there in his steaming wet clothes, not saying a word. There was a long silence and then Buteau said jeeringly:

'I knew you wouldn't have the guts.'

Fouan remained rooted to the spot, inscrutable, not opening his lips to say a single word.

'All right, Lise, give him his grub since he's come back now he's hungry.'

Lise had already stood up and fetched a bowlful of soup. But Fouan grasped the bowl and went away to sit down on a stool, as though refusing to sit down at the table with his children. He greedily ladled up big spoonfuls of soup, so overcome by hunger that his whole body was quivering. Buteau himself finished off his own meal at leisure, rocking to and fro on his chair, picking up pieces of cheese with the point of his knife and putting them into his mouth. The old man's gluttonous feeding intrigued him. He was watching the movements of the spoon with a grin on his face:

'Well, well, it looks as if your little walk in the fresh air has given you quite an appetite. But I shouldn't indulge in it every day, it'd cost too much to feed you.'

His father continued loudly gulping down his soup without a word. His son went on:

'Well, you dirty old man, I suppose you spent the night with a tart? That's why you're so hungry, I expect?'

Still no reply, merely the same obstinate silence and fierce gulps as he stowed away spoonful after spoonful of soup.

'Look, I'm speaking to you,' shouted Buteau crossly. 'You might have the good manners to answer.'

Fouan did not even raise his staring, bewildered gaze from the bowl of soup. He did not seem capable of hearing or seeing anything, miles away in his own thoughts, as though trying to say that he had come back just to eat and, although his stomach was present, his heart was far away. He was now roughly scraping the bottom of the bowl with his spoon, to finish the last drop.

Touched by this display of hunger, Lise ventured to intervene:

'If he wants to lie low and say nothing, why not leave him alone?'

'Then he's not to start buggering me about again,' Buteau went on angrily. 'Once, I don't mind. But are you listening, you obstinate old bastard? Let what's happened today be a lesson to you! If you play me any more tricks, I'll let you starve in the gutter!'

Having now finished, Fouan rose painfully to his feet and, still without a word in a silence which seemed increasingly like the silence of the grave, he turned on his heels and dragged himself wearily to his bed under the stairs, where he flung himself down without bothering to undress. He immediately fell into a leaden slumber and did not stir again, as though knocked unconscious. Lise went to look at him and came back saying that perhaps he was dead. Buteau took the trouble to go and look himself. He shrugged his shoulders. Dead? Good God, do you think people like him die as easily as that? But he must really have got around to be in such a state. The following morning, when they peeped in again, the old man had not stirred; he was still sleeping that evening and he did not wake up until the morning of the second night. He had been unconscious for thirty-six hours.

'So there you are again!' remarked Buteau with a sneer. 'I was thinking that if you went on like that you wouldn't be needing any more bread!'

The old man did not look at him, made no reply and went to sit outside by the road to take the air.

And now Fouan really showed how obstinate he was. He seemed to have forgotten the bonds that they still refused to return, or at least, he now said nothing about them and no longer tried to find them, maybe through indifference or at any rate resignation. But he shut himself off completely from the Buteaus and remained buried in silence. He refused to speak to them for any purpose or in any circumstance whatsoever. They continued to live together, he slept and ate there, he saw them and crossed their paths; but there was never a look or a word, he dragged himself wearily around like a spectre amongst the living, as though stricken dumb and blind.

Once they had grown tired of concerning themselves with him without succeeding in extracting one single sound from him, they left him to his own obstinate devices. Buteau and even Lise both stopped talking to him as well, tolerating him around the place like a piece of perambulating furniture and eventually being hardly aware that he was there. The horse and two cows were of greater account.

In the whole house, Fouan had only one friend left, young Jules, who was just coming up to his tenth birthday. Whereas

Laure, who was four, saw him through the pitiless eyes of her mother and father and would slyly struggle out of his arms as though she too already resented having a useless mouth to feed, Jules liked the old man's company and he provided the last link between Fouan and the others; when a positive yes or no was required, he was the messenger-boy.

His mother would send him to bring back the answer because he was the only person for whom his grandfather would break his silence. And in addition, now that Fouan was being abandoned by everyone, the little lad would help him with his household chores, such as making his bed in the morning and seeing that he had his ration of soup, which he would eat on his lap in the corner, for he still refused to sit at table. Then they would play together. Fouan enjoyed taking the little fellow by the hand and walking along together; and on such occasions he would unburden himself of all his woes; he kept talking interminably, bewildering the little boy and finding it difficult to express himself, for now that he was talking less and less he was losing the use of his tongue. But the bumbling old man and the lad who could think only of nests and blackberries got on well together and would chat for hours. He taught Jules to set snares and built a little cage for him to keep crickets in. This tiny child's hand, which he held in his as they walked through these deserted byways where he now had neither land nor family, was his only remaining solace and it gave him some joy in living a little longer.

In any case, Fouan had ceased to be considered as a living person. Buteau acted on his behalf, drew his money and signed for him, on the pretext that the old fellow was going dotty. Monsieur Baillehache paid the one hundred and fifty francs annuity owing from the sale of his house directly to Buteau. The latter had run into trouble only with Delhomme, who refused to pay over to him the two hundred franc pension; but hardly was his back turned than Buteau pocketed the money. That made three hundred and fifty francs which, as Buteau kept moaning, would need doubling and more before he could even cover the cost of his food. He now never mentioned the bonds; let sleeping dogs lie, that would come out in the wash. As for the interest payments, he claimed that he always went round to honour the contract with old Saucisse, fifteen sous every morning as the annuity on his acre of land. He announced loudly that too much money had already been paid for him to give up that commitment. But rumour had it that Saucisse, after being terrorized and threatened with unpleasant consequences, had agreed to break the contract and return half the money he had received, one thousand francs out of two thousand, and that if the old shark was saying nothing about it, it was because, crook that he was, he was too vain to admit that he had been outcrooked. Buteau sensed that a gentle tap would be enough to knock him over for good.

A year went by and, although declining every day, Fouan still held on. No longer was he the neat old farmer, immaculately clean-shaven with carefully trimmed side-whiskers, always wearing new smocks and black trousers. In his gaunt and haggard face there remained from the past only his long, large, bony nose pointing earthwards; each year his stoop had grown more pronounced and now he went along bent almost double, with only a little time to go before he finally toppled over into the grave. He hobbled about on two sticks, his face covered in a long dirty white beard, wearing out his son's clothes, full of holes and so unsavoury under the warm sun that people would keep upwind, as when meeting some squalid ragged old tramp. And in this decaying human wreck only the animal still survived, obstinately clinging to life. He would fling himself on his bowl of soup like a ravening wolf, never satisfied and even ready to steal Jules's slices of bread if the youngster did not protest. As a result, they cut down his rations and even put him on short commons, on the excuse that he would eat himself to death. Buteau accused him of having gone to the dogs during his stay up at the Castle with Jesus Christ, and it was true : this formerly sober old farmer, who had never spared himself and lived on bread and water, had become used to fine living, to eating meat and drinking spirits, for bad habits are quickly acquired, even when it is a son debauching his father. Seeing that the wine kept disappearing, Lise had to lock it up. On those days when there was a meat stew, little Laure was sent to stand guard over it. Ever since the old man had owed Lengaigne for a cup of coffee, he and Macqueron had been warned that they wouldn't get their money if they offered him tick. He still never broke his tragic silence, but sometimes, when his bowl was not filled or the wine was removed before he had been given his share, he would sit glaring at Buteau in hungry impotent rage.

'Keep on staring, old man,' Buteau would say. 'Don't imagine that I feed my livestock for doing fuck all! If someone likes meat, he must bloody well earn it, greedy guts! Aren't you ashamed of falling into disgusting habits at your age?'

Fouan had not gone back to the Delhommes because he was too proud and obstinate after the insulting remark made by his daughter; and he now had to suffer everything the Buteaus inflicted on him, abuse and even bodily harm. He gave no further thought to his other children but submitted in such a state of weariness that the idea of trying to escape never entered his head: it wouldn't be any better elsewhere, so what was the point? When Fanny met him, she would never be the first to speak to him. The more kind-hearted Jesus Christ, after bearing him a grudge for the unfriendly way in which he had removed himself from the Castle, had greatly enjoyed watching him become abominably drunk at Lengaigne's and leaving him in that state at Buteau's door: a dreadful business, with everything turned upside-down, Lise having to scrub out the kitchen and Buteau swearing that next time he'd make him sleep on the dungheap. The old man had now become so timorous and distrustful of his elder son that he even had the strength of will to refuse further offers of refreshment. He also often saw La Trouille with her geese as he sat out by the roadside. She would stop and scrutinize him with narrowed eyes as she chatted for a second while her flock stood watching behind her, perched on one leg with their necks on the alert. But one morning he discovered that she had stolen his handkerchief; and after that, as soon as he caught sight of her in the distance, he would brandish his sticks in the air to keep her away. She thought this funny and amused herself by setting her geese on him and not running away until some passer-by threatened to box her ears if she didn't leave her granddad alone.

However, till now Fouan had been able to walk and this consoled him, for he was still interested in the land and would constantly be going up to look at his former fields, like old men still obsessed by passionate memories of former mistresses. The old man would hobble slowly and painfully along all the roads, stopping at a field and standing for hours propped up on his sticks; then he would crawl along to another one and start daydreaming again, like a dried-up old tree by the roadside. His vacant staring eyes no longer clearly distinguished wheat from oats or rye. His head was in a daze; confused memories kept rising from the past: in such and such a year that piece of land had produced so many bushels. Even the dates and the figures eventually became uncertain. Only one feeling, albeit an empty one, still dogged him: the thought of the land, that land which he had coveted so much and owned so proudly, the land to which he had sacrificed his all for sixty years, his arms, his legs and his heart, his very life; that thankless land which had passed into the hands of another man and was continuing to produce without reserving any share for him. And his heart ached at the thought that this earth now knew nothing about him, that he had retained nothing of her for himself, not a penny-piece or a mouthful of bread, and that he had to die and he would rot while she, with no care for him, would become reborn and fruitful through his old bones! No, it was hardly worth the candle to have burnt himself out in a life of toil and then stand naked and infirm at the end! And when he had prowled around his old pieces of land like this, he would topple into bed so wearily that they could not even hear his breathing.

But his failing legs were depriving him of this last reason for living. Soon, walking became so laborious that he hardly moved beyond the village. On fine days he had three or four favourite stopping-places: the pile of beams in front of Clou's smithy, the bridge over the Aigre, a stone bench near the school; and he would creep slowly from one to the other, taking an hour to cover a couple of hundred yards, dragging his clogs as if they were heavy carts as he creaked along, lurching lopsidedly on his worn-out old hip-joints. Often he would stay daydreaming for a whole afternoon, squatting on the end of a beam, absorbing the sun. He would sit stock-still in a stupor, staring blankly. People went by now without greeting him, for he was turning into a mere thing. Even smoking had become too much of a chore and he was giving it up, for quite apart from the fact that he found the labour of filling and lighting his pipe exhausting, it was too heavy for his gums to hold. His life now revolved round one desire only:

to stay put. In the burning midday sun, he would shiver, icy-cold, as soon as he moved. His will and his authority were already in ruins and in his final decline he was no more than an abandoned old beast of burden afflicted with the memory of having once been a man. However, he did not complain, inured as he was to the idea that a worn-out horse, having served its purpose, must be put down once it can no longer earn its keep. An old man is useless and he costs money to feed. He himself had longed to see his father die. That his children in their turn might want him to die, too, caused him neither surprise nor resentment. Such things had to be.

A neighbour would say to him:

'Well, old Fouan, you're still keeping going.'

And he would grunt:

'It takes a blasted long time to peg out and it's not for want of trying.'

He was telling the truth, for what peasant would not stoically and willingly accept death once he has been stripped of his belongings and the earth is waiting to reclaim him?

Yet one further tribulation was in store for him. Urged on by his little sister Laure, Jules turned against him. Laure seemed jealous when her brother was with his grandfather. The old man was a nuisance, they'd have much more fun playing together. And if Jules would not go off with her, she clung round his neck and carted him off. Afterwards, she made herself so agreeable that he forgot his household duties towards old Fouan. Gradually she won him over completely, already practised in womanly wiles and having set out to achieve that aim.

One evening Fouan had gone along to the school to wait for Jules, already so weary that he was relying on the youngster to help him up the slope. But Laure came out with her brother, and as the old man was stretching out his trembling hand to catch hold of the little boy's, she gave a sneering laugh:

'There he is, bothering you again. Don't let him!'

Then, turning round towards the other young ragamuffins, she shouted:

'Don't you think he's a sissy to let himself be mucked about like that?'

Embarrassed by their yells of scorn, Jules blushed and, wanting

to show what a big boy he was, he jerked his hand away, copy-
ing his sister's words as he shouted at the old man who had
accompanied him on so many walks:

'Stop bothering me!'

Dazed and blinded by tears, Fouan stumbled as though the
ground were slipping from beneath his feet and he felt the little
hand tugging itself away. The others laughed even louder and
Laure forced her brother to dance round the old man singing the
childish refrain:

> It's raining, it's pouring,
> The old man's snoring,
> He got into bed and bumped his head
> And couldn't get up in the morning.

Weak and trembling, Fouan took nearly two hours to reach
home on his own, scarcely able to drag one foot after the other.
And that was the end: the little boy stopped bringing him his
bowl of soup and making his bed, the straw mattress which he
barely turned from one month's end to the next. He no longer
had even this youngster to talk to; he sank into complete silence.
Now he was utterly alone: not one single word to anyone or
on anything at all ever passed his lips.

Chapter 3

THE winter ploughing was drawing to a close, and on this cold and gloomy February afternoon Jean had just arrived with his plough at his big Cornailes field where he still had a good two hours' work. It was one end of the field which he was intending to plant with wheat, a Scottish variety of cone wheat which his former employer Hourdequin had advised him to try and of which he had even promised him a few bushels for seed.

Jean immediately set the ploughshare where he had stopped the day before and, leaning on the plough handles to start a new furrow, he set the horse going with his usual rough growl: 'Gee up there!'

Heavy rain following on a great deal of sunshine had packed the clay so tightly that the coulter and ploughshare had difficulty in slicing through it. You could hear the heavy lumps of earth grinding against the mouldboard as they curled over and buried the manure which had been spread across the field. Now and then, the plough would jerk as it hit a stone or some other obstacle.

'Gee up there!'

Jean tensed his arms to ensure that his furrow was straight as a die, while his horse, with lowered head, its hooves sinking into the ridge between the furrows, kept pulling steadily onward. When the plough started to become choked Jean shook off the mud and grass with a jerk of his wrists and pursued his course, leaving the rich earth heaped up behind him, still quivering, like some live thing with its very vitals exposed.

When he reached the end of the furrow, he turned and started another. He soon became as though intoxicated by the reek of the earth which he was stirring up, the reek of the damp dark corners, seething hotbeds of growth. The effort of walking and concentrating his vision completed the confusion of his mind. He would never become a real peasant. He wasn't a son of this soil, he was still the urban worker which he had been before, the trooper who had fought in Italy, and he could see and feel things which peasants neither see nor feel, the vast melancholy peace of the plain and the mighty breathing of the earth under sun and rain. He had always had thoughts of retiring to the country. But how silly of him to imagine that, when he laid down his rifle and his plane, the plough would satisfy his need for peace and quiet! If the earth was restful and good to those who loved it, the villagers contaminating it like vermin, those human insects battening on its flesh, were enough to disgrace it and blight any approach to it. He could not recall being so unhappy since the time, already distant, of his arrival at La Borderie.

Jean lifted the handles slightly to make the going easier. He was annoyed to see a slight curve in the furrow. He turned and urged his horse on, determined to be more careful:

'Gee up there!'

And what trials and tribulations he had had in these last ten years! First, having to wait so long for Françoise; then the fight with the Buteaus. Not one day had passed without some trouble or other. And now that Françoise was his and he had been married for two years, was he really happy? Even if he still loved her, he had realized that she did not, and never would love him in the way he would have liked to be loved, body and soul. They both lived amicably together and they were doing well, working hard, saving money. But things were not right between them, and when he held her in his arms in bed he felt that she was cold and that her mind was on other things. Now she was five months pregnant with a child conceived without pleasure, the sort who are nothing but a nuisance to their mothers. Even this pregnancy had not brought them closer together. Above all, more and more, he was becoming painfully aware of something which he felt the night they had taken over the house, the feeling that his wife thought him a stranger, a man from another world, born and bred in foreign parts, God alone knows where; a man who didn't think like people from Rognes, who seemed to be a different sort of person from her and with no possible connexion with her, even though he had given her a baby. One Saturday after their marriage, in exasperation at the Buteaus, she had brought back a sheet of official stamped paper from Cloyes, in order to make a will leaving everything to her husband, because it had been explained to her that the house and land would revert to her sister if she died before having a child, since only money and goods and chattels entered into her marriage contract with Jean. And then, without a word of explanation, she seemed to have changed her mind and the blank sheet of paper was still lying in her chest of drawers; and apart from his personal interest in the matter, inwardly he had felt deeply hurt because it seemed to him to show lack of affection. Now that they were going to have a baby, what did it matter anyway? All the same, he felt sad at heart each time he opened the chest of drawers and saw the now useless sheet of official paper.

Jean stopped to give his horse a breather, while he himself threw off his worries in the icy air. Slowly he let his gaze wander over the empty horizon and the immense plain, where in the far distance other teams were dimly discernible in the grey light. He was surprised to recognize old Fouan, who had come up from Rognes by the new road, impelled by some memory of the past or the need to cast eye over one of his former pieces of land. Then he looked down and for a minute he was absorbed by the sight of the open furrow, the bowels of the earth which lay exposed at his feet; yellow and strong at the bottom, it looked like fresh young flesh which had been laid bare by turning over the soil, while the manure buried underneath formed a rich and fertile bed. His mind again grew confused; what an odd idea, to burrow into the soil like this in order to be able to eat bread; and then there was the worry of Françoise's failure to love him; and other thoughts as well, even dimmer, on what was growing there, on his baby soon to be born, on all the work which people did, often without being any the happier for it. He took hold of the handles again and growled:

'Gee up there!'

Jean was just finishing his ploughing when Delhomme, who was walking back from a neighbouring farm, stopped beside his field:

'I say, Corporal, have you heard the news? Looks like war.'

Jean let go of his plough and jerked upright in shocked surprise.

'War? Who with?'

'Well, with the Prussians, from what I can tell. It's in the papers.'

With a set face, Jean's thoughts went back to Italy again and all the fighting there, the slaughter from which he had been so delighted to escape unscathed. In those days, how he had longed for a life of peace, in some quiet corner! And now when he heard the word war shouted to him by this man passing by on the road, the thought of it set the blood coursing through his whole body.

'Well, if the Prussians are buggering us about, we can't let them take us for mugs!'

Delhomme did not share this view. He shook his head and pointed out that it would be the end of the countryside if the Cossacks came back, as they did after Napoleon. There was nothing to be gained by knocking each other about: much better to work something out together.

'What I'm saying doesn't affect me. I've deposited some money with Monsieur Baillehache. Whatever happens, Nénesse won't be called up. The draw's tomorrow.'

'Of course,' said Jean, calming down. 'It's the same with me. I've done my stint and now I'm married. I don't give a damn for their fighting! So it's the Prussians, is it! Well, we'll give 'em a thrashing, that's all!'

'Goodbye, Corporal.'

'Goodnight.'

Delhomme went off, stopping to call out the news further on and then for a third time; and the threat of approaching war sped over the plain of Beauce under the vast, sad, ashen sky.

His task completed, Jean thought he would go off straight away to La Borderie and pick up the promised seed. He unhitched, leaving the plough at the end of the field, and jumped onto the horse. As he was going off, he remembered Fouan and looked for him, but without success. No doubt the old man had taken shelter from the cold behind a stack still standing in the Buteaus' field.

At La Borderie, after tying up his horse, Jean called out but nobody replied: everybody must be working outside. He went into the deserted kitchen, rapped on the table and at last heard Jacqueline's voice coming from the cellar in which was the dairy; a trap-door opened directly at the foot of the stairs, so awkwardly placed that there was always a serious risk of an accident.

'Who's there?'

He was squatting at the top of the steep flight of steps and she looked up and recognized him.

'Oh, it's you, Corporal!'

He could see her too, in the half-light coming from the ventilator. She was working down there amidst her pans and basins, from which the whey was dripping into a stone trough. Her sleeves were tucked up to her armpits and her bare arms were white with cream.

'Come on down. You're not afraid of me, are you?'

She still used her familiar form of address, as in the old days, and she was laughing in her usual forthcoming way. He was embarrassed and stayed where he was.

'I've come for the seed that the master promised me.'

'Oh yes, I know, wait a second, I'll be up.'

And when she came up into the light, he thought how fresh she looked, with her bare white arms, and smelling of fresh milk. She was watching him with her charming, shameless eyes and finally asked him with a saucy look:

'Aren't you going to give me a kiss? Being married's no excuse for being rude.'

He pretended to give her two smacking kisses on her cheeks, to make it plain that they were just friendly ones. But he found her disturbing and past memories sent a little thrill through his body. He'd never felt that with his wife, whom he was so fond of.

'Come along with me,' Jacqueline continued. 'I'll show you the seed. Just think, even the servant's away at the market.'

She crossed the yard into the wheat barn and went behind a pile of bags. The wheat was stored against the wall, held in by planks. He followed her, a trifle oppressed at finding himself alone with her like this, in this quiet corner. He immediately pretended to be interested in the seed, a fine Scottish variety of cone wheat.

'Isn't it big!'

But she gave her husky gurgle and quickly brought him back to the subject that interested her.

'Your wife's pregnant, isn't she? So you can let yourself go, eh? Tell me, what's it like with her? Is it as nice as with me?'

He went very red and she laughed, delighted at having disconcerted him. Then a sudden thought seemed to strike her and her face clouded over.

'You know, I've been having a lot of trouble. Fortunately, it's all over now, and I've come out on top.'

In fact, Hourdequin's son Léon, who had not been seen for years, had suddenly dropped in at La Borderie; and on the very first day Léon, who had come to see what was happening, had received his answer when he realized that Jacqueline was occupying his mother's bedroom. For a moment, Jacqueline was scared because she had set her mind firmly on marriage in order to inherit the farm. But the captain made the mistake of trying on an old trick: he attempted to extricate his father from his dilemma by being caught by him in bed with Jacqueline. It was too obvious. She made a great display of virtue, shrieking and sobbing, telling Hourdequin that she was going to leave because no one treated her with respect any more, and there was a dreadful row between the two men when the son tried to open his father's eyes, which only made matters worse. Two hours later, he went off himself, shouting as he went through the door that he preferred to give up the lot and if he were ever to come back it would be to kick that bitch out.

In her triumph Jacqueline made the mistake of thinking that she could get away with anything. She informed Hourdequin that in view of all these mortifications, which were the talk of the district, she owed it to herself to leave him if he wouldn't marry her. She even began to pack her bags. However, still upset at having parted from his son, the more so since he was also full of grief because he secretly felt himself to be in the wrong, Hourdequin nearly knocked her unconscious with a couple of slaps in the face, which stopped any further talk of leaving and made her realize that she had been in too great a hurry. In any case, she was now in complete charge, openly sleeping in the marital bedroom, eating separately with the master, giving the orders, settling the accounts, holding the keys of the safe and so autocratic that he would consult her when any decision had to be taken. He had greatly aged and she had high hopes, in his decline, of eventually overcoming his resistance and persuading him to marry her when she had finally succeeded in wearing him down.

Meanwhile, as in his fit of rage he had sworn to cut his son off with a shilling, she was trying to prevail on him to make a will in her favour. She could already see herself as the mistress of the farm because she had extracted a promise from him one night in bed.

'All these years I've been working like a slave to give him fun,' she said. 'You must realize that it's not because of his looks!'

Jean could not help laughing. As she was talking, she had unthinkingly been plunging her bare arms into the wheat, then lifting them out and putting them in again, so that her skin was covered in a fine, soft powder. He stood watching her and then made a comment that he regretted afterwards:

'And what about Tron and you? Still going strong?'

She did not seem offended but spoke out openly, as though confiding in an old friend.

'Oh, I'm quite fond of that big softy but he really is a bit of a nuisance. Just imagine, he's jealous! Yes, he keeps picking rows with me, the only man he doesn't object to is the master, and even then... I think he comes and listens at the door to make sure we're asleep.'

Jean laughed again. But she was not joking, because secretly she was afraid of this giant of a man, who, she claimed, was sly and untrustworthy like everybody from the Perche. He had threatened to strangle her if she deceived him. So now she was terrified when she went with him, despite her weakness for his sturdy limbs. She herself was so slim that he could have crushed her between his thumb and forefinger.

Then she gave a pretty shrug of her shoulders, as though to say that she had coped with others like him before. She went on with a smile:

'I say, Corporal, it was nicer with you, we got on so well together!'

Without taking her quizzical gaze off him, she had started to turn the wheat over again with her arms. And once again he felt himself weakening, forgetful of the fact that he had left the farm and not thinking of his wife and their unborn baby. He grasped her wrists plunged deep in the wheat and ran his hands up her velvet-soft, floury arms, until he reached her girlish bosom which too much fondling seemed to have made all the firmer. This was

426

what she had been wanting ever since she had looked up at him crouching down beside the trap and felt a sudden revival of past affection, as well as the sneaking pleasure of taking him away from another woman, his wife. He had seized her in his arms and was pressing her backwards onto the heap of wheat while she was already sighing in ecstasy when the tall, lean figure of the shepherd Soulas appeared from behind the sacks, coughing violently and spitting. Jacqueline jerked herself upright, while Jean stuttered breathlessly :

'Well, that's it, I'll come back and pick up a dozen bushels. Isn't it big, really big !'

His ardour cooled, Jean hurriedly made his way out of the barn and unhitched his horse in the yard, ignoring Jacqueline's signs; she would rather have hidden him in Hourdequin's bedroom than forgo her lust for him. But he was anxious to escape and repeated that he would come back the following day. As he was going off leading his horse by the bridle, Soulas, who had gone out to wait for him by the gate, said to him :

'So there's no decency left anywhere when even you go back and do it, like the others ! Well, do her the favour of warning her to keep her trap shut if she doesn't want me to open mine. Ah, there'll be ructions, you'll see !'

But refusing to have anything to do with the matter, Jean thrust his way past. He felt thoroughly ashamed and irritated at what he had just been prevented from doing. He thought that he was fond of Françoise but never had he felt such wild bursts of desire for her. Could it be that he was fonder of Jacqueline? Was his desire for that shameless little hussy so deep? And as his whole past came back to him, his anger increased when he realized that, despite his struggles, he would still go back and see her. His mind in a turmoil, he flung himself on his horse and galloped off to reach Rognes as quickly as possible.

It so happened that on that very afternoon, Françoise thought she would go and cut a bundle of lucerne for her cows. This was one of her normal tasks and she imagined that she would find her husband up there ploughing, since she did not much care to go there by herself, for fear of running into the Buteaus, who were furious at no longer owning the whole field and kept continually trying to pick a quarrel as a result. She took her scythe

427

with her : the horse would be able to bring the bundle of grass down on his back. But as she came up to Cornailles, she was surprised at not seeing Jean, although she had not warned him of her plans : his plough was there, where on earth was he? Her final shock came when she recognized Buteau and Lise standing beside the field, angrily waving their arms about. They were in their best clothes and were carrying nothing in their hands; no doubt they had just stopped on their way back from a visit to a near-by village. For a moment she was on the point of turning back. Then she felt annoyed with herself for being scared : she had every right to go and visit her own land. So she continued on her way, carrying her scythe over her shoulder.

The truth was that whenever Françoise met Buteau like this, particularly on his own, she became completely flustered. She had not spoken to him for two years; but she still could not look at him without a thrill running through her whole body. It could have been a thrill of anger but it might have been something else as well. Several times when she had been going along this self-same road on her way to her field of lucerne, she had caught sight of him in front of her. He would turn his head two or three times to look at her through his grey eyes flecked with yellow. A shiver would run through her and despite herself she would quicken her pace while he slowed down; and as she had passed beside him for a second, their eyes had looked deeply into each other's. And then she had had the uncomfortable sensation that he was behind her; she felt stiff and awkward and could not walk properly. The last time they had met she had been so put out that, in trying to jump off the road into her own field, unbalanced by her swollen belly she had fallen flat on her face. He had burst out laughing.

That evening when Buteau gleefully told Lise how her sister had tripped over, their eyes glinted with the same thought : supposing the little bitch had been killed and her brat with her, then her husband would have been left with nothing and the land and the house would have come back to them. La Grande had told them all about the business of the unmade will, which would now be pointless, in view of Françoise's pregnancy. But they'd never had any luck, there was no chance of some mishap removing the mother and her child for their sake! But they returned to the subject as they were going to bed, just to talk about it, because discussing a person's death never killed anybody. Supposing Françoise died without leaving an heir, wouldn't that be wonderful, a real godsend! In her venom, Lise even went so far as to swear that she didn't consider Françoise as her sister anymore; she would hold her head on the block if necessary, so that they could get back their home which that slut had driven them out of in such a disgusting way. Buteau was not quite so greedy, he said he'd be quite happy if the baby died before it was born. It was the pregnancy that stuck in his throat, because any child would put an end to the hopes that he was still harbouring, for in that case he would lose the property for good and all. Then, as they were both getting into bed and she was blowing out the candle, she gave a strange little giggle and said that as long as babies haven't actually come, they may never come. There was silence in the dark and then he asked why she was saying that. Lying close beside him she made a whispered confession: last month, she'd been annoyed to discover that she'd been caught out again, so that without saying anything to him she'd gone off to see a woman from Magnolles, an old witch called Sapin. No more pregnancies, thank you very much! Buteau would've given her a hot reception! So the Sapin woman had quite simply got rid of it for her with a needle. He listened without expressing either approval or disapproval; the only sign of satisfaction was the jocular way in which he said that she ought to have got a needle for Françoise. This amused her too, and, cuddling up to him, she whispered that the Sapin woman had told her about another way, such a queer one! What was it? Well, what a man had done, a man could undo, all he had to do was to have the woman and while having her make three signs of the cross on her stomach and say three aves backwards. And then, if there was a baby, it would go away like wind. Buteau stopped laughing and, although they pretended not to believe it, the superstition bred in their bones sent a little shudder through their frame, because everybody knew that the old woman from Magnolles had changed a cow into a weasel and brought a dead man back to life. If she said it, then it must be true. Then Lise coaxed him to try it out on her and recite the ave backwards and make the sign of the cross three times to see if she felt anything. No, not a thing, that meant that the needle had done the trick. But what a lot of harm that would have done to Françoise! He grinned and wondered if he could. Well, why not, since he'd already had her once? No, he never had! He denied it while Lise, now feeling jealous, dug her nails into his flesh. They went to sleep in each other's arms.

Ever since then, they had been haunted by the thought of this child growing bigger every day who would take their house and land away from them for good; and every time they met their young sister, they immediately looked straight at her waistline. When they saw her coming along the road they would measure her with their eye, shocked to see how her pregnancy was proceeding and realizing that it would soon be too late.

'Bloody hell!' shouted Buteau, coming back to the ploughed field which he had been examining. 'That thief has gone a good foot over into our field. Look, you can see from the boundary stone!'

Françoise had continued to walk calmly towards them, disguising her fear. Then she realized the meaning of their furious gestures. Jean's plough must have encroached on their piece of land. This was a continual source of dispute between them; not a month would pass without some question concerning their shared boundary setting them at loggerheads. It could only end in blows and lawsuits.

'Do you hear?' he went on, raising his voice. 'You're on our land, I'm going to straighten you out.'

But without bothering to look round, the young woman went on into her field of lucerne.

'We're talking to you!' shouted Lise, beside herself with rage. 'Come and see the boundary stone if you think we're lying. Come and see the damage you've done.'

And infuriated by her sister's deliberate and contemptuous silence, she flew into a rage and went up to her, clenching her fists.

'Look, are you trying to have us on? I'm your elder sister, you ought to show proper respect. I'll make you ask pardon on your knees for all the dirty tricks you've played on me!'

She was standing in front of her, furious with resentment and so purple with anger that she could scarcely see:

'Get down on your knees, you slut!'

Still not saying a word, Françoise spat in her face, as she had done on the day they had expelled her from her house. And as Lise was shrieking, Buteau intervened, pushing her violently aside.

'Let me handle this, I'll see to her.'

Oh, she'd certainly let him see to her! He could bend her and break her back like a rotten tree; he could make cat's-meat of her, treat her like the slut she was, she'd certainly not stop him, she'd even help him! And now she craned her neck and started peering round to make sure that no one would disturb him. And all around, under the gloomy sky, the vast grey plain stretched out with not a soul in sight.

'Go on, there's no one about!'

Buteau was advancing towards Françoise and from the set of his face and the taut way he held his arms, Françoise thought that he was going to give her a thrashing. She had kept hold of her scythe but she was trembling; in any case, he now caught hold of the handle, wrested it from her and flung it into the lucerne. All she could do to keep him at a distance was to retreat. So, still facing him, she walked backwards into the next field and made for the stack which was standing there as though she hoped to use it as a shield. He came slowly on and seemed even to be shooing her in that direction, gradually opening his arms while his face relaxed into a silent laugh, revealing his gums. And suddenly she realized that he was not going to beat her, he was after something else, something that she had been refusing him for so long. And now she was even more terrified, for she felt her strength deserting her, whereas she had hitherto been so plucky, so ready to give tit for tat, swearing that he would never succeed. Yet she was not a little girl any more; she had had her twenty-third birthday at Martinmas and she was a real woman now, still red-lipped and with eyes as round as saucers. But now she felt all soft and melting and her limbs seemed to be turning to water.

Still forcing her to retreat, Buteau at last addressed her in a low, passionate voice:

'We've not finished with each other and you know it! You know I want you and I'm going to get you!'

Having succeeded in backing her up against the stack, he caught hold of her shoulders and flung her onto the ground. But now she started struggling desperately, spurred on by memories of her obstinate resistance in the past. He was holding her down and dodging her kicks.

'What's the objection now you're pregnant, you silly little bitch? I won't give you another one, that's for sure.'

She burst into tears and seemed to become hysterical; she no longer tried to defend herself, swinging her arms about wildly, with her legs twisting and turning convulsively; and each time he tried to take her, he was flung off sideways. In his fury, he lost all restraint and, turning to his wife, he called:

'For Christ's sake, don't just stand there watching! If you want me to do it, come and hold her legs, can't you?'

Lise had been standing motionless some thirty feet away, scrutinizing the horizon and then looking down at the pair of them without the flicker of an eyelid. When her husband called out to her, she did not hesitate for a second; she came up, seized hold of her sister's left leg, dragged it sideways and sat down on it, as though trying to crush it. Pinned to the ground, her spirit broken, Françoise closed her eyes and submitted. Yet she had not lost consciousness and, after Buteau had possessed her, she was seized in her turn by such a violent spasm of pleasure that, uttering a long cry, she clasped him tightly in her arms, squeezing the breath out of his body. Some passing rooks took fright and behind the stack there emerged the livid face of old Fouan, who had been sheltering from the cold. He had seen everything and doubtless took fright too, for he hid himself once again in the straw.

Buteau had stood up. Lise was watching him narrowly. She had had but one thought in her mind, to make sure that he did the job properly; but he had gone at it so eagerly that he had forgotten everything else, the sign of the cross and the ave spoken backwards. She was shocked and beside herself with rage. So he'd done it just for the pleasure of it.

But Françoise gave her no time to tackle her husband. For a second she had remained lying on the ground, as though overcome by the violence of her orgasm, which she had never enjoyed before. Suddenly she had realized the truth: she loved Buteau, she had never loved and would never love anyone else. This discovery filled her not only with shame but, since it upset all her ideas of fairness, with fury against herself as well. Here was a man who was not hers, who belonged to her sister whom she loathed, the only man in fact whom she could never have without forfeiting all respect. And she had just let this man have his will with her and she had held him so tightly that he knew she was his! She jumped to her feet, distraught, her clothes disordered, breathless and stammering in her distress.

'Pigs! Beasts! ... You're both just pigs and beasts. You've ruined me. They send people to the guillotine for less than that. I'll tell Jean, you dirty pigs! He'll know what to do with you.'

Buteau merely grinned and shrugged his shoulders, delighted that he had finally succeeded.

'Oh, stuff it. You wanted it badly, I could feel you wriggling. We'll do it again sometime.'

For Lise, these jocular remarks were the last straw; and in her growing exasperation with her husband she vented all her rage on her young sister.

'It's true, you trollop, I saw you. You caught hold of him and forced him. Didn't I say that all my troubles came from you? Just you try to deny that you didn't seduce my man, yes, even as soon as we were married, when you still needed me to blow your nose for you!'

It was strange to see such an outburst of jealousy when she had been an accomplice, but it was jealousy inspired less by the act itself than by the fact that her sister had taken half of everything that belonged to her. If this girl hadn't been her sister, would she have had to share everything with her? She detested her because she was younger and fresher and more desirable.

'That's a lie!' Françoise shouted. 'That's a lie and you know it!'

'So I'm lying, am I? So it wasn't because you wanted him that you kept going after him, even when he went down into the cellar?'

'Me? Me? And that was me a moment ago, was it? Who was the old cow holding my leg? You might have broken it! And let me tell you, I can't understand something like that, you really must be quite disgusting or else you wanted to kill me, you dirty bitch!'

Lise's immediate reply was a smart slap in the face. Losing

control of herself, Françoise rushed at her sister. Buteau was standing there grinning with his hands thrust in his pockets, refusing to intervene, like a vain cockerel being fought over by two hens. And the fight proceeded, viciously and mercilessly, with bonnets torn off, blows and bruises exchanged, each woman trying to find some vital spot with their fingers. As they pushed and lurched, they had come back into the field of lucerne. Suddenly, Lise gave a scream: Françoise was sinking her nails into her neck. She saw red and the thought sprang into her mind, sharp and clear, that she might kill her sister. She caught sight of the scythe, to the left of Françoise, its handle lying across a tuft of thistles with its point in the air. Like lightning, she tipped Françoise sideways with the whole strength of her wrists. The poor girl stumbled, swung round and fell on her left side with a dreadful shriek. The scythe was slicing into her flesh.

'Christ Almighty!' stammered Buteau. And that was all. It was over in a flash and there was nothing more to be done. Aghast that what she had wanted had happened so suddenly, Lise watched the blood gushing and staining the slashed dress. Could the blade have cut into the baby, to cause such a flow of blood? Behind the stack Fouan's pale face was emerging again. He had seen what had happened and his dim eyes were blinking.

Françoise was now lying motionless and, when Buteau came nearer, he did not dare to touch her. An icy gust of wind chilled him to the marrow and his hair stood on end in horror.

'She's dead. Christ, let's get away!'

He had taken Lise's hand and they ran off along the deserted road, their feet barely touching the ground. The low, gloomy clouds seemed to be pressing down on their skulls; the clatter of their feet sounded like a crowd pursuing them; and they ran across the flat empty plain, he with his smock billowing in the wind, she dishevelled, carrying her bonnet in her hand and both repeating the same words, grunting like hunted animals:

'Christ, she's dead. Christ, let's get away!'

As they lengthened their stride, their cries turned into rhythmical, involuntary grunts, a sort of breathless snuffling sound in which you could distinguish the words:

'Christ, dead! Christ, dead! Christ, dead!'

They vanished from sight.

A few moments later, when Jean came trotting back on his horse, the sight was horrible to see.

'What's up? What's happened?'

Françoise opened her eyes, still without stirring: she gazed at him earnestly with her large eyes full of suffering. But she made no reply, as though already far away, thinking of other things.

'You're hurt, there's blood, do tell me what it was.'

He turned towards old Fouan, who was just coming up.

'You were here, what happened?'

Then Françoise said slowly:

'I'd come for some grass. I fell on my scythe. Oh, it's the end of me!'

Her eyes were looking into Fouan's, telling him all those other things, the things which only the family should know. Dazed though he was, the old man seemed to understand and he repeated:

'That's right, she fell and hurt herself. I was over there and saw it.'

They hurriedly fetched a litter from Rognes. On the way back, she fainted again. It was feared she might not reach home alive.

Chapter 4

IT so happened that on the following day, a Sunday, the young men of Rognes were due to go to Cloyes to draw lots, and as La Grande and Frimat's wife quickly rallied round to undress and put Françoise to bed with infinite care, outside in the street below the drum roll was sounding in the gloomy, fading light, a real death-knell for the poor.

Almost out of his mind, Jean was on his way to fetch Dr Finet when he met the veterinary surgeon Patoir near the church; the latter had come to look at old Saucisse's horse and, despite his reluctance, Jean forcibly insisted on his coming to look at the injured young woman. But when Patoir saw the gaping wound he bluntly refused to have anything to do with it: what was the point when there was nothing to be done? When Jean came back with Monsieur Finet two hours later, the doctor reacted in similar fashion. All he could do was to make the patient's last two hours less painful with drugs. The five months pregnancy was an added complication, for the baby could be felt stirring restlessly as it died together with its mother in the womb which had been perforated at the very moment when it was bearing fruit. After trying to apply a dressing, before he left the doctor declared that the poor woman would not survive the night, although he promised to call in again the following day. But she did survive and was still alive when, at about nine o'clock, the drum began to beat again to assemble the conscripts in front of the school.

All night the skies had dissolved into rain and, sitting in a daze in the bedroom, his eyes brimming over with tears, Jean had listened to the water pelting down in torrents. Now, through the damp, warm morning air, he could hear the drum as though muffled in crape. The rain had stopped but the sky remained leaden and overcast.

The drum roll continued for a long time. The drummer was new, a nephew of Macqueron's who had done his military service and was beating away as though leading his regiment into battle. The whole of Rognes was in a stir because the news of the threat

436

of war which had been circulating in the last few days made the drawing of lots this year even more harrowing than usual. Oh, no, not to go and get bashed about by the Prussians, thank you very much! There were nine youngsters from the village who were drawing lots, something which had perhaps never happened before. And amongst their number were Nénesse and Delphin, who, after being bosom pals, had been separated when the former had gone to work in a restaurant in Chartres. Nénesse had slept at his parents' farm the night before and he had changed so much that Delphin hardly recognized him: a proper gent with a stick, a silk hat and a sky-blue tie, fastened in a ring: he wore tailor-made clothes and made fun of Lambourdieu's suits. The second lad, on the other hand, clumsy in build and with a weather-beaten face, had thickened out and looked as sturdy as a young tree. All the same, they had lost no time in renewing their friendship. Having spent part of the night together, they turned up in front of the school, arm in arm, when they heard the roll of the drum which kept up its persistent, relentless ratatatat.

Parents were standing about in the square. Gratified at Nénesse's distinguished appearance, Delhomme and Fanny had come along to see him leave; moreover, their minds were at rest, because they had insured against any eventuality. As for Bécu, he had polished up his gamekeeper's badge and was threatening to give his wife a clout because she was crying: why shouldn't Delphin be fit to serve his country? The lad himself expressed indifference: he was sure, he kept saying, that he would draw the right number. When the nine had assembled, which took a good hour, Lequeu handed over the flag to them. There was discussion as to who should have the honour. It was usually the tallest and strongest, so they finally chose Delphin. He seemed very put out by this, because, despite having fists like hams, he was a shy young man and uneasy about anything he was not used to. What a long, awkward bit of gear to lug about! Let's hope it wouldn't bring him bad luck.

At the two street corners, Flore and Coelina were each giving the final spit and polish to their respective tap-rooms, ready for the evening. Macqueron was gloomily looking on from the doorway when Lengaigne made his grinning appearance in his. It must be explained that the latter was exultant because two days ago the government inspectors had seized two casks of wine secreted in his rival's woodpile, and this unfortunate mishap had forced the latter to send in his resignation as mayor; and no one doubted that the anonymous letter denouncing him had certainly been sent by Lengaigne. To complete his discomfiture, Macqueron was in a state of fury over another matter: his daughter Berthe had so compromised herself with the wheelwright's son, whom he did not want as a son-in-law, that he had at last been obliged to agree to their marriage. For the last week, the women fetching water from the fountain had been talking of nothing else but the daughter's marriage and her father's trial. He would certainly be fined and perhaps even gaoled. So, faced by his neighbour's offensive laugh, Macqueron preferred to go back into his shop, embarrassed by the fact that other people were also beginning to laugh.

But now Delphin had taken the flag and the drummer struck up again, Nénesse fell in behind him and the seven others followed, forming a small platoon which made its way along the level road. Little urchins ran beside them, while a few parents, the Delhommes, Bécu and a few others, accompanied them to the end of the village. Having got rid of Bécu, his wife hurried up the hill and furtively slipped into the church, where, after making sure that she was quite alone, although she was not religious she knelt down in tears, pleading to God to see that her son drew the right number. For more than an hour she knelt there mumbling her heartfelt prayer. The flag had gradually faded from sight in the distance along the Cloyes road and the sound of the drum had finally been swallowed up in the open air.

Dr Finet did not call until about ten o'clock and he seemed greatly surprised to find Françoise still alive, for he had been expecting to have nothing more to do than sign the certificate. He examined the wound, shaking his head and slightly bothered by the story he had been told, although he had no suspicions. He asked to hear about it again: how on earth could the poor woman have managed to fall on the point of her scythe like that? He left, full of indignation at such clumsiness and vexed at having to come back for the death certificate. But Jean was still in a sombre mood and kept looking at Françoise who silently closed her eyes every time she felt her husband's questioning gaze resting on her. He suspected her of lying and of trying to hide something from him. At daybreak he had slipped away for a moment and hurriedly gone up to the field of lucerne to have a look, but he had not been able to see anything clearly, only footprints washed out by the torrential rain during the night and, in one place, trampled ground, doubtless where she had fallen. When the doctor had gone, he sat down again beside the dying woman's bed, alone for once, as Frimat's wife had left for lunch and La Grande had gone off to see if all was well at home.

'Are you in pain?'

She kept her eyelids tightly closed and made no reply.

'Françoise, are you hiding something from me?'

Apart from the little gasping breath in her throat, she seemed already dead. Ever since last night she had been lying on her back, motionless, as though frozen into silence. Although burning with fever, she seemed to have found inner reserves of will-power to prevent herself from becoming delirious, for fear of blurting something out. She had always had a peculiar character – pigheadedness, they called it – the pigheadedness of the Fouans, refusing to be like other people and full of ideas that amazed them. Perhaps she was moved by a sense of family solidarity stronger than hatred or desire for revenge? What was the point since she was going to die? These were things reserved for your kith and kin, kept buried in that little territory where you had all grown up together, things which must never, in any circumstances, be divulged to strangers; and Jean was a stranger, the young man whom she had never been able to bring herself to love, whose child she was taking with her, without giving birth to it, as though she were being punished for having conceived it.

Meanwhile, ever since he had brought her back home to die, he had been thinking of the will. All that night he had been unable to banish the thought that, were she to die now, he would have only half the furniture and the money, the hundred and twenty-seven francs in the chest of drawers. He was fond of her, he would have given his own blood to save her, but the thought that he might lose not only her but the land and the house as well increased his sadness. Till now, however, he had never dared to raise the subject; it was so awkward, and also there had always been other people present. Finally, seeing that he was not going to learn anything further about how the accident had occurred, he decided to broach the other matter.

'Perhaps there are some things that you'd like to settle?'

Françoise became tense and did not seem to hear him. With her eyes closed and her face set, she made no sign.

'You know, because of your sister, in case something were to happen to you. We've got the official paper in the chest of drawers over there.'

He fetched the sheet of stamped paper and continued in an embarrassed voice:

'Here we are. Would you like me to help you? Are you still strong enough to write? It's not that I'm interested for myself. It's just the idea that you won't want to leave anything to people who've done you so much harm.'

Her eyelids twitched, proving that she had heard him. So she refused? He was shocked and uncomprehending. Perhaps she herself would not have been able to say why she was shamming dead even before she was nailed in her coffin. The land and the house didn't belong to this man who had chanced to come into her life, like someone passing in the night. She owed him nothing, their baby was going away with her. By what right would this property have left the family? Her obstinately childish ideas of fairness protested: this is mine, that's yours, so let's say goodbye and that's that! Yes, these were some of the things and there were others as well, less clear, her sister Lise who now seemed so far away, lost in the distance, and Buteau alone remained, loved despite his brutality, desired and forgiven.

But Jean too had become infected by this dread virus of lust for land. In exasperation, he raised her from her pillow in an attempt to make her sit up, at the same time trying to thrust a pen between her fingers.

'Look, it's not possible, surely? Do you really prefer them to me? You'd let that gang take the lot?'

At that Françoise opened her eyes and the look she gave him went straight to his heart. She knew that she was going to die; in her large staring eyes you could see her bottomless despair. Why was he torturing her like that? She wouldn't, she couldn't do it. A muffled cry of pain and grief escaped her and that was all: she fell back in bed, her eyes closed again and once more her head lay still in the middle of the pillow.

Ashamed of his brutality, Jean was so upset that he was still sitting there with the sheet of official paper in his hand when La Grande returned. She realized what was happening and drew him aside to ask him if there was a will. Stammering as he lied, Jean explained that he had been hiding the piece of paper in order not to cause Françoise unnecessary anxiety. La Grande seemed to approve; she was still on the side of the Buteaus, for she could foresee dreadful events taking place if they were to inherit. And sitting down at the table, she started her knitting again, saying loudly :

'Well, as for me, I'll never do any harm to anyone. My affairs were cut and dried a long time ago. Oh yes, everyone will have his share, I'd be ashamed to favour one more than the other. You've all been remembered, you'll get it all one day !'

This was exactly what she told the members of her family every day and she was repeating it at her great-niece's deathbed out of sheer habit. And every time she would laugh to herself at the thought of this famous will which would make them fly at each other's throats once she was gone. Every single clause contained a potential lawsuit.

'Oh, if only you could take it all with you,' she added in conclusion. 'But since you can't, we must let others enjoy it !'

Now Frimat's wife came in and sat down at the table facing La Grande. She was knitting too and the afternoon passed with the two old women quietly chatting, while Jean, unable to settle, kept walking up and down, going out and coming in again in an agony of suspense. The doctor had said there was nothing to be done, so they did nothing.

First, Frimat's wife deplored the fact that no one had been to fetch Maître Sourdeau, a professional bone-setter from Bazoches, who knew about wounds as well. He would say some words and he could close them up by just blowing on them.

'A wonderful man !' confirmed La Grande, in a voice now full of respect. 'He put the Lorillons' breastbones straight. Old Lorillon's breastbone caved in and weighed down on his stomach, so that he started to go downhill fast. And the worst thing was

441

that then old Lorillon's wife began to suffer the same thing, it's catching, of course, as you know. And so they all got it, their daughter, their son-in-law, all the three children. My word, they'd've all died if they hadn't sent for Monsieur Sourdeau who put it right by rubbing a tortoiseshell comb on their stomachs.'

The other old woman sat approvingly, nodding her chin at every detail. There was no doubt about it at all, everyone knew. She herself added a further fact:

'It's old Sourdeau who cured the Budins' little girl of fever by slitting a live pigeon open and applying it to her head.'

She turned her head towards Jean, who was standing in a daze by the bed.

'I'd ask him to come if I was you. Perhaps it's not too late even now.'

His reply was an angry gesture. He was too much of the supercilious townsman to believe in such things. And the two women went on and on, exchanging remedies, parsley under the mattress for kidney trouble, three acorns in your pocket to cure any swellings, a glass of water blanched by moonlight and drunk on an empty stomach to get rid of wind.

'I say,' Frimat's wife suddenly exclaimed, 'if no one's going to fetch old Sourdeau, perhaps someone ought to ask the priest to come.'

Jean made his same angry gesture and La Grande pursed her lips.

'What earthly good could he do?'

'What could he do? He'd bring God's comfort, that's not a bad thing, sometimes.'

La Grande shrugged her shoulders as if to say that that sort of thing didn't cut much ice any more. Each to his own: God in his heaven, people on earth.

'Anyway,' she remarked after a pause, 'the priest wouldn't come, he's ill, Bécu's wife told me just now that he was leaving by carriage on Wednesday because the doctor said that if they didn't get him away from Rognes he'd certainly peg out.'

And indeed, during the two and a half years that Father Madeline had been parish priest, he had been steadily failing. Homesickness, a desperate longing for his mountains in Auvergne, had been slowly but surely gnawing at him every day at the sight of the flat plain of Beauce stretching to infinity, a sight which over-whelmed him with sadness. Not a tree or a rock, and brackish pools instead of fresh mountain streams cascading from the heights. His eye grew dimmer, his frame more gaunt than ever, people were saying that he had consumption. If only he could have taken some consolation from his parishioners! But this timid, uneasy soul, coming as he did from a very devout com-munity, was appalled by the lack of religion of the villagers, who were interested only in the externals of their faith. The village women bewildered him with their shouting and squabbling and took advantage of his weakness to run church affairs for them-selves, leaving him worried and full of qualms, constantly terri-fied of unwittingly falling into sin. One final blow lay in store for him: on Christmas Day, one of the Daughters of Mary was taken with labour pains in church. And ever since this scandal he had had difficulty in keeping going and they had become re-signed to having him taken back to Auvergne, a dying man.

'So we're going to be without a priest once more,' said Frimat's wife. 'Who knows if Father Godard will want to come back?'

'That old curmudgeon!' exclaimed La Grande. 'The very thought would kill him.'

Fanny now came in and the conversation came to an end. She had been the only member of the family to come the previous day and she had returned to see what was happening. Jean merely pointed towards Françoise with a trembling hand. A sympathetic silence followed. Then Fanny asked in a whisper whether the sick woman had asked to see her sister. No, she hadn't said a word about it, it was as if Lise didn't exist. This was very surprising because, however much they were at loggerheads, death is death. When else could you make your peace if not before you had to leave?

La Grande thought that Françoise should be asked about it. She stood up and leant forward:

'Well now, Françoise, what about Lise?'

The dying woman did not stir. Her closed eyelids gave a barely discernible tremor.

'Perhaps she's expecting someone to fetch her, I'll go.'

At that, still without opening her eyes, Françoise said no by gently rolling her head on the pillow. And Jean insisted that her

443

wish should be respected. The three women sat down again. They were surprised that Lise herself hadn't thought of coming now. Members of families were often terribly obstinate.

'Oh dear, there are so many things to worry about,' Fanny went on. 'Take me, for example. I've been on tenterhooks all this morning because they're drawing lots. And it's silly, really, because I know that Nénesse won't have to go away.'

'Ah, yes,' said Frimat's wife, 'you get worked up all the same.'

Once more the dying woman was forgotten. They talked about the luck of the draw, of the young men who would have to go and those who wouldn't. It was three o'clock and, although they were not expected back until five o'clock at the earliest, rumours from Cloyes were already circulating, carried by the sort of bush telegraph that links village to village. The Briquets' boy had drawn number 13, no luck there! The Couillets' had drawn 206, he'd surely be safe! But the others were more doubtful, there were contradictory reports and excitement was rising to a high pitch. No news of either Delphin or Nénesse.

'Oh, I'm all of a flutter, isn't it silly,' said Fanny again.

They called out to Bécu's wife, who was passing. She had gone back to the church and now was wandering about like a lost soul, feeling so harassed that she would not even stop to talk.

'I can't stand it any longer, I'm going to meet them.'

Jean was staring vacantly out of the window, not listening. Ever since that morning he had several times noticed old Fouan hobbling around the house on his two sticks. Suddenly he saw him again with his nose stuck to the window, trying to see into the room. He opened the window and the old man, looking quite taken aback, faltered: 'How is she?' Very low, it was the end. So he craned his neck and looked at Françoise from a distance, for such a long time that he seemed unable to tear himself away. When they saw him, Fanny and La Grande came back to their idea of sending for Lise. Everyone had to do his bit, it mustn't end like this. But when they asked him to run the errand, the old man gave a shiver of fright and made himself scarce, grunting and mumbling between his toothless jaws, his voice slurred from lack of practice.

'No, no, I can't possibly, not possibly.'

Jean was struck by his frightened look and the women made a

gesture of helplessness. After all, that was something that concerned the sisters themselves, they couldn't be forced to make their peace. And at that moment, a sound was heard, faint at first like the buzzing of a blowfly, then louder and louder, booming like a gust of wind blowing through trees. Fanny gave a start.

'Is that the drum? Here they are, goodnight all!'

She disappeared without even stopping to give her cousin a farewell kiss.

La Grande and Frimat's wife had gone to the doorway to look. Only Françoise and Jean were left, she obstinately still and silent, perhaps hearing all that was said but determined to die like an animal which had crawled into its den; he standing in front of the open window, racked with doubt and plunged in grief caused, so it seemed to him, by both people and things. The whole vast plain of Beauce. How loudly this drum was echoing through his whole being, this never-ending drum roll which mingled his present sorrow and past memories of barracks and battles, of that dog's life of poor bastards who haven't a wife or children to love them!

As soon as the flag appeared in the distance on the flat road, gloomy in the fading light of day, a throng of urchins started running along in front of the conscripts and a group of parents formed at the entrance to the village. The whole nine as well as the drummer were already drunk, bellowing out a song in the melancholy evening light and wearing favours of red, white and blue ribbons; most of them had their number pinned to their hats. When they came in sight of the village, they bawled even louder and swaggered in like conquering heroes.

Delphin was still in charge of the flag but now he was carrying it slung over his shoulder like a cumbersome, useless piece of rag. His face looked drawn and hard and he was not singing; nor had he a number pinned to his cap. As soon as she caught sight of him, his mother rushed trembling towards him, at the risk of being knocked over by the marching group.

'Well?'

Without slackening his pace, Delphin furiously thrust her aside:

'Go to hell!'

Bécu had come up, all agog like his wife. When he heard his

445

son's remark, he did not enquire further and, as his wife started sobbing, he had the greatest difficulty in holding back his own tears, despite his earlier patriotic claptrap.

'What the bloody hell good is that! He's a goner!'

Left behind on the deserted road, they both made their way laboriously back to the village, he recalling his hard life as a soldier while his wife turned angrily on the God to whom she had twice gone to plead and who had not heard her prayers.

On his hat Nénesse was wearing the number 214, superbly daubed in red and blue. This was one of the highest numbers and he was exultant at his good fortune, flourishing his stick to beat time for the wild singing of the rest. When she saw the number, instead of being delighted Fanny gave a sorrowful moan : if only they had known, they wouldn't have put one thousand francs into Monsieur Baillehache's lottery. But she and Delhomme embraced their son, all the same, as if he had just escaped from a grave danger.

'Don't fuss me!' he cried. 'It gets on my nerves.'

The band of young men stamped their way through the village, to the dismay of the inhabitants. And now their parents took care to steer clear of them, realizing that they would be told to go to hell, for all the lads were using the same foul language, those who would be going as well as those who were staying. In any case, they were incapable of speech, with their eyes popping out of their heads, and drunk as much from their bellowing as from their drinking. One wag who was blowing his trumpet with his nose had, in fact, picked a losing number, while two others, looking wan and with rings round their eyes, were certainly amongst the successful ones. If the enthusiastic drummer had led them into the depths of the Aigre they would gladly have toppled in.

Finally Delphin handed over the flag at the town-hall :

'Christ, I've had enough of that bloody rag. It brought me nothing but bad luck!'

He took Nénesse by the arm and led him away while the others took Lengaigne's tap-room by storm, surrounded by parents and friends, who finally learnt the facts. Macqueron appeared in his doorway, his heart aching to see that all this custom was going to his rival.

'Come along with me,' repeated Delphin laconically. 'I'm going to show you something funny.'

Nénesse followed him. They'd have time for a drink later. The damned drum was no longer battering their eardrums and it was a relief for them to go off together along the road which was now steadily sinking into darkness. And as his friend said nothing, plunged in thoughts which were doubtless not very cheerful, Nénesse started talking to him about a big business opportunity. The day before yesterday he had gone to the Rue aux Juifs for a bit of fun and he had heard that the Charles' son-in-law Vaucogne was intending to sell the establishment. With a skunk like that at the mercy of his women, the place couldn't possibly keep going! But what a chance to put the house on its feet and what a juicy prospect for an energetic, intelligent young man who was tough and had a good business sense! And the moment was just right, too, because in the restaurant where he was working he was in charge of the dancing and had to see that the tarts behaved themselves, so you can imagine! Well, the trick was to scare the Charles, make them see that No. 19 was within an inch of being closed by the police because of the unsavoury things that were happening, and acquire it for a song. Eh? That'd be better than being a farmer, he'd become a gentleman straight away.

Absorbed in his own thoughts, Delphin was not listening very attentively and he jumped as the other lad gave him a friendly dig in the ribs.

'Lucky people are always lucky,' he said quietly. 'You're going to be your mother's pride and joy.' And then he fell silent again while Nénesse, like a young man who knows all about such things, started explaining in advance all the improvements he would introduce at No. 19 if his parents could put up the necessary funds. He was a bit young but he felt that he had a real vocation for the job. And at that very moment he caught sight of La Trouille hurrying by in the dark on her way to meet one of her boy friends; so to show his familiarity with women he gave her a smart slap on the bottom as she passed. La Trouille was just going to hit him back when she recognized the two of them:

'Oh, hello, it's you two. Haven't we all grown up!'

She was laughing as she remembered the games they used to

get up to in the past. She had changed least of all, because even at twenty-one she was still a simple little tomboy, as slender as a young poplar, with her tiny girlish breasts. She was glad to see them and she gave them both a kiss.

'We're still friends, aren't we?'

And she would have been willing to start their old tricks if they had wanted to, merely for the pleasure of seeing them again, like old friends having a drink together.

'Listen, La Trouille,' said Nénesse, pulling her leg. 'I may be going to buy the Charles' shop. Will you come and work there?'

At that, she stopped laughing and burst into indignant tears. She disappeared, swallowed up in the shadows, desperately stammering in her childish way:

'Oh, that's dirty, that's dirty, I don't like you any more.'

Delphin had not said a word and now he set off again with a determined air.

'Come along. I'm going to show you something funny.'

He walked quickly ahead and left the road to make his way through the vineyards to the house which the council had let his father have ever since they had given the priest the presbytery. He lived there with his father. He took his friend into the kitchen and lit a candle, pleased to see that his parents had not yet come home.

'Let's have a drink,' he said, putting a litre of wine and two glasses on the table.

Then, after his drink, he rolled his tongue round his mouth and went on:

'So, I just wanted to tell you that if they think they've got me with that beastly number, they're mistaken. When I had to go and spend three days in Orléans on the death of Uncle Michael, it nearly killed me, because I felt so rotten at not being at home. You think that's silly, don't you, but what can I do, I can't help it, I'm like a tree that dies if you uproot it. And they want to take me off to God knows where, to places that I've never even heard of? No, they never will!'

Nénesse had often heard him talking like this. He gave a shrug.

'People say that and then they go off just the same. Don't forget the gendarmes.'

Without answering, Delphin turned round and with his left

448

hand picked up a little hatchet beside the wall, used for splitting sticks. Then he calmly laid his right forefinger on the edge of the table and, with a sharp blow, chopped it off.

'That's what I wanted to show you. I want you to tell the others whether a coward could have done that.'

'You silly bugger,' exclaimed Nénesse in dismay. 'People don't mutilate themselves like that. You're not a man any more!'

'Bugger that! Now the gendarmes can come if they like, I'm certain not to have to go.'

And he picked up the finger he had chopped off and threw it into the log fire. Then he shook his hand, dripping with blood, and roughly bandaged it in his handkerchief, which he then tied with a piece of string to stop the bleeding.

'We mustn't let that stop us knocking off the bottle before we go back and join the others. Cheerio!'

'Cheerio.'

By now, with all the smoke and shouting, you couldn't see or hear a thing in Lengaigne's tap-room. Apart from the lads who had just drawn lots, the room was packed: Jesus Christ and his friend Canon were busily leading old Fouan astray with a litre bottle of spirits between the three of them; shattered by his son's bad luck, Bécu had slumped into a drunken slumber, head on table; Delhomme and Clou were playing piquet; not to mention Lequeu, who had his nose stuck in a book and was pretending to read despite the din. Another scuffle amongst the women had caused feelings to run high: Flore had gone to the fountain to fetch a jug of water and there met Coelina, who had flung herself at her to scratch her eyes out, accusing her of taking money from the revenue-men so as to split on her neighbours. Macqueron and Lengaigne had rushed up and nearly come to blows as well, the former swearing that he would catch him out wetting his tobacco while the latter grinned and taunted him about his enforced resignation, and everybody else joined in, just for the fun of waving their fists about and bawling, so that for a moment there seemed a danger of a general brawl. It had ended without blows but there was still pent-up anger and a quarrelsome mood in the air.

First, there was nearly a row between Victor, the son of the house, and the conscripts. He had done his time and he was showing off in front of these youngsters, outbawling them, challenging them to idiotic wagers, such as holding a bottle of wine up in the air and emptying it straight down your throat or pumping a full glass of wine out with your nose without a drop going through your mouth. All at once, on the subject of the Macquerons and the imminent marriage of their daughter Berthe, young Couillet started laughing and cracking jokes about the old story of Not Got Any. They'd have to ask her husband next day: had she got any or not? They'd been discussing it for so long, it really was stupid.

And people were surprised when Victor suddenly flew into a rage, for he had always been keenest to claim that she hadn't got any.

'Look, shut up, she has got some!'

This statement created an uproar. So he'd seen her, had he? Been to bed with her? But he formally denied it. You can see without touching. He had worked out a plan, one day when he hadn't been able to put the idea out of his head and wanted to make sure. How had he done it? That was his business.

'She has got some, word of honour!'

There followed a terrible row when young Couillet kept asserting loudly that she hadn't got any, knowing nothing about it but refusing to back down. Victor was shouting that he used to say that, too, and he hadn't changed his mind because he wanted to support those lousy Macquerons but because truth is truth. And he flung himself on the conscript and had to be dragged off.

'Say that she has, Christ Almighty, or I'll do you!'

A lot of people still remained doubtful. Nobody could explain Victor's exasperation because he was normally very hard towards women and had publicly renounced his sister, who had had to go into hospital as a result of her loose living. Suzanne was rotten through and through. It was a good thing she had kept away and not come and infected them with her filthy body.

Flore fetched up some more wine and everybody started drinking again, but, despite this, insults and punches were still floating about in the air. No one would have thought of deserting the bar to go and eat. When you're drinking, you don't feel hungry. The conscripts struck up a patriotic chorus to the accompaniment of such a banging of fists that the three paraffin lamps on the table flickered, emitting trails of acrid smoke. It was stifling. Delhomme and Clou decided to open a window behind them. At that moment Buteau came in and slipped into a corner. He did not have his usual aggressive look and his little eyes slid furtively round the room, looking at everyone in turn. He had doubtless come to satisfy his need to discover what news there was, unable to remain any longer in his house where he had been shut up since the day before. He seemed to be so taken aback by the presence of Jesus Christ and Canon that he did not even tackle them for making old Fouan drunk. He also scrutinized Delhomme at length. But it was the sleeping Bécu, oblivious of the frightful din, who particularly intrigued him. Was he really asleep or just shamming? He nudged him with his elbows and was somewhat re-assured when he noticed that he was dribbling down his sleeve. He then concentrated his whole attention on the schoolmaster, struck by the extraordinary look on his face. Was something wrong? Why wasn't he looking normal?

Indeed, although he was pretending to be concentrating on his reading, Lequeu kept giving violent jerks. The conscripts' songs and mindless joviality were putting him beside himself.

'Bloody clodhoppers!' he said in a low voice, still trying to restrain himself.

In the last few months his situation in the commune had been deteriorating. He had always been rough and coarse towards the children, boxing their ears and telling them to go home to their dungheap. But his outbursts of temper had been growing worse, and he had run into serious trouble by splitting open a little girl's ear with a ruler. Some parents had written asking for him to be replaced. And on top of it all Berthe Macqueron's marriage had just destroyed a long cherished hope and calculations for the future that he thought were coming to fruition. What a miser-able lot these peasants were, refusing him their daughters and now taking the bread out of his mouth all because of a stupid girl's ear.

Suddenly, exactly as though he had been in his classroom, he slapped his book with his hands and shouted to the conscripts:

'Can't you pipe down, for Christ's sake! Do you really think it's as funny as all that to get your mug bashed in by a Prussian?'

They stared at him in astonishment. No, of course it wasn't

funny, everyone agreed on that, and Delhomme produced the old argument that everyone should defend his own bit of land. If the Prussians came to Beauce, they'd soon see that the people there weren't cowards. But to have to go and fight for other people's bits of land, that certainly wasn't funny at all.

And at that very moment Delphin came in, very red in the face and with a feverish look in his eyes. Nénesse followed him. Delphin heard the last remark and, as he sat down with his friends, he cried out:

'That's the stuff, let 'em come, those Prussians, and we'll have 'em for breakfast!'

They had noticed his handkerchief tied round his hand and asked him about it. It was nothing, just a cut. The table shook as he thumped his other fist down on it and ordered a litre of wine.

Canon and Jesus Christ were watching these young men with a pitiful, patronizing look. They too were thinking that you had to be young and pretty stupid, and even Canon's heart began to soften as he thought about his formula for future happiness. Resting his chin on his hands, he said out loud:

'Yes, war's bloody awful and, by Christ, it's time we took over. You know what I think. No more military service, no more taxes. Complete satisfaction of everybody's appetites for the least possible amount of work. And it's going to come, the day's not far off when you'll be able to hang onto your children and your money if you follow us.'

Jesus Christ nodded approvingly; but, unable to restrain himself any longer, Lequeu exploded:

'Oh, yes, you bloody humbug, you and your earthly paradise, forcing everyone to be happy in spite of themselves. What a joke! Do you think that's possible with us? Aren't we already rotten to the core? What we need is for some savages or other to come and clean us up first, Cossacks or Chinks!'

This time everyone was stunned into complete silence. So this slyboots could talk, this spineless little man who'd never shown anyone the colour of his opinions before and used to make himself scarce as soon as he might have to stand up and be counted, for fear of his superiors. They were all agog, particularly Buteau, who was anxiously listening to hear what he would have to say, as if these questions could have some relevance to the other matter. Opening the window had cleared the room of smoke and the dank, warm night air was coming in, there was a feeling of great peace extending far out over the dark, slumbering countryside. And with his ten long years of timidity bottled up inside him and so angry that he no longer cared a damn for compromising his career, the schoolmaster at last vented the hatred which had been stifling him :

'Do you take people for geese when you tell them that plums fall straight into your lap off the tree? Long before you can get your thing going, the land will have packed up and everything will be buggered up.'

In the face of such a vigorous attack Canon, who had never yet met his match, was visibly shaken. He tried to launch out into all the tales he had picked up from his fine Paris friends, such as state-owned farms and scientific agriculture. The other man cut him short :

'I know all that claptrap. By the time you get round to your scientific agriculture, the plains of France will have already been submerged under a flood of American wheat. Look, this little book that I was just reading gives all the details about it. Christ, the French peasant can pack up. The show's over !'

And as though giving a lesson in his classroom, he talked about the wheat across the ocean. Immense plains the size of a kingdom in which Beauce would have looked like a little lost lump of dry earth, land so fertile that instead of fertilizing it you had to reduce its fertility by a previous harvest, which didn't prevent it producing two crops a year; farms of eighty thousand acres divided into sections and each section divided into smaller sections; the large ones each having their own overseer, the smaller ones under a foreman with whole camps of hutments for man and beast, the kitchens and the equipment; battalions of agricultural workers taken on in the spring, organized like a campaigning army, living in the open with free board and lodging and laundry and medical care and dismissed in the autumn; furrows several miles long to be ploughed and sown; oceans of wheat to be cut stretching so far that you couldn't see where it ended; the worker needing merely to see to the working of the machines, double ploughs equipped with cutting discs, sowers and weeders, combine-harvesters, self-propelled threshing machines with straw elevators and automatic sacking; peasants were mechanics, a whole platoon of workers following each machine on horseback, ready to dismount to tighten a screw, change a bolt or make a spare part; in a word, the land had been turned into a bank, operated by financiers, exploited and cropped to the limit and giving ten times as much under such impersonal, scientific, material care than it would deliver, even reluctantly, in response to the loving handiwork of a man.

'And you hope to compete with your tuppenny ha'penny equipment,' he went on, 'when you don't know anything and don't want to, just stuck in your rut. Yes, you're knee-deep in wheat from America! And there'll be still more of it yet, it'll be waist-high, shoulder-high and up to your mouth and then cover your head! A river, a torrent, a flood which'll swallow up the whole lot of you!'

The peasants were listening round-eyed, panic-stricken at the thought of this flood of foreign wheat. They could already imagine it with horror; were they going to be carried away and drowned, like that devil promised? It was almost as if it were happening already. Rognes, their fields, the whole of Beauce would be submerged.

'No, it'll never happen,' choked Delhomme. 'The government will protect us.'

'A fine thing, the government,' replied Lequeu with a sneer. 'It needs protection itself. What's really funny is that you elected Monsieur Rochefontaine. At least the proprietor of La Borderie was logical to want Monsieur de Chédeville. Neither of them are of any earthly use, anyway. No parliament would ever vote an import duty of that size, so protectionism won't help you. You're buggered, you might as well shut up shop.'

At that there was uproar, with everybody talking at once. Couldn't they stop this miserable wheat coming in? They would sink the boats in the harbours, they'd shoot anyone bringing it ashore. Their voices were trembling and they would have wept and begged on bended knee for someone to save them from this abundance of cheap bread which was threatening the country. And with a derisive laugh the schoolmaster replied that nothing like that had ever been seen before: in the old days the only fear was famine; people had always been afraid of being short of wheat, so they must be really sunk to have reached the stage of being afraid of having too much. He was becoming drunk with his own words as he shouted down their wild protestations.

'You're a breed that has reached the end of its tether, you've been eaten up by your idiotic love of the land, that miserable bit of land which has got you by the short hair, which prevents you from seeing any further than your noses, which you'd commit murder for! You've been wedded to the land for centuries and she's made you into cuckolds. Look at America, the farmer is master of all his land there. There's nothing to attach him to it, no family link, no memories. As soon as his field is exhausted, he moves on. If he hears that five hundred miles away they've discovered more fertile plains, he ups and settles there. He's free and he's making a lot of money, whereas you're just poverty-stricken prisoners.'

Buteau had gone pale. Lequeu had looked at him when he mentioned murdering. He tried to put a bold face on it.

'People are what they are. What's the point of getting annoyed, since you say yourself that it wouldn't change anything?'

Delhomme nodded and they all began to celebrate again, Lengaigne, Clou, Fouan, even Delphin and the conscripts, who had been watching the scene with amusement, hoping that it would end in blows. Nettled at seeing this ink-shitter, as they called him, shouting louder than they, Canon and Jesus Christ pretended to roar with laughter too. They had reached the point of siding with the peasants.

'It's stupid to get annoyed,' asserted Canon with a shrug. 'We need organization.'

Lequeu made a savage gesture:

'Well, let me tell you what I think. I'm in favour of demolishing everything.'

He was livid with rage and he flung the words in their faces as though hoping they would flatten them:

'What bloody cowards peasants are, yes, all peasants. When you think that you're in the majority and that you let the townsfolk and the workers bugger you about. Christ, there's only one thing I regret and that's that my mother and father were peasants. Perhaps that's why I dislike you even more. Because there's no doubt about it, you could be the masters. But the fact is that you don't really get on well together, you're isolated and suspicious and ignorant: you save all your dirty tricks for each other. Well, what have you got hidden in all that stinking stagnant water? Are you like those duck-ponds covered with weed that look deep and which you couldn't drown a cat in? Fancy being the secret force that could shape the future and then just sticking in the mud! And believing in priests. So if there's no God, what's holding you back? When you were held back by fear of hellfire, then it's understandable that you grovelled. But now just go ahead: loot everything, burn everything! And meanwhile go on strike, that would be easier still and funnier too, you've all got a bit of money, you could hang on as long as you needed. Produce just enough for your own needs, don't market anything, not one sack of potatoes, not one bushel of wheat. How all those Parisians would starve! What a spring-clean that would be, by Christ!'

From the remote depths of the darkness, a gust of cold air seemed to be blowing through the window. Long trails of smoke were rising from the flaring paraffin lamps. Nobody felt like interrupting their rabid schoolmaster, despite all the uncomplimentary remarks he was addressing to them.

He concluded at the top of his voice, banging his book on the table till the glasses tinkled:

'I'm telling you all this but I'm not worried. Cowards though you are, it's you who'll finally overturn everything when the time comes. It's often happened and it'll be the same again. Just wait until your hunger and poverty make you fling yourselves on the towns like ravening wolves. And this wheat that's being brought in may spark it off. When there's too much of it, there won't be enough, we'll have shortages again. It's always wheat that causes revolts and killings. Oh, yes, the towns will be burnt down, razed to the ground, the land will become a desert overgrown with brambles and there'll be blood, streams of blood, so that the land will once again be able to provide bread for those who'll come after us!'

He tugged the door open and disappeared. In the general stupefaction, a cry was heard; the dirty scoundrel, they ought to have his blood! Such a quiet man up till now! He must be going mad. Delhomme, normally so calm, said that he would write to

456

the *préfet* and the others urged him to do so. But Jesus Christ and his friend Canon seemed particularly enraged, the first because of his ideas about 1789 and his humanitarian motto of liberty, equality and fraternity, the second with his authoritarian social and scientific organization. They were pale and exasperated at not having found any reply to him and more indignant than the peasants themselves, shouting that people like that ought to be guillotined. Hearing mention of blood, the rivers of blood which Lequeu had been calling down on the world in his frenzy, Buteau, with all sorts of strange ideas churning around unconsciously inside his head, had stood up with a nervous shudder, as though he were in agreement; and then he slid along the wall, furtively glancing to see if he was being followed, and disappeared in his turn.

The conscripts immediately started celebrating again. They were vociferously demanding sausages from Flore when Nénesse shut them up by pointing to Delphin, who had just collapsed with his head on the table. The poor devil was as white as a sheet. His handkerchief had slipped off his injured hand and was becoming stained with blood. So they yelled at Bécu, who was still asleep; he woke up at last and looked at his son's mutilated hand. He must have understood because he picked up a bottle, screaming that he would brain him. In the end, when he had taken the boy away, stumbling, they heard him bursting into tears in the middle of his oaths.

That evening, having heard of Françoise's accident at dinner, Hourdequin came into Rognes to ask Jean about it, as a friendly gesture. He was smoking his pipe and preoccupied with all his troubles as he walked along in the deep silence of the dark night. Feeling somewhat calmer, before calling on his former farm-hand he decided to prolong his walk by going down the hill. But when he was at the bottom, the sound of Lequeu's voice, which seemed to be carrying through the open window of the tavern into the shadows of the night, brought him to a sudden halt in the darkness. Then, deciding to walk up the hill again, the voice pursued him, and even when he had reached Jean's house he could still hear it as clearly as ever, as if it were sharpened by distance, like the cutting blade of a knife.

Jean was standing outside beside his door, leaning against the wall. He was so distressed that he could no longer remain at Françoise's bedside, for he was stifling.

'I'm sorry, Jean,' said Hourdequin, 'what's the news?'

The poor man made a heartbroken gesture.

'Oh, Monsieur Hourdequin, she's dying !'

Neither of them said anything more. Deep silence fell again while Lequeu still went ranting on in his grating voice.

After a few minutes, the farmer, who was listening in spite of himself, could not resist saying angrily :

'Can you hear that man bawling away? Isn't what he's saying funny when you're feeling sad?'

Once more he was plunged in his sorrows at the sound of that frightening voice and at the thought of the woman dying in the next room. He loved his land so dearly, sentimentally and almost intellectually : and now the last harvests had dealt him the final blow. He had squandered all his fortune and soon La Borderie would not even be able to feed him. Nothing had been of any use, his enthusiasm, his new methods of farming, his fertilizers, his machines. He blamed his disaster on lack of capital; but even then he wasn't certain, because everyone was in the same boat, the Robiquets had just been turned out of La Chamade for not paying the rent and the Coquarts were going to have to sell their farm at Saint Juste. And there was no possible escape. Never had he felt more fettered by his land than now, for every day the money and effort he had poured into it had shortened the chain. Catastrophe was looming round the corner, to put an end to the age-old struggle between the smallholder and the big landlord by destroying them both. It was the beginning of the times he had predicted, with wheat at less than sixteen francs and thus sold at a loss; the land was bankrupt as a result of social factors which were obviously stronger than the will of man.

And suddenly, heartbroken at his failure, Hourdequin found himself siding with Lequeu:

'Christ, he's right ! Let everything go to pot and we'll all pack up and brambles will take over the land, since the earth's exhausted and people of our sort are finished.'

And thinking of Jacqueline, he added :

'Fortunately, I've got another trouble that'll settle my hash before that happens !'

But at that moment they heard La Grande and Frimat's wife walking about and whispering indoors. Jean shivered and ran in. It was too late. Françoise was dead, and had perhaps been dead for some time. She had not opened her eyes or her lips again. La Grande had simply noticed that she was no longer alive when she had touched her. Very white, she seemed to be sleeping, her face sunken and obstinately set. Standing at the end of the bed, Jean looked at her, bewildered, his head swimming, thinking of his sorrow, his surprise that she had not wanted to make her will, the feeling that something in his life had been broken and was coming to an end.

At this moment, as Hourdequin, once again despondent, took his leave in silence, he saw a shadowy figure slip away from the window and scurry off into the darkness. He thought it might be a prowling dog. It was Buteau, who had come up to keep watch and was hurrying away to announce to Lise that her sister was dead.

NEXT morning, just as they had finished putting the corpse into the coffin, which was resting on two chairs in the middle of the room, Jean was surprised and outraged to see Lise come in, followed by Buteau. His first reaction was to turn them out; what a heartless couple, who had not even bothered to pay their last respects to their dying sister and who were finally making their appearance now the lid had been nailed down and there was no danger of meeting her face to face. Only the presence of other members of the family, Fanny and La Grande, held him back. Quarrelling in the presence of the dead was unlucky; and anyway, no one could stop Lise from making amends for her unkindness by deciding to sit with her sister's body.

So the Buteaus, who had been relying on this respect due to the dead, settled in. Without saying that they were taking over the house again they just did so in the most natural way in the world, as though it were the obvious thing now that Françoise was no longer there. True, she still was there, but all packed up to set off on her longest journey and no more of an encumbrance than a piece of furniture. After sitting down for a minute, Lise absent-mindedly started opening cupboards to make sure that no articles had been removed during her absence. Buteau had already started prowling round the cowshed and stables, like the owner who knows his way about. By evening they seemed to be completely at home again, hampered only by the coffin blocking the middle of the room. In any case, they needed to be patient for only one night: that floor space would be free early next morning.

Jean walked about uncertainly amidst all the family like a man in a daze, not knowing which way to turn. At first the house and furniture and Françoise's body had all seemed to belong to him, but as time went by they seemed to be slipping away into other people's hands. By nightfall, no one was troubling to speak to him any longer; he was merely an intruder whose presence was tolerated. Never had he felt such a disagreeable sensation of being an outsider, of not having a single friend amongst all these people who formed a united front, at least where he was concerned. Even his poor wife was ceasing to be his, so much so that when he expressed a wish to sit by her body, Fanny tried to send him away on the grounds that there were too many people there already. But he had stuck to his guns and had even taken the hundred and twenty-seven francs which were in the chest of drawers in order to ensure that they did not disappear. As Lise had opened the drawer soon after her arrival, she must have seen them, as well as the sheet of official paper, because she had quickly whispered something to La Grande. It was after this that she had settled down again with such assurance, knowing that no will had been made. No, she mustn't get the money; apprehensive as he was of what the morrow might bring, Jean said to himself that at least he'd make sure of that. Then he spent the night on a chair.

Next morning the funeral took place early, at nine o'clock, and Father Madeline, who was leaving that evening, was just able to take the service and go to the graveside; but once there, he collapsed and had to be carried off. The Charles had come, as well as Delhomme and Nénesse. It was a decent funeral, with no trimmings. Jean was crying. Buteau was wiping his eyes. At the last minute, Lise had protested that she felt weak in the knees and would never be strong enough to accompany her poor sister's body on its last journey. So she remained behind on her own, while La Grande, Fanny and Bécu followed the bier. And on their way home, all of them deliberately stayed on in the square in front of the church to witness the final scene which everybody had been anticipating for the last twenty-four hours.

Up till now the two men, Jean and Buteau, had avoided each other's gaze, afraid of a fight developing over Françoise's dead body before it was barely cold. Now they both made their way determinedly back towards the house, watching each other out of the corners of their eyes. Now we'll see! At first glance Jean realized why Lise had not joined the funeral procession. She had wanted to stay behind in order to move in at least all their most bulky articles. She had done it within the hour by throwing her bundles over Frimat's wall and carting the breakables round on a wheelbarrow. And finally, with a clout round the ear she had sent Laure and Jules packing into the yard where they were already scuffling, while old Fouan, whom she had also hustled in, was sitting recovering his breath on the bench. The house had been recaptured.

'Where are you going?' Buteau asked Jean abruptly, stopping him in the doorway.

'I'm going into my house.'

'Your house? Where's that? Anyway it's not here. This is our house.'

Lise rushed to join Buteau and with her hands on her hips started screaming insults at him, more foul-mouthed even than her husband.

'What's that he said? What's that dirty shit want? He'd been making my poor dear sister's life a misery long enough; but for him she wouldn't have died from her accident and she showed what she thought of him by not leaving him anything in her will. Smash him, Buteau, he'll contaminate us all if he gets in!'

Choking with rage at this savage attack, Jean still attempted to reason with them.

'I know the house and land will be yours now, but I still own half the furniture and the animals.'

'Half? What a bloody cheek!' shouted Lise, cutting him short. 'You dirty pimp, you'd have the nerve to take half of something when you'd only got the shirt on your back when you came here, you didn't even bring your own curry-comb, you lazy layabout. So you want to make your living out of women, do you, you dirty pig?'

Coming to her support, Buteau swung his arm to push Jean away from the door.

'She's right, clear off. You had your jacket and trousers, you can keep 'em, but now get out!'

The family seemed to be giving silent approval, above all the women Fanny and La Grande, who were standing watching some thirty yards away. But now, livid with rage at so outrageous an accusation and stung to the quick at the suggestion of such a foul calculation on his part, Jean lost his temper and shouted as loudly as the rest:

'Oh, so that's it, is it, you want a row? Well, you'll get it. And first of all, I'm going in, it's my house until the property's been properly divided up. And then I'll go and fetch Monsieur Baillehache, who'll seal everything up and put me in charge. It's my house, so you just sod off!'

He stepped forward with such a terrifying air that Lise moved away from the doorway. But Buteau hurled himself on him and they grappled with each other in the middle of the kitchen. And the dispute was now resumed indoors, this time to decide which of them would be ejected, the husband or the sister and brother-in-law.

'Show me a paper giving you the right to this house.'

'You can wipe your arse on any paper. It's good enough just to have the right to be here.'

'Well, bring the bailiff along and the police, like we did.'

'The bailiff and the police can go and get stuffed! Only twisters need them, honest folk settle their accounts privately.'

Jean had taken refuge behind the table. He was desperately eager to hold his ground because he could not accept the idea of leaving the house where his wife had just breathed her last and which seemed to represent all the happiness he had known in life. But Buteau was likewise furious at the thought of having to give up the place he had just won back; and he realized that the matter must be settled. He said:

'And that's not all: you're just a pain in the arse!'

He leapt over the table and once more hurled himself on Jean. However, the latter picked up a chair and flung it at his legs, tripping him up. As he was taking refuge in the next room, hoping to barricade himself in, Lise suddenly remembered the money, the hundred and twenty-seven francs which she had seen in the chest of drawers. Thinking that he was rushing in to take them, she slipped ahead of him, opened the drawer and gave a scream of anguish.

'The money! That bugger stole the money last night!'

And now Jean had no chance, for he had to keep guard over his pocket. He kept shouting that the money belonged to him, that he would be glad to settle up and they would certainly be left owing him some money. But neither the man nor his wife was listening and she rushed at him, hitting harder than her husband. Fiercely they pushed him out of the bedroom into the

463

kitchen where all three of them swirled round in a confused mass, bouncing off the furniture. He kicked himself clear of Lise but she came back at him and sunk her nails into the scruff of his neck while Buteau rammed him with his head and sent him sprawling on the road outside. They stood blocking the doorway and yelling:

'You thief! You took our money! You thief, you thief!'

Painfully, Jean picked himself up, stammering angrily.

'All right, I'll go and see the judge in Châteaudun and he'll make sure I can get in here and I'll sue you for damages! You've not seen the last of me!'

And shaking his fist as a parting gesture, he disappeared in the direction of the plain. The family had prudently made themselves scarce when they saw that blows were being exchanged, for fear of possible trouble with the law.

And now the Buteaus could utter a cry of triumph. At last they had succeeded in throwing this outsider, this usurper, out into the street! They'd got their house back, as they'd always said they would. Their house! Their own house! The thought that they would now be back in their old family home, built by one of their ancestors, filled them with a sudden mad joy, as they raced through the rooms, yelling at the tops of their voices for the sheer pleasure of shouting in their own home. Laure and Jules ran in, drumming on an old frying-pan. Only old Fouan remained sitting on the stone bench, showing no sign of elation as he followed their antics through his dim eyes.

Suddenly Buteau stopped still.

'Christ! He went off up the hill, suppose he tried to do something to our land?'

It was absurd, but this impassioned cry threw him into a turmoil as his mind suddenly came back to his land, in a frenzy of joy and apprehension. Ah, that land was even closer to his heart than the house; that spit of land up there which filled the gap between his own two plots and gave him back his seven and a half acre field, such a splendid field, even Delhomme hadn't got one like it. His whole body started quivering with pleasure as though a woman you loved and whom you thought lost had suddenly come back to you.

He was seized with a wild urge to see his land straight away, together with the mad fear that the other man might make off with it. He set off at a run, grunting that he'd have no peace until he was sure.

Jean had in fact gone up onto the plain to avoid the village and was making his way towards La Borderie through force of habit. When Buteau caught sight of him he was just walking past the Cornailles field, but he did not stop and the only glance he gave this piece of land which had been such a bone of contention was one of sorrow and distrust, as though accusing it of having brought him bad luck. His eyes had filled with tears at the memory of the first time he had spoken to Françoise : wasn't it at Cornailles that the cow Coliche had dragged her into the field of lucerne when she was little more than a child? He walked slowly away, hanging his head, and Buteau, who was spying on him, still uncertain whether he might be up to some trick or other, followed behind him up to the field and stood for a long time contemplating it : it was still there and it seemed to be in good heart, nobody had harmed it. His heart overflowed with joy at the thought that it was his again, and forever. He stooped and picked up a lump of earth in both hands, crumbled it, sniffed it and let it trickle through his fingers. It was his own good earth, and he went home humming a tune, as though intoxicated by its smell.

Meanwhile, Jean was walking vacantly on without knowing where his feet were leading him. At first he had intended to hurry over to Cloyes to see Monsieur Baillehache in order to regain possession of his house. Then his anger had subsided. If he were to gain possession today, he'd only have to leave tomorrow. So why not swallow the bitter pill straight away, since it had already happened? Anyway, those swine were right : he was going off as poor as when he'd come. But the thing which took away his will to fight and made him decide to accept this situation was, above all, the thought that Françoise must have wanted things that way since she hadn't left him her property. So he abandoned the idea of doing anything straight away and as he strode along, if his anger boiled up again, it was directed against the Buteaus, whom he swore to bring to justice in order to claim his rightful share of the inheritance, which belonged to him as Françoise's husband. They'd see if he would let himself be plucked like a chicken !

He raised his eyes and was surprised to find himself at La Borderie. A half-conscious impulse must have brought him back to the farm for shelter. And indeed, if he didn't want to leave the district, wouldn't he find work and bed and board here to enable him to stay on? Hourdequin had always thought well of him and he had no doubt that he would take him on, then and there.

But he was disturbed to see Jacqueline crossing the farmyard in great distress. It was just striking eleven o'clock and he had arrived in the middle of a terrible catastrophe. That morning the young woman had got up before the maid and found the trap-door of the cellar, the one situated so dangerously at the foot of the stairs, left wide open; and Hourdequin was lying down below, dead, his back broken by the edge of one of the steps. She had screamed, people had come running in; and now the farm was in a state of turmoil, the farmer's body was lying on a mattress in the dining-room while Jacqueline, in despair, was in the kitchen, dry-eyed, but looking completely distraught.

As soon as Jean came in, she unburdened herself in a voice choking with emotion.

'I'd always said something would happen. I wanted them to put the trap-door somewhere else! But who on earth can have left it open? I'm sure it was closed last night when I went upstairs. I've spent the whole morning trying to work it out.'

'The master came down before you, did he?' Jean asked, stunned by the accident.

'Yes, the sun was just coming up. I was asleep. I thought I heard a voice calling him from downstairs. I must have been dreaming. He'd often get up like that and always went down without a light, to catch the farm-hands just when they were getting out of bed. He can't have seen the hole and he must have fallen into it. But who can have left the trap-door open? Oh, it'll be the death of me!'

A suspicion flashed into Jean's mind which he immediately rejected. She had no advantage to gain by his death; her despair was quite genuine.

'What terrible bad luck,' he muttered.

'Yes, it is terrible bad luck, terrible bad luck for me!'

She sank into a chair, prostrate with grief, as though the house were collapsing all around her. And she'd been relying on at last marrying her master! And her master had sworn to leave everything to her in his will and now he'd died without having had time to sign anything. And she wouldn't even get her wages, his son would be coming back and he'd boot her out, just like he'd promised. Nothing at all! A few trinkets and clothes, only what she'd got on her back! It was a crushing blow, a real disaster.

Something that Jacqueline had not mentioned, for she had forgotten about it, was that the day before she had succeeded in having the shepherd Soulas dismissed. Enraged at finding him always spying on her behind her back, she had accused him of being too old and no longer competent; and although Hourdequin did not share her view he had given in to her, by now cowed and cravenly submissive and ready to accept any humiliation in return for the pleasures of her bed. He had dismissed Soulas with kind words and promises while the shepherd stared at his master through his pale eyes. Then, slowly, he had started to tell the whole truth about the slut who was the cause of his misfortune: a whole string of randy males, with Tron bringing up the rear, together with all the details about him, so shameless and arrogant and lustful that everyone knew about it and everybody in the district used to say that the master must like his farm-hands' leftovers. In vain the farmer tried, desperately, to interrupt him, because he valued his ignorance and was so terrified at the thought that he might have to get rid of her that he no longer wanted to know the truth: but the shepherd had gone steadily on to the bitter end, not leaving out one single occasion when he had caught them together and relieving himself of some of his resentment by being able at last to unburden his heart. Jacqueline knew nothing of the shepherd's denunciation of her. Hourdequin had rushed away into the fields, fearing that he might strangle her if he were to meet her; when he came back later on, he had merely dismissed Tron on the pretext that he had been leaving the farmyard in a state of indescribable filth. At that she had begun to suspect something and, while not daring to defend the cowherd, she had persuaded Hourdequin to let him stay one more night, relying on being able to find some way of keeping him on next day. And now everything was in the balance as a result of this fatal blow which had destroyed ten years of laborious calculation.

Jean was alone in the kitchen with her when Tron appeared. She had not seen him since the previous day, while the other farm-hands had been wandering anxiously around the farm with nothing to do. When she caught sight of this giant, childlike, stupid animal from the Perche and saw how furtively he came in, she gave a cry:

'It's you who opened the trap-door!'

Suddenly everything became clear as he stood there aghast, pale and trembling.

'It's you who opened the trap-door and called out to him so that he'd stumble into it.'

Jean recoiled, horrified at what he saw, although the other two in their emotion and confusion seemed not to notice his presence. Hanging his head, Tron mumbled a confession.

'Yes, I did it. He'd sacked me and I wouldn't have been able to see you any more. I couldn't bear it, and then I'd been thinking that if he died we'd be free for each other.'

She listened coldly, with every nerve strung to breaking-point as he mumbled blissfully on, disclosing all the feelings which he had been harbouring in his thick skull, the humble, savage jealousy of a servant towards the master whom he had been forced to obey and his sly plot to commit this crime in order that he alone would have complete possession of the woman he desired.

'I thought you would be pleased once it'd happened. If I didn't tell you anything about it, it was so's not to embarrass you. And now he's gone, I want you to come away with me so we can get married.'

Jacqueline burst out harshly:

'Marry you? But I don't love you and I don't want to! So you killed him so as to have me? You must be even more stupid than I thought. What a crazy thing to do, when he hadn't married me and made his will. You've ruined me, you've taken the bread out of my mouth. It's my back you've broken, do you understand, you bloody idiot? And so you think I'll go off with you? Just look me in the face, do you take me for a complete imbecile?'

Now it was his turn to listen, open-mouthed, at this unexpected reaction.

'Because we'd had fun and games together, do you imagine I could put up with a crass idiot like you forever? Marry you?

Oh no, I'd pick someone a bit sharper than you if I wanted a husband. Look, clear off, will you, you make me sick. I don't love you and I don't want anything to do with you. Clear off!'

Tron was shaken by anger. What was wrong? Had he committed his murder for nothing? She belonged to him, he'd take her by the scruff of the neck and carry her off.

'You're a first-class slut,' he growled. 'All the same, you're coming with me or else I'll settle your hash like I did his.'

Jacqueline strode up to him with clenched fists:

'Just try!'

He was a powerfully built, tall, thickset man, and she was very weak, as slim and graceful as a girl. But so frightening was her attitude, with her teeth ready to snap, her eyes sharp and glinting like daggers, that it was he who stepped back.

'It's all over, clear off. I'd sooner never have anything to do with a man again than go away with you. Clear off, clear off, clear off!'

Like a cowardly, savage beast, Tron retreated, cowed but already secretly thinking how to take his revenge later. He looked at her and said once again:

'I'll get you, dead or alive.'

When he had left the farm, Jacqueline gave a sigh of relief: good riddance! Then, still trembling, she turned round and, unsurprised to see Jean still there, she exclaimed in a sudden burst of frankness:

'How I'd like to set the police on that swine if I wasn't afraid of being picked up as well!'

Jean was still standing there chilled to the marrow. Moreover, the young woman was now seized by a nervous reaction: fighting for breath, she flung herself sobbing into his arms, saying how unhappy she was, so unhappy! Her tears flowed on and on, she wanted to be pitied and loved, she kept clinging to him as if she wished he would carry her off and look after her. And he was beginning to become very irritated with her when a gig drove into the farmyard and the dead man's brother-in-law, the lawyer Baillehache, who had been fetched by one of the farm-hands, sprang down. Jacqueline ran over to him to pour out her troubles.

Jean slipped out of the kitchen and once more found himself on the bare, flat land under a rainy March sky. But he was too upset by everything he had just learnt and by the shock he had received, on top of his own sorrow, to notice anything. He had had his full measure of bad luck and, despite his sadness at his former master's fate, he selfishly quickened his pace and hurried away. It was hardly up to him to denounce the Cognet girl and her lover, it was for the law to keep its eyes skinned. Twice he looked round, imagining that someone was calling him and feeling almost like an accomplice. He did not breathe freely until he had reached the first houses of Rognes. By then, he was saying to himself that the farmer had suffered for his sins and he was turning over in his mind that great truth that men would be much better off if women didn't exist. He had started thinking of Françoise once again and he was choking with emotion.

When he reached the outskirts of the village, Jean remembered that he had gone to the farm in search of work. He immediately started worrying and wondering whom he could approach at such a time. The thought occurred to him that the Charles had been looking for a gardener for the last few days. Why not go and offer his services? After all, he was still a sort of member of the family and that might be a recommendation. He set off for Roseblanche straight away.

It was one o'clock and the Charles were just finishing lunch when the maid showed him in. Élodie was serving the coffee and Monsieur Charles made his cousin sit down and offered him a cup. He accepted, although he had eaten nothing all day; his stomach felt all contracted, the coffee might help to relieve him. But when he found himself seated at the table with these middle-class people, he did not feel like asking for the gardening job then and there: perhaps later on, when he could think of a way to introduce the subject. Madame Charles had started condoling with him and mentioning her own grief at poor Françoise's death, and he was feeling emotional. The family must have thought that he had come to take his leave.

Then, when the maid announced the visit of Delhomme and his son, Jean was forgotten.

Since that morning, important business was afoot for the Charles. After leaving the churchyard, Nénesse had gone along with them back to Roseblanche and, while Madame Charles went in with Élodie, he had stayed behind with her father and bluntly offered to take over No. 19 if an agreement could be reached. According to him, the brothel, which he knew, was going to be sold for a ludicrously small sum. Under Vaucogne, it had reached such a parlous state that he wouldn't get five thousand francs for it; everything needed changing, the shabby furniture as well as the unsuitable staff, who were so hopeless that even the military had started going elsewhere. For a good twenty minutes, he had slated the establishment, to the bewilderment of his uncle, quite taken aback by his grasp of the whole business, his bargaining skills and the extraordinary gifts he showed for one so young. What a fellow! He'd certainly be able to cope! And Nénesse had said that he'd come back with his father after lunch to discuss the matter seriously.

Monsieur Charles went in to talk it over with his wife and she too was amazed at the young man's talents. If only their son-in-law Vaucogne had had half his gumption! They'd have to go carefully to make sure he didn't take them in. The point was that Élodie's dowry was at risk. But beneath all their fear was their irresistible liking for Nénesse and their wish to see No. 19 in the hands of some skilful and energetic owner who would restore its prestige even if they lost money by it. So when the Delhommes came in, they greeted them very cordially.

'You'll have some coffee, won't you? Fetch the sugar, Élodie!'

Jean pushed back his chair and they all sat down round the table. Freshly shaven, his tanned face quite inscrutable and full of diplomatic caution, Delhomme did not utter a word, whereas Nénesse, all dressed up in patent leather shoes, a mauve tie and a waistcoat with a gold floral design, seemed very much at his ease and full of ingratiating smiles. When Élodie blushingly offered the sugar-bowl, he looked at her and tried to pay her a compliment:

'What big lumps of sugar you've got, cousin.'

She blushed even more and in her innocence could not find anything to say, so put out was she by this remark from such a charming young man.

That morning, Nénesse, sly fox that he was, had put only half his cards on the table. Ever since the funeral, when he had caught sight of Élodie, his plans had become more ambitious: not only would he get No. 19, he wanted the girl as well. The transaction was a straightforward one in the first place; no money need change hands, he'd only take her with the brothel as dowry: furthermore, even if her only dowry for the moment was this house, a speculative proposition, later on she would be inheriting a lot of money from her parents. And so he had brought his father along, determined to make his proposal straight away.

For a moment, they talked about the weather, which was extremely mild for the time of year. The pears had plenty of blossom but would it set? Their coffee was almost drunk, the conversation flagged.

'Élodie my pet,' said Monsieur Charles suddenly, 'why not go for a little walk in the garden?'

He wanted to get rid of her because he was anxious to discuss business with the Delhommes.

'Please, Uncle,' Nénesse interrupted, 'I wonder if you would mind very much if Élodie stayed here with us? I've got something to say which concerns her and it's always better not to take two bites at a cherry, isn't it?'

And then he stood up and made his proposal, like a well-bred young man:

'I just wanted to say that I'd be very happy if I could marry my cousin, if you gave your consent and she agreed, too.'

There was great surprise. But Élodie in particular seemed completely taken aback and so scared that she rushed over to Madame Charles and flung her arms round her neck, her ears crimson with modesty. Her grandmother made a great effort to calm her.

'Come along, come along, my darling, that's enough, do be sensible! No one's going to eat you just because someone's proposed to you. Your cousin didn't say anything unkind, look at him, don't be silly.'

But soft words were not enough to make her show her face.

'Well, young man,' Monsieur Charles said eventually, 'I didn't expect your proposal. Perhaps it would have been better to have mentioned it to me first, because you see how sensitive our little pet is. But, in any case, let me assure you that I have a high opinion of you because you seem to me a fine young man and not afraid of work.'

Delhomme, whose features had not moved one iota throughout, uttered two words:

'Of course!'

And realizing that he must be polite, Jean added:

'Yes, he is indeed!'

Monsieur Charles was collecting his thoughts and had already reached the conclusion that Nénesse was not a bad match: he was young, active and the only son of rich peasant smallholders. His granddaughter wouldn't find anyone better. So, after exchanging a glance with his wife, he went on:

'It's a matter for her to decide. We would never go against her wishes, she must make up her own mind.'

So Nénesse gallantly repeated his proposal:

'Cousin, will you do me the honour and pleasure...?'

Still burying her face in her grandmother's chest, she did not give him time to finish but nodded vigorously three times, tucking her head still further down, no doubt keeping her eyes hidden gave her courage. The whole company was struck dumb, amazed at the speed with which she had said yes. So she must be in love with this young man, whom she hardly knew? Or was it that she wanted any man, as long as he was good-looking?

Madame Charles smilingly kissed her hair, saying:

'Bless her little heart! Bless her little heart!'

'Well,' said Monsieur Charles, 'since she's willing, so are we.'

But a misgiving crossed his mind. His heavy eyelids drooped and he added with a gesture of regret:

'Of course, my dear young man, we shall have to give up the other idea, the one you suggested to me this morning.'

Nénesse looked surprised:

'Why should we?'

'What do you mean, why should we? Well, because, well really, you must understand that ... we didn't leave her to be brought up in a convent until she was twenty for her to... No, it wouldn't be possible.'

He was blinking uneasily and chewing his lips in his efforts to express his meaning without being too explicit. His little girl in the Rue aux Juifs! A young lady who had been so well educated, who was so completely innocent, who'd been brought up knowing absolutely nothing!

'I'm sorry,' said Nénesse bluntly, 'that's not how I see it. I'm getting married in order to set myself up, I want my cousin and the house at No. 19.'

'The confectioner's!' exclaimed Madame Charles.

Once this word had been uttered, the discussion seized on it and it was bandied about to and fro between them. Really, was it reasonable to include the confectioner's shop? The young man and his father insisted on it as the dowry, pointing out that it was the bride's one really valuable possession and they couldn't possibly give it up; and they appealed to Jean to support them, which he did with a jerk of his chin. In the end, they all began to shout and, forgetting themselves, started to spell out the details in crude terms, when they were silenced in a most unexpected way.

Élodie finally revealed her face and stood up, looking as always like a tall slim lily planted in some shady corner, pale, bloodless and virginal, with her vacant look and mousy hair. She faced them all and said quietly:

'My cousin's right, we can't let it go.'

Aghast, Madame Charles faltered:

'But my little pet, if you knew...'

'I do know. Victorine told me all about it a long time ago, the maid you dismissed because of her men. I do know about it and I've thought about it and I'm absolutely sure we can't let it go.'

The Charles sat down dumbfounded, rooted to their seats, staring at her with wide-open eyes, completely bewildered. So she knew about No. 19, what took place there, the money they earned from it, the whole business in fact, and she could still speak about it so calmly? What wonderful innocence, shrinking at nothing!

'We can't let it go,' she repeated. 'It's too good and too profitable. And anyway, how could we let a house like that, which you've built up with hard work from nothing, go out of the family?'

Monsieur Charles was completely dumbfounded. But underneath the shock he could feel an indescribable emotion welling up inside his heart and bringing a lump to his throat. He stood up, swaying and steadying himself against his wife, who had also stood up, trembling and choking with emotion. They both thought that their granddaughter was sacrificing herself and distractedly started trying to dissuade her :

'Oh you darling, no, dearest, you mustn't !'

But Élodie's eyes filled with tears and she kissed her mother's old wedding-ring which she wore on her finger, the wedding-ring scratched and worn by all her toil in No. 19.

'Yes, I will, you must let me do what I feel. I want to be like Mummy. If she could do it, so can I. There's no disgrace in it, since you did it yourselves. I'm looking forward to it, I promise you. And you'll see how I'll help cousin Nénesse and how quickly we'll put the house on its feet again, the two of us together. We'll get it going, you don't realize what sort of person I am !'

At this they could restrain themselves no longer and tears poured down their cheeks. Completely overcome by emotion, they sobbed like children. They had hardly brought her up with such a thing in mind, but what could you do? Blood will out. They could recognize a vocation when they saw one. It was exactly the same with Estelle : they'd shut her up, too, in the convent with the Sisters of the Visitation and left her ignorant and imbued with the highest principles of morality; and she had still turned out to be an incomparable brothel-keeper. Upbringing wasn't all that important, it was intelligence which mattered. But even more than that, the Charles' deep emotion and their uncontrollable tears sprang from the glorious thought that No. 19, their own creation, flesh of their flesh, was going to be saved from ruin. With the enthusiasm of youth, Élodie and Nénesse would hand on the torch. And they could already see it restored to public favour, in all its pristine brilliance, as in the finest hours of their own régime.

When Monsieur Charles was at last able to speak, he took his granddaughter into his arms.

'Your father caused us many anxious moments, but you've consoled us for everything, my little angel.'

Madame Charles hugged her too, and they stood in one single group, mingling their tears.

'So it's a deal?' asked Nénesse, anxious for a firm commitment.

'Yes, it's a deal.'

Delhomme was beaming, like a father delighted to have set up his son in a way he could scarcely have expected.

With his usual caution, he stirred himself to express his opinion:

'Well, that's that! And if you never regret it, I know we shan't. No need to wish the young couple good luck. As long as the money's coming in, everything's always all right.'

And on that conclusion everyone sat down again, to discuss the details in peace.

Jean realized that he was in the way. During these sentimental outbursts, he had been embarrassed to be there and would have slipped away earlier if he had known how to do so. Eventually he drew Monsieur Charles aside and asked about the gardening job. The wealthy man immediately froze: offer a job to a relative? Impossible! It's never any good employing a relative, you can't tell them off! Anyway, he'd filled the job the day before. So Jean went away, hearing Élodie saying in her toneless voice that if Daddy was going to be naughty she'd make him see reason.

Once outside, he walked slowly away, not knowing where to turn now for work. Out of his one hundred and twenty-seven francs, he'd already paid for his wife's funeral, the cross and the surround at the graveyard. He was not left with much more than half the sum; but he could still manage for three weeks on that and afterwards he'd see. He was not afraid of hardship, his only worry was being unable to leave Rognes because of his lawsuit. Three o'clock struck, then four, then five. For a long time, he wandered aimlessly about the countryside, with strange, confused notions churning around inside his head, going back first to La Borderie, then to the Charles'. It was the same story everywhere, money and women, the kiss of death and the breath of life. It was not surprising if they were the source of all his troubles. His legs began to flag and he remembered that he hadn't yet eaten. He went back to the village, deciding to put up at the Lengaignes', who let rooms. But as he was crossing the square in front of the church, the sight of the house they had driven him out of that morning awakened his wrath again. Why should he let those swine have his two pairs of trousers and coat? They were his and he wanted them, even if it meant another fight.

Night was falling and Jean could barely distinguish old Fouan sitting on the stone bench. He was just coming up to the kitchen door in which there was a lighted candle when Buteau recognized him and rushed out to block the way.

'Christ Almighty, it's you again. What do you want?'

'I want my coat and my two pairs of trousers.'

A furious quarrel arose. Jean stood his ground and wanted to look inside the wardrobe cupboard while Buteau picked up a bill-hook and was swearing he would slit his throat if he tried to come in. In the end Lise's voice was heard shouting inside the house:

'Oh, go on, let him have his old rags. You'll never wear them, he's contaminated them!'

The two men stopped shouting. Jean stood waiting and at that very moment, behind his back, he heard old Fouan, dreaming to himself and rambling in his mind, mumble out loud:

'Get away quick! They'll be after your blood just as they were after the girl's.'

In a blinding flash, Jean understood everything, Françoise's death as well as her obstinate silence. He already had his suspicions and now he no longer had any doubt that she had saved her family from the guillotine. His hair stood on end and he could find nothing to say or do when Lise flung his coat and trousers straight at his face through the open door.

'Here, take your filthy rags! They're so foul they'd've stunk the place out!"'

He picked them up and went off. And not until he was out of the yard and on the street did he wave his fist at the house, shattering the silence with one single word:

'Murderers!'

Then he disappeared into the darkness. Buteau was shaken to the core. He had heard old Fouan muttering and rambling and Jean's last word struck home like a bullet. What now? Were the police going to start interfering just when he thought that the affair had been buried with Françoise's dead body? He had been breathing freely ever since he had seen her disappearing into the earth that morning and now the old man knew everything! Was he just pretending to be stupid in order to keep them under observation? This thought added the final drop to Buteau's cup of bitterness and made him feel so ill that he left half his supper, and when he told Lise, she started shivering too and could not eat anything either.

They had both been looking forward to their first night in their newly won home, but it turned out to be a night of horror and misery. They had put Laure and Jules to bed on a mattress in front of the chest of drawers, until such time as they could find somewhere else, and had gone to bed and blown out their candle before the children were asleep. But they could not sleep a wink themselves and lay tossing and turning as though on hot coals. Finally they started talking in an undertone. What a burden this old father of theirs had become since he'd fallen into his second childhood! A real burden who could ruin them with what he cost to keep. You couldn't imagine the amount of bread he ate and a real glutton as well, picking his meat up in his fingers, spilling his wine all over his beard and so filthy it made you sick to look at him. And now he always went about with his trousers undone, he'd been caught exposing himself to little girls like a worn-out, half-dead animal. What a disgusting obsession for an old man who in his youth hadn't been any filthier than anyone else in his habits. Really, it was enough to make you want to pole-axe him, for he didn't seem ready to go of his own accord.

'When you think that he'd topple over if you blew on him,' muttered Buteau. 'And he won't give up, he doesn't care a damn about mucking us up! Those old buggers, the less they work and the less they earn, the harder they cling on! He's never going to kick the bucket.'

Lying on her back, Lise added:

'It's a bad thing for him to have come back here. He'll be too comfortable, he'll take on a new lease of life. If I'd had anything to say about it, I'd've prayed God not to let him sleep a single night here.'

Neither of them mentioned their real concern, the thought that their father knew everything and could give them away, quite innocently. This was the last straw. The fact that he cost them money, that he was an encumbrance, that he was preventing them from freely enjoying the stolen bonds, was something they had been putting up with for a long time. But the thought that one word from him could bring them to the guillotine, that was really going too far. They'd have to do something about it.

'I'm going to see if he's asleep,' Lise said suddenly.

She relit the candle, made sure that Jules and Laure were sound asleep and slipped along in her shift to the room where they stored the beetroot and where they had set up the old man's iron bedstead again. When she came back she was shivering, her feet frozen by the tiled floor. She slid under the blanket again and snuggled up to her husband, who held her in his arms to warm her.

'Well?'

'Well, he's sleeping with his mouth wide open like a trap-door because he can't breathe properly.'

Silence fell but, although they said nothing as they lay in each other's arms, they could sense their thoughts in the beating of their hearts. This old man who always had difficulty in breathing would be so easy to finish off, some little thing pushed gently into his throat, a handkerchief or just fingers, and they'd be rid of him. They'd even be doing him a favour. Wouldn't he be better sleeping peacefully in the churchyard than being a burden to everyone, himself included?

Buteau was still hugging Lise in his arms. Now they were both burning hot as if desire had set their blood on fire. Suddenly he let go of her and sprang out onto the tiled floor in his bare feet.

'I'm going to take a look myself.'

He disappeared, candle in hand, while she held her breath and listened wide-eyed in the dark. But minutes went by and no sound came from the room next door. In the end, she heard him come back without a light, his feet padding softly on the floor, his breath coming in gasps. He came up to the bed and reached for her, whispering:

'You come, too, I'm afraid to do it by myself.'

Lise followed Buteau, holding her arms out in front in order not to bump into him. They no longer noticed the cold and felt uncomfortable in their nightclothes. The candle standing on the ground in the corner of the old man's room showed him lying on his back with his head beside the pillow. He was so stiff and gaunt with age that but for the painful rasping breath issuing from his gaping mouth you might have thought he was dead. He was toothless and his mouth looked like a black hole into which his lips seemed to be falling; and the two of them bent over and peered into it as if to see how much life remained at the bottom. For a long time, they stood looking side by side, with their hips touching. But their arms had lost their strength; it was so easy and yet so difficult to pick something up and stuff it into that hole. They walked away and came back again. Their mouths were too dry to say anything, they could speak only with their eyes. She was staring at the pillow as though to say: Go on! What are you waiting for? But he stood there, blinking and pushing her into his place. In exasperation, Lise suddenly caught hold of the pillow and clapped it down on her father's face.

'What a skunk you are! Why has it always got to be a woman?'

At this, Buteau ran forward and pressed with all his might on the pillow while Lise climbed onto the bed and sat her bare rump down with all her weight like some dropsical old carthorse. As though demented, they leant on him with their hands and thighs and shoulders. Their father gave a violent jerk and his legs shot up with a sound like a breaking spring; he looked like a fish squirming about on the grass. But not for long. They were holding on to him too tightly and they could feel him subsiding underneath them as his life ebbed away. A long shudder, a final quiver and all that was left was a piece of limp rag.

'I think that's it,' grunted Buteau breathlessly.

Lise stopped bouncing up and down and remained sitting hunched up, waiting to see if she could feel any quiver of life underneath her.

'That's it, he's not moving.'

She slid to one side, her shift rolled up round her hips, and lifted off the pillow. But then they gave a grunt of terror.

'Christ Almighty! He's gone all black, we're sunk!'

Indeed, it would have been impossible for him to have got into such a state by himself. They had pounded away at him so savagely that his nose had been pushed right down into the back of his mouth; and he was all purple, like a real black man. For a second, they could feel the ground swaying beneath their feet, they could hear the thundering hooves of the gendarmes, the clink of handcuffs, the thud of the guillotine. The sight of their botched handiwork filled them with horror and remorse. What could they do about it now? It would be no good washing his face with soap, they'd never succeed in making him white. And this terrifying, sooty hue gave them an inspiration.

'Suppose we set fire to him?' muttered Lise.

Buteau heaved a sigh of relief:

'That's right, we can say he set light to himself.'

Then he thought of the bonds and he clapped his hands as his face lit up and he gave an exultant laugh.

'By Christ, that's it! We'll make them think that the papers went up in flames with him. There'll be no accounts to settle!'

He quickly rushed over to fetch the candle but she was afraid of setting everything alight and at first refused to let him bring it too close to the bed. In the corner behind the beetroot there were some straw ties; she picked one up, lit it and began by setting fire to her father's hair and his long white beard. There was a sizzling sound, with little yellow flames and a smell of spilt fat. Suddenly they recoiled in horror, open-mouthed, as if some icy hand had pulled them back by their hair. Under the dreadful pain of his burns, their father, not completely smothered, had opened his eyes and this hideous black countenance, with its big broken nose and blazing beard, was staring at them. It took on a fearsome expression of pain and hatred and then collapsed. The old man was dead.

Buteau was panic-stricken, but at this moment he uttered a yell of fury as he heard sobbing at the doorway. It was the two children, Laure and Jules, in their nightclothes, who had been woken up by the noise and had come in through the open bedroom door, attracted by the glare of the flames. They had seen what was happening and were screaming with fright.

'You blasted little vermin,' shouted Buteau, rushing towards them. 'If you ever say a word, I'll strangle you. And here's something to remind you.'

He gave them both a clout that sent them sprawling. They picked themselves up, dry-eyed, and ran away, to curl up on their mattress, where they did not stir again.

Now anxious to finish, Buteau, despite his wife's objections, set light to the palliasse. Fortunately the room was so damp that the straw burned slowly. Big clouds of smoke swirled up and they opened the skylight, half asphyxiated. Then it began to flare up until the flames reached the ceiling. In the middle their father was crackling and the unbearable stench, the stench of burning flesh, grew stronger. The old house would all have gone up in flames like a haystack if the straw had not started smoking again, damped down by the bubbles dripping from the body. All that remained on the cross-pieces of the iron bedstead was a half-charred corpse, disfigured and unrecognizable. One corner of the straw mattress was still intact, with a tiny corner of cloth hanging down.

'Let's go,' said Lise, who was shivering again, despite the tremendous heat.

'Wait a minute,' Buteau replied. 'Got to make things look all right.'

Placing a chair beside the bedhead, he knocked the old man's candle off it, to make it seem as if it had fallen onto the palliasse. He was even artful enough to set light to some paper on the ground. They would find the ashes and he would explain that the day before the old man had found his bonds and kept them by him.

'That's that, let's get to bed!'

Buteau and Lise left the room, jostling each other in their haste to hurry back to bed. But the sheets were icy cold and so they once more clung desperately to each other to warm themselves up. Dawn came and still they could not sleep. They said nothing, but shudders ran through them and they could hear the pounding of their hearts. They had left the door of the next room open and it was this that so troubled them; but the thought of closing it disturbed them even more. They dozed off, still clasped in each other's arms.

Next morning, hearing the Buteaus' desperate calls, the neighbours hurried round and Frimat's wife and the other women were able to see the upset candle, the half-burnt straw mattress, the papers reduced to ashes. They all exclaimed that it was bound to happen, they'd predicted it dozens of times before, because the old man was in his second childhood. And what a stroke of luck that the house hadn't burnt down as well!

Chapter 6

Two days later, on the very same morning old Fouan was to be buried, Jean woke up very late, tired after a sleepless night in the little room which he had rented in Lengaigne's house. He had still not gone to Châteaudun to see the magistrate, although this was his only reason for not leaving Rognes; every evening he kept putting off his decision until the following day, even more hesitant as his anger cooled; and it was a final, anxious struggle with himself to reach a decision that had kept him awake.

Those Buteaus! What murderous beasts they were, killers whom any honest man ought to try to send to the guillotine. As soon as he had heard of the old man's death, he had realized the foul deed they had committed. That disgusting pair had roasted him alive to shut his mouth. First Françoise, then Fouan. Killing the one had forced them to kill the other. Whose turn next? And he reflected that it was his turn: they knew he was in on the secret and they'd surely pick him off in some lonely corner if he persisted in remaining in the district. So why not denounce them to the police straight away? He had almost decided to do so; he'd go and see the police as soon as he got up. Then once more he was gripped by indecision, full of misgivings at the thought of such a matter of life or death in which he'd have to be a witness and frightened that he himself might suffer as much as the guilty ones. What was the point of stirring up more trouble for himself? Of course, he was not behaving very courageously, but his excuse was, as he kept reassuring himself, that by keeping quiet he was respecting Françoise's last wishes. A dozen times during the night he had swung to and fro, on tenterhooks at the thought of this duty which he dare not face.

When Jean finally sprang out of bed at around nine o'clock, he dipped his head in a basin of cold water and suddenly reached a decision: he would say nothing, he wouldn't even start a lawsuit to get back half the furniture. The game would certainly not be worth the candle. His pride came to his rescue: he was pleased not to be one of such a band of rogues, to be an outsider. Let them

483

devour each other if they wanted: it would be a good riddance if they all destroyed themselves. All the suffering and disgust he had experienced during his ten years in Rognes surged up inside him in a flood of anger. To think that he had been so blissfully happy the day he left the army, after the Italian campaign, because he wouldn't be a sabre-rattler or a killer any more! And ever since then he had been living amongst savages, surrounded by foul play of every sort! Immediately he'd got married, he'd felt sad at heart; and now there were thieves and murderers about! Real wolves prowling around over such a vast, tranquil plain! No, he'd had enough of all these ravening beasts; living in the country was impossible. What was the point of tracking down one couple, one male and female, when they ought to exterminate the whole pack? He'd sooner leave.

At that moment, Jean's eyes fell on a newspaper that he had picked up in the bar the night before. He had been interested by an article on the imminence of war, for the war rumours which had been circulating during the last few days had been causing much alarm and despondency; and an unconscious, half-extinguished flame now suddenly flared up, rekindled by the news. His last motive for hesitation, the thought that he had nowhere to go, was suddenly removed, swept away as though by a gust of wind. That was the answer. He'd go and fight, he'd join up again. He'd paid his debt but so what? When you've got no fixed job any more and life is unpleasant and you're fed up at being harassed by enemies, then the best thing is to go off and smash 'em! He felt suddenly relaxed and exhilarated. While he was dressing, he loudly whistled the bugle call which he had followed into battle in Italy. People were such swine and the hope of demolishing a few Prussians cheered him up; and since he had found no peace in this corner of the world where families were all out for each other's blood, he might just as well go in for real slaughter. The more people he could kill, the more bloodstained the earth, the more he would feel he was getting his revenge for this god-forsaken life of misery and suffering that mankind had reduced him to.

When Jean went downstairs, he ate two eggs and bacon served by Flore and then called to Lengaigne to settle his bill.

'You leaving, Corporal?'

'Yes.'

'But you'll be back?'

'No.'

The innkeeper looked at him in surprise, keeping his thoughts to himself. So this big clot was going to give up his rights?

'And what are you going to do now, then? Taking up carpentering again?'

'No, soldiering.'

On hearing this, Lengaigne's eyes nearly popped out of his head and he could not restrain a contemptuous snigger. What an idiot!

Jean was already on the road to Cloyes when, seized by a sudden emotion, he stopped, and went back up the hill. He could not leave Rognes without taking a final farewell of Françoise's grave. And there was something else as well, the desire to take a last look at the immense sad plain of Beauce which he had come to love during his long solitary hours working there. The church-yard lay at the back of the church, surrounded by a small broken-down wall, so low that as you stood amongst the graves your gaze could range from one end of the horizon to the other. Under the pale March sun, the hazy sky had the delicacy of white silk, enlivened by the merest touch of blue; and under this gentle light, still numbed by winter frosts, Beauce seemed to be pro-longing its slumber like a drowsy woman no longer properly asleep but not stirring, luxuriating in her laziness. The far hori-zon was misty and the plain seemed all the more immense with its square fields of autumn wheat, oats and rye already green, while on the rest of the arable land, still bare, spring sowing had already begun.

In every direction men could be seen moving along with a steady sweep of their arms sowing the rich earth. The golden seed could be seen as a living cloud slipping from the hands of the nearest sowers; and then, as their figures became smaller and were lost in the infinite space, the seed swirled around them until, in the far distance, it seemed like a sheer quivering of light itself. For miles around, at every point of the boundless plain, the life of the coming summer was raining down in the sunlight.

Jean stood beside Françoise's grave. It was in the middle of a row and old Fouan's grave was already dug next to it. The cemetery was overgrown with weeds, for the parish council had never been able to bring itself to vote the fifty francs needed for the gamekeeper to keep it tidy. Crosses and surrounds had rotted where they stood; a few stained old stones still remained, but the charm of this solitary corner lay in its very neglect and its deep calm, barely disturbed by the cawing of the ancient rooks wheeling around the steeple of the church tower; here, away from the world, you could sleep in humility and forgetfulness; and filled with this peace of the dead, Jean was standing gazing with curiosity over the vast plain and the sowing which was bringing it new life when the bell began to toll slowly, three times, then twice, then a full peal. It was Fouan's body starting on its last journey. The bandy gravedigger came up with his rolling gait to take a quick look at the hole.

'It's too small,' Jean remarked. He felt suddenly emotional and anxious to stay and watch.

'Not a bit!' the lame man replied. 'He's shrunk in the roasting.'

The previous day the Buteaus had been very apprehensive until Dr Finet had called. But the doctor's only worry was to expedite the signing of the death certificate to save himself unnecessary journeys. He came, looked, expressed his indignation at the stupidity of families who leave old men who are wandering in their minds alone with lighted candles, and if he did harbour any suspicions, he took good care to keep them to himself. Good God! Suppose they had crisped their old father a bit, since he was in no hurry to die! He'd seen it all; such things hardly mattered. In his indifference, born of contempt and resentment, he was content merely to shrug his shoulders: a dirty rotten lot, these peasants!

Relieved, the Buteaus now had only the ordeal of meeting the family, which they had foreseen and faced resolutely. As soon as La Grande appeared, they burst into tears, to put up a front. She scrutinized them in surprise, thinking it rather unwise to cry quite so bitterly; in any case, she had only come round out of curiosity, for she had no claim on any of the estate. It was more dangerous when Fanny and Delhomme appeared. He had just been appointed mayor to replace Macqueron and this had given his wife such a swollen head that she was in danger of bursting with pride. She had kept her word; her father had died without any reconciliation between them; and she was still smarting so much with indignation that she shed no tears over his corpse. But someone was sobbing: it was Jesus Christ making a very drunken entrance. He wept buckets of tears over the body, bellowing that it was a blow from which he would never recover.

However, Lise had set out glasses and wine in the kitchen and they got down to business. They started by excluding the annuity of one hundred and fifty francs from the sale of the house, because it had been agreed that this should go to the one who was looking after their father at the time of his death. However, there remained the nest-egg. Hereupon Buteau told his story of how the old man had taken his bonds from underneath the marble top of the chest of drawers and how it must have been for the pleasure of looking at them that night that he had set light to his hair and beard; they had even found the ash of the papers; there were people who would bear witness to it, Frimat's wife and Bécu's wife, amongst others. They all eyed him while he was telling his tale but he remained unperturbed as he crossed his heart and swore blind. Obviously the family knew and he didn't give a damn as long as he was left in peace with the money. Moreover, with her usual high-handed bluntness, Fanny did not mince her words, calling them thieves and murderers: of course they had set light to their father and robbed him, it was as plain as a pikestaff! The Buteaus responded with violent insults and monstrous accusations. So she wanted to stir up trouble for them, did she? And what about the poison in the soup that had nearly made the old man kick the bucket when he was living with her? They'd have plenty to say about everybody else if anyone said anything about them. Jesus Christ had started whimpering and howling again, grief-stricken that such dreadful crimes were possible. Heavens above! His poor father! Were there really sons who were such inhuman beasts as to roast their own father? When they ran out of steam, La Grande added a few words to stir the pot. Then, uneasy at the row they were all making, Delhomme went and closed the doors and windows. He had his official position to think of now and, in any case, he was always in favour of sensible solutions. So he ended by saying that such things ought not to be mentioned. A fat lot of good it would do them if the neighbours were to hear! There would be legal proceedings and the innocent would perhaps lose more than the guilty. They all fell silent: he was quite right, there was no point in washing your dirty linen in public in a law-court. They were terrified of Buteau; a crook like that was capable of ruining them. And underlying all this – their acceptance of crime, their deliberate silence over murder and theft – there was even the sense of collusion peasants feel for the outlaws of their society, for poachers and killers of gamekeepers whom they may fear but will never betray.

While La Grande stayed behind to drink the coffee provided for the wake, the others left rudely, as a sign of their contempt. But the Buteaus were grinning to themselves now that their money was safe and they knew that their troubles were over. Lise started putting on airs while Buteau, deciding to do things properly, ordered the coffin and went to the cemetery to make sure they were digging the grave in the right place. It must be explained that in Rognes peasants who have thoroughly detested each other in their lifetimes do not fancy lying side by side when they are dead. The rows are filled up as space is needed, at random. So when it happens that two enemies die in quick succession, it causes the authorities considerable embarrassment because the second family will say that they will hang on to their body rather than let it rest next to the other one. In fact while Macqueron was mayor he had taken advantage of his position to buy a separate plot of land, out of the normal order; unfortunately this plot was next to the grave of Lengaigne's father, where Lengaigne had booked a plot for himself. The latter had borne a grudge ever since, for the thought that his corpse would be rotting next to that of that bastard added fuel to their long-standing rivalry and was poisoning the remaining years of his life. Similarly Buteau was furious when he inspected his father's plot. It was to the left of Françoise's, which was right and proper, but, by sheer bad luck, in the row parallel to hers, just opposite, was the grave of the wife of old Saucisse, who had reserved the next plot for himself; so when that old rogue Saucisse finally pegged out, his feet would be on top of old Fouan's skull. Could such a thought be entertained for one single second? Two old men who had loathed each other ever since that dirty trick over the annuity; and now the scoundrel of the piece, the one who'd diddled the other, would be able to kick him about for all time! Christ Almighty! If the family was feeble enough to put up with that sort of thing, old

Fouan's bones would turn in their grave against old Saucisse's. Boiling with fury, Buteau went raging down to the town-hall and descended on Delhomme to force him to allocate another plot since he was in a position to do so. Then, when his brother-in-law refused to depart from custom, quoting the deplorable example of Macqueron and Lengaigne, he called him a coward and a traitor and stood shouting in the middle of the street that he was the only good son of the family because the others didn't care a bugger whether their old father would rest quietly in his grave or not. He collected a sympathetic crowd and then went home bursting with indignation.

Delhomme had just had to handle a more serious embarrassment. Father Madeline had left two days ago and once again Rognes was left without a priest. The attempt to provide one of their own, an expensive luxury for the parish, had in fact been so unsuccessful that the town council had voted to cancel this item of expenditure and return to the former arrangement of sharing the parish priest of Bazoches-le-Doyen. But despite his bishop's persuasion, Father Godard refused ever to take the sacraments in Rognes again, infuriated at his colleague's departure and accusing the villagers of having half-killed him purely in order to force him, Father Godard, to come back. He was going about saying loudly that next Sunday Bécu could toll the bell until Vespers when suddenly Fouan's death had complicated the issue and brought it to a head. A funeral's not like a Mass, you can't put it off indefinitely. Secretly pleased at the opportunity, Delhomme, whose judicious nature did not exclude a touch of malice, decided to go to Bazoches to see the priest personally. As soon as the latter caught sight of him, his face went purple and started swelling at the temples. Even before Delhomme opened his mouth, he waved him away. No! Absolutely not! Never! He'd sooner give up his own parish. And when he learnt that it was for a funeral, he stuttered with fury. Ah, so those heathens were deliberately dying because they thought that was the way to force his hand! Well, they could bury their own dead, he was hanged if he would help them on their way to heaven! Quietly, Delhomme waited for the first outburst to subside before putting forward his own point of view: only dogs died without a blessing and you couldn't leave a family with a dead man on their hands, and, finally, he drew attention to his personal reasons: the dead man was his father-in-law, the father-in-law of the mayor of Rognes. Now, how about tomorrow at ten o'clock? No! Never! Spluttering and floundering, Father Godard stuck to his guns, and the farmer had to leave without persuading him to change his mind but in the hope that he might think it over.

'I'm telling you: never!' the priest flung at him for the last time from his doorway. 'Don't toll the bell. There's no point! Never!'

Next morning, Bécu was told by the mayor to start ringing at ten o'clock. They would see. At the Buteaus', everything was ready; the body had been coffined the night before, under the expert eye of La Grande. The bedroom had already been washed and no sign of the fire remained, except their father in his wooden overcoat. And the bell was tolling when the family, assembled in front of the house for the funeral procession, saw Father Godard coming up Macqueron's street, out of breath from running and so red and furious that he had taken off his hat and was vigorously fanning himself with it for fear of having an attack. He looked neither right nor left but disappeared into the church, coming out a moment later in his surplice, preceded by two choirboys, one bearing the cross and the other the holy water. He gabbled a few hasty words over the corpse and, without bothering to see if the bearers were following him with the coffin, he went back into the church, where he started to say Mass at top speed. The bewildered Clou with his trombone and the two startled choristers were hard pressed to keep up with him. The family sat in front: Buteau and Lise, Fanny and Delhomme, Jesus Christ and La Grande. Monsieur Charles was honouring the funeral with his presence and had offered his wife's apologies: she had gone to Chartres two days before with Élodie and Nénesse. As for La Trouille, just as she was setting out, she had noticed that three of her geese were missing and had slipped away to look for them. Behind Lise sat her two children, Laure and Jules, as still as mice, with their arms folded, dark-eyed and staring. And there were many acquaintances in the other pews, especially the women, the wives of Frimat and Bécu, Coelina and Flore; in a word, it was a really good turn-out. Before the preface, when the priest turned towards the congregation, he stretched his arms out wide in a terrifying gesture, as if about to strike them in the face. Bécu, very drunk, continued to toll the bell.

On the whole, it was a reasonable Mass, even if it was taken too fast. People were being tolerant, smiling at the priest's anger and excusing him; after all, it was natural for him to be upset by his defeat, just as everyone was delighted at Rognes's victory. Faces were beaming with amused satisfaction at having had the last word in this matter of the sacraments. They had certainly forced him to bring the word of God to them, even if, in their heart of hearts, they didn't give a damn for Him.

When the Mass was over, they passed round the aspergillum and the procession reformed : the cross, the choristers, Clou and his trombone, the priest breathless with haste, the coffin carried by four peasants, the family and the other mourners. Bécu started tolling the bell again so violently that the rooks all flew out of the belfry, cawing in distress. The procession had only to go round the corner of the church to reach the graveyard. The singing and music rang out more loudly against the profound silence of Nature, amidst the weeds peacefully fluttering in the breeze, warmed by the misty sun. And in the open air the coffin seemed suddenly so small that everyone was struck by it. Jean, still standing there, was quite startled. Poor old man, so emaciated by age, so reduced by his wretched life, that he fitted comfortably into this toy box, such a tiny little box, hardly any size at all! He wouldn't take up much room, he would be no great encumbrance in his corner of this vast expanse of land which had been his sole passion and which had burnt his body to a cinder. The body had arrived at the edge of the gaping grave and Jean's gaze followed it and looked beyond, over the wall, from one end of Beauce to the other; and on the ploughed lands sweeping away into the infinite distance, he could once more see the sowers, swinging their arms in the same steady gesture, and the living cloud of seed raining down into the open furrows.

When the Buteaus caught sight of Jean they exchanged an anxious glance. Was that bastard waiting there in order to make a fuss? As long as they felt that he was in Rognes they would never sleep peacefully. The choirboy holding the cross had just set it down at the foot of the grave and, standing beside the coffin resting on the grass Father Godard was rapidly reciting the last prayers. But the mourners were distracted by the late arrival of Macqueron and Lengaigne, who kept on looking up towards the plain. They followed their gaze and were intrigued to see a large cloud of smoke billowing up into the sky. It must be at La Borderie, it seemed like haystacks on fire behind the farmhouse.

'*Ego sum*,' the priest snapped angrily. Their faces turned back towards him and their gaze returned to the coffin; only Monsieur Charles continued talking in an undertone to Delhomme. That morning he had received a letter from Madame Charles and he was in the seventh heaven of delight. Hardly had she arrived in Chartres than Élodie had shown herself outstanding, as energetic and crafty as Nénesse. She had diddled her father and was already in charge. A sheer gift, that's what it was, a sharp eye and plenty of drive! And Monsieur Charles talked sentimentally about settling into a happy old age in his Roseblanche estate with his collection of roses and carnations, now flourishing better than ever before, his birds, all quite recovered and singing merrily, so that it did your heart good to hear them.

'*Amen!*' said the choirboy with the holy water sprinkler, very loudly.

Father Godard immediately launched into the *De profundis clamavi ad te Domine*, still in the same angry voice. And he continued while Jesus Christ drew Fanny to one side and started fiercely attacking the Buteaus again:

'If only I hadn't been so drunk the other day. It's really too idiotic to let ourselves be done down like this.'

'Well, we certainly have been,' agreed Fanny, keeping her voice low.

'Because in fact,' he went on, 'those swine *have* got the bonds. And they've been enjoying the proceeds for a long time, they'd come to an arrangement with old Saucisse, I know all about it. For Christ's sake, aren't we going to take them to court?'

She drew away from him and said fiercely:

'Oh no, not me! I've got other things to do. You can do it if you like.'

It was Jesus Christ's turn to look scared and hold back. If he was unable to persuade his sister to take the lead, he was not at all sure about his own relationship with the law.

'Ah well, I suppose I'm imagining things. Anyway, when you're honest at least you have the consolation of being able to walk with your head high.'

La Grande, who was listening, saw him straighten his back with an air of dignified respectability. She had always accused him of being a simpleton for the beggarly existence he led. She thought it pitiful that a strapping fellow like him didn't go and make a row at his brother's to claim his share. And happy to be able to lead him and Fanny up the garden path, quite irrelevantly, with an innocent air, she repeated her usual promise:

'Well, you can be sure that I'll never do any harm to anyone, I've got it all settled a long time ago. Equal shares for all, I'd not die happy if I didn't treat everyone alike. Hyacinthe's there and you too, Fanny... I'm ninety, my turn will come one day!'

She did not believe a word of what she was saying, being quite determined to go on enjoying her possessions without end. She'd bury the lot of them. And now she'd seen one more on his way, her brother. Everything that was happening before her eyes, this corpse beside the open grave, the final ceremony, seemed something put on for the neighbours' benefit, not for hers. Tall and thin, with her stick under one arm, she stood bolt upright amidst the graves, feeling nothing except curiosity at this tiresome business of dying which affected others.

The priest was gabbling the last verse of the psalm:

'*Et ipse redimit Israel ex omnibus iniquitatibus ejus.*'

He took the holy water sprinkler and shook it over the coffin, raising his voice as he said:

'*Requiescat in pace.*'

'*Amen,*' replied the two choristers.

And the coffin was lowered into the grave. The gravedigger had attached the ropes and only two men were needed, for it weighed no more than the body of a little child. Then they all filed past, handing the sprinkler from one to the other, each making the sign of the cross over the grave.

Jean came up and took the sprinkler from Monsieur Charles: he looked down into the hole. His eyes were dazzled by gazing for so long over the vast plain at the sowers burying the future bread, from one end of Beauce to the other, until their figures were lost in the distance on the bright, hazy horizon. However, down

493

below, in the earth, he could discern the coffin, looking even smaller with its plain narrow wooden lid the colour of golden wheat; and lumps of this rich earth were sliding down, half covering the coffin so that he could see only a pale mark at the bottom, like a handful of that wheat which his former fellow farm-hands were casting into the furrows out there on the plain. He shook the sprinkler and handed it to Jesus Christ.

'Father Godard! Father Godard!' Delhomme called discreetly, running after the priest who, having finished the ceremony, was storming away, forgetting the two choirboys.

'What is it now?' he asked.

'I wanted to thank you for your kindness. So next Sunday we'll ring the bell for Mass at nine o'clock, as usual, shall we?'

And as the priest glared at him without replying, he hurriedly added:

'There's a poor woman here, very sick and quite alone and penniless... You know her, it's Rosalie, the one who mends the chairs. I've sent her a bowl of soup but I can't do everything.'

Father Godard's face softened and relaxed into an expression of tenderness and charity. He rummaged desperately in his pockets but could find only twenty-five centimes.

'Lend me five francs, I'll let you have them back next Sunday. Till Sunday, then.'

And once more he rushed breathlessly away. Well, they might be forcing him to bring God's word to Rognes again but the good Lord would condemn them all to everlasting hellfire, there was no doubt about that. But there was nothing he could do and that was no reason for letting them suffer too much on earth.

When Delhomme came back to the others, he became involved in a terrible squabble. First of all the mourners had watched with interest the spadefuls of earth which the gravedigger was throwing onto the coffin. But finding himself by chance side by side with Macqueron, Lengaigne had bluntly tackled him on the subject of the plot. The family, about to disperse, stayed to watch and soon became involved in the battle, which was punctuated by the steady thud of the spadefuls of earth on the coffin.

'You hadn't got the right to do it!' Lengaigne was shouting. 'You shouldn't have jumped the queue, even if you were the mayor. It was just to annoy me that you wanted to get a place

494

next to my father, wasn't it? But you're not there yet, by God!'

'Oh, for Christ's sake leave me alone!' Macqueron retorted. 'I've paid for the plot and it's mine. And there I'll go and no dirty pig like you is going to stop me!'

They were jostling each other as they stood beside their concessions, the few feet of earth where they would sleep for ever.

'But doesn't it mean anything to you, you low bugger, that your bloody carcass will be next to mine, just as if we were real friends? It gets my goat. We've always loathed each other's guts and now we're supposed to make our peace and lie side by side happily ever after. No, not for me, I'm never going to make it up with you.'

'I don't give a damn! You can lick my arse and go on licking it beside me as far as I'm concerned!'

This contemptuous remark was the last straw for Lengaigne. He stuttered angrily that if he pegged out last he'd sooner come along at night and dig Macqueron's bones up. The other man sneered that he'd like to see that: and then their wives intervened. The thin and swarthy Coelina furiously contradicted her husband.

'You're wrong, I've told you you're heartless. If you persist, you can lie in your hole by yourself! I'll go somewhere else where I won't be messed about by that bitch over there.'

She jerked her chin in the direction of the peevish and spineless Flore, who retorted sharply:

'We'll see who does the messing about. Don't get worked up, dearie, I don't want your stinking corpse contaminating mine.'

Bécu's and Frimat's wives intervened and separated them.

'Come on, come on,' Bécu's wife kept saying. 'You're both agreed, you won't be side by side! Everyone's got the right to his own ideas, you're free to choose your own company.'

Frimat's wife approved.

'Of course, it's natural. Look, my old man who's going to die soon, I'd sooner keep him with me than let him be put next to old Couillet, he'd had words with him in the past.'

Tears had come to her eyes at the thought that her paralysed husband would perhaps not survive the week. The day before, trying to put him to bed, she had stumbled with him and certainly, once he was gone, she would not be long following him.

But Lengaigne suddenly tackled Delhomme, who had just come up.

'Look, you're a fair man, you must make him move out and send him back to the end of the queue, like the others.'

Macqueron shrugged his shoulders and Delhomme confirmed that, seeing that he had paid for his plot, it now belonged to him. Nothing like it must happen again, that was all. At this, Buteau, who was trying to restrain himself, blew up. The family had felt obliged to observe a certain discretion as the spadefuls of earth continued to thud down onto the old man's coffin, but Buteau was so indignant that, pointing to Delhomme, he shouted to Lengaigne:

'You needn't rely on this young bugger to have any family feeling! He's just had his father buried next to a thief!'

There was uproar; the family took sides. Fanny restrained her husband by saying that the real mistake had been in not buying a plot for their father next to Rose when they had lost their mother; while Jesus Christ together with La Grande set about Delhomme, both protesting violently that it was inhuman and inexcusable to put the old man next to Saucisse. Monsieur Charles was also of this opinion but expressed it more mildly.

Nobody was able to hear what anybody was saying when Buteau's voice suddenly rose above the din, shouting:

'Yes, their bones will turn in their graves and they'll eat each other up!'

At this, everyone joined in, relatives, friends and acquaintances. What he said was right, their bones would turn in their graves. The Fouans would finally gobble each other up; Lengaigne and Macqueron would squabble as to who would rot first, the women, Coelina, Flore and Bécu's wife would keep going at each other with tongue and claw. You couldn't rest, side by side, even in your grave, if you loathed each other. And in this sunny graveyard, under the peacefully sprouting weeds, the dead old ancestors fought fiercely on with no quarter given, from coffin to coffin, as fiercely as the fight waged by their living descendants above them amidst the tombstones.

But a cry from Jean drew them apart and everyone turned to look:

'La Borderie's on fire!'

There was no longer any doubt, flames were bursting through the roofs, flickering and pale in the daylight. A large cloud of smoke was wafting gently northwards. And at that very moment La Trouille came into sight, running at top speed from the farm. While looking for her geese she had noticed the first sparks and had stopped to enjoy the spectacle until the thought of being the first to come and tell the story had sent her running back to Rognes. She straddled the little wall and shouted in her shrill boyish voice:

'It's burning like mad! It's that dirty louse Tron who came back and set fire to it, in three places, in the barn, the stables and the kitchen. They pinched him just as he was setting light to the straw, the drivers have half-killed him. And the horses and cows and sheep are all being roasted alive. You should just hear them squealing! There's never been anything like it!'

Her green eyes were sparkling and she burst out laughing:

'And then there's the Cognet girl! You know, she'd not been well since the master died. So they'd forgotten all about her, lying in bed. She was already being toasted and she only just managed to get out in her shift. Oh, she looked so funny dashing round the countryside with bare legs, dancing up and down and showing everything she's got, front and back, and people were shouting "Gee up, neddy," to help her along, 'cause no one really likes her. One old man said: "There she goes just like she came, with only a shift to cover her arse!"'

Once again she squirmed with delight.

'Come and see, it's so funny. I'm going back!'

And she jumped off the wall and dashed away at full speed towards the blazing farmhouse.

Monsieur Charles, Delhomme, Macqueron and almost all the villagers followed her, while the women led by La Grande also left the churchyard and went out onto the road to have a better view. Buteau and Lise stayed behind and the latter detained Lengaigne for a moment, anxious to ask him about Jean without making it too obvious. Had he found work since he'd taken lodgings in the village? When the innkeeper replied that he was leaving and going to join up again, Lise and Buteau felt a great weight lifted from their minds and both made the same remark:

'What an idiot!'

It was all over now, they could look forward to settling down happily again. They glanced at Fouan's grave, which the grave-digger had nearly finished filling in. And as the two children were lingering to take a look, their mother called to them:

'Come on, Jules and Laure. And be good and do what you're told or else that man'll come and bury you too!'

The Buteaus went off, pushing their Jules and Laure along in front of them. The two children, who were in on the secret, looked as good as gold with their large, dark, silent, knowing eyes.

Only Jean and Jesus Christ were left in the churchyard. The latter, not greatly interested in the fire, was continuing to watch it from a distance. Standing motionless between two graves, with a vacant dreamy expression in his eyes and looking like a drunken crucified Christ, he seemed to portray the ultimate sadness of all philosophizing. Perhaps he was reflecting that all life is just smoke. And as solemn ideas always excited him, he absent-mindedly lifted his thigh, in his vague dreamy way, and let out three farts, one after the other.

'Good God!' exclaimed Bécu, very drunk, as he was going through the graveyard on his way to the fire.

A fourth one came so close to him as he went by that he could almost feel the blast on his cheek. So as he went away, he called out to his friend:

'If that wind keeps up, there'll be some shit on the way.'

Jesus Christ gave an experimental squeeze.

'Well, I'm damned, I do want to shit, in fact.'

And stepping deliberately and holding his legs carefully apart, he hurried away and disappeared round the corner of the wall. Jean was alone. In the distance, swirling above La Borderie, now largely burnt out, vast clouds of reddish smoke were casting shadows over the ploughed fields and the scattered sowers. And slowly his gaze came back to the two fresh mounds of earth at his feet, under which Françoise and old Fouan lay in their last sleep. The anger and disgust with people and things which he had felt that morning was melting away, leaving behind a deep sense of peace. Despite himself, he was pervaded by a feeling of gentleness and hope, perhaps because of the warm sunshine.

Yes, his former master Hourdequin had given himself a lot of fuss and bother with these new inventions of his and he hadn't reaped much benefit from his machines and fertilizers, all this new science which was still not properly understood. And then the Cognet girl had finished him off and he too was sleeping in the churchyard; while all that remained of his farm was ashes whirling away in the wind. But what did it matter? The walls might be burnt down but you couldn't burn down the earth. Mother Earth would always be there to feed those who sowed her. She had space enough and time, until people learned how to make her produce more.

It was like all those stories of revolutions and political upsets that people kept prophesying. It was said that the land would pass into other people's hands and harvests from other countries would overwhelm ours and all our fields would be overgrown with brambles. So what? Can you harm the earth? She'll still belong to someone who will be forced to cultivate her in order not to starve. If weeds grew over her for years, it would give her time to rest and become young and fruitful again. The earth doesn't take part in our petty, spiteful, antlike squabbles, she pays no more attention to us than to any other insects, she merely goes on working and working, eternally.

And then there was pain and blood and tears, all those things that cause suffering and revolt, the killing of Françoise, the killing of Fouan, vice triumphing, and the stinking, bloodthirsty peasants, vermin who disgrace and exploit the earth. But can you really know? Just as the frost that burns the crops, the hail that chops them down, the thunderstorms which batter them are all perhaps necessary, maybe blood and tears are needed to keep the world going. And how important is human misery when weighed against the mighty mechanism of the stars and the sun? What does God care for us? We earn our bread only by dint of a cruel struggle, day in, day out. And only the earth is immortal, the Great Mother from whom we spring and to whom we return, love of whom can drive us to crime and through whom life is perpetually preserved for her own inscrutable ends, in which even our wretched degraded nature has its part to play.

Such were the confused notions swirling through Jean's head. But a bugle call resounded in the distance as the firemen of Bazoches-le-Doyen arrived at the gallop, too late. And as he heard it, Jean straightened his back. It was the sound of war breaking through the smoke, with its horses, its cannon, its murderous howl. He choked with emotion. Well, since he no longer had the heart to plough this old land of France, by God, he'd defend it!

As he left he cast one final glance at the two grassless graves and at the infinite expanse of the rich plain of Beauce swarming with sowers, swinging their arms in the same monotonous gesture. Here were the Dead, there was the Seed; and bread would be springing from the Good Earth.

MORE ABOUT PENGUINS, PELICANS, PEREGRINES AND PUFFINS

For further information about books available from Penguins please write to Dept EP, Penguin Books Ltd, Harmondsworth, Middlesex UB7 0DA.

In the U.S.A.: For a complete list of books available from Penguins in the United States write to Dept DG, Penguin Books, 299 Murray Hill Parkway, East Rutherford, New Jersey 07073.

In Canada: For a complete list of books available from Penguins in Canada write to Penguin Books Canada Ltd, 2801 John Street, Markham, Ontario L3R 1B4.

In Australia: For a complete list of books available from Penguins in Australia write to the Marketing Department, Penguin Books Australia Ltd, P.O. Box 257, Ringwood, Victoria 3134.

In New Zealand: For a complete list of books available from Penguins in New Zealand write to the Marketing Department, Penguin Books (N.Z.) Ltd, Private Bag, Takapuna, Auckland 9.

In India: For a complete list of books available from Penguins in India write to Penguin Overseas Ltd, 706 Eros Apartments, 56 Nehru Place, New Delhi 110019.

Zola in Penguin Classics

THERÈSE RAQUIN

Translated by L. W. Tancock

The immediate success which *Thérèse Raquin* enjoyed on publication in 1868 was partly due to scandal, following the accusation of pornography; in reply Zola defined the new creed of Naturalism in the famous preface which is printed in this volume. The novel is a grim tale of adultery, murder and revenge in a nightmarish setting.

NANA

Translated by George Holden

An evocation of the glittering, corrupt world of the Second French Empire, where prostitution played an important part at all levels. Prompted by his theories of heredity and environment, Zola set out to show Nana 'the golden fly', rising out of the underworld to feed on society – a predetermined product of her origins. Nana's latent destructiveness is mirrored in the Empire's, and they reflect each other's disintegration and final collapse in 1870.

LA BÊTE HUMAINE

Translated by Leonard Tancock

'Love and death, possessing and killing, are the dark foundations of the human soul' – this pessimistic view haunted Zola when he was writing this taut thriller of violent passions and sexual jealousy. But the book, whose main characters are railwaymen and their women, is also a fascinating study of the criminal mind and a bitter attack on the French judicial system with its fatal flaw that magistrates, being poorly paid government servants, are subject to blackmail, corruption and political pressure. In fact truth and justice themselves must toe the party line.

Zola in Penguin Classics
From the Rougon–Macquart series:

L'ASSOMMOIR

Translated by L. W. Tancock

'I wanted to depict the inevitable downfall of a working-class family in the polluted atmosphere of our urban areas', wrote Zola of L'Assommoir (1877), which some critics rate the greatest of his Rougon-Macquart novels. In the result the book triumphantly surmounts the author's moral and social intentions to become, perhaps, the first 'classical tragedy' of working-class people living in the slums of a city – Paris. Vividly, without romantic illusion, Zola uses the coarse argot of the back-streets to plot the descent of the easy going Gervaise through idleness, drunkenness, promiscuity, filth and starvation to the grave.

GERMINAL

Translated by L. W. Tancock

Germinal (1885) was written by Zola to draw attention once again to the misery prevailing among the poor in France during the Second Empire. The novel, which has now become a sociological document, depicts the grim struggle between capital and labour in a coalfield in northern France. Yet through the blackness of this picture, humanity is constantly apparent, and the final impression is one of compassion and hope for the future, not only of organized labour, but also of man.

THE DEBACLE

Translated by Leonard Tancock

The climax of Zola's great Rougon-Macquart series, The Debacle (1892) takes as its subject the Franco-Prussian war of 1870, which brought about the collapse of the corrupt and vulgar Second Empire, transformed France and left scars which have remained unhealed to this day. While Zola's account of these tragic events is remarkably factual, The Debacle is much more than a documentary. It is at once one of the greatest war novels ever written and a grimly prophetic vision of our time.

Flaubert in Penguin Classics

MADAME BOVARY

Translated by Alan Russell

The central character of *Madame Bovary* is the bored wife of a provincial doctor, whose desires and illusions are inevitably shattered when reality catches up with her. In the book, which established the realistic novel in France, Flaubert vents his profound contempt for the *bourgeois* mentality, but betrays a certain sympathy for the human frailty of Emma Bovary.

SENTIMENTAL EDUCATION

Translated by Robert Baldick

This story of a young man's romantic attachment to an older woman, is regarded by many to be the greatest French novel of the last century. Flaubert's insight into the realities of life – rather than the remorseless exposure of its illusions, as displayed in *Madame Bovary* – enables him to reconstruct in one masterpiece the very fibre of his times.

SALAMMBO

Translated by A. J. Krailsheimer

A tale of epic grandeur and appalling savagery which tells of the aftermath of the First Punic War, when the Carthaginian army is forced to contend with a revolt by their unpaid mercenaries. Here Flaubert was able to give full rein to his love of the gorgeous, the voluptuous and the bizarre.

BOUVARD AND PÉCUCHET

Translated by A. J. Krailsheimer

Liberated from a humdrum existence, Bouvard and Pécuchet make a series of ill-fated sorties into vast areas of experience. Their comic and poignant misadventures make variations on one of Flaubert's favourite themes, that of human stupidity in general, and bourgeois stupidity in particular.

and

Three Tales